THE COLD JENA GRAY TRILOGY

COLD JENA GRAY

JENA PARKER RETURNS

JENA PARKER

"THE FINAL RESOLUTION"

JENA PARKER

"THE FINAL RESOLUTION"

LIFE IS A MYSTERY AND THEN YOU DIE!

BETTY SWEM

JENA PARKER "THE FINAL RESOLUTION"
LIFE IS A MYSTERY AND THEN YOU DIE!

iUniverse books may be ordered through booksellers or by contacting:

iUniverse
1663 Liberty Drive
Bloomington, IN 47403
www.iuniverse.com
844-349-9409

ISBN: 978-1-6632-0603-9 (sc)
ISBN: 978-1-6632-0800-2 (hc)
ISBN: 978-1-6632-0604-6 (e)

Print information available on the last page.

iUniverse rev. date: 03/22/2021

For my brother McKenley,
*I always wanted to do something extraordinary, and
I think I did …*

COLD JENA GRAY

PROLOGUE

As a child, I used to dream of being someone famous, someone so important that people would watch me constantly, focusing on every move I made, but things change when you get older. Maybe it's because people don't notice you as much or maybe you just don't notice yourself. As I was transitioning, I didn't notice the change in myself right away, but then slowly, it began to take form, and I suddenly saw myself as a creature of the night, a creature that appeared innocent and harmless at first, but as you moved closer to it, you began to notice small bits and pieces of evil and ugliness. I saw the dark side of myself in the mirror many times, but I looked away and pretended that I wasn't that person, that I wasn't that unforeseen shadow that people would love from a distance but hate up close. They'd hate me. They'd hate everything about me, but did I really care? No. I really didn't care, because deep inside of me, I knew the truth, and I had embraced it a long time ago subconsciously. Deep inside, you know the truth too.

Am I cold? Well, I'm wearing a coat, hat, scarf, and even gloves. Yet, I feel cold and empty. There's a chill running through my bones that is constant, a chill that makes me want to feel the warmth of something other than your hands, those ugly hands that touched me. I hate them! Please go away! I long for a feeling of something red and hot like blood. How it flows like a river when it streams from a lifeless body. How I love it when it drips from my eyes, down my arms to the tips of my fingers, and then to the floor with each drop magnified by my obsession with it. I imagine my face being splattered with it. Am I cold? Yes, I'm cold, but not because of my body temperature or because it's below zero outside. No! That's not the kind of coldness I feel inside. It's the kind of coldness that a person feels after all the good in her is gone—after you've taken all you could, and your mind begins to project its own images of the world you built that is far from the accepted reality seen by the eyes of the righteous ones.

CHAPTER ONE

Three people are standing out in the middle of the hot, windy desert. The wind is blowing fiercely, and Jena is handcuffed to a police officer's car. Tears are streaming down her cheeks. Her clothes are torn, and she is bleeding through her pants from a gash in her left knee. Jena screams out, "Were you there?"

A young boy with dark hair and sky-blue eyes stands across from her. He gives Jena a discontented look and hangs his head in shame. He bites his lips. "Where?" he asks.

Jena struggles to get loose from the handcuffs. She screams out again, "Were you there? ... When he was!" Jena starts crying.

The police officer stands with his gun pointed at Jena and then at Jake to signal that no one should move. He leaves his gun pointed at Jake and turns to him. "Did you see who did this to her, young man?" Office Reyes asks.

Jake looks away and breathes hard. Then he throws his hat to the ground in frustration. The police officer walks up to him and sticks his gun in his face. "Oh, you're a tough guy? You think throwing your hat down gonna help you?" He digs his gun into Jake's left cheek. "You look at me when I'm talking to you, boy!" Officer Reyes cocks his weapon.

Jena starts to cry and screams loudly while still struggling to get loose. She pleads with Officer Reyes. "Look at what he has done to me!"

Officer Reyes turns to look at her. His face turns beet red. He turns back to look at Jake with an angry expression on his face. Jake remains silent and steps back from the officer's gun.

Jena bursts into tears. "How could you let them do this to me, Jake?"

He doesn't answer.

"You answer me!" She yells louder.

Jake looks down and rubs his head in panic. He looks up at Jena. "Yes. Yes, I was there. I was watching. I was watching him do this to you, and I couldn't stop him."

Jena looks at Jake with a disgusted, evil look on her face. Her eyes are as red as fire, and her tears are streaming harder down her cheeks. "You bastard! I'll kill you!" Jena screams. "I'll kill you. You just wait and see! I'll make you pay!"

Officer Reyes grabs Jena by the arm. "Watch your head, lady." He helps her into the police car. He puts his gun back in his holster and points at Jake. "You meet me at the station." Officer Reyes opens the driver's side door and hops inside. He sticks his head out the window. "I have some questions for you, kid. So, you get your ass down to the station now."

Jake nods his head. Officer Reyes slams the car door. He stares at Jake from the car's rearview mirror. He talks to himself in the mirror. "Don't you try any funny shit either because I'll find you and I'll do worse than she'll do to you. So, if you decide to not show up, boy, I'll surely kill ya."

Jake stands at the back of the car and watches as Officer Reyes drives away. Dust hits him in the face as the car spins out of the desert. Jena turns around and stares at Jake from the back of the police car. She doesn't take her eyes off him as the car drives quickly out of the desert. Jake just continues to watch the car disappear. He stares up at the night sky, gets into his car, and then heads to the police station. Jena is sitting silently in the back of the police car when she hears a soft voice calling her.

"Jena? Jena, wake up, honey. It's time for school."

Jena suddenly awakes from her dream. "Mom?" she says in a groggy voice. "How late am I?"

Mrs. Parker stands up. "Not that late, but late." Her mother smiles and kisses her on the forehead. Jena quickly showers and begins to get dressed for school. She stands in front of her dresser mirror and stares at her red and teary eyes. She looks deep into the mirror and slowly touches her eyes. She quickly picks up her makeup kit and begins applying small dots to hide the dark circles around her eyes. The mirror has four pictures on it and a cross necklace that dangles from the top of it. She looks at her makeup and frowns. "You look ugly," she says to herself as she removes the wet towel and throws it over the mirror. She pulls her hair back into a ponytail and slips into a light-blue shirt and a checkered skirt, grabs her books, and then quickly rushes downstairs. Stumbling down the stairs, she smells the breakfast her mom is cooking. "No time for breakfast, Mom!" She yells out as she grabs a piece of candy from the jar near the door. "I gotta run."

Mrs. Parker quickly tries to catch up with her. "Jena!" she calls in a disappointed voice.

"Sorry, Mom, I love you, but I gotta go," Jena says as she slams the front door. The school bus pulls up, and the door swings open. Ms. Amy, the bus driver, is smiling at Jena. "I see you barely made it this morning, Jena."

Jena smiles back and walks up the bus steps. Her longtime friend Jake is waiting for her. "Hi, Jake," she says as she sits down next to him.

"Hi, BFF," Jake says sarcastically.

"Oh, Jake, you're Mr. Silly today, huh?" she says and punches him on the shoulder.

"Jena, you look like you didn't get any sleep last night." He stares into her eyes.

"I didn't," she replies. "I had another dream, and strangely, it was about you." Jena stares at Jake.

"Well, I hope it was a good one." He smiles.

"It was surely interesting," Jena replies.

Sliding closer to Jena, he asks, "So, Jena, have you made any decision about my request?"

"What request, Jake?" Jena smiles and turns away.

"Ah, the request to go with me to the dance this Saturday."

Jena laughs. "Come on, I can't go to the dance with my best friend. What would people say? They'd laugh at the both of us." Jena smiles and pinches his cheek.

He turns away, his expression serious, and then he turns back to look at Jena again. "Jena, who cares about what people will say? I want to take you." He slides closer to her and slightly nudges her. In a serious voice, he says, "I want to take you to the dance, so what's wrong with that?"

Jena flashes back to her dream when Officer Reyes had her handcuffed to the police car, and tears are streaming down her cheeks while Jake stands staring at her. The bus pulls up to the school just as the first bells rings. Jena stands up. "Jake let's talk about this after school. I got to get to class."

He stands up. "Okay," he says. Jake watches as she walks away. Two boys, Ken, and Mark, walk up behind Jena and begin making obscene gestures. "Jena, you look good today, but you'd look even better with that skirt off." They both start laughing.

She turns around with her mouth open in surprise. "Leave me alone, Ken!" she says. "I'm just trying to get to class. Can't you see that?"

Ken has a malicious grin on his face. "I know, and I'm just trying to get into your panties."

Jena looks at Ken in disbelief that he just said that. Jake walks up. "Man, you better get away from Jena, because you don't want me to kick your ass."

Ken stands, looking tough, and then walks up to get in Jake's face. "Okay, tough guy, then after school, we'll see who kicks whose ass," Ken says and walks off.

Jena watches the clock throughout the day. She is tired and bewildered by her dream.

Jake and Jena pass each other throughout the day, but they barely speak. Ken passes Jake in the hallway and points at his watch. The bell rings, and Jake walks out to the bus stop. Ken walks up to him. "Are you going to kick my ass, Jake? Because if you are, then let's go."

Jake brushes up against Ken.

Principal Ricky walks out toward the bus stop. "What's going on, boys? What's the problem with you two?"

Ken steps back from Principal Ricky and adjusts his jacket. "Nothing, sir." He holds his hands up. "No problem here."

Principal Ricky puts his hands on his hips and eyes both boys. "Good, because you know Maplesville is a small town, and we small-town folk like to keep things peaceful." Principal Ricky stares at both boys. "You two got it?" Jake walks toward the bus. Jena follows. Principal Ricky steps on the bus too. "This is why today I'm riding the school bus." Everyone stares at him. The bus driver closes the door and smiles as she stares out the bus's front window. Principal Ricky stands up in front before the bus driver pulls away. "Students, I'm riding the school bus to let you kids know I'm here to support you and that I'm not going to tolerate any violence at Maple Landing High," he says while eyeing Jake and Ken. Principal Ricky sits down. The bus driver pulls away.

Jake and Jena sit next to each other on the bus.

"So?" Jake says.

"So what?" Jena replies.

"So, have you decided about the dance?"

"Jake, I don't want people to laugh at us."

Jake touches Jena's hand. "You mean you don't want people to laugh at you."

They both laugh. "You're a funny guy."

Jena turns and looks out the bus window. Jake begins to fantasize about Jena—just the way Jena turns her head and the sparkle in her beautiful eyes as she smiles, the softness of her neck, and even how he would kiss her if he had the chance. He fantasizes about how he'd romance Jena. He imagines himself walking to her door; she suddenly opens it wearing only an unbuttoned shirt, her long hair swaying in the wind. He slowly caresses one of her breasts while kissing her passionately. Without words being spoken, Jena motions with her finger for Jake to follow her into the house. Like a hypnotized maniac, he follows her into her house, leans her up against a wall, and then gently kisses her. "I want you to take me right here, Jake," he imagines Jena whispering. "I want you to take me right here, right now, Jake." He moves his hands underneath her blouse, but suddenly he is thrown back into reality when Jena's voice echoes on the bus, calling his name.

"Jake? Jake?" she calls. "Are you all right?"

Jake looks around the bus and then back at Jena. "Yeah, man, I don't know why I went into the zone, but I'm back now."

"Good," she says. "Because for a moment there, I thought you were turning into a zombie," Jena says in a creepy voice. The bus stops, and Jena gets up. "I'll see you tomorrow, zombie." "Yeah, sure," he replies.

Principal Ricky stands up as Jena passes him. He gives her a strange look and a creepy smile and winks at her. "You have a good night now," he says as he nods his head.

Jena has an uneasy feeling. "Thanks, Principal Ricky," Jena says as she hurries off the bus.

Mr. Parker is out in the front yard playing with the dog. Jena tries to walk quickly past her father. "Something wrong, Jena?" Mr. Parker looks back at Principal Ricky standing in the bus doorway.

"No, Dad. I just had a long day at school." Jena looks back at the bus. Principal Ricky is still standing in the bus doorway, and for moment, it seems like every male on the bus is staring at her. She runs into the house and closes the door quickly.

Mrs. Parker is in the kitchen cooking dinner. Jena tries to walk upstairs without her mother noticing her. "Jena?" Mrs. Parker calls. "Jena, honey, could you come into the kitchen?"

"Yes, Mom."

Mrs. Parker is bleeding from a small cut on her hand she'd gotten while chopping chicken. Jena walks into the kitchen and sees the blood running slowly from her mother's hand. She rushes over to her. "Mom, are you all right?"

"Yes, honey. It's just a small cut," she replies while wrapping her hand with a kitchen towel. "Jena, could you go upstairs and get me the first-aid kit?"

Jena turns and runs to the upstairs bathroom to get the first aid kit while her mom puts pressure on her wounded hand. She runs back downstairs. "Mom, you're bleeding very badly."

"Oh, it's not that bad, hon," Mrs. Parker replies. "I've had worse."

"Just hand me a big Band-aid, and I'll be just fine." Jena gets a Band-aid out of the can and helps her mom put it on. The bleeding stops. "Now, see? I'm okay." Jena and her mom laugh.

Mr. Parker walks into the kitchen. "Well, it looks like someone cut themselves again." He puts his hand on Mrs. Parker's shoulder. "I guess I'm cooking tonight," Mr. Parker says.

"Either that, or we're not going to eat," Mrs. Parker says with a smile.

Mr. Parker kisses her hand. "You know I'll cook, honey." He gives her a hug. "Now, it might not taste like much." "Dad, I'll cook," Jena says.

"No, honey, you go do your homework. I'll cook," Mr. Parker says. "But thanks for the offer."

Jena's mom kisses her. "Yeah, honey, thanks for offering. You go on up and start your homework, and we'll call you when dinner is ready."

"Okay, Mom."

Jena walks up the stairs and stops. She glances from the top of the stairs back down at her parents. Her dad is holding her mom in his arms and kissing her. Then he kisses her cut hand again. She listens while her parents laugh as her dad scrambles around the kitchen trying to cook dinner. Jena walks to her room and picks up a picture of her parents from her dresser mirror. It is an old picture of the two of them taken when Jena was three years old. The wind blows through her bedroom window as she walks to it so she can place her face in the blowing wind. Her window curtains are blowing from side to side as she gazes out at the night sky. The wind tosses her hair around her face. She stares across the street where the McNeil's live. The house is dark, and there are no cars in the driveway. She closes her window and curtain and walks back into the room. She sits on the bed.

A car horn blows loudly outside. Jena runs to her window and stands to the side so she can peek out without being observed. A car is waiting for two kids to move out of the street. Standing in his dark driveway is Mr. McNeil, staring up at Jena's window. At first, Jena isn't sure Mr. McNeil is looking at her, but the distance can't stop Jena from noticing his cold black eyes glaring at her. Jena quickly moves away from the window.

She turns off her room light, slowly walks back to the window, and peeks out again. Mrs. McNeil's car is now in the driveway. The lights in the house are on, and McNeil is no longer standing near his car. Jena slightly opens her window, and she can hear Mrs. McNeil calling for Mr. McNeil, but she gets no answer. She looks around the house, steps back in, and closes the front door. Jena continues to peek out her window, standing out of the way so no one can see her. At the edge of the house is where she spots Mr. McNeil kneeling down, hiding from his wife and peeking around the corner of the house to see if she is coming. Jena watches him carefully, trying not to be seen. She backs away from the window and sits down on her bed again. She turns on her desk lamp and opens up her math book. The phone suddenly rings, and Jena jumps. She picks up the phone, but Mrs. Parker had already answered it. Jena listens in. It is Jake's voice. She feels at ease.

"Hello?" Mrs. Parker says.

"Hi, Mrs. Parker, can I speak to Jena?"

Mrs. Parker calls for Jena, "Jena, telephone!"

Jena answers quickly, "Hi, Jake. What's up?"

"Not much," he says. "I just was thinking about you. I wanted to hear your beautiful voice."

"Oh." Jena blushes. She tries to act normal and break the ice.

"Jake, don't you have some homework to do?" Jake doesn't answer.

"Jake, are you there?"

In a disappointed voice, he says, "Yeah, I do, but I just wanted to talk to you for moment. I just wanted to check on you. I thought if I talked to you before you went to bed, you'd possibly dream about me again."

"Ha, ha, Jake. Very funny." Jena tries to peek out her window again while listening to Jake talk. "Jake, I like hearing your voice, but you're really, really getting weird on me. What's getting into you? You're starting to act like my creepy neighbor," she says, trying to be funny. "Are you sniffing glue again?" Jena asks with a smirk.

"Jena," Jake calls her name.

"Yes?" she replies while still peeking out the window.

"I've known you since we were in the second grade, right?"

"Yeah."

"And ever since the second grade, I've always …" He pauses.

"Well, I've always thought you were a very special person."

"Jake, I know. You're special to me too."

Stumbling on his words, Jake continues, "What I mean, Jena, is that …" Jake pauses again. "Never mind." "Jake, what are you trying to say?" "Jena!" Mrs. Parker yells.

"Jake, wait a minute. Mom is calling me." Jena puts the phone down.

"Five minutes to dinner, Jena!" Mrs. Parker yells.

"Jake, my mom just yelled for me. It's dinnertime." Trying to make him feel more comfortable, she adds, "And can you believe my dad cooked? So, what were you going to say?"

"I just wanted to tell you I appreciate your friendship."

Jena plays with the telephone cord. "Yeah, well, me too. Jake, I have to go. Mom is only giving me a few minutes to get downstairs. If you hurry, you can eat with us."

Jake is quiet. "Ah no, I think I'll pass on dinner tonight, although your mom is a great cook."

"Remember I just said my mom didn't cook tonight; she cut her hand, so my dad cooked."

"No! I'm definitely not coming," Jake says jokingly.

Jena and Jake laugh.

"Well, I have to go, Jake. I'll talk to you at school tomorrow."

"Okay, bye, Jena."

Jena hangs up the phone and heads downstairs. To her surprise, Mr. McNeil is sitting on the couch in the living room. She hesitates but walks slowly toward the kitchen.

"Hello, Jena." Mr. McNeil stands up. "Nice to see you again."

Jena stares at him. "Hello, sir," she answers. She walks into the kitchen.

Mr. Parker begins talking to Mr. McNeil. Mr. McNeil's eyes fixate on Jena as she walks toward the kitchen. He stares at her ass. Mr. Parker glances curiously at him. "Miles!" Mr. Parker says, giving Mr. McNeil a harsh look.

Trying to play it off, Mr. McNeil pats his head, "I'm just surprised at how much Jena's grown up. She's really grown into a lovely young lady."

"Yes, she has," Mr. Parker replies. "I'm very proud of her. Miles, it was nice of you to drop by, but it's dinnertime for the family."

Mr. McNeil chuckles as he tries to peek into the kitchen through the front door on his way out. Jena stands next to Mrs. Parker trying not to look in the living room. Mr. McNeil stands outside the front door but still has his body leaned up against it.

"I'll be leaving now, but let's get together for golf or catch a game," Mr. McNeil says.

"Yeah, sure, Miles, just let me know, and I'll check with the missus to see if I can get a guy's night out."

Mr. McNeil grins and pats Mr. Parker on the shoulder. "Still the dedicated husband, huh?"

"Oh yeah." Mr. Parker smiles.

"He better be!" Mrs. Parker yells from the kitchen. "It's either that or Ms. Couch tonight."

Jena makes her plate. She quickly glances from the kitchen as her father talks to Mr. McNeil through the door. She tries not to but locks eyes with Mr. McNeil. Mr. McNeil gives her a lecherous stare. Mr. Parker closes the front door and walks into the kitchen.

"That Miles hasn't changed since high school," he says. "He's still the same old jerk he's always been."

Jena sits down at the kitchen table. Mrs. Parker struggles with one hand to put the food on the table.

"Let me get that, hon. Come on, you know you can't do that."

"Yeah, Mom, you sit down, and we'll put the rest of the food out."

The doorbell rings. Mr. Parker heads for the front door. "I'll get it, Dad," Jena says. Jena goes to open the door, and it's Mr. McNeil again. Jena is a little uneasy. "I forgot my keys. Can't get in the house without those things." Mr. McNeil walks past Jena and lightly touches her. "Just let me get them really quick," he says.

"Who is it, Jena?" Mrs. Parker asks.

"It's just me, Kitty," Mr. McNeil says. "I forgot my keys."

"Well, get them, and get out; we're trying to eat dinner here."

"Sure thing, boss."

Jena stands in the doorway waiting for Mr. McNeil to get his keys. He grabs his keys, walks out the door, turns around, and winks at her. Mr. McNeil drops his keys on the ground intentionally to stare at Jena's legs. He tries to make conversation with her, but Mr. Parker walks up and stands next to her. He picks up the keys from the ground. He locks eyes with Mr. McNeil. "Here you go, Miles. Now good night." He slams the door in his face.

CHAPTER TWO

Jena stands still for a moment at the front door. Mr. Parker grabs her and hugs her tightly, trying to make her feel better.

"What a nuisance of a neighbor, huh, Jena?" He tries to make her laugh. "I made your favorite tonight." "What? Chicken?" Jena smiles.

"Ah, no, sweet peas!" He hugs Jena and smiles.

"Oh, Dad, that's not my favorite; that's yours." Jena doesn't eat much of her dinner. She plays with the sweet peas and lets her mashed potatoes drip from her folk.

"Jena, are you all right? You barely touched your food."

"Yes, Mom. I'm all right. I'm just tired from school today, and I still have homework to do."

"Jena, why don't you just try to eat something." "Okay, Mom," she replies.

As Mr. and Mrs. Parker talk at the dinner table, Jena remains quiet. She picks at her food, trying not to make it too obvious to her parents that she is feeling uneasy about Mr. McNeil. She thinks back to when Jake called her. What was he really trying to say to me? she wondered. Today has been a weird day. It's like I woke up in another universe.

Jena eats a spoonful of her dinner and heads upstairs. Her parents are too preoccupied with each other to notice that she hadn't touched any of her dinner. She opens her bedroom window.

A cool breeze is flowing through the room. The papers on her bed begin flapping around as if there were a small storm brewing up in her room, and then rain begins to fall. Jena sits on her bed just staring out her window. She listens to the rain as it hits the windowpane and the rooftop of her house. She tries to start her homework, but the wind starts to blow very hard. She lies on her bed and gently places her head on her pillow. Jena loves the rain because it always makes her sleepy. She begins to drift off to sleep. When Jena wakes up, it is 5:00 in the morning and she can hear her dad getting ready for work. He is humming the tune of a favorite song of his and her mother. She gets out of bed quickly to move her school papers and books from her bed to her nightstand before her dad comes into the room to wake her. She pretends that she is sleeping when her dad opens the door to her room.

"Jena?" Mr. Parker calls.

Jena pretends to wake up. "Yeah, Dad?" "Jena, it's almost time for school," he whispers.

"Yeah, okay," she says back.

Mr. Parker is a simple, hardworking man. He is up every morning at 4:00 and always peeks in to wake Jena for school.

"Thanks, Dad," Jena says gently. "Love you. Have a good day at work."

Mr. Parker closes Jena's door and continues to hum as he walks downstairs to the kitchen to get his lunch. He opens the refrigerator and remembers that he'd forgotten to make his lunch. "Damn, I forgot Kitty's hand," he says. "I forgot to make my lunch."

Jena can hear her dad stumbling around in the kitchen trying to make his lunch quickly. She tries to get out of bed, but she is so tired she instantly falls back to sleep. She begins to dream.

She is on an airplane, and the man sitting next to her is just staring at her. He won't speak to her. She tries to ask the man questions, but all he does is stare at her. The plane begins to wobble and spin out of control and then stabilizes. Throughout the tumble of the airplane, the man just stares at her. Jena looks around the airplane, and she realizes that there are only men on the airplane. Even the flight attendant is a man. She begins to cry, and one of the men walks up to her. "What are you doing on this airplane, young lady?" Jena just stares at him tearfully in her in confusion.

He asks again, "What are you doing on this plane?"

"I don't know," she answers. "I don't know how I got here. I was in my room, in my bed, and now I'm on this airplane. Can you tell me how I got here and how do I get off?"

The man doesn't say a word to Jena. He stands up and walks backward, away from her. He begins shaking his head no in fear. "No, I can't because once you're on this airplane, there is no getting off. I have been trying to get off. But once you're on this plane, you will never get off. I couldn't find a way out, and you won't either." The man continues to speak, "You'll find out why one day, and by that time, it will be too late."

Jena just stares out the window of the plane and then jumps up from her seat. The man sits back down in his seat and doesn't utter another word. He sits completely still as if nothing were going on. The plane begins to spin out of control. She panics and races to the emergency door.

She begins frantically trying to open the door by beating and shaking it. "Let me out! Let me out!" she yells. She pushes harder and harder while all the men on the plane just stare at her. No matter how hard she pushes, she can't get the door open. She turns around and leans up against the door. Sweat is pouring down her face. She takes a deep breath and then walks toward the front of the plane.

All of the men on the plane just stare at her with blanks looks on their faces. A sudden calmness comes over her. The men begin growling at her and clawing the seats of the plane. Jena stands and stares at the men without blinking an eye. She walks down the plane's aisle and stares each and every one of the men straight in the eyes. Jena can hear a voice calling her. "Jena! Jena!" Jena doesn't know where the voice is coming from. She sits back down in her seat and doesn't say a single word.

"Jena!" Mrs. Parker calls as she shakes her to wake her up. "Jena, wake up! You're late for school." "What time is it?" Jena asks.

"Honey, its six thirty, and you have to be at school at seven. You need to get up and get moving. Are you feeling all right?" Mrs. Parker feels Jena's forehead.

"Yeah, Mom." Jena gets up. "I just had this weird dream. I mean weird. I woke up earlier when Dad was getting ready to go to work; I must have fallen back asleep. I'm sorry."

"It's okay, hon. Just get ready, and I'll take you to school."

Jena rushes to the shower. She leans one arm against the shower wall. Water runs down her face and body. Her body is tired from the night before. What's wrong with me? she thought.

She flashes back to her dream when she first realized that she was on the airplane: how she felt so confused and lost and then at the end of the dream, how she felt powerful and changed. She lathers soap all over her body, rinses, and dries off with a towel. There is yelling outside. Jena glances out of her bedroom window. Mrs. McNeil is yelling and pointing as she walks behind Mr. McNeil. He is walking swiftly to his car. "You're an asshole!" she yells.

Mr. McNeil turns around. "You shut your mouth!" he yells. "You're always starting something." He gets into his car and slams the door. He sits in his car. Mrs. McNeil walks back into the house. Jena quickly closes her window curtains and starts getting dressed for school.

"Jena, honey, let's get moving!" Mrs. Parker yells. "I'll get the car running and ready to go."

"Okay, Mom." Jena finishes getting dressed and throws her books into her bag. She runs downstairs.

The doorbell rings. Mrs. Parker opens the door. Mr. McNeil is standing out front wearing a light-gray suit. "Hi, Kitty. How are you this wonderful morning?"

Mrs. Parker stands in the doorway surprised. "Good morning, Miles, and I'm fine. Something wrong?"

"Uh, I was on my way to work, and I saw your car running. Going somewhere?"

Mrs. Parker sighs. "Well, Jena is running late for school, so I'm going to take her."

"Kitty, you look like you hurt your hand last night."

"Yes, I cut it slightly while cooking dinner."

"Look, I'm on my way to work; why don't you just let me drop Jena off on my way? It'll save you some gas."

Jena walks down the stairs just as Mr. McNeil is offering to take her to school.

"Jena, is that all right with you? Miles said he doesn't mind dropping you off on his way to work."

Jena stops and doesn't say anything for second. She stares down and then straight at her mom. She tries not to let her mother know she is not okay with it. "Sure, Mom; it's all right."

"Great then, I'll just turn the car right off. Thanks, Miles."

Grinning, he says, "Kitty, we all went to school together and we're neighbors. Well, come on, Jena." Mr. McNeil waves. "Let's get going and get you to school."

Jena walks cautiously across the street to Mr. McNeil's car. Mrs. McNeil walks out, and Mr. McNeil gives her a sour look.

"Hi, Jena!" Mrs. McNeil yells and waves. She walks up to the car. "Getting a ride to school?" Mrs. McNeil glances at her husband. He doesn't look at her.

"Yes, ma'am," Jena answers. "I slept late this morning."

"Oh, honey, I remember those days when I was late for class," Mrs. McNeil begins to ramble. "Ah, those days were so long ago."

Mr. McNeil becomes impatient listening to his wife. "Okay, well, we're running late." Mr. McNeil hurries his wife up.

"Don't be a stranger, Jena." Mrs. McNeil gently touches Jena's hand. "I know being a teenager can be an awkward time, but we all get through it and then we get married. What a great combination, huh?" Mrs. McNeil steps away and stares as the car drives away.

Jena sits in the car still and silent. Mr. McNeil taps his fingers on the steering wheel. Jena tries to remain quiet to get through the ride. Mr. McNeil's eyes roam down to her legs. He continues driving down the street. "So, Jena, how are things at school?" Mr. McNeil tries to make conversation.

"Good, sir."

"You don't have to call me, sir," he answers.

Jena moves slightly closer to the passenger door. Mr. McNeil makes a turn on an unfamiliar street. "Mr. McNeil, this isn't the street that goes to my school," Jena says quietly.

He looks at Jena. "Don't worry; this is just a different route I take." He looks over at her. "When I want to avoid a lot of traffic."

Jena stares out her window. He is looking at her with dirty old-man eyes. "Don't worry, I will be at your school in no time."

Jena can see him moving his hand closer to hers. Her eyes widen. She clears her throat. He moves his hand back. "Jena, I've known your parents for a very long time. If you ever need anyone to talk to ..." A car pulls in front of Mr. McNeil almost causing an accident. "What an asshole!"

Jena swallows and puts her hand over her chest.

"Are you all right?" Mr. McNeil touches Jena's leg. She moves away quickly.

"Yes," Jena says in a panic.

Mr. McNeil pulls into the school drop-off zone. The school bell has just rung, and kids are rushing to get to class. "Here we are."

Jena quickly gets out of the car and closes the door. She walks away from the car without saying good-bye to Mr. McNeil. Mr. McNeil yells, "Jena!" She turns around. "Have a great day!" he says. She shakes her head and pulls her bag up on her shoulder.

"Thanks. Sorry, I was being rude," she says. "I'm just in a rush. Thanks for giving me a ride."

Mr. McNeil smiles and watches as she walks away. Not looking where she is going, Jena bumps into two girls strolling to class. The three girls drop their books and begin picking them up.

"Sorry, guys," Jena says. "I wasn't looking where I was walking."

"No shit," Carol says.

"Carol be nice; she didn't mean it. Hi, my name is Chance, and this is Carol."

"My name is Jena, the girl who can't seem to look where she's walking."

All three girls laugh.

"Are you new here, Jena?" Chance asks.

"No." Jena looks at Chance strangely. "I'm not new; I've been going to this school for the last four years."

"So, have we," Carol says rudely. "Where have you've been?"

"Hiding behind a rock."

"This is a big school," Carol says. "I'm sure we've passed each other at least a hundred times and just didn't know it." "A hundred times?" Chance says.

"At least," Carol replies.

"Yeah, this is a big school," Jena says. "Well, I gotta go, guys." Jena picks up one of her books from the ground. "I'm already late." She begins walking toward her class.

"Hey, Jena!" Chance yells. "Want to hang out after school?"

Jena stands and thinks for a second. Realizing that she doesn't have many friends, she replies, "Sure."

"We'll meet here at the hit spot," Carol jokes.

"Okay!" Jena yells.

The school bells rings, and Jena begins running to her class. She's one minute late, and Mr. McDuffery isn't too happy about that. Jena tries to close the classroom door quietly. "No need to be quiet, Jena, the entire class can see that you're late," Mr. McDuffery says.

"Sorry, Mr. McDuffery."

Jena moves toward her seat. "I woke up late, and I—"

Mr. McDuffery cuts her off. "Okay, Jena, thanks, but for now, just have a seat."

Jena sits next to Jake, who's grinning because she's late. There's a white rose on her desk. Jena looks at Jake and starts smiling. "Thanks, for the flower."

Mr. McDuffery catches Jena talking to Jake. "Jena, so you want to be late and talk in my class during no-talking time?" Mr. McDuffery asks. "Please be quiet. Everyone please turn to page fifty-five, chapter ten; this is where we will start today—or should have started two minutes ago." Mr. McDuffery just looks at Jena with a disapproving look on his face. Everyone in the class turns to page 55, except Jake.

Jake raises his hand.

"Yes, Mr. Paterson?"

"I apologize, Mr. McDuffery. I accidently left my book at home," Jake says.

"Accidently?" Mr. McDuffery replies.

"Yes," Jake says. "What if I accidently give you a failing grade for today?"

The class laughs.

"Just look on with Jena, please," Mr. McDuffery replies.

Jake moves his desk closer to Jena's and smiles. The class seems to last forever. Jake flirts with Jena with his eyes throughout the class. The bell rings, and everyone can't wait to get out of Mr. McDuffery's classroom. "Jena!" Mr. McDuffery calls before Jena leaves his room. "I didn't mean to embarrass you today. We all have our bad days, and yours happened to be today." Mr. McDuffery hands Jena a paper he had graded with an "A." "Maybe this will cheer you up," he says.

"Thanks, Mr. McDuffery." Jena smiles and continues walking out of the room with Jake.

"What did he say to you?" Jake asks.

"He just wanted to apologize," Jena replies.

"At least he didn't give you a late slip to take to the office like I got. "When I was late, he gave me detention," Jake says.

"Jake, you came to class when it was almost over," Jena says. "I, on the other hand, was only one minute late. I don't think you can compare the two."

They both laugh and walk toward their next class. Jena stops laughing and gets a serious look on her face "Jake, do you dream? I mean, do you have, like, weird dreams? Dreams you don't understand?"

"Sometimes, Jena."

Jena looks away, trying not to remember the horrible dream she had. Jake can see that the dream she had worries her. He tries to change the subject. "So, what are you doing after school?" "I've been invited out," she replies.

Shocked, he asks, "By who?"

"By two girls I accidently bumped into before class. Well, let's get to class before I'm late for this one too." Jena rushes off. "See you after school, Jake."

Jake waves good-bye. Jena walks into the classroom and for the first-time notices Chance sitting in the far back of the room. She walks to the back. "Hi, Chance. I never noticed that you were in this class," Jena says.

Chance stands up. "I never noticed you either."

The two girls stand there with nothing else to say. "I'm just going to take my seat." Jena points in the direction of her usual seat.

"Okay." Chance sits back down.

The school day seems to drag on, and Jena can't seem to get the dream she had out of her mind. After school, Jake is standing by the bus stop waiting for her. Jena walks up to him. "I'm so happy this day is over," she says. "Where's the bus?" "Late, as usual," Jake says.

Principal Ricky walks out and starts yelling at some kids for fooling around.

"Jena, are you all right?" Jake asks.

"Did I tell you that I got a ride with Mr. McNeil this morning?"

"No," Jake replies.

"That guy is weird."

Jena starts telling Jake about her experience with Mr. McNeil on her way to school. Her voice fades out as he just focuses on her lips and eyes. "So that's what happened," Jena says.

Trying to act like he had been listening, he says, "Yeah, you're right; he's a real weirdo."

CHAPTER THREE

The school bus pulls up, and Jena and Jake get on the bus. Ken makes a joke from the back of the bus. "Jena, why don't you come back here and sit with us?"

"No, thanks, Ken." Everyone on the bus starts laughing.

Jake turns around. "Man, just leave her alone."

Ken backs down. "Oh, Jake, come on, we're just joking around."

Jake looks around the bus. "Who are we? Because you're the only one talking." Jake turns back around. "Okay, man. I'll leave your girlfriend alone." Jake stands up.

"Jake, stop." Jena touches his arm.

The bus driver yells out to Jake to take his seat and for Ken to shut his mouth. Jake sits down, and Jena sits next to him. "Hey, do you think it was Ken who gave me the flower?" she whispers.

"Maybe it was Principal Ricky," Jake says in a joking tone.

"What?" Jena replies. "What would make you think it was Principal Ricky?" Jena asks.

Jake shrugs his shoulders. "It was what he said to you before we got on the bus. Do you remember?" Jake replies. "And the fact that he's creepy. Just look at him."

"Just think of what you're saying, Jake? You think that Principal Ricky has a crush on me?"

"Yeah," Jake replies. "A big, huge one." Jake starts laughing.

"Stop laughing, Jake." Jena tugs on his shirt.

"So, it could be him or not, but if it is him, I'll take care it, Jena, if you want me to."

"What are you gonna do?"

"Well, I can walk up to Principal Ricky and say, 'Hey, leave Jena alone; she's my girl.'"

Jena starts laughing. "Jake, Principal Ricky knows we aren't dating; he was our second-, third-, and fourth-grade teacher, and now he's our principal. He knows we're just good friends."

"Yeah, but … maybe that will make him back off."

"Just don't do anything, Jake," Jena says. "Because I still don't know for sure if it was Principal Ricky who sent me the flower, and I don't want to get you in trouble. Besides, look at this flower. They both look at the flower on her lap. "It's beautiful, and I'm just glad someone out there is thinking of me." She looks up at him with a smile.

Time suddenly freezes for Jake for a moment; he is mesmerized by her smile. He examines every curve of her mouth, every dimple on her face, and those eyes, those beautiful eyes just keep him hypnotized. Jena snaps her fingers. Jake bounces back to reality. "Even if it's Principal Ricky who sent them, so what? I have a secret admirer who finds me attractive." Jena grabs Jake by the nose and squeezes.

Jake just looks at Jena and nods his head. He thinks to himself; I love you, Jena. If only I could tell you that I sent the rose and if only I could tell you how much I want, you and how much I love you. The bus stops. Jena stares at her house. "Okay, here's my stop." She stands up. "See you tomorrow, stud. I gotta go in to do some serious homework. Oh wait!" Jena stops.

"What?" Jake asks.

"I was supposed to be hanging out with those two girls I met, Chance and Carol. I forgot about it because of the whole flower thing. Oh well." Jena walks off the bus. "I'll see tomorrow. Bye, Jake."

Jena gets off the bus and walks toward her house. Mr. McNeil is standing in his front yard. He has a dozen roses in his hand. The bus driver pulls away, and Mr. McNeil waves and walks toward Jena. Jena tries to hurry inside. "Hey, Jena!" Mr. McNeil calls. He runs to catch up with her.

"Hi," she answers, out of breath.

"Wow, I haven't seen you since when?" he says, trying to make a joke. "Oh, I know, since I dropped you off this morning." Mr. McNeil stands and speaks to Jena while tightly gripping the dozen roses in one hand. He holds his briefcase in the other. Jena stares at the roses, which look similar to the rose she has.

"Nice flowers, Mr. McNeil," she says in a hesitant voice. "These are for my wife." Jena sighs with relief.

"I thought I'd make up for our fight this morning."

Jena stares intently at the roses Mr. McNeil is holding. The roses seem similar to the rose left on her desk, and it looks like one of the roses is missing from the bunch. "Mr. McNeil, it looks like the flower shop may have shorted you one rose."

Mr. McNeil looks at the rose bunch. "Oh, damn, you're right, Jena. I paid for a dozen, and I got eleven." He widens his eyes at her. "Well, hopefully the little missus won't look as hard as you did and notice the missing rose." Mr. McNeil's eyes zoom in on Jena's rose. "Looks like someone was thinking of you today too, huh?" Mr. McNeil points a finger at Jena's flower.

"Yes, someone left me a rose on my desk. I don't know who it was, but I'm sure whoever it was, was only trying to be nice."

Mrs. McNeil pulls up in her car. Mr. McNeil tries to hide the flowers behind his back. Mrs. McNeil gets out of the car, and Mr. McNeil walks over to her and hands her the roses. They begin kissing and walking away toward the house. They pay no attention to Jena. She just watches the two laugh and cuddle as they walk into the house.

Jena thinks to herself, There is no way it could be Mr. McNeil. Wow, just this morning, she was a raging bull, and he was the biggest jerk, but look how in love they seem to be! Jena walks away shaking her head. "It wasn't him. Why would Mr. McNeil want to give me a flower?"

The mystery of the flower stays on Jena's mind. As she starts to walk toward the house, a car pulls up and starts honking its horn very loudly. A voice yells out to Jena, "Hey, Jena! You stood us up!" It was Chance and Carol.

Very surprised, Jena says, "Hey, guys, how did you know where I live?"

"Jena, this is a small town. Everyone knows where everyone lives," Chance replies. "So, are we still on?"

"Yeah, sure. Just let me put my stuff in the house and tell my mom I'll be back later." Jena walks into the house. She can smell the aromas of her Mom's great cooking coming from the kitchen.

"Mom! Mom!" Jena yells.

"I'm upstairs," Mrs. Parker yells back.

Jena quickly runs upstairs. "Mom, can I go out for a little while? I met these two girls at school, and well, you know, I don't usually go anywhere, so I told them I would hang out today."

"Sure, Jena, it's okay with me," she replies. "I'm sure your dad will be fine with it too, so go have some fun for a change. Just make sure you're home by dinner."

Jena runs up to her room quickly to put her stuff away. She glances into the mirror, brushes her hair, pats on a little makeup, and then runs back downstairs. "See ya, Mom!" she yells.

Jena hops into the backseat. Chance turns the music way up, and the two girls in front start singing along with the song. Chance yells to Jena over the music, "Jena, do you like this song?

This song really rocks." Jena just nods her head.

Chance tries to speak over the music. So, you like pool?" "What?" Jena replies.

Chance turns the radio down. "Do you like playing pool?" "Oh yeah, it's cool," Jena replies.

"Jena, I'm so glad you could hang out with us," Chance says.

"So where are we going?" Jena asks.

"We're going to a place called Topaz. It's like a bar but kids our age can hang out there. Do you know how to shoot pool?" "I've never played pool before," Jena replies.

"We'll teach you. Right, Carol?" Chance looks over to Carol.

Carol looks back at Chance with a smirk. "You mean Ken will teach her; he's the expert."

Jena leans forward. "Why is Ken going to be there?"

Chance and Carol ignore her. "Hey, Chance, maybe we'll see that hot guy again too."

The two girls start laughing. "Maybe he can teach all of us a thing or two."

"You're bad, Carol," Chance says.

The two girls start laughing louder. Jena just sits quietly for a moment and then laughs lightly, pretending to get the joke. Chance pulls up to Topaz; it is a biker club located across town. Several older male and female bikers are standing around their bikes drinking and smoking cigarettes.

Jena has a frightened look on her face. "Guys, is this place safe?" Jena asks.

"Is anywhere safe?" Carol replies. "Yes, it's safe, Jena," she continues. "We come here to hang out all the time." Carol looks back at Jena with a disappointed look on her face. "Are you scared?"

"No," Jena replies.

"Do you think we would bring you to an unsafe place?" Carol is trying to intimidate Jena. Jena just stares at her.

"I don't see any other kids our age here." Jena looks at the older bikers.

Carol tries to get confrontational. "Maybe there are inside, Jena."

"Carol, please just shut up." Chance points a finger at her.

A crowd of high school guys walks out of the building. "See, look, there's Ken and his friends." Oh great, Jena thinks.

"What's wrong, Jena?" Chance asks.

"Oh, Ken is just the only person in the world who doesn't like me. He picks on me almost every day," Jena replies.

"Not today, Jena." Chance grabs Jena and pulls her closer to her. "Because you're my friend now and you're with us. Besides, Ken's my boyfriend, and I'll kick his butt if he does or says anything bad to you."

Jena is surprised. She thinks to herself, I never saw Ken with Chance, but I guess I never really paid attention either, because I never noticed Carol and Chance at school. How is that possible? I mean, where have I been for the last four years?

Ken walks up to the car and kisses Chance on the lips. "Hi, babe."

Carol tries to make him take notice of her. "What about me, Ken?"

In a low voice, he says, "Hi, Carol," while still kissing Chance. He's trying to ignore her. He glances in the backseat and notices Jena. "What is she doing here?" Ken asks.

"We asked her to hang out with us," Carol replies quickly.

Chance grabs his face. "And you better not say one damn thing to her, or I'll kick your ass."

"Calm down, Chance," Carol replies. "He's not going to do anything."

Chance kisses Ken on the cheek. "Ken, she's our friend, so that means you be a nice little boyfriend, or I may become an enraged girlfriend, and you don't want that." Chance grabs Ken's jaw and shakes his head. Then she kisses his lips really hard.

"Of course not, babe. You know I don't want my lady being mad at me." Ken gives his buddy standing next to him a thumbs up. "I'll be nice tonight."

"No, Ken, you will be nice always. Got it?" Chance says.

Ken kisses Chance on the forehead. "Got it," he says. Trying to be friendly, he says, "So what's up, Jena?" He reaches his hand out to her.

She lightly touches him.

"Don't worry, I promise I will be a complete gentleman."

Ken's other friends yell out to him. "Hey, man, let's go inside!"

"Hold on, guys!" He yells back. "Let's go, babe."

Carol quickly gets out of the car, and Ken just stares at her. He opens the door for Chance. "You too, Jena. Let's roll." Ken keeps the car door open for Jena. He puts his arms around Chance and whispers something into her ear. Chance smiles and kisses him again. Carol becomes angry. Inside the building, country music is playing, and two drunken bikers are trying to dance without falling down.

"Look at those two freaks!" Ken says. He starts laughing out loud.

"Is there something funny, kid?" one of the drunken men asks.

"No," Chance says quickly to avoid a confrontation.

"Well, yeah," Ken says.

"Ken, stop!" Chance yells. She doesn't want him to start a fight.

He continues, "We're laughing at your stupid asses trying to dance," Ken says to the man.

One of the drunken men walks toward Ken. The club bouncer begins to move closer to him, ready to intervene. "Hey, Ernie, just cool it man, because you know I'll put your ass out," the bouncer says, holding a pool stick. "And kid?" The bouncer points at Ken. "Shut up because I'll put your ass out too. You're lucky I let you stay. If I didn't know your bro Mark, you and your monkey friends would be out of here. So, don't say another damn word, all right?"

"Got it."

The bouncer walks away and knocks one of the drunken bikers down. "Get up, you jerk."

Ken wraps his arms tightly around Chance and tries not to say anything. The two drunken bikers continue to dance. Ken reaches for the pool stick. "See, I told you that those two bikers were freaks," Ken says.

"Well, if they're freaks, and they're in this bar, then what are we?" Carol asks.

"We are a group of high school seniors that makes this place feel like gold," Ken replies.

All of them except Jena start high-fiving and laughing.

"Now, let's shoot some pool," Carol says.

Ken pays for the pool table and grabs the pool sticks.

"Okay, who's going to teach Jena how to play pool?" Chance asks. Everyone stares at one another. Chance and Carol stare at Ken.

"Come on, guys." Ken raises both his hands up to gesture that he doesn't want to teach Jena.

"It's okay, guys; I really don't want to play," Jena says. Chance gives Ken a dirty look.

"You're playing pool, young lady. Come here, Jena." Ken reaches for her. "You get in front, and I'll stand behind you and show you how to play pool."

"Don't get too happy, Ken." Chance folds her arms. Ken blows her a kiss and smiles. He stands behind Jena with his body close enough to embrace hers. Jena feels a little uncomfortable, but she continues to allow Ken to teach her. Ken puts his hand on Jena's and shows her how to shoot a ball into the pool table pocket. Just then, Jake walks in and is instantly angry that Ken is embracing Jena. Jake goes crazy with the thought of Ken touching Jena. In his mind, Ken is pretending to teach her how to play pool only to get close to her. Jake stares angrily at the both of them, and he walks up to the pool table. Jena looks up at Jake in surprise. Ken backs away from Jena.

"Jake, what are you doing here?" Jena asks in a surprised voice.

"Jena, the question isn't what am I doing here, but what the hell is this jerk doing touching you?" Unable to hold back his anger, Jake yanks the pool stick out of Jena's hand. Ken pushes Jena out of the way and picks up a pool stick. The two boys stand face-to-face, ready to fight.

CHAPTER FOUR

Jena tries to get in between Ken and Jake. "Stop! You guys we're all eighteen, but you two are acting like you're two years old." Jena walks closer to Jake. "Jake, I came out here with Chance and Carol. I didn't know Ken was Chance's boyfriend." Jake looks over to Chance.

"What are you doing here? How did you know I was here?" Jena asks.

"I went by your house, and your mom told me you had left with two girls. I figured it was Chance and Carol, and since I knew where they hang out, I decided to come by to surprise you, but I guess I got the surprise with Ken's arms all wrapped around you."

"Jake, it's not like that," Jena tries to calm things down. "Ken was just showing me how to play pool." "I bet," Jake replies.

"Man, why don't you get the heck out of here?" Ken says, as he moves closer to Jake, pushing Jena out of the way.

"You're being silly, Jake." Jena tries to intervene again.

"Am I?" Jake stares back at Ken.

"Yes, you're being silly." Jena grabs the pool stick out of his hand. "Jake, let's just leave, okay?"

Jena tries to grab Jake's arm, but he pulls it away.

"Ken walks over to Jake. "What's your problem, man? I mean, do you really want to start some shit in this place?" Ken gets closer to Jake's face.

"Do you?" Jake replies,

"Look, I was just showing her how to play a simple game of pool, and here you come, trying to play the hero, as if you were rescuing someone."

"Ken, stop! We don't want a fight!" Chance breaks in.

Ken turns and looks at Chance with an angry face. "Look, Chance, he's the one who came here and interrupted our pool game, and you want me to stop?"

In a panicked voice, she says, "Yes, I do."

Ken pokes Jake in the chest. "Well, I'm not going to. I gonna shut this guy up once and for all," Ken replies.

"Jena, get out of the way before you get hurt!" Carol yells.

Chance grabs Jena and pushes her out of the way. "Guys, stop!" Jena yells, trying to keep the two boys from getting any closer. "Jake let's just go; let's just leave this place and go home," Jena says, her voice shaking with fear. "You don't have to fight."

The bouncer comes out from his boss's office in the back of the club. "Hey, you two!" he yells. "You fight in this bar, and I'll kick both of your asses."

Neither Jake nor Ken back down. The bouncer walks over. "You think I'm kidding? I will mess the both of you up!" He's getting angry. "You know what? All of you get the hell out of here!" A sudden noise of glass breaking comes from the other side of the room. Two bikers are about to fight. One of the bikers punches another one in the stomach and then the face, picks him up, and throws him over the bar. The bouncer runs over to try to stop the two bikers from fighting. Chance grabs Ken's hand to pull him away, but he jerks away from her. Jena is still in the middle of the two, and she puts her hands on Ken's and Jake's chests to try to stop them from getting any closer, but Ken pushes her out of the way, and she falls to the floor. Jake throws a punch and hits Ken in face, and the two boys start fighting. Ken picks up a chair and hits Jake over the back. Jake falls to the floor, and Ken begins punching him in the face and stomach. Chance runs over and tries to stop Ken, but Ken's friends pull her back.

"Let them fight," one of the guys says.

The bouncer is still trying to stop the two bikers from fighting. He begins fighting with the both of them. Chairs and glasses are broken everywhere. One of the bikers pulls out a knife. He stabs the other biker in the stomach and cuts the bouncer on the arm. The bouncer stares down at his bleeding arm. He walks up to the biker, grabs his neck, and chokes him up against a wall. The biker stabs the bouncer in the shoulder. The knife sticks there, and the bouncer continues to choke the biker, who's still pressed against the wall. The bouncer lifts the biker up in the air by the neck and throws him over the bar. The biker slams into the liquor bottles behind the bar before hitting the floor. The stabbed biker lies bleeding on the floor. Ken is still beating on Jake. Jake is unable to move. His face is bruised, and his nose is broken. Jena, Chance, and Carol are all screaming for Ken to stop, but Ken's friends hold the girls back. The bouncer turns around; he still has the knife in his shoulder. He runs over to Ken, picks him up by his jacket, and throws him over a table. Ken hits his head and is knocked unconscious. Jake is on the floor still in pain from all the hits he took from Ken. Chance runs over to Ken. Carol calls 911 for an ambulance.

Jena kneels down to help Jake, and she starts crying. "Jake, oh my God! Jake, please be all right! I'm so sorry, Jake."

Chance tries to talk to Ken, but he does not answer her. Tears are flowing down Jena's face. "Jake, please say something, please," she pleads.

Jake tries to open one of his eyes. The police and paramedics come rushing into the room. One of the EMS teams checks Ken, and the other checks Jake's vitals. Ken is still unconscious. The EMS team quickly puts Ken on a stretcher to take him to the hospital. Jake is put on another stretcher. Both of the boys are hauled in the same ambulance to the hospital. EMS then checks the stabbed biker on the floor. The biker is pronounced dead at the scene. Another team is called in to treat the bouncer for the stab wound and the other biker, who is knocked out behind the bar.

A police officer interviews Chance, Carol, Jena, and the bouncer to find out what happened. It is Officer Reyes, but Jena doesn't recognize him from her dream. He walks over to the bouncer who is being treated by one of the paramedics. "So, what happened here, Ernie?" Officer Reyes asks.

The bouncer looks around the room with the knife still lodged in his arm. "Well, it looks like we had a fight. Isn't that obvious, Reyes?"

"Look, just because you've been stabbed doesn't mean I won't haul your ass downtown," Officer Reyes replies. "So, while we are waiting for an ambulance to come get your sorry ass, how about telling me what the hell happened here?"

Ernie sighs. "We had several fights, and as you can see, I got stabbed trying to break up the fights." He continues, "That's all I'm going to say. If you want more, you'll have to talk to my lawyer."

Officer Reyes looks around the room. He stands quietly staring at the bouncer. "I'll see you again." He calls for the ambulance to come get the bouncer and take him to the hospital. Officer Reyes walks over to Jena, who is still in shock. "Hello, my name is Officer Reyes," he says.

Jena doesn't say anything. "What's your name, ma'am?" Jena has tears in her eyes. "My name is Jena." "Jena what?" Officer Reyes asks. "Jena Parker."

"Okay, Jena Parker, can you tell me what happened here?"

Jena tries to talk though her sobs, but she can't get the words to come out. "Ah … Well …" She struggles to speak.

Officer Reyes stands and stares at Jena with a pen and pad in his hand.

"Ken and Jake were arguing over me, and then they got into a fight. Ken hit Jake with a chair. Jake fell to floor and …" Jena begins crying harder. "And I don't know … I don't know."

Trying to comfort Jena, he says, "Okay, Jena, just take your time; everything will be all right." Officer Reyes pats Jena on the shoulder.

Chance and Carol walk over to Jena and Officer Reyes. "Were you two young ladies here when the fights broke out?" Officer Reyes asks.

Chance and Carol look at one another. Before Chance can answer, Carols says, "Yes, but we didn't see everything that was going on. I mean, we just don't know who started the fight," she adds.

Jena just stares at both Chance and Carol in disbelief. "Okay, so what did you see?" Officer Reyes asks.

"Well, Officer, there was so much going on at the same time that we just don't know what happened," Chance repeats.

"Yes, Officer, there was just too much going on, and, well, we couldn't keep track of everything," Carol says.

Officer Reyes taps his pen on his head. Chance stares at Carol and Jena. Jena looks at Officer Reyes with tears in her eyes. She shifts her gaze to Chance and Carol. "Can we leave?" Chance asks. "One of the guys who got hurt is my boyfriend, and I'm very worried about him," Chance pleads.

"I will need both of your full names and parents' phone numbers," Officer Reyes says. "I'm Carol Jones."

"I'm Chance Middleton."

"And what are the names of the boys who were fighting?" Officer Reyes asks.

"Ken Stewart and Jake Paterson," Chance replies. "Now can we leave?"

"Okay, you girls can go, but you are directed to go straight home to your parents first," Officer Reyes replies. He walks away to speak to the other officers on the scene.

"Let's go, guys. We need to get to the hospital."

"Didn't you hear what that police officer just said? We have to go home first," Jena says, still sobbing.

"He said we should go home to our parents, not that we had too. He's not my dad," Carol says.

"He's going to tell our parents," Jena replies.

"So what? I need to see Ken, and you need to see Jake," Chance replies.

"So? He's gonna tell our parents anyway," Carol says.

"Let's just go to the hospital for a second, and then we'll go home," Chance insists.

"No," Jena says in an angry voice. "You guys take me home first. I'm not gonna get myself into any more trouble."

"Okay, we will drop you off, and then we'll go," Chance says.

The three girls walk out of the building. It is getting dark outside, and the parking lot is empty except for their own car, the police cruisers, and the owner's car. Jena quickly jumps into the car's backseat. Sitting quietly in the backseat of the car, Jena is upset about Jake getting hurt. She thinks back to the funny conversation they'd had on the bus earlier about the mysterious flower and how close Jake and she had become over the years. She can see Chance looking back at her in the rearview mirror. She becomes angry thinking about when Officer Reyes asked Chance and Carol what happened in the club and they both lied and how she felt pressured not to tell Officer Reyes that Chance and Carol were liars, that they saw everything, and they knew what really happened. Chance pulls over to the curb in front of Jena's house.

Jena gets out and begins to walk away.

"Jena, I'm sorry."

Jena turns around. Tears flow down her cheeks. She doesn't say anything. Chance drives away. Mr. McNeil is standing in his front yard watering his plants. He stares at the two girls as they drive away. Jena walks into her house, closes the door, and then turns around to look through the door peephole. Mr. McNeil is standing in his front yard staring over at Jena's house. He grips the water hose tightly as the water runs down his pants to his shoes. Jena breathes quickly and panics. She looks down to the floor and turns around to lean against the door.

CHAPTER FIVE

Jena can feel her heart beating out of control. She takes in a deep breath and then turns around to peek through the hole again.

"Jena, what are you doing?" Mrs. Parker asks. She's standing in the kitchen doorway waiting for her. Jena turns around quickly. Mrs. Parker walks toward Jena. She can tell Jena is scared.

"Jena, are you all right?" Mrs. Parker touches her forehead. "We got a call from an Officer Reyes that some high school kids were involved in a fight at a bar. What's going on?"

Jena just breaks down in tears. Mrs. Parker puts her arms around her and walks her to the living room couch. Mrs. Parker sits Jena down on the couch and takes a seat next to her. "Jena, what happened, honey? The officer said Jake, Ken, and some other people at the bar got hurt, that they're both on their way to the hospital."

"Yes, Mom, they're both hurt, and it's all because of me! It's all my fault!" Jena cries.

"What do you mean it's your fault?" Mrs. Parker asks. "How do you have anything to do with these two boys being in the hospital?"

"Because they were fighting over me, Mom!" Jena yells. "I went to this place with Chance and Carol, and Ken was there. Mom, I didn't know Ken was going to be there, but then Jake showed up and he saw Ken helping me learn how to play pool, and I guess he got mad and jealous. They got into an argument, and then it led to a fight. Oh, Mom, it was just so terrible, Jake getting hurt." Jena wipes the tears from her eyes and cheeks.

Mrs. Parker pats Jena on the back. "Oh, Jena, it's not your fault. You didn't make those two boy's fight. They decided to fight on their own. You can't take responsibility for someone getting hurt if you didn't cause it. I'm sorry Jake and the other kid got hurt, but both of them made a choice to fight." Mrs. Parker stands up. "I'm sure Jake will be all right."

Jena stands up too. "Mom, I need to go see Jake. Officer Reyes told all of us to go home first, but I really need to know Jake is all right."

"Jena ..." Mrs. Parker answers in concerned voice.

"Mom, I have to go see him. Please take me," Jena pleads.

"Jena, I think I should speak to your father about what happened today first."

"Mom, please! If you tell Dad now, I'll never see Jake. Please, Mom, just take me up there. Can't we just tell Dad later?" Jena runs and hugs her mom tightly.

"Okay, Jena, I'll take you to see Jake. First, let me call Mrs. Paterson to let her know we are going to the hospital to see Jake."

"Mom, Mrs. Paterson is probably at the hospital with Jake."

"Yes, you're right. Well, let's go." Mrs. Parker grabs her purse and her keys, and they both head outside to get into the car.

Mr. McNeil is still standing in his yard. Jena gets into the car. Just as Mrs. Parker opens her car door, Mr. McNeil calls to her, "Hey, Kitty! Is there something going on, something wrong with Jena?"

Trying to avoid him, she says, "No, we're just headed out. Be back later." Mrs. Parker quickly gets into her car to head to the hospital.

The hospital emergency parking lot is crowded. Mrs. Parker turns in. "Oh, Jena, this doesn't look like a good night for the hospital." They walk into the hospital building. Several friends of

Ken's and Jake's are standing outside. Jena holds her head down as she walks into the hospital building. "Jena!" Chance calls. "What's up?"

"I'm here to see Jake," Jena answers softly.

"I went to see Ken, but his mother wouldn't let me see how he was doing." Chance grabs Jena's hand. "I don't think she likes me very much."

Jena puts her hand on Chance's shoulder. "If I see or hear anything, I'll let you know."

"Thanks, Jena," Chance replies.

Jena and Mrs. Parker walk to the hospital emergency room counter. The nurse is sitting at the desk reading a magazine. Mrs.

Parker taps on the counter.

"Yes, may I help you?" the nurse asks.

"Yes, we are friends of Jake Paterson. Could you tell us what room he is in?"

The nurse types in Jake's name. "He is on the second floor, room 201."

"Thank you." Mrs. Parker reaches for Jena's hand. "Come on, Jena, let's go upstairs."

Mrs. Parker and Jena walk to the elevator and get in. Jena notices that a man has followed them onto the elevator. The elevator doors close. The man stands next to the wall and stares at Jena. Trying not to look at the man, Jena pushes the second-floor button and then turns to the man. "I'm going to the second floor as well," the man whispers to Jena. The elevator door opens at the second floor, and Jena and Mrs. Parker walk off the elevator. Jena looks back, but the man isn't there.

"Mom, what happened to the man that was on the elevator?" she asks.

"What man, Jena?" Mrs. Parker replies as she looks back. "It was only you and I on that elevator." She gently grabs Jena's face. "Are you all right, honey? Are you up to this? Maybe we should go home. You've had a very stressful day. Why don't you just lie down and see Jake tomorrow."

"Mom, we're already here, and I have to see Jake tonight," Jena insists. "I'm sure he is waiting for me to come see him. If I were hurt in the hospital, I know he would do whatever it took to see me."

Feeling sympathy for Jena's pain, she says, "I understand, honey. I know you care about Jake."

"I'm all right, Mom. I mean, I was upset earlier, and I still am a little, but Jake and I are friends and I need to be here for him now," Jena replies.

Jena and Mrs. Parker walk down the hall toward Jake's room. Jake's father is standing in the hallway speaking to his doctor. Mr. Paterson stops what he's doing to speak to Mrs. Parker and Jena as they walk toward him. Mr. Paterson walks up and gives Jena a hug.

"Jena, are you all right?" Mr. Paterson asks.

"Mr. Paterson, I'm so sorry for what happened to Jake," Jena replies.

"It's okay, Jena. Jake is barely speaking, but he told us it was his fault and not yours." Mr. Paterson hugs Jena again.

Mrs. Paterson walks out of Jake's hospital room. She hugs Jena too. "Jena, are you all right, honey? Hi, Kitty," she says as she hugs Mrs. Parker.

Mrs. Parker reaches for Cindy Paterson's hand. "Jena and I wanted to come and see how Jake was doing. Jena is very worried about him."

"Well, Jake's doing okay," Cindy replies. "As well as can be expected."

Jena walks closer to Jake's room door. Jake is hooked up to several tubes and machines. His eyes are closed. "Can I see him?" she asks.

"Sure," Cindy answers. "His eyes are closed, but he's kind of awake. The nurse just gave him a mild sedative to help him sleep through the pain. I'm not sure how long he will be awake."

She walks through Jake's hospital room door and up to his bedside. Jake's eyes are closed, and the television in the room is on. His face has some bandages on it, and one of his arms is in a sling.

Jena gently touches his hand. Jake doesn't move. She stands over him, watching him sleep. Jake smiles, and in groggy voice, he tries to speak. "I bet you thought I was asleep," he says. "I just wanted to feel your hand on mine without saying anything, just for a moment."

"I'd squeeze it if I thought it wouldn't bring you more pain."

He barely whispers back, "Hi, you." Jake slightly and painfully smiles at Jena.

"Jake, I'm so sorry."

Jake shakes his head slowly. He whispers to her, "No, don't be." His eyes begin to close. The medicine the nurse gave him is beginning to take full effect. He falls asleep.

"Rest, my sweet Jake." Jena gently reaches over to kiss Jake on the forehead, and then she turns to walk out of the room. Jena overhears Mrs. Paterson speaking to her mother.

"Jake's doctor said that he may be in the hospital for at least a week."

Jena walks toward them. "He fell asleep on me, but I think he'll be all right," she says in a relieved voice. Mrs. Parker and the Paterson's continue to talk.

Jena notices a girl from her school dressed as a candy striper.

She walks over to speak to her. "Susan, is that you?" Jena asks.

"Hi, Jena," Susan replies.

"What are doing here, and why are you dressed like that?" Jena asks.

"I'm a volunteer for the hospital, Jena. You know, a candy striper." Susan turns away to show off her work outfit. "Like my outfit?"

"So, you're here all the time?" Jena asks.

"No, just sometimes after school and on the weekend, if they need me."

"Can anyone be a candy striper?" Jena asks.

Susan lifts one of her eyebrows. "Yeah, I guess so. Just go see Ms. Louis," Susan says. "She's our warden." The girls laugh.

"Well, I have to get back to work. See ya." "Yeah, see ya." Jena waves good-bye.

Susan turns back around. "Hey, don't worry, Jena. I'm working this floor tonight. I'll keep an eye on him."

"Thanks, Susan," Jena walks back over to where her mother and the Paterson's are still talking.

"Ready to go?" Mrs. Parker asks.

"Yes, I guess so, Mom."

"Don't worry, Jena; everything will be all right," Mrs. Paterson says as she and Mr. Paterson walk back into Jake's hospital room.

"Good night, guys," Mr. Paterson says.

Jena and Mrs. Parker begin walking toward the elevator. "Feel better now?" Mrs. Parker asks as she hits the button on the elevator.

"Yes, I do, Mom. Thank you for bringing me."

Jena and her mother step into the elevator. Jena looks at her mom and for the mysterious man who got on with them earlier. The man never shows up again. I know I saw him, Jena thinks. Maybe I'm just stressed. "Mom, what do you think about me becoming a candy striper?" Jena asks. Mrs. Parker just stares at her with a surprised expression on her face.

CHAPTER SIX

Mrs. Parker smiles at Jena.

"Mom, what are you smiling about? Is there something wrong with me wanting to help in the hospital?"

"No, but it does seem kind of sudden, Jena. This wouldn't have anything to do with Jake being in the hospital, would it?"

"Well, yes and no," Jena replies. The elevator door opens, and Jena and Mrs. Parker walk to the hospital parking lot. Jena continues to try to convince her mother. "I mean, I want to see Jake and I want to do something good at the same time. So, what could be better than volunteering in the hospital to help sick people?" Jena says.

"You had a traumatic experience, and now you want to do something good. I think you wanting to help others can be a noble thing. My answer is yes."

Jena jumps up and down. "I still need to speak to your father about it, okay?"

"Yes," Jena confirms.

"Yes," Mrs. Parker answers again, this time with a bigger smile.

"Mom, could we stop by to see Ms. Louis about me volunteering before we leave the hospital?" Jena asks.

"Sure, honey, let's find out where her office is located." Jena and Mrs. Parker walk the hospital halls to find Ms. Louis. They stop several hospital staff members who instruct them to go to another person for the information. Jena and her mother stop by the hospital patient information desk to try to find Ms. Louis's office. A young male nurse is sitting behind the nurses' station desk, talking on the phone.

They stop to ask him for the location of Ms. Louis's office. "Sarah, if you leave the house this time, I'm not taking you back!" the man speaks angrily into the phone. "I mean it!"

Mrs. Parker stares at him. He slams the phone down. "Can I help you?" he asks in a rude voice.

Stunned, Mrs. Parker is silent for second. "We are trying to find Ms. Louis's office. Can you help us?"

"Behind you."

"What?" Mrs. Parker has a puzzled looked on her face.

The male nurse points. "Her office is right behind you."

"Thank you," Mrs. Parker says. Jena just doesn't say anything.

The male nurse slams the phone down again. He gets up and walks away from his desk. "Damn woman."

"Sam? Sam?" Ms. Louis walks out and calls for the male nurse who just keeps on walking.

"I'll be back, Ms. Louis. Just going to the bathroom!" the male nurse yells.

She turns to Jena and Mrs. Parker. "How may I help you?" "We are looking for Ms. Louis," Mrs. Parker says.

"I'm Ms. Louis." She looks directly at Jena. "Let me guess, you want to be a candy striper." "Yeah," Jena replies. "Well, come in, young lady." Jena is nervous.

"Have a seat." Mrs. Parker stands in the hallway to wait for Jena. "Well, I only have one question that I ask before my volunteers start, and it is: why do you want to be a volunteer?" Ms.

Louis smiles as she leans over her desk a little.

Jena turns around to look at her mother and then back at Ms. Louis. "Well, the reason why I want to be a volunteer is because …" Jena stops for a second. "It's because I …" Ms. Louis stares intently at Jena. "The truth is someone I care about very much just got hurt, and it made me realize how important life is, so I want to do something to help," Jena replies.

Ms. Louis nods her head in agreement. "Jena, that was a very good response. The hospital is always looking for good people. I would be happy to have you as a volunteer," Ms. Louis says. "I just have one more question." Jena stares at her curiously. "Can you start tomorrow?"

Mrs. Parker sticks her head in the door.

"Mom, can I start tomorrow?"

"Yes. Why not? I'm sure your dad will be all right with it." Ms. Louis walks out of her office with Jena and Mrs. Parker. Sam, the nurse, still hasn't returned to the nurses' station. "Where the heck is Sam? It was nice meeting you both." She shakes Jena's and Mrs. Parker's hands. Then she walks off searching for Sam in the hallways. Jena and her mother walk out of the hospital to the car. They talk and laugh while walking to the car.

Mrs. Parker's cell phone rings. "It's your dad," she says.

"Mom don't tell Dad yet," Jena pleads.

"Okay," Mrs. Parker replies and answers the phone. "Hi, honey. ... No, no, everything is all right. We're actually on our way home right now. ... Okay, I'll see you when we get there. ... "Love you too." Mrs. Parker winks at Jena. "I got him in the bag, but I do have to tell him everything. You do understand right?"

Jena smiles as she gets into the car. "Yes, Mom." Chance waves down the car as they are driving off. "Mom, it's Chance. Can you stop?" Jena asks.

Mrs. Parker stops the car. "Jena, did you see Jake?"

"Yes."

"What about Ken?"

"I just saw Jake; I didn't see Ken. I'm sorry," Jena says in a sad voice.

Chance suddenly becomes extremely upset. "I thought you were going to see how Ken was doing too!" Chance yells.

"Calm down, Chance," Jena replies. "I'm sure he's all right."

Chance runs away from the car and gets into her car where Carol is waiting and speeds away. Jena opens the door to get out and stop Chance. "Chance!" she yells. Jena stands in the parking lot and then slowly gets back into the car. "Hopefully, Ken's parents will let her see him." Jena closes the car door.

Mrs. Parker begins to drive home. She stops for an elderly couple walking to their car. On the way home, the main highway traffic is slowed down by a traffic jam. Police officers are directing traffic. Mrs. Parker drives slowly with the traffic. A car has flipped over a little further up the road.

"Mom, what do you think is going on?" Jena asks.

"There seems to be a car accident up ahead," Mrs. Parker replies. "Here comes a police officer. Maybe he can tell us what's going on."

"Hi, ma'am, there's been an accident, so please drive slowly as we try to get the injured individuals to the hospital. I'll be directing you past the accident. Please try to keep moving," the officer says.

"Thank you, Officer," Mrs. Parker replies. She drives slowly past the overturned car. Ambulances and police cars surround the accident area. Jena notices as their car passes that it's Chance's car.

"Mom! Mom! It's Chance. It's Chance and Carol!" Jena yells. "Stop the car, Mom!" Jena yells.

"Jena, I can't stop. I have to keep moving. You heard the officer," Mrs. Parker replies.

Jena stares out the car window in fear. The EMS team is carrying two people on stretchers to the ambulance. Jena's mother continues driving to their house.

CHAPTER SEVEN

"**M**om, what if something terrible has happened to Chance and Carol? I mean, what if they're really hurt or dead?"

"Jena, I'll try to contact Chance's mother. Both the girls were on stretchers. I mean, if they were dead, I'm sure we would have heard something by now."

"But Mom!"

"Jena, calm down; you've had a rough day. First Jake and now these two girls. You need to just relax and take a deep breath."

"Okay." Jena breathes in deeply several times. She starts panicking again. "But, Mom, please try to call Chance's mother."

They both get out of car and walk into the house. Jena's father walks into the room. "What' going on? Cops are calling, and there's a car accident on the main highway that's got traffic backed the hell up!" Mr. Parker says in an angry voice.

Jena looks at her mom. Mrs. Parker looks at Jena. "Jena, go upstairs so I can speak to your father." "Mom!" Jena whines.

"Jena, please, just go upstairs, so I can speak to your father. I promise I will let you know if I speak to Chance's mother." "Okay, Mom." Jena walks slowly upstairs. She stops just at the top of the stairs to try to listen to what her parents are talking about.

Mr. Parker walks toward his wife. He gently grabs her arm and looks deeply into her eyes. "What's going, Kitty?" Mr. Parker asks.

Mrs. Parker walks toward the kitchen. She sighs. "Well, first, you might want to have a seat."

"Okay," Mr. Parker replies. He walks toward the couch and sits down. "So, what's going on?" he asks again.

"Jena went to a club."

"A club? What kind of club?" Mr. Parker asks.

"It's not really a club; it's a biker bar."

Mr. Parker jumps up off the couch. "What?"

"Okay, calm down," Mrs. Parker says. "Let me explain. Apparently, Jena was just trying to make new friends with Chance and Carol."

"Who?" he replies.

"These two girls from school," Mrs. Parker says quickly. "They invited her to hang, just like girls do. They took her to this biker bar place, and things were going okay for a while until Jake showed up."

"What the hell was Jake doing there?" Mr. Parker asks.

"Jake came by here earlier looking for Jena, and I told him that she wasn't home and that she left with two girls from school," she answers, sounding impatient.

"Okay," Mr. Parker replies. "I guess he knew where they were and went there."

"Ken was there too."

"Oh, I don't believe those two boys really like each other."

"Yes, that's true." Mrs. Parker nods her head yes. "Jake and Ken got into a fight, a real bad one, and now the both of them are in the hospital."

"Wow, now I can see why Jena is so upset," Mr. Parker says.

Mrs. Parker walks around the room in a circle. "One more thing," she says.

"There's more?" Mr. Parker replies.

"Yes, there's more," Mrs. Parker says sharply. "On our way home from the hospital, Chance and Carol were being escorted to the hospital in an ambulance. They are the ones that got into that car accident on the main highway. It appears they got into a car accident leaving the hospital." Mrs. Parker continues, "Chance left the hospital parking lot in spinning rage when Jena didn't have any information on how Ken was doing."

Mr. Parker looks up the stairs, and he notices Jena's shadow on the stairway. "Jena, come downstairs!" Mr. Parker calls. Jena stands frozen for moment. "Jena, come here. I can see you on the stairs."

Jena walks slowly down the stairs and stops on the last stair. "Dad, I'm sorry I didn't know all of this was going to happen today," Jena says slowly. "Please, don't be mad. I was just trying to make new friends, and I didn't know Jake was going to come or get into a fight."

Mr. Parker walks toward Jena. "It's okay, Jena. We're not blaming you for all of this." He gives her a hug. "I'm just a little shocked to hear about everything that happened today. I'm just very happy that you're not hurt." Mr. Parker gives Jena a bigger hug. "If something were to happen to you, Jena, I just don't know what I'd do. Jena, you are the only child I have." Mr. Parker squeezes her tightly and then turns to reach for Mrs. Parker's hand. "You and your mother …" He looks at Mrs. Parker with tears in his eyes. "You both are all I got."

"I know, Dad," Jena replies. "I decided that I want to be a volunteer at the hospital. I hope you will let me."

Mr. Parker turns to look as Mrs. Parker. She nods her head yes. "Well, if it's okay with your mom, then it's okay with me," Mr. Parker says. Jena gives her father a great big hug and runs upstairs. "Remember, everything I just said, Jena."

Jena stops at the top of the stairs. "I will, Dad. I promise." Jena walks to her room with a great big smile on her face. Her window is open. She walks slowly to it. The neighborhood streets are silent. She sees her next-door neighbor's cat roaming the neighborhood.

She gets ready to go outside to get him when she hears a noise across the street. The living room light is on at the McNeil's' house. Jena can see Mr. McNeil's shadow pacing back and forth in the living room. Mrs. McNeil is just standing still with her hand on her hip. Jena continues to stare curiously at the McNeil's' shadows. Mr. McNeil walks toward Mrs. McNeil and grabs her neck. Jena stares with surprise. Mrs. McNeil is struggling to get loose. Mrs. McNeil raises her hand back and slaps Mr. McNeil in the face very hard. Mr. McNeil walks away quickly. Mrs. McNeil follows him and turns the living room lights off. Jena stands and leans over in her window surprised and shocked at what she has just witnessed. Jena hears another noise on the side of the McNeil's' house. She looks harder to try to see what is moving in the dark. It is Mr. McNeil; he is standing next his house with a shovel in his hand. Jena tries to close her window quickly, but it is too late; Mr. McNeil looks up and sees her in the window. He stands still and stares at Jena. He smiles at her and then turns around to walk to his back door as he holds the shovel tightly gripped in his hand. Jena closes her bedroom window, puts on her pajamas, and tries to forget what she has just seen. Exhausted from the long day, Jena falls asleep quickly.

During the night, she tosses and turns in her sleep. She begins to dream she is back on the plane. This time, she is the pilot. Jena dreams that she is flying the plane and all of the men on the plane are sitting silently. Jena makes an announcement to the male passengers aboard. "This is announcement from your pilot," she says. "I'm about to crash this airplane into the sea. Everyone, please stay calm and seated." The men on the airplane don't move. "Once I crash the plane, we are all going to die, so please buckle your seat belts and don't bother saying your prayers, because you're all creeps and you all deserve to die!" Jena flies the plane into the sea.

She wakes up suddenly from the dream breathing hard and drenched in sweat. The morning sun is beaming through her window. I wonder why Mom didn't wake me up, she thinks. She hears a door close and two people talking and laughing outside. Jena runs to her window and sees Mr. and Mrs. McNeil kissing in their driveway. Jena rushes to get ready for school. She can smell the aroma of pancakes as it fills the room. She goes to the stairs and hears Mrs. Parker in the kitchen singing. Her mother's happy mood makes Jena feel at ease, but she is still confused by what she'd seen at the McNeil's' house the night before—how just yesterday, they were such a happy couple, and then last night, he had a shovel in his hand like he was going to murder someone. Jena peeks out of her bedroom window. Kids are walking to school; the neighbor's dog is barking; and both of the McNeil's' cars are in the driveway. Maybe I was seeing things, Jena thinks. Maybe I'm just going crazy.

CHAPTER EIGHT

Jena rushes down the stairs and slips on one of the steps on the way down. Mrs. Parker hurries out of the kitchen. "Jena are you all right?" she asks.

Jena stumbles as she gets up. "Yes, Mom, you know, clumsy me," Jena answers.

"Well, next time, be careful. You know your dad's been meaning to repair those darn stairs. You could get hurt if you're not careful."

Jena walks to the kitchen door. "Mom, I'm sorry; I'm going to have to skip breakfast this morning. I had another bad night's sleep, and I'm running late," Jena says in a hurry.

"But, honey, I made all of your favorites," Mrs. Parker says in a whiny voice. "Jena, just sit down and have a few bites, and I'll take you to school," she insists.

"Okay, Mom," Jena says as she sits down at the kitchen table. She starts eating breakfast, and Mr. Parker comes downstairs.

He sits at the table next to Jena and Mrs. Parker and opens the morning newspaper. "Aren't you supposed to be getting along to school, young lady?" he says.

Jena looks up at her dad with sad, sleepy eyes.

"She's running a little late this morning; you know, bad night's sleep again," Mrs. Parker says, "I'm going to be taking her to school today. After all of the excitement from yesterday, I can understand how Jena might not sleep well."

Mr. Parker raises one of his eyebrows at Mrs. Parker. Jena quickly finishes her breakfast. "Well, Mom, we better get going."

Looking down at her watch, her mom says, "You're right, Jena. It is getting late." Mrs. Parker grabs her purse and car keys, and Jena grabs her book bag. Mrs. Parker leans over and gives Mr. Parker a kiss on the cheek. "Now, you be good today," she says with a smile.

Jena walks quickly to the front door. Mr. Parker turns around from the kitchen table. "Ah, Jena, no kiss for Dad?"

"Dad, you know I'm not a little kid anymore," Jena replies.

"Just kidding, honey, but every once in a while, you can at least give your old dad a hug." Mr. Parker smiles as he turns back around to read his paper. Jena goes back to the kitchen and hugs her dad, and then she and Mrs. Parker head to the car. Mrs. Parker backs out of her driveway just as a delivery truck is passing by. The delivery truck almost collides with Mrs. Parker's car. She stops quickly. The delivery driver gets out of his truck. He walks with a limp, and it takes him a few seconds to get to the car. Mrs. Parker is in a rush, so she blows her horn. The delivery driver walks up and taps on her window.

"Are you all right, ma'am?" he mumbles.

Mrs. Parker rolls down the car window. "Yes. Sorry, I didn't see you," Mrs. Parker says.

"It's all right, ma'am. I believe it was my fault. I wasn't paying attention like I should, but please don't call the boss."

Jena and Mrs. Parker look at each other. The delivery driver leans over to look at Jena. "I'm just glad you and the young lady are all right," he says. Trying to make conversation with Jena, he asks, "So what's your name, young lady?"

Mrs. Parker answers quickly, "I'm Mrs. Parker, and she is Jena. I'm so sorry, sir, but we are in such a rush."

"Oh, sure, sure," he answers. "It was nice meeting the both of you, and you two have a good day now, you hear?" The delivery driver limps back to his truck and continues driving down the street. Mrs. Parker backs out of her driveway and begins driving Jena to school.

"Mom, that was a close call. He was a strange one, wouldn't you say?" Jena says.

"Yeah, it was. There must something in this town that spurs car accidents," Mrs. Parker replies.

"Mom, remember you have to pick me up today so I can start my first day as a hospital volunteer."

"Oh yeah! Today is the big day for you to somewhat start a job."

Jena and her mother both laugh.

"And of course, you get to see Jake." Mrs. Parker turns and looks at Jena.

"I hope he's all right, Mom."

"I'm sure he's doing well, Jena."

"He's my best friend, and I still feel a little responsible for what happened at that club," Jena replies.

"Jena, it wasn't your fault." Mrs. Parker continues to drive. "I'm sure Jake didn't want to get into a fight, but he did, and he has to take responsibility for that. I know he didn't mean to get hurt, but Jake knew that he and Ken haven't gotten along since middle school, so maybe he should have left the bar or not have gone at all."

"Mom, Jake and I have been friends since grade school. You know he's like a brother to me. I know he was just trying to protect me," Jena replies. "I mean, I don't really like Ken either, but he's Chance's boyfriend, and I couldn't exactly ignore him at the club, although I wish I had now," Jena says as she puts her head down.

Mrs. Parker pulls up at the school. "Jena, I know Jake is your friend, but are you sure that something else isn't going on there?" she asks.

"Yes, Mom, nothing." Jena opens the car door and closes it. She leans over into the passenger's car window. "Don't forget to come pick me up after school," she says to her mother.

"I won't," Mrs. Parker replies.

Jena smiles at her mom, throws her book bag over her shoulder, and walks toward the school. Other students are standing around everywhere, and everyone is whispering as Jena passes them. One student stops Jena. "Hey, aren't you the girl who got in a fight at that club last night?"

Jena keeps walking. Another student stops her. "Jena, did Jake really get knocked out? I heard that Ken knocked his ass out, and then Ken got stabbed by the bouncer. Is that what happened?" the kid asks.

"No!" Jena replies harshly. She continues to walk to her locker. Ken's brother Mark stands next to Jena in the hallway.

"Jena!" Mark calls.

Jena turns. "Mark how is Ken?" she asks. "I'm sorry about what happened to him and Jake. I didn't want anyone to get hurt."

"I know, Jena, it's not your fault," Mark replies. "I know my brother isn't innocent, although my parents think he's a saint. Don't worry; Ken is doing okay. He's still a little banged up, but I think he'll live. I also heard that Jake is doing okay too," he says.

"Yeah, I think Jake will be all right," Jena replies. "What about Chance and Carol?" she asks.

Mark moves closer to Jena. "Well, I heard that Carol is in real bad shape, but Chance is doing okay," Mark replies.

"How bad is Carol?" Jena asks. "What do you mean?"

"Not physical, but mental. She's upset about something. Who knows what's going on with her?" Mark says. "I just can't believe that everyone is in the hospital in this town. It almost feels like we're living in a cursed town. Maybe we're in the Twilight Zone, huh, Jena," Mark adds as he backs away to go to class. "My parents are pissed, not at Ken, but at me for not being there to stop the fight. Can you believe that? You know, my dad being a preacher and all, this type of news isn't good for the church." Mark backs into a group of Ken's teammates.

"Hey, Mark, so how's Ken doing?" Bobby, one of Ken's hangout buddies asks. Several of the other guys glance over at Jena. "He's doing well. I gotta go," Mark replies quickly.

Bobby glares at Jena from the corner of his eye to make sure she is paying attention. "It's too bad that Ken didn't kick Jake's ass a little harder." Bobby smirks at Jena.

Mark gets in his face. "Look, man, what's too bad is that either of them got hurt fighting just to see who's got the bigger head when I can clearly see you do," Mark says.

"Yeah?" the guy replies.

"Yeah," Mark says.

One of Ken's other teammates pulls on the guy's arm, and they all walk away. Mark turns to Jena. "Jena, don't worry about those jerks."

"I won't." She slams her locker door and walks to her classroom. Talking to herself, she says, "I just want everyone to get out of the hospital."

Mark catches up with her. "Mark, we better go to class, or we're going to be late, and you know how Mr. Jamison gets when we're late for his class." Before walking into the classroom, she adds, "Hey, Mark, after school, I'm going to volunteer at the hospital. Hopefully, I'll get to see everyone while I'm there." They both take their seats in the class.

The school day goes by very quickly for Jena. The last school bell rings, and she rushes outside to wait for her mother. Ken's teammates are all standing around laughing, joking, and staring at her. She ignores them and sits down on the bench outside the school building. Jena opens a book and begins to read. A delivery truck pulls up, and it's the same guy who almost got into an accident with her mom that morning. The deliveryman gets out and limps toward the school. He notices Jena on the bench and walks up to her. "Hey, aren't you the young lady from this morning?" he asks.

Jena looks up slowly. The sun is shining in her eyes. "Yes, I am," she answers reluctantly.

The delivery driver stands over Jena blocking half of the sun behind him. Jena begins to feel uncomfortable. She stands and pretends she is looking for her mother. The delivery driver moves closer to her. "You're a pretty young lady," he says.

Jena moves away from him and notices her mother. She grabs her things and quickly walks toward her mother's car. The delivery driver just stands and stares as she walks away. "Hey!" he yells.

Jena slowly turns around and stands in a frozen state. He limps over to Jena holding one of her books in his hand. Jena watches as he slowly limps toward her. She prays that he will move a little faster, but for some reason, she just can't move herself.

"You forgot your book."

Jena slowly reaches for her book. The driver smiles: his teeth are crooked and dirty. He hands Jena the book. Jena looks at him and swallows. "Thank you," she says quietly and then turns away quickly. Mrs. Parker begins blowing the car horn.

The delivery driver yells, "And by the way, my name is Joe! Joe Johnson! It was nice to meet ya!" He lowers his voice and adds, "And I'll see you again, I hope."

CHAPTER NINE

Jena gets into the car. She looks back at the delivery driver, who is still standing near the bench staring at her. Mrs. Parker begins driving away.

"So how was your day?" Mrs. Parker asks.

Jena doesn't answer. She is preoccupied with the delivery driver.

"Jena, did you hear me?"

"Yeah, Mom. Today was fine," she replies.

Mrs. Parker drives to the hospital. Jena gets out. "Call me, Jena, when you're almost done," Mrs. Parker says.

"I will, Mom, and thanks again." Jena walks into the hospital.

An emergency situation is going on as she walks through the door. She goes to Ms. Louis's office to pick up her uniform and to find out which floor she will be working on for the day. Jena walks into Ms. Louis's office. Ms. Louis is scanning her computer screen. She looks up. "Hi, Jena. Welcome to your first day as a hospital volunteer," she says.

Ms. Louis appears to be in a rush. She hands Jena her uniform. "Well, here's your new outfit," she jokes. Jena takes her uniform. "You will report to Ms. Cook, who will be your supervisor for today. She is located on the second floor. So, do you have any questions?" she asks.

Jena shakes her head no. "Well then, good luck." Ms. Louis rushes out of her office, giving Jena a quick wave. Jena walks out behind her. She goes to the elevator door. The door opens, and she sees a man inside. Jena walks into the elevator. No one but the man is in the elevator. He is silent. Jena steps into the elevator, and then the door closes. The man reaches for the number two button. Jena stands back feeling a little frightened. The elevator door opens to the second floor. She looks back at the elevator. The tall, suited man is still there. She sighs with relief. The elevator door closes. She walks to the nurses' station. A nurse is sitting at the computer looking over what appears to be notes on a chart.

"Excuse me?" Jena speaks softly. "My name is Jena, Jena Parker, and I'm looking for Ms. Cook."

The nurse points to her name tag. "I'm Ms. Cook, and I'm assuming you're my volunteer for today."

"Yes, ma'am."

She looks at Jena with wide eyes and one hand on her hip. "Well then, go change into your work clothes. Come back, and I'll tell you what to do." Jena changes and then returns with her clothes in her hand. "You can put those in a locker in the back," Ms. Cook says.

Jena does so and returns again. "Now, the first thing I would like you to do is to go to each room on this floor and visit the patient. Ask each patient if there is anything they need." Ms. Cook sits downs and begins working on her computer as she is giving Jena instructions.

"Yes, ma'am," Jena replies.

She walks down the hall to the first patient's room. The door is closed. Jena opens the door slowly. The patient is turned on his side. "Sir, my name is Jena, and I'd like to see if there is anything, I can do for you today?"

The patient turns over. It is Ken. Jena is surprised. "Hi, Jena," Ken says slowly, in a low, raspy voice.

Jena walks closer to Ken's bedside. "Ken, how're you doing?"

"Oh, I'm doing all right, I guess," Ken replies trying not to look directly at her. "I'm getting stronger every day."

"Well, that's great." Jena sits down in the chair next to Ken's bed. "I'm glad you're doing well," she says.

"Yeah, I think I'll be getting out of the hospital real soon," Ken replies. "So, what are you doing here dressed like that?" Ken asks.

Jena tugs at her shirt. "I'm a volunteer," she replies.

Ken smirks a little. "A volunteer? Here at the hospital?" He looks at her in disbelief. Then he turns away. "You volunteered to see Jake, didn't you? I heard he's in a room right down the hall from me," Ken says in an angry voice.

"He is," Jena answers with excitement.

"Yes, well, don't let me hold you up."

Jena stands up from the chair. "Ken, I'm really sorry about what happened," she says. "I didn't mean for you or Jake to fight.

I certainly didn't think you guys would take it this far." "Yeah, well, shit happens," Ken replies.

Jena shakes her head and begins walking out of Ken's room. She turns around. "Ken, did you know that Chance and Carol are in the hospital too?"

Ken tries to sit up in his bed. "What happened to them, Jena?"

"On the way home yesterday, my mom and I saw a car accident. It was Chance and Carol. I believe Chance was upset, because I guess your mom wouldn't let her see you and I went to visit Jake, but I didn't get any information about you, so she was mad."

Ken remains quiet. Jena moves closer to him and touches his hand. "But I'm here to check on the both of you today." Ken squeezes her hand.

"Damn, why is everything so messed up right now? I have to find out where she is!" Ken says in a concerned voice. "Jena, please tell me when you find out anything else about what's going on."

"Sure, I will."

Jena walks out of Ken's hospital room. She continues down the hallway looking in every room trying to locate Jake. He isn't where he was last night. She finally finds him in the last room down the hall. Jake's room door is open, and he is watching a football game.

Jena walks in, and Jake smiles at her. "Look at you. You're a candy striper, right?" Jake says in a joking voice.

"Very funny, it's called a hospital volunteer outfit," Jena replies.

"Oh, that's what they call it now? You look like an oversized candy cane."

Jena walks closer to Jake's bed. He starts laughing again. Jena stops and looks around the room. "I'm glad you're so happy. Don't laugh too hard; you may break your stitches, or I may cause you to get more."

Jake laughs again. "That's why I love you, Jena." An awkward silence fills the room.

"Ah," Jena replies. Trying to change the subject, she says, "So is there anything I can get you? Anything you need?"

"Yes, you can get me the hell out of here; I'm bored to death," Jake replies.

Trying to fix Jake's pillow, Jena says, "You know I can't do that, Jake, but what I can do is get you something to drink or maybe another pillow?"

Jake sits up in his bed. He stares at Jena with a serious look on his face. "How about you come over and give me a kiss? That'll make me feel better."

"Jake, I think you really are sick. Why are you talking this way? I know you think you're okay, but you still need rest," Jena says. "Stop joking around. What's gotten into you lately?"

Jake has a serious look on his face. "I'm not joking, Jena. I'm serious. There is something I have been wanting to tell you for a long time now, but I just couldn't," Jake says.

Jena stops and stands still with an uncertain look on her face. "Jake, don't."

"No, Jena, I have to. I have to tell you now. First, please sit down. If I don't tell you now, I may never tell you. Jena, I know we have been friends since kindergarten." Jake pauses and then reaches for

Jena's hand. "We're in high school now, and ever since the eighth grade, I've had these feelings for you. This is crazy, I know," Jake says in a shy voice. "Jena, I love you."

Jena moves her hand away from Jake's. "What?" she responds, surprised.

"I love you," Jake's says again in a more confident voice. "You're my best friend, and I love you so much. I know I love you because you're all I think about. That's why I went so crazy when I saw Ken's arms around you—that and the fact that I can't stand him. It drove me crazy to see him touching you. That's why I reacted the way I did. I was out of my head." Jake licks his lips. "It was weird, but all I wanted to do was kill him."

Jena stands up from the chair. She walks toward the door and then turns around. Tears begin to flow from her eyes. She opens the door. "Jena, don't go." She stops with the door in her hand, halfway open. "Jena, please don't go." She walks out and closes the door gently behind her. She walks slowly down the hospital halls with her arms folded and tears flowing. She goes to the women's bathroom where she stands and stares at herself in the mirror. Tears runs down her cheeks. The reflection changes in the mirror, and for a split second, she looks evil and angry.

"Who are you?" she asks herself. The reflection of herself smiles back at her. She passes out. When she awakes, she is on the floor facedown. Her leg are crooked, and she has scraped her knee on a piece of broken tile on the floor. Her knee is bleeding slightly. She gets up and splashes water on her face, cleans her knee, and then leans closer to look in the mirror again.

"What are you, and who are you?" she whispers.

CHAPTER TEN

The dark illusion in the mirror lightens again. She continues to stare at herself. Her tears stop. She gently splashes water on her face again and then takes a paper towel to dry it. She walks back toward Jake's room, but there is a nurse in his room. Jena stands and watches through the room door's narrow window. Jake leans over and stares back at her. He smiles. She smiles back at him and then places her hand on the glass to signal to him that she is all right. She turns and goes to complete her welcome rounds with other patients. Jena heads back in the direction of the nurses' station to check in with Nurse Cook. Nurse Cook appears preoccupied with responding to patient requests and out-of-control room buzzers. Jena walks up to the counter. Nurse Cook is overwhelmed.

"Jena, I need to go to the fourth floor to room 406 to check on a patient who is buzzing every five seconds. She has been buzzing me for the last few minutes, but I can't leave the nurses' station." Feeling overwhelmed, she says, "They all have been buzzing."

"Okay, Ms. Cook, I'll go straight there." Jena rushes to the elevator, pushes the button, and waits. The elevator seems to be stuck on the first floor. Jena looks around for the hospital staircase. Opening the stairway exit door, she finds the stairway is empty and creepy. Jena walks up to the fourth floor to room 406; the door is cracked open and the room dark. Jena can hear a girl crying.

"Hello?" Jena says as she slowly opens the door. "My name is Jena, and I'm a hospital volunteer. I'm here to help you." Jena reaches for the light switch. "I'm just going to turn on the light, so I can see you," she says softly.

The girl tries to speak through her tears. "Don't turn on the lights!" she says in a voice harsh from crying.

Jena slowly steps back toward the room door. "Hi, I'm not sure if you heard me, but my name is Jena. I'm here to help you." "Jena is that you?" the girl asks.

Jena recognizes the voice. "Carol?" she replies.

"Yes, it's me, Carol."

Jena slowly walks toward Carol's bedside. She sits on a chair next to her. "Carol, it's dark in here. Why do you want the lights off?"

"No! No lights!" Carol screams. "I like crying in the dark." She snuffles. "I know it sounds crazy but crying in the dark makes me feel better."

"Carol, I'm so sorry for what happened to you and Chance. I saw you guys on the highway. You were on stretchers. Why are you crying?" Jena asks. "What's wrong?" Jena looks around the dark room. "Besides being here in the hospital."

"Jena, I've been friends with Chance for a long time, but there's something I haven't told her, something I haven't told anyone." Carol turns around in her bed. "Jena, turn on the bed's overhead light? It's not as bright." Jena turns on the light and sits back down. Carol's eyes are red and puffy. Carol reaches for Jena's hand. She has a serious look on her face. "Jena, I'm in love with Ken." Jena shifts in her chair. She doesn't say anything. Carol squeezes her hand. "I'm in love with Ken, and Ken's in love with me, I know it. We have been secretly seeing each other behind Chance's back for over a year now. I don't know what to do. He's hurt, and he won't speak to me. I went down to his room, and he wouldn't even look at me. You're the only person I have told about my true feelings for Ken." Jena sits in silence and continues to listen to Carol. Carol sits up in her bed and raises her voice. "I mean, do you have any idea what it is like to be in love with someone who thinks they're in love with someone else?"

Jena has a stunned look on her face. "Carol, I …" Jena stops. "I don't know what to say. I haven't known you and Chance that long, but you two seem like very close friends. Maybe you should just tell her."

Carol begins to cry a little. "I can't tell her." She gives Jena a weird look. "This is why I'm telling you. I have to talk to someone about this. Just promise me, Jena, promise me you won't tell Chance or Jake. Please," Carol pleads. "This is has been very hard for me."

Not sure if she should keep the secret, Jena tells Carol what she wants to hear. "I promise, Carol, but you shouldn't be worried about them right now," Jena says. "You should be concentrating on getting better. I'm volunteering at the hospital for a while. Is there anything you need right now?"

Looking away, she says, "No. … Yes." Carol changes her mind. "I need Ken, but I know you can't do anything for me." Carol leans back down in her bed. She curls her arm under her head and pillow. "Jena, do you know what it's like to love someone who doesn't even notice you? Someone you know may never love you the same way?" Jena thinks about Jake. "Jena, I love Ken so much that sometimes I think I could die for him. Having to my hide my feelings hurts so much inside. I'm so tired of pretending." Sounding delusional, she continues, "I want to be with the man I love!" Carol starts to cry again. Jena just sits quietly while Carol sheds tears of pain. She thinks back to just moments earlier when Jake confessed his love to her and how she couldn't tell Jake she loved him back because she wasn't sure of her feelings. Carol continues to cry, and Jena continues to think about Jake. Carol stops crying and notices Jena is thinking to herself. Feeling sorry for Jena, she says, "Jena, I can tell that you will find an incredible love someday. This person will love you so much that it will overwhelm you," Carol says.

Jena stands up and leans over to Carol with a sad, grim look on her face. "Carol, I know it must hurt you to love a person who is in love with someone else. I'm sorry you have to pretend that you don't, but you have to ask yourself if it's really worth it. Is it worth it for you to lose yourself when you're so young?"

Carol looks away from Jena in disappointment. "Jena, please leave!" she screams.

Jena nods her head and begins walking out of the room. She stands by the door for a second and then opens it and walks out. She walks slowly down the hospital hallway. Carol starts screaming very loudly, "I love him!" She screams over and over again, but Jena just keeps walking.

A nurse stops Jena in the hallway. "What's going on? What's wrong with that patient?"

Jena stares at the nurse. "She's heartbroken," she replies. Jena can't believe the sudden change in herself; she feels no compassion for Carol. She stares at the nurse again. "And you can't heal a heartbroken person when they don't want to be healed," Jena says as she walks down the hallway. The nurse just looks at Jena strangely and then rushes off to Carol's room.

Jena takes the elevator back down to the first floor to Ms. Louis's office. She is sitting in her office reviewing paperwork. Jena stands in the doorway. Ms. Louis looks up from her computer and notices Jena standing near her office door. She stands up from her chair and puts the paper down on her desk. "Jena, is something wrong?" Jena just stands with a blank look on her face. Ms. Louis walks over to her and grabs her shoulders. "Jena, can you speak? Did something happen with one of the patients?" Ms. Louis asks.

Jena looks at Ms. Louis with a lost look on her face. "I don't think I can do this job, Ms. Louis." She starts to shake. "I don't think I'm cut out to be a hospital volunteer."

Ms. Louis walks Jena into her office and sits her down. "Jena, not everyone is meant to do this job," she replies. "This job certainly requires a strong and willing individual who is open to all that can occur in a hospital. Some people have physical, mental, and social needs. You're just starting out; give it some time." Ms. Louis sits back down at her desk. "Let me try to explain to you why I became a nurse." Jena sits quietly in the chair waiting to hear Ms. Louis tell her story. "Jena, when I was a young lady, I sat and watched while my mother struggled with cancer. We were poor, and she couldn't afford to go to the hospital all the time or seek medical treatment every single time she got sick. I remember my mother working all day and then coming home tired and sick. She would vomit blood and lay still on the bathroom floor for hours. Even as a young child, it was painful to watch. After she'd lay there for hours, she would get up, take a shower, and still make dinner. I grew up watching her struggle with this disease; yet she was the strongest woman I've known. My mother died when I was fifteen, and my brother and I ended up going to stay with my aunt and uncle. They were nice people, but it wasn't the same as having my mother's love and comfort. My father wasn't a part of our lives, so she was all we had. When I was seventeen, my brother was shot in the chest." Ms. Louis begins to cry. "Right in front of me. I felt hopeless and helpless in trying to save his life. I screamed for help, but in the neighborhood, we lived in, no one cared. He died in my arms. Blood was everywhere, and I was so angry and hurt that I'd lost the only two people I truly loved. The day my brother was buried, I saw a young girl dressed as a hospital volunteer. That is when it hit me, what I wanted to do. So, I also became a volunteer for a local hospital. Since that time, I've seen many deaths and many happy outcomes for patients who had severe illnesses. Both moments have had an impact on my life, which has made me a better person inside and in a lot of ways healed me from my mother's and brother's deaths. I understand now that being a nurse is not just saving lives and healing people's bodies, but also their spirits. So, you see, Jena, this is my reason for being a nurse. You have to ask yourself what's yours? Becoming a nurse is not always something you choose to do, but something that chooses you."

Jena looks up at the room ceiling and then back at Ms. Louis and smiles. "I can do this." Jena sits up straight in the chair. "Maybe I can't be you, but I certainly can try." Ms. Louis stands up and gives Jena a big hug. Jena smiles with confidence. "Well, I better get back to work before Ms. Cook calls down here looking for me," Jena says.

"Jena, why don't you just go home for the day? Think about what I said, and then if you still want to be a volunteer, come back tomorrow. Call your mother to pick you up, go home, think, and then come back tomorrow," Ms. Louis says. "I realize that you have a lot going on in your life. You're about to graduate, possibly go to college, and you have several friends who have unfortunately ended up in the hospital recently." Ms. Louis smiles a little. "That could raise anyone's blood pressure. I'll speak to Ms. Cook. What we spoke about here today is just between us."

"Okay … Okay," Jena replies. Jena walks out of Ms. Louis's office; she sits outside on the hospital bench and takes her cell phone out to call her mother. "Mom, I'm done for the day. Could you come pick me up?" Jena asks.

Jena hangs up and waits for her mother to pick her up. The hospital's automatic doors open, and Mr. McNeil emerges. He has a hold of a woman's arm, and he seems angry. The woman has a paper in her hand. He lets her go, and she waives the paper in his face and then slaps him. Jena can't hear what they are saying, but she notices that they are having a really serious argument. The woman throws the paper in Mr. McNeil's face and walks off quickly. Mr. McNeil picks the paper up from off the ground, crumbles it up, lights up a cigarette, and then walks to his car in the parking lot. Jena sits still on the bench, confused about what she just saw happen between Mr. McNeil and a woman who isn't his wife. Mr. McNeil throws his cigarette down on the ground, gets into his car, and slams the door. He drives past the hospital doors and notices Jena sitting on the bench. He stops his car, gets out, and walks up to Jena.

"What did you see?" Mr. McNeil asks. Jena sits frozen on the bench. He speaks to her in an angry voice. "I said, 'What did you see?'"

Mrs. Parker drives up and sticks her head out the car window. "Hi, Miles. Come on, Jena. Let's go. I'm in a rush. Dinner is on the stove."

Mr. McNeil turns around quickly, trying to change the angry expression on his face. "Hello, Kitty." Mrs. Parker gives him a strange look. Feeling guilty, he adds, "Oh, I'm just getting some results, but nothing to worry about." Mr. McNeil fixes his toupee. Jena stands up and rushes to get into her mother's car. Mrs. Parker drives off, and Mr. McNeil waves at them. Jena watches out of the passenger's side mirror as the car is driving away. Mr. McNeil is standing near the bench and staring at the car as it drives away.

Jena sits in the car scared to death.

CHAPTER ELEVEN

Jena sits quietly in the car while Mrs. Parker goes on and on about how badly her day went, starting from when the trash truck almost hit Mr. Chester's dog. An old lady, Ms. Barber, went missing for a few hours because of her Alzheimer's disease. Mrs. Parker keeps talking, but Jena zones out. She tunes in for a moment just in time to catch her mother saying, "Can you believe everyone in the neighborhood was searching for her and she was sitting in her backyard the whole time? Not to mention that your grandma keeps calling me to come see her."

Jena zones out again. She flashes back to her dream when she was on the airplane with all those unknown men. She thinks back to when she saw Mr. and Mrs. McNeil arguing that one day and then them making up as if nothing had happened, and now this strange encounter when she caught Mr. McNeil arguing with an unknown woman? Who was that woman? What a strange thing to see, Jena thinks. Mr. McNeil seemed so different when he saw her watching him and that woman. He was mean and scary. He was still creepy, but something in his actions made Jena feel fearful of him. Interrupting her mom's bad-day sermon, she says, "Mom?"

Mrs. Parker pauses. She turns toward Jena slightly. "Do you think that Mr. McNeil acts strange sometimes?" Jena asks.

Mrs. Parker leans back in her seat. "I've known Miles since high school," she answers. "He always made me wonder; that's all I can say. Jena, why would you ask such a strange question?" Jena doesn't reply. "Did he say or do something to you, Jena?" "Never mind, Mom," Jena says.

Mrs. Parker shrugs Jena's strange question off. Silence fills the car. Trying to break the silence, she says, "He's an all-right person, Jena, except when you get trapped in a conversation with him, and then that's when you're doomed." Jena laughs a little. Then the both of them burst out in laughter. Mrs. Parker pulls up in the driveway. Mrs. McNeil is already home and is standing by her car talking on her cell phone. Jena and Mrs. Parker peek over at her as she waves her hand and paces angrily up and down the driveway. Jena wonders if Mrs. McNeil is angry because she knows something? She looks back on how Mr. McNeil was so quick to approach her after she caught him with the unknown woman. Mrs. McNeil is crying and screaming on her cell phone. "How could you do this to me?" she screams. "You said you would never do this again!" she screams even louder.

Jena and Mrs. Parker sit in the car and listen. "I should go and check on her," Mrs. Parker suggests with concern. Mrs. McNeil goes on and on, screaming and yelling at the caller, and then she throws the phone in the backyard and walks into the house. She slams the door. Mrs. Parker gets out of the car. "I'm going over there; she seems really mad."

Mrs. Parker walks over to Mrs. McNeil's house. She knocks on the door and calls out for Mrs. McNeil, but she doesn't answer. Jena stands and watches while her mother tries to get Mrs. McNeil to open the door. Mrs. Parker walks back toward her house. Jena is outside the car looking curiously with her bag hanging off one shoulder. Mrs. Parker walks toward her. "She won't open the door."

"Mom!" Jena calls. Mrs. Parker passes her. "Do think she'll be all right? What do you think is going on?" Jena asks.

Mrs. Parker just shakes her head and walks toward the house. Jena follows her into the house and sits down on the couch. Mrs. Parker walks into the kitchen. Jena puts her hands over her face and rubs her eyes, and then she stands up and peeks out the living room window to see if Mrs. McNeil has come back to get her phone. Jena opens the front door. The wind is blowing hard, neighborhood kids are playing in the street, and there is no sign of Mrs. McNeil outside. Mr. McNeil pulls into his driveway. Jena closes the front door quickly. Mrs. Parker is starting dinner in the kitchen and doesn't notice Jena peeking outside. Mr. McNeil gets out of the car and strolls to the house. His work briefcase is swinging in one hand, and he has a dozen roses in the other. Mr. McNeil puts his key in the doorway, but Mrs. McNeil has already opened the door. They began to argue in the doorway. Mrs. McNeil pushes him outside as he tries to push his way into the house. He hands her the flowers, but she snatches them out of his hand and throws them out the front door. Mr. McNeil continues to try to force his way into the house. He pushes her as he struggles to get through the front door. Jena can no longer see Mrs. McNeil, only Mr. McNeil standing in the doorway with his briefcase lifted up as if he were going to hit her. He turns to look to see if anyone is watching him, and then he slams the front door. Jena watches with her mouth open. She grips the living room curtain watching as she waits to see what happens next, but she can't see any movement in the house. She runs upstairs to peek out her bedroom window. She stands there for at least a half hour. Night begins to fall, but she continues to stand there, peeking out the window hoping to get a glimpse of something. As the dark moves in, there are still no lights on at the McNeil's' house.

Mrs. Parker walks into Jena's room. "Jena, why are you standing by the window?"

Jena is startled. She turns around and then smiles at her mother. She lies. "Oh, I was just watching the kids playing out in the street. I was just caught up in the moment, remembering what it was like when I was a kid and played outside all night long. Do you remember that Mom?"

Mrs. Parkers walks up to Jena's window. She lightly moves Jena's curtain back. "Of course, I remember," she replies. "How I could I forget." She turns around to pat Jena on the shoulder and then continues to peek out of the window. "No lights are on," she whispers to herself as she peeks out the window concerned about her longtime friend Jane McNeil. She wonders why Jane doesn't turn on any lights in the house when both cars are parked in the driveway.

"Jena, did you see Jane and Miles leave with someone else?" Trying to rationalize the situation, she adds, "Maybe they went to dinner with the Carson's." She stands and stares out the window. Jena is silent. Mrs. Parkers turns to look at her.

Jena has a blank look on her face, and then she lies to her mother. "No, Mom, all I saw was the kids."

Mrs. Parker walks out of Jena's room and back downstairs. She stops and peeks out the living room window. Her obsession with finding out what is going on is growing. She stands and watches the McNeil's' house. Car headlights turn the corner into their driveway. Mr. Parker gets out of the car and walks into the house. Mrs. Parker has a sad look on her face. Mr. Parker walks up to her. "What's wrong, Kitty?" He grabs her and pulls her close to him. He sits her down on the couch.

"Ah, I'm just worried about Jane. She and Miles had a fight again. I hope she is all right."

Mr. Parker peeks out the window. "Well, it looks like Miles is home, but I don't see any lights on in the house. Maybe I should go over there to see what's going on."

Mrs. Parker stands up. "No, honey, don't go over there," she replies. "Maybe they just need a little time alone."

Mr. Parker hugs Mrs. Parker. "Maybe we need a little time alone." He kisses her. "Is Jena home?"

Mrs. Parker starts giggling. "Yes, she's upstairs," she whispers.

"Well then, we are just going to have to be quiet," Mr. Parker says playfully.

"You bad boy," Mrs. Parker replies. "Let's just wait until Jena goes to sleep."

They both giggle. A light finally comes on at the McNeil's.

"Kitty, the lights just came on," Mr. Parker says. He walks over to the window. Mr. McNeil's shadow is pacing back in forth in the living room window. Mrs. Parker joins him at the window. They both stand and stare through their window and watch Mr.

McNeil pace back and forth.

"What do you think is wrong with him?" Mrs. Parker asks.

"I don't know, Kit." He gives Kitty a concerned look. "Do you think I should go over there?" he asks again. Mr. Parker begins pacing. "I think I should go over there," he says.

Mrs. Parker is silent for a moment. "Ah, I don't know," she replies reluctantly. "I tried to speak to Jane earlier, but she wouldn't open the door. Maybe we should let them work it out."

Mr. Parker turns and walks around the room. "I don't know, Kitty," he says in an uncertain voice.

"This looks like something serious. I know you're concerned," Mrs. Parker says. "I am too, but you know those two have been at it since we were in high school. I'm sure they'll find a way to work it out."

"Yeah, you're right," Mr. Parker replies. "So, what's for dinner?" he asks.

Smiling, she answers, "I was making your favorite today."

A surprised look crosses his face. "Really?" Mr. Parker runs to the kitchen. "You made meatloaf?"

"No," Mrs. Parker says, "because just when I was getting ready to make dinner, Jena called. So, I ran out and picked her up, and dinner is not ready yet." Mrs. Parker taps Mr. Parker on the shoulder. "Besides, you're home early today, so you'll just have to wait." Mrs. Parker walks to the kitchen and removes a pan from the kitchen cabinet. Mr. Parker just stands in the living room still peeking out the window at the McNeil's'. Mrs. Parker yells from the kitchen. "And I'm not making meatloaf, because it'll take too long."

Peeking out the window again, Mr. Parker answers, "Uhhuh."

Mrs. Parker yells from the kitchen again, "I'm just going to make some beans and rice!"

Still distracted by Mr. McNeil's pacing shadow, Mr. Parker answers slowly, "Okay, hon, anything you make is fine with me."

Jena is still upstairs staring at the McNeil's' house from her room's window. She pulls a chair up from her desk, turns off her lights, and then sits down to stare at the McNeil's' house. She peeks through her window as if she were a spy. Mr. McNeil is still pacing back and forth. Jena stares at the McNeil's' house for an hour. He paces back and forth, but now, he has something in his hand.

Mrs. Parker calls for Jena, "Jena, time for dinner!"

Jena is mesmerized by the McNeil's'. She doesn't want to leave the window. Mrs. Parker yells again, "Jena, dinner!"

Jena quickly turns on her room lights, puts her chair back, and then runs downstairs. She walks into the kitchen. Mr. Parker is sitting at the table reading a newspaper. "So, Mom, what's for dinner?" Jena asks.

Mr. Parker looks up from the paper. "Beans and rice," he says in a disappointed voice.

Mrs. Parker gives him a mean look. "You said you didn't care."

He smiles at Mrs. Parker and begins reading his paper again. Jena sits down at the table. "I like beans and rice, Mom." Mr. Parker puts his paper down. "I like beans and rice too, but I pay a terrible price later."

Mrs. Parker laughs. She turns off the stove. There is a knock at the door. Mr. Parker puts his paper down and goes to open it. Jake is leaning in the doorway. "Hi, sir. Is Jena around?" Jake asks.

Jena hears Jake's voice and, surprised, stands up from the kitchen table and walks toward the front door.

CHAPTER TWELVE

J ake leans over in the door, gripping the doorknob tightly. "Jake, what are you doing here?"

Jake leans further in the doorway. He walks into the house. "I came here to see you. I wanted to know how you were doing." Mr. Parker gently grabs Jake's arm to help him into the house. He walks Jake slowly to the couch. Jake puts his hand on his forehead. "Jake, are you all right?" Jena reaches over to him.

He looks up at her. "Now I am," he says with that smile he always gives Jena. Mr. Parker smiles a little himself and walks back into the kitchen.

"Well, I'll give you two kids a moment together, but, Jena, your dinner is on the table, so don't take too long," Mr. Parker says.

Mrs. Parker peeks her head into the living room. "Jake, would you like to have some dinner?"

"Well, I am a little hungry," he says. "Mom, could I have a few minutes with Jake?" "Sure," Mrs. Parker replies.

Jena sits down next to Jake on the couch. "What are you doing out of the hospital? Did they release you, or did you just leave?" Jena asks.

Jake puts his hand on Jena's knee. "The doctor told my mom it was okay for me to go home, but I'm supposed to be in bed." Jake laughs. "I had to see you, Jena. I know you were a little shocked about my confession earlier today, so I had to know you were okay."

Jena looks down and then over at the house clock. Jake reaches over and gently lifts her face up to look at him. "Jena, I do love you. I really do," he says. "I love you as a friend, as a sister type, sort of … and if one day, something more could happen, I'm sure I'll love you even more." Jake is silent for a second. "Our friendship means more to me than anything, and a part of being a friend is telling the truth." Jake gently touches Jena's face. "Now our friendship can truly grow." Jake tries to stand up. Jena helps him. "Well, I better be getting back home before my mom sends a squad car looking for me."

Mrs. Parker walks into the living room. "Jake, why don't you come in and have some hot food?"

Jena nods her head at Jake. Mrs. Parker insists. Jake takes a look at Jena. "All right," he replies. He takes his time walking into the kitchen. "Mrs. Parker, can I use the phone to call Mom to let her know where I am?"

"No worries, Jake. I've already talked to her. Now, have a seat." Mrs. Parker pulls a chair out for Jake.

Jena wraps her arms around Jake's and slowly helps him into the chair. Mr. Parker is sitting at the table picking at his food.

"So, what's for dinner tonight?" Jake asks in an excited voice.

Mr. Parker stares up at Jake from his plate. "Huh, good question, Jake," he says in a sarcastic voice. "You have a right to know." He continues to poke fun. He leans close to Jake and tries to whisper, "Have you ever heard of a noloaf? Ever heard of that?" Mr. Parker smirks. Mrs. Parker gives him a quick glare. Jake shakes his head. "Well, son, it's the alternative to meatloaf, but don't let me spoil the fun."

Mrs. Parker hands Jake a plate, and he begins digging in. Jena, Mr. Parker, and Mrs. Parker stop and stare at Jake. Mrs. Parker turns and smiles at her husband. "You see, hon, someone likes my noloaf kind of cooking."

They all laugh. Jena reaches over to touch Jake's hand. "Slow down." Jake finishes his plate and licks the spoon. Mr. Parker just stares. "Mrs. Parker, this was one of the best meals I've had in a long time," he says. "I really mean it; this was great."

"Thanks, Jake." Mrs. Parker grins from ear to ear. Jena helps Jake get out of the chair. "Now you try to make it on home before your mom really sends out a squad car looking for you."

Jake kisses Mrs. Parker on the cheek. "Yes, ma'am." Jena walks Jake out to his car.

They both stop in front of his car. Jake turns toward her. "So, we're good, right?" he asks. "I mean we're still best friends?"

Jena smiles at him. "Of course, we're still best friends, jerk," she says. "What kind of stupid question is that?" She stops and stares at the McNeil's' house. It only has one light on. There is a dark figure standing in the doorway staring back at her. It's Mr. McNeil. Jake turns around and sees Mr. McNeil standing in the doorway.

"Why is their house so dark?" he asks. "And why is Mr. McNeil standing in the doorway like some creeper?"

Jena stands closer to Jake. "I know, it's creepy, right? They were fighting earlier," she says.

"Who?" Jake asks.

"Them. The McNeil's," Jena tries to speak quietly. "I also saw Mr. McNeil fighting with another woman at the hospital. I couldn't hear what they were saying, but she seemed pretty pissed at him. Then he came home, and Mrs. McNeil dug into him. The house has been dark for hours now," she says.

Jake looks back over, and Mr. McNeil is still standing in the dark doorway. "Now he's standing staring at us in his doorway like some crazy man. Maybe you guys should call the cops," Jake says. "I mean, who stands in a dark doorway for over five minutes? This guy has got to be nuts." Jake can see the fear in Jena's eyes. "Do you want me to say something to him, Jena?" Jake asks. "I mean if this creep is bothering you, I will go over there and kick his ass," he adds in a loud voice.

"Please stop." Jena puts her hand over Jake's mouth. "Look at you, you're barely getting around, and you want to kick someone's butt." Jena looks at Jake. "Okay, no more ass-kicking for you; it's time for you to go home and get to bed."

Jake gets into his car. "Yeah, you're right, but Jena …" Jake tries to talk, but Jena is distracted.

"He's gone." Mr. McNeil is no longer standing in the doorway. The house is still dark, and there is no movement from Mrs. McNeil. Jena continues to be distracted by the darkness of the McNeil's' house.

"Hey." Jake tries to get Jena's attention. "I'll see you at school tomorrow."

"Of course," Jena replies. "Wait, you're going to school?"

Jake sticks his hand out his car window. "Of course. Good night, banana head," Jake says as he backs out of the driveway. "And, oh, don't forget, you're still my prom date."

Jena shakes her head, smiles, and then walks toward her house. I can't believe we're graduating in two weeks; Jena thinks to herself. She opens the door. She hears a noise and turns around. Mr. McNeil is standing in the doorway with something in his hand.

Jena rushes into the house and slams the door behind her.

CHAPTER THIRTEEN

Mr. and Mrs. Parker rush into the living room. "What in the hell is going on, Jena?" Mr. Parker yells. "Why did you slam the door?" he shouts as he opens the door.

Jena stands in a state of panic. She tries to speak, but fear has gotten the best of her. Mrs. Parker grabs Jena's arms. "Jena, speak to us. Is there something wrong with Jake?" Mrs. Parker asks. Mr. Parker rushes to open the front door to see if Jake is all right, but the car is gone. Mr. McNeil is still standing in his doorway, but Kitty doesn't notice him. The house is still dark, and Mrs. McNeil is nowhere to be found. "Jena, what is it?" Mrs. Parker continues to ask.

"It's Mr. McNeil; he just keeps on staring at me." Jena's hands start to sweat and shake. Mr. Parker stands next to Jena. "I saw him today." Jena says.

"Who?" Mr. Parker ask. "Miles?"

Jena nods her head yes. "I saw him arguing with another woman at the hospital."

Mrs. Parker folds her arms. "Is that why you rushed into the car?"

Jena sits down. "Yes, Mom." Jena has a terrified look on her face. "Mom, he seemed so mad at me," she says. "At first, he didn't see me, but when he was about to get into his car, he saw me on the bench, and then you drove up, Mom, and I hurried to get into the car."

Mr. Parker is furious and heads upstairs to his bedroom closet to grab his shotgun. He mumbles as he walks up the stairs. "God damn piece of shit gonna scare my daughter!" Mr. Parker rumbles upstairs searching for his gun and bullets. "If that asshole thinks he can terrorize my daughter, well, he's got to deal with me first."

Mrs. Parker runs up the stairs. "Now look, Jim, there's no need to get violent. I mean, he hasn't done anything."

Mr. Parker paces back and forth around the bedroom. "Oh yes he has, Kitty. Didn't you hear Jena downstairs? This asshole has been watching her like a creepy criminal standing in a dark doorway." Mr. Parker loads up his gun.

"We don't know that for sure."

Mr. Parker replies, "Are you calling our daughter a liar, Kitty?" he yells even louder. He pulls the window curtain back. He puts it back. "For all we know, Jane could be dead. I'm going over there to see what the hell is going on." Mr. Parker loads more bullets into his gun, quickly walks down the stairs, and heads out the front door to the McNeil's'.

Jena and Mrs. Parker stare frantically out the living room window, and Jena turns to grab and hug her mother. "Mom, you've got to stop him!" Jena says.

Mrs. Parker opens the front door. "Jena, if you know anything about your father, there's one thing you can't do, and that is stop him from doing whatever the hell he wants to do."

Mr. Parker places the gun on his shoulder as he walks across the street. Mr. McNeil is standing still in his dark doorway. Mr. Parker walks up to Mr. McNeil. "What the hell is wrong with you, Miles? Why are trying to scare Jena?" He points the shotgun at Miles and tries to bully his way into the house. "And where in the hell is Jane?" he yells. Mr. McNeil just stands and stares at him. "What the hell is wrong with you, Miles? Are you deaf? I said, 'Where is Jane?'"

Mr. McNeil tries to take advantage of the darkness. He pulls Mr. Parker into the dark house. The two men begin to wrestle around the dark living room. Mr. McNeil reaches for a baseball bat he hides behind the door and starts swinging at Mr. Parker. Mr. Parker points his gun in the dark room and fires two times. "Miles, you don't want to do this. I'll shoot you. I'll shoot you dead. You want to mess with my baby girl." Mr. Parker trips over something in the dark. He falls and realizes it's a body. Mrs. McNeil's dead body lies under Mr. Parker. The gun falls out of his hands. He manages to get a grip on the gun. Mr. Parker is in shock as he feels Mrs. McNeil's blood-soaked dead body lying beneath him. He tries to get up but slips on her blood. "What the hell have you done, Miles?" Mr. McNeil manages to turn on the living room lamp. He stands with a bat in his hand and a blank face. His shadow flows over him like an overgrown giant. The bat rises. "Put it down, Miles!" Mr. Parker yells.

Mr. McNeil swings the bat at him, and Mr. Parker fires two shots; one hits Mr. McNeil in the arm and the other hits him in the leg. Mr. Parker manages to get up but slips again on Mrs. McNeil's blood. He stares down at Mrs. McNeil stiff body. She has been bleeding from the neck. He yells, "Kitty, Jena, call the police! Hurry! Call the police!" Mr. Parker tries to hold back his tears. He looks over at Mr. McNeil, who is bleeding heavily from his wounded arm and leg.

Mrs. Parker rushes into the house. She sees Mrs. McNeil's bloody body on the floor. "Oh my God! He killed her! You killed Jane!" she yells. She yells for Jena from inside the house. "Jena, call 911 now!"

Jena picks up the telephone to dial 911. The operator answers.

"Nine-one-one, how can I help you?" "Help." Jena's voice seems weak at first.

"Ma'am, I need you to speak up. This is the 911 operator; how may I help you?"

Jena screams, "You have to help us! He's crazy!"

"Ma'am, please calm down; we have your address. Is this where the problems is?"

"Next door."

"Ma'am?"

"Next door, she's dead."

"Who's dead, ma'am? Just hold on; we're sending a car," the operator assures her.

"Please hurry, my mother and father are next door, and they could be hurt. There's a crazy man next door. He's crazy, and I think he's going to kill my father."

"Okay, ma'am, we are sending a police car over right away. Please stay on the line and stay calm."

Jena stands in the doorway with the cordless phone. Mr. Parker keeps the gun held on Mr. McNeil. Mrs. Parker runs over to Jena. "Mom, they're coming!" Jena says.

"Okay, Jena, I'm going back over there," Mrs. Parker replies.

"No, Mom. Don't!" Jena pleads. "Please don't go back over there. I'm sure Dad is all right."

Mr. Parker leans over to see if Mrs. McNeil is still breathing. He puts down the gun and tries to perform CPR but stops when he realizes she is dead. He turns to look at Mr. McNeil, who is still in the corner bleeding. "How could you kill your own wife?" Mr. Parker slips again in Mrs. McNeil's blood. The gun is flung out of his hand and over near the front door. Mr. McNeil reaches for the gun from the floor. He points it at Mr. Parker. "The same way I'm going to kill you and your damn nosey daughter," Mr.

McNeil replies.

"You bastard!" Mr. Parker yells.

Mr. McNeil slowly aims the gun. Mr. Parker tries to get up, but his feet can't get traction on the wet floor. Mr. McNeil also struggles to get up. He finally manages to stand up, and he points the gun barrel down at Mr. Parker and fires twice. Mrs. Parker stands silently in the McNeil's' doorway in shock at what she just saw. She is frozen in shock and horror. Mr. McNeil wobbles and holds the shotgun in his hand. Mrs. Parker stares as her husband lies with two gunshots to his head. Mrs. Parker screams and runs to him. "Honey, please don't die on me! Please," Mrs. Parker begs through her tears.

Mr. McNeil points the gun at Mrs. Parker and fires, but there're no bullets left. Mrs. Parker lies there holding Mr. Parker in her arms. Blood runs down her hands and arms. She uncontrollably cries, "No, please! Please don't take him, God!"

The police arrive. Kitty is holding her husband in her arms. She tries to shake him awake, but in a moment of silence, she realizes there is no hope. She pleads to God anyway, "Please don't take him."

Jena drops the telephone to the floor and rushes out the front door to the McNeil's' house. Police squad cars are surrounding the McNeil's' house. Mrs. Parker's grip on her husband is so strong that the police officer has to pry her hands loose. She pulls away from the officer with blood dripping from her hands and tears streaming down her face. She walks slowly to the McNeil's' front yard and then falls to her knees. Jena walks outside, but she stops in the middle of the street. Mrs. Parker looks up at her with tears pouring down her face. Jena puts her hands over her eyes, hoping that when she removes them, this whole thing will have been just a nightmare. She stands still as if she were frozen in time. One look at her mother's face and she knows. She knows that her life will never be the same. She stands still in the middle of the street. Mrs. Parker cries hopelessly on her knees. She reaches for Jena to comfort her. Jena knows what horror lies in the house. It isn't something she can bear. It isn't something her reality can handle. She begins running, and tears stream down, falling behind her as the wind blows in her face. How far should I run? she wonders. To the ends of the earth? To the sun and back? Or do I just stand here and let the pain disintegrate me until I'm dust or until I'm no more? She keeps running and running until she reaches a dark neighborhood street. Out of breath, Jena leans over coughing and breathing hard. She looks over at a house sign swinging from a fence. The sign reads "Beware of Dog." Jena tries to catch her breath, but she can't stop her thoughts of her mother's face and bloody hands. She begins to walk slowly down the dark street. The street is silent. No dogs are barking; no lights are on; and no people are walking or talking—just nothing. She continues to walk until she reaches Jake's house. Somehow, she can't remember how she got to Jake's house or how she knew where to find his house in the dark when she didn't even know where she was running to. Jake's house is dark, except for the TV in his room. He's asleep. Jena climbs up to Jake's bedroom window. She taps on the window very lightly. Jake doesn't move. Her hopelessness begins to set in again, but she knows he is the only person who can help her. She gives the window a harder tap. Jake wakes up and slowly walks toward his window. Jena is standing close to the window's edge. Jake opens the window, and Jena crawls in. Her eyes are red, full of tears.

Jake grabs her close to him. "Jena, what's wrong?" Jake whispers. Jena doesn't say a word. She just crawls into his bed. Jake doesn't ask her any more questions. He places his blanket over her body and watches while she falls asleep. Jake lies close to her, comforting her throughout the night. He places his arm around her body. He gently rubs her arm and then kisses her on the cheek. He whispers words of comfort to her. "Whatever it is, no matter what, I will be here for you." Jena lies motionless next to Jake. Her body is still chilled from the outside air. He keeps her close to him throughout the night. He stares at her, wishing he knew what or who had hurt her. Jake finally falls asleep from sheer exhaustion.

The morning sunlight shines through Jake's window and casts a shadow. Jena is standing in the window staring at the sunlight. Her body is exhausted from the night before. She turns around and realizes that Jake has just awakened. They stare at each other for a moment, and then Jena turns around to stare back at the brilliant sunlight.

CHAPTER FOURTEEN

Jake slowly removes the covers; the sunlight blinds him as he slides to the edge of the bed. Jena is still staring out the window. She doesn't move but stands still in front of the window slightly shadowing Jake. Jena speaks softly from the window. "Isn't the sun a beautiful thing, Jake?" she asks. "I mean, it rises without a sound, and then it disappears the same way." Jena speaks in a sad voice. "Without making sound. Yet we go on all day without noticing it sometimes. Without really appreciating how beautiful the sun, the moon, and the stars really are."

Jake stands up and walks toward Jena. "Jena, what's going on?" he asks. He touches her shoulder. "What's wrong?" Jena says nothing. She just stares at the sun. "You come to my room in the middle of the night upset and crying. I wanted to say something, but I didn't know what to say. All I know is that whatever it is, I want to be there for you." Jake moves closer to Jena.

Jena turns around and rushes into his arms. She begins to cry and presses her face into Jake's neck. Her tears fall down his neck to his shirt. "Jake, my father was killed last night by Mr. McNeil," Jena answers in a tearful voice.

Jake squeezes her body into his. He doesn't say anything at first. "What do you mean your father was killed last night?" he finally asks. "I just saw him at dinner." He is almost speechless.

Jena cries harder. Her body is limp, and hopelessness fills her world. Jake holds her tight and tries to comfort her. Jena releases Jake and walks to the bed to sit down. "I know, Jake, but that was then; now, he's gone. He's dead and my mother …" Jena falls silent, trying hard to hold back more tears. "Oh God, the look on my mother's face when I saw her was too much for me to bear," Jena says. "So, I ran. I ran before she could tell me what I already knew. I ran so I could be with you."

Jake kneels down next to her and lays his head on her knees. He then sits next to Jena on the bed. "So, your mother doesn't know where you are right now?"

"No, she doesn't."

Jake reaches for her hand and places it in his. "Jena, you have to call her to let her know where you are and that you're all right," Jake says. "Ah damn, this is horrible." Jake stands up from the bed. "I can't believe what you're saying. Your dad is dead." Jake turns around. "What in the hell happened last night?" Jake asks.

Jena tries to wipe the tears from her eyes. She snuffles. "Mr. McNeil just flipped out. I saw him earlier yesterday at the hospital arguing with another woman. She seemed pretty pissed off at him. He knew I saw him, and I was scared. Then later that day, when Mom brought me home, I saw Mrs. McNeil on the phone arguing with someone. She seemed pissed too. I watched out of my window to find out what was going on. I lied to Mom. I lied and told her I didn't see anything … but I did. I was staring from the living room window, and then I went upstairs to stare from my bedroom window." Jena looks up at Jake. "The house was dark and creepy. I saw Mr. McNeil come home, but when Mom asked me if I'd seen anything, I told her no. I just didn't want her to know that I'd been watching the McNeil house. I should have told her about what I saw at the hospital." Jena starts to cry again. "I should have told her that I saw him come home and that he was standing in the doorway in the dark just staring over at my house watching me and that this wasn't the first time. If I'd just said something, then maybe …" Jena stops speaking and starts crying very hard. Jake tries to comfort her. "Jake, if I'd said something, maybe my dad would still be alive and maybe Mom would of have called the cops earlier. I was just too afraid to say anything. Now, my father's dead." Jake's door suddenly opens.

Mrs. Paterson stands in the doorway. "I've been listening to you two talk," she says. She walks over to give Jena a hug. She hugs her and starts to cry. "Your mother just called. I'm so sorry, Jena. I told her not to worry, because I just knew that you would be here with Jake. She has been trying to call all night, but I guess our phone was not working. I don't know. Please call your mother because she is extremely worried about you."

Jake says he'll get the phone from downstairs and bring it to Jena. "Jena, you need to call your mother now." Jake goes downstairs to get the living room cordless phone. Jena stands in his room with Mrs. Paterson, who has a terrified look on her face.

Jena notices that Jake is walking better. "He's doing a lot better, huh?"

Mrs. Paterson tries to speak, tries to talk through her tears. "Yes, he has been doing great since he left the hospital. Didn't you see him last night?" Mrs. Paterson asks.

Jena has a puzzled look on her face. She remembers Jake hardly being able to walk. Jake makes it back upstairs and hands Jena the telephone. She slowly takes the phone out of Jake's hand. "Come on, Jake, let's give Jena some privacy."

Jena dials her house number. Mrs. Parker answers the phone in a sad and sober voice. "Hello."

Jena is silent at first, and then she speaks. "Mom."

In a relieved voice, her mother says, "Jena, sweetie, I'm so happy to hear your voice."

"Mom." She tries not to cry. "Mom, I'm …" Jena cries. "I'm sorry I ran away, but when I saw your face, I just couldn't … I just couldn't bear to hear you say it. The look on your face made my heart drop, and all I could to do was run, run as fast as I could."

"I know, honey," Mrs. Parker says. "It's okay. I know that's why you ran." She sighs and then starts crying.

"Mom, I'm coming home."

"Jena, take as much time as you need. Right now, I don't know if I can hold an entire conversation without crying. I want you to come home, but I know you're grieving too. Let Jake comfort you."

"Mom, I need to be there to comfort you."

"Jena, come when you can …" Mrs. Parker's voice fades into tears.

Jena can tell that her mother is no longer there with her but tries to talk her back to the conversation. "Mom, I'll be there soon." Mrs. Parker hangs up the phone. "Mom … Mom!" Jena calls, but Mrs. Parker has already gone.

Jake walks back into the room. Jena sits on his bed without any words to say. She looks back up at the sun and then closes her eyes. Jake walks toward Jena, but she can't face him.

"Jena, I'll get dressed and take you home," Jake says.

"Thanks," she replies.

Jake takes his clothes out of the drawer and then leaves the room to get dressed. He returns to his room and finds Jena still sitting silently on the bed. "Are you ready?" Jake reaches his hand out to her.

"No, but let's go," she replies. Jena gets up from the bed. Jake puts his arms around her, and then they both walk out of the house to his car. They get into the car. Jake starts it up and backs out of the driveway. Trying not to look over at the McNeil's, Jena stares straight ahead without moving. Jake pulls into her driveway. "I'm sorry that I got you out of bed. I know you're not quite recovered," Jena says.

"Jena, I would do anything for you," Jake replies. "Anything." He gets out to open the car door for her. There are police officers still investigating the crime scene at the McNeil's' house. Jena turns away from the McNeil's' house as she gets out of the car. "Jena, I have something to say before you go into the house. I have to tell you that I heard on the news that Mr. McNeil is still alive," Jake explains.

"Your father shot him twice, but somehow, he managed to survive. I thought you'd rather hear this from me than from someone else," Jake continues to explain.

"Jake, isn't this supposed to be a good year? This is our senior year of high school. My best friend in the whole world just confessed that he's in love with me, my dad gets killed, and now I find out that the man who killed him lives? I don't know how I'm going to make it through this. I've always tried to do the right thing. Be a really … really good person." Jake grabs Jena's hand. "My dad always taught me to be the best person that I can be in this world, because he always said that there's enough evil and the world doesn't need any more. This is what he always taught me, and now look, his friend, our neighbor, was the very evil he was talking about. This evil lived right next door to us." Jena starts crying again. "Why couldn't he see that evil?" She looks over to Jake. "Huh? Why?" She walks to the front door. Jake calls to her, but she keeps on walking. She opens the door and then closes it behind her. Jake watches. He gets back into his car and drives away.

CHAPTER FIFTEEN

Jena walks into the house. It's quiet except for the cuckoo clock ticking. She gently closes the door behind her and then peeks out the living room window to watch as Jake drives away. Family photos are scattered throughout the house. Jena leans down to pick up a picture from the floor. "Dad," she quietly whispers. "Why?" She holds a picture in her hand of her dad teaching her how to play baseball when she was three years old. Jena stares at the photo and tears begin to flow from her eyes. She suddenly hears the rustling sounds of boxes, drawers, and closet doors opening and closing from upstairs. Mrs. Parker is mumbling as she scrambles to look for more pictures and anything her late husband had given her. Jena stands and stares at her mother as she rambles, throwing boxes and searching for photos and other mementos. "Mom!" Jena calls.

Mrs. Parker turns around for second to look at Jena, but she frantically continues to search for any pictures of her husband. Pretending like everything is fine, she says, "Oh, Jena, I'm glad you're home, because I need your help, dear." Jena looks around the disaster of a room. "We have to find all the pictures in the house that have Daddy in them." Mrs. Parker sounds a little crazy. "You see, we have to gather all these pictures so we will never forget all the wonderful things he's done for this family." She paces around the room. "You know, all of our happy times—"

Jena interrupts her. "Mom, maybe you should just relax."

Mrs. Parker gives her an angry stare. "I can't relax right now," she replies. "I have too much to do," she says, sounding even more frantic. "I have to find these pictures, plan a funeral, and heck, your graduation is only weeks away." Mrs. Parker walks up to Jena. "You silly girl, I don't have time to relax." She lightly touches Jena's face. "You always make laugh. Ever since you were a little baby, you've made me laugh." Her voice cracks. Tears begin to run down her cheeks. "Jena, don't ever stop laughing in life." Jena hugs her mother. Mrs. Parker begins crying in Jena's arms. Speaking through her tears, she says, "Jena, please promise me you'll always laugh. Don't turn into a person who gives up on life." Trying to sound convincing, she says, "Jena, somehow or someway, we will get through this and we will go on."

Jena embraces her mother while she cries. Jena doesn't know what to say, so she just holds her mother close. "Mom, you're exhausted. You need to get some sleep." Jena sits her mother down. "We can look for the photos of Dad tomorrow, but today, you have to rest." She leans down toward her mother. "I know this is very rough for you, Mom, for the both of us, but like you said, somehow, we will get through this … somehow, someway." Jena helps her mother lie down. She pushes the boxes of pictures, gifts, and other items her mom dug out to the other side of the bed. Mrs. Parker is exhausted and instantly falls asleep. Jena puts a blanket over her, kisses her on the forehead, and begins cleaning up her mom's room. She picks up a photo from off the floor. It's a photo of her dad when he was in the army. She kisses the photo and says, "Don't worry, justice will be served. One day, the sun will shine brighter than it's ever shone and that will be the day Mr. McNeil will pay."

Jena walks to her room. Her window is open, and there is a slight breeze blowing. Jena lies down on her bed and falls into a deep sleep.

She begins to dream she's back on the airplane standing in the front row staring at all the faceless men.

Jena struts down the aisle waving a gun in her hand. Mr. McNeil is sitting in the back of the plane reading a newspaper. His face is visible to Jena. She points the gun at him. "What are you doing on this plane?" Jena asks.

Mr. McNeil puts the newspaper down. "Do I know you?" he asks.

"You must know me since you're on my airplane," she says.

Mr. McNeil looks around the airplane at the other passengers. Trying to talk tough, he says, "Look, lady, why don't you go and harass someone else. Can't you see I'm busy reading my paper?" Mr. McNeil raises his newspaper up so he can ignore Jena.

Jena pulls the top of the paper down with the gun. "So, you don't remember, do you?" she says. Jena points the gun at Mr. McNeil's head. "Don't you know who you are?" she asks. "You're the evil that lives next door."

Jena fires the gun in her dreams. She suddenly wakes up and falls out of her bed to the floor. She places her hand over her face in disbelief. She walks to her mother's room to see if the abrupt fall woke her up. Mrs. Parker is still sound asleep. Jena begins cleaning up the house. She moves from room to room, cleaning the floors and walls, and she places the pictures back where they came from. She goes back upstairs to check on her mother. Mrs. Parker is still asleep. Jena takes a long shower and washes her face and hair. The steam from the shower fogs up the mirror in the bedroom. She wipes the steam away with her hands. She puts on fresh clothing, puts her robe over it, and slips into her night shoes. Then, she goes downstairs to start dinner. The doorbell rings, and she walks over and opens the door. Detective Martin is standing in the doorway.

"Sorry to visit your house so late, ma'am, but is Mrs. Parker available?" Detective Martin asks.

Jena closes her robe a little tighter. "My mother is asleep," she answers.

Looking in the house curiously, he says, "Well, okay, but when she wakes up, could you tell her that Detective Martin stopped by and I need her to answer a few more questions concerning the murder of her husband, your father." Jena looks worried.

Detective Martin tries to comfort her. "I know this is a terrible time for you both, but the investigation must continue in order for us to bring your father's killer to justice."

Jena nods her head. "I understand, Officer," she replies. "I will tell my mother as soon as she awakes."

Detective Martin tips his hat. "Thank you, ma'am, and have a good night."

Jena closes the front door. She walks back into the kitchen and opens the cabinet door. Cans of sweet peas are lined up perfectly and take up most of the space on one of the shelves. Jena reaches for one of the cans. She holds the can tightly in her hands. "Dad's favorite ... sweet peas," Jena says with a smile.

Mrs. Parker awakes. She calls for Jena. Jena closes the kitchen cabinet door and puts the can of sweet peas on the counter. "Coming, Mom!" she yells. She walks through the living room, up the stairs, and then to her mother's room.

Mrs. Parker is lying in the bed turned sideways toward the room's door. Jena stands in the doorway. Her mother waves for her to come closer. "I see someone took a shower." She smiles.

Jena moves closer to her mom. "Yes, I thought it was time I stopped torturing my nostrils," Jena says with a smirk.

"What were you doing downstairs?" Mrs. Parker asks.

Jena sits on the bed. "Well, I was attempting to make dinner," she replies.

"Dinner? You?" Mrs. Parker says in a sarcastic voice.

"Uh, yeah, Mom, I think I can manage making something for dinner for us," Jena replies.

"Okay then, the kitchen is yours."

Jena stands up and starts to head back downstairs. She turns around quickly. "Oh, Mom, there was a police officer who came by; it was Detective Martin. He came by to speak to you, but I told him you were asleep."

Mrs. Parker remains silent for moment. She removes the covers and jumps out of bed. She looks over to Jena. "Well, just as well. I'm really not in the mood to talk to anyone except you, Jena." She touches Jena's face. "I have his card; I'll give him a call tomorrow."

Jena can see the sadness and disappointment on her mother's face. She listens as her mother begins to mumble words to herself as if she were talking to her dad. Mrs. Parker walks out of the bedroom and passes Jena without saying a word to her. Jena knows her mother is very upset by the death of her father, but there is also something strange about her, something different. Jena knows her mother isn't the same person she was yesterday or even the person she will be tomorrow.

CHAPTER SIXTEEN

Jena walks down the stairs holding her head low, thinking about her dad and the wonderful times they'd had when she was little. She walks into the kitchen, pulls out a pot from the bottom shelf, and then grabs two cans of sweet peas from the kitchen cabinet. Yeah, that's what we'll have tonight, Dad's favorite, sweet peas, Jena thinks to herself. We'll have Dad's favorite, and I bet I'll make Mom smile. Jena starts to hum while making dinner.

Mrs. Parker walks into the kitchen. "Ah, I know that smell." She sounds excited.

Jena and her mother sit down to dinner and talk for hours. Jena tells stories about her father from when she was a kid. They laugh, cry, and then laugh again throughout the night. "Jena, you know your dad loved you so much," Mrs. Parker says. "He really wanted the best for you, and so do I. I know he would want you to graduate high school and then to go straight to college." Mrs. Parker grabs Jena's hand. "I want you to go to college." She puts her head down and then raises it up again. "We've been saving for college since you were born. Your dad worked day and night for us to have a good life and for you to go to college." She looks away with uncertainty on her face. "We will get through this terrible time, but when it's all over, you can't stay here with me; you have to go to college," she insists.

"You have to go on with your life. I will be right here whenever you need me, honey."

Jena walks over to give her mother a great big hug. She puts her forehead against her mother's and then kisses it. "Thank you, Mom," Jena says tearfully. "Thank you."

Jena and her mother spend the entire week planning her father's funeral. Family, friends, and co-workers of Mr. Parker stop by the house to offer their condolences. The funeral takes place on a Saturday. Jena and her mother both cry tears of disbelief. Mr. Parker's longtime friend and his sister eulogized him. Jena fell to her knees when they opened her dad's casket. Mrs. Parker fainted and had to be carried out of the church. Jena reaches for her mother's hand as they carry her out of the church, but her mother is totally withdrawn from sheer sadness. At the grave site, Jena and her mother hold hands as the pallbearers lower her father into the ground. Autumn leaves blow through the mid-evening air. Mr. Parker's sister Denise reaches for Mrs. Parker to walk her away from the grave. Jena refuses to leave. Jake stands next to her. There is a silence at first, and then Jena speaks.

"Sorry, I haven't spoken to you in a week, but I've been trying to spend time with my mother. She has been trying to pretend that she is all right, but as you can see, she has fallen completely apart. I know a large part of my mother died with my dad." Jena turns to look at Jake. "Some people can go on, I suppose, but I think my mother might not be able to withstand the loneliness," she says. She looks up at the sky.

Jake turns Jena around to face him again, stares her deeply in the eyes, and then squeezes her close to him. "I'll do whatever it takes to make sure you're happy again," Jake whispers in her ear. "Whatever it takes. Jena, you mean the entire world to me." He kisses her gently on the cheek.

Jena takes one last look at her father's grave site. "Let's go, Jake." She reaches for his hand. They both walk away from the grave site to his car and then drive away. Jake turns on the radio in his car.

The radio news broadcasts an all-points bulletin that a man alleged to be the murderer in the killing of Mr. Jim A.

Cold Jena Gray Parker, Mr. Miles McNeil, has escaped from St. Mary's Hospital. Jena turns the radio up. The radio announcer continues to speak. "Police officers are asking that everyone keep their doors locked and eyes out for this man. If you see him, please contact the Maple County Sheriff's Department." Jena turns off the radio. Jake puts his foot on the gas. He pulls up to Jena's house.

Police officers are surrounding the house. Jena opens the car door and begins to get out. "Jena, wait." Jake leans out the car window. "Jena, I want to come inside even if it's just for a little while just to make sure you and your mother are all right." "All right, but I'm not afraid of Mr. McNeil," Jena replies.

"I know, but I'd like to come in just the same," Jake pleads. Jake and Jena walk into the house. Mrs. Parker is sitting on the couch watching the news.

The news is reporting the escape. Jena walks over to turn the TV off. "I guess you already heard?" Mrs. Parker says.

"Yes, Mom, but we're not going to let that maniac run our lives." Jena turns around to look at Jake. "We aren't going to let this control our lives."

Mrs. Parker gets up from off the couch and walks upstairs. Jena turns to Jake. "Jake, I'm not afraid of him, and I'm not letting him control our lives," she repeats. Jena walks into the kitchen and grabs two waters out of the refrigerator. She sits down on the couch. Jake sits next to her. "Here." Jena pushes a water bottle toward Jake. "I'd offer you something stronger, but neither of my parents drink," Jena says.

Jake plays with the water bottle for a moment. Surprised at how Jena is acting, he says, "Water is fine."

Jena stands up. "Jake, I'm coming to school tomorrow."

Sounding surprised, he replies, "Okay."

"We are graduating soon, and I plan on walking down the aisle to get my diploma," she says. "I've earned it, and my father would be proud of me." In an angry voice, Jena continues, "And neither Mr. McNeil nor anything else is going to stop me from being the person that my father wanted me to be." Jena opens her water bottle and then takes a sip. She leans over.

"Jena, are you all right?" Jake asks.

"I'm fine, Jake," Jena answers softly. "I'm just fine." She gets up from the couch. "Look, thank you for bring me home and for being here for me. You are an incredible friend." She walks toward the front door signaling that it's time for Jake to leave. Jake places the water bottle on the living room table and then walks toward the door. Jena opens the front door. The police officers are outside laughing and smoking cigarettes. Jena gives them a mean look. Jake starts to walk out. On impulse, Jena grabs him and kisses him fiercely on the lips. "See you tomorrow."

Jake is surprised. He licks his lips and then shakes his head. "Yeah. See you tomorrow," he replies. Jena closes and locks the door, grins a little, and then turns off the downstairs lights and walks upstairs.

CHAPTER SEVENTEEN

Jena passes her mother's room. Her door is slightly ajar, and she can see her kneeling down praying. Jena quickly walks away to her own room. She lies down on her bed and falls into a deep sleep. Jena awakes suddenly the next day.

Mrs. Parker is standing over her bed. Startled by her mom's presence, Jena asks, "Mom, what are you doing here?"

"Jena, I was thinking that maybe I should sell the house and move somewhere up north, near Grandma."

Jena moves closer to the edge of her bed. "Mom, I'm still here with you. I mean, I haven't gone to college yet. And besides, you and Grandma don't really get along too well."

Mrs. Parker shakes her head. "Yeah, you're right," she replies. "But maybe it's time that I try to make things right with her. Maybe I should try before something else happens." Mrs. Parker walks out of Jena's room. She gently closes the door behind her.

Jena gets out of bed and stands in front of her mirror. She looks deeply into the mirror at herself. "Who are you?" she asks herself.

Mrs. Parker rushes back to Jena's room and opens the door.

"Mom, what's wrong? You scared me." Jena says.

Mrs. Parker's strange behavior is starting to worry Jena. "Sorry, honey," Mrs. Parker replies. "I just wanted to tell you not to be late for school."

Jena stands in front of the mirror feeling uneasy about her mom's sudden burst of energy. Jena hesitates to reply. "I won't be late, Mom."

Mrs. Parker slams the door. Jena walks away from the mirror, takes a shower, and then gets ready for school. She slowly walks down the stairs. Mrs. Parker is humming in the kitchen while cooking breakfast. Jena slowly opens the door and then sneaks out. She stops outside to stare at the McNeil's' house, and then she continues to walk to school.

A car pulls up behind her and honks its horn. Jena turns around. Jake sticks his head out the window. "Want a ride, pretty lady?"

Jena turns around and then smiles. "Maybe," she replies. She stands near the car door.

"Okay then, girl, let's go," Jake says.

Jena gets into the car. Jake turns up the radio and then drives off. Jena turns the radio down. "Jake, I think my mother is having a nervous breakdown," she says.

"Why? What's up?" he asks.

"Well, she's just acting strange. I mean she popped into my room and scared the living hell out of me," Jena says. "I know that popping into someone's room isn't enough to call 911 or anything like that, but it's just the way she did it. It's like she's not herself. Do you know what I mean?" Jena asks.

"Yeah, I guess, Jena," Jake replies. "I'm sure your mom is just going to through some changes. She'll come around to being her old self." Jake pulls into the school's student parking lot. "Jena, she just lost her husband, so maybe she's just trying to pull herself back together," Jake adds.

Carol, Chance, and Ken are all standing in the parking lot talking. Jake pulls into a parking space. "So, it looks like everyone got released from the hospital at the same time," Jena says sarcastically.

Jake turns off the car engine and then glances over at Ken. "I guess so."

Jake and Jena get out of the car.

"Hey, Jena!" Chance calls. "Hey, Jena, come over here!"

Jena yanks on Jake's coat. "Come on, you."

Jena and Jake walk over to Chance. "So, look." Chance wraps her arms around Ken.

Carol gives Jena a big hug. "Jena, I'm so sorry about your dad," she says.

"Yeah, Jena, that was bullshit what Mr. McNeil did, and now he's running around free somewhere." Ken says.

Jena looks down at the ground. "Hey, guys, can we change the subject?" Jake says.

Chance jumps up from where she is sitting on Ken's car. "Well, I see we all made it out of the hospital." She laughs. Carol puts her arms around Ken. Chance reaches to take Carol's arms off and puts her arms around Ken instead. "Yeah." Looking over at Carol, she says, "And we're all out just in time to graduate from high school. Isn't that great?" She kisses Ken on the lips.

Carol backs away with a frown on her face. "So, Jena, what're your plans after high school?" she asks.

Jena glances over at Jake. "I plan on going to college," she replies.

"Hey, me too!" Chance says. "Ken and I got accepted at Northwest University."

"Wow, that's great, so did I!" Jena replies in an excited voice.

Carol stares at Chance and Ken with a disappointed look on her face. "Jake, where did you get accepted?" she asks.

Jake looks away, trying to avoid the question.

"Well?" Carol asks again.

"Just about every college I applied too," he replies in smart voice. "What about you, Carol?" he asks.

Carol kicks her foot around. "Well, I don't have any acceptance letters yet, but there's still time, right, guys?" Carol answers in a skeptical voice.

Jena turns to Jake. "Well, we have to go," she says. "I can't be late for class."

Chance nudges Ken to say something. Jake and Jena begin walking away. "Hey, you guys?" Ken calls. Jena and Jake turn around. "I'm having a graduation party next week. I know we've had our differences, but you are welcome to come."

Jake walks back to Ken. "Thanks, man." He reaches out to Ken. They shake. Jake turns around, and he and Jena walk to class.

"Huh." Jena begins to speak.

"Jena don't say anything," Jake replies.

"Okay, I won't." She smiles. Jake walks Jena to her class, kisses her on the cheek, and then rushes off to his class. "See you second period!" Jake yells as he races down the hallway.

Not looking where he is going, he accidentally bumps into Principal Ricky. "Slow down, kid," Principal Ricky says. Jena walks into her class and closes the door.

Ms. Pickens walks up to Jena before she sits down. "Jena, sweetie, I'm so sorry about what happened to your father," she says. "If there's anything I can do or if you're having difficulty concentrating on class, please let me know. The school does understand that you're in the grieving process." She touches Jena's shoulder.

"Thanks, Ms. Pickens, but I'll be fine," Jena replies. She sits down at her desk.

The national anthem comes over the intercom, and afterward, Principal Ricky makes an announcement. "To our high school seniors, you will be graduating in just two weeks. Make sure you do your best to maintain the fine quality of statesmanship you have demonstrated throughout the year. Certainly, our school has its ups and downs like any other school, but at Maple Landing High, we are fighting, and we don't quit," Principal Ricky continues. 'No!" he screams into the intercom. "No, we keep going. So, seniors and the rest of the school, keep going. Thanks to you all!

This is a message from your principal. Have a great day!"

The entire class starts laughing out loud. "I think Principal Ricky is a freak," one student says.

"No, he's just straight-out crazy," another student replies.

"I think I'm going to puke!" another student yells out.

"Okay, class, settle down, and let's get started for the day," Mrs. Pickens says.

Jena sits at her desk thinking about her mother, graduation, and Jake, the three most solid things she has in life.

The student sitting behind Jena leans over in his chair and whispers in her ear, "If I was you, Jena, I'd track down Mr. McNeil and kill him."

Ms. Pickens walks around the class with a stack of papers in her hand. "All right, everyone, it's pop quiz time."

"Aww, man!" echoes throughout the classroom.

Jena stares off into the classroom. Ms. Pickens hands Jena her test and leans over to whisper in her ear. "Don't worry, Jena, if you have difficulty, just let me know."

Jena nods her head. Ms. Pickens puts the test face down on her desk and then continues handing the test out to the rest of the class.

CHAPTER EIGHTEEN

J ena completes her test within fifteen minutes. She spends the rest of time thinking about her father and mother. She thinks back to the night her father died and the devastated look on her mother's face after McNeil shot him in cold blood, how she ran and ran until she couldn't run anymore, and the pain and the total mental exhaustion she felt as a daughter who'd lost one of the greatest dads in the world.

Principal Ricky enters the classroom just before the school bell rings. He speaks to Ms. Pickens privately, and then Ms. Pickens calls Jena over to them. "Jena, Principal Ricky would like for you to see him in his office."

She feels immediate concern for her mother. "Is there something wrong?" Jena asks.

"We'll talk about it in my office," Principal Ricky replies.

Jena follows Principal Ricky to his office. He walks swiftly, leaving Jena a little behind. He tries to make Jena feel comfortable. He turns to look at her before opening his office door. Touching Jena on the shoulder, he says, "The office tried to call Ms. Pickens' room, but the phone apparently isn't working." Principal Ricky allows Jena to walk into his office first.

Officer Reyes is standing near a corner in the office. "Come in, Jena, and have a seat," he says. Principal Ricky closes his door behind him. He sits down in his chair. Officer Reyes sits in the chair next to Jena. He gives her a concerned look. "First, Jena, I want to say I'm very sorry about your father." Jena looks away, as if she's fed up with hearing people say they're sorry.

"I know you and your father were very close. I grew up with John, so I understand your pain. This is a sad time for all of us, dear," Principal Ricky says.

Officer Reyes faces Jena. "Jena, someone has reported seeing Mr. McNeil in this area."

Jena stands up. "But my mom—"

Before Jena can finish, Officer Reyes speaks. "Jena, please have a seat."

Jena sits back down. "We're keeping a close watch on your house and you. That's why I asked Principal Ricky to call you to the office. If you see Mr. McNeil or if he contacts you, please call the police right away. Again, your mother is fine. We have a car at the house and a police officer checks on her every hour. We will be here for the both of you and this community for as long as it takes to get this killer."

"Jena, I'm recommending that you be released from school early today," Principal Ricky says. "Officer Reyes will escort you home."

Jena stands up and throws her book bag over her shoulder. Officer Reyes opens the door. Jena begins to walk out and then stops. She turns around and stares at the two men. "I'm not going to let Mr. McNeil, or anyone make me live my life in fear," she says. "He's already taken my father, and I'm not going to let him control my life too." Jena walks quickly and fiercely to Officer Reyes's car. She gets in the car and slams the door.

Officer Reyes stares back at Jena in the rearview mirror. "Are you all right, young lady?" he asks.

Jena ignores him and stares off out the window. Officer Reyes continues to drive Jena home. He pulls into the driveway. There are two officers sitting in the police car in front of the house. Jena quickly gets out and walks into the house without saying a word. When she enters the house, she finds Mrs. Parker asleep on the living room couch. Jena tries to walk softly up the stairs, but a creak from one of the broken stairs wakes her mother.

"Jena?" Mrs. Parker calls.

Jena stops. "Yes, Mom?" She kneels near her mom on the couch. "Mom just go back to sleep," she whispers. "I know everything, and I don't want you to worry about me." Mrs. Parker doesn't reply. She drifts back to sleep. Jena walks around the living room. She tries to be quiet, but Mrs. Parker wakes again.

"Jena?"

"Mom, I'm here," she says quietly.

Mrs. Parker falls back to sleep again. Jena walks upstairs. She falls asleep on her bed. In the morning, she gets up and finds Mrs. Parker still asleep on the couch.

At school, Jake approaches her at her locker. "Hey, you," he says.

"Hi," Jena says in a sad voice.

"Crazy times, huh?" Jake asks.

"Yeah, crazy times."

Jake tries to cheer Jena up. "Well, at least we have prom in two days," he says.

"We?" Jena acts surprised.

"You know 'we,' as in me and you?" Jakes jokes.

Jena closes her locker door. "Of course, silly."

Jake tries to hold back his excitement and quickly changes the subject. "So, are you going to Ken's party tonight?" he asks. "I'm thinking about going."

"I don't think that would be a good idea, Jake." Jena stands still for a moment. "I mean you and Ken just had a fight that landed the both of you in the hospital."

"Yeah, I know." Jake reaches for Jena's books.

"What are you doing?" Jena is surprised.

"I'm being a gentleman."

Jena walks closer to Jake. "Jake, I can carry my own books," she replies. "You know, maybe going to the party would be a good idea, because then maybe you guys could find a way to move past this. You know … act like adults."

"Yeah, maybe we should go," Jake says in a hesitant voice.

"Well, I'll be there, so if you want to see me, then you'll be there," Jena teases Jake, gives him a flirtatious smile, and then walks away.

Carol stops Jena on her way to class. "Going to the party tonight, Jena?"

Jena nods her head and keeps walking. Carol walks next to her. "Well, that's good news," Carol says.

"Yeah, sure, why not?" Jena replies.

Carol walks with Jena to her class. "Jena, I'm going to tell Chance how I feel about Ken tonight." Jena stops. "I really feel it's time I stop pretending that I don't love Ken." Carol gently touches Jena's shoulder and then walks to class. Jena stands in the hallway with a shocked look on her face.

In homeroom, Chance sits in the desk next to Jena's. "Hi, Jena."

Jena sits down. "Hi."

"So, Ken's party is tonight. I hope you and Jake will be there."

Jena hesitates a little. "I'll be there. I don't know about Jake."

"I understand," Chance says. "Jake may need a little more time to get over things."

The homeroom teacher walks in, and Chance and Jena don't speak to each other again until after class. Chance gathers her things and catches up with Jena before she leaves. "Jena, why don't you come to my house to get ready for the party? I have a closet full of clothes, so I'm sure you'll find something. Carol will be there too."

Jena swallows. Feeling sorry for Chance, she says, "Oh, okay, sure, why not?"

The school day goes along as usual. In every class, Jena is bored and can't wait for the end of the day. Carol and Chance are waiting for Jena after school. The three girls head to Chance's house. They try on clothes and makeup. Jena watches while Chance giggles and jokes with Carol. Chance's mother calls for her from downstairs. "Coming, Mom!" Chance yells back. "Gotta go see what Mom wants. I'll be back." Chance admires one of her dresses on Jena. "Jena, you look great." Chance leaves the room.

Jena tries to talk Carol out of telling Chance the truth. "Carol, are you sure you want to reveal your love for Ken tonight?" Jena asks.

Without blinking an eye, she says, "Yes." Carol continues to try on Chance's dresses.

"But you and Chance are best friends," Jena says. "How could you do something like that?"

Carol just stares at Jena. She throws Chance's dress on the floor. "Yes, we are friends, Jena, but I love Ken and I want to be with him. Don't you think that Chance deserves the truth? Haven't you ever been in love before? Don't you love Jake?"

Before Jena can reply, Chance returns to the room. "So, girls, have we found the perfect dress? We've got to show our asses off tonight." Chance has huge smile on her face. Jena looks at Carol with a disappointed expression on her face. All she can think is, How can a person be so cruel by pretending to be a best friend when she is just a straight backstabber? The girls continue to get dressed, but Jena is uneasy about Carol's true intentions. Jena wants to tell Chance the truth about Carol's motives, but she just can't. She watches as Carol continues to carry on as if she were a real friend to Chance. If only Chance knew how evil Carol is, I know she would get her revenge, she thought.

CHAPTER NINETEEN

The girls leave Chance's house to head to Ken's party. They pull up to the house. Ken is standing outside with two other guys smoking a cigarette. Chance pretends to run Ken over with her car. "You better get out of my way or suffer my hot wheels on your hot ass!" she yells out the car window with a smile, and then she bursts into laughter. Carol turns to her and gives her a mean look. Ken walks up to the car. He peeks in the backseat and smiles at Jena.

"Hi, Jena," he says. Noticing Jena has one of Chance's dresses on, he adds, "Hot dress." Ken's eyes are glued on Jena.

"Thanks, Ken," she replies.

Chance waves her hand in Ken's face. "Hey, lover, I'm the only girl you're supposed to be admiring," she says jealously.

Trying to get noticed, Carol says, "Hi, Ken," with a big, bright smile.

Not even looking at her, he ignores her and kisses Chance on the lips. Ken opens the driver door for Chance. "Let's go, baby. It's time to party." They all rush to get into Ken's house where the party is jumping. Jake is across the street watching them from behind a tree. He stands in the dark where no one can see him. The DJ in

Ken's house is rocking the music. Jena walks to the kitchen where it's quiet. Ken follows her.

"So, Jena …" He circles her. "What's going on?" Ken moves closer to her.

Trying to ignore him, she says, "Not much, Ken. I'm just chillin', waiting to graduate just like you."

Carol stands behind the kitchen door to eavesdrop on their conversation.

"Jena, I know you don't think I like you, but it's really the opposite."

Carol opens her mouth wide. Ken smirks a little. He leans closer to Jena. "Why do you think I don't like Jake? Hmm?" Ken asks. "I don't like Jake because he's always been able to get close to you when I couldn't." Ken moves closer.

Jena steps back from Ken. "Ken, I think you've had a little too much to drink," Jena replies.

He grabs Jena's arm. "No, Jena." Ken leans in to kiss her. She moves back from him. "I'm just being honest," he replies. "I like you." Ken moves even closer to her. "I like you a lot."

"What about Chance, Ken?" Jena says in a dismissive voice. "How do you think she'll feel about your feelings toward me?" Jena tries to walk away.

Ken grabs her arm again. "Chance and I are just a high school fling." He pushes Jena up against the kitchen counter.

Carol bursts into the kitchen. "Ken, what are you talking about?" she yells in pissed-off voice. The music stops. Chance and a group of people rush into the kitchen. "What do you mean you like her?" Carol points to Jena. Carol pushes Jena out of the way. "Ken, I've loved you for all this time and watched while you cuddled up to Chance, and now you like Jena?" Carol says in a nasty tone.

Chance walks further into the kitchen. "What's going on here, guys?" Chance pushes Ken. A crowd of people pile up in the kitchen doorway. "What's going on in here?" Chance repeats.

Carol walks up to Chance, gets in her face, and points at her. "I'll tell you what's going on. I'm in love with Ken, and he likes Jena while at the same time, he's dating you."

Chance moves closer to Carol. She pushes her. Carol pushes her back. The two girls begin to fight. They tussle on the floor, and Ken and Jena try to break them up. Ken pulls Carol off Chance. Carol punches Ken in the face, gives Jena a dirty look, and then runs out of the kitchen, crying, shoving, and telling them to get out of her way. Chance sits on the floor with a busted lip and black eye. Her hair is tangled, and her clothes are torn. Ken reaches to help her up, but Chance slaps his hand away. She stands up and slowly walks out of the kitchen through the crowd.

Jena walks up behind her. "Chance wait!" she calls. Chance turns to look at Jena. "Don't say anything to me." "Chance, it's not my fault!" Jena yells.

Chance walks out of Ken's house, gets into her car, and slams the door. She drives off in a rage. Jake steps out from the shadow of the tree. He tries to stop Chance, but she just keeps on driving. Jena walks outside with Ken. A crowd of people from school follow them. Jake stands in the middle of the street wondering what happened.

Carol comes from out of nowhere. "Jake, you should kick Ken's ass," she says angrily. "He just admitted that he's in love with Jena."

Ken has an angry look on his face. "I never said I was in love with Jena!" he yells. "I just said I liked her." Carol just gives him a mean look.

"And what's wrong with that?"

Jake is pissed off. "Oh, dude, you really are a piece of work."

Jena stands in between the two boys. "Look, there's not going to be any more fighting tonight." She pushes the two boys back. "Everyone, just calm down." She reaches her hand out to Jake. "Jake, let's go."

Jake doesn't move an inch. Jena tugs on his coat. Jake and Ken stand and stare each other down. "Jake, let's go," Jena says again as she pulls harder on his coat.

Jena starts walking, and Jake follows. They begin walking down the dark street quickly. "I thought you said you weren't coming, Jake," she says.

"I wasn't there," he answers. "I wasn't there. I was hiding behind a tree."

"Hiding?" Jena yells.

"I was waiting outside for you, but it looks like all the action was going on inside the house." Jake stops. "What's going on, Jena?"

Jena stops walking.

"Why is Carol so mad?"

Jena is hesitant to answer. She puts her hand on her hips. "Well, Carol overheard Ken saying that he likes me, and then Carol and Chance got into a fight." Jena raises her hand in the air. "Carol has had a secret crush on Ken. So does this sound like a soap opera to you?" Jena asks.

"No, it sounds like I should've kicked Ken's ass."

Jena leans over as if she feels sick. "Carol was going to confess her love tonight, but Ken crushed her heart when she overheard him telling me he likes me." Jena runs her hand through her hair.

"What a jerk," Jake says. "You know I've never liked him, and now I know why. How can you be friends with someone that you just want to beat the crap out of every single day?" Jena sits on the street curb. "I guess now we know what prom's going to be like. "Jake sits next to her. "Hey, you want to blow off prom and just go to dinner or just hang somewhere else?" he asks.

"You know, after tonight, that actually doesn't sound too bad," Jena says. "At this point, I don't think that prom is going to be much fun." Jena kicks a piece of paper lying on the ground. Sighing, she says, "Jake, we can't just miss prom. It's our senior prom. Why don't we just walk in and walk back out?" Jena glances at him. "Just to say that we went." She shrugs her shoulders. "Just a suggestion."

Jake stands up. "Well, we better head back to Ken's house," he says.

"Why?" Jena asks.

"Because that's where my car is parked," Jake replies in joking voice. "Did you think we were walking to your house?"

Jena and Jake both starts laughing. She shoves Jake a little. Jake stops to lean over to hug her, but she turns away. "Hey, remember when you stole my lunch and tried to blame it on poor Steve?" Jake laughs.

"Oh, come on, you know I didn't do it."

"What I know, Jake, is that you had peanut butter all over your hands and shirt and your mom didn't make you that for lunch." Jena smiles. "I was so mad at you."

Jake puts his arm around Jena. They begin walking back to his car. No words are spoken. Jena glances over at Jake just to see the expression on his face. He is smiling, and for a moment, Jena feels like she is in love with him. Jake leans over and kisses her on the forehead.

"You're the bestest friend a guy could have," he says.

Jena smiles. "You too," she says.

He stares at her. They finally get to Jake's car, and he drives her home.

CHAPTER TWENTY

On the phone, Jena asks, "Okay, so you're wearing what?" "I have on a duck suit, carrot-head wig, Charlie Chapman hat, and I'm wearing a weird beard."

"Ah … yeah, that sounds crazy, Jake." "And you?" he asks.

Jena looks in the mirror. "Well, I'm … dressed like a clown."

Jake laughs uncontrollably. "A clown? Come on, you couldn't have been something a little sexier?"

"Look, you said we're just going to walk in and walk out, so what does it matter what I wear?" Jena's doorbell rings. "Hold on, Jake, someone's at the door."

Jena opens the door, and it's Jake standing in the doorway.

"Oh, that's unique," she says.

"Ha! You fell for it," he replies.

They both stare each other and laugh. Jena peeks out into the driveway. "Let's get out of here before my mom catches me and makes me take this clown suit off. I told her we were skipping the prom and going to your house to watch movies because what school has prom right before graduation?"

He says, "Hurry up," and closes the door. He stops and stares at Jena before she gets into the car. "You know you still look good even in that clown suit."

Surprised, she smiles. "You think so?"

"No, I was just being nice; you're a clown for goodness' sake." Jake chuckles.

"Oh, but a carrot-head wig is something to brag about?" Jena says. In the car, they both poke fun at each other.

"Clown."

"Carrot Head."

CHAPTER TWENTY-ONE

Two weeks pass, and it's only one day away from graduation. "Wanted" posters of Mr. McNeil are plastered all over the neighborhood and surrounding areas. Police officers continue to keep a watchful eye on Jena's house, while still searching for clues to where Mr. McNeil could be hiding. Mrs. Parker has not said a word for two weeks. She sits in front of the window daily just staring out. Jena hasn't spoken to Chance, Carol, or Ken since the night of the party. The day of graduation is joyful yet gloomy for Jena. Jena helps her mother get dressed for the graduation ceremony.

Jena hasn't spoken to any of her friends other than Jake about her father's murder by a man who still can't be found. She stands in front of her room mirror adjusting her cap and gown. She removes a picture of her parents from her mirror. The smiles on her mother's and father's faces make her feel sad. She remembers how happy her parents were back then. She thinks back to the many nights she sat on the stairway out of sight and watched while they cuddled and danced quietly. How her dad had held her mother in his arms and the gentle kisses he gave her on her cheeks while they danced to their favorite song. "If I Can't Have You, I Don't Want Nobody, Baby" by Yvonne Elliman. Jena remembers thinking at the time that her parents were the happiest people on earth and that she hoped to one day find a love like theirs. Jena puts the picture back on her mirror. She walks to her mother's room, but she isn't there.

"Mom!" Jena calls.

Jena walks downstairs, and Mrs. Parker is standing by the door holding her keys in her hands. Jena tries to take the keys from her mother's hand. Mrs. Parker grips the keys tightly. "Mom, you can't drive," Jena says. "Jake's mother is going to pick us up. They will be here in a few minutes. Just have a seat until they get here."

Mrs. Parker lets go of the keys. Jena puts the keys down on the living room table. She peeks out the living room window. Jake's mother is just pulling up in the driveway. She reaches over to give her mother a hand. "It's time to go, Mom."

Mrs. Parker stands up and gently touches Jena's face. She has a proud, but sad look on her face. Jena knows what she is thinking, even if she doesn't say a word. Jake rings the doorbell, and Jena opens the door. She grabs her mother's purse on the way out the door. The graduation ceremony is crowded. There are students, parents, and proud grandparents everywhere. Mrs. Paterson takes Mrs. Parker to the seating area. Jena and Jake take their chairs for the ceremony. Chance, Ken, and Carol all pass them by, but no one says a word. Everyone seems eager for the ceremony to be over, but Jena cherishes the moment. This is the moment her dad talked about for months before he died: the moment that she would reach for her diploma when the principal called out the name "Jena Parker," she whispered quietly to herself.

"Jena Parker!" Principal Ricky calls.

Jena realizes she is being called. Time must have passed her by as she daydreamed. This is the moment; the moment Jena's been waiting for. Jena stands tall and walks up to get her diploma. People in the audience are standing up cheering and clapping for her. Jake jumps out of his seat and cheers the loudest.

Jena looks out into the crowd to find her mother. Mrs. Parker is standing with one arm up in the air trying to wave at her. Jena stands next to Principal Ricky, who is holding her diploma. Her smile is as bright as the sun. She reaches for her diploma, shakes Principal Ricky's hand, and walks off the stage. Jake is called next. Jena turns around to watch Jake get his diploma. His moment seems just as exciting and special as hers. After all diplomas have been given out, Principal Ricky makes a final speech. The crowd cheers, and then hats go up in the air. The moment seems almost overwhelming for Jena. She turns to Jake and gives him the biggest hug ever. Ken, Chance, and Carol can't contain their excitement either, and for the first time in two weeks, everyone seems happy to finally be moving on past high school. Carol gives Jena a big hug, and Ken shakes Jake's hand. Chance and Carol had made up a week before and didn't tell anyone until now. Everything finally seems to be coming together for everyone.

Principal Ricky walks up to Jena. "Jena, I know this has been a tough year for you." He turns to speak to all of them. "But you guys have made it through high school, so be the best you can be as you all go to college. I'm really proud of all of you."

Jena thinks that all these years she has never seen Principal Ricky this way. He isn't just a principal; he is also a nice man, a man who really cares about his students. Mrs. Paterson and Mrs. Parker walk down to where Jena and Jake are standing. Jena hugs her mother. Mrs. Parker tries to whisper in Jena's ear, but her words just won't come out. She just nods her head and leans it next to Jena's. It is like she hasn't heard her mother speak in years. Jena is really hoping to hear her mother's voice, that sweet voice that woke her for school when she was late, that voice that told her father she loved him. Jena longs to hear her speak, but her mother won't say a word. Uncontrollable tears stream down Jena's face from the hurt she knows her mother is still feeling from her father's death. She hugs her mother again just to see if she will say anything, but Mrs. Parker doesn't. She just holds Jena tightly in her arms. Jake hugs the two of them together, and in a second, it seems like everyone is locked in a group hug. Jena hugs Mrs. Paterson. The moment couldn't be more perfect. Yet, Jena thinks for second that this isn't a perfect moment, because her father isn't there to share it with them. Jena doesn't let on to anyone, not even Jake, how much her mother not speaking really hurts her. For weeks now, she's just been acting like an alien had taken over her body. If I could take away your pain, Mom, I would, Jena thinks to herself.

Jena tries to brush off her sad thoughts, so she can enjoy the moment. In a few weeks, she will be leaving for college with all her friends. She will be starting a whole new chapter in her life. On the way home, Jena glances out the car window trying to relive the moment she was handed her diploma, the hugs and the emotions that swirled in the air. What a perfect moment! Nothing could have been more perfect, Jena thinks to herself, other than her mother speaking again and having both of her parents together holding hands, dancing to their favorite song, or her mom in the kitchen making Dad's favorite sweet peas.

CHAPTER TWENTY-TWO

As the days go by, Jena continues to prepare for college. Jake stops every once in a while, to check on her and Mrs. Parker. He often stays for dinner to keep Jena company and preoccupied so she will not worry so much about her mother. Jena feels very guilty leaving her mother in the state she is in. Although Mrs. Parker isn't totally helpless, it is her mother's total silence that worries Jena the most. The first day of college finally nears. Mrs. Parker helps Jena pack the night before. Jena desperately wants to express to her mother how excited she is that she is finally going to college, but she can't.

Mr. and Mrs. Paterson and Jake finally arrive at the house to pick Jena up. Mrs. Parker doesn't want to go. She helps put Jena's stuff in the car, and then she hands Jena a letter. Jena goes to open it, but Mrs. Parker signs not to open it yet. Jena hugs her mother tightly. Mrs. Parker starts to cry.

"Mom, I don't want to leave you," she says. "Not like this."

Mrs. Parker shakes her head and gives Jena a look that says, "You must go. You have to go." And with no words spoken, Jena knows that her mother won't have it any other way. She turns away and gets into the car. Mrs. Parker hugs Mr. and Mrs. Paterson. She reaches over and gives Jake a hug too. Jake kisses her on the cheek. She then walks into the house and closes the door behind her. This will be the last time Jena will see her mother for a while.

She begins to sob softly in the backseat. Jake holds her tightly while Mr. Paterson drives to the college.

"It's going to be all right, Jena," Jake whispers. He grabs Jena's hand and pulls her tightly to him. He tries to comfort her. "Maybe this will turn out to be a good thing, Jena. You're going to college, and you know your mom wouldn't have it any other way." Jake continues to try to comfort her.

Jena sits up. She lets go of Jake's hand and turns to stare out the car window. She turns back to Jake and nods her head in agreement with him. "Maybe you're right," she says in a cracked voice. "Maybe a new beginning will help the both of us." Jena tries to convince herself that everything is going to be all right, that maybe her mother could come back to normal and maybe she would have the time of her life with Jake and her other friends at college, but the certainty of it all still seems so far away from her. Mr. Paterson pulls up to the Northwest University visitor parking lot, and students and parents are everywhere. Flyers and school banners hang all around the university.

"We're here!" Jake yells in an excited voice.

Jake and Jena are the first to get out of the car. Carol is walking around the college campus alone. She walks over to Jake and Jena.

"Hey, guys!" Carol screams and waves.

"Hi." Jena gives Carol a hug. "So, I see you made it here too." "Yeah." Carol looks around in surprise that she got into college. "But I appear to be bit lost," she says.

"Well, it's our first day, Carol, and I'm sure we all will be struggling to find our way around this place," Jake says. He grabs Jena's bags.

Mr. and Mrs. Paterson both get out of the car. "Okay, Mom and Dad," Jake says as he prepares for them to leave, "I think Jena and I can make it from here."

Mrs. Paterson walks up to Jake. "Oh, honey, come on. I'm not going to see you for a while," she says in a teary voice. "You could at least let your mother walk you to your room."

Mr. Paterson hugs Mrs. Paterson closely. "Come on, hon," he says to his wife. "We have to let go someday." Mr. Paterson gently pulls her away from Jake.

She looks up at her husband. "Oh, just one more hug, please." Mrs. Paterson gives Mr. Paterson a quick glare. Jake puts his bags down to give his mother a huge hug. Mrs. Paterson kisses Jake on the cheek and begins to cry. She hugs and squeezes him tight. She can see Jena is about to cry, so she reaches her hand out to her. "Jake will take care of you," she whispers to Jena. "So, don't worry, we will look after your mom." Mrs. Paterson blows her nose and wipes her tears with a handkerchief from her purse.

Mr. Paterson wraps his arms around her and comforts her. "Okay, you guys, go on to your rooms and get settled in," he says.

Jena and Jake begin walking away. They wave good-bye. Jake walks Jena to her dorm room. He turns to her. "Well, this is your home for a while." He sets Jena's bags down on her bed.

"Don't put those on my bed, stupid." Jena pushes Jake a little.

"Sorry." Jake puts the bags down on the floor.

A short, black-haired girl stumbles into the room carrying two heavy bags.

"Here, let me help you with that." Jake reaches to help her.

"No, no, no. I can do it myself, thank you!" the girl yells. "I'm a strong woman. I'm a liberated woman, and I don't need a man doing anything for me."

Jake looks back at Jena. "Okay then. Jena, I'm going to go get settled in my room. I'll hook up with you later so we can hang out." Jake turns around. "Oh, by the way, we have orientation today at three, so let's grab some lunch at twelve." Jake walks out of the room.

The freaky girl is talking to herself as she rummages through her bags. Jena looks at her strangely. "Everything all right?" she asks.

The girl looks up and gives Jena an annoyed look. "Yeah, everything is all right. I'm a strong woman," the strange girl repeats. "I know I can do this," she says. "I know I can find what I'm looking for; I just got to keep searching; that's all."

Jena turns away. Wow, what crazy chick! she thinks to herself. And I thought I had problems! Jena starts unpacking. There is a light knock at the door. Ken is standing in the doorway. Jena looks up at him.

"Hi, Jena," he says. He walks into the room.

"Ken," she replies quickly.

He reaches for her bag. "Need some help unpacking?" he asks.

Jena puts her head down. "No, Ken, I think I got it." He sits down on Jena's bed. She just looks at him.

"What's up, Jena? Are you mad at me?" he asks.

Jena looks up. "No, not at all," she answers politely.

Feeling unwelcome, Ken stands up. Jena's roommate is standing in a corner with her arms folded staring at him. "Okay, well then, I'm going to go hang out," he says. "I guess I'll see you around?"

"Yeah, Ken, I'll see you around," Jena replies. She continues to unpack. Her strange roommate begins rifling through her bags again, searching for this unknown item. Jena unpacks and leaves the room. She tries to close the door behind her. Her strange roommate stops her. She grabs the door before Jena can close it.

"Please. Please, don't close the door right now," the roommates asks.

"What? Why?" Jena asks.

"Because it's not time to close the door," the roommate answers. "The time to close the door is when we're settled in this room and we're ready for the night to end. The day hasn't ended."

Jena stands in shock for moment. "Ah." She is caught off guard. "Okay, well, but when you leave the room, could you close the door anyway, because I really don't want my stuff to be stolen?" Jena asks.

The roommate opens her mouth in shock. "Sure," she answers sharply, rolls her eyes, and then walks away. Jena walks down the halls of the girl's dorm. She explores the other halls.

Chance and Carol are in a hallway talking. Jena tries to walk away without being seen, but Carol spots her. "Jena!" she calls.

"Jena, where are you going?"

Trying to not answer, Jena keeps walking.

"Oh, I get it; you were trying to sneak away," Carol tries to make a joke.

"I didn't want to interrupt you guys, since you seem to be in deep conversation."

"Well, we were talking about going to a party after the orientation today," Chance says.

"The orientation is supposed to last at least two hours, but the best is the party right after," Carol says. "Do you want to go?" Chance asks.

Jena holds her head down. "No, not really guys," Jena answers. "Parties just don't seem to work out that well for us, huh, guys?" The two girls laugh. "Jena, those were high school parties," Carol replies. "No sweat, chick, we're in college, so the party life here is going to be fun and exciting, not lame like in high school."

Jena puts her hand on her hip. "Carol, it wasn't high school that started the party fights; it was us," she replies. "It was always someone from our group, so no, I'm not going. Let's just start our college friendship off on a good note. No parties."

Jena laughs out loud, and then all three girls laugh together. "I think I'm just going to hang out at the library tonight," Jena answers. "Maybe read some books and then kind of lay low until Monday when the official first day of classes begins." The girls hug. "Sure, Jena, we understand," Chance says.

"Yeah, no worries, girl." Carol echoes.

"Now that that's settled, Jake and I are meeting for lunch before orientation," Jena says. "Do you guys want to hang out too?"

The girls stare at each other and laugh. "I think we'd rather go to get ready for the party tonight," Carol answers.

"But you have orientation first," Jena says.

"Yeah, we know, but we're going to orientation dressed for the party, so we don't have to come back," Chance says in her happy-girl voice.

The two girls give Jena another hug and walk away to their rooms. Jena goes back to her room. She checks the time on her phone; it's 11:00. She decides to wait for Jake in her room. When Jena reaches the room, she sees the room door is closed. She slowly opens the door, and her strange roommate is hanging up her clothes in her closet.

She turns around. "Oh, you're back." She walks over to greet Jena. Jena looks surprised. "Before you say anything or think I'm crazy," the roommate starts to explain, "I just want to say that I'm hanging up your clothes because I felt you and I got off on the wrong foot earlier, and I just wanted to make peace with you since we're going to be roommates for a while." The roommate puts out her hand. "My name is Theresa."

Jena slowly extends her hand. "My name is Jena. Jena Parker."

"Nice to meet you, Jena Parker."

"The same." Jena smiles. "Nice to meet you too, Theresa. Theresa?" Jena waits for her to say her last name.

Theresa doesn't say anything. She just stares at Jena. "Oh, sorry, my name is Theresa Henderson," Theresa finally answers. "Sorry, I'm not good with making friends." She quickly turns around.

Jena touches her shoulder. "It's okay, Theresa. We'll get to know each other."

Theresa has a contented look on her face. She rushes back over to Jena's closet. "Now before you kill me, do you like your blue pants in the same row as your red ones? Or how about do you like your pants and shirts to be on the same hanger? I know that's weird, but some people are picky, like me." Theresa grins.

Jena stares.

"Well?"

Jena jokes, "That's a complicated question."

The two girls burst out in laughter. They both begin rearranging Jena's clothes in her closet, and just for a moment, Jena forgets her troubles. For moment, her world seems less painful and more forgettable. The two girls help each other rearrange each other's closet. It was a really fun time for Jena. She has made a new friend, and the world doesn't seem as closed to her.

Just maybe, maybe I can live a normal life, Jena thinks to herself.

CHAPTER TWENTY-THREE

Jake came by Jena's room and watched while Jena and Theresa laughed with one another. "You two seemed to be having fun," Jake says. "I guess all the weirdness is over with, huh?"

Jena and Theresa just stare at one another. Jake feels awkward and silly. Jena closes her closet door. She grabs Jake by one arm. "Let's go, silly."

Jake grabs the doorknob to close the door. Jena stops him. "Jake, you can't close the door; the days hasn't ended yet," Jena says.

"What?" Jake replies.

"Never mind, let's just go."

Jake stops in the hallway. "Was I a jerk back there?"

Jena taps one finger against her lips. "Hmm, maybe just a little." She grabs Jake's arm again. "Now let's go eat," she says. "I'm hungry."

Jake pretends to put his ear to Jena's stomach. "Yeah, I can hear the beast rumbling away in there."

Jena and Jake eat lunch at the campus café. The café is crowded with college students. They talk and laugh for hours up until the time for new student orientation. They both walk to where the orientation is to take place. When they arrive, the three-hundred seat auditorium is almost full. Jake and Jena find a seat in the back of the room. They pass Ken on the way up to their seats. Ken smiles at Jena and nods at Jake. Five minutes before the orientation starts, Chance and Carol stand in the doorway showing off their skimpy outfits. Dean Philips stands in front of the class with an old gray suit on. His glasses hang off the tip of his nose. He looks down through his glasses, his eyes patrolling the auditorium to politely signal to the two girls to please find a seat so that the orientation can begin. Chance and Carol take advantage of having the entire room watching them as they find a seat. They walk slowly and seductively in order to get attention from all who are watching, which is just about everyone in the room. The dean's eyes follow Chance and Carol as well. Two guys in the front row can't contain their excitement for the two girls and stand up to offer them their seats.

"Welcome, new Northwest students. Hello, everyone, and welcome. I'm Dean Philips." Dean Philips's voice echoes throughout the entire room. "Welcome to your first day at an outstanding university."

The orientation lasts for hours. Various student orientation instructors speak. They talk about the university and take questions from the students. There are laughs and school spirit cheers. The sound of the instructor's voice starts to fade away for Jena. Her thoughts drift to her mother and how lonely she must be feeling alone in the house all by herself. Jena feels guilty for leaving her mother alone. Five o'clock finally comes, but the instructor is still talking. Chance's and Carol's patience is beginning to wear thin, thinking about how boring this orientation is and all the fun they are going to have at the party. The final instructor finally speaks and wraps up the orientation. The students are released.

One student yells out, "Let's party!"

Everyone cheers. Each sorority and fraternity group has planned their own party. Chance and Carol stay seated to be the last to leave the room. What they really want is what they get: every male student staring at them and every female student envying them. Ken stops to try to speak to Chance, but she ignores him. Carol smiles at him. He walks away with the crowd. Jake and Jena get up to leave.

"Are you going to any of the sorority parties, Jena?" Jake asks.

"No. I think I'm going to spend my evening at the library," Jena replies.

"Library?" Jake responds in a disappointed voice. "Jena, we will have plenty of time to study; let's go hang out and have a good time." Jake insists. "I really would like to spend some time with you." He gives Jena a sad look.

"No, you go and have fun," she says. "I'm not in the mood for a party. Like I said, I'm going to the library." "Well, I'll go too," Jake tries to respond.

"Alone," Jena replies.

Jake is disappointed, but he tries not to show Jena how much. Jena starts walking out of the orientation room. "I'm just going to call my mom really quick and then head to the library. I'll catch up with you later, Jake." She reaches for his hand. Jake nods his head in a disappointed way.

"Sure," Jake says. "I understand. But, Jena, please don't shut me out. I'm here for you."

Jena smiles. "I know, Jake." She walks out.

Chance and Carol finally get up. Several guys are waiting for them. They just soak up all the attention they are getting from the guys. They walk away with ten to twelve male students following them. Jena walks slowly to the campus library. There are only the librarian and two other students in the entire building. She walks to the literature section. She picks up a book and begins reading it. Four hours has passed without Jena noticing. And at nine o'clock, the librarian taps Jena on the shoulder.

"Hi," the librarian whispers in the lowest voice Jena has ever heard. Jena moves closer to hear what she's saying. "The library is now closed."

Jena nods her head okay. She looks around and sees the library is completely empty. Trying to speak as softly, Jena barely moves her lips or makes a sound. "Yes, ma'am." Jena leaves. Outside the library, it's dark and cold. The wind is blowing briskly. Jena tries to bundle her jacket as tightly as she can. She forgets the exact way to her dorm. She walks down a path that looks familiar to her. Three guys are standing outside talking. Their faces aren't clear to Jena. She just keeps on walking. The boys follow her. Jena tries to run. One of the boys grabs her, and then they all drag her behind the library building. Jena screams, "Help!" No one hears her. One of the boys stuffs her mouth with something to shut her up. He punches Jena in the face twice. She becomes dizzy, almost unconscious. Dark figures are all Jena can see. Her vision is blurred. One of the boys is wearing strong cologne, something she had never smelled before. The strong odor from the cologne is all Jena can smell besides the alcohol on their breaths. Their hands are mostly rough; one of them is soft. The wind howling and the depths of her fear grow but dim away as she fades in and out of consciousness. The boys never say a word; they just hand gesture as if they know exactly what each is to do. While two boys hold Jena down, the other two take turns, two savage beasts invading her most precious place. The one who seems to be the leader cuts Jena's pants. He rips her pants off, removes her panties, and begins brutally raping her. The boys take turns raping Jena. Tears run down one of her swollen eyes. Panting is all Jena hears before she completely passes out. The boys leave her there unconscious and with her clothes ripped off. She lays there bleeding and cold, so cold that her body is numbed.

Jena's roommate reports her missing, and that's when campus police find her behind the library raped, unconscious, and unaware of her surroundings. Campus police immediately call for an ambulance. Late in the night and into the early morning, Jena is transported to the nearest emergency room. Jena lies on the hospital stretcher with one eyed beaten closed. The bright light from the hospital lights burns her eyes. With one closed completely, she keeps the other closed tightly to help stop the stinging and burning from her tears.

CHAPTER TWENTY-FOUR

Jena can vaguely hear what is going on around her. The nurse gives her a shot. "It's okay, Jena; you're in the hospital, and we're going to take good care of you," the nurse says.

Jena can feel herself drifting away, far away to a place she is all too familiar with.

She is back on the airplane standing in the middle of the aisle. She's wearing a red leather coat and red hat and gripping a knife tightly in her hand. All of the men on the airplane are still faceless, reading newspapers and smoking cigars. Mr. McNeil sits in the back still reading his paper. Jena walks up to him. "I see you're still here," she says.

Mr. McNeil looks up through his glasses. "Why are you bothering me, ma'am? What have I done to you?" Mr. McNeil asks. "I've done nothing that I know of." Jena stands closer to him. She puts the knife to his neck. Mr. McNeil sits still. "Please, please, don't kill me whoever you are," Mr. McNeil pleads for his life.

All of the faceless men turn to stare at Jena. Jena puts down the knife. She walks with briskness and confidence back to the front of the plane. She holds the knife in next to her side. Each of the faceless men put their newspaper down as she passes. Their eyes focus on her and then back on Mr. McNeil. The men speak simultaneously to Mr.

McNeil. "Do you know who she is?"

"She's Jena."

Jena slowly tries to wake up from the dream when she hears a voice. "Jena?" a nurse calls. "Jena, hi, I'm Elaine. I'm your nurse." Jena slowly opens one of her eyes. "Jena, you're in the hospital. Something really awful has happened to you, but we are taking very good care of you. Jena, if you understand what I'm saying, please lift a finger from either hand." Jena lifts her right index finger. "Great," the nurse replies. "Jena, we want to contact someone from your family, but we don't have a number or any information. I know you probably don't want to talk right now, but I'm sure your mother, father, or someone would like to know where you are and how you're doing."

Jena sits silent for moment. She blinks one eye. She slowly tries to speak. "Don't," Jena whispers in a cracked and wounded voice.

"Jena, I can't hear you," the nurse replies.

"Don't," Jena tries to speak again. "Don't call anyone, please."

The nurse stands still for a moment. "I understand," Nurse Elaine replies.

Nurse Elaine leaves Jena's room. She falls back to sleep and begins to dream again. This time, she's standing in the middle of nowhere.

There's fog everywhere. Someone taps her on her shoulder. Jena turns around. A foot away from her stands her father. He stands in the middle of the fog. Jena runs to him and hugs him tightly.

"Dad, I'm so happy to see you," she says.

Mr. Parker stands without saying anything. Jena pulls back to look at him. He smiles at her. "Dad, are we in heaven? I know you're in heaven. Where else could you be?" Jena asks. Mr. Parker begins to back away. Jena tries to follow, but her body can't move. "Dad, please don't go!" Jena cries out. "Please don't go!" Jena cries out again, but

Mr. Parker fades away in the fog. "Dad!" Jena screams out loud. Her voices echo through the dark. "Dad!"

Jake stands over Jena's bed and sees her struggling in her dream. He touches her lightly. "Jena!" he calls. "Jena, wake up! Jena, you're dreaming! Wake up," Jake says.

Jena stares at Jake. She looks away, ashamed. Tears stream down her face. "Jake, go away." Jena turns away. "Please just go away," Jena says.

"Jena, I know you might not want to see anyone right now, but I'm not leaving you," Jake says. Jena keeps her face turned away from Jake. She cries and reaches out for his hand. Jake kisses hers. "It's all right," Jake says as he kisses and caresses Jena's hand. He begins to cry. "Jena, it's all right. I'm here for you. I'm going to find out who did this to you, and I'm going to kill them. I'm going to kill them, Jena." Jena screams out uncontrollably. Jake runs to get the nurse.

Nurse Elaine and the two doctors run into Jena's room. Jake walks quickly out of Jena's room. Jena is yelling, "Let me out." She tries to tear out the needles and oxygen tube connected to her.

"Ms. Parker, please calm down," one says, trying to hold Jena down.

Another nurse comes in quickly and injects medicine into her arm. Jake, frantic, stands in the doorway and watches. He starts pacing back and forth past her room door. Jena begins to calm down slowly. Her body relaxes back into her bed. Her eyes slowly close, and then she falls completely out into a deep sleep. Nurse Elaine fixes Jena's oxygen tube and puts her IV needle back in. Jake walks back into the room.

"She should rest comfortably now," Nurse Elaine says. "Maybe you should come back in a few days to allow her to adjust to what has happened to her. Do you know who her parents are?" Nurse Elaine asks.

"Yes, I do," Jake replies.

"She doesn't want the hospital to contact her parents, but she really needs to have someone here for her."

Jake wipes the tears from his eyes. "Jena's father was murdered not too long ago, and her mother is not well right now," he answers. "I'm her only family." Jake stares at Nurse Elaine. "The only person she can count on right now." Jake walks over to Jena's bedside. "I'm going to stay here with her for as long as it takes. I'm going to leave now, but I'll be back with my bags."

Nurse Elaine can hear the hurt in Jake's voice. "I'll be here for her until she recovers." He begins to cry again. "I'll be here for her forever." Jake stands up from the chair.

Nurse Elaine walks out of the room with tears in her eyes. She closes the door behind her to give Jake some privacy.

Days and weeks go by. Jake comes to the hospital when Jena is asleep and awake. Sometimes, Jena will cry in her sleep, cry for help, and then she'll fall back to sleep as if she somehow finally manages to find a peaceful place. While awake, Jena won't speak a word to anyone, not even Jake. Day by day, Jena gets better, but her silence worries Jake because he just can't reach her to bring her back to the Jena he knew. He can't reach her. The police come to Jena's room to try to talk to her, but she won't say a word.

One night, after Jena has been in the hospital for over a month, she is lying awake staring at the wall in her room while Jake is asleep. Jena quietly arises from her bed. She slips on her clothes and packs the few items that belong to her. She drapes her bag over her shoulder and watches Jake as he sleeps soundly in the chair. She slips away from the hospital without being noticed by anyone. In the middle of the night, Jena heads back to her dorm room to get some cash she had hidden in her closet. When she enters the room, her roommate Theresa is asleep. Theresa suddenly wakes.

"Jena, what are you doing out of the hospital?" Theresa asks. She removes the covers and walks over to Jena. Jena doesn't say a word. "Jena, are you all right?"

Jena goes straight to her closet and begins searching for her hidden cash. She grabs her hats and pulls out the hidden money. The letter her mother gave her falls off a shelf in her closet to the floor; she slowly picks it up and puts it in her bag. Theresa quickly switches on the room lights.

"Turn off the lights!" Jena screams.

Theresa just stares in shock. Jena looks up at her and then stands up. "Now!" she screams. Theresa rushes to turn off the lights. "Jena, you're really freaking me out." Theresa panics. "I mean you come here in the middle of the night. You're not talking." Theresa begins to cry. "What's going on?"

Jena turns to Theresa and gives her a chilling, eerie look. "You might want to stay out of my way," she says abruptly. She gives Theresa an evil look, opens the door, and then walks out of the room.

CHAPTER TWENTY-FIVE

J ena thinks to herself as she walks out of her dorm room. She catches a cab to take her somewhere, anywhere. She stares out the cab window thinking about her rape. Her thoughts zone in and out, and a voice in her head speaks to her. "Are you cold? Do you feel a chill running through your bones that makes you stand so still as if you're lifeless? Almost dead. Frozen. Sometimes, that's what I feel when I think of what he did to me. How he changed my life in a way that I will never be the same again."

The cabdriver is impatient. "Where to, lady?" he asks. Jena gives him a blank glare. "Take me to the nearest hotel." "You got it," he answers.

Jena gets out and pays the cabdriver. She walks through the front door and drops her bag on the counter. There's a fat man eating a hotdog with mustard running down his cheeks to his shirt. Jena watches with disgust. Jena clears her thought. The TV is loud, and the hotel clerk is yelling at it while watching his favorite show, Fat Slobs Are People Too.

"Ah, look at that jerk?" a voice in Jena's head says.

The clerk throws his French fries at the television and begins to scream, "Who does this asshole thinks he is? Fat people need love too."

Jena rings the bell on the counter. The man just sits and ignores her. She continues to ring the bell. Finally acknowledging Jena, he says, "Just a minute." He raises one finger up at Jena, but he doesn't look at her. She gives him a deep, dark stare.

You lazy piece of shit. Low life. Creep, she thinks to herself.

Finally, he struggles to stand up out of the chair. He appears to weigh about three hundred pounds, and his shirt barely covers his stomach as his jeans sag in back. Jena rolls her eyes and then grabs her bag from off the counter.

"Well, hello there, young lady," he says, trying to flirt. He raises one of his eyebrows at Jena. There is mustard spattered all over his shirt. Jena fixates on the mustard. Trying to wipe the mustard off his shirt, he says, "I like your red hat." He leans over the counter. "It's hot."

Jena looks up at the man. She doesn't blink. "How much for a room?"

He tries to prolong the conversation. "Well, we have all sorts of different types of rooms, especially for a pretty lady like you. Just about any size … you like." He tries to lean back so Jena can look at his personal area. "What size would you like?"

Jena puts money on the counter. "Anything," Jena replies.

"Well, I have a cozy room on the second floor. It'll give a whole lot of privacy if you know what I mean." The clerk smiles at Jena.

"Hmmm …" she mumbles.

"That will be thirty dollars, little lady." "All I have is twenty-five," she says.

"I'll take it." he hands her the room keys.

Jena begins walking out the door. The man tries to push his way around the corner. "Hey, we got cable and coffee … and breakfast in the morning," he says, breathing hard, as Jena walks out. Jena doesn't turn around or wait for him to finish. She walks to her room, puts down her bag, and turns the television to the news. She paces up and down the hotel room listening to the news. There is a knock at Jena's hotel room door. Jena pulls the curtain back. The front desk clerk is standing at the door holding a wine bottle and two glasses. She gets angry but opens the door. The fat clerks stands in the doorway.

"Hi, it's me again, you know, the front-desk guy," he says.

Jena just stares. He starts to walk in, but Jena stops him. "Well, we aren't much of a hotel here, but we do like to show our guest good hospitality." He hands Jena the wine bottle and a glass. Looking into Jena's room, he asks, "Can I come in?"

Jena hesitates at first but then backs away to let him in. She snatches the wine bottle out of the clerk's hand and opens it with her teeth. "Oh, you're quick." The clerk strolls into the room. His butt crack is showing. Despite Jena being angry, she pretends not to care and just pours the clerk a glass of wine and then herself some. She puts the wine bottle on the table.

Trying to make conversation, he asks, "So are you from around here?"

"No," Jena replies. "I'm just passing through."

The clerk flops himself onto Jena's bed. She pushes out her lips in disgust. "We have nice, comfortable beds here." The clerk pats his hand on the bed. "Why don't you lie down next to me and check it out?" Jena walks toward the bathroom. "Hey, where are you going?" the clerk asks.

Jena turns on the water in the tub, takes off all of her clothes, and then stands naked in the bathroom doorway. The clerk's eyes widen. He begins to chuckle. "I see you and I are going to be good friends. Huh?" He struggles to get off the bed. The fat clerk undresses and rubs one of Jena's breasts on his way into the bathroom. "You're nice and firm. I like that," he says in a panting voice. Jena pretends to be excited.

"Why don't get in the tub and I'll join you?" she says.

The clerk gets more excited by touching Jena. "Oh, you're nice and firm," he says over again.

He turns to get into the tub. Jena pushes him hard. He slips, falls, and hits his head on the toilet. The clerk's head is busted and bleeding. "What the hell? Help me." He reaches out for Jena's hand.

She walks back into the bedroom, reaches for the lamp, removes the shade, and then walks back into the bathroom. The clerk tries to scream louder, but Jena begins beating him on the head over and over again. Blood spurts from the clerk's head and splatters all over Jena's body and the bathroom. Jena continues to hit him over and over again. The clerk's body slumps in the corner of the bathroom. Blood from his head spills out furiously. Jena puts the lamp down. She's breathing hard with no expression on her face. Then she begins to smile while staring at the clerk's cold, lifeless body lying on the floor. She kneels down to touch the streaming blood on the floor. Staring at the blood reminds her of the night her father died. She whispers to the dead clerk, "You go now. You go now and tell somebody." She stands and poses her body firmly. "You go and tell Mr. McNeil I'm coming." The water in the tub is almost overflowing. Jena turns off the water. She steps over the dead clerk and gets into the tub to take a bath. Then she dresses and leaves the clerk dead in the room.

At the hospital, Jake sleeps through the night. He awakes the next morning and finds Jena's bed empty. He walks down to the nurses' station. Nurse Elaine is working on clinical papers. Jake walks up to the counter. "Hi, does Jena have some tests? Because she's not in the room, and I was just wondering ..." Jake asks.

The nurse reviews Jena's chart. "No, none that I ...I'm aware of," Nurse Elaine stutters. She begins checking all of the clinics for appointments for Jena. She calls security to the floor, but no one can find her. "Jake, I believe that Jena may be gone," Nurse Elaine says in an uncertain tone. "I guess she slipped out in the middle of the night."

Jake runs back to Jena's room and then outside the hospital. He frantically searches for Jena everywhere. Jake goes back to the college to search for Jena. He goes to her room. Theresa is just leaving. "Theresa, have you seen Jena?" Jake asks.

Theresa just stands still, afraid to answer.

"Theresa, answers me!" Jake yells.

"Jake, she was here last night." Theresa pauses. "She's not herself." She begins walking, almost running, away. "Look, I have to go, but you need to find her and help her. She really needs help." Theresa walks quickly away. Jake speaks to anyone he can find to find out if anyone has seen Jena. He calls Mrs. Parker, but she doesn't answer the phone. He finally goes to the police department to report Jena as a missing person.

CHAPTER TWENTY-SIX

J ena takes a cab to the train station. There are hundreds of
people there. She waits to board the train that will take her
home, take her back to a place where pain lies waiting for her, to
a house where her father once lived and loved and where her mother
once spoke and lived a life with meaning and hope. The idea of going
home to see her mother made her feel good and bad at the same time.

There in the graveyard will be my father. And the man who
killed him still walks free—free to kill again and free to make me
feel unfree, she thinks to herself. Jena boards the train. She shares
a car with a traveling doctor, a tall, slim, old man who carries a
medical bag with him everywhere. He sits across from Jena reading a
newspaper. His glasses hang from the tip of his nose, and he snuffles
to suggest he has allergies. Jena stares out the train's window. The
old doctor continues reading his paper. The doctor puts his paper
down. Jena is staring at him.

"Is there something wrong, young lady?" the doctor asks.

"No," Jena answers quietly and then looks back out the window.

Feeling a little uneasy, the doctor clears his throat. "So, what's
your name, young lady, and where are you headed?" he asks in a
curious voice.

Jena continues to stare out the window for a moment and then looks back at the doctor. "My name is Jena." She pauses for second. She knows she is no longer the innocent young lady who laughed and felt sorry for things she couldn't change. She doesn't feel sorry anymore. She isn't even sure if she feels anything at all. She just knows she isn't the same person and will never be again. "My name is Jena." Jena pauses. "Jena Gray. I'm going home to see my mother."

"Ah, home," the old doctor replies. "You must be a college student." Fixing his paper, he says, "Well, I'm sure your mother will be very excited to see you."

Jena nods. "Yes, she'll be very excited."

"Well, I guess it's not a secret with me carrying this bag and all, that I'm a doctor. I've been practicing medicine for over fifty years. So, what are you studying in college? What do you want to do when you graduate?" he asks.

All Jena can think about is finding and killing Mr. McNeil. "I don't know what I want to do," she answers. "Not yet." Jena gets an angry look on her face.

Feeling Jena's uneasiness, the doctor backs off on asking Jena any more questions and begins reading his paper again. The old man begins to slump to get comfortable in his chair. Jena just stares at him with a devious look. She stares at his medical bag. The old man dozes off to sleep. Jena watches him. She reaches for his medical bag. In the bag, there are all sorts of medical instruments, pills, and a sharp cutting medical knife. Jena removes the pills and the knife, and she watches while the old man sleeps peacefully. The newspaper he had been reading lies on his lap. Jena looks the doctor up and down. She wonders what he's dreaming about or if he's even dreaming at all. He's been a doctor for fifty years. I wonder how many deaths he's seen or caused. She stabs him in the stomach while he sleeps. The doctor bleeds out quickly. Jena watches as he bleeds to death. He wakes briefly.

"Are you cold?" he whispers to Jena. "Is it cold on this train?"

Jena sits across from him and just stares. "Yes," she answers. "It is very cold on this train."

The old man closes his eyes and dies. The last hours of the train ride, Jena sits watching the old man's dead body. Blood drips from his stomach to the floor. The old man lies still with his mouth slightly open. His glasses hang from his nose while his body sways back and forth with the train's movement. Jena wonders how a body can still move even when it is dead. She thinks to herself, I'm still moving, and I believe I'm dead too.

The train stops. Jena is finally home. She grabs her bag and leaves the old man's dead body lying in the train car. A cab takes her home. Mrs. Parker is in the house watching television. Jena rings the doorbell. Mrs. Parker opens the door, and Jena rushes into her mother's arms. "Mom," Jena says gratefully. Mrs. Parker doesn't say a word, but Jena can tell that she is happy to see her. Mrs. Parker touches Jena's face gently. The smile on her face is like Christmas to Jena. Jena walks into the house, and everything seems the same. She feels so relieved. The living room, kitchen, and even her room— nothing has changed. Jena feels peace for the moment. She feels right being home. Her family picture still hangs on her dresser mirror. The breeze from her window is still flowing. Everything seems perfect, but everything isn't perfect. Out of Jena's room window, she can see the McNeil's' house. Her mother still isn't speaking, and the haunting memories of the night her father was murdered make it seem like it was yesterday. The horrible feeling of that night her father was killed comes rushing back to Jena instantly. The breeze that once felt warm now feels cold and empty. Jena lies on her bed for the moment, and then she goes downstairs. Mrs. Parker is in the kitchen trying to make dinner. Jena walks up to her. "Mom, are you ever going to speak again?"

Mrs. Parker stares at Jena with disappointed eyes. She shakes her head with uncertainty and then walks up to Jena to hold her. "Mom, you have to speak to me," Jena says. "I need you to speak to me. So much has happened since I left home, and now more than ever, I need the comfort of my mother." Mrs. Parker can see the hurt in Jena's eyes. She tries to speak.

"What's …" Mrs. Parker tries to speak again. "What's wrong …?"

Jena can tell her mother is trying to speak, but how can she tell her that she's just been raped and that she's killed two people. How would her mother understand? Could she even cope with any more pain in her life? Mrs. Parker rushes to grab a piece of paper and pen. She writes quickly on the paper. "What's wrong, Jena?" Mrs. Parker stares at Jena.

Jena doesn't say a word, but the tears begin to stream from her eyes.

Mrs. Parker grabs her. She struggles to speak again. "What's wrong?" Mrs. Parker holds Jena tightly. Through Jena's pain, the sound of her mother's struggling voice makes her feel some happiness. Finally hearing her mother's voice reminds her of when she was a kid and her mother would speak to her all the time, helping with her homework, making dinner, and most of all, talking to Dad. Watching her mother struggle to speak, Jena doesn't have the heart to tell her mother the truth.

"Don't worry, Mom." Jena touches her mother's face.

"Everything will be all right. I just miss Dad; that's all."

Mrs. Parker smiles and nods to say, "Me too."

"Now let's see what you're cooking." Mrs. Parker smiles.

Jena puts her arms around her mother's shoulders. They sit, eat, and mostly Jena talks throughout the evening. Mrs. Parker manages to say a few words here and there, but the happiness on her face is more than enough for Jena. This is one of the best nights for the both of them. They laugh at family pictures and even play a game. "Mom, you look tired," Jena says. "Why don't you go up and get ready for bed, and I'll clean up down here," Jena says as she looks around the kitchen.

Mrs. Parker heads upstairs. Jena stands and stares at the bottom of the stairway and watches while her mother slowly walks up. "I'll come up and talk to you before I go to bed, Mom." Mrs. Parker turns around, gives Jena a slight smile, and then nods her head.

CHAPTER TWENTY-SEVEN

Downstairs is quiet. The still of the night fills the room as Jena stands and stares off at an old antique her grandmother had given her mother when she was a little girl. How old and precious that antique is to Mother, Jena thinks to herself. How much she loves it and how heartbroken she would be if anything were to happen to it. Jena sits down on the couch in the living room. How soft this couch feels, she thinks to herself. Suddenly, a crackling sound comes from upstairs.

Mrs. Parker is walking around getting ready for bed. Jena flashes back to the last time she saw her father, just before he was killed. That horrible night comes rushing back to her, and all she can think about is the look on her mother's face after her father was shot and murdered. Jena rises from the couch and walks up to the old antique that Grandmother gave her mother. She touches it gently. She stares at it and wonders what her mother would think if she broke the antique. Just above that antique was the family photo of her mother, father, and herself smiling as if nothing could go wrong. Yet, at this very moment, everything that could be wrong is wrong, Jena thinks. Jena reaches in her coat pocket. She grabs the pills she stole from the doctor on the train, and then walks to the kitchen. Mom always loved a glass of warm milk before she went to bed.

Jena thinks back to when her mother made her warm milk to help her sleep. She makes her mother a tall glass of warm milk and then walks upstairs. Mrs. Parker is lying in her bed almost asleep. Jena walks into the room with the glass in her hand. Mrs. Parker slowly awakens and sits up in the bed with a smile of joy on her face like a little child when a mother comes to tuck her in. As she walks toward her mother's bedside with the glass of milk in her hand, her parents' favorite song repeats over and over in her head. "If I Can't Have You, I Don't Want Nobody Else, Baby."

"If I can't have you," Jena begins to sing the song to her mother as she walks toward her. "If I can't have you, I don't want nobody, baby. If I can't have you …"

"Ah, oh," Mrs. Parker is thrilled. Jena continues to sing her and her father's favorite love song. Jena sits down on the edge of her mother's bed and hands her the glass of warm milk. Mrs. Parker begins drinking the milk. Jena watches with silence in her eyes. She drinks all the milk and then puts the glass on the table next to her bed. Her eyes instantly begin to get very heavy.

"I love you, Mom," Jena whispers quietly to her mother. Mrs. Parker tries to stay awake. "I know how much you loved Dad." Her body begins to go limp. "I know that your life will never be the same without him." Jena rubs her mother's hair and face as she lies there. Mrs. Parker tries to reach for Jena, but her body is very weak from the pills. "I remember the painful look on your face, Mom, when you knew Daddy was gone forever. It is a look I will never forget." Mrs. Parker goes quietly and peacefully into a deep sleep that she will never wake from. Jena watches as her mother drifts away. She had laced her mother's milk with a sedative she found in the doctor's medical bag.

"Good-bye, Mother," Jena says while she covers her mother's body with a blanket. "You go now," Jena says. "You go and you tell him. You tell him I'm coming for him." She kisses her on the forehead and walks downstairs to clean the kitchen. She cleans the entire kitchen and even cleans up the living room. On her way out, she grabs her bag and then takes one last look upstairs where she knows her mother lies dead. "Tell Dad I said hello and that I love him," Jena says as she turns to open the front door to leave. She leaves all the lights on. As she opens the door, Jake is just beginning to ring the doorbell. Surprised, Jena stands still in the doorway.

"Jena!" Jake calls as he grabs her body tightly in his arms. "Are you all right?" he asks.

"I'm fine, Jake," she says. "What are you doing here?" she asks.

"I'm looking for you," Jake replies in a concerned voice. "I've been so worried. I mean you left the hospital without saying a thing to me. Why? The hospital's looking for you too." Jena stares upstairs. "What's going on, Jena?" Jake asks. Jake looks past Jena into the house and up the stairs. "Is your mother all right?" he asks.

Jena walks out and stands on the porch with the door open signaling for Jake to follow. Jake walks out. Jena closes the door. "Yes, she's fine," Jena replies. "She's asleep though, and I don't want to disturb her, so why don't we leave and go somewhere?"

"Somewhere?" Jake answers. "Where?"

"I don't know, just anywhere but here," Jena says. She glares across the street toward the McNeil's' house.

Jake turns and looks too. "I understand," he says. He wraps his arm around Jena, and they walk back to the car.

Jake opens the door for her, and Jena sits down quickly in the car. She takes one last glance at the house she called home as Jake drives away. She turns to him. "Jake, let's go to New York."

Jake pulls over to the side of the road. "Jena, New York?" Jake acts surprised.

"Yes, New York," she replies. "I want to get away to somewhere new and exciting. All you have to do is drive me there, and then you can come back." Jena gets a little angry. "If you don't take me, I'll find a way to go anyway."

Jake pulls back onto the highway. "Jena, you know I'll do anything for you." Jake turns to her. "I'll take you, and I'll stay with you as long as you need me to. Besides, there's no class this week."

Jake drives all night to New York. Jena barely speaks to him. They arrive in New York, and the streets are still lit up. Jake and Jena stare at the Statue of Liberty in amazement.

"I think I'll try this hotel," he says. He gets out of the car. "You wait here, Jena. Let me check this place out." Jake pays for a week's stay at the nice hotel. They are both exhausted from the long drive. "Are you hungry, Jena?" he asks. Jena nods her head yes. "You can go up and get settled in the room, and I'll go get us some food."

"Okay," Jena replies.

"Do you want me to take your bag in first?" Jake reaches for Jena's bag.

Jena grabs it quickly. "I got it, Jake," she says abruptly.

"Okay, well then, I'll be back shortly."

Jake hands her the key to the room. She walks in and hides her bag under the bed and then lies down on the bed. Mentally exhausted, Jena falls asleep on the bed.

She is back on the airplane still wearing the red leather jacket and the red hat. Mr. McNeil is at the back of the airplane still reading his paper. Jena walks up to him again. She puts the knife back to his neck. He panics. "Why are you doing this?" Mr. McNeil asks. "What do you want from me?"

Jena looks closely into Mr. McNeil's face. "I want you to die," she answers. "I want you to bleed like you made him bleed."

Mr. McNeil starts to sweat. "Who are you talking about?" he asks.

Before she can answer, she wakes up and stares up at the ceiling of the room. Jake knocks on the door. She opens it, and he's standing in the doorway with two greasy bags in his hand. The bags are dripping. "Did you kill something?" she asks. "It's about time you got back," Jena says as she swings the door open.

She grabs Jake and gives him a kiss on the lips.

"Let's go shopping?" Jena asks.

Jake is surprised but is secretly delighted by Jena's sudden attention to him. He puts the bags on the table. "I thought you were hungry?" he asks.

"I am." Jena grabs one of the bags, pulls out a sandwich, and then takes a bite. "But I want to go shopping," she says. She turns around and around in the room "This is New York; there's shopping everywhere." She stops and stares at Jake. "So, let's go." Jena pulls Jake's arm.

He grabs a sandwich and takes a bite as Jena pulls him out of the hotel room. "We're in New York, Jake." She starts to giggle as she glances over at him. "This is the place, Jake, where you can start over, where anyone can get a second chance."

Jake is mesmerized by Jena. His love for her is obvious. Just watching her happiness makes him feel good inside. Jena's sudden burst of excitement thrills Jake. He can't wait to take her shopping. He would do anything to make her happy again. They go to several stores. Jena buys shoes and a purse, but she can't find the perfect dress. "Jake, I want to find the perfect dress." She is just about to give up. Jake stops to look at hats from a vendor parked on the sidewalk. Jena leans against a building disappointed. "I want the perfect dress," Jena says out loud.

Cars pass back and forth on the busy street. People are walking around everywhere. Across the street in the window is a dress. Jena stands up straight. She smiles as she looks across the street at the dress that is displayed in the boutique window. I've found you; she thinks. "I've finally found you."

CHAPTER TWENTY-EIGHT

Jena runs across the street without thinking. Cars honk their horns, but she doesn't care; she just keeps running. Jake chases her, trying not to get hit by a car. Jena stands in front of the boutique window. Her eyes glaze over as she stares at the dress in the window. She turns to Jake. "Jake, this is it! This is the dress I've been hoping for." A red dress is displayed on a mannequin in the window. The dress sways close to the mannequin's body. The front hangs low, and the dress fits close and has a mermaid shape. Jena walks into the store. An old woman sits on a stool waiting for a customer.

"Hello and welcome," the old woman says in an eager voice. Jena stands and stares at the dress. The old woman struggles to stand up. "How may I help you, young lady?" she says slowly.

Pointing at the dress in the window, Jena says, "I want that dress. The red one in the window. I want it." "Oh, that dress," the old woman replies.

"Yes, please; I have to have it," Jena says.

The old woman walks toward the window. "Well, that's the only one I have. Nobody has ever tried it on. If you want it, I'll sell it to you, and I'll even throw in that red hat from over there." The old woman points to a red hat that hangs on a hat rack. Jena walks slowly toward the hat. She touches it. The hat is a high-top shape.

Jena puts it on her head and then stands in front of the mirror. The old lady and Jake stand next to her and look in the mirror. "See, that hat fits you perfectly."

Jena stares at herself in the mirror. A flashback from her dream of her wearing a red hat crosses her mind. "Yes, it does," Jena says.

The old woman walks away to get the dress off the mannequin. "Let me help you, ma'am," Jake says. Jake removes the mannequin from the window. He takes it in the back. The old woman follows. "I thought I'd bring her back here," he says. "I don't want her naked in the window."

The old woman smiles. "You're nice, kid." Then she gives Jake a long stare. "But be careful," she tells him like a fortune-teller.

Jake pays for the dress and hat. Standing out in front of the store, Jake holds Jena's hand. "Are you happy?" he asks.

"Yes, I'm so happy, Jake," Jena says and kisses him on the cheek.

"Now can we eat?" Jake asks.

"Of course, let's go," Jena replies.

Walking on the streets of New York, Jena feels bold, empowered. There are so many people in New York, she thinks. So many people like me, people who are confused, happy at times, maybe they have someone they love, someone like a father or a mother. A woman passes Jena and stares at her in a fearful way. Jena mumbles to herself. And even someone who may have killed. Killed just like me. They all are maybe just like me. Searching for something. Something we don't know even exists.

"Here." Jena stops in front of a café. "This is where we'll eat."

Jake takes a peek inside. "Looks decent," he says. He opens the door for Jena, and they walk in. A man seats them at a table. Two kids around their same age sit next to them at a table. "Dude, we're in New York and that club is hot," one of the guys says.

Jena listens in on their conversation. "Are you sure, man?" the other guy asks. "Because if there's not a lot of hot women there, I'm going to kick your ass."

They both start laughing. A tall, slender waitress walks up to Jake and Jena's table. "What'll you have?" she asks in a rough Jersey accent.

Jake looks at Jena. Jena shrugs her shoulders. Jake feels a little intimidated. "We'll take the special with two Cokes. All right?" Jake says.

"Two specials, Earl," the waitress yells as she walks away.

She brings back the food. The two guys get up from the table. Jena stops one of them. "So, where's the party tonight, guys?" she asks. "I overheard you talking about a club.

"Yeah, it's supposed to be hot. It's called New House Club," one of the guy's answers.

The other guy stares at Jena and smiles. "You guys should come." He winks at Jena. Jake gives him a jealous look. The two guys leave.

"So, what do you say, Jake? Up for a little clubbing tonight?"

Jake stares into Jena's eyes. He can't say no. He takes a bite of his sandwich. His cell phone vibrates. "That's weird," he says.

"What's weird?" Jena asks.

"My mom called, but I didn't even hear the phone ring the first time. I should get this."

"No." Jena grabs the phone. "Let's just have some fun."

The phone stops ringing. Jena hands him back the phone.

"Looks like she left a message, but I'll check it later."

"Yeah, check it later," Jena replies. She starts to eat and smiles at Jake. "I'm sure she'll understand. So, what about tonight?" Jena asks again.

"Why not?" Jake replies. In his mind, all he can think about is how much he loves her and that every moment spent with her is all he has ever wanted. "I'm out of school for a week, and hell, we're in New York," he answers. "So why not have some fun?"

Everything seems great between Jake and Jena. Jake is starting to believe that Jena will make it through her problems. She seems happy for the first time since the death of her father and the horrible rape she endured. Jake never brings up the rape because he wants her to forget about it. All he wants is to be close to her, to see her smile, and to fantasize about her. I want to love, Jena, he thinks to himself. I'm so in love with you.

Back at the hotel, Jake dozes off in a chair while watching TV. Jena watches over him while he sleeps. Her face goes blank as if she feels nothing for him. She knows that she is just pretending to be happy, to be all right, but inside, she is dead, cold, and empty. And Jake's presence can't bring her back to the Jena he knew. She opens Jake's wallet and takes out his credit card. At a corner store down the street, she buys hair dye and a pack of cigarettes. As the store clerk rings up the cigarettes, she speaks to Jena.

"You know smoking is bad for you, young lady."

Jena snatches the cigarettes from the clerk's hand and moves her face closer to the clerk's. "Yeah, well, so is hell," she replies. "You ever thought about that?"

The clerk stands back. Jena walks back to the hotel. There is a homeless man sitting in a corner near an alleyway. Jena stops and kneels down. She blows smoke in the homeless man's face. "Can I have one?" he asks.

Jena just stares at him. "I should kill you," she says. "Put you out of your misery. But looking at you, I can tell you're already dead. You're walking dead, just like me."

The homeless man is speechless. "Can I still have a cigarette?" he asks.

Jena stands up. "No. Just die quicker, and then you won't need to smoke or be homeless ever again." She walks away.

Upstairs, Jake is still asleep when she returns. Quietly opening the hotel room door, Jena is able to slip back into the room without Jake noticing. She puts Jake's credit card back in his wallet and goes straight to the bathroom where she spends hours getting ready for the club. Tonight, will be a new beginning for me, she thinks. She stands in front of the mirror for hours staring at the red dress Jake bought her. She colors her hair red. With the red dress, red hair, the shoes, and the makeup Jena is wearing, she looks like a completely different person. She feels like a mature woman who just grew up from being a little girl. She stands in front of the mirror and makes poses like a woman who no longer thinks of herself as a child, but a person on a mission to make her life as meaningful as possible—even if it means killing someone else.

"Are you going to take all night?" Jake says, as he knocks on the bathroom door.

Jena doesn't reply. She stands without moving, without sound. The red hat sits on the side of the bathroom sink. She slides the hat over her head and slightly tilts it down so that it covers one side of her face. She opens the bathroom door and stands to the left of the door. Jake looks up from playing a game on his cell phone. He stands in complete shock at how beautiful Jena looks. The expression on his face tells her he is in total awe. He swallows. "You look …" He can't speak for a moment. "Jena, you look so beautiful. You don't even look like you."

I'm not me, Jake, she thinks. "It is me, Jake," she says, trying to convince him. She walks toward Jake in a sexy and seductive way. "It's the new me." Jake wraps his arms around Jena's tiny waist. "Get dressed and ready so we can go."

Jake shakes his head. "Well then, let's go burn up the town," he says.

They catch a cab to the club. Outside the club is a line that wraps around the building. When Jena gets out of the cab, she looks like a celebrity. Everyone is staring at her. Too impatient to stand in a long line, Jena walks straight up to the door bouncer while Jake pays the cabdriver. The bouncer holds a guest list in his hand. "And who are you, miss?" the bouncer asks.

Jena looks the bouncer deeply in his eyes. "My name is Jena."

The bouncer stares at Jena's beautiful, red lips. "Jena Gray."

The bouncer is taken by her beauty and pulls the line divider back to let Jena enter the club. She looks back and points. Jake's running to catch up with her. "He's with me," she tells the bouncer. They both walk into the club like celebrities. Jena's confidence level is high. She no longer thinks of herself as Jena Parker, a shy young lady from a small town. She is now a high roller, an undiscovered, a member of the walking dead. Inside, the club is packed. People are practically breathing down each other's necks. The crowd ranges from young college students to middle-aged adults. When Jena walks into the room, all eyes are on her. Her beauty is stunning, and she knows that all the attention is on her—at least for tonight. Jake stands close to her.

"This place is crowded," he says. Jena stares around the room. "Hey, I have to go to the men's room." Jake taps Jena on the shoulder. She turns to him. Jake tries to yell over the music, "I have to go to the men's room!"

"I'll be at the bar," Jena replies. She walks to the bar and stands in the center with both arms bent back on the bar as she scans the dance floor. The music is blasting, and people are dancing everywhere. Jena leans on the bar and stares seductively at the dance floor. A middle-aged man and a young girl are dancing provocatively. They catch Jena's eye. That man looks familiar, she thinks to herself. The man dances closely with the young girl on the dance floor. He's wearing a tight polyester blue suit and a colorful shirt from the '70s. His hair is flopped over on one side. His belly flops over his pants, and he is completely drunk. Jena stares intently at the dance floor. Her face darkens. Her flush deepens with anger. Her eyes grow as black as a coal, and the hunger to kill sparks in her eyes like a lightning bolt when it strikes to kill anyone in its way. It was Mr. McNeil! It's him! It's him! she repeats over and over in her head.

CHAPTER TWENTY-NINE

Mr. McNeil had tried to change his looks slightly, but Jena knows who he is. She stands staring at the drunken Mr. McNeil and the young girl from the bar. Her expression grows angrier. Her face displays a horrible frown. She strolls to the dance floor. People are dancing, but just like a phantom, she moves smoothly through the crowd. Her parents' favorite song comes on, and the moment feels right. She pushes the young girl dancing with Mr. McNeil out of the way and starts dancing with him. She touches Mr. McNeil and herself all over as she dances. Mr. McNeil doesn't recognize her. He tries to move the hat, but Jena slowly moves his hands to her breasts and then up her dress. Mr. McNeil smiles. Coming on to Jena, Mr. McNeil tries to kiss her, but she pretends to push him away. She grabs his arm from behind her and dances him off the dance floor and out of the club.

Jake looks for Jena at the bar. He spots Jena leaving the dance floor with a man. He yells for her, but she doesn't hear him. Jena's total focus is on Mr. McNeil. She wants him dead in the way that a lover wants sex, in a way that a woman wants her dead husband back. The passion she feels for Mr. McNeil is far beyond the love Jake feels for her. It's far beyond the earth. Outside the club, Mr. McNeil waves for a cab. Jake is seconds too late to stop Jena from leaving.

Just as he runs out of the club, the cab pulls off. "Damn it!" he says. He waves for a cab to follow them. Jena and Mr. McNeil's cab pulls up to a five-star hotel. With so much traffic, Jake's cabdriver falls a little behind. "Don't lose them, please." He panics. Sweat is dripping from his face. His cell phone rings. "Hello?" he answers.

"Jake!" His mother is on the other end. "Jake, honey, are you all right?"

"Yes, Mom, what's wrong?" he asks.

"How come you haven't been answering your phone or calling me back?"

"Mom, I'm in New York."

"New York? What are you doing in New York?"

"I found Jena, and well, she—"

Mrs. Paterson cuts him off. "You're with Jena? Jake, Jena's mother has been murdered. Kitty's dead." Mrs. Paterson starts to cry. "The police believe that Jena killed her, and she may also be involved in two other murders." Jake drops his cell phone. "Jake!" Mrs. Paterson calls. "Jake!" Her voice echoes from the cell phone on the cab floor.

"Drive faster!" Jake yells at the cabdriver.

Jena flirts with Mr. McNeil, and she touches his leg and moves her hands up his pants. Mr. McNeil kisses her chest and neck. She breathes out loudly. "I want you," he says. His very presence sickens Jena, but it isn't enough to stop her from getting revenge. Nothing and no one can stop her. In the hotel room elevator and hallway, Jena plays with McNeil. She gives him every impression that she is his for the night, that she wants him—and she does, dead.

Jena watches while a drunken Mr. McNeil searches for his room key. "Here, let me help you." She reaches in his pants pocket and finds the room key. He leans on the door and falls into the room as she opens it. She pushes Mr. McNeil on the bed. "Take off your clothes," she says in a sexy voice. Mr. McNeil removes his belt, pants, everything. He walks up to Jena to help her remove hers. "No, not yet" Jena whispers. Jena teases him.

He smiles and stumbles to the bathroom. "I have to go to the little boys' room," he says. "But when I get back, I want you naked in my bed," he says drunkenly. Jena begins to remove her dress. Mr. McNeil stumbles into the bathroom. Jena paces up and down the room quickly to try to find something to kill him with. She opens the hotel room drawer and finds a gun. She quickly takes off her clothes and stands naked in only her red high heels with the pistol held in her hands behind her back. Mr. McNeil stumbles out of the bathroom and tries to walk toward Jena but falls on the bed.

"That's good," she says. "I want you on the bed."

"Do you?" Mr. McNeil says while trying to sit up.

"Now, push your way up so I can see all of you clearly," Jena says.

"Come join me?" Mr. McNeil asks.

Jena pulls the gun from behind her back. "What are you doing?" he asks in a panicked voice.

"I'm not a little girl. I'm someone you know," Jena says. "Someone you took something from."

Mr. McNeil squints his eyes. "Jena?" He recognizes her. "Jena Parker? Is that you—"

Jena shoots Mr. McNeil once in the head. "No! My name is Jena Gray." Then she shoots him again in the face and twice in the chest.

Jake is in the hotel hallway and hears the gunfire. He opens the room door and tries to grab the gun away from Jena, but it's too late. "Jena, what have you done?"

Mr. McNeil's body lies dead and bleeding on the sheets. Jena stares at him. "Get out, Jake," she says.

"Jena, hurry up and get dressed!" Jake yells. He stares at Mr. McNeil. "We have to get out of here. The cops will be coming." Jake stares at Jena's naked body. His passion for her grows, and although Mr. McNeil is lying on the bed dead, all he can think about is making love to her. Jake hands Jena her dress. "Put it on; we have to go!" He tries not to stare at her naked body. Jena gently puts on her dress. Jake grabs her hand, and they rush out of the hotel room into a cab and head back to their hotel.

Both of them remain silent in the cab. Jake holds the gun in his hand. "No matter what you think, Jake, he deserved it. I'd kill him over and over again if I ever had the chance to. He murdered my father, and he murdered me."

Jake holds the gun and doesn't say a word. Finally, he asks, "Did he touch you, Jena?"

"You mean did he touch me? No."

Jake turns away and breathes a sigh of relief. The cab finally gets to the hotel room. Jena goes to the bathroom and stands in the doorway. "I'm going to take a bath." She slams the bathroom door.

Jake sits down on the bed and lays the gun on the table next to the bed. He begins to cry. He is torn between knowing the hideous things Jena has done and his obsession with her. He removes his shirt and sits on the bed. Jena walks out of the bathroom naked. She walks up to Jake. "Do you want me, Jake?" She lays him down on the bed and kisses him—first, gently on the lips and then down his chest to his pants.

She removes his belt; he turns her over. "Are you sure?" he asks.

"Take off your pants, Jake," Jena replies.

Jake removes his pants. He kisses Jena from her belly to her breast. His hot tongue gently licks her all over. Jena caresses his body and gives in to him. He stops for a moment. Hesitating and wanting her at the same time, breathing hard, he asks, "Jena, did you kill ..." Jake puts his head on her shoulder. Still breathing hard, he asks, "Did you kill your mother and those two other—"

Jena kisses Jake on the lips to stop him from finishing. She puts one finger over his lips. "Jake, please don't ruin this moment. Take me," she says. "I want you now, and you've wanted me forever."

He begins kissing and caressing her again. Jake's passion overtakes him. He doesn't care if Jena has just murdered a man or even if she murdered her mother. He stops and stares deeply into her eyes. "I love you, Jena," he says in a soft, passionate voice. "I love you so much." Jena doesn't say a word back. He continues to make love to her. She moans passionately. Jena begins to think back to the night she went to the library. Jake's body sways back and forth like a ship on the ocean.

His body movement takes her back, takes her back to the night she was raped. His body movement feels so familiar. His cologne smells so familiar, Jena thinks to herself.

"I love you, Jena," Jake whispers again.

She remains silent. That smell, she thinks. That familiar smell, Jena continues to think to herself as Jake makes love to her. I remember that smell, these tenders, but eager hands touching me. I remember. Jena tries not to believe it could have been Jake. She flashes back to when they were playing as kids in the park and at school, to middle school when Jake always teased her, and to high school when he confessed his love to her. That night at the library, she thinks. The librarian taps me on the shoulder and whispers that it's time to go. The red cup, Jake. It's all foggy. No. Jake was there. He met me at the door. "Drink this," he says. I remember now. Jena thinks. "It's really good," he says, so I drank it all. This moment, his body movement, and this familiar smell, I can't … remember … but wait. He held my hand and guided me to his room. I was dizzy, and then I felt my body fall to the bed. Were there three men? I don't know. Was it him? One face, two hands, his breath. What's wrong with me? It can't be Jake. A voice speaks. "It's him, Jena. He did it. Don't you remember his obsession with you? The constant drooling over you. Always hanging around trying to pretend he wanted to just be your friend, but all the while he only wanted one thing: all men want one thing, Jena. It's him!" the voice yells.

Her body jerks. Tears run down Jena's cheeks as Jake continues to make love to her. After they make love, Jake kisses Jena gently on the lips. He pulls her next to him in the bed. He begins stroking her hair. "Jena," he whispers. "I've always loved you." Jena stares off into space. "I've always wanted you, but I didn't think you would ever want me this way. Making love to you is like making love to an angel."

Jena leans up in the bed. She reaches for the gun and points it at Jake. "Except, Jake, I'm not an angel," she says. "I know it was you. I remember now."

"Jena, no! Please, let me explain!" Jake yells.

Jena fires a shot. It hits Jake in the head. She watches while Jake dies. She sits up in the bed for a few minutes and then gets up to get dressed. She never looks back at Jake, but she doesn't have to; she knows he's dead. She can hear the blood drip from Jake's body onto the floor. Before leaving the room, she stops at the doorway. "Now you go. You go and tell somebody." She opens the hotel room door and closes it behind her. "Are you cold? Do you feel a chill running through your body? Well, I do. And I'll never be the same again."

THE END

JENA PARKER RETURNS

CHAPTER ONE

"No!" Jake screams. Two bullets hit him, one in the chest and the other in the head. "Stop, Jena! It wasn't me!" She hears Jakes voice echo in her head as she tosses and turns.

"Wake up, Jena." Jake shakes her. "Wake up. You're dreaming." Jake pushes Jena. She opens her eyes.

"Jake?" Jena stares at Jake in disbelief that he is still alive. She's breathing hard. "Oh, Jake." Jena looks around the room. The gun she used to kill Mr. McNeil is on the table next to her. She looks back at Jake, and then she gets out of the bed slowly. "You're alive, but …"

Jake removes the covers. "Yes, you killed Mr. McNeil … and possibly a few other people."

Jena shakes her head. "My mom?" she asks.

"She's dead, Jena," Jake replies.

Tears run down Jena's face. "No! God no!" Jena looks at the bed, blankets, and sheets. "Did we?" she asks.

"Yes, we made love last night and, Jena, it was perfect."

Jena sits on the bed. "I killed you last night, Jake." She looks back at Jake.

"You were dreaming, Jena," Jake says. Jake touches her on the shoulder. He tries to hug her.

"No! Stop! Get away from me," Jena screams.

"What's wrong, Jena?" Jake asks.

"What's wrong? I'm a damn killer, Jake. I killed my—" Jena stops. "I killed my mother … Why would I do that?"

Jake rubs his hands through his hair. "I don't know, Jena, and I don't care. I love you."

"Oh, you love a killer? A person who could kill her own … mother."

Jena begins to remember her father's horrible death. She gets angry and remembers why she killed Mr. McNeil. He deserved every bullet he got; she thinks.

Jake walks over to Jena's side of the bed. He sits down next to her. "Jena, I don't have all the answers," Jake says. "I don't know what happened to make you do the things you did. What I do know is that I love you and I'll do anything for you." Jake kisses Jena on the cheek and then tries to kiss her on the lips.

"Don't!" Jena gets up from the bed. "I have to go," she says quietly.

"Go where?" Jake asks.

"I don't know, Jake, just away from you. From this place." Jena picks up the gun.

Jake stands up. "Jena, please put the gun down."

She points the gun at Jake. "You don't know who I am, Jake. Who I've become." Jena has both index fingers on the gun's trigger. Jake steps toward her. "Stop! Don't move, Jake," she says.

"Jena, you don't want to do this," Jake pleads.

"Really? I don't? You don't know what I want or what I care about." Jena walks closer to Jake. She puts the gun to his head.

"Jena, I love you," Jake says.

"Love. Me. You love me. I don't think you do. I think you've been obsessed with me since we were kids. I think you've wanted to have sex with me, but you don't love me. How could you love someone who has killed her own mother and is capable of killing you? No, you don't love me … and that's why you have die."

"Jena, no!"

"Yes, Jake, with everything that's happened, you have to die. I can't have you constantly reminding me of the things that I'm not proud of."

"Jena, please. Don't, Jena, please—" Jena fires two shots into Jake's head. He falls backward to the bed.

Jena suddenly wakes from her dream. Jake is lying next to her, still asleep. She pulls the covers back and realizes that they are both naked. She looks around the room, fearing that this moment is also a dream. The blowing wind from the hotel room window convinces her that this moment is real. The gun that killed Mr. McNeil is still on the table next to her bed. She slowly gets up and dresses, staring at Jake the entire time. She grabs the gun from the table and places it in her bag and then slips on her shoes and coat. The wind blows her hair from side to side. She reaches back into the bag for the gun and points it at Jake. With the wind still whipping at her hair, she stands firm and continues to point the gun at Jake. Exhausted from the night before, Jake doesn't stir. Jena puts the gun down.

Jena remembers spotting Mr. McNeil at the dance club. She remembers how she flirted with him in the cab and in the hotel room—and how she killed him just before Jake rushed into the room. The look on his face. The look of love and fear.

Jena puts the gun back into her bag. She backs away, slowly opens the hotel room door, walks out, and gently closes the door. A couple is kissing in the hotel hallway as Jena passes. The girl stops and stares at Jena as she walks past. Jena gives her an evil look. She stops.

"Is there something wrong?" Jena asks. The couple just stares at Jena, and then the girl shakes her head.

"Get out of here," the guy says to Jena.

Jena pulls out her gun. "You talking to me?" Jena points the gun in the guy's face. "I don't think you're talking to me."

"No, I wasn't talking to you," the man says. "I was talking to myself."

Jena looks at the girl. "Are you scared?" Jena asks. The girl looks at the man, afraid to speak. "I asked are you scared?" Jena raises her voice. The girl nods her head. "What's your name?"

"Candy," she reply.

"Candy," Jena says. "Your name is Candy?"

"Yes."

"Well, Candy, get the hell out of here." Jena points the gun at Candy and pushes her. Candy runs down the hall. Jena points the gun at the man. "What's your name?"

"My name is Paul."

"Paul … Well, Paul, today is your unlucky day." Jena fires a shot at Paul's left leg. Paul falls to the floor. People begin peeking out of their hotel rooms. Jake opens the door. Jena sees him and runs.

"Jena! Jena come back!" Jake yells and tries to run behind her, but Jena is gone. Jake goes back to help Paul.

Candy is standing over Paul. "Don't help him," she says. "He's an asshole." Candy kicks Paul.

"Well, talk about kicking a person when they're down," Janice, one of the guests, says.

Jake rushes back to the hotel room. I have to find Jena, he thinks. He frantically gets dressed, quickly grabs his things, and leaves the room. Jena, my love, I know you're confused, and I know you're not yourself, but I will find you. Jake stops. I will find you.

Jake rushes out to the New York streets and screams Jena's name. "Jena!" He cries out. "Jena! Where are you?" People pass Jake by and stare, but he doesn't care. He is desperate and willing to do or say anything to be with Jena again.

Jake searches for Jena for days, but there is no sign of her anywhere. He passes a police station and stops, but he realizes he can't report Jena as a missing person because of the murders she has committed. He doesn't know what to do. Just then he looks up and notices a flashing sign advertising a psychic palm reader. Jake contemplates his options as the flashing lights blink back and forth. He finally walks in the door.

A lady with a wrinkled face and a scarf wrapped around her head is sitting at a table. She looks at Jake, glaring at him with her dark eyes. "My name is Jaslin. How can I help you?" Jake just stands there and doesn't say a word. As if she could sense Jake's desperation, Jaslin stands up and gestures to Jake with one of her arms. "Please, have a seat." Jake sits down in the chair.

The two of them sit and stare at one another for at least a minute. "I know why you're here," Jaslin says. Jake looks away to avoid Jaslin's eyes. "Please look at me," she says. "Look at me and know the truth," she continues. "Know the truth about the one you love." Jake's eyes widen. "That's what you seek?" she asks quietly. "You seek the one you love … and the one you fear." Jake doesn't speak. "Your lips don't move, but your eyes," Jaslin glares at Jake, "yes, your eyes tell me all the truth I need to know. You want to know where she is, don't you?" Jake shakes his head. "You want to know if she is," Jaslin pauses, "bad?" Jake swallows. "I must tell the truth," Jaslin says. "You may not be satisfied, but the truth is all I know and is all I will tell anyone. The truth in itself can be a lie. A lie and the truth can be one in the same. She is good, and she is bad. She is a woman scorned and a woman who has no path. The pain in her is deep … too deep for you to reach. She is falling—falling slowly. Just like a bird flying through the sky, she is free."

"Will I find her?" Jake asks.

"Yes," Jaslin answers. "You will find what you want to find, but it may not be real."

Jake stands up. "Oh, come on. You haven't told me anything," he shouts. "Just a bunch of nonsense." He slams his fist on the table. "Where is she?"

Jaslin stands. "I've told you a lot, but you are not open to listening. She is here."

Jake looks around the room. "Here? Where?"

"Wherever you are, Jake, that's where she is."

"How did you know my …" Jake pauses.

Jaslin continues. "Wherever you are, Jake, she is with you. You will always be able to find her. Find your Jena."

Jake is shocked. He reaches in his pocket.

"Don't," Jaslin says. "I don't want your money. You will pay a price, but it will not be here."

Jake stands with his head down for a moment. "I don't know what price I have to pay. I love her," he says. "Love has no price."

"Everything has a price," Jaslin says.

Jake rushes out of the building. He walks down the deserted street. I will find her; he thinks to himself. I will find you, Jena.

CHAPTER TWO

Jena sits on the city bus with her bag in her lap. She stares out the bus window and flashes back to a memory from when she was five years old.

"So, Daddy, what kind of animal is that?" Jena asks her father.

"Oh, Jena, this isn't an animal. This is just a ladybug." Mr. Parker picks up the bug and hands it to Jena. "Here—see, it won't harm you," he says.

Jena slowly reaches for the ladybug. "Are you sure, Daddy?" Jena asks. Mr. Parker smiles at her and nods his head. Jena holds the ladybug gently in her hands. She grins at her father. "It's just a little old tiny bug looking for a friend. I'm holding it, Daddy," Jena says. "I'm holding it!" The young Jena smiles at her father. "I love it, Daddy. It doesn't want to harm anyone. It's just a little old bug." Suddenly she's back on the bus.

"Do you mind if I sit here?" Jena looks up and discovers an old lady with a cane staring at her. Jena shakes her head then turns back to stare out the bus window.

"My name is Joan," the old lady says. "What's yours?"

Jena turns to her. "Jena," she says.

"Jena," Joan says. "I like the name Jena. It sounds so sweet." Jena turns away. "I bet your mother was just beside herself trying to come up with a name for you," Joan continues. "I remember when my daughter was first born. I didn't quite know what to name her, but as soon as looked into those big baby-blue eyes I knew. I knew she had to be called Lucille. You know, like Lucille Ball?" Jena continued to stare out the window. Joan got quiet. "I lost Lucille about six years ago." Jena turns back to look at Joan, whose eyes begin to well up with tears. "Yeah, she left me. Here. She was such a nice young lady, although she wasn't really young at all. She was sixty-five."

The bus stops, and Jena stands up to get off. "So, this is your stop?" Joan asks. Jena stares at her. "You don't say much, do you?" Joan asks.

"No," Jena replies, and then she walks down the aisle of the bus and steps off. Joan stares out the bus window as Jena walks away. Just as the bus is getting ready to leave, Jena turns around and looks back at Joan. She walks up to the bus window so Joan can read her lips. Jena whispers, "Lucille is better off." Joan moves back from the window with a surprised look on her face while the bus pulls away.

"Papers! Anyone need a paper? How about you, ma'am—would you like a paper today?" Jena walks past without saying a word. Scott, the paper guy, gets upset. "Oh, what does a guy have to do these days to get someone to buy a paper?" he yells.

Jena stops, turns around, and walks back toward Scott. "Shut up!" she yells. Scott looks shocked. "Do you think that anyone wants to buy your pathetic paper?" Jena asks. "Why would anyone want to read this paper? It's depressing and loaded with columns of bad news and poor advertising. Someone's always trying to sell you something—someone like you."

"Look, lady—" Scott tries to speak.

"I said shut up!" Jena says.

Scott stares at the coldness in Jena's eyes. He quickly packs up his newspapers. "I'll just find me another corner," Scott says.

"Yeah, you do that," Jena says. Scott hurries up and leaves.

Jena reaches in her bag for a piece of paper with an address on it. This is it; she thinks. In front of her is a cathedral church. Jena stands in front of the building and stares for a moment. She begins walking up the long steps of the church. Statues of angels and godly figures surround the church entrance. When Jena walks inside, she sees it is full of beautiful paintings of Christ, angels, and other holy figures. There is a red carpet leading up to the altar. Two altar boys stand at the front entrance.

"May we help you?" they both say simultaneously.

Jena shifts her gaze back and forth between the two boys and realizes they are twins. "Yes," she says, "I'd like to see the priest. I'd like to attend confession."

One of the altar boys turns. "Follow me, and I will take you to him." He walks slowly in front of Jena; Jena patiently follows. He takes Jena to a booth located near the front of the church. "Here," the altar boy says. "He is in here." The boy slightly bows his head and then slowly walks back to the front of the church.

Jena walks into the booth. There is a priest sitting inside, but Jena can barely see him. She opens the window to speak to him. She doesn't say anything for a moment. The priest doesn't say anything either. Jena blinks her eyes.

"Forgive me, Father, for I have sinned."

A deep voice echoes through the confession booth window, "Yes, my child."

"I have sinned, and I'm here to confess," Jena says quietly.

"My name is Father John, and I will hear your confession," he says. "Go on, my child."

"Father, I committed a horrible act of revenge on the man who killed my father." Jena pauses. "I don't have a family anymore, Father. My father is dead. All of them are dead. Some by the hands of another, and …" Jena pauses again.

"Yes—go on, child," Father John says.

"Father, will the Lord forgive me?"

"The Lord forgives everyone who confesses and ask for forgiveness."

Jena leans forward. She remembers the gun fire echoing in her head when she shot Mr. McNeil, and the feeling of contentment rushes back to her. She peeks through the confession booth window. "Father, what if a person isn't truly sorry?"

Father John pauses before answering, "You mean you aren't sorry you shot me?" Jena stares closely and realizes that the priest is Mr. McNeil. Mr. McNeil leans closer to Jena's face. His nose presses against the confession booth window. Jena looks at him with fear. "Of course, you're not sorry. You meant to kill me, and you'll kill again and again because you're a killer, Jena. You were a killer long before I killed your father."

Jena is eye to eye with Mr. McNeil. "I killed you once, and I'll kill you again."

"You can't kill a ghost, Jena." McNeil begins shaking the confession booth. "You can't kill me anymore." He is laughing— harder and harder. Jena suddenly wakes up on the bus. Old lady Joan is sitting next to her.

"So, see, dear, that's my life summary in ten minutes," Joan says. Jena stares at her and looks around the bus with a startled expression on her face. She is breathing hard. The bus stops, and Jena rushes to get off. Still breathing hard, she hurries to exit the bus. The bus driver doesn't say a word as he opens the door. Jena's bag falls to the ground. She reaches to pick up her bag and glances back at the bus. Old lady Joan gives her an evil grin, and then everyone on the bus stands up and stares at her. The driver steps off the bus. Jena begins to run down the street.

She runs until she reaches a corner store. There is a Chinese woman working behind the counter. Jena goes inside. A bell rings. A man wearing a long leather jacket enters the store behind Jena. Jena walks over to the drink cooler. The man moves toward the counter and points a gun at the woman.

"You give me everything you got!" the robber says. The woman freezes in fear. Jena leans back against the cooler. The man turns to Jena and says, "You better not move." The robber turns back to the

Chinese woman and points the gun at her face. "Move faster, lady. You're in America. This is America, and you better give me what I want," the robber says. The scared Chinese woman scrambles to get the money out of the cash register. She is so nervous that she drops most of the money on the floor. "Pick it up!" the robber yells.

A gun fires. The robber is shot in the shoulder. He quickly turns toward Jena as she fires the next shot through his head. Blood spills over the store counter and on the Chinese woman's face. The woman screams. Jena points the gun at her. "Shut up! I don't want to kill you," Jena says. "At least not today." The Chinese woman continues to scream as she falls to the floor in fear. Jena puts her gun back in her bag, grabs a cola from the cooler, and walks out of the store.

CHAPTER THREE

Jena, where you? Jake ponders as he desperately searches New York's streets, stores, and alleys. He is physically and mentally exhausted, so he walks back to the hotel room, plunges onto the bed, and falls asleep.

Police officers begin to surround the corner store where Jena shot the robber dead. Jena manages to wave down a cab driven by a Middle Eastern man wearing a white turban on his head.

"Where to?" the cab driver asks. Jena hands the driver a piece of paper. "Okay," the cabby says as he presses heavily on the gas pedal. He eventually pulls up to the hotel where Jena and Jake had stayed. "That'll be fifteen dollars and ninety-four cents," he says. Jena hands him a twenty, gets out of the cab, and closes the door without saying a word.

There are several people walking past the hotel. Jena quietly looks around to make sure there are no cops in the area. A man is entering the elevator. He sees Jena coming and holds the door, but Jena walks past the elevator straight to the stairs. The man gives her a strange look, shakes his head, and then lets the elevator door close.

The hotel is quiet. While Jena ascends the stairs, she remembers the night she and Jake made love, the horrible dream she had about killing him, and the moment she left him. She wonders to herself,

Why am I going back to that room? Am I hoping that Jake will be there waiting for me to return? If he isn't, is he out pounding the streets searching for me? Can he possibly understand why I killed?

Exhausted from searching for Jena, Jake is crashed out on the hotel room's bed. Jena uses her room key to open the door. She sees Jake lying motionless on the bed. He doesn't hear the door opening. She slowly closes the door and walks to the edge of the bed, puts her bag on the floor, and gently lies down on the bed next to him. Facing him, she watches him sleep. She studies his face, his lips, and the movement of his eyes under his eyelids. I wonder what he is dreaming about, she thinks. Her thoughts begin to wander back to when they were ten-year-old playing at the lake; that was when she first knew in her heart that Jake loved her. In her mind, she is transported back to when the two of them were sitting near the lake, tossing rocks, and talking.

"Tim was a jerk today," Jena says.

"Yeah, he's always a jerk," Jake says. "I never wanted to be his friend, but Mom was friends with his mom so ..." Jake pauses. "Well, you know how that goes." Jake stares over at Jena. Jena looks away.

She sighs and then looks back at him. "It's not your fault, Jake." Jena reaches over to touch Jake's hand. "You didn't know that he was going to tell the whole school your secret."

Jake throws a rock in the lake. "Yeah, now the whole world knows." He throws another rock.

"It's not that bad," Jena says.

Jake stops throwing rocks. "No, I guess not," he says. "I mean, it's not a real big deal that I accidently wet the bed," he quietly says.

Jena shakes her head and tries not to laugh. She moves closer to Jake. "Jake, everybody wets the bed at least once."

Jake looks over at Jena and says, "Yeah, but the whole school doesn't know about it. I knew I should never have let him spend the night ..." He pauses again. "Jena, have you wet the bed before?"

Jena's mind says no, but her lips lie. "Of course, Jake," she says. "Once I had this really weird dream that I was going, but in my dream, I was on the toilet and when I woke up, I was in my bed."

Jake smirks. "You thought you was on a toilet?"

"Yeah, the dream seemed so real."

Jake begins to feel better. "Yeah, yeah," he mutters and then turns to Jena. The sunlight beams in Jena's eyes, and Jake can't take his eyes off her. Jena stares back at him, and the two of them lock eyes for over a minute. Jake finally turns his head, and Jena puts her head down. "So …" Jake stands up and reaches for Jena's hand, "we better get back before your mom calls my mom," he says.

Jena stands up and brushes the dirt off her shorts. "Yeah, I guess so," she says.

"Jena, you know you're my best friend?"

"Of course, I know that Jake."

Jake smiles at Jena, and Jena smiles back. They both begin walking toward home.

Jena shoves Jake. "I bet you can't outrun me," she yells and begins to sprint.

"Oh, no fair! You're cheating!" Jake screams as he tries to catch up. They both run through the wooded field, leaping over flowers, and zigzagging through trees.

Jake opens his eyes to discover Jena staring at him, smiling. He is shocked and mesmerized by her presence. "Am I dreaming?" he asks.

"No," Jena replies. She begins to lean toward him.

"Please don't move, Jena," Jake asks. "I just want to look into your eyes. Those beautiful eyes." He gently reaches over to touch her face. He brushes her hair back. "You're beautiful, Jena."

Jena blinks her eyes and has a sad look on her face. She leans forward. "You still think I'm beautiful after everything I've done?" She looks down at Jake.

Jake leans forward. "Yes, I do."

Jena stands up and reaches for her bag. "Jake, we have to leave New York. There are police officers all over the place, and I killed a man earlier."

"Jena!" Jake stands up. "What happened?"

"He was robbing a store, and clearly he was going to kill me and the clerk—so I did him in first." Jena turns around. "And I can't say I didn't enjoy it, because I did."

"How did you know I would still be here?" Jake asks.

"Jake, I knew you wouldn't leave New York without me, and I couldn't just leave you here to wonder. So, I came back for you. I've put you in a terrible position." Jake turns around to face the hotel door. "Jake, we have to leave now! I'm surprised the police don't have this place surrounded." Jake walks closer to Jena.

"Maybe that's because this is New York and there's probably five million other murders going on," he says.

"Maybe," Jena replies.

"Where are we going to go, Jena?"

Jena reaches in her bag and pulls out the letter her mother had given her right before graduation. "Home," Jena says. "It's been only a few days. I'm sure my family hasn't buried my mother yet." Jena speaks sharply, "So you're going to take me home, Jake." Jake turns to look at Jena, but then he puts his head down. Jena pauses. She walks slowly toward him. "Are you afraid of me, Jake?" She smiles at him.

"No," he answers as he moves closer to her. He touches her face. She tries to look away. "Don't look away from me," he says in a soft voice. He kisses Jena gently on the lips. "Despite everything, Jena, I love you."

Jena breaks his gaze and walks away from him. "Jake, we have to go," she says in a demanding voice. "I don't want to miss my mother's funeral." Jena walks out of the hotel room and heads toward the car.

Jake turns and walks to the car with his hands in his pockets. He stops to stare at Jena as the wind blows through her hair and brushes her long coat open. He thinks back to the days when they were on the school bus together and he couldn't stop staring at her and daydreaming about her.

Jena opens the car door. "Are you coming, Jake?" she asks.

Jake snaps out of the daydream. He smiles at her as he walks to the car, gets in, and starts it up. "Jena, before I drive you back home, please promise that you won't run away again." Jake looks over at her. Jena looks away. "Promise me."

Jena is silent. Jake's voice fades away, and she is back in the hotel room pointing the gun at Mr. McNeil as he lies on the bed, filled with terror and fear. She hears his voice. "Jena … Jena Parker," he says.

"No. My name is Jena Gray." She can hear her name Jena Gray repeat over and over again in her mind. Then all of the thoughts of the tragic memories of the past sink in like a deep stab wound as she finally accepts the person she has become.

CHAPTER FOUR

She isn't Jena Parker anymore; she is Jena Gray. Nothing Jake or anyone else could do or say can change that now, she thinks. "The police are looking for me?" Jena turns to Jake and asks.

"Yes," he hesitatingly answers. "Yes, they are, Jena. My mother has already been questioned over ten times about my whereabouts ..." he says as he turns to Jena, "and yours. They're even trying to link me to the murders you've committed."

Jena frowns and turns away. "You had nothing to do with it," she says in a hard, rushed voice.

"As long as I'm missing, they'll assume I'm with you and they'll assume I played a part in the murders."

"Jake, you don't—"

Jake quickly pulls over to the side of the road and stops the car. He stops so quickly that they both bounce around in the car. "What were you gonna say, Jena? Were you gonna say, 'Jake, you don't have to be here' or 'Jake, you can leave'? If you were gonna say that, then you might as well save your words because I'm not going anywhere." He squeezes the steering wheel and pushes down hard on the gas pedal, propelling the car back on the highway.

Jena sighs and rolls down the car window. The wind blows her hair sideways as Jake stares off down the road. The two of them remain silent for hours, Jena staring off at the side of the road as Jake drives. Jake steals glances at her while trying hard not to lose his focus. What is she thinking about? he wonders to himself. Does she even think about me at all? Does she remember our friendship, how much I love her? How much I've always loved her? Jake peeks over at Jena. Jena is still staring out the window, almost as if Jake no longer existed and she was just traveling in some soundproof capsule. The woman I love is a killer—not a born killer, yet a killer just the same. She's a young, beautiful girl who once had a bright future ahead of her. Now she's torn and transformed. Just as Jake has this last thought, Jena turns and stares him directly in the eyes without saying a word. Jake quickly looks away. Jena turns back and resumes staring out the window.

"Are you hungry?" she asks.

Jake pauses and then breathes hard. "A little," he answers.

"Well, let's stop," she says.

"Okay," he replies. They pass a road sign. "Well, the nearest food and gas is in ten miles." He looks over and discovers her gazing at him with cold eyes.

"I guess we're stopping in ten miles," Jena says. She continues to stare at Jake as he drives. "Don't be afraid of me, Jake," she says as she scoots closer to him. She touches his leg and runs her hand up to his crotch and squeezes it. "I'll never hurt you."

Jake shakes his head. "Jena, you have a strong grip."

She smiles at him. "So, does that mean you want me to stop?"

"Umm, yes … no, I mean I …" Jake is caught off guard by Jena's boldness.

Jena lets go of Jake's crotch and then whispers in his ear, "We'll finish this later." She turns and scoots back to her side of the car. Her hair blowing in the wind again, she goes quickly back into her own time capsule. Again, there is nothing but silence in the car between them—at least in spoken words.

Jake's thoughts about Jena are out of control. He can't think of anything but holding her gently in his arms and making love to her like he had before. His mind returns to when he was in bed with Jena. He fantasizes about her laying there naked. Her body so beautifully formed. His hands all over her soft skin. He leans down, kisses her, and begins caressing her breast. She turns her head to the side as he kisses her neck, breasts, stomach, and between her thighs. As his tongue massages her inner lips, Jena moans with excitement and grabs his head, pulling it closer to her. Jake kisses her thighs again, her stomach, her neck, and then he passionately kisses her on the lips as he slowly penetrates her. Jena breathes out softly and then lets out a harder breath. She grabs him tightly as he penetrates slowly and softly.

Jake tries to focus on driving, but his mind keeps drifting back to that night. He grips the steering wheel tightly.

"Jake!" Jena yells. "Watch out!" Jake's focus returns to the highway in time to see the deer in front of them. He swerves almost off the road to avoid hitting the deer. He pulls off to the side of the road. Jena is staring at him with a shocked look on her face. She gives him a mean look. "What the hell is wrong with you?" she asks him.

Jake is breathing hard—less from the almost-fatal accident than from the thoughts of him and Jena. Jake sits silently for several seconds before even looking at Jena. "I'm sorry." He looks over at her and then looks to the other side of the road, where the deer was standing. "I'm sorry I wasn't paying attention."

"Really," Jena snaps at him.

"I had something very important on my mind, Jena," he answers back.

"Yeah—what?" she asks. He drives back onto the road. "What were you thinking about, Jake?" Jena refuses to let it go.

Jake doesn't answer right away. He spins back onto the road and starts driving again. Jena looks back out her window. "You," he finally answers. "I was thinking about you and me last night." Jena looks over at him, looks down, and then looks back out the window. "I was thinking about how lovely you looked—tender, sweet—and how much I really …" Jake swallows. "How much I love you, Jena. I love you so much."

Jena doesn't say a word. She leaves Jake hanging on his thoughts of her without her expressing any thoughts of him. Jena suddenly leans forward. Jake is looking her. "Jake. Jake!" she yells. "Stop the car!"

"Why?" he asks.

"Because there's a guy walking out onto the highway, and I don't want you to hit him." Jake looks back to the highway. A young guy with a backpack on his shoulders, a jacket in his arms, and an iPod in his hand is waving them down. Jake speeds up. "What the hell are you doing, Jake?" Jena yells.

"I'm speeding up. I'm not going to stop."

"Why not?"

Jake slows down and stops just inches from hitting the walker. "So, you want to pick up a hitcher?" Jake asks her.

"Yes," she answers. Jena opens her car door, gets out, and walks up to the hitchhiker. The two stand in the middle of the road and stare at each other. Jena grabs his bag. "You need a ride?" she asks.

The man gives her a flirty look with a slight come-on smile. "Yeah. I would say me walking out in the middle of the highway would be a great indicator of that."

Jena frowns and tosses his bag back to him. "Really? I would say that you almost got your ass killed. If it weren't for me telling Jake"—she points at Jake—"to stop, you would be spread out across this highway and we would be halfway down this road. Now I'll ask you again." She leans her head slightly to the side. "Do you need a ride?"

The hitchhiker quickly answers, "Yes!"

Jena waves for him to get in the car. The hitchhiker pulls the backseat down to hop in. Jena grabs him. "No. I'll get in the backseat. You get in the front."

He looks at her strangely. "Okay, will do," he says. The hitchhiker hops in the front. Jena gets in the back.

Jake looks back at her and then at the hitchhiker. "You got a name, guy?" Jake asks.

"Yeah—Matt."

Jena leans up. "Matt what?"

"Matt Ross." Jena leans back. Matt asks, "Where are you guys headed?"

"Home," Jena answers. "We're headed home."

Matt shakes his head. "And … umm … where's home?"

"Where are you headed, Matt?" Jake asks.

Matt pauses. "Well, I'm not really headed anywhere. I'm kind of a loner—a drifter." Matt puts his bag on the car floor. "So, wherever you guys go or however far you're willing to let me ride is where I'm going." Matt looks back at Jena and then looks at Jake.

Jake puts the car in gear and drives off quickly. "We've got to make a food, gas, and whatever-else stop," Jake says. "So, you cool with that?"

Matt nods his head. "Yeah, man, I'm cool with whatever you guys do. I mean, I'm the one hitching a ride." Matt leans back comfortably in his seat. "Hey, man, when you hitch you got no complaints."

Jake peeks at Jena in the rearview mirror; she stares back at him and winks.

CHAPTER FIVE

"Five miles to the next gas and food stop," Matt says as he gets comfortable in his seat.

Jake drives a few more minutes and then the five-mile sign appears. "How did you know that Matt?" Jake asked.

"Oh, I've traveled this road a few times," Matt says causally. Jena remains silent. Jake glances at her in the rearview mirror.

"Well, here's our stop," Jake announces. "I'll get the gas first and then we'll eat." Jake pulls into the gas station, gets out, and begins pumping gas.

Matt turns around to start a conversation with Jena. "So, that's your boyfriend?" Jena just gives him a blank stare. Matt is persistent. "You are a very beautiful girl. I'm sure that's your boyfriend."

Jena leans up and stares Matt right in the eyes. "So, what if he is?" she answers. "What are you going to do about it?" The look in her eyes makes Matt a little uneasy. Jena leans back in her seat just as Jake gets back into the car. Matt turns around. He makes quick conversation with Jake.

"Hey, umm, I'm a little low on cash, but when we get to the restaurant, I'll hit up an ATM."

"Yeah," Jake replies, clearly unconvinced. Jake drives to the diner.

"Oh, look. We're at Kyler's Diner—the home of the best hot and fresh breads and all-you-can-eat soup," Matt says in a sarcastic voice. "Wow, only in the middle of nowhere would a bunch of hicks think that all-you-can-eat soup could be a delightful meal." Matt continues to make jokes. "You know, I once ate at this place that said they had the best burgers in town. Turns out they were serving up ground-up rat meat. Man, I ate one of those rat burgers and puked for an entire week." Jake and Jena both remain silent. "Man, just thinking of that makes me want to puke."

"Can we not talk about rat burgers right now?" Jake asks as he gets out the car and lets Jena out from the back.

Jena walks over to Matt's windows and leans in and whispers to him, "Maybe you would have been better off being spattered all over the highway."

Jake grabs her. "Let's eat, Jena."

She opens the car door for Matt. "Yeah, Matt, let's eat some nice rat soup."

Jena and Jake walk into the diner. Matt grabs his bag and follows them. Jena, Jake, and Matt find a table. Five huge truckers walk in behind them, laughing and joking.

"So, what are you carrying today, Bob?" one of the truckers asks.

"Oh, just some hot items," Bob says. They all sit down.

"Hot items? What hot items?"

"Hot like your momma, boy ..."

"Oh, we doing 'your momma' jokes?" The biggest guy in the group suddenly stands. "Oh, don't any of you talk about my momma. Don't say anything about my momma." The biggest trucker has a serious look on his face. The entire table is quiet. Jena, Jake, and Matt overhear the truckers' conversation.

"Good lord, Big Papa, calm down," Bob says. "No one said anything about your momma." Big Papa sits back down while eyeing all of them. "Yet ..." Bob laughs, and the other three guys chuckle real hard. Big Papa begins getting up again. "Oh, sit down and get some all-you-can-eat hot soup in this hot-ass desert." Big Papa sits down, and they all laugh, joke, and chuckle some more.

The restaurant has ten tables, all filled with waiting customers. There's only one waitress, and the owner, Kyler, is the cook and the cashier. There's a TV right on the cashier's counter. Its signal flickers in and out, and Kyler has to pop it a few times to get the picture to come back into view.

"Damn it, Kyler," Big Papa yells out. "Every time we come in this place we have to wait. You say you're going to get more help, and here we are again—and here you are with just one damn waitress."

"Calm down, Big Papa. I'm just trying to run a local business," Kyler yells back. "I leave the truckin' to you guys, so you leave the cooking to me."

"You call soup cookin'?" Big Papa yells back. "Hell, I can make a can of soup. Besides, it's hot as shit in this desert. Who the hell wants soup, anyway?" Big Papa says loudly.

"Obviously, you, Big Papa, because you're back again," Kyler yells. "So just wait until Rosa gets to your table."

Big Papa gives Kyler a dirty look. "I better get some hot and fresh bread too," he yells out. The truckers start laughing. Rosa finally gets to the truckers' table.

Jena eyes the entire diner, watching everyone talk and wait patiently for Rosa to take their orders. Matt looks at her. "You looking for someone?" he asks.

Jake quickly butts in. "So, Matt, how long have you been just wandering around the world?"

Matt scratches his neck. "For a while, man. I mean, I don't really have a home," he says. "I'm a loner, and I like it that way." Matt focuses back on Jena. "Jena, you are the quietest female I've ever met." He laughs. "I mean, most the women I've been around—and that would be a lot—couldn't shut up. But you, you are so calm and quiet," he says.

Jena gives Matt a mild smile. "You ever heard of the quiet before the storm?" she asks while giving Matt a devilish look. Matt backs off.

Rosa finally reaches their table. Jena and Jake order while Matt looks nervously around the diner. He watches while Kyler cashes out his customers. His eyes lock in on the exchange of cash.

Rosa asks Matt, "What'll you have?" Matt is still distracted by the cash out of the customers. He quickly reaches in his bag and pulls out a gun just as Kyler cashes out another customer. The customers are all frantic, whispering and crowding around each other. Kyler tries to reach for the shotgun he keeps under the counter.

"Don't reach for that gun," Matt yells. "I know where you keep it, and I'll blow you away."

Big Papa and all the other truckers stand up, ready to fight. "You don't want none of this, son," Big Papa says with his fist clenched. Matt points his gun back and forth from between Kyler and the truckers.

Matt's a little nervous, but he tries to act tough. "No, you don't want none of this," Matt says. "Now sit down and shut up." He points the gun around the room. Jake has an angry, intense look on his face, but Jena is calm.

A man yells, "Put down the gun!" Matt points the gun at him, back at Kyler, and then around the room.

"Give me the money, man," Matt yells.

"I ain't giving you shit," Kyler yells back, still reaching for his shotgun. Matt feels trapped. He glances down a little, and in that one second Jena is standing behind him with a gun pointed at his head.

"Put it down, Matt," she says in a calm voice. Matt is still pointing his gun at Kyler.

Kyler grabs his shotgun and points it at Matt. "I'm going to blow you away, son."

"Shoot 'em—shoot 'em!" Bob the trucker yells. The tension in the room grows: Jena pointing her gun at Matt, Matt pointing his gun at Kyler, the truckers all ready to fight, and Kyler ready to shoot off his shotgun.

The TV clears, and there's a news bulletin. As the newsman begins to speak, Kyler peeks up at the TV. The entire restaurant is suddenly listening in. Jena's picture is flashing on the TV. "Wanted for multiple murders in—" the picture flickers off and then on again "—and New York, Jena Parker." Everyone in the room stares at Jena. Kyler cocks his shotgun. Jake stands up. The truckers move in closer.

Bob yells out, "That's her! That's Jena Parker."

"Oh my God, we're all going to die!" a woman yells out while clinging to her daughter.

"Don't kill me!" Matt says as he panics.

"Girl, you better put down that gun," Kyler says.

Jake grabs Matt's gun from his hand and points it at Kyler. "Put it down, man," Jake says in a commanding voice.

Another news flash comes on the TV, and Matt's picture flashes across the screen. "Also wanted in Larmont and Fairmand Counties for burglary and murder is Matthew Ross." Everyone in the diner looks over at Matt. Kyler is ready to shoot. Jake stands next to Jena.

"Oh shit, we got two mass murderers in this restaurant!" Bob yells out.

"I just hit the button. The cops are on the way," Kyler says.

"Jake, let's go," Jena says while scoping the room. Jena and Jake back out of the diner together with their guns pointed.

Matt turns toward them with his arms in the air. "Please don't leave me here!" Matt pleads.

"Leave 'em or let 'em stay—either way, all three of you are going down," Kyler says.

"Put down the weapon," a woman pleads. "For the love of God, just let them go." Kyler ignores her.

Jake and Jena back out the door. The truckers are ready to jump Matt. Matt continues to plead with Jena. "Jena, please don't leave me here. They're going to kill me."

Jena glances over at Jake. A woman jumps in front of Kyler. "Back up, Matt," Jena says. "Let's go."

Matt grabs his bag and rushes out with Jena and Jake. Jake rushes to start the car while Jena covers them. The truckers follow them slowly. Kyler rushes out from behind them. Matt jumps in the passenger seat, and Jena gets in the backseat. Jake drives off quickly.

Kyler and some of the truckers jump in his truck, two in the front and two in the back. Jake is driving over a hundred miles an hour. Kyler is behind him, and so are the cops.

"Drive man, drive!" Matt yells. Jake steps on it and manages to get a speed advantage over them. Matt puts his head down in relief. "Oh, man, that was close," he says.

"Pull over, Jake," Jena says.

"What?" Jake answers.

"Pull over!" Jena yells.

Matt turns around. "What the hell?" he says to her.

"Jake, pull this car over now!" Jena yells.

"Man, don't pull over." Matt tries to grab the wheel. "Don't pull over. She's crazy." They spin out along the side road. Jake manages to stop.

"Get out!" Jena tells Matt.

"What? But you just saved me!" Matt looks confused.

"Get out!" Jena points the gun at him.

"You're not going to shoot me," Matt tests her. "I don't care what that TV said. You're not a killer."

Jena shoots a bullet through the front passenger window, right past Matt's face. "Really?" she says.

Matt runs out of the car. Jake spins off. Kyler and the cops manage to catch up, but they stop to capture Matt. Kyler holds a shotgun on Matt while the truckers hold him down and the sheriff handcuffs him.

"Matthew Ross, you have the right to remain silent. Anything you say …" the sheriff reads Matt his rights as he handcuffs him. Jake drives off as fast as he can. Jena lies down in the backseat, puts the gun on the car floor, and stares out the back window.

CHAPTER SIX

J ake tries to calm down. "Shit! Shit!" he grips the steering wheel tightly. "What the hell was that?" he says out loud. He peers in the mirror at Jena, worried about her. She is calm and staring out the back window. "Jena, are you all right?" Jake says in a panicky voice.

"I'm fine," she says while continuing to stare out the window. Jena's thoughts drift off, away from Jake's panic. Jake is like a blur in the mirror. It's almost as if they're sharing the same space in two alternative worlds.

As a child, I used to dream of being someone famous. Jena sees herself as a child playing with her dolls and smiling with her dad. Now I am, she thinks to herself. All that I was seems like a distant memory. A hoax. A clown laughing at me, taunting me. I saw my dark side several times, but I looked away and pretended that it wasn't me … How could I become this person? She asks herself.

Jake is still talking in the background. His words are like bubbles popping in the air. Jena doesn't hear his voice anymore. She doesn't even believe she is sitting in a backseat of a car. When she looks back at Jake, she sees herself in a transient state with the road being just a black image of a gateway and her body floating toward it. There is a force pulling her into this black hole—a force she can't stop. It pulls her back in slow motion, past her shooting of Mr. McNeil, past her sitting with the doctor on the train, past her opening the door for the hotel clerk, and past her father as he stood there in the fog in her dream.

"Daddy …" Jena reaches out for him as the force takes her. "Daddy …," she calls. She can feel her body drifting further into the darkness of the force. Her eyes begin to get heavy, her body limp. She is exhausted, paralyzed, and drifts into a deep sleep.

Jena is ten years old, sitting at the top of their house stairs watching her parents slow dance to their favorite song. "If I can't have you, I don't want nobody baby. If I can't have you," Jena's father whispers in Kitty's ear as they dance. He kisses her softly on the lips. Kitty smiles and rests her head back on his shoulder. He kisses her on her forehead, and the two of them dance romantically as Jena watches. Jena smiles at the gentleness her parents share together and dreams of one day having a love like theirs—so passionate, so tender.

Jena gets up and begins to walk to her mother's room, but Jena is now a teenager. She stops and stares at her mother's empty bed and tries to walk into her mother's room, but the force won't allow her to. She is instantly pushed backward. She can feel her body swaying back and forth while she giggles with excitement.

Jena, age five, swings back and forth as her dad pushes her higher and higher. She giggles loudly. Her hair sways in the cool breeze, legs lifted high in the air. Her mom claps her hands and smiles at the two of them. The swing stops and Jena runs off into her mom's arms, reaches to kiss her on the cheek, opens her eyes, and she's in seventh grade and kissing Jake's cheek.

Jake had picked up her books after Ken knocked them out of her hands. He gently handed the books back to Jena, and she leaned over to give him a kiss on the cheek. "You're my hero," she whispers to him. Jake smiles at her. After school that day, they walk down to the lake where they always meet to talk. The cool, warm breeze blows through Jena's hair while Jake sits next to her, gazing at her long eyelashes, her lips, her slender shoulders, and her legs. She turns slightly toward him and smiles as the sun reflects off her smooth lips, wet from her lip gloss.

"Thank you for picking up my books," she says while smiling.

Jake is shy and only smiles and tries to distract himself from her by throwing rocks in the lake. He glances over at her. Her body starts to levitate. He is amazed, caught off guard, and tries to grab her legs to stop her from leaving. "Jena! Jena!" he yells. "What's happening?" The sun suddenly turns dark, and Jake struggles to hold on to Jena's legs. Jena looks down at him frantically holding on to her. She tries to reach for him, but the force is pulling her away. "Jena!" Jake cries. "Jena, please don't go." He grips tightly to her, but his hands begin to slip. "Please!" He can no longer hold on and is forced to let her go. She drifts away into the darkness. Jake stands there with his arms raised up high, crying, and then he falls to his knees. Jena is gone.

She floats somewhere in the darkness and just drifts. There is no one and nothing around her: no sound, no people, no mother or father, and no fear. A tiny light, as small as a pinhead, shines through the darkness. She fixates on the light and lies in transit watching it. She has is no sense of time. Eventually, her body begins to drop. She reaches for the only thing she has—the tiny light—but the faster she falls, the less the light is in sight, until it's gone and only darkness surrounds her. The darkness and Jake's voice blurs together a little. When she can hear him clearly, she opens her eyes.

"Jena," Jake calls. He has pulled over to the side of the road, out of sight, and he gently touches Jena's arm. "Jena, are you all right?"

Jena is silent, but she feels relieved and happy that it's Jake's face she awoke to. She reaches for him, pulls him closer, and begins kissing him softly and squeezing him tightly. "I've been waiting for this moment all day," she whispers softly in his ear.

Jake kisses her gently on the lips, and then they both gaze deeply into each other's eyes. He reaches for her face, touches it, and rubs his hands down her cheek, along her neck, to her breast while gently caressing and kissing her. Jena stops for a second and navigates Jake on to his back in the backseat. She sits on top of him, removes her blouse, and throws it in the front seat. He reaches for her breasts and gently squeezes them and leans up to bury his lips in between them while removing her bra. He pulls her to him, his hands conforming to her like soft butter, rubbing every inch of her body, every sensual part of her. She breathes softly as he kisses her neck and smoothly removes her pants and panties and his own. She grips him tightly, and he assists her, squeezing her deeper into him. Jena moans softly, harder, and then harder. Her nails dig deeply into his skin, lightly piercing it just enough to induce a little pain and unforgettable pleasure. Jake gently turns Jena around on to her back. He stops to stare at her. Her eyes blaze up at him like the moon shining on a bright night. Her hair is pushed back, showing off her lovely shoulders. Her naked body is exposed to his obsessed eyes. Every movement is an enchanted feeling for him, like horses running in slow motion, pushing them together. He leans into her and they both hear the angels' music. Nothing but music—soft, angelic music—in rhythms that pulse as slowly as the heart of Sleeping Beauty. The motion of their bodies is like ripples of ocean waves flowing over and over again. Though all is silent, to them it is like roaring thunder a hundred times over, nonstop hard raindrops, and then back to sun all in one moment that seems to last for hours and hours.

"I love you, Jena," Jake moans and murmurs through his passion. "I love you so much."

"Jake," Jena says softly. She reaches for his hand. "Squeeze me … squeeze me … hold me, please. Oh, I … I …"

"Jena, are you all right?" Jake asks. "Jena? Jena?"

Jena slowly wakes up. "Jake?" She looks around the car. She breathes out. "Wow. It was so real."

"What was real?" he asks.

"I was dreaming, and then I woke up and we started …" She looks out the car window.

"We started what, Jena?"

"We were making love." She reaches for Jake's face. He is surprised. "I thought it was real," she says. "I mean, I had just woken up, and then we started … but …" Jena stops talking.

Jake kisses her. "It can be real, Jena," he says. "It can be real right now."

Jena stares at him. She leans in close to his face. She stares at him as if it were the first time, she had ever seen him. "You're right, Jake. It can be real." She kisses him and then slowly removes her shirt. Her brushed-back hair accentuates her beautiful shoulders. Jake's eyes shine as bright as the moon. She whispers in his ear, "Yes, it will be as real as I dreamed it—even better. I'll make sure of it."

CHAPTER SEVEN

J ake resumes their drive home. The car is once again silent, as Jena stares off out the window.

"This has been a long ride, huh?" Jena says while waving her hands out the car window, the wind pushing it back while she defies it.

"Yes, but we are almost home," Jake says quietly. "Jena, we're going to have to be careful. The police are looking for you … and me. We can't afford to be seen. We are very lucky to have gotten this far without getting caught," he says while looking around the road suspiciously. They pass a road sign: fifty miles to Maplesville.

Jake utters, "Jena, last night was … so beautiful. You're beautiful. I'm not leaving you, so don't ask me too." Jena is silent. "We have to find somewhere to hide until we can sort all this out," Jake says.

"Jake, I'm going to my mother's funeral. I think about her. I think about what I did. I know murder is an awful thing to do to your own mother, but my mom died the moment my father left her—the moment that gun fired and killed him. I would have run a hundred miles to avoid seeing her face. I knew she would never be the same again, no matter how much I wanted and needed her to be. Watching her suffer was like watching her fall from a hundred-story building in slow motion." Jena reaches in her bag. Jake watches her.

She pulls out the letter her mother gave her after graduation—a letter she never opened. Jena holds the letter lightly in her hand, looks up at the car ceiling, and then puts it back in her bag.

Jake comforts her. "When you're ready, you'll open it."

Jena looks over at Jake as they pass the next highway sign: thirty miles to Maplesville. Jake reaches for Jena's hand, but she pulls away. "I'm not afraid, Jake. I'm not afraid anymore. If anything," she looks out the window, "they should all be afraid of me."

Jake turns off onto a side road. "We have to find another car. The police are looking for us, and by now they have to know what we're driving. Jena, I'm sorry, but I'm going to steal a car tonight."

Jena shakes her head. "Wow, you're worried about stealing a car when I've just killed a few people only a few days ago." She sighs.

Jake pulls slowly into a wooded area. There is a house sitting by itself. The lights on the porch are dim and flicker on and off. A pickup truck sits under an outside garage, and an old car is parked on the grass near the house. Jena and Jake sit still and stare out at the lonely, broken-down house.

Jake slowly opens the car door and steps one foot out. He glances back at Jena. "This is it," he says as he steps out of the car and then gently closes the car door. Jena follows him. They both stand staring out at the house. A slight wind is blowing, and Jena's hair sways in the breeze. Her coat is brushed back by the motion of the wind. Jake looks over at her, swallows softly, and reaches for Jena's hand.

She turns to look at him, squeezes his hand, and kisses him gently on the lips. "What a boy will do for love," she whispers to him.

He softly touches her face, the wind blowing both of them closer. "Not a boy, Jena—a man. I'm a man now. I was a boy a long time ago, but now I'm a man in love. So deeply in love. A love like those told about in fairy tales, movies, and books. But this is no fairy tale or movie. This is me and you, my love." He leans into kiss Jena, but he stops to just watch her with her eyes closed, her beautiful hair swaying in the wind, and her soft lips waiting for his embrace.

She opens her eyes. "No kiss," she says.

He hugs her tightly. "I just wanted to look at you. Look at your beautiful skin, your face—everything about you is my armor." He places his forehead on hers. "We'll take this journey together." He grabs her hand and walks toward the truck. Jena stands on the lookout as Jake searches for the keys. While Jake continues to search for the keys, Jena wanders off closer to the house. She walks to a window and peeks in.

There is a man standing in the doorway of a room. He is angry and yelling at someone. Jena can barely see the other person. The man grips his fist and walks swiftly toward someone. A woman with her clothes half torn off runs from the end of the room, trying to get away from the man. She is crying and begging for him to stop. He hits her, and the blow from his fist knocks her to the floor.

"Please stop!" she screams. "Please don't do this, Carl. Please stop," she says again.

"You shut up, Maggie." He reaches over and grabs her up by the neck. "You shut up now!" He pushes her against the wall and begins hitting her over and over again, and then he tries to kiss her.

She begs, "Please. STOP IT!"

"You asked for it, Maggie," he says in a deep, mean voice. He rips her dress; one side is hanging almost completely off. Her nose is bleeding, and her face is battered and bruised from his hard fist. He reaches to hit her again. A gun cocks. He turns around with hand ready to strike. Jena is holding a gun on him.

"Don't do it," Jena says in low voice.

"Who the hell are you?" Carl yells. "Get the hell out of my house, you little bitch." He lets go of Maggie. She crawls into a corner, as he walks toward Jena. Jena fires a shot and barely misses.

Jake runs toward the house screaming Jena's name. "Jena! Jena!"

Jena holds the gun on Carl. She looks down at Maggie, who is curled up in the corner crying. Her face is almost beaten in, her clothes torn off, and there are bruise marks all over her body.

Carl walks, big and bad, toward Jena. "You think you can come in someone's house and pull a gun on them? Huh?"

Jena walks toward him, pointing the gun directly at his head. "Yes. I do," she replies. She peeks over at Maggie, who is too afraid to look at her.

Jake reaches the room. "Jena, put the gun down."

"No, Jake. If anyone deserves to die, it's definitely this creep." Jake looks over and sees Maggie crying in the corner.

The room is still and then, just like a circle, the room winds around and around. Maggie in the corner, Jake at the door, Jena with the gun pointed at Carl, and Carl standing defiant. The room spins around and around. Maggie in the corner, Jake at the door, Jena with the gun pointed at Carl, and Carl's face changing to Mr. McNeil's. Jena's eyes grow black as coal. The room darkens. Maggie in the corner, Jake at the door, Jena with the gun, Carl on his knees.

"Stand up, Maggie," Jena speaks gently to Maggie as she looks over at her. "Stand up, and don't be afraid." Maggie stares at Jena. Carl looks back at Maggie to intimidate her. "Don't be afraid, Maggie." Jake moves toward Maggie. "No, Jake, don't," Jena says. "Let her do it on her own."

"Maggie, don't you listen to her," Carl says. Maggie stops crying. She looks over at Jake and Jena.

Jena keeps the gun on Carl. "Come on, Maggie, stand up. It's okay. It's okay." Maggie looks around the room at the broken lamp, down at her torn clothes, and then back at Carl. She slowly manages to stand on her feet, her body shaking and fragile from the beating. She fixes her clothes the best she can. Jake looks away. She walks to the mirror and begins to cry of shame. "It's okay, Maggie," Jena says.

"Maggie, look at you," Carl taunts her. Jena lets him stand while still holding the gun on him. "Yeah, look at you," he continues. "You're ugly. You're fat. You're hopeless." Maggie breathes in hard and stares at herself in the mirror in horror and in shame. Carl looks back over at Jena.

Jena walks a little closer to him, still holding the gun tightly. She begins to tell a story. "There once a man named Mr. McNeil, who lived next door. He was an awful man, a terrible soul who stole the heart of a little girl." Jena walks closer and closer to Carl. Carl stands still while listening closely to Jena's story. "Mr. McNeil was a man of the unknown, a nameless figure, faceless, and destined to face justice. He had no future, because he was a man on a plane—on a plane to nowhere, to destination unknown. How do I know?" Jena is face-to-face with Carl. "I know because I was on the plane with him, and I made sure he never, ever landed …"

Jake steps close to Jena. Maggie is right beside Carl. She grabs the gun from Jena and shoots Carl twice. He stares her in the eyes as he falls to the floor. Maggie stands holding the gun over his still body. Jake is in shock and doesn't move. Jena stands alongside Maggie—both of them standing over Carl's bleeding body, both of them with emotionless stares on their faces.

A cool breeze flows through the room. Jena and Maggie both sway as they glare down at Carl. Jena kneels down toward Carl and whisper to him, "Now you go. You go and tell them that I'm coming." She looks up at Maggie, the gun still gripped tightly in her hand. Jena slowly stands up and gently takes the gun from Maggie's hand.

Maggie blinks twice. She is focused and is in her right mind. "Will you help me bury him?" she asks, looking at Jena and then Jake. Jena looks over at Jake. He steps slowly toward them. Jena, Jake, and Maggie lift Carl's heavy body and carry it to the backyard and lay him down. Jake grabs a shovel and digs a grave for Carl as Jena and Maggie watch.

CHAPTER EIGHT

J ake is exhausted from all of the shoveling. He climbs to the top of the grave, lays the shovel down, and gives Jena a look as if to say it's time to put Carl's body in the grave. Carl's dead body lies still on the cold, black ground. Maggie is watching the night sky, avoiding looking at Carl lying there with blood streaming down from his shirt to his pants. Jake reaches for Maggie's hand as Jena stands near her and touches her shoulder. Maggie turns to stare at Carl, walks slowly toward him, and kneels down. Jake walks away in disappointment with himself for being a part of Carl's death.

Jena stands over Maggie. "Maggie," Jena calls.

Maggie stands up. "I'll do it." She looks at Jena. "I'll do it by myself. He's my problem." Maggie reaches for Carl's arms. She tries to drag him, but his body is too heavy. Jena turns to look at Jake; he walks farther away. Jena leans down, grabs Carl's legs, and both she and Maggie struggle to carry Carl to the grave. They throw him in. Jena grabs the shovel and begins to cover Carl's body with the dirt Jake had dug. She lays the shovel down when she is done.

Maggie stands next to her. "Thank you," she says to Jena. Maggie begins to cry. "I'm not crying because I'm sorry," she says. "I'm crying because I'm so happy. Happy that my beatings will stop. That I won't have to look at another blooded face in the mirror.

That I won't have to hide from my family and friends because I'm too ashamed to tell them the truth." Maggie continues to break down in tears.

Jena doesn't cry or show any emotions, she just points out into the night. "Can you see that Maggie?"

Maggie looks out into the night. She is confused. "She what?" she answers in a sobbing voice.

"Freedom," Jena says as she turns to walk away. Maggie turns to watch Jena leave. The wind blows, her body movement flows in sync with the wind, and Jake waits for her as he always has, his hands reaching for her, waiting, and longing to hold her, no matter the consequences. No matter the risk or what the end holds. He wasn't thrilled about what he had done, but he wasn't going to leave Jena. Maggie saw in Jena's body movement Jena's sheer confidence that the man she was walking toward was a man that loved her, adored her, and would do anything to keep her—even dig a grave for a woman's lowlife husband whom he didn't even know.

"Wait!" Maggie yelled. Jake and Jena turn around. Maggie walks toward them. "The keys to the truck are hidden under the door mat," she walks toward the house. Jake and Jena follow. "I hide them there just in case one day I'd ever get the courage to leave this hellhole of a place." Maggie gets the keys. "I want you two to take the truck." Maggie looks off to the long, winding road that leads to her house. She hands Jake the keys. "Take the truck and drive. Drive and drive to wherever you two want to go." Maggie smiles as she looks at Jena and Jake. "You two drive on. Drive."

She's inspired by the love Jena and Jake have for one another. A tear drops from one eye. She gets a sudden burst of energy and runs toward her front door. "I'm getting out of here," Maggie says loudly. "I'm going to my sister's, and I'm getting out of here. I'm burning this damn place down to the ground. Everything …" she stops to look around her yard, "everything … Now, you two, come on in, wash up, and be on your way. Don't you worry about me." She wipes the tear from her eye. "No, don't worry about me. I'm getting out of here." Maggie runs into the house, calls her sister, slams the phone down, and runs around the house packing whatever she can take with her.

Jena and Jake wash up in the kitchen. Jake turns to Jena. "You think she'll be all right?" he asks.

Jena watches as Maggie packs her things. She is no longer crying, and her face has a glow of light to it. Just like a child being born, Maggie is living life for the first time in a long time. Jena turns to Jake. "She'll be fine. Let's go."

They both walk out of the house without saying good-bye to Maggie, and they jump into the truck. Jake drives away down the road. Jena puts her arm out the window. The cool breeze runs up the sleeve of her coat, up her arm, and a burst of wind flows through to her hair. She closes her eyes. Mr. McNeil's face flashes through her mind. She opens her eyes quickly.

A car speeds past them on the road. The driver honks the horn twice to alert Jake to get out of the way. It's a woman wearing a black hat, an angry look on her face, driving like a drunk who's had way too many beers. The woman spins the car's tires and drives out of control. The dust and wind kick up as she zooms past Jake and Jena.

Jake stops the truck. "Whoa …," he says. Both he and Jena get out of the truck, stand in the middle of the dusty road, and watch as the woman's car roars up to the house. She leaves the car running and gets out carrying two cans of gasoline. Maggie runs to the car, throws her stuff in, and grabs a gasoline can. They both start sprinkling gasoline all over the place. They both act like two children running loose in a kids' park, laughing, and talking loudly. The woman lights a fire all around the house area.

Jake begins to run toward the house; Jena holds him back. "Let it go, Jake," she says. "Let it go." They watch as Maggie and her sister burn down the house, burn the car, and burn everything else in sight. Black smoke fills the air, and Jena knows the firemen will soon come … and then the cops.

She turns to Jake. "Jake let's get go. There's nothing else we can do here. This is Maggie's moment." Jena glances over at Jake and speaks firmly to him. "This is her moment, and she's earned the right to celebrate it the way she chooses." Jena gets back in the truck. Jake follows. He puts the truck in drive and spins off down the road.

Jena glances back at the burning house in the rearview mirror. Maggie and her sister are jumping up and down and hanging onto each other as everything burns. And although a man is dead, a woman is somehow alive again—and for Jena, justice is done. Jena continues to watch until she can no longer see the burning house in the mirror. She rests her head back, breathes softly, and then closes her eyes.

Jake drives cautiously to avoid being noticed and stopped by the cops. The highway is dark and empty; ten- or fifteen-minutes pass between them meeting any other car. Jake turns on the radio just as Jena doses off. The radio announcer makes an all-points bulletin: "The Maplesville police have apprehended Matthew Ross, who is wanted for burglary and murder in several other counties. They are holding Matthew Ross without bail." Jena opens her eyes widely. "The Maplesville police department is also looking for Jena Parker, wanted for multiple murders, and Jake Paterson, who is considered an accomplice to those murders. We will keep you updated as we receive news on these two murderous individuals." Jake turns the radio off. Jena closes her eyes tightly. The inevitable outcome seems to strike both of them at the same time, and neither of them utter a single word.

Jena dozes off again. Just when she gets comfortable sleeping, a car races past them, honks the horn three times, and a woman sticks her head out the window. It's Maggie. She is smiling and waving out the passenger window of the car. Jena's eyes began to get heavy as Maggie's sister's car fades out of sight.

Jena's eyes blink slowly as Maggie's hand wave becomes a reoccurring event in slow motion. Even when Jena closes her eyes, she can see Maggie's hand waving, her smile, and her sister's car speeding past in slow motion. Everything in slow motion. Jake turns to look at them and then back at her in slow motion.

Jena's eyes blink in and out, watching the world around her resist gravity and pull her away from reality until she is no longer in the car. She is back on the plane, where she sits next to a man who has a strong resemblance to Mr. McNeil. He sits next to Jena, who is trying to recognize her surroundings. The man laughs out loud.

Jena looks at him. "You're dead." She smiles.

"Am I?" he says as he chuckles.

"Yes, you are," she answers.

"Well, I'm here. You're here," he says.

Jena stands up and turns toward him. "Yes, we are both here, but only one of us is leaving." She leans down to get close to his face. "And it's not you."

Mr. McNeil is quiet for a moment, and then he laughs again. "Maybe that's a good thing," he says. "Maybe I like it here. Maybe it's you who's the unfortunate one." He laughs again. Jena stares at him. "Look at you. You killed me, and you still don't have any peace. You still wander in and out of this fictitious plane. Why do you come back?" Jena struggles to answers. She looks around the plane. The man gets confident. "Yeah, why do you come back?" He picks up a newspaper that was sitting in the back of the seat in front of him. He crosses his legs and begins reading the paper. "Let's see what's happening today. Oh," he says, "Matthew Ross was caught by the Maplesville police department. Ha, ha." He laughs. "And look, murderer Jena Parker is still on the loose. Oh, if the police department could just get on this plane. Ha, ha. Jena Parker?" He chuckles hard, looks up from the paper laughing, and stares at Jena. "Don't they mean Jena Gray? Ha, ha." He laughs uncontrollably.

Jena snatches the paper from his hand and rips it up. "No," she says. "They mean Jena Parker." She leans close to him. "I'm leaving." She walks to the front of the plane. "You want to know why I come back here?" She looks around the plane, and all the passengers disappear. She turns around to look at Mr. McNeil with a mean expression on her face. "I come back here because this is my plane, my rules, and you're just a simple man trapped here," she says in a commanding voice. Mr. McNeil stands up. He tries to move, but he can't. "See," Jena says. "You're not like me. You're nothing. You're my nothing, and that's what you'll always be to me."

Jena wakes up. Jake is out of the truck, standing next to the lake where they used to meet as kids. Jena sits up, looks around in amazement, opens the truck door slowly, and steps out. She knows that she is home.

CHAPTER NINE

Jake is throwing rocks into the lake. He has a depressed look on his face. Jena walks toward him. He doesn't look at her; he just continues to throw rocks. Jena suddenly remembers all the moments she and Jake shared together at the lake when they were children. She remembers waiting for Jake at the lake one day after school, and she is transported back to that day.

Jake is running late. Jena looks around while she waits for Jake. When Ken taps her on the shoulder, she is startled.

Jena stares at Ken. "What are you doing here?" she shouts.

Ken smiles while circling her. "Umm, I guess you're waiting for Jake?" Jena walks away. Ken follows her. "So, you can't speak to me?" he says.

"Yes, I'm waiting for Jake. But you didn't answer my question. What are you doing here?"

"Well, I just wanted to say hello. What's wrong with that?"

Jena smirks. "Well, we don't really speak to each other, and neither do you and Jake, so I'm just wondering."

Ken stops and begins to back away from Jena. "What, you think no one knows about you and your lover boy's favorite spot?" Ken says in an angry voice.

"He's not my lover boy," Jena says. "He's my best friend."

"Oh … friend." Ken laughs. "Anyway, your friend has after-school detention, so I thought I'd be nice enough to come all the way out here to tell you. Well, so much for niceness." Ken walks away.

Jena just stares at the lake. She kneels down, picks up a few rocks, and begins throwing them in the lake. She is back, and Jake is still throwing rocks in the lake. He kneels down.

Jena stands over him. "What's wrong?" she asks. Jake turns his head and looks off into the distance. Jena kneels down next to him. She gently touches Jake on the shoulder.

He looks down at her hand, back up into her eyes, and then kisses her hand. "My mom called." He sighs. "She left me a message. My dad is in St. Mary's Hospital. He passed out at work, and right now the doctors don't know what's wrong with him." Jake stands up. "My mom is pleading for me to come home." Jake almost breaks down. A tear drops from one of his is eyes. He turns to Jena. "Jena, my mom said your mother's funeral is tomorrow." Jena turns around quickly. She tilts her head down slightly and closes her eyes. Jake walks close behind her. "Jena, I have to go see my father." Jake grabs her. Tears begin to flow from his eyes. He puts his head on her shoulder.

"I understand, Jake," Jena says softly. She turns around to face him. "I'm so sorry." She looks down at the ground. "I'm so sorry that you have to be here with me when your family needs you. You have to go now." She pulls away from Jake.

"No," he says. "We will go together."

Jena turns around with a surprised look on her face. "Jake," she says. "The cops. We can't."

Jake walks quickly behind her. He grabs her arm. "Yes, we can." He holds her tightly. "I won't leave you behind. Never, Jena." He squeezes her. "Never." Jake looks deeply into her eyes. He kisses her softly on the lips. They lock eyes for more than a minute. No words. No movement. No sound. Just the locking of their eyes. Jena reaches for his face with both hands and, just like the wind, she rushes to kiss him. She kisses him like never before. Long, deep kisses. Jake is lost in her. "I love you," Jake says to her. Jena stares him down. She kisses him again, over and over again. "You're my family too, and I will take care of you until the world stops for me—and even then, I'll spend the reminder of the time searching for you until I find you again so I can take care of you and love you." He holds her closely. "My world will never stop, for you are my everything—my every moment and my only reason."

Jena is taken by Jake's words. "What will we do?" she asks. "Where will hide?"

"We'll go to my parents' house and hide in the basement. My mother is at the hospital, so she won't be around." Jake looks off again. He grabs Jena's hand to lead her to the truck.

Jena suddenly stops. Jake turns around. She lets go of Jake's hand. "Jake, I will go to my mother's funeral."

"Jena, you—" Jake begins to speak.

"No. Don't say I shouldn't go, because I will go." She walks past Jake and turns back around. "I will go to her funeral, and no one—not you, not the cops—no one will stop me." She gets into the truck.

Jake leans on the truck's hood. He puts both hands on the truck and stares through the front window at Jena. "Okay," he says while nodding his head yes. "Okay." He walks over to Jena's door, opens it, and kisses her on the cheek. "Okay." He kisses her hand, closes the truck's door, and walks with his head down to the driver's side. They both take one last look at the lake. The stillness of the moment sets in, and they both can feel that their journey will begin a new chapter the moment they leave the lake. Jake drives away.

Darkness has set in, and Jake manages to drive through his neighborhood without being noticed. The streets are empty. Only the wind shares the space with him and Jena. His house is dark, and his mother's car is gone. Jake passes his house and stops.

"There's a car garage down the street. We'll park the truck there and walk back." He looks over at Jena and smiles. "Maybe this would be a good time for you to wear that famous red hat of yours."

Jena doesn't find the humor in Jake's joke. "Yeah," she says as she looks away.

Jake pulls up to the parking garage window. There's a tall, slim man sitting in the booth reading a newspaper. Jake slowly pulls forward. The man doesn't look at him, he just sticks his hand out the window and shoves the parking ticket in Jake's face. Jake quickly snatches the ticket and drives off. Jake parks the truck on the highest level in the parking garage. He shuts off the engine and sits still for a moment. He turns to speak to Jena, but she grabs her bag and opens the truck door before he can say anything.

Jake gets out, walks up to her, and reaches his hand out to her. "Everything will all right," he assures her. "You'll see."

Jena just stares at his hand for a moment, her heart slightly racing. The inevitable awaits as she looks up to gaze off into the night. She takes Jake's hand, and they both begin to walk back to his house, cutting through backyards and alleyways just as Jake had done when he was a kid.

Jena and Jake stop in the dark near his neighbor's house. Jake checks out the area. "Looks clear." Jake reaches for the extra key, hidden under a plant near the back door. He opens the door. The house is dark and quiet; no one appears to be inside.

Jena reaches for his shoulder. "Find some lights before we trip over each other," she says.

"I'm looking." Jake manages to turn on the living room lamp. He stares around the room. Jena stands close to him. She walks up to look at the pictures on the mantle: Jake's father and mother, his brother and him, and him and Jena as children.

Jena looks back at Jake. "We were once kids," she says softly. "Innocent kids, young and full of life's energy. Just dreaming of being teenagers, graduating high school, going to college." Jena walks away from the mantle. She shakes her head. "But now look at us. I'm a killer, and you're wasting your life chasing after me."

Jake walks over to her. "I'm not chasing after you, Jena. I'm standing by you." He reaches for her, but she shies away. "It doesn't really matter what you say or do, I'm not leaving you." He turns Jena around. "I know you're afraid."

Jena jerks her arm away. "I'm not afraid, Jake," she says abruptly. "I just don't want you to let your life go to shit for me. Look around. This is your home, your family … and what are you doing? You're playing Bonnie and Clyde with me." Jake looks down. Jena walks upstairs to Jake's room. He follows. She opens his door, walks in, and circles the room. Jake stands in his doorway. Jena sits down on his bed. She remembers the night her father was shot and killed by Mr. McNeil. She closes her eyes tightly. A small tear falls from one of them. Jake sits next her.

"I remember everything," Jena says. She lies back on his bed; Jake lies back alongside her. "I remember, Jake. I was so torn, broken, and ripped apart. It was the most unbelievable moment in my life." Jena's tears begin to fall. "That night … that night was the end of my life the way I knew it." She quickly sits up.

Jake follows and grabs her shoulder. "Jena …," he calls.

"No. Please." She sobs. "I miss him so very much. I try to forget, but my father … my mother …" Jena's tears are flowing like a waterfall out of control. "What happened to us, Jake?" She stands up. "What happened to my family? Why were we so cursed?"

Jake wipes a tear from Jena's face. He soothes her by caressing her face. He hasn't seen her vulnerable in such a long time. Somehow, the old Jena had come back; Jena Parker had returned. Jake knows that this is a moment that has to be savored. It marked the moment that Jena had returned home, had returned to being the girl around the corner. The best friend. The crush. The love of his life. He caresses her cheeks, hair, and shoulder. He can see and feel the pain and confusion in her eyes. Her tears are like a bullet lodged in his heart. He wants nothing more than for her to know that he would do anything to put her pain in a box and throw it away in the deep ocean, a hidden treasure meant to never be found again. "I love you, Jena," he says. "Please tell me now that you love me too."

Jena looks at him. She sees the compassion in his eyes, his sincere emotions, and the death of his own life in order to make her happy. She looks away.

"Jena, please—I need to hear you say it." Jena turns her eyes down. Jake moves in closer to kiss her. She doesn't say anything, but she doesn't turn away from his kiss. His lips enfold hers like soft pillow feathers or cotton candy. Jake's room door opens wider.

"What are you doing?" Jake and Jena both look up in sheer surprise to see Ted, Jake's brother. He had been asleep and was awakened by their voices. Jake stands up. Ted's face is red. They both just stand and stare at each other like two men ready to brawl in the Wild West. Ted quickly runs up to his brother and gives him a hug. His eyes watch Jena as she stands and stares.

"I'm so happy to see you, brother," Ted says as he hugs Jake harder. "Man, I just thought something really bad happened to you." Ted looks up at Jena.

Jake hugs Ted back. "I'm good, man," he says. "I'm good."

Ted stands back a little, still taken by the moment. "Dad, man." Ted rubs his hand on his head.

Jake turns around to look at Jena. "I know, man. Mom called."

Ted breaks down. "Man, he just passed out." Ted tries to hold back his tears.

Jake walks over to him, squeezes his brother's shoulder, and hugs him again. "It's okay, man," Jake consoles him. "It's okay."

Ted looks over at Jena. "I can't believe you brought her here, Jake."

"Back off, Ted." Jake stands in front of Jena.

"Look, it's not that I don't like you, Jena." Ted leans past Jake to look at her. "I do. I mean, I don't know whether to believe the shit I heard or not, but it's Mom." Ted walks around the room. "Mom broke down over Kitty's death, and now Dad is in the hospital." Ted continues to explain, "I mean, man, things around here are just wicked. I just think Mom is going to lose it if she finds out Jena is here. This whole thing is falling apart." Ted sits down on Jake bed. "Hell, I'm falling apart, and I'm still in high school."

Jake tries to console Ted. They both continue to talk about their dad, their mom, Jena, and where Jake has been the last couple of days.

Jena wanders out of the room. She walks around the upstairs, remembering when she was little, and her mom would bring her over to play with Jake. She remembers her, Jake, and Ted running through the house as their moms chatted downstairs in the kitchen while baking cakes, pies, and cookies. The aroma from the chocolate chip cookies baking in the oven would fill the entire house, and the three of them couldn't wait for the cookies to be done. Gooey chocolate morsel sticking to their fingers and faces, the three of them would laugh uncontrollably at cartoons or at the silliness of their parents' crazy clothes and conversations.

Jena wanders into the Paterson's bedroom. There is a black dress, hat, and shoes laid out. Pictures of Jena's mom and Mrs. Paterson are pasted all over the bedroom mirror and dresser—pictures of when they were little girls, of them as teenagers, and of the Paterson's and Parkers as couples at the local bowling alley. Jena walks up to the dress. She touches the fabric. She looks back at the pictures of her mom and then back at the dress and shoes.

CHAPTER TEN

Jena walks back to Jake's room. Ted and Jake are still talking. She stands in the doorway.

Ted stands up, walks over to her, and gives her a big hug. "I've missed you, girl." He squeezes Jena really hard. Jena smiles a little and hesitates, but she eventually gives in and squeezes him tightly back. "I don't know what really happened, Jena, but I know you, so I'm gonna just be the friend I've always been to you." Ted gently pinches her cheek. Ted turns to Jake. "Hey, you guys, you don't have to worry too much tonight. Mom won't be back until early morning." Ted looks at Jena. "She's ... umm ... coming back to get ready for the funeral tomorrow morning." Jena stares out Jake's window as the darkness of her murderous actions dawns on her.

Jake won't let her slip back into a deep depression again. He walks over to her. "We're going to the basement now."

Ted watches as they both head down toward the basement. "Hey," Ted calls. "Umm ... I'll make dinner."

Jake gives him a weird look. "You—make dinner?" He laughs.

"Umm ... well, I don't know, man. Hey, I'm a decent cook now," Ted says in a joking voice.

"Sure," Jake says as he smirks at Jena and then walks down the steps. "I guess we really don't have a choice." Ted laughs as he shrugs his shoulders and closes the basement door.

The basement is a little chilly, dimly lit, and full of the Paterson family's old furniture, toys, clothes, and other household items. Jake flops on the couch and laughs; he almost falls over the side to the floor.

Jena laughs out loud. "You klutz! Ha, ha." They both laugh loudly. She flops down next to him. "So, this is home?" she says smiling.

"I guess." Jake chuckles. He starts bouncing up and down on the couch, trying to keep Jena in a cheery mood. "Remember, Jena?" Jake keeps bouncing. "Remember when we were kids and how we just bounced and played on our parents' furniture?" Jena's body is shaking from Jake's bouncing. She tries not to laugh, but she can't help herself. "Oh, come on, Jena—bounce with me."

Jena thinks back to when she and Jake were children. His words echo from the past. Little Jake's voice flashes through her mind. "Come on, Jena—bounce with me." Jena starts bouncing up and down on the couch. The two of them together, acting like little children, bouncing up and down on the couch, laughing, giggling, and being playful with one another.

Suddenly the basement door swings open. Jake and Jena quickly stop. It's Ted. "Hey, what are you guys doing?" Ted asks.

Jake and Jena are relieved that it's Ted and not Mrs. Paterson. They look at each other and burst out into loud laughter. "You trying to scare us, guy," Jake asks.

Ted starts laughing. "I realized you guys didn't want to add me in the fun, so I thought I'd add my own fun." The three-start laughing together just like they had when they were kids, splattered with chocolate chip cookie dough all over them, bouncing up and down on their parents' furniture.

Jake's eyes beam with excitement as he watches Jena laugh out loud. He stops everything to watch her. He studies each and every detail of her smile, the way her hair flows, the widening of her eyes. The bus rides, the talks at their school lockers, and the afternoons at the lake all flash before him. He understands that life isn't just pieces of moments; it's every moment—and his moment is lost in Jena's eyes and her smile. His smile fades, not because of sadness, but because he wants to freeze this beautiful moment just like a red rose frozen in the winter woods. Still red, still beautiful, and still alive, even if the cold had stopped its moment. It still wants to be noticed. To live. To breathe. Jake is convinced that Jena wants to live again. He can hear it in her laughter, feel it in his heart. He is ready to battle anyone and anything that gets in the way of her happiness.

Trying to rush Ted off, Jake says, "Aren't you supposed to be cooking us something, dude?"

"Oh, now you're longing for my cooking?" Ted jokes. "Just a minute ago, you weren't sure if I could cook." Jake and Jena stare each other with smiles on their faces. "Okay, I get it—you just want to be alone with Jena." Ted heads up the stairs and peeks down at them as the door closes. He raises his eyebrows just before the door shuts.

Jena gives Jake a shy look as he moves in close to kiss her. The basement door swings back open just before Jake lands the kiss. Ted does a funny little dance and closes the door again. Jake tries to move in for the kiss again.

Jena stands up. "I think I'm going to take a shower while it's safe." She laughs to herself as she walks up the basement steps.

"Yeah … umm … me too." He walks behind her. "You go use the bathroom in my room, and I'll hit the hallway one."

"You like to follow me, don't you, Jake?" Jena laughs.

"I'm not following you. I just happened to need a shower, just like you."

"Yeah, yeah. You just make sure you stay in your shower," Jena says playfully.

"I'll try." Jake leans in his room's doorway.

Jena sniffs his armpit. "You stink."

Jake sniffs his armpits. "Yeah, I guess it's not sexy, huh?"

Jena laughs. "Not really."

Jake watches as she enters his bathroom and closes the door. He thinks to himself, Jena's back. My Jena is finally back.

Jena turns on the shower. Steam fills the bathroom. She carefully steps into the shower. The hot water races down her skin. She stands under the showerhead with her hand braced against the shower wall. The water drills down her on her hair, body, and feet. She looks up. "Shampoo and a razor," she utters. "Just what I need." She stares at the shampoo and razor before grabbing them. I guess I should probably ask Jake what he is doing with a razor in his shower, she thinks as she laughs to herself.

The hot shower makes Jena think about Jake. The heat of the water reminds her of the heat they shared when they made love. The soap suds slowly glide down her body, just like Jake's hands when he gently caressed every inch of her. Jena touches her own body just as Jake had—first the neck, chest, breast, stomach, thighs, and then her vagina. She heats up just thinking of Jake. She closes her eyes and imagines him on top of her. His movement … his motion … like a hard ocean wave crashing up against a rock, over and over again. She tightly closes her eyes and imagines him thrusting into her, tossing her over, playing with her, and giving her everything. All of him, over and over again. Like a caged tiger, her face is filled with desire as both hands press up against the shower wall.

Jake pulls back the shower curtains. He is naked, and his body is dripping wet. Breathing hard, he stares at Jena's naked, wet body. The hot steam surrounds them. He steps into the shower and presses his body up against hers. He begins kissing her softly and then harder. Jena parents' song jiggles in her mind. Jake looks at her as he gently plays with her nipples, squeezes her breasts, and leans down to kiss both of them. He licks her neck with the tip of his tongue, kisses down her chest, her stomach, and then gently kisses between her thighs. His hands smoothly slide up her thighs, waist, and back to her breasts. He grabs her to him like a man in charge who knows what he wants. He kisses her deeply. They are locked in a deep, passionate kiss as he hands discover every intimate inch of her.

There's a knock at the bathroom. "Hey?" a voice calls. "Jena? Time for dinner." It's Jake. He leans his face up against the bathroom door. "Are you all right?"

Jena comes back to reality. She turns off the water. "Yes. I'll be out in a minute." Jena grabs a towel.

"Okay," he answers softly. "I've put some of my clothes out for you."

"Okay, Jake. Thanks."

Jake can see the steam roll out from underneath the door. He places his hand on the door.

Jena can still feel him standing outside the door. She places her hand on the door. "I'll be downstairs soon." Jake smiles as he walks away.

Jena slips into a towel. Jake has laid out some of his clothes on the bed: black sweatpants and his favorite football team T-shirt. She slips on a pair of his socks and fantasizes for a moment that she's Jake's wife, in their room, in their house. Everything seems so perfect, but she knows it isn't. Jake's father is in the hospital, her mother is dead, and she is a fugitive on the run from the cops. She knows no matter how much she wants things to be perfect, it never will be.

Jena walks toward Jake's room window, opens it, and sticks her head out to feel the cool breeze. If only snow would fall right now, she thinks. Beautiful white snow crystals and shooting stars all at once. What a fantasy, she thinks. What a gift that would be to brighten the world I live in now. Jena closes the room window. Her tension is back. All that was so happy, so peaceful disappeared out the window the moment she opened it. An upside-down world is what she sees and feels. Even the magical moment that she and Jake so recently shared felt like it happened a lifetime ago when it happened only an hour ago.

She looks around Jake's room, walks out to the hall, and then looks once more into his room—as if it would be the last time, she sees it. She slowly walks down the hall past Jake's parents' room. She stops to glare at Mrs. Paterson's dress for her mother's funeral. What an ugly dress, she thinks. Just hanging there, waiting to be worn by a warm body. Why should a warm body wear that dress? she thinks. Why? That dress should be worn by someone cold. Someone not worthy of wearing it. Someone whose heart is as black and cold as that dress. Jena walks into the Paterson's' bedroom, removes the dress from the hanger, and grabs the shoes. She quickly heads to the basement to hide the outfit.

Jake and Ted are waiting for her at the kitchen table. Jake stands up. "What took you so long?" he asks.

"I was just thinking about some things. Life." Jena glances at the food on the table. She remains standing. "There is so much in life that is unexplained. The dark tunnels of life. The dungeons and lost chambers. In the blink of an eye, anything can change your life—for better or worse. Either way, you have to be ready. Ready for it all. Ready for a showdown." Jena looks at Jake and Ted. "You two have a father in the hospital, a mother that needs you, and a world that is still capable of offering you both something." She sits down. "And I ... well, I have a funeral to attend tomorrow." Jake has a worried look on his face. Jena reassures him. "The world is still spinning, Jake, and tomorrow I must face my own doings—and I must face them alone."

None of them have an appetite, although they all pretend, they are still hungry. The sun had set, the rain had come, and the wind had blown everything around in the room. The truth could not be hidden—not by laughter, not by memories, not even by love.

CHAPTER ELEVEN

Jena sits at the dinner table with thoughts of her life moving backward like a horrible hurricane ripping through a small town. Jena at the dinner table, in the shower, on the couch laughing with Jake, at the lake, at Maggie's, in the car with Jake, at the hotel with the gun pointed at Mr. McNeil ... running to Jake's ... her mother's bathroom ... frozen across the street, watching her mother on her knees cry with blood on her hands ... the murder of her father. Walk backward, she thinks, and then maybe it'll all be a horrible nightmare. Maybe I'm not a murderer. Maybe my father and mother are still alive, and Jake and I are back at school, laughing and playing as we did when we were children. No, forward. There is no walking backward for me.

Jena distances herself from Jake and Ted for the rest of the night. When the morning comes, she knows exactly what she has to do and the demon she has to face.

Jena stands looking in the mirror the morning of her mother's funeral. She is wearing Mrs. Paterson's black dress, shoes, and black hat with a veil that covers her face. The day of her mother's funeral has now arrived, and it's time for her to face the truth—that backward is really forward and the time has come for her to walk through the pitch-black door.

She grabs the truck keys off the dresser, slips out of the house, and heads down the street to the parking garage. The garage is almost empty. Only the truck and two other cars, which look abandoned, are parked there.

From red to black. The red dress she had worn was so provocative. Red, the color of blood. The color I dreamed of when I thought of Mr. McNeil's vicious ways. Now a black dress—so black, so cold, and so fitting for a person like me, she thinks to herself while walking toward the truck. She gets into the truck and glances in the side mirror. Is my heart really as black as this dress, as this hat, as these shoes? Could I be so cold? So heartless? Or is my heart just hidden, buried underneath the world, and I somehow have to find my way back home?

Jena turns on the truck engine. The radio instantly plays coverage of a police officer taking questions from a local reporter. "Officer Reyes did Matt Ross confess to the robbery and murder he allegedly committed?" the news reporter asks.

"This information can't be revealed at this time, because the investigation is still pending," he replies.

"Officer, is Matt Ross being charged by the Maplesville's police?"

"We are working with the other counties as we continue to investigate," he answers quickly.

"Officer Reyes, there has been a rumor circulating that Matt Ross is an accomplice of Jena Parker, also known by the alias Jena Gray. What can you tell us about that?" Jena turns the radio up.

"Though we are not ready to confirm or deny that relationship, I can say that we have received information from this arrest that has aided in our search of Jena Parker. We believe that Jena Parker may currently be either close to or in Maplesville. We will be ready for Ms. Parker if she tries to return to Maplesville. She will be arrested or captured the moment she hits this town."

Jena turns off the radio and spins out of the parking garage. She drives past the ticket booth without paying. The ticket attendant yells as Jena passes, calls it in, and then tries to run after her. Jena speeds off. The attendant stands in the middle of the busy highway, winded and exhausted from chasing the truck. The attendant is hit by a car and is knocked unconscious.

Jena continues to drive to the funeral. She doesn't know exactly how she will attend the funeral without being noticed. She knows her grandmother will be there along with uncles, aunts, cousins, and other family members. The police will probably be circling the funeral site waiting to arrest her and undercover detectives will be watching out for her. She also knows that soon Jake will discover she is gone, and he'll come running after her like a tiger chasing a lamb.

Jake awakens, calls out for Jena, but no answer is sent in return. He can feel the emptiness in the room. There is not a sound or a whisper of her voice. The evidence is clear that she is gone. He hears footsteps upstairs and his mother's voice as she tries to wake up Ted.

"Ted. Ted." Mrs. Paterson shakes Ted to wake him.

"What, Mom?"

"Where's my dress?"

"What?" Ted opens his eyes wide.

"Where is my dress for Kitty's funeral?" Ted sits up. He looks at his doorway. Mrs. Paterson turns around. Jake is standing there with his eyes locked on his mother. "Jake," Mrs. Paterson utters softly in shock. She crosses the floor slowly, trying not to stumble as she walks toward her son. Mrs. Paterson looks up at him as if she has seen a ghost. Her tears drop, one by one, onto her pinstriped blouse and then like hard rain drops her tears flow as she rushes into Jake's arms. "Jake, your father ..." She is at a loss for words.

"Mom, it's okay." Jake holds her tight.

"Jake, you have to see him." Mrs. Paterson squeezes him tighter. "He's not good. He's not good at all, Jake."

"It's all right, Mom. We'll go." Jake rubs his mom's back as he stares at Ted. "We'll go together."

Mrs. Paterson calms down for a moment, breathes a deep breath, and then let's go of Jake. She bites her bottom lip, runs her fingers through her hair, and swallows. "Where is she?" She looks at Jake.

"Mom, please."

"Where is she, Jake!" she screams.

"I don't know."

"Yes, you do. She took my dress." Mrs. Paterson circles the room. "My shoes! My hat!" Jake is quiet. "Jake, she's a killer!" She yells louder, "She's a killer! How could you bring her in my house?" Mrs. Paterson sits down at the end of Ted's bed. She looks up.

"She's going to Kitty's funeral," Jake says.

She rushes off the bed and tries to pass Jake. "She's going to Kitty's funeral! Oh, my God! What is she doing?"

Jake grabs his mom's arm. "Mom, please calm down."

She pulls away from him. "Calm down? Calm down!" She struggles to pass Jake.

"Mom stop it! You don't have the facts," Jake pleads with her.

"Yes, I do!" she yells. "She killed three people—and her own mother." Mrs. Paterson begins to shake. "I thought she killed you, too, Jake. Now you're an accessory to murder! Running from the cops and linked with this Matt Ross!" She pushes Jake. "Get out of my way. I have to call the cops."

"No!" Jake yells back. "No, mom, you can't do that."

"Why not?" She stands back from him.

Jake slowly answers, "Because I love her." He walks toward his mom. "I love her, Mom."

Mrs. Paterson looks back at Ted, who has a terrified look on his face. She sits down on the bed. "How could you love a killer?" she asks.

"I love her, Mom, and that's that. I love you too. I love Dad. I even love Ted." Ted lifts his eyebrows surprise at what Jake just said. Jake sits down next to his mom. "I don't want to hurt or disappoint you, Mom. I've been with her, and the journey we've shared together has been unbelievable."

Mrs. Paterson stares at Jake with a shocked and disappointing look. "You killed too?" She shakes her head and begins to cry.

"Mom, please don't cry."

"Jake, the cops are looking for her—and they're looking for you too. I don't want you to go to jail. Your fathers in the hospital. Ted's here alone all the time. You're on the run. I ... I just can't take it anymore." Jake holds his mom to try to console her. "I just can't."

Jake gets on his knees in front of his mother. "Mom, let's go see Dad." He holds her hand in his. Mrs. Paterson looks deep into his eyes. Jake's eyes beam bright like the sun. The last time she had seen him, he was a boy going off to college. But in front of her is a man. A man on the run with a woman who is a killer. A man who is still her son, no matter what the circumstance. And she is a mother who wants to protect her young. She glances into Ted's and Jake's faces and decides she has to conceal her anger for Jena from Jake in order to destroy the hold Jena has on him.

"All right," she agrees. She stands up. "Get ready, guys." She slowly starts walking out of the room, eyeing Jake, and thinking, I'll make Jena pay. Thoughts of Kitty race through her mind. I'll make her pay for everything she's done. She stops at Ted's doorway. "I won't go to Kitty's funeral today—not because I don't have a dress or anything to wear, but because I'm too damaged. What little piece of me is left," she turns to face them, "I must give to you two and your father."

She walks out of the room and goes straight to the kitchen to call the police.

Officer Reyes answers the phone. "Maplesville Police Department. Office Reyes speaking."

Mrs. Paterson tries to disguise her voice. "Hello, I won't say who I am, but I have information to report."

"Yes, ma'am. Go ahead." Officer Reyes listens closely.

"I believe that Jena Parker may attempt to attend her mother's funeral." Mrs. Paterson quickly hangs up the phone, leaving the officer listening to only a dial tone.

She places her hands together in prayer. "This one's for you, Kitty. Rest in peace, my dear friend. Rest in peace."

Jake walks into the kitchen. "Mom, you all right?" He hugs her. "I'll be ready soon, Mom." She is quiet. He kisses her on the cheeks before walking away.

Is life really so complicated? Jena wonders. How can a girl go from being so innocent, sweet, and curious to being a stone-cold killer? What a vicious act of faith, that I could be the one to create such darkness.

Jena stands in the mist in the woods across the street from the funeral grounds. She watches as people dressed in pitch-black clothing and sunglasses begin to get out of cars and the family limo. No one notices her. She is a dark figure aligned with the woods, just waiting for the right moment to step out of the dark and into the light where everyone can see her, but no one will know who she is and where she came from. She lifts the veil from her face just as the hearse passes by. The shock of seeing the hearse gives her an unsettling feeling—an emotion that is as quiet as the woods she stands in, but causes a deep, thundering thump in her heart. It's like someone had just walked up to her and ripped all of her clothes off to shame her. She is powerless to move while stones, leaves, and tree branches begin to fall on her. Her palms lift to the sky, expecting what she feels she deserves—the true reality of the pain rooted so deep in the vessels of her heart. "Mom," she utters as tears begin to fall from her eyes. The pain of knowing that it is her mother lying in that hearse awakens a spirit in her, just like a swimmer coming up for air from the waters, or like a mother viewing her baby for the first time, or a child looking at her father's smiling face while her hair blows in the wind as he pushes her back and forth on the swings. Jena walks out to blend in with her family. She passes a family car just as her grandmother, Kitty's mother, steps out. Jena looks at her, an old woman with tears running down her face, wearing a big black hat and carrying a big black purse. Granddad Donaldson and Uncle Norman walk alongside her.

"It's all right, Mom," Uncle Norman comforts her as he holds her arm tightly. All of the family is gathered at the funeral site. Cousins, great aunts, and uncles, even Jena's dad's sister, Aunt Denise. Jena walks alongside all of her family. With no one saying a word or asking who is who, she manages to find her way through the funeral crowd to a front row seat right next to her grandmother.

CHAPTER TWELVE

I was five when I last saw my grandmother, Jena silently reminisces. Her and Granddad came down to help celebrate Mother and Father's ten-year anniversary. My grandmother was always very nice to me. She always sent me beautiful pageant-like dresses and shoes, along with really bright hair bows. I loved getting gifts from my grandmother. My grandfather lost one of his arms in the war. He was a kind person, but I was always frightened to see him walking around with that one arm. I would just hide behind my mother when he'd try to talk to me, and I couldn't keep my eyes off that missing arm. Even now, looking at him, I remember the fear I felt in thinking, "What monster stole my grandfather's arm?" How awful that must have been for him to be a one-armed man. My mother was very close to my grandfather, but she never really got along with my grandmother. She would tell me, "My mother is so judgmental. I can't stand the way she talks about other people. I'm not like her, Jena. She always gave me this look. I never will be like her," my mother used to say to me all the time. She said she would raise me differently than her mother raised her. Looking at my grandmother with uncontrollable tears running from her face, anyone would have thought she and my mother were closer, but I guess the past doesn't matter—even if we lived it with the one, we loved in patches or pieces. We still love the ones who are dear to us as a whole, especially when all that's left is a casket staring back at you.

Jena's aunt Denise sits next her. She is also wearing a veil over her face. She doesn't look at Jena, just straight ahead with a black handkerchief in her hand to wipe the tears away from her eyes. Jena can hear her aunt sniffling every few seconds. With her grandmother falling apart on the right side of her, her aunt Denise's unbearable emotional state to the left of her, and the other family members crying and moaning all around her, she is truly trapped to endure it all. She can feel the buildup of emotions raise like the heat from a volcano about to erupt. She wants to stand up, yell at the top of her lungs, and run … run to her mother.

The time has come. She can't hold back her tears any longer. They begin to drop like hail—hard, long, and everlasting. She takes a deep breath and puts her head down to let her tears fall to the ground. She lets them fall … fall … "My mom," she utters through the tears. "My mother." Jena is trembling, lost in sorrow. All of her family, the friends of her mother, and even the entire area itself just fades away from her. It is just her, her mother, and the ugly truth; that's all she can allow herself to see.

Beautiful birds begin to fly over her mother's casket. One of them lands, flaps its wings, and stares directly at Jena. Its eyes are as blue as the sky, and its feathers are as white as the snow. The bird sits quietly on the casket and stares at Jena, and then it flies up in the air and lands on her lap. Jena's tears fall on the bird's wings. As it opens its wings, what seemed to be a small bird ends up being a bird with big, beautiful white wings that glow like pearls and are capable of soaring like an angel. The bird flies off of Jena's lap toward the sun. Its shadow grows large over the funeral as it flaps it wings, flying farther and farther away into the sky.

Jena is overwhelmed by the presence of the bird. It somehow calms and excites her at the same time. She reaches her right hand up to remove the veil from her face, but right before she does Jena's aunt slowly taps Jena's leg. She looks at Jena with tears streaming down her face. She looks into Jena's eyes, but she doesn't say a word; they both just stare at one another. Jena's and her aunt's tears drop at the same time. Their tears fall simultaneously as they look deep into each other's eyes. Jena stops, puts her hand down, and looks back at her mom. Her aunt Denise looks back toward the casket without saying a word to Jena. Jena glances over at her grandmother, who is leaning over, barely able to keep from fainting. Her grandfather and Uncle Norman try to keep her from falling completely apart.

The minister walks to the podium to begin the service. The family who are seated stand up. Her aunt Denise slowly stands up. Her grandmother is too distraught to stand on her own. Jena's grandfather and her uncle try to help, but she is so traumatized that her legs are weak and heavy. Other family members try to console her by talking to her, patting her shoulder, and wiping her tears. The minister watches and doesn't speak until the family has Grandmother Donaldson to her feet. Everyone is standing, including Jena. Her aunt Denise glances at her. The minister is ready to start.

Just as he begins, a police car pulls up to the funeral site. Two men get out: one wearing a police officer uniform and the other in a dark-blue suit, a long black coat, and dark shades. They talk as they stand by the police car. Uncle Norman looks over at them. He signals to the minister to start without him. The minister begins to speak to the family.

Norman approaches the police car with an angry, depressed look on his face. "Why are you guys here?"

Officer Reyes and Detective Martin walk over to Norman. "We got a call."

Norman gives them a much angrier look. "About?" he asks sharply.

Officer Reyes steps in closer to him. "Someone called the police department with a tip saying that Jena Parker may be attempting to attend this funeral." Officer Reyes scopes out the crowd.

Norman looks back at his family and then back at the officers. "Look, this is a funeral." He holds his head down in despair. "A funeral. A goddamn funeral." He holds his hands up in the air. "My mother doesn't need to see cops at her daughter's funeral."

Officer Reyes gets mad. He puts his hand on his gun. "This is official business."

"No," Norman says loudly. "This is a funeral. So please leave." Norman points at the officer.

Detective Martin gives Officer Reyes a quick look. Officer Reyes moves in closer to Norman. "You're not going to tell us how to conduct this investigation."

"Investigation of what?" Norman yells.

"The murder of Katherine Parker by her daughter, Jena Parker."

Norman steps up to Officer Reyes. "There's no proof that Jena killed her mother." He points at the officer.

"Put your hand down, mister."

Norman frowns. "Don't tell me what to do." He clinches his fist.

Detective Martin steps in between the two men. "We are here to follow a lead," Detective Martin pleads. "That's our job." He gives Norman a meaningful look. "Your niece is wanted for multiple murders. And it is a fact that she is a suspect in the murder of own mother."

Officer Reyes pipes in, "That's right. So, what proof do you have that your niece didn't kill her own mother?"

Norman pushes Officer Reyes. "Just as much proof as you guys have that she did!" he yells.

Officer Reyes and Norman begin swinging at one another. They both scramble around fighting in the dirt. Detective Martin does his best to break up the fight. Some of Jena's other uncles run over to help break up the fight. Jena's great-uncles Paul and Ray grab Norman and pull him off of Officer Reyes.

"You're under arrest, pal, for assaulting an officer of the law!" Officer Reyes yells.

"You interrupted my sister's funeral." Paul and Ray are holding Norman. The minister has stopped speaking, and the family is standing, staring at the fallout. "What are you going to do," Norman yells, pointing at his family, "check all of my family looking for her?"

Officer Reyes stares over at the family. Almost all of the women have black veils over their faces. He looks over at Detective Martin.

Norman, breathing hard, starts crying. "For the Lord's sake, this is my sister's funeral." He breaks down crying, falling to his knees. "Have some respect for my family. For her. Please ... please," he pleads as he cries. "Have some respect for my family."

Officer Reyes brushes himself off. He tries to calm himself, but he's still angry. He looks over at Detective Martin and then gets in the car.

Detective Martin looks over at the crowd. He sees Jena, but he doesn't know it's her. He feels bad and wants to apologize to Grandmother Donaldson. He walks over to her. Jena is still sitting next to her. "Ma'am," he speaks to Grandmother Donaldson. "Ma'am," he speaks to Jena. "Ma'am," he speaks to Denise. "I just want to apologize for coming here today."

Jena stands up. Denise stands up next to her. Jena's grandmother is crying and doesn't answer or responds to Detective Martin's apology. Jena walks past Detective Martin. "Excuse me," Jena politely asks. Detective Martin steps back to let her pass. She walks to her mother's grave, stops, and stares at the casket. Detective Martin turns around and stares at her. He begins walking toward her, but Grandmother Donaldson grabs his hand. She stands up.

"Thank you, but please leave now," she sobs. "I'd like to bury my daughter in peace."

Detective Martin nods his head. He steps back. Jena remains at her mother's graveside, just staring at the casket. Her aunt Denise walks over to be with her. She pretends to talk to Jena. Detective Martin walks to the car, and he and Officer Reyes leaves the funeral.

The wind picks up just as the funeral ends. Jena is still standing next to her mother's casket, and Aunt Denise is standing alongside her. To the side of where Jena's mother will rest is Mr. Parker's grave. Denise is so overwhelmed by Kitty's funeral and her brother's grave that she leaves without saying good-bye to the family or Jena. The family members all begin to leave the funeral, but Jena is still standing, staring at her mother's grave. Jena's grandmother stays behind and stands next to her, waiting for Kitty's body to be placed in the ground.

"You want to say something to me?" Jena asks her grandmother.

"We all know it's you," she answers. "I knew it was you the moment you sat down next to me."

"Then why didn't you speak to me?" Jena asks.

"Well, I was never very close to your mother, so I'm sure she told stories about me. I decided that I'd let you be."

"And the cops?" Jena looks at her.

"They say you killed her. Did you kill your mother, Jena?" her grandmother asks.

Jena is silent. She removes the veil from her face. "I set her free. One may call it murder, but my mother died …" Jena gets choked up. "She died the moment my father was murdered. But you wouldn't know that, would you, because she never spoke a word after that night. You two never spoke to each other anyway, so you will never truly understand how silent and distant she became after my father died. I have to live with my demons," her tears begin to fall, "and, well, you have to live with yours."

Jena kneels down to touch her mother's casket one last time. "Good-bye, Mom," she utters softly through her tears. She walks away, leaving her grandmother standing alone.

CHAPTER THIRTEEN

In the air. Up in the sky. The plane flies and flies. Sit down in your seat quietly, because where the plane takes you can be unpredictable, so you have to ready for anything. In flight, the plane begins to fall. Everyone's afraid. Everyone grabs hold of something or someone. We tighten our seat belts, floatation devices in hand, as the roof of the plane rips off and people, one by one, are lifted out of their seats into the sky, into the cold air. Lifted up like air balloons drifting away to an unknown destination. Everyone but me. I'm still in flight, waiting for my plane to land—waiting for Jake to save me. What if I loosen the seat belt? I let the floatation device float away, and I just run up and down the plane like a child playing in a playground as it continues to go down. I go down with it when it crashes and burns to the ground. I'm still in flight. Jena Gray. Jena Parker. Jena Gray. Jena Parker.

"Wake up, Jena," Jena's mother's voice whispers to her. Jena quickly wakes up and finds herself in the truck. She's in the middle of the woods just two miles from the funeral site. She looks at herself in the mirror, grabs her bag, and changes her clothes. Her mother's letter falls out of the bag. She picks it up from the ground and grips it tightly in her hand. "Mom," she says as she puts the letter back in her bag.

Jena walks around the woods barefoot. She admires the trees, weeds, and small animals roaming around. "Nature at its best," she says. Jena hears a buzzing noise coming from the truck. She walks back to the truck, leans in to reach under the seat, and grabs the cell phone. She answers it.

It's Jake's voice on the other end. "Jena." She is silent. "Jena," he calls her name again.

"Jake," she finally answers.

"I'm at St. Mary's hospital with mom and Ted." Jena remains quiet. "Mom is a mess ... and Dad ... he's not responding." Jake is quiet. They both refrain from speaking. "Where are you?" Jake finally asks.

She looks around. "I'm in the woods."

"Oh. Well, when are you coming back?"

She hesitates to answer. "I don't know. I don't think I'm coming back, Jake. It's not that easy. We've both been running from the cops, so it's probably better we remain apart." She walks with the phone. "There only looking for me, anyway."

"Jena, they're looking for both of us. Heck, I'm wearing a hoodie, sunglasses, and a hat trying to disguise myself. Look, I know you're at your mother's funeral—"

She stops him. "Jake, I don't want to talk about it. I'm going my own way, so let me go."

"No," he replies.

She hangs up the phone on him. She stands tall, looking around at the forest again. Thoughts of Jake run through her head. Thinking of his smile—so bright, so alive—makes her shed a tear and a few moments of sadness. But she knew that she had to let him go, because he would never let her go. Ever.

Jake calls for Jena, but the ringing of the phone is all he hears. His mother is standing behind him. She touches him on the shoulder. "Let her go, Jake." He turns around and gives her a surprised look. "Just let her go. She comes with too many issues, and right now your father needs you. Your family needs you."

"Mom, do you love Dad?" She is surprised at his question. "Do you love my father?"

"Yes."

"Then don't tell me not to love Jena, because that's like me telling you not to love Dad—and I know that's completely impossible. I can't do the impossible. You can't do it, and neither can I." He pauses and turns around. "You're right that I do need to be here with my family. I'm here, and I'm sorry I wasn't here sooner. I'll be here for you, Mom. But don't ever ask me to stop loving Jena, because that is like asking me to die." Jake walks away from his mother to cool off. He tries calling Jena back, but she doesn't answer the phone.

The phone has been discarded on the ground in the middle of the forest. The forest is dark, with only the light from the moon to illuminate it. Jena is alone, hungry, sad, and confused. She knows she has to remain in hiding but also that she has to find somewhere to go. She cranks up the engine, rolls up the passenger window, and drives out of the woods onto a one-way highway toward town. She drives the highways and back roads in hopes that it will lessen of a risk of her being noticed by anyone, especially the cops—particularly Officer Reyes, who is out to get her at all cost.

She drives and drives until she ends up at the hotel where she once stayed. It is the place where the rude, fat clerk saw his fatal end. Now she is about to step back into what seems like a time bubble. She sits in the truck in the parking lot. The "open" light flash on and off. Not much has changed since she was last here; the place is still run down, and there are cats everywhere. Surely it was a refuge for the wanted, the ones who are hiding or running from something. A dark, hidden spot filled with secrets; each room shared by strangers who lie to themselves at night and pretend to be normal, self-righteous people in the morning.

Jena steps out of the truck. She reaches for her bag, tosses it on her shoulders, and walks slowly toward the hotel entrance. She hesitates before she opens the door. The glass door is cracked. A tiny bell hangs off the handle. Everything seems quiet, still—not like the last time when the clerk had the television blaring for the entire hotel to hear. She opens the door and walks to the counter. There is a book lying on the counter titled Cold Reda Gray: Life Is Filled with Mysteries and Then There's Death. Jena found the title of the book very interesting. The TV is in same spot. The counter and everything else inside looks exactly the same except there is no clerk. Jena visualizes the fat clerk sitting there eating while staring at the loud television, mustard clinging to his shirt. She stands and stares around the hotel's trashy lobby.

A tall man, wearing a wrinkled red silk shirt and a gold chain, walks from the back. He is smiling as he approaches Jena. "Hello, there." The clerk seems overexcited to see a customer. "How can I help you?"

Jena is taken aback. "Umm, I would like a room."

"That's wonderful." The clerk starts searching for his paperwork. "That's great. We love, love people at "The Palm Lee Inn hotel." Jena shakes her head. "Yep. We have the best hotel in town." The clerk looks around and so does Jena, both trying to believe his bullshit. "We offer cable TV, comfortable beds, and ... breakfast." Jena looks at the small concession stand. "Just coffee and donuts, nothing special." The clerk laughs. Jena has a serious look on her face, but she finds the clerk quite funny. "So, young lady, what floor do you want?"

"Second floor."

He looks at the keys. "Well. Second floor. Let's see. Second floor." There are only three keys left, so Jena can't understand the clerk's prolonged tally count of his available rooms. "Umm." He looks at all three keys. "Well, it looks like all of the rooms left just happen to be on the second floor."

"Great." Jena tries to be patient and polite. The clerk scrambles around to search for more paperwork. Jena's patience is running thin. "Could I just have the key?"

"Sure, sure." He gives Jena a pleasant smile and hands her a key. "But wait—I have to get you to sign some papers, you nice young girl." He grabs the paperwork, and his book falls to the floor. "Oh, sucks." He reaches down to pick it up. Jena stares at the poster hangings on the wall behind where he had been standing. There's a scratched picture of her with big "WANTED" posted on it. The clerk catches her staring at the picture. "Yeah, that's Jena. Jena Parker." The clerk looks at the picture and then back at Jena. "Hey, you look like her. You guys could be twins. Yeah, twins."

"Twins?" Jena says.

"Yeah," the clerk says as he stares at Jena. "Ah, but no way you're her. I mean, what are the chances of her returning to same place where she committed murder?" The clerks laughs. "I'm not that lucky. I mean who am I? I'm nobody. Just a silk shirt–wearing hotel clerk who wants to be a writer."

"A writer?" Jena seems curious.

"Yeah, see." He shows Jena the book. "This is my book. Cold Reda Gray: Life Is filled with Mysteries and Then There's Death. Isn't that a catchy title?" Jena nods her head. He starts rifling through his paperwork. "Man, I just love this book. I mean it's my own work, but I just love it." The clerk looks back at Jena's picture posted on the wall. "You know, I'd love to write a book about her."

Jena looks up at herself on the wall. "Why?"

"I mean, she is so mysterious. She kills the clerk at this hotel, kills a doctor on the train, and—oh, she was obsessed with that McNeil guy who killed her father." The clerk stares starry-eyed at Jena's picture. "But most intriguing of all, I just heard that she killed her mother too." He hands Jena the paperwork. "Can you imagine that?"

"Are we finished?" Jena asks in a subdued voice.

The clerk keeps talking. "I'd write a good book about her. I'd name it Cold Jena Parker. Although that would have to wait because I'm currently working on my sequel to this book." He holds his book proudly in his hand. "You know what I'm going to call it?" Jena lifts one eyebrow. "Cold Reda Gray: Reda Jones Returns. She returns to get revenge on all the ones she didn't kill." The clerk smiles at Jena. "By the way, my name is Franklin." He reaches out his hand to Jena.

Jena reaches her hand out to shakes his. "Franklin, good luck with your book." He shakes Jena's hand. Jena signs the paperwork, hands it back to him, and opens the door to leave.

"Oh, and thank you for choosing our lovely hotel!" He yells as she starts to walk off. Jena closes the door.

"Geez, I finally found someone crazier than me," she says to herself as she walks to her room. Jena finally reaches the hotel room. She slides the key in to open the door. The room is an exact replica of the room where she once stayed. The room where she caved-in to her impulse to see the sight of blood. Where the coldness in her heart began. Where the light dimmed to dark and then to pitch black. Jena throws her bag on the bed and waits. Was the clerk going to come to her room? Was his niceness just a way to soften her up so she could bare her innocence? He doesn't really know me; she thinks as she undressed. She stands in the bathroom doorway naked, staring at the tub and visualizing the fat clerk splattered with blood, dead on the floor and herself naked in the tub. She stands and thinks, Life is a mystery, filled with the unknown. It's a mystery that can take you far away from your reality. It is almost like there's an insane part of you that is only revealed when you actually look at yourself in the mirror for more than one minute; there it is, that creature that lives inside you—even when you laugh and try to hide it. I stand as proof of that mystery and the unknown. I'm proof that the dark does live among the light. I'm dark, and I'm light. The only thing is … I don't which one I will be tomorrow.

CHAPTER FOURTEEN

Jena watches as her other self submerges herself in the tub full of bloody water. Looking through an hourglass of suppressed memories, it was time to come face-to-face with her true self. It was here, in that tub. It was here that she murdered that clerk and left him lying on the floor, bare naked and bleeding from every corner of his flesh. She glances at the clerk on the floor and then back at herself in the tub. Jena watches herself stare off at the bathroom wall. She's staring at herself staring out into the nowhere, the nothing, the black space corner of the bathroom. Then it happens, in the flicker of the eye. Jena's body begins to slide deeper down into the tub. Her body—still, lifeless, and as cold as the clerk on the floor. Her hair submerges in the bloody water, then her face, and then her entire body is goes under. Jena watches as her other self-sinks completely under the water. She doesn't do anything to stop her. She wants her to die. She knows if she had died right there, then that is where this horrible story would have ended. But it wasn't where the story ended.

Jena emerges from the water, laughing and giggling to herself. She starts playing with the water, washing her body and her hair. She looks at the clerk on the floor and laughs at him, even throwing bloody water on him. Jena watches herself show no mercy, no fear, and no regrets. She gets out of the tub and walks over and stops to look at her present self. "Now it's your turn," she says as she walks past. "It's okay. A little bit of blood won't hurt you. Go on—touch him, feel him. He's not alive, and neither are you. You're dead inside, and there's no coming back from it." They both stand naked watching the blood flow from the clerk. They stand face-to-face. "Get dressed," Jena tells herself. "We have a guest coming."

The two Jena's put on identical dresses: the unforgettable red dress. So spectacular on her—well fitted, and perfectly made for a master of murder. It empowers her to be who she wants to be outside the world of the simple Jena. It is the dress of death, worn along with the red hat of doom.

Someone is coming; both Jena's are ready for him. There's a knock at the hotel room door. They look at one another, smiling back and forth at each other. They have very much anticipated this moment, and the Jena's can hardly wait to invite their guest inside. Both of them take one last look in the mirror, readjust their red hats, and blow kisses at themselves in the mirror.

Jena walks confidently to the door. She opens it, and there is a man standing in the doorway with red flowers in his hands. He's wearing a dark-blue suit, red tie, white shirt, and black shoes. The roses cover his face as he attempts to surprise Jena. She smiles and leans to the side to peek at him. He pushes the roses toward her to play at hiding his identity for just a while longer. Jena reaches for a rose. She removes one and turns to hand it to her other self, but there is no one there. She turns around, and it's Matt Ross standing in the hotel room doorway. He is grinning, waiting to be invited in. His face is smoothly shaven, his curly blonde hair nicely cut, with his big baby-blue eyes daring her to say no. She gives a seductive look, smells the beautiful red roses, smiles, and waves to signal him to come in.

"They're beautiful," she says while smelling the roses.

He looks at her. "You're beautiful."

Jena blushes. She walks closer to him, looks him up and down, and then softly touches his red tie with the edge of her fingertips. "I like this color."

He looks at her dress, admiring her tall, slender figure and slightly exposed cleavage. "I like the dress." He brushes his hand smoothly over her waist. "I also like what's in it." Matt puts one hand in a pocket and slowly walks around the hotel room. Jena watches him. He stands in front of the mirror admiring himself, adjusts his tie, and then blows a kiss at himself. He turns to Jena. "Are you disappointed, surprised, or happy to see me?"

Jena looks down. "Well, I'm not surprised. I kind of knew you were coming." She lays the roses on the bed. "I'm definitely not disappointed. I wanted you to come." She walks over to him. "So, I would say I'm happy to see you." She runs her hand down Matt's face.

Matt circles her slowly. "Happy?" he questions her motive. "Are you sure?"

She begins to circle him. "Yes. I'm completely and utterly sure." She kisses him on the cheek.

"Show me," Matt says. "Show me just how happy you are to see me."

She stares at him as his big blue eyes try to trap her and his mischief begins to settle into her. "You don't trust me?" she asks.

"It's not that I don't trust you, Jena. I just know a lot about you."

"You do?"

"Yes," he says. "I know that you and I are a lot alike. We both like the color red, and we both have mysterious behaviors." He gets up close to her face. The blue in his eyes deepens. "But mostly the similarity comes from the fact that we both love to murder people." He grabs Jena's arm. She snatches it away from him.

"You're wrong about me, Matt. I don't like to murder people. I'm just a simple girl trying to find her way through life." Matt looks confused. She reaches her hand out toward Matt. "Come with me." Jena takes hold of Matt's hand and tries to show him who she is inside—her true inner self—not a murderer, not a wicked person, just a simple girl wanting to live a simple life.

Matt appears to be interested and mystified by her. They lie side by side on the bed. Matt gazes into her eyes. Jena tells him a story. "When I was a child, I dreamed of flying a plane."

Matt looks over at her and smiles. "You?"

Jena laughs. "Yes, me. I wanted to be a pilot." He laughs. "Why do you find that so funny?"

"You're a beautiful girl and, well, you can be anyone you want to be. I just find you wanting to be a pilot kind of ... funny."

Jena smiles. "Well, I did. Flying a plane to me is like getting to be a bird flying in the sky. Just imagine yourself being a pilot of a plane with all those people in it. All aboard awaiting their arrival at their destination, and you're the one responsible for getting them there. Flying high up the sky." Jena daydreams. "Just cruising along the skyline in the clouds, above the world, above the world below where ..." she hesitates.

Matt looks at her. "Where?" Matt gives her a curious look.

Jena sits up. "In the sky above the world of people full of hatred. A world where a man could kill another man for no apparent reason at all." Matt sits up as Jena continues. "A world where a girl sees her mother on her knees, hands bloodied, crying her heart out because her husband has just been murdered by scum." Matt gently touches Jena's shoulder. Jena's voice deepens. "A world where a man stands in the middle of a highway to stop a car so he can catch a ride as he plots to commit robbery." Jena gets to her feet and looks over at him. Jena looks around the room. "A world like this, Matt. The world you and I live in." Jena leans down to stare him straight in the face. "Your world. I wanted to be a pilot so I could fly above your world." She turns around. "And now my world. I never wanted to be in this dark, cold cave. And now that I am, I don't know how to escape." Matt walks slowly to Jena. He hugs and holds her tightly. "Do you understand, Matt?" she whispers to him. "Do you understand what I'm saying to you? I wish you could have seen my life as a child, laughing with my parents, at the lake with Jake ... my childhood. I wasn't always like this. I wasn't born to be this way. I was meant for something better. My father was meant to be alive. Everything that happens to you is a domino effect with the consequences only ending up being a circle. A maze." A tear drops from Jena's eye onto Matt's suit coat. "Here I am, back at the hotel where it all began—where my life shattered into blood droplets of never-ending rain."

Matt kisses her on the cheek. "I'm here for you, and I'll never leave your side. You and I are meant to be together. Jake doesn't understand who you are, but I do."

Matt's magical hold instantly fades from Jena. "Jake," she whispers. "You're not Jake," she says.

"No, I'm not, but I can love you just as much if you'll let me. You won't have to worry about protecting me or if I'm judging you. We're the same, Jena."

Jena walks to the mirror. "I don't want to be this way, Matt."

Matt frowns. "Why not? What's wrong with the way we are?"

"Everything is wrong with the way we are!" she yells. "Everything! I was supposed to live a simple life, not be on a murderous quest."

Matt feels rejected. He carries on in an angry tone, "This is who we are, and you're going to play the role of queen of the murderers as I play king." They both circle each other, and the rooms follows them—spinning around and around. Matt's anger grows. "I do know you, Jena. I know you killed that clerk. Look at him lying there with blood spilling from him as though he's been beaten to death. Beaten to death by a murderer. I know you killed that helpless doctor on the train. Stole his medical bag and took it to off your own mother." Jena's face grows as red as her dress. "I know that your obsession led you to go to New York to chase down Mr. McNeil, just so you could murder him for revenge. Yeah," Matt bites his bottom lip, "I also know that you'll kill again, and again, and again, because that's who you are. That's the kind of freak you've turned yourself into."

Jena tries to take control of herself. She turns around to stare at herself in mirror. Her dress doesn't seem as bright and sexy as it was before. Her hat is crooked, so she removes it. Self-pity springs instantly over Jena's mood. Jena reaches her hand out to Matt. He is skeptical at first. Jena seems sincere. "Please take it." Matt submits to her despite his distrust. Jena guides Matt from the hotel room to another place. "Sit, please."

Matt looks around in disbelief. "Why are we on a plane?" He gives Jena a strange look as she walks slowly toward him. "How did we get here?"

"Matt, all of those things you said about me may be true," she adjusts her red hat perfectly on her head, "but there is one thing you don't know—something that you're just not quite aware of at this moment. You don't know that this is just a dream. I'm dreaming about you. This whole thing isn't real." She laughs as she walks closers to him. "Even so, it is still a fact that you're such a creep—such a low, desperate person—to have the gall to come into my dream to try to seduce me to your level of amateur, manipulative ways. I wanted to be the old Jena," she walks closer and closer to him, "the Jena that I once was. It seems just yesterday, but that's the thing—yesterday is gone. I don't know if I'll come back, but what I do know is that I'm going to find you … and I'm going to kill you." She backs Matt up until he fumbles and takes a seat. He sits down next to a man reading a newspaper. He's face is covered. Jena leans up close to Matt's face. "And you're right—you're not Jake. You'll never be him, so consider yourself forewarned."

The man puts the newspaper down. "Sit tight, young man, because once you're on the plane, you're never getting off." He puts the newspaper back up.

"Now go. Go and tell them, Matt," Jena says. "Tell them I'm coming. I'm coming to get you, Matt Ross—and I'm coming for them too."

CHAPTER FIFTEEN

Jake is frantic, almost beside himself worrying about Jena. Hidden by the hoodie and sunglasses, Jake sits by his father's bedside hoping that he opens his eyes and praying that his love is somewhere safe. The room is quiet. Jake, his mother, and Ted are motionless and silent as they watch Mr. Paterson lie like a corpse in the hospital bed.

Ted stands up. "Mom, I have to step out. I need some air." He looks at Jake.

"I'll come with you, man," Jake says. Jake and Ted leave the room and head down the back stairway. "I don't know how much longer I can keep up with hiding my identity." Jake stops in the stairway. "Sooner or later ..." he sighs, "sooner or later they are going to come looking for me at this hospital."

Ted looks depressed. "Man, Mom can't take any more bad news. Dad's life is on the ropes."

"I'm not sure if I'm much help sitting around here just waiting to be captured, and Jena is out there somewhere."

Ted steps down one flight of stairs. "Face it—your life is shit, man."

Jake steps behind him and takes off his shades. "Yeah, my life is shit—but I've got to find her. Ted, give me your cell."

Ted gives Jake a sour look, reaches in his pocket, and passes Jake the cell. "Meet me outside when you're done, man." Ted walks outside the hospital's back door. Jake holds the cell in his hand. He searches for a number, finds it, and hits dial.

Five guys are standing outside of a night club eyeing some college chicks when one of them receives a call. "What's up, Ted?" Silence.

"Not Ted. Jake."

"Jake? What the hell, man." Ken walks away from the crowd. Where the hell have you been? Where's Jena? Did she kill all those people? Her mother? That guy on the train?"

"Cool down, man. I need to talk with you. Now isn't the time to play twenty questions. I've been to hell and back. Right now, I need your help." Silence.

"With what?"

"I know we aren't best friends ... I'm not sure if we are friends at all ... but I'm in hiding, man, and so is Jena."

"Where is she, Jake?"

"She's here in town somewhere. I have to find her before the cops do." Jake pauses. "After I find her, we need a place to hang. My dad is in the hospital."

Ken speaks quickly, "I heard, and I'm sorry. Your dad is a real cool guy. My dad and mom went to see him yesterday." Silence.

"Can you help me?"

"Yeah," Ken doesn't hesitate. "Yes. I'll do what I can. Look there's a masquerade party going on at the campus tomorrow."

"Party?" Jake says. "How's that going to help me? Help Jena?"

"Hey, come see me tonight. We'll find Jena, and then you guys come to the party tomorrow," Ken tries to convince him. "I mean, you'll be all dressed up. Everyone's going to be here—Chance, Carol ... everyone—but no one will know who you guys are." Ken turns to look at his friends. "This is a way for you two to stop running for a moment. Have a normal atmosphere for a moment. I'll find you a place to hang, but I want to see you guys. We'll get some costumes, sit back, and enjoy some real fun." Ken waits for

Jake to respond. When he doesn't, he continues to try to convince him. "We'll worry about the cops and everything else later. Jake, if Jena is going crazy, then maybe she needs to be around teenage kids her age. Maybe this will snap her back to reality. Meet outside the college library in an hour."

"That's an hour away. And I don't have a clue as to where she is." Jake is frustrated.

"Meet me here, Jake." Ken ends the phone call and holds the phone tightly in his hand.

Jake walks up to Ted. "Take me to the college library."

Ted hands him the keys. "Take yourself." He walks away.

"Ted?" Ted stops. "I love her. Take care of Mom and Dad. I'll be back."

Ted turns around. "I know. Just put gas in the car." He walks inside.

"Ted?" He turns around. "I'm out of cash."

Ted shakes his head. "Man, the cash is in the dash. Jake? I love her too, man. I hope this all is just a bad dream." Ted walks inside.

Jake rushes to the car. He begins the hour drive to reach the college campus. Thoughts of Jena race through his mind. He remembers the night they first made love, after she had murdered Mr. McNeil in cold blood. The fear he felt watching her point the gun after her murderous act. Realizing how sexy and attractive she was when he finally saw her in the nude. Watching the shapes of her body—nipples hard, tall, and slender legs. So, dominate, so beautiful, and so deadly. At that moment, he didn't know if she was going to turn and shoot him too or not. All he could do was believe that the love he felt for her would make her recognize him and remember their life leading up to this tragic moment. Somehow this released her into his arms, where he bared himself to shed light on the darkness she felt. He was overwhelmed with passion, held up to that point deep within a part of him but never recognized by the brightly lit yet dark eyes, which flooded the gates like red roses falling from a dead tree. The moment of the death somehow became the moment of life for Jake. It was the first time his love was truly revealed, no longer hidden from her, and expressed in the most profound way possible: hot, unexplained, and unbelievable, passion.

On a dark road in the middle of nowhere, Jake finds himself lost in deep thought. He is so aroused by the mere thought of Jena that he stops in the middle of the highway. Time slips away from him. He feels powerless and anxious about finding Jena. Where could she be?

Suddenly there's a knock on Jake's car window. A middle-aged man wearing a red wig, donning awful painted makeup, and dressed in a clown suit peeks in the car. "Hey, you all right?" Jake keeps his hand on the steering wheel and shakes his head. The man moves in closer. "You realize that you're parked in the middle of the road," he looks around, "in the middle of nowhere?" The man seems confused at Jake's silence. "Are you hurt? On weed? Umm ... what's wrong with you? You're parked in the middle of the road—like I said—in the middle of nowhere." He takes off his wig.

Jake thinks back to the prom night when Jena dressed as a clown. He breaks his silence. "Do you realize that you're parked in the middle of nowhere dressed up as a clown?"

"Yeah. I realize that. So, what! I'm trying to help you. I'm headed to a masquerade party." He starts wiping his face and gets makeup on his hand. "Damn, now my makeup is screwed!" the man yells.

"What if I told you the party was tomorrow night?"

"Really? Come on?"

"Yep," Jake says. "Tomorrow."

"So, I'm dressed up as a clown, in the dark, in the middle of highway, in the middle of nowhere, and there's no party?"

"Nope, not tonight."

"Damn." The man walks back to his car swearing, "Damn. Damn. Damn." He gets in his car and zooms up beside Jake. "No party?"

"None," Jake replies.

"Damn. All this work I put into my makeup. Damn. Damn. Damn. Well, I guess I'm headed to the nearest hotel." He walks back to his car and throws his wig off to the passenger side of his car. Jake looks back at the man's car. The man spins off, stops, and backs up. "You sure? These kids called me. They said the party was tonight."

Jake shakes his head. "I know—damn, right?" Jake says smiling.

"Yeah. Damn." The man spins off.

Jake follows behind him and laughs to himself. His thoughts swing back to the prom night when Jena was dressed up as a clown. He remembered that even as a clown she was still beautiful to him. Stunning. Even a clown suit couldn't hide her natural beauty, the beauty the shined from her heart when she burst out in laughter. That night was one of the best nights of their lives, even though they brushed off the traditional celebration of horny heads dancing at the prom. They wanted to make a stand against the ridiculous fighting among friends over cheating and backstabbing and rebel against the typical high school ballroom gowns and the boring bow ties that are found in the trash within one hour of the event starting. What a night that was, Jake thinks. First picking Jena up at her house, cracking jokes as they anticipated the facial expressions of their friends when they walked into prom. The jaws dropping, the fingers pointing, the fake outburst of laughter when the room full of pranksters was pranked. Jake remembered how Jena tried to back out of it at the last minute.

Jake is driving and can't stop fidgeting with his hat in the mirror. Jena stares at him with a strange look from her clown made-up face.

"That hat isn't going to change. Stop messing with it."

"It has to be straight, Jena. I can't go in there with a crooked hat—I'd look stupid."

Jena grins. "Jake, you look stupid anyway—with or without the hat … or the outfit." They both laugh. "Maybe crashing the prom isn't smart." Jena takes off her clown nose and plays with it in her hand. "I mean, our friends being all mad at each other is no real reason for us to just blow off the prom." Jake is quiet. "That was a very horrible night, watching Chance and Carol fight over Ken,"

Jena's voice saddens. "Chance was so heartbroken, finding out Carol was cheating with Ken."

Jake rolls his eyes. "Well, that's not all that happened that night." Jena looks over at him. Jake's voice changes, "Ken came on to you, confessing his undying love for you." Jake is jealous. "I never trusted him. Even in middle school, he was just a freaking asshole. I probably didn't like him when we were babies either. I bet we were in the same baby room at St. Mary's hospital." Jake frowns. "He was probably crying, and I was probably telling him to shut the hell up."

Jena is amused by Jake's jealous behavior. "Do you think he was wearing a clown's suit? Why didn't you get out of your little baby crib and show him some muscle, muscle head?"

Jake laughs. They both get quiet for a moment.

"Breaking the ice, clown face."

"Weirdo."

"Fake nose."

Jena looks over at Jake. "Ridiculously tall and uncalled for hat."

Jake laughs and thinks of a comeback. "Peanut head."

They both laugh at each other as Jake pulls into the high school gym parking lot. "I take it you just couldn't think of anything else?" She laughs loudly.

The moment had come: the prom. The stars are blazing in the night sky as they both sit quietly in the car watching their peers drag themselves into the prom like robotic zombies all looking for brains they don't have. Yet somehow walking into those doors made them think they made a smarter decision than them. For a moment, Jena, and Jake's zombie outlook on two teenagers who had been dating since the ninth grade changed to recognizing a romantic couple full of sincerity and gentleness for one another. They were sharing this moment together, walking into the prom like a prince escorting his princess. Jena couldn't help but think that that could have been her and Jake. Jake was obviously having the same thought. He glances over at Jena, watching her gaze starry-eyed at the couple.

"That's Ann and Rich," Jena says.

Jake nods his head. "Yeah. Wow, they have been dating since we were in ninth, right?"

"Yeah," she says slowly. She looks over at Jake, who takes has hat off. "You don't want to go in, do you?"

Jake looks out his window. "Not really." He touches Jena's hand. "The truth is that I wanted to take you to prom. I wanted to share this night with you, to make you feel like a princess."

Jena gently squeezes his hand. "Jake, proms, props, and people all gathering together were never important to me. This is prom. This is our prom. We didn't choose to celebrate it the traditional way. We chose to give each other a long-lasting gift of laughter in these ridiculous, sweaty, hot outfits." She looks into Jake's eyes. "I feel like princess—even in this clown's suit. There are many different ways of feeling beautiful, feeling free. I'm as free as a bird right now because I have such a caring and wonderful friend like you."

Jake is mesmerized by Jena's words. He gently presses his thumb against her cheek. He starts the car. "Jena," he calls.

"Jake, I know. I truly do know, and that is why I will always, always have a special place for you in my heart."

Jake tries to hold back his emotions. "Well," he puts the car in gear, "you're still a peanut head." They both laugh.

"After all that?" She laughs.

He grins from ear to ear. Never had he believed that Jena would break the cold ice to give him a little hope that one day she could love him just as much as he loved her—deeper than the earth's core, higher than the sky will allow the human eye to see, and farther than man has ever walked toward the end of the never-ending earth then back around to do it all over again. I'd do this all over again for her. Live this life again just to have her speak those words to me that commends me with the highest gold medal for my boyish crush. Gosh, I love her, he thinks. I love her so much.

He starts to back out of the parking spot with the biggest smile on his face. Jena is his girl/friend/everything else to him, and no prom dress or Saturday Night Fever outfit would change that. Love is love. Life is love lived in the face of another who loves you back, and that's what he has this night with Jena—a shot at love. Jake's mind is in a twilight state. He backs out without looking and almost runs down someone.

"Hey!" someone yells from behind the car. It's Ken, all dressed with no one to prance inside the prom with. He has his hands on the back of car as if he were Superman and could stop it from leaving tire tracks on his polished getup. He walks swiftly up to Jake's window and leans in, smiling. "Trying to turn me into a zombie, dude?" He peeks at Jena's and Jake's outfits. "Wow," laughing out loud, "you two look like freaks." He laughs.

"Umm, you want something?" Jake asks.

"Yeah, just wanted to say hello. We are somewhat friends."

Jena doesn't look at Ken. "I don't know about being friends."

"Come on, guys." Ken stands back from the window. "We are most likely going to college together, so we might as well be friendly. I know I'm a jerk."

"Really?" Jake says sarcastically.

"I shouldn't have cheated on Chance. And Jena … I'm sorry for coming on to you." He pats the window seal and walks away. Jake watches him as he walks into prom like a lonely pimp who just realized the power he felt was only in his head. For once, Ken looked human to him. Just seeing him alone, sorrowful, while still dressed up for a night of entertainment suddenly shined a bright light on him. It made Jake remember when he, Ken, Chance, Carol, and Jena were all hanging out laughing when they were younger—when high school's ruthless competition to be popular or to be a fantastic lover wasn't important, and when friendship came naturally without everyone pushing for the best stooge's award.

Jake tunes back to reality. He continues his drive toward Northwest University to meet Ken. His only mission is to find Jena, hold her in is arms tightly, and keep her safe within the world they've built—their prom night, their sacred love. "Jena," Jake softly utters her name as he drives on down the road.

CHAPTER SIXTEEN

The loneliness from the long ride traps Jake deep in thought. How can all of this be happening? he thinks. It seems like we were all just in high school waiting for the big graduation day, and now I'm hiding from the cops, the love of my life has left me, and I'm stuck looking at a broken taillight belonging to the worst clown I've ever met. What a life. He laments his decision to take Jena to New York. If only he'd have said no, he could've just taken her into hiding somewhere where no one would have found them, where he could have loved her for eternity without fear of losing her or, even worse, having her captured by the cops and taken away forever to live as prisoner. I have to find her. He presses down harder on the gas pedal. Where could she be? He passes a road sign: two miles for hotel, gas, and food. Hotel? He thinks hard. Would she go back to where it first started? What are the chances? The road exit is coming up. Jake quickly turns off the road.

He pulls into a rundown hotel's parking lot. The lights are flashing "Vacant Rooms." I don't remember the name of the hotel, he thinks. Oh well, it's worth a shot. He gets out, puts his hands in his pockets, and looks around the parking lot for the truck. There's a truck, but it's not Maggie's. It's a red, beat-up truck, parked on the curve like a drunk just decided, "Here, this is where I'll park." He walks toward the hotel.

The clerk is standing at the front desk reading a newspaper. Jake opens the door and hears the sound of a cheap bell attached to the doorknob. He stands at the counter for at least thirty seconds before the clerk acknowledges him. Jake notices a wanted sign with a scratched photo of Jena on it. The photo is upside down, but he can tell it's her.

"You know her?" the clerk suddenly asks.

Jake looks back at the clerk. He shrugs his shoulders. "No."

The clerk walks over to put the photo right side up. "I guess more people would recognize her if the damn picture was posted right." He has a smoker's laugh, yellow teeth, and a bald spot on the top of his head.

Jake tries to make small talk. "So, you got vacant rooms, sir?"

"Sir? Just call me Clark."

"Okay. Clark, you got vacant rooms?"

"No," he grins. "All the rooms are taken."

"But your sign says—"

Clark cuts Jake off. "That sign is broken. It always says vacant rooms."

Jake folds his arms. "But your parking lot is empty."

Clark looks out the window. "Yeah, so what? Not everyone has a fantasy car. Some people walk. Hell, on this road, hitchhike," he rambles. "Hell, nowadays that's the way to go. Just live like there's no tomorrow. No car, no house, no bills," he stares Jake in the eyes and lifts his eyebrows, "no wife … now that's the life for me. That's the good life." He starts snapping his fingers, echoing his words, "That's the good life."

Jake glances back at the wanted poster. He tries to be clever. "That girl, who is she?"

"Oh man, she's, umm, some chick who killed a few people." Clark leans over the counter. "They're just making a big shit out of what she did, but I don't buy it. Hell, my photo should be posted up there, because I've done a lot of shady shit in my lifetime. A lot." Clark scratches his bald spot.

Jake has a sympathetic look on his face. "She looks like an ordinary person—just a simple young girl."

Clark stares at the photo. "Yeah, I guess. But if she's anything like me, looks can be deceiving."

"So, she hasn't come through here," Jake fishes for information.

"Nope. If she had, there would be photos of me and her posted on that wall right next to that stupid wanted poster sign." Clark gets heated. "I wouldn't turn her in. Heck, I'd probably join her in getting even with some people."

"Well, I've gotta go find me a hotel." Jake backs away.

Clark follows him out the door. "There's another hotel at the next exit. It's not too far from the university. A lot of kids go there to hang out, you know."

"Thanks." Jake gets into the car.

He drives off, gets back on the road, takes the next exit, and pulls into the hotel parking lot. There are several cars, trucks, and campers parked at the hotel. "The Palm Lee Inn," Jake whispers to himself. Jake walks inside.

A clerk wearing is standing at the counter with a big smile on his face. "Hello. How are you?" He's extremely polite—the total opposite of the last clerk, whose negative outlook on life seemed to ooze out of his pores. Jake sees that Jena's wanted photo is pinned up on the wall. The clerk runs up and shakes Jake's hand. "Wow, it's great to see you."

Jake is surprised. He's never had anyone great him with such enthusiasm, let alone a hotel clerk. "Hi," Jake says as he shakes the clerk's hand quickly and then puts his hands in his pockets.

"So, looking for a room? Oh, by the way, my name is Franklin Bosler."

Jake thinks he's funny, but he tries to stay focused on finding Jena. "Frank," he thinks out loud.

"Yeah, Frank. What a name, right?" Frank walks back to the counter. "Yeah, my mother and father named me Franklin. I think it's a good name. I'm named after a great man." Frank stands with a huge grin on his face. "Hey, I know the parking lot looks full, but I've got rooms left. Yeah, nice rooms." Frank's grin shows all of his teeth. Frank catches Jake glancing at Jena's wanted poster on the wall. "She's a beauty, huh?" Frank sighs. "A killer beauty."

"Yeah, she's quite good looking." Jake tries to look away. His eyes zoom in on Frank's book lying on the counter. "Cold Reda Gray? That's an interesting name for a book." Jake picks up the book.

"You like to read?" Frank is excited.

Jake puts the book down. "Yeah, some books interest me."

"Well, you're going to like this book. It's about a girl who has all these tragic things happen to her that it ultimately turns her into a killer."

Jake nods his head. "Sounds interesting."

Frank starts scrambling for paperwork. "So, what floor do you want ... first ... second?" Frank hands Jake the paperwork and a pen.

"I'll take the second floor."

"Well, the second floor is the most popular floor. Earlier I had a young lady request the second floor, too, and a few other college students. Oh, these college students always seem to love the second floor. Must be something special about that floor." Frank eyes Jena's picture. "Oh, I know—that's the floor where Jena Parker murdered the previous clerk that worked here. Those kids are going to that room thinking that there's some sort of supernatural powers there or something." Franks pops his hand on his forehead. "Dumb me. I should've figured that out since I'm so fascinated by murder mystery. Hey, that's why I wrote this book."

"I'm curious about the girl. The girl, was she good looking?" Jake steps closer to the counter.

"Oh, yeah." Frank puts his book under one arm and walks up to Jake. Jake stares at the book tucked tightly under his armpit. "She was sort of strange, but certainly she was good looking. She looks a lot like this girl who's wanted for multiple murders."

Jake has a wild look in his eyes. "What girl?"

Franks points at the poster of Jena. "That girl. Jena Parker, the notorious murderer, wanted by the cops, wanted by the FBI, wanted by me because I want to interview her for my next book. She's popular." Jake reaches in his pockets. Franks backs up slowly. "Hey, you don't have a weapon, do you?" Frank says, obviously scared. "I mean, there's not a lot cash here. Just maybe a few bucks."

Jake has a puzzled look on his face. "What? I don't have a gun. I was just looking for my money for the room."

"Oh, yeah." Franks laugh out loud. "Man, it's these murder mystery books I'm writing. They make me paranoid—although the last clerk did meet his doom at this very place."

Jake pulls out cash he'd nabbed from Ted's car dash. "How much?" Jake puts the cash on the counter.

"Twenty-five dollars for a luxury hotel night stay." Frank picks up the cash and starts counting.

"I don't need luxury," Jake says. "I just need a room."

Franks hands Jake a five-dollar bill. "You gave me too much. Now sign that paper. Here's your key. You've just got yourself the best room in town!"

Jake scribbles his initials on the paperwork: JP. He dashes out the door to find Jena, frantically looking at the rooms, trying to figure out which one she is in.

Franks steps outside, his book still tucked under his armpit. Jake looks at him. "She's in room 201." Frank hands Jake his book. "Here, take this too. I'm sure after a good, hot night of fun, you'll probably want a good book to read."

Jake snatches the book and runs like a tiger chasing a deer in the wilderness. He stops and stands still at the door with the book under his arm. His heart is racing like a clock ticking out of control. He taps on the door, whispers Jena's name, knocks louder, and then plays with the doorknob.

Jena awakens slowly from her dream. She still isn't sure if she is still dreaming or if the knock is real. She lies still for moment, trying to balance her reality from her dream. "Matt Ross?" she utters. "How did he find me?" She quickly gets up from the bed to face herself in the mirror. This is it. This is my dream. Matt Ross is coming to face me down. She wonders if she should use this moment to take Matt out or use this moment to redeem herself. She opens the door. "Jake?"

He rushes her into his arms, and the book falls to the floor. Jena is shock, relieved, and confused all at once. "Jena, please put your arms around me." He starts to cry. "Please put your beautiful arms around me."

She squeezes him back tightly. "You found me," she says, still shocked. "You found me." Without a moment to spare, Jake kisses her lips. All of the worry, fear, and uncertainty fade as he pours all of his soul into a long passionate kiss. Jena can't break free of his passion; it cages her up like an animal stuck in a cage with another animal that is protecting its territory and nurturing it, as it rules the land it stands on. Jake wants to take control of Jena's passion, to let her know that running isn't going to stop his love from existing, that it is only going to make it grow bigger and stronger and resistant to even her efforts to push it into the shadow. Nothing could break the kiss. It is a moment within a moment that has its own timing, not determined by destiny or circumstances, yet a simple point of love.

"I had to find you." Jake's face is drowned with tears. "It was no choice to me." He kisses Jena's face. "No choice."

Jena begins to cry. "What are we going to do?" she asks.

Jake pulls her close. "Nothing tonight except be together. I don't care what's going to happen tomorrow." He caresses her hair. "Because all I care about is right now, finally finding you and holding you again." He grabs her face. "Looking into those beautiful eyes, I don't care about tomorrow, Jena. I'll deal with tomorrow, tomorrow."

Jena gently kisses him. He slowly removes her jacket; it falls to the floor. The moment was perfect, the timing just right, and the mood bolstered by the oasis of tranquility. Jake removes Jena's clothes. He kneels down to kiss her feet, legs, and thigh. She looked like a goddess to him, and he is her slave to do as she wills. She watches as he takes off his clothes, never taking his eyes off of her. He throws his clothes to the floor. He takes her in his arms and leads her to the bed. He stares deeply into her eyes. "I don't want anyone else or anything else except you." He kisses her gently on the lips. "Even the moment before this moment is done. I'm just taking every moment with you like it is the only moment."

Jena smiles with passion as she guides his head to her face. Jake massages her entire body with his lips. He gently inserts himself, penetrating Jena with the slowest motions possible without breaking a stride in every level of his strokes.

"Oh, Jake," Jena softly calls.

"Yes—call my name again. I love it when you say my name when I'm making love to you."

Jena's fingernails clutch Jake's back. He tosses her up until she sits upright on top of him. She leans in, her hair swaying in front of his face as she moves her body with his, like waves running smoothly down a river on a warm, sunny day. Jake's eyes close, hands squeezing her waist, leaving his fingerprints deep in her skin. Jena leans her head back. Her hair flows backward as they both move in a consistency reaching the highest peak that any men or women could encounter together as their minds, hearts, and souls merge into an unbreakable bond.

Jena sighs. Jake falls silent, as if he's been given a tranquilizer that just took effect as their bodies, once in limbo, were reborn back to the world. They lie in each other's arms, eyes heavy, bodies worn, and minds at peace.

The hotel is quiet, and there's a light, warm breeze outside. It's three o'clock in the morning, and Franklin is gathering his paperwork together for the shift change. He's in a good mood, singing, until he comes across the signature of one of the hotel guests. A familiar name: Reda Jones. Franklin's face turns beet red. He grabs the paper in both hands and almost rips it in half from his excitement. "Reda Jones. My Reda Jones? Jena Parker?" he utters as he stares back at the wanted poster on the wall.

CHAPTER SEVENTEEN

Jena reaches over to put her arms around Jake. He turns to hold her and glances at the radio clock on the table behind her. "It's five o'clock," he says.

Jena breathes in. "Five?" she says and turns to get out of bed. She sits on the side and turns to look at him. "We should get an early start before the sun rises."

"Sure," Jake says. Jena moves slowly to the bathroom, turns on the shower, and steps in. She lets the hot water roll down her hair and body. The door opens slightly. Jena can see the steam rushing out of it. She turns around just as Jake steps in the shower to join her.

Jena grins and then shyly turns around. "Umm, there's a thing called privacy." She laughs a little.

Jake moves closely behind her, reaches for her waist, and then moves in even closer to her. He holds her tightly as the water runs down both of their bodies. Whispering in her ear, he says, "There's also a thing called love." She reaches her arm up behind to Jake's face and neck. She gently caresses his neck as he holds her tight and whispers, "I don't want to go outside this room. I don't want this moment that we've captured in a bottle to be broken."

Jena closes her eyes and wishes too that they didn't have to leave, but reality set ins. She knows that the world is waiting for her. She has to leave the room in order for both worlds to unfold. "I wish we could stay here, Jake, but we can't." She turns around and hugs him tightly and then steps out of the showers, brushes her teeth, and leaves the bathroom.

Jake is left standing under the hot water, feeling a bit isolated from her but determined to never let her leave his sight again. He finishes in the bathroom and leaves to get to dress. Jena is dressed, looking in the mirror, combing her hair. He watches her every move.

"I like your hair red." Jena looks at him, then back in the mirror.

"I guess it's okay," she says. Maybe it's time I changed it back. She watches through the mirror as Jake is getting dressed. His bare, naked chest is toned like a body builder whose only goal is to make a woman understand that he would be Tarzan and she would be Jane. His jeans are perfectly fitted around his toned abs. He slides on his shirt. Jena turns around, leaning on the small dresser. "I didn't know that you were such a gym fanatic."

Jake blushes. "I wouldn't say I'm a fanatic." He walks to her. "I'd say I was trying to do whatever it took to get your attention."

She checks out his body. "Well, I'd say you got it." She looks over at her bag sitting on a chair near the bed, walks over, and takes out the letter her mother wrote to her. Jake walks over to her. Jena plays with the letter, tempted to open it.

"You should open the letter," Jake tries to convince her. He puts his hand on her shoulder.

"I should … but I won't. Not now." She puts the letter back in her bag. It's six forty-five in the morning; daylight breaks through the window shades. Jena and Jake are ready to leave.

Jake reaches in his pocket for Ted's cell phone. "Where is my phone?" He looks around the room. "I must have left it in the car. Kens probably pissed."

Jena stops. "Ken?" She picks her bag up. "Why would he be pissed?"

Jake pauses. "I asked him to help me find you." He gives Jena a pitiful look. "I needed help. I was desperate."

Jena blows it off. "Okay. Let's go."

Jake opens the hotel door. The parking lot is almost empty; just Ted's car and two other cars are outside. Jake looks back at Jena before stepping out and asks, "Where's the truck?"

"It's out back. Do you really think I would have parked it up front?"

He smiles at her. "No, of course not." His foot snags on a newspaper lying in front of the room's door. He picks it. Jena and the stories of the murders she committed are the front-page news. Jake doesn't want her to see. He looks around at the other hotel room doors, and there aren't any newspapers in front of them.

"Let me see, Jake." Jena grabs the paper from him. "Jena Parker wanted for multiple murders," she murmurs. She closes the paper and sticks it in her bag.

Jake gives her a look. "Why are taking this garbage?"

She pushes past Jake out the door and stops. "It's not garbage. It's the truth. You can't run from the truth, Jake. It'll always find you. No matter where you go or what you do, the truth will always be there waiting for you to face and conquer it. I must face my truth." She puts her head down. "And maybe someday I'll be able to conquer it." She walks to the car.

Jake follows. Tension fills the air. Jake can feel the enchanted moment they shared last night slipping away. He is crushed and wants nothing more except to make the entire situation go away and for last night's unforgettable love making to be every night for the rest of their lives. Jena gets into the car and closes the door. Jake stands out by the driver's side, peeking in, trying to break the tension. "Are you all right?"

"Yes, Jake, I'm fine." Jake gets inside the car, cranks it up. Just as Jake starts to drive away, the front office door opens. It's Franklin. He's holding up a big poster sign with words written in red: "You're Famous, REDA JONES!" As the car passes, he holds the sign up high. Jena stares at him; her and Franklin lock eyes. He knows and she knows what the sign really means. Franklin doesn't say a word yet smiles uncontrollably at Jena. The car jets off onto the long highway—Jena's hair swaying in the wind, one hand out the window, gazing off into the early morning sky. "I'm famous," she utters to herself. Jake is quiet. He doesn't ask questions about Franklin or the sign.

Jena is silent. Thoughts of her mother, father, and the funeral drift through her mind as the wind blows against her face. Sometimes the sun can be too bright; sometimes it is not bright enough. Sometimes the blue skies aren't as blue as I'd wish they would be, but that's life. The sky isn't always going to be painted blue, and the sun isn't always going to shine just right. Either way, I'm still going to be that girl who killed her mother. Who killed an innocent man on a train. Who killed two men who deserved it, a slob, and a father killer. Mr. McNeil took my father's life, and somehow—in the midst of it all— he managed to take my life with him. He ruined me, and I let him. And now the man that I love, Jena looks over at Jake, he's ruined too. Both ruined, wrecked, and in love. We are that love story in the movies, written in books, and portrayed by average people who see the movies, read the books, and think to themselves, "Hey, that's us." We are those lovers, but my life is much more complicated than a movie or book. I don't think Jake and I are the modern Romeo and Juliet because I'm not going to let it end that way.

"What kind of help did you want from Ken?" Jena says as she gives Jake a mean look.

"To help find you. Like I said, I was desperate." The cell phone rings. Jake looks around for it while still trying to keep one eye on the road; Jena ignores it. In a sad voice, Jake says, "It's under the seat, Jena. Please get it for me. It could be my mom or Ted." Jena reaches for the cell and pulls it from under the seat. Ken's name and number are flashing on the cell phone.

"It's Ken," Jena says in a rough voice.

Jake ignores the call. He takes the phone from Jena. There are at least six missed calls and messages from Ken. A seventh missed call appears on the phone. "Jena, please don't withdraw from me. I need you right now. And you need me."

She doesn't want to treat him badly. "Okay, where are we going?" she asks.

"Hold on." Jake presses down to listen to the messages. Message one: "Jake, where the hell are you? I'm out in front of the library. Call me back." Message two: "Jake, come on, man. It's getting late—let me know what's up." Message three: "I'm about to leave. If you're still coming, call me." Message four: "Hey, I'm headed back to the room. I'm starting to get worried. Hopefully, Jena didn't off you too." Message five: "Hey, man, I'm back in the room. Sorry about that Jena crack. I was just kidding. I want to help you find her, so call me back." Message six: "Man, it's two in the morning. I got class tomorrow and a hot chick sleeping next to me. Hopefully, you're all right. Maybe you've already found her, which would explain why I can't find you. Anyway, man, the party is still on tomorrow. I've got some costumes for you guys. There's gonna be drinks, hot chicks—Chance and Carol will be there—it's going to be kick-ass, so call me back." The seventh messages pops up: "Jake, man, it's the next day, meaning the last I spoke to you was yesterday. I called your mom—whoa, bad idea. Now she's worried. If you don't contact me today, I'm calling the police—because shit, man, I don't know what else to do." Jake clicks the off button. The phone rings. It's Ken. Jake picks up.

"Yeah. Goddamn." Ken sounds excited. "Oh, thank goodness, man. You're alive! What's up."

"I'm with her," Jake says in a sober voice.

"That's good news because I was going to call the cops. Your mom called me at least six times. I didn't tell her about Jena. I just told her you were coming here to cool off—clear your head." Silence.

"We're on our way," Jake finally responds. "Where do we meet?"

Ken thinks. "Let's meet at this place called Kings. It's the exit right before the college. We'll meet there to plan. Tonight's the night man—party night!" Ken shouts. His friends in the background start cheering.

"Look, I don't know if we're going," Jake shoots the idea down, spying Jena as she stares out the window. "A party maybe too risky."

"We're going," Jena answers without looking at Jake. "We're going to go to that party, Jake. Maybe we need a little fun."

"Is that Jena?" Ken yells. "Is that her? Oh, man, I know what people have been saying about her, but I'm not judging. I just can't believe I'm about to see her," Jake is quiet, "and you too," Ken redeems himself.

"Hey," Jake says in a firm voice. "No one except you, Ken. We don't need the entire school knowing where we are and where we are going to be."

Ken laughs. "I got it." Ken hangs up the cell.

Jena stares out the window. She's not in the mood for small talk, yet with every passing moment in the car her curiosity grows, wondering what lies ahead for her at Kings. A party? And what dark fields of unfinished business lie ahead?

CHAPTER EIGHTEEN

"This is it." Jake pulls into King's Café's parking lot. He looks around the parking lot, across the street, and in the café for any signs of cops. "Doesn't appear to be any police officers here." He looks over at Jena. "Ready?"

She puts on her hoodie jacket and dark sunglasses. "Yep." Jake puts on his hoodie and dark sunglasses as well. Jena opens her car door first, grabs her bag, and then they both walk in together.

The café has a few stragglers, truck drivers, and one family with a little two-year-old. Jena walks ahead; Jake follows her. They both look around the café for Ken. He's sitting in the back corner of the café alone. Jena spots him and walks over. Ken watches her in amazement. Ken seems nervous as Jena stands near the table. Jake's standing behind her, holding her arm, looking around the room. Ken gestures to them to sit down. He looks suspiciously around the café.

"Are you looking for someone?" Jena asks. Chance walks up to the table. Jena looks at her.

"Don't blame him. I followed him," she says. She pushes Ken over and sits down. The four of them sit for minutes just staring at one another without saying a word. Jena stares directly at Chance and then at Ken. Chance picks up the menu. "Are we going to sit here and say nothing?" She signals to the waitress. "Let's at least order some food. If not, we'll really look suspicious."

The waitress walks over. "Hi, ya'll. Welcome to Kyler's … Oh, I mean welcome to King's café. We have a great special." The waitress points at the menu Chance is holding. "Eggs, bacon, and ham for only $4.95. Comes with a side of biscuits or bread." She smiles at Jake. "We even have raisin bread, too."

They all look at each other. The cook yells from the back. "Tell them about our soup special!" Jena peeks at the cook. She nudges Jake on the shoulder.

"It's that guy from the other restaurant!" Jake whispers to her.

"We'll all have the special," Jena quickly says to get rid of the waitress. "And coffee."

The waitress takes all the menus, smiles, and walks away. "Four SPs," she yells back to the cook.

"What about soup?" the cooks yells.

The waitress gets testy. "Hell, Kyler, nobody wants any damn soup." Jake stares at Jena.

"Wow, you guys are real serious looking with the shades and hoodies on." Ken grins. "I really feel like I'm involved in some espionage shit."

Jena gives him stare. Even through the shades, Ken can tell she means business. "You are." She pulls down her shades for a second. "Ken, we don't have a lot of time to chat."

Jake takes off his hoodie but leaves on his shades. "Tell us the plan," he says.

"Wait," Chance interrupts. "Where have you guys been?" She looks over at Jena and then lowers her voice to merely a whisper. "Jena, did you kill those people?"

Jena keeps her cool. "Chance, we don't have time to discuss my life right now. Jake and I came here to get away from the madness. Ken said there is a party tonight. I'd like to go to it."

Chance glances at Ken. "It's good to see you, Jena." Chance tries to balance her feelings.

"Here's the plan—" Ken begins to speak just as the waitress comes back with the coffees.

"What plan?" the waitress inquires. They all look at her. She politely puts the coffees down and walks away.

"I didn't know nosy came with the waitress job," Ken says sarcastically. "Anyway, here's the plan." He moves in closer, lowers his voice. "I've got a friend named C. A. T. Tyler." Chance frowns at him. He looks back at her and then back at Jake. "He's a good guy. Cool."

"He's a drug dealer, Ken," Chance says in rude voice. Jake and Jena look at each other.

Ken sits back, just looking at her. "Chance, I would hardly call him a drug dealer. He only sells weed. Nowadays, weed is medicine. So, he sells medicine." Chance rolls her eyes. "Now, C. A. T. has agreed to let you guys hang out at his house." Ken gets excited. "He's got a nice, badass house. Hot chicks there all the time." Chance is embarrassed.

Jake smirks at Chance's reaction. "I take it by your reaction, Chance, that you and Ken are back together."

Ken hugs her close to him. "Yeah, man." He kisses her cheek. Jena stares at them both. "She's my babes. Then and Now." Ken gets cocky.

Jena feels a rage at the mere thought that Chance would even consider taking Ken back after he cheated with Carol. Jena clinches her bag. "Give us directions," she tells Ken. Ken slides the directions across the table. The waitress is just coming with their food. Kens and Jena's hands touch as Jena reaches for the paper. The waitress tries to be nosy. Jena snatches the paper and puts it in her bag.

The waitress is assisted by another waitress. "Here you guys go. Four SPs." The four of them give her a strange look as if to say "Okay, really?" She looks at them. "That's our code word for the today's special." She has a creepy smile on her face, and she stares at them for a second before putting the plates down.

The other waitress gives her a nasty stare. "I do have other tables, Ann."

Ann looks at her. She gets upset. "Just because I have more tables than you don't mean that you can insult me in front of my customers." The other waitress shoves the plates at her and walks off. Keeping a smile on her face, Ann gently puts the plates down.

Kyler, the cook, rings the pickup bell. He yells loudly from the kitchen, "Ann, soup's ready!"

Ann smiles at them. "I am so tired of soup." She walks away.

"We have to get out of here," Jena says as she looks over at Jake, who is just getting ready to eat. Bob, Big Papa, and two other truck drivers walk in the door. Jake looks over at them. He drops his fork, gets up, and reaches for Jena.

Chance butts in; she seems desperate to say something. "Can we talk to each other first? Jake? Ken? Could you guys leave me and Jena alone, just for a minute? I think that it would look less suspicious if you guys sit at a different table." She glances at Jena. "This way, Jena and I can talk."

Jena turns to her. "Talk about what?"

Chance stands up to let Ken out. "Just to catch up," she says.

"We don't have time, Chance."

She gives Ken a look. "Jena, please," Chance pleads.

Jena relents. "Jake, I'm going to give her five minutes."

Ken stands up, looks around the room, and walks off with Jake. The two of them stroll to a table at the front of the café. Jake keeps his eyes on Jena.

Chance sits down, eyes to the floor, picks up a spoon, and then puts it back down. She looks up at Jena. Jena makes a bold move, completely removing her shades. "You look different," Chance says.

"I am different."

Chance shows compassion for her. "I'm sorry about your father ... and your mother. I won't ask if you really killed her."

"You just did."

Chance looks out the café window. "I'm really not with him—not really." Jena looks at her, lets her confess. "Mr. McNeil is dead, right?" Chance continues to prod.

Jena answers boldly. "Yes. He is dead."

"I do understand, Jena. I understand how anyone could get to a breaking point."

Jena tests her. "So, you could kill someone?"

Chance looks out the window again and then back at Jena. "I could?" She sounds unsure. "I'm sure I could." She thinks back to the night she found out about Carol. "I know I could. I could have killed Ken for cheating on me." She looks directly at Jena. "I could have killed Carol for what she did." Jena tries to believe her. "I could have killed you, Jena, after Ken confessed that he'd had a crush on you all that time." Jena sits and listens to her. "I was crushed. Broken. It was the worst betrayal I'd ever felt."

Jena goes back to what Chance said about her. "So, you could have killed me?"

Chance backs out of her words. "Not really killed you, but I felt rage. I felt like I could have easily spun out of control. This is why I think you should turn yourself in."

Jena looks up at the café ceiling, tapping her fingers together. "This is why you wanted to talk to me? So, you could tell me a past that I already know and then woo me with your cries and humbleness—just so you can convince me that turning myself in is what's best for me? That somehow my teenage life is over because you've got all the answers?"

Chance gets angry. "Jena, you're just prolonging the inevitable. Sooner or later, you'll get caught," she looks over at Jake and Ken. Jake is staring at them, paying little attention to Ken. "And Jake—he'll get caught, too, and go to jail. You two won't be in the same jail, you know."

Jena plays with her. "What's this really about, Chance? Is this about my murderous actions ... or your jealousy? Either way, you don't matter. What you're saying to me is like water running off a cliff—such a long way for it to go until it hits the bottom, and when it does, all that happens is that it splatters everywhere. Does that seem like a scenario I'm interested in?" Chance looks away. Jena pounds her fist on the table. "You might want to look at me." People in the café turn around to look at them. Jake stands up. Jena gives Chance a mean, angry look. "The person you knew years ago, or even that awful night, is not the person sitting at this table with you." Chance begins to shake, tears begin falling. Jena stands firm. "What? Are you afraid? Do you feel my fire? How hot it burns? Think of when you may have accidently burned your hand on the stove, the pain you felt, and then imagine my life's pain now— that fifty thousand times over. Feeling pain—whether inflicted intentionally or unintentionally—either way, I've claimed it."

Chance sobs, fearing Jena may hurt her. "Jena, you weren't the only one hurt." Her eyes well up and tears fall from them as she frantically runs her fingers through her hair. "I was too. I was ruined. So, I … I do know how fire can burn deep. How we can dig our own holes to bury ourselves in. Hide from shame felt that was not meant for us, but meant for someone else—someone like Mr. McNeil, who may have deserved to have never-ending pain, to fall without ever landing, or just to land and …" she wipes her face, "and just to have you there to fire two bullets into his chest. He deserved it." She raises her face through the tears.

"I'm the victim of an eternity of burning fire. I pray for rain." Jena has listened, but she shows little compassion for Chance. She doesn't want to remember that night when she was beaten and raped. She gives Chance a cold look, almost as if she has a light shining directly on her. She pulls Chance into her world. "You feel powerless, don't you? Scared? It's a feeling like no other—not knowing what to do, where to turn, or who to trust. Then there are times you just want to pick up something and throw it across the room or even at yourself as you stare at the reflection you see in the mirror. It can be overwhelming." Chance stops crying for a moment, breathing hard as she listens. "Revenge is what you're really sobbing about. That is what this whole conversation is about. You have the urge to break loose from being a caged animal trapped within your own pain, forced to accept it, fighting hard to run from it. You want my secrets. You want to feed off my fire, learn from me, so you can tailgate my journey." Jena is cold. "That's not going to happen. My advice to you is to let your fire burn until it can't burn anymore. Let it light you up until you're so consumed by it that you begin to feel coldness run through your mind, until it numbs your hands, feet, and then all of you. Once you reach that point, you won't need my fire." Jena stands up. Chance's eyes are red, and they follow Jena's every move. She is shaking and obviously fears Jena. Jena turns to walk away.

"Jena," Chance's voice cracks, "I don't want that kind of coldness. There's warmth still out there for you and for me."

Jena turns around. "Really? Where is it?"

Chance looks over at Jake. "Jake is your warmth."

Jena stares at Jake with compassion and then walks to him, leaving Chance drowning in her tears. Kens rushes over to console Chance, who pulls away from him and dashes out of the café.

CHAPTER NINETEEN

J ena walks toward Jake. She can see his face is filled with hope, fear, and love for her. Why does the light always seem brighter when it's farther away? Just until you get close to it. Then you realize it wasn't a light at all, just the reflection in your eyes of what you had hoped to see—what you wanted to see most—which was something that shines so bright that it melts the cold, hardened ice from your soul.

Jena and Jake begin to walk out. "Stop!" Kyler is holding a shotgun on them. "What—you think you can come into my café and I wouldn't remember who you two are?" He cocks the gun; customers scream. Ken stands up. "You two aren't going anywhere." Bob, Big Papa, and two other truck drivers stand up, giving Jake tough looks. "This is going to go down a little different from the last time." Bob points at Jake. Ann calls 911. "You two come in my café—eating, talking, and plotting—after you cause me to lose my restaurants in Donner's County."

Ann yells out, "Police got me on hold."

"Sit down!" Kyler yells at both of them. Jake and Jena stand still. Jake tries to walk forward. Kyler points the gun at him. "I said sit down." Ken is speechless; he doesn't know what to do.

Jena walks forward. "I'm not sitting down."

Kyler points the gun back at her. "Girl, you won't be missed." Kyler walks closer. "The cops are looking for you in Maplesville, New York, and now Donner's County—not to mention that I've been waiting to catch up with you and that Matt Ross. He's lucky he's in jail. You're wanted for murder, so who's going to care if I shoot you?" Kyler points the gun around the café. People duck in fear. "Anyone in here care if I shoot Ms. Jena Parker—also known as Jena Gray—killer of four people, including her own mother?" He points the gun around the café again. "Anyone?"

A man in the corner booth stands up and points his gun at Kyler, ready to shoot. "I care," he yells from the back. It's Franklin, the clerk from the hotel. Kyler points his gun on Franklin. Franklin walks closer, pointing his gun directly at Kyler. "I care. I'm not going to let you kill my Reda Jones."

"Reda Jones?" Kyler is confused. "This isn't Reda Jones," Kyler yells. "This girl is Jena Parker."

"Jena, you and Jake leave." The friendly face Jena remembered has been transformed; Franklin looks sullen and mean. He seems out of control.

Jena turns to Franklin. "This is my battle. There's no need for you to get involved." Franklin and Kyler stand face-to-face, guns ready to light up the room.

"No, that is where you're wrong, Jena. You're my Reda Jones—and if you die, she dies. I plan on writing my next book, and Reda Jones ain't dying today."

"You are one crazy, nutty bar fool," Kyler says as he tries to keep his shotgun on Franklin and Jena. Ann is still holding on the phone. Bob stands up. Jena pulls a gun on him. Kyler screams at Franklin, "Do you have any idea of what the hell you're talking about?"

Franklin gets sentimental. His eyes get dreamy, teary. "I know exactly what I'm talking about." Jena is drawn to him as he speaks. "There's only a once in a lifetime chance that you will find a character who can take you out of your simple world of hotel clerk. A character who is so charismatic, beautiful, torn," he looks over at Jena, keeping the gun pointed at Kyler, "full of energy ... dark. And most of all ... deadly." He focuses back on Kyler. "You create a character like that only once in a lifetime. Once. But what are the chances that you will actually get to meet that very same character in real life? Jena Parker is Reda Jones, and I'll kill you before I let you harm her." Jena can see that there is a bit of darkness in Franklin. Behind the cheery face, pleasant attitude, and overexaggerated hotel hospitality, there is a man filled with his own mystery. His obsession with a fictional character has led him to brand me as a mentor, Jena thinks.

Jena glances over at Ken, trapped in the back of the café. "Ken, Chance, let's go," Jena yells to him.

"Don't you move, son," Kyler yells back.

Jena swings her gun away from Bob and points it directly at Kyler. "Don't tell me what to do." She points her gun at a window and blows a bullet through it. The window glass shatters over a café table. "Get the hell out of here, Ken!" Ken, Chance, and two other people rush to jump out the window.

Bob jumps to grab Jena's gun. Kyler fires off, hitting Bob in the chest. Franklin fires, hitting Kyler in the shoulder. As he falls backward the shotgun goes off, shells hitting Ann in the stomach. Franklin holds his gun down on Kyler, Jena on the truck drivers. Two waitresses run over to help Ann. Jena walks slowly over to Kyler, who is holding his bleeding arm on the floor. Franklin points his gun at the truck drivers. Jake is standing holding the door open, waiting for Jena in amazement of her instant change. Jena points down at Kyler. "I told you I wasn't going to sit down." She looks around the café and feels a slight uneasiness with the gun in her hand. She puts her gun away. "Everybody, my name is Jena Parker. I've been accused of many crimes, and I can't tell you right now if those crimes were justified or not. What I do know is this isn't the last time you're going to hear my name or see my face. As it haunts you, even when you reflect on painful memories in your life that doesn't involve me, but when you do think of me try to remember someone that hurt you deeply." Franklin listens closely. Everyone gives Jena their attention. "Someone that hurt you so deeply that it made you pause, sit for hours, question everything you ever believed in. Who you are? Why is this happening to you? Why me?" she screams. "Why me?" she screams again, spying the entire café. "Think about anyone who made you feel that way, and then think of me. Then try to judge me." She turns to look at Jake, who's surprised to see this side of Jena that he's never seen before. This is the very first time he feels disconnected from her, that he sees her as a different person. He can feel her rage, an unsettling feeling amplified by the scene around him: Kyler shot in the arm, Ann shot in the stomach, Bob shot in chest, Ken jumping out the busted window, and Franklin possessed by his own obsession. Jake's hand braces on the door. Witnessing the truth makes him fear the future.

Jena can see the dissolution in his emotions for her, but she doesn't care. She walks quickly past him out the door and gets in the car. Jake follows and gets in the car. Chance gets in her car and spins out the parking lot. Just as Jake is ready to pull out, Ken pulls up next to them and rolls his window down. He's sweating and excited. "Holy shit." He rolls the window up and zooms off. Jake follows.

Jena rolls the window down so she can breathe in the wind. She tries to calm her emotions. Wind blowing in her face, she turns to look at Jake and wonders, Did I lose my love? My warmth? The one person who'd give it all up to ride forever with me to hell. Knowing that's where we're headed, he still drives as though heaven lives in these eyes when he looks at me—at least he did until a moment ago, when I know he finally saw the fire that's been burning in me. Is that enough for him to finally leave? "Now you know," Jena says.

"Know what?" Jake answers quickly.

"Who I am."

"Jena, I saw you after you shot Mr. McNeil, but I—"

She cuts in. "I know you felt he deserved it … but today I revealed myself."

"I know that is not who you are or who you want to be. Don't you want to be with me?"

"Jake, it's either going to be that you're going to live in my hell or I'm going to live in your heaven. I don't know if both can exist."

"Both can't exist. That's why I'm going to give everything I've got to give you heaven, forever happiness, because I know an eternity of my love being draped over you will take away your pain. I refuse to accept anything else. I'm with you all the way. There's no turning back for me now. I love you. That's never going to change. We've just got to figure out a way to get through this, and then we can leave. Maybe get out of the country—hide out in Mexico. I don't know, but I know I want you with me and I want you to want me too." He looks at her. "Do you want me?"

Jena is quiet. "I do want you, but I don't know if your fantasy can be reality." Jake is disappointed, but he still hasn't given up on their future.

Ken pulls up to the gateway of a huge house. He has a code to open the gate, but it doesn't work. He buzzes.

"Yep," a voice answers.

"It's me." Ken sounds frustrated. "The code is not working again."

"Yeah, I know. I just changed it." The gate opens. Ken rolls in; Jake follows. Ken gets out of his car and raises his arms in the air. "Hey, hey—we're here!" Jake goes to talk to him. Ken is still in shock and pumped up over what happened at the café. He and Jake talk in private while Jena sits in the car and ponders whether to leave and never be seen again. She finally gets out.

Ken stares at her. "I'd say you're a badass, but I think you already know that." Ken says as he smiles and winks at her.

Not entertained by his comment, Jena asks, "Can we go now?" She puts her shades back on.

"Sure, but first let me show you guys something." Ken clicks a button on his keys, and his car trunk pops opens. There are four costumes in the back. "Hey," he points, "these are the picks for tonight."

Jena is spying the red dress, shoes, and face mask. She gives Ken a distasteful look. "I guess the red outfit is mine?"

Ken reaches for the dress. "I thought you liked the color red?" Ken hands her the dress, shoes, and mask. Jena folds the dress and sticks the shoes and mask in her bag.

Jake rifles through the trunk, looking over the two male outfits. The Phantom of the Opera was one of his choices. "I'll take this one." Jake grabs the outfit, shoes, and mask.

Ken closes his trunk. "Excellent," he whispers. Ken lays out the rules. "Now, here's the deal. C. A. T. owes me a favor, so I'm cashing in on it by asking him to let you two stay at his house without any questions asked of who you are or what you're doing here. He's a real nice, cool guy—or man, I guess, because he's a little older than us—but he's cool with all the high profilers at the university so no one bothers him, if you know what I mean."

"So, he sells weed to staff," Jena says sarcastically.

Ken pauses. "Something like that. Anyways, you guys go on to the room, chill, eat, shower, and change to get ready for the party of your lives!" Ken starts walking. "It's that simple."

Jena looks at Jake. She has on shades, but he knows what she's thinking. No party they have ever attended was ever that simple, and what would make them think that this party would be any different? Ken turns around, waves both his hands forward. "Let's go."

Jena walks first. Jake lags behind, checking his costume for the party. The front door is open, but there's no one there to greet them. Jena stands and stares at the house from the outside. It looks like a white castle, with beautiful angel statues, tall glass windows, and palm trees aligned with the sides of the house. They all step inside, amazed at the beauty of this house. Marble floors, classic paintings, modern inside decor, leather couch and chair. If selling weed can get you a place like this, then I'm in the wrong business, Jena thinks. She isn't completely sold on the idea that this guy is just a simple drug dealer. They all turn to admire the living room. C. A. T. has his arms stretched out over the back of the couch. He's just staring at a painting on his wall. No music, no television, no one else in the room—just him staring at a painting of two horses.

CHAPTER TWENTY

"**W**elcome to my house." He doesn't turn around. "I hope you find everything here to your liking. My servants, Moishe and Mary, will assist you with all of your needs."

"Man, you have servants?" Ken is surprise.

"Of course," he answers back in a low, raspy voice. "What kind of food do you two like?" Jena and Jake look at Ken. "Moishe and Mary can make anything from any country. Would you like silk or satin sheets? Moishe and Mary can provide you with the sheets of your choice. This house has six bedrooms. Please feel free to pick your choice." He pauses. "But I have a feeling that you two may be shacking up together." C. A. T. grins.

"Man, I said no questions." Ken waves to Jena and Jake to make their way to a bedroom.

C. A. T. smirks. "I hardly think that asking about food, sheet, or room preferences can be considered asking questions." He laughs. "At least not the questions you were referring too."

Jena raises her eyebrows at Ken as she and Jake start walking quietly to their room. Jena stops. "Thank you for letting us stay at your house."

C. A. T. is quiet for a second. "You are most very welcome. Feel free to stay as long as you two wish." C. A. T. remains seated, still staring at the painting of the two horses.

Ken walks to the back of the couch, leans down, and whispers to C. A. T., "This is a big favor. Thanks for helping my friends."

C. A. T. turns around. There's a large scar over his left eye. "You helped me, so I'm helping you. What would this world be like if we didn't all help each other? Now you and I are back at the beginning of the favors … I may need you again … to do me a favor," C. A. T. emphasizes. "When the time comes, I hope that you will not ask any questions either." Ken stands, gives C. A. T. a nod, and walks out of the house. C. A. T. turns around and goes back to staring at the horses.

Jena and Jake walk room to room admiring all the unique decor, statues, paintings, lamps, and furniture. Everything looks expensive. They pass Moishe and Mary on the way to their room, carrying towels and blankets. They both wear servants' uniforms, but they are fancy. Moishe is wearing a black butler's suit. It almost looks like he is dressed to go out. If it weren't for the fact that he is carrying sheets and towels and is wearing a name tag, he could have been mistaken for the owner of the house. Mary is wearing a beautiful dress that still has the maid style to it, but it looks like she could be going to a ball or a party. Both look straight ahead but acknowledge Jena and Jake with quick nods. They look like they are just coming from cleaning the rooms, but there aren't any other guests in the house and neither of them appear dirty or tired from cleaning.

Five of the bedrooms are all on the same hall, but so far apart that privacy wouldn't be an issue. Jake leads them down the hall, choosing the middle room facing the side entrance. "I think this room would be best. That way we can get in and out without having to go to the front entrance." Jena nods.

Moishe passes them again in the hallway. He doesn't look at them, just walks straight ahead, turning left down another hall into a room. Jena is curious, and instead of following Jake into the bedroom, she follows Moishe. He is standing in the room dusting off the bookshelf. The room is a large office with a table, leather chair, a small leather couch, and a large bookshelf that seems almost impossible to clean by one person.

Jena stands behind Moishe as he cleans each book delicately. She breaks the silence between them. "Do you like cleaning bookshelves?" Moishe is shocked. He keeps cleaning, never turning around. He is quiet. Jena steps forward. "Books are a great way to get lost in another world." She touches and admires the bookshelf. "Are you a butler or a bodyguard?"

Moishe continues to clean. "Both," he says. "I clean the house, and—if needed—I clean the house." Jena understands.

She walks closer and then stands where she can see the side of his face and body. His suit is perfectly clean, nails manicured, jet-black hair groomed with a stylish haircut. "You look more like a bodyguard," Jena presses.

"I'm whatever C. A. T. wants me to be. Today I'm a house cleaner, tomorrow I may be a cook," he looks at Jena, "and the next day I may have to kill someone. It's a job." Moishe begins cleaning the shelf again.

Jena looks around the room. There's a large window with beautiful satin curtains in front of it. She walks slowly to the window and opens it. The warm breeze brushes against her skin, her hair sways back. Moishe turns to watch her. He steps down from cleaning the bookshelf, walks slowly toward her, and joins her in feeling the warm breeze.

"The night is coming," Jena says. "It is easing its way, but it's coming. The warm breeze here reminds me of being home, in my room. I used to stare out the window feeling the warm breeze against my skin. My neighborhood was always dark, quiet … at least at night. My parents would be downstairs dancing to their favorite song, and I'd be upstairs feeling the breeze, smiling, and listening as they laughed and sang to one other." Moishe stands still, just listening to her. A silence comes over Jena.

"I, too, like the breeze," Moishe speaks. "It calms my spirit. It reminds me of home too. My home far, far away. Sometimes I wish I were back home, listening to the loud music, the kids playing in the street, and my wife yelling at me, 'Moishe! Moishe! Come help in the kitchen.'" Moishe is quiet. "But those days are gone. They are far, far away, just like my home. Now my home and my memories are one. There's no need to go back. My wife and children are dead, and so is my home." Moishe walks away, leaving Jena with her thoughts. He finishes cleaning the bookshelf, and then he walks out of the room.

Jena walks back to the bedroom. Jake is in the adjacent bathroom, singing in the shower, "If I can't have you, I don't want nobody, baby ..." Jena listens to his horrible singing. She smiles, sits on the bed, pulls out the red dress, and stares at it. She thinks back to the last time she wore a red dress. She was in New York and spotted the dress in the window at a little boutique store owned by an old, wise woman. A dress once seen in a dream. A dream that came true, true as the blue in the sky and red as the blood that runs through her veins. It was the chosen dress. The dress to be worn to capture the eye of a cold one. To capture the eye of the coldest one of all: Mr. McNeil.

She puts the dress down and lies back on the bed. Now the dress has found me again. She looks over at the dress. Begging to be worn, tempting me not to wear it ... knowing I can't resist the power it has over me. She reconsiders the script running through her head. If I believe that a dress could hold such power over me, then that would mean I'm powerless to stop what will happen tonight ... or tomorrow. The dress doesn't hold any powers, she thinks. It is just a part of the meaning. What is meant to be. What will be. It didn't show up to tempt me; I'm the temptation of it. I choose to wear it, use it, make it a part of my plans. Jena reaches for the dress. She lays it across her body as she drifts off.

She is on the plane. For the first time, there is a woman sitting in the back, laughing with a man. Their identities are blurry to her eyes. She walks slowly toward them. Their voices get louder and louder until Jena is standing in front of the two of them. The woman and man play no attention to Jena as they laugh and joke with one another. It's like she is invisible to them. Jena watches in surprise and in disappointment. It's her mother laughing with Mr. McNeil like they were lovers. Like they were husband and wife. Jena grows angry.

"Where is my father!" she yells at her mother. Kitty doesn't answer, ignoring her. Jena leans forward, yelling louder. "Mom, where is my father!" Mr. McNeil touches Kitty's face. She kisses him. "Mom, stop!" Jena yells louder. "Stop it! Stop it!" She reaches for Mr. McNeil but can't touch him. Like she is frozen in time, in a dream she had no control over, Jena realizes she can't be seen or heard. She is left to be tortured by their laughs, their happiness, and she's forbidden to move or stop it. She feels like crying but can't. Only rage covers her thoughts.

"Painful to watch?" a voice speaks to her. Jena looks around the plane. No one is there. "I know it's very painful to watch, but what can you do?"

Jena thinks to herself, Where is this voice coming from?

"You can't do anything," the voice continues to torment her.

"I can do something." Jena screams louder to her, "Mom! Please stop!"

Mrs. Parker looks at her. "I can't, Jena." She smiles at Jena. "I can't stop. I don't want to."

Jena doesn't understand. "What? What are doing? He killed Dad. Why are you sitting here laughing with him? He killed him. He's the cause of all of this."

Mrs. Parker stands up and reaches out to Jena. "I know," she says to her. Jena closes her eyes in disbelief.

She wakes up with real tears running down her face. She sits up quietly, wiping away the tears. Jake is standing over her with a towel wrapped around his waist. She grabs her bag and dress and dashes past him into the bathroom. She stands staring at herself in the mirror. What the hell was that? she thinks. What was my mother doing with Mr. McNeil? He's trying to torture me. He can't get to me in the real world, so now he's going after my mother.

Jena frantically searches through her bag to find the letter her mother had given her. "Mom," she utters softly. "What's in this letter?" The envelope is slightly dirty, wrinkled from being carried around. She stares at the letter, her tears dripping on it. She lays the letter on the bathroom counter next to the red dress and stares at them both.

Jake knocks on the bathroom door. Jena cries quietly. "Jena, what's up? Let me in." She doesn't answer. "We don't have to go to this party. We could just stay here." She stares at the letter again, reaches for it, and turns it around to open it. "Jena, please talk to me." She puts the letter on the counter.

She wipes the tears completely off her face and opens the door. "I'm going to this party." She closes the door, leaving Jake standing dripping wet with a towel wrapped around his waist.

CHAPTER TWENTY-ONE

Jena walks out of the bathroom and checks Jake out as he dries off. "You look refreshed."

He smiles at her. "I feel great." He takes off his towel and catches Jena staring at him. He takes advantage of the moment, walking around in the nude. "Can you believe that bathroom? It's phenomenal in there. Marble shower, tub, sink. It has everything—toothbrushes, body washes for him and her." Jena keeps her eyes on Jake as he gets dressed.

"Yeah, I think I'll go get ready."

"Jena." She stops. "Where were you?"

She turns around. "I was just roaming around." She walks into the bathroom again.

Jake stands at the door. "We don't have to go tonight." He stands, waiting for her to respond.

"I want to go." She turns to look at him. "I know you do too. Besides, Ken has done us a huge favor, asking his friend if we can stay here ..." Jena smirks, "almost getting killed. I think he'd be really disappointed if we didn't show up." Jake is silent. "Anyway, we are wearing costumes. No one is going to know who we are." She reaches in her bag, searching for her lipstick. "I don't see any reason for us not to go."

Jake reaches for the door to close it. "Then we'll go," he says in a Dracula voice. "I must go now and get dressed."

Jena yells through the door, "You're not going as Dracula—you're the Phantom of the Opera!"

Jake laughs. "Ha, ha. Just making sure you're paying attention."

Jena listens to Jake's unique laugh. She pictures how his eyes twinkle as he smiles and laughs hard. He is such a wonderful person. So sweet, so kind, and so loving toward me. Not to mention patient. I wish he weren't so hell bent to be caught-up in my nightmare, but what would I do without him, without his unconditional love? What friend or lover would stand by a killer? He believes in me, but is he being foolish by denying himself the ultimate feeling in life—freedom?

Jena stares at herself in the mirror until it grows dark, and she zones out in deep thought. Mirrors foretell so many things about ourselves. What do I see when I look at myself? A young girl with long, reddish hair and blue eyes, tall and slender. Is that all I see? If I look longer into the mirror, I believe I'll see something beyond the human eyes, something deeper, something that once slept but now awakens. It wants to come out, to see the light outside of you. It wants to break free, see the world, learn it, understand how to maneuver its way around, and then take it from you—your life—and make it its own. While you seek to find answers to calm the spirit and ease the soul, it's already taken you. Now you must succumb to it or be ready to battle with it until you or it dies—maybe both.

She visualizes herself wearing the red dress, walking barefoot in the hot desert, sun beating down on her, feet blistering, mouth dry. She passes many people: the men on the plane, Sam the delivery driver, Principal Ricky, Jake, Ken, Carol, Chance, her mother, her father. She stops in front of Mr. McNeil. He's dressed all in black. She pushes him, but he doesn't move or respond. She picks up a rock and throws it at him; it bounces off. She fights him, but nothing works. He just stands there without moving or responding to her. Jena turns around and sees that everyone is lined up looking at her all tired out, clothes torn, hot, sweaty, breathing hard. They all turn away from her to walk away like a wounded soldier waving the white flag to end the battle. She is disappointed, sad, feels powerless, and wants to cry, but something inside of her won't let her. She turns to Mr. McNeil, who is still standing there waiting for her. He reaches his hand out to her. She hesitates and then turns to walk away, but he grabs her legs. She screams and kicks, as her body slides farther into the dark sand. Somehow, he holds her without even touching her. Her fingers dig deep in the sand while she screams and kicks for help—just screaming without sound. She looks up, and everyone is still walking away, no one helping, no one talking, no one stopping Mr. McNeil.

Then suddenly it stops. He is gone, and so is everyone else … everyone except Jake. He is standing with his hand on hers, pulling her back. Why couldn't I see him before? she thinks. Was he always here? Jake doesn't look like Jake to her; something is different about him. The way he looks at her is different. It isn't with those loving, dreamy eyes that want her and would never leave her. He is just someone who is helping her but doesn't love her. She can feel the distance between them the moment he lets go of her hand. Just then, the wind kicks up the dust; his hand is there, and then it is gone. Gone forever. She can see that in his eyes. The emptiness. The coldness. Why didn't he just let me fall instead of allowing me to see his revulsion with me. Or is that my punishment—for him to help me and then let me see him walk away while I stand here looking like a beast? She yells for him to come back, but he doesn't. He just keeps on walking and walking until he is out of her sight.

She wipes her dirty hands on her red dress and starts walking. She walks until she comes to the end of the desert, where she can't walk anymore. Falling to her knees, she collapses. She lies still, with no willingness to go on—nothing left to fight for, nothing left to lose. There is nothing, no one; even the sun has retired.

When life's endurance of pain conquers you at the same time that love abandons you, it can cause instant paralyzation of your emotions. Your soul and spirit break free and leave the body there to wait until the dust covers your eyes and your mouth open prays, they return to give you one more chance to go on. Even the will to try can slip slowly away while you tell yourself, "This isn't how I want my life to end. I want to live. Oh please, spirit, come back. I want to live. I want Jake."

She focuses back on herself in the mirror. I can change things, she thinks. I can make my life different and make sure that I never lose Jake's love and forever put this dark feeling back where it belongs—as only a reflection in the mirror.

Jena opens the bathroom door. Jake is in his costume; he stares at her with a dreamy look as she stands in the doorway. Tonight, I'll prove to Jake that I can break free, that I can be the woman he wants and needs. That I love him just as much, if not more, than he loves me. Tonight, I'll tell him. She reflects back to her wearing the dirty red dress, how she felt when Jake let go of her hand and walked away. I don't want to be alone, just wearing a dirty red dress, lying in the desert, waiting for my soul and spirit to return. I'm alive right now, looking at my heart beating right in front of me—Jake. He's everything a woman could want, and I don't want to long for him when he's right where I can feel his strong, muscular body embracing mine; his tender lips pressing against mine, using them to caress my entire body; and his hands wrapped over me, trapping me, so nothing or no one else can even attempt to stop our passion. To watch him walk away from me would tear my entire being into millions of pieces … and I'd kill anyone who tries to take him away from me.

"You look beautiful, just stunning," Jake tells her.

"Thank you." Jena picks up the bright-red mask, the color so opposite of what she is feeling. She puts it on. "How do I look now?"

He walks up to her, takes off the mask, and kisses her softly on the lips. "You look beautiful with the mask on or off."

She says to him in a seductive voice, "I bet you prefer off, don't you?"

"I do prefer it off." He takes the bait. He puts the mask down on the bed and squeezes her tightly to him. "I prefer everything on you off." He presses his hands in the middle of her back, pushing her closer to him, and kisses her. He runs his hand down the side of her neck, continuing down to her breasts, and kisses both of them. Looking up at her with those irresistible eyes, he raises her hand to his lips and kisses it up her arm, her neck, and then back to her lips. He whispers in her ear, "I want you right now." Jena is pulled like gravity into the moment. Her emotions are captured like a beautiful butterfly in the jar, and instantly the world outside the room doesn't exist to her; only here is her presence required. "I want to hear you say you love me," he says. "I need to hear you say it. Let's get naked and lie on this bed like there's nothing to bother with in this world." He lifts her in his arms, her feet slightly dangling from the floor as she drapes her arms around his neck, holding on tight as if her life depends on it. He slowly puts her down, rubs his hands down her back, and begins sliding her dress off.

There's a knock at the door. "Open up! Up, up?" Ken's knocking spoils the mood. Jake tidies up Jena's dress and then opens the door with a disappointed look on his face. Ken strolls in. "Hey, hey." He spins around like a showroom model. "So, what do you think?" he says, pointing at himself dressed as a James Bond agent.

Jake closes the door, checks him out. "Not bad. So, you bring the Phantom of the Opera suit for me, and you get to be James Bond?"

Ken struts around the room, trying to be cool, one hand in his pocket. He recites a few James Bond movie lines. Jena smiles. He walks over to her. "Oh, my lady." He kisses her hand. "Looks like James Bond is stealing someone's woman tonight," he jokes.

Jena quickly pulls her hand away. "I don't think so."

Jake stands in between them. "That's a negative, dude. The Phantom will kick Bond's ass if he tries to take his girl."

Ken turns around, pointing his finger like a gun. "I'm just kidding, man. Too many ladies will be at this party for me to worry about Jena—although she is looking very beautiful tonight."

Jena grabs her bag and mask. "Let's go." She walks out the door. Moishe is standing in the hallway. He reaches for her coat. She stares at him. "You don't have to carry my coat." She walks off, with Jake and Ken following behind her. Moishe follows them outside.

There is white limo out front. Ken does his James Bond impression. "This is a masquerade party, not the prom," Jena jokes.

"Not my idea, Jena. This car is compliments of Mr. C. A. T. Tyler. Moishe is our limo driver."

Jake walks around the limo. "This is a sweet ride." Ken and Jake act like little kids getting ready to go to the playground.

Moishe holds the door open for Jena. "You're not going to tell me that I can't open the door for you, either are you?" She shakes her hand and smiles at him. Jake and Ken get into the limo. Jena starts to step in.

"Wait!" She stops. "I forgot something." She turns around and dashes back into the house; she had left her mother's letter by the bathroom sink. She quickly walks to their room. She hears voices coming from the office where she had earlier spoke with Moishe. Two people are talking. She quickly goes into the bathroom, picks up the letter, and hurries out of the room, but she stops in the hallway when she hears one of the men mention Matt Ross. She turns around, walks slowly to the office door, and stands outside and listens. It's C. A. T. and another person talking.

"Matt Ross owes me a lot of money." C. A. T. is angry.

"He's in jail," the other person says.

C. A. T. looks at him. "Not anymore. I just received word through a third party that the police in Maplesville released him today." C. A. T. strolls around his office. "So that means he's out there roaming around with my money." He points at the other person. "I want my money," C. A. T. pounds his hand on his desk, "tonight!" Jena backs away slowly. "You find Matt Ross—that thief—and you bring him here to me. Tonight. Not tomorrow. Not the next day … tonight."

Jena quickly hurries out of the house. She doesn't let Moishe open the limo door for her this time. Ken is riding in the front with the limo driver; Jake is in the backseat waiting for her. She sits down with a concerned look on her face and utters a name she thought she'd never say again, "Matt Ross."

CHAPTER TWENTY-TWO

The look on Jena's face worries Jake. "What happened in the house?" Jena looks up and shakes her head. He slides over to her. "What happened, Jena?" He forces her to speak.

"Matt Ross," she says sternly.

"Matt Ross?" Jake is confused. "What about him?"

"He's out of jail and most likely is going to be here tonight."

"He is here in town?"

"Maplesville."

He rubs her knee. "So what? He's no one, just some guy we gave a ride to."

Jena stops him from rubbing her. "He's also the guy who tried to make us accessories to a robbery. That's why that Kyler guy is so angry with us. You don't know what Matt told the cops. He probably told them that it was our idea to rob Kyler's. Why is he out of jail?" She ponders. "He is supposedly wanted for multiple robberies and murder, so why would police let him go?"

Jake backs away. "Why do you care, Jena?"

She looks at him strangely. "Why? Because I do, and that's all you need to know right now."

Jake is angry and disappointed. Every time it seems that things are going great with him and Jena, something happens. Something gets in the way. He begins to doubt himself. Am I ever going to truly make her happy? Jena pays little attention to him.

A voice speaks over the limo car intercom. "Hello, back there. This is your captain speaking." Neither Jake nor Jena is in the mood for Ken's pranks. "Hello? Come on guys, we're almost at the party."

Jake is angry and so is Jena, both for different reasons. Jake is angry because destiny will not live up to its promise. It keeps teasing him with tidbits of intimate moments with Jena that appear promising, yet end up being a fluke, a dirty trick, like a man who went all-in with his fortune and walked away from the table with nothing. The more he thinks about how horrible the night was going, the more his angry grows, mostly from his disappointment and heartbreak. The prospect of him and Jena sharing another beautiful night tonight seemed dead.

Jena's anger stems from something different. She, too, wishes that everything around her and Jake would just crumble, leaving them there with a piece of earth just big enough for them to stand on. But it isn't that simple for her. Matt Ross represents more than a hitchhiker looking for a ride or a deadbeat thief traveling from town to town. He is her rape, her father's death, the clerk, the doctor on the train … her mother; he is the reminder of it all. And if she is to put it all behind her, she'll have to take on Matt Ross too.

Jena hits her hand on the window. Jake looks over. She's hurt herself. He slides over, takes her hand, and rubs it in his. She can see the rejection in his eyes, just like in her thoughts; he was ready to walk away. "I'm sorry, Jake."

Looking into her eyes melts him. He caves in. He has nowhere to put the love he has for her except in her hands, for her squeeze it, crush it, or even massage it back to life—like she just did. He kisses her wounded hand and reaches for her face. "I don't give a damn about Matt Ross or anyone else right now. I just want tonight to be about us." He kisses her. "I don't want anything to ruin it."

The limo stops. Jake and Jena look outside into another world—a world full of costumed characters. Jena realizes that she can be anybody she wants to be tonight. She doesn't have to walk in those doors fearing that someone will recognize her. She has her mask, her man—the moment is hers if she'll take it … if she can listen to Jake and leave it all behind, at least for tonight, and let the moment take them to places they couldn't without masks. Jena smiles at Jake. "I—"

She's interrupted. The limo doors swing open, and Ken sticks his head in. "Hello, it's your captain." They both laugh at him. "Don't laugh just yet," Ken whispers. "The limo driver just gave me a heads-up that there are uncover cops here tonight. Some of them are from Maplesville, some from Donner's County, and there are local cops here." He looks at Jena. "They're looking for you, Jena. Both of you put your masks on, be careful," he smiles, "and by all means, guys, let's have a rocking, kick-ass time!"

Jena puts her mask on; its fits like it was made for her. "Wait." She grabs Ken's arm. "Where's Chance? Carol?"

Ken takes her arm and helps her out of the limo. "They're here … somewhere." Jena eyes the crowd of college kids dressed up in their fantasy outfits, diamonds and pearls, suits, and ties. There are lots of girls wearing similar red dresses. The three of them walk through the crowd, Jake's arms wrapped around Jena's waist, holding her as if their bodies were born together. Ken walks off to flirt with two girls.

Where is Chance? Jena wonders. She eyes the crowd and locks in on a girl. It isn't clear to her where Chance is, but it is obvious where Carol is; she is the girl stalking Ken, watching every move he makes as her anger grows with each smile he shares with another girl. Carol walks up to Ken and argues with him. The two girls he was flirty with stand there and watch, giggling. He blows Carol off. Her face is red, eyes bulging like they are about to explode, and she's breathing hard as she storms away to go inside the university's party room. She is dressed as Cat Woman, and it is apparent that right now she feels like tearing Ken's heart out. Now I know what Carol is wearing, she thinks, but where is Chance?

Jake guides Jena inside. The place is beautifully decorated with diamond chandeliers, rose petals scattered in various places, waterfalls, tiny elves, and every costume imaginable: Cinderella, Snow White, Dracula, Jason, Michael Myers; some scary and some enchanted, but all pleasing to Jena's eyes. She's in a room full of people who, for one night, want to be someone other than who they are. It's an amazing feeling for Jena, who once again feels a sense of normalcy among her peers. Maybe that's because they are all dressed in costumes and masks, no one really portraying themselves—no one except her. She is the only one who came as she is: a killer.

Jake grabs her, twirls her around on the ballroom floor, bows to her, and then they dance. He pulls her close, and they dance slow, his face pressed closely to hers, eyes slightly closed, his hands braced tightly around her waist. Strolling with the music as if they were dancing on air, dancing in soft wind as gravity collapses, taking them both higher above the crowded dance floor. He spins her around and around, pulling her in close, kissing her, playing with her, caressing her, and then spinning her back out again. Freedom.

"I have to go to the ladies' room," Jena whispers softly.

"I don't want you to leave me." Jake holds on to her.

"I'm not leaving you. I'll be back."

"I'll walk you there."

"I can walk myself," Jena says. Jake holds on to her arm, releasing it slowly while passionately staring at her as she walks away. Jena seductively walks through the crowd. She's alive and free from her past, floating on air, so filled with enthusiasm that she embraces the laughter and happiness of everyone around her. She doesn't feel like an outcast. She feels like a part of it—maybe even, in some way, the reason for it. She passes by Ken dancing with a girl wearing a sparkling blue dress, blue satin gloves, a crown with shiny crystals, and a mask painted like the blue sky with white clouds. What a beautiful costume, Jena thinks. So unique, peaceful, and calm. Ken plays and flirts with the girl. Jena can't see her face. Chance? Jena smiles. Although her last encounter with Chance wasn't pleasant, because of the happiness she feels being with Jake, feeling like a normal person in an enchanted setting, she wanted nothing but happiness for Chance too. She wants her to feel the freedom of being in love with a man who can see past the outer layers of the human soul to the find the black pearl, a treasure that has possessed his heart. She turns around; Jake is still watching. What an incredible feeling to have that man love you back without setting conditions that aren't achievable, even under circumstances such as hers. Jake is truly the most wonderful and loving man I'll ever meet in my life. Jena stands still as the motion of the world surrounds her: people drinking, dancing, engaging in intimate kisses. She smiles at Chance and Ken as they dance with a romance-filled life promise that anything is possible if they try.

Jena walks through the crowded room. A tall man watches and then follows her. Jena stops a young girl who is laughing with a friend. "Where's the restroom?" The girl points to two double doors.

The man steps up to the three of them and grabs Jena's arm. "Would you like to dance?" he asks. Jena politely pulls her arm away, shaking her head no.

One of the girls shoves her purse to the other and then grabs the tall man's hand. "I will dance with you." She drags him out onto the dance floor.

Jena uses both her hands to open the double doors leading to the bathrooms. The women's bathroom is on the left, and the men's is on the right. She opens the women's door and steps into the bathroom. The bathroom is large with pink-and-black heart designs over the wall, a marble black-and-white floor, high ceiling, with tiny crystal lights surrounding the entire room. The sinks are gold with pieces of black marble chipped inside, and there is a large mirror that runs almost as high as the ceiling of the room. She walks slowly into the bathroom, taking tiny footsteps with taps that sound like Cinderella slippers brushing the floor. Jena spins around like a princess while watching herself in the mirror, smiling in sheer happiness and excitement. As she stops and stares at herself in the mirror, which suddenly turns dark.

There is crying coming from one of the bathroom stalls. She walks over and tries to gently push the door open, but the person inside stops it. It's Carol, crying and sobbing over Ken. She doesn't reveal herself. "What is wrong?" Carol is silent, sobbing frantically. "Has someone you loved hurt you?"

Carol breathes hard. "Yes," she utters through her tears.

"Is he with someone else?"

"Yes."

"Why don't you just leave him alone? Find someone to love you—someone who deserves you."

"There is no one else," she says in a louder, painful voice. "No one I want. He is everything to me. Have you ever loved someone so much that you can't sleep or think of anything else except his hands all over your body, squeezing you, caressing you until his body feels like it's pierced in yours, mounted together, forever making love in a white room with no sound except your sexual cries of pleasure, known to no one except the two of you?" Carol's voice is louder and strong. "His kiss more powerful than a winter ice storm—never cold, but hot as the sun burns when nakedness is expose to it without fear of time or pain. Don't you tell me that you know anything about that kind of love, because you don't know. You have no idea how still a room can be when you see the man you love holding someone else … kissing her. It's almost like I stood there watching my death." Carol stands up and opens the door. "You don't know anything." She tries to walk past the woman standing in the doorway.

"Don't I?" The woman pushes Carol. "Don't I know, Carol?" Carol tries to push back, but she shoves Carol up against the bathroom toilet; she hits the wall. The woman drags her out of the bathroom, locks the door, and pushes her up against the wall.

Carol is in shock, but she tries to fight back. "Who are you?" Carol screams. The woman throws Carol up against the bathroom sink and begins to choke her. Carol grabs her hands, but her grip is too tight.

"You think you can steal someone's love and make it your own? Pretend to be someone's friend and then backstab and take the only love she ever knew?" The two-woman struggle. Carol tries to grab the vase from the bathroom counter. The woman yanks it from her, struggling Carol down to the bathroom floor. "You think you're the only one who's loved someone like that?" She begins strangling her. Carol's face turns red as the life slips from her. "No, you're not." The woman laughs. "I was told that I should let my fire burn," she strangles Carol until there are only seconds of her life left. She removes her mask. It's Chance. She leans down with a mean, angry look on her face and whispers in Carol's ear, "You're my fire." The life slips away from Carol's eyes. She is lift lying on the bathroom floor.

CHAPTER TWENTY-THREE

C hance stands up, unlocks the door, and leaves Carol's stiff on the floor with her eyes and mouth wide open.

Jena washes her hands, smiles in the mirror, and leaves the bathroom. A girl dash past her. "Oh, thanks goodness this bathroom isn't locked. The other one down the hall was locked, and I had to go really bad." She pushes past Jena, who is too happy to care if the girl shoved her.

As Chance is putting her mask on, she can see the back of herself standing in the mirror. She sees herself closing the other bathroom door, smiling, and laughing. But it isn't a mirror; it is Jena. Jena turns around, and there is Chance staring back at her. The two girls stand face-to-face. Same dress, same hair, same shoes, same mask. Chance stares at her. Jena is shocked.

Chance moves closer to Jena. "You said to find my own fire. Now I have." Chance smiles, puts her mask on, and walks off.

A scream comes from the other bathroom. A girl runs by screaming, "Murder! Someone has been killed in the bathroom!" Other people run to the bathroom. Jena bullies her way through the crowd. She sees Carol lying there dead, lifeless. She rushes back toward Jake while people rush in to see the murdered body lying on the floor.

Jena spots Chance and runs to catch up with her. Chance sees her struggling to get to her. She laughs and manages to push her way through the crowd, leaving Jena stuck. Jena knows she can't scream or say anything without exposing herself.

She bumps into the Ken. He grabs her arms. "What is going on?" he shouts.

"Carol's dead." Jena pushes away from him to find Jake.

Ken rushes off to the bathroom, but he can't get through the crowd. He yells, "Carol! Carol!" The uncover police try to get a handle on the out-of-control crowd.

Jake finds Jena and pulls her to him. "What the hell is going on?" Jena grabs his hand to lead him out of the party.

Moishe is standing out in front of the limo. He sees them coming and opens the back door. Jena and Jake hurry in. Before closing the door, the driver asks, "Are we waiting on Ken?"

"No!" Jena shouts. "Get us out of here!" Moishe rushes to get in and drives off. Jena takes off her mask. She wants to cry, but she can't.

"Jena!" Jake shakes her. "Jena! What's happening?"

Jena's eyes are red. "Chance killed Carol."

Jake gives her a shocked look. "What ... what do you mean, 'Chance killed Carol'?"

"That's what happened, Jake. Chance is dressed up exactly like me. I saw her! She has on the same dress, shoes, even her hair is just like mine."

Jake leans forward and says, "I can't believe that Carol is dead, and that Chance killed her."

"She must have planned this all from the beginning," Jena says. "She had to have put my outfit in Ken's car."

Jake leans back in the seat. "This is unbelievable ... I can't believe this is happening."

"Well, it is." Jena looks out the car window. "She looked crazy—probably as crazy as I looked. This is revenge." Jena closes her eyes for a moment. "She wanted revenge on Carol for cheating with Ken ...

and I guess she wanted revenge on me, and that's why she dressed like me. I'm living in a nightmare within a nightmare. Chance has taken on my darkness and made it her own. I never thought I could feel as happy as I was tonight, or I would never have told her those words."

"What words?" Jake asks.

Jena pauses. "To find her fire. To let her fire burn until it couldn't burn anymore, until she was cold …" she looks over at Jake, "cold-blooded, that is. And I think killing Carol surely proved she is."

"This is unbelievable." Jake puts his head down. His cell phone rings. "Yeah. What's going on? What are the cops saying?"

Ken is upset. "They're looking for a woman wearing a red dress, red shoes, and a mask. That sounds like someone we know, doesn't it?"

"Look, Jena didn't kill Carol. It was Chance."

"Where's the proof?" Ken gets loud. "People are saying that they saw a woman in red leave the bathroom. Jena is in red!"

Jake yells, "So is Chance! She dressed up like that to frame her. She's gone crazy." Jake gets angry. "Crazy over you."

"What?"

"Yeah, man, she's gone nuts. She was heartbroken when she found out you cheated with Carol, her best friend."

Ken is in disbelief. "No, man, that can't be true. Chance and I broke up before we started college. I was kidding around at the restaurant earlier about her being my babes. She was dating someone else."

"Did you ever see her with the other guy?"

"No."

"Then how do you know?"

"Because she told me that she was over me—had forgiven me."

"Well, she lied. Now Carol is dead, and the police, no doubt, are going to try to blame this murder on Jena. I'm not going to let that happen." Jake speaks low, "Ken, you have found Chance before

Jena does. Because if she finds Chance first, I think …" Jake pauses, "I think she'll kill her."

"I'll do what I can, but I don't know. She's probably looking for me. She probably wants to kill me next." Ken looks around frantically.

Jake yells. "Don't be a damn coward. Find her!" he slams off the phone.

Jena stares out the window. "Ken doesn't have to find her because I'll find her. And you're right—I'll kill her."

A pickup that had been following closely behind the limo slams into it. Jake and Jena are kicked forward. Jake hits his head on the window. "What the hell?" Jake looks back. There are two shadows in the truck and a shotgun in the middle of them. The truck slams into the limo again, causing Moishe to swerve into the bushes off the road.

The two men get out of the truck. One grabs the shotgun, walks up holding the gun, and opens the back limo door. "Get out!" He points the shotgun at Jena. Big Papa opens Jake's side and yanks him out to the ground. He cocks the gun. "I said get out!"

It's dark and only the truck light is beaming on them, but the silhouettes reveal who they are: it's Kyler and Big Papa the truck driver. Kyler shoulder is wrapped up in bandages. "I got you now, girl," Kyler says. "No more running, killing people, costing people their businesses. Your time is up. Now give me that bag." Jena hands Kyler her bag.

"Haven't you had enough?" Jena asks.

"Not yet." Kyler points the shotgun with his good arm at her face. "Not until you're dead. You and your boyfriend."

Moishe gets out of the limo, shoots Big Papa, and then points his gun at Kyler. "Give her back her bag." Kyler fires his shotgun at Moishe, but he misses. Jena's bag falls to the ground. She picks it up and ducks as Kyler and Moishe fire back and forth at each other. She sees Jake lying on the ground, but she can't move because of the gunfire.

"Jake," she calls, but he doesn't move. "Jake!" She crawls through the limo's backseat, keeping her head down. Jake moans: he's hurt. Big Papa stabbed him with his knife before kicking him to the ground. Blood is coming from Jake's upper shoulder. Jena's eyes grow big. "No!" She races over to Jake and sits him up. Moishe and Kyler are still firing it out.

"I'm all right," Jake speaks, and Jena is relieved. She wraps her arms tightly around Jake, his blood draining on her red dress.

I've never felt so helpless, Jena thinks. I was so scared that he left me here to deal with this world that doesn't understand me and wants nothing more than to make me pay for my crimes—and everyone else's. If this was it, then this was going to be it! Jena gently lays Jake down. The warm night breeze flows through her hair and ruffles her dress. It dawns on her that she can't change who she was or the past that haunts her. In spite of the romance, the glamour, and the glitz of the night, her destiny had found her. The red dress, the truck, the light, Moishe and Kyler shooting it out in the middle of the road: it was all a part of the entire plan … and now the plan must be completed.

Jena reaches in her bag, grabs the gun, points it at Kyler, and shoots him. Kyler falls down to the ground, shotgun rising high in the air. Moishe stares at her as she walks toward Kyler. She stands over him and shoots him two more times in the chest. Moishe slowly puts his gun down. Jena stands over Kyler, the warm night breeze blowing, her grip firm on the gun—as if it were made for her to use. Kyler is barely alive, coughing up blood, facing imminent death. Jena kneels down close to his ears. Tears run down his face. She whispers, "Now you go. You go and tell them I'm coming."

Jena's face is the last thing Kyler sees before he closes his eyes. His end had come, and now he was among the rest of them. Mr. McNeil, the hotel clerk, the doctor on the train …

Jena looked over at Moishe. She puts the gun down by her side, griping it tightly, and then turns and runs to Jake's side. She holds him in her arms, kisses his face, and tries to put him in the limo.

Moishe walks over to help. Once Jake is in the limo, Moishe and Jena walk back to Kyler's body. Jake sits up and peeks out the window to watch, pressing on his shoulder to slow down the bleeding.

The warm wind blows as Jena watches Moishe drag Kyler's body to the ditch. Kyler's head slumps over, bleeding, lifeless. Moishe goes back for Big Papa's body, drags it to the ditch, and lays it on top of Kyler's like two sacks of potatoes. He walks back and stands next to Jena. He puts his gun in the back of his pants. Jena watches him. Such a professional move, she thinks.

Moishe breaks his silence. "I told you." He looks at Jena, who's still staring at the dead bodies. "Some days I'm the butler, the cook," he looks back the limo, "the limo driver, but today I'm the killer— and so are you." Moishe walks back to the limo, gets in, and puts his hat on. He cranks up the car, turns on the lights, and waits for Jena.

When the moment comes, I'll have to answer to all of my sins, but until then I will have to serve out my time living as the person I am. The judge and jury has not yet been formed, so let me prepare them a plate fit for a court, fit for a queen who will soon sit on the throne of death. Matt Ross, I'm coming for you. Soon you'll know what they know: that the dark in the day is no different than the dark at night. Jena gets into the limo. She holds Jake close to her. The thought of losing him sparked alive the part she tries so hard to hide, but she knows that you can't hide behind your own shadow. You have to stand out in front of it, take its hand, and lead it, because you both can't hide from the truth—so why not let both shine? Moishe spins off, leaving only dust on the dead bodies.

CHAPTER TWENTY-FOUR

"Y ou're free to go." Office Reyes hands Matt Ross a bag with all of his belongings in it. He grips the bag tightly, stopping Matt from taking it. "But not for long. We'll be watching you, waiting for you to make your next mistake—and that's when I'll put you away forever. Not even the rats will want you." He lets loose of the bag. Matt grabs his things and walks out. Officer Reyes follows him. "You know you're not going to get away with the crimes you committed." Matt keeps walking. "You hear me?"

Matt turns around to face Officer Reyes. "I understand."

Officer Reyes walks up to him, poking his finger in Matt's chest. "Just what do you understand, creep? Do you understand that I won't rest until I get you back behind bars? Do you understand that I hate punks like you who commit crimes in our society, but somehow get away with it?" Officer Reyes moves in closer to Matt's face. "Do you understand that I'm going to track you down like a dog? Soon as you make another mistake, I'll be there to lock your ass up!"

Matt's looks him straight in the eyes. "I understand." He backs up. "But I also understand that I'm free right now and you're harassing me, officer." Matt turns away and walks out the door.

Officer Reyes walks to door, opens it, and stands staring at Matt as he walks away. He yells for one of his deputies.

"Yes, sir?" Deputy Paul's answers with excitement. "You follow him." He turns to the deputy with an evil look in his eyes. "You find out everything that kid gets himself into and report back to me ASAP! I want him and Jena Parker behind bars for the rest of their lives! You got that?"

"Yes, sir." Deputy Paul's puts on his hat and runs out the door, almost slipping on a rock. He looks back. Officer Reyes is shaking his head. Paul's is embarrassed, so he quickly gets into the police car.

"Idiot," Officer Reyes says as he walks back to his desk.

Matt is walking around, looking for some action—something to keep him out of trouble, but a way for him to make money or steal it. He walks into a pawn shop. A worker name David is standing behind the counter. Matt walks up.

"What do you need?" David asks as he leans on the counter, eyeing Matt.

Matt wraps his bag around his shoulder. "I need a job."

David stands up. "Work is slow around this town. You'd be better off going up near the university." David smiles. "That's where the jobs are—and the hot chicks."

Matt puts one hand in his pocket, eyeing the cash register. "Well, I don't have a ride. That's why I need a job, you know, to pay the bills." Matt eyes the jewelry lying in the case.

David spots him. "You like jewelry?"

Matt smiles. "If I can afford it, but right now I'm completely busted. So how about helping me out with a job?"

David waves for Matt to move in closer. "Check this out. I hate the owner at this place. He's fired me more than once, but since my old lady is his daughter, she makes him hire me back. He claims I've been stealing from him."

"Well, have you?" Matt's curiosity grows.

"Maybe?" David laughs. "But he doesn't have cameras or any type of surveillance, so he doesn't know shit. He just thinks he knows." David looks around the pawn shop to see if anyone else is listening to him. "Let's step outside." Matt follows him. "Here's the deal." David folds his arms. "I get you a job here, and you help me rob the son of a bitch. What do you say?"

Matt is cautious. "Look, I just got out of jail. I ain't trying to go back. That asshole Officer Reyes ain't going to give me a moment's peace in this town, so I'm just looking for a job for a couple of weeks and then I'm out of this town for good."

David's face grows angry. He unfolds his arms and steps up to glare in Matt's face. "You don't go along with this plan, and I won't give you a moment's peace—and you won't have to worry about leaving this town, because you'll come up missing. So again—are you in or out?"

"I'm in," Matt agrees. "Not because you threatened me, but because I want half of everything." Matt gets close to David's face, showing no fear. "Half of the jewelry. Half of the money." He stares David in the eyes. "Everything. You got that?"

David walks away laughing. "Deal. And, by the way—your hired."

Matt quickly turns around. "So, you're the boss?"

"Yes, when that old fart isn't around, I'm the boss—and I just hired you. So put your shit in the back, and let's get to work." Matt follows him. As he's walking in, Deputy Paul's slowly passes the pawn shop staring at him. Matt's not sure how long he's been watching. He politely waves and then walks in behind David.

The pawn shop phones rings. David answers it and then walks to the back. Matt walks around the pawn shop calculating how much money he'd make off the jewelry, TVs, and other items that are worth something. He begins to formulate a plan for how he is going to murder David so he can take his half too.

David hangs up the phone. "That was the old lady. I told her that I hired someone so now her dad can't complain that work isn't getting done and I'd have more time to show her who's boss," David winks, "if you know what I mean."

Matt doesn't turn around; he continues to calculate. "Yeah, man, I know what you mean. Got to keep the ladies satisfied."

David walks over to Matt. "Aye, so you got a lady?"

Matt is silent. "No. Not anymore."

"Oh, drama." David laughs. "Well, I have drama with my woman at times, but all it takes is me going home and laying it on real hard and then she's a happy little baby after I rock that ass to sleep." David gets serious. "Now, enough with small talk. Let's get down to business on how we're gonna pull this job off."

Matt puts his bag down and walks over to David. "So how are we going to do this?"

David rubs his chin. "Well, I got a van out back. That's where most of this stuff will go. I got a friend a few towns over who's willing to buy everything we bring him that's worth something." David continues to plot. "There's a safe in the back that has a lot of cash in it. That old man won't tell me the combination, but I've been watching him, and I think I know what it is now. We're going take every cent from that safe and the cash register." David has a devious look on his face. "We're going to rob this place tonight."

Matt's greed grows. "You did say I'm getting half, right?"

"Sure, man, half. It's you and me doing the job—so, yeah, you get half. But if you try to cross me, you'll get more than your fair share."

Matt's not afraid of David's puny threats. He thinks to himself; I've been up against men far more important than this small-town trash, but I'll let him think he's running something until the moments comes when he realizes he's out of his league.

Matt and David work on cracking the safe open. David tries every combination he can think of, even his girlfriend's birthday, but they are all wrong. He gets frustrated. "Damn it! I thought I had that old man figured out, but he is cleverer than I thought." He hits his hand on the wall. "He must have known I was watching him."

Matt looks at the safe. "What about his wife?"

"Tory's mother died ten years ago. She barely spoke to her."

Matt eyes the safe. "Yeah, but what about her mother's birthday?"

David's eyes grow wide. "Wait." He remembers Tory talking about her mother and how devastated her father had been when she passed away. David tries the safe again. "I don't know when Tory's mother was born," he grins, "but I do know the day she died." He tries the combination on the safe; it unlocks. "Bingo." He opens the door, and coins fall out. There are stacks and stacks of twenty-, ten-, and hundred-dollar bills. David jumps up and down. "Hell, yeah! We hit the jackpot, man. We're rich!" Matt is silent. He lets David enjoy the moment, but he knows all that money will be his before the night is over. David yells, "Grab that bag, man. Let's load it up with all this cash." Matt grabs the bag and helps David load the cash, coins, and jewelry.

Nightfall was all they were waiting on to load the van. David backs the van closer to the pawn shop's back door. He and Matt begin loading up as many items as they can. TVs, camcorders, cameras, DVDs, video games, and everything they thought might be of value. Matt picks up his bag. "Man, I think we got everything." David slaps his hands together. "Hot damn—we did it, man. I'm finally leaving this damn town." David gets emotional while Matt just pretends to care. "I've waited so long to leave this place. It's been hell living in a town where you just can't get nowhere in life. I was a nobody here. No one cared about me." David puts his head down, tearing up. "I thought I'd never see the day when I could leave all of this behind me." David walks up to Matt. "I don't know you, but I'm damn sure grateful you walked in that door."

Matt gives David a blank and uncaring stare. "Me too." He pulls a pocket knife out of his bag, rushes David, and stabs him with it in the stomach.

David turns around to run. "What the hell are you doing?"

Matt chases him down and stabs him again and again until he lies still on the floor. Matt picks up a TV.

David pleads from the floor, "Please, man. Please don't do it." Matt raises the TV high and drops it over David's face. David's body convulses and then is still.

"I guess you're never leaving this town now," Matt utters. He leaves the TV on David's face, grabs his arms, and drags him to the back of the pawn shop. Reaching into David's jean pocket, Matt grabs the keys, his bag, and the bag of money and jewels. "Sucker," he says as he walks out the back door. Matt gets in the van and hits the main highway leading out of the town.

They had forgotten to lock the pawn shop's front door. Deputy Paul's walks in. "Hello?" he yells out. "David?" He walks around the half empty pawn shop, turns around the counter, and see's David dead body lying in the back with the TV covering his face.

Deputy Paul's makes a call on his radio. "This is Deputy Paul's, come in." He repeats himself, yelling, "This is Deputy Paul's, come in!"

The dispatcher responds, "Go ahead, Deputy Paul's."

"Send backup. There's been a murder at Levy's Pawnshop." He looks around. "There's also been a robbery." He looks out back. "Looks like David's van has been stolen as well. Possible suspect—Matt Ross. Send an ambulance and put out an APB to all available officers for a roadblock to all main highways. And contact Officer Reyes immediately."

"Deputy Paul's, Officer Reyes was listening in to this dispatch. He's on his way."

Deputy Paul's squeezes his walkie-talkie's talk button. "Copy that."

Officer Reyes doesn't show up on the crime scene. He is too busy racing down the road attempting to track down Matt Ross.

Matt manages to make it to the main highway. He speeds in the van in his effort to get out of town. A black car with black tinted windows is following him close. He tries to speed up; he floors the van. The black car speeds up behind him and bumps the back of the van. Pulling up next to van, someone slightly lowers car the window.

A woman's hand, wearing a ruby-red ring, signals for Matt to pull over. He doesn't. He tries to run the car off the road by slamming into it. The car swerves off the highway, but it comes roaring back and slams into the van. Matt runs off the highway, but quickly gets back on. The woman's hand reaches back out the window; this time she is holding a gun. She fires two shots at the van's tires, blowing them out, which causes Matt to run off the highway into a utility pole. The front of the van is completely smashed in. Matt head hits the steering wheel, and he's knocked unconscious.

A man opens the driver's door of the car, and a woman gets out of the back. They both step slowly toward the van. Matt is still unconscious, bleeding from the head. The man grabs Matt, his bag, and the bag of money.

The woman checks out the stolen items in the back of the van. "Nice," she says. She closes the van's back doors and walks over to Matt as he's being dragged out of the van. Matt slowly opens his eyes. His vision is blurred. He tries to focus in on the woman. She smiles at him. "Matt Ross," she says.

Matt's vision clears. "Mary?"

Mary grabs his face. "Yes, Mary." The man picks Matt up and carries him to the car. Mary gets on her cell phone. "We got him … and also, send someone out to Route 45. There's a van out here filled with all sorts of goodies. I'm sure it'll make up for some of our losses." She clicks off the cell phone and jumps in the car's backseat.

Matt is barely conscious. He looks over at Mary and tries to speak, "Mary … why?"

Mary looks over at him. "You know why. And in an hour, you'll have to answer to C. A. T. So, go to sleep." Matt completely blacks out. Mary lights up a cigarette as the car spins away.

CHAPTER TWENTY-FIVE

You don't really understand the truth about life until your heart experiences its first emotional breakdown. That's when it all becomes clear to you that night and day can both be the same if your heart is broken down, cold, and left in a forest where even you can't find it. Everything gets confused; the truth becomes the lies, the lies become the truth, and in between is nothing to hold onto except your insane rationalizations as to why you feel so empty inside.

Jena holds Jake tight as she struggles with her inner self. The heart is resilient; it can be broken into many, many pieces and somehow still find its way back to total completeness. But this can happen only if you have the courage to let love in, let love prove itself to be true—so that lies and the truth can be obsolete, canceling themselves out to allow the heart to feel true freedom. Jena presses down hard on Jake's bleeding chest while he lies still in her arms. Tears run down her face onto his, tears frozen in the air like mini snowballs that instantly melt the moment they touched his beautiful, warm skin. She never knew she could love someone so much that even the thought of anything ever happening to them would cause her to feel uncontrollable rage—rage that can only be satisfied by death of the person who brought out the ugly force in her. The force she felt when Mr. McNeil killed her father, and the force brought on by that horrible night when she was brutally raped.

Jena knew she loved Jake very much, but she hadn't been sure that the love she felt for him would be stronger than the hate she felt inside. Jena leans down to kiss Jake. He slowly opens his eyes and smiles at her. I want to give him all of the love I have inside, every ounce of it, she thinks. She reflects back to when Big Papa stabbed Jake and the anger she felt. When the heart feels threatened it bleeds of sorrow, especially when it comes to someone you love. When the one you love hurts, you hurt. If they feel pain, you feel pain. And if someone tries to harm them—you kill them.

Moishe drives as quickly as he can. He pulls up to the house and then rushes around to help Jena carry Jake into the house. Blood drips from Jake's chest. They manage to get Jake safely in the house. Moishe gives him strong medicine to ease the pain, and then he begins to stitch up the bleeding wound. Jena watches as Jake struggles to keep his eyes opened. Moishe carefully finishes stitching up the knife wound. Jena sits quietly on the bed as Jake falls asleep.

Moishe runs to the car to get Jena's bag. He brings it back, and hands it to her. "Here—you may need this."

Jena looks up at him. "Thank you."

He turns around. "I have something else for you." He hands Jena a gun.

"I have a gun."

"Yes, I know, but a person in your circumstances should have at least two." Jena hesitates. She reaches for the gun and puts it her bag. She looks back at Jake. "He will be fine," Moishe comforts her. "I've had many stab wounds, so I know he will survive." Moishe leaves the room, quietly closing the door behind him.

Jena lies next to Jake, lightly rubbing his body, wishing she could take away his pain. She rests her head on his stomach, listening to his breath flowing in and out. She feels at peace knowing that he is healing, feeling no pain. Hopefully when he awakes, he won't remember the other her, the one who fired a shot without regret …

the one who would do it again. She reaches for his hand and places it into hers, and then she drifts off to sleep with her arms draped around Jake.

Jena is back on the plane, but this time there is no one there except her—no pilot, no passengers, and no Mr. McNeil. Where has everyone gone? She thinks. Why do I feel so alone? She walked the plane searching each section for something she has lost, but she can't remember where she's put it. She searches and searches, but she can't it find it. She sits down, exhausted from searching and sad that she is alone and that even her worst nightmare, Mr. McNeil, is gone.

There is a light touch on her hand. She looks over and sees the touch came from a little girl, who is sitting next to her brushing a doll's hair. The girl has long, blonde hair and she's wearing a light dress and no shoes. Jena watches her as she quietly brushes the doll's hair.

"Do you know why little girls cry?" The child asks. Jena doesn't say anything, just continues to stare at her. The little girl stops brushing the doll's hair and looks up at Jena. "Here. Take my doll." Jena reaches for the doll, but before she can take it the little girl snatches it back. "I asked you a question, but you didn't answer me. Why do little girls cry!" she shouts.

Jena is shocked. She doesn't know the answer. "I don't know why, little girl. Maybe someone hurt them." Jena looks away.

The little girl stands up on the plane seat. She starts jumping up and down screaming, "No! No! No! That's not why little girls cry."

"Then why?"

The little girl stops jumping and leans close to Jena's face to whisper in her ear. She has a sad look on her face. "They cry because they don't have a mommy or a daddy." She looks behind her and smiles and starts jumping up and down again. Jumping higher and higher.

Jena watches in amazement. "Stop that!" she yells at the girl. "Stop it! You're going to fall." The girl continues to jump higher and higher. Jena tries to reach her, but she can't. "Stop it! Please! You're going to fall and hurt yourself."

She stops jumping, grabs her doll by the hair, and gets down from the chair, giving Jena a mean look. "So?" She walks away with her head down, and then she turns around. "You want to know why else they cry? They cry because Mr. McNeil is behind them." Jena stands up quickly and turns to find Mr. McNeil sitting behind her, grinning.

Jena wakes up breathing hard. She hears loud talking and rumbling going on in the house.

"Shut up! Where's my money!" C. A. T. yells.

"I don't know," a voice mumbles. She hears a punch and then a grunt.

"What do you mean, you don't know? Maybe this will help you remember." Two more punches back-to-back.

"He says he doesn't know," Mary tries to help Matt. "Besides, here's a bag of money. I mean surely this is enough to make up for what he stole from us."

"Us!" C. A. T. screams. "Us! You mean what he stole from me. You were his lover and obviously mine too." Mary points her gun at C. A. T. The driver, Lance, points his gun at Mary. C. A. T. laughs. "Oh, I see, you guys think you're going to have a shoot-out in my house? Take it outside! And take this asshole to the back room and beat him until he talks."

"What about the van C. A. T.?" Mary says as she slowly puts her gun down.

"The money is mine. The hell with the van. It's probably just a bunch of junk."

Lance puts his gun back. "It wasn't junk. It was a lot of good shit."

"Okay then, Lance, you go get it. Take the van from the back, drive it out there, load up all the good shit, and bring it back."

Lance looks stressed. "What!" he yells. "All by myself? Are you crazy, C. A. T.?"

"Yes, I'm crazy—so get the hell out of here. But first take this loser to the back." C. A. T. turns to Mary. "Mary, you watch him. See what information you can get out of him." He walks up to Mary slowly. "I said watch him, not make love to him."

Mary grabs Matt, who's barely standing. She and Lance drag him to the back room. Jena listens as they pass the bedroom door. Lance and Mary tie Matt to a chair. Lance puts his gun to Matt's face and asks, "So where are the millions?" Matt's face droops down, blood oozing from his nose. Lance cocks the gun.

Mary cocks her gun, pointing it straight at Lance. "Leave him," she demands.

Lance points his gun at her. "What? You feel sorry for him? Look at him. Your lover's useless." He puts his gun away and tries to seduce Mary. "I'm a better lover than him any day."

"Yeah, maybe any day but today. Frankly, not ever. I've seen you in action, and I don't think your drill has enough power."

Lance laughs. "Drill. Power. You're funny. That just goes to show just how much you've been lacking a real man. Why would I need a drill," he laughs, "when I can hammer you all night long?"

Mary gets angry. "Don't you have a van to pick up? A lot of shit to carry? I'm sure that will take you—oh, let me think—the rest of night. So, get lost." Lance walks out of the room.

Matt tries to speak. "Let me go, Mary."

Mary kneels down. "Where's the millions, Matt? Tell me."

Matt is quiet. "I've gained some consciousness. Mary, why don't you just come with me? We can spend the millions."

"Where is the money, Matt?"

"It's hidden in a place where no one will find it—especially if I'm dead. Just untie me. Let's kill C. A. T. and Lance and get the hell out of here. We can have a beautiful life together. Kids. Lots and lots of money."

Mary steps away. "What about getting married?"

Matt pauses. "Married? Why do we have to get married?"

Mary turns to him. "Because I love you, and if you marry me then I'll know you're ready to commit."

Matt gets angry. "Untie me, Mary." He screams, "Untie me!"

Mary pulls her gun on him. "I'll do no such thing until you say you will marry me and until you tell me where the money is."

Matt laughs. "I'm not getting married."

Mary slaps his face. "Then you're not getting untied, and you'll die in this chair." She shoves the gun really hard into his face. "I'll be one to kill you." She leaves Matt tied to the chair, walks to the door, and turns of the lights. The room is dark with only the moonlight shining in.

Matt pleads, "Mary, don't leave me." She opens the door. "Mary, please don't leave me. You know you love me. You won't kill me." Mary closes the door, leaving Matt tied to the chair.

Matt leans his head back to control the bleeding from his nose. He drifts off, coming in and out of consciousness. The door opens. He can hear a woman's high-heeled footsteps walking behind him. He sits with his eyes closed, grins a little, and starts talking. "Mary, we've been together for a long time, and I do love you. You know that. I just wasn't the kind of guy that wanted to get married, but I thought about it, and well … if I were to marry anyone, it would be you. I love you, Mary." A woman's soft hands untie the ropes from his hands and legs. He leans forward. The woman puts a gun on the table, walks to the window, and looks out at the moonlight. Matt stands up and manages to turn on the lamp on the desk. There's a gun in front of him and a woman wearing a red dress standing in front of the window. He stares at her, but he's not sure who she is. "Mary?" Matt picks up the gun. He grips it tightly in his hand. "Mary?"

She walks slowly around the room. "Do you know why little girls cry?" She talks with her back to Matt. Matt is silent. "I asked you a question."

"I don't!" Matt hesitates to answer. Jena cocks her gun. Matt hears it and points his gun at her back.

She slowly turns around. "Little girls cry because they don't have a mommy or a daddy."

"Who are you?" Matt asks, holding the gun firmly. Jena walks slowly toward him with only the moonlight shining slightly off her face. Her shadow moves in closer to Matt. "Don't come any closer, or I'll shoot you." Matt walks backward. He turns on the room light. Jena is pointing her gun at him, and he points his at her. They both circle the room, eyeing each other. "Jena Parker," he utters.

"Matt Ross," she utters. "I've been waiting for you." Jena walks a little closer.

Matt licks his lips. "Yeah."

Jena smiles. "Oh, yeah. I knew when I saw the moon shining bright that this would be the night, I'd kill you."

Matt laughs. "I don't think that's going to happen." He mocks her. "Not tonight. Not ever."

Jena fixates on Matt. "Do you know what it's like to feel hot stones sunk in your belly? To get so angry and frustrated that all of your good emotions shut down and all that's left is a cold shell covered by skin, barely attached, not sharing any particular connection yet occupying space together?" Jena moves closer to Matt. "I feel that same anger and frustration when I look at you."

Matt tries to seduce her. "Jena, you're a beautiful girl. I felt something for you the first time we met out there on the highway. I know you felt it too. You felt the sensation of two heroic individuals with the same common interest—to rebuild our lives, separate from the pain that was forced on us. You want the same things I want. You want to conquer. You want to make them pay for the life you have to live now. I'm sure every one of them deserved to die." Jena stares at Matt. "You and I can run this world that we've created. We can walk it together, side by side. No one would be able to stop us." Matt grins. "Hell, they can't even catch us."

"Do you know why little girls cry, Matt?"

Matt laughs. "Jena, you've already given me the answer—because they don't have a mother or a father."

Her eyes are cold. "No, not always. Because sometimes when they are crying inside, they are really laughing." She shots Matt in the chest. "And that's why you have to die." Jena watches while Matt's body falls limp to the floor. His eyes focus on Jena as he falls. Jena leans down near him. "Do you feel it? That cold feeling that runs through your body when it knows the end is close? Now coldness meets coldness." She smiles. "How ironic is that? But the difference is you're leaving and I'm staying." Matt tries to speak as tears run from his face. She whispers to him, "Now you go. You go and tell them that I'm coming." Jena stands up, stares down at Matt as he lies stiff on the floor.

The room door flies open. Mary stands in the doorway in shock as she witnesses the death of the man she loves. She instantly falls to her knees, crying over Matt. "Matt!" She shakes him, but his body flops with no life. She looks up at Jena in rage and then down at the gun Jena is holding in her hand—the gun that killed her love. She stands up, points her gun at Jena, and screams through her tears, "You bitch!"

CHAPTER TWENTY-SIX

Mary points her gun at Jena, hands shaking, tears running down her face. C. A. T. yells for backup and runs down the hallway into the room. Moishe is behind him.

C. A. T. sees Matt bleeding from the chest and yells out. "What the—"

Mary turns and shoots him in the head. He falls backward into the hallway wall. She starts firing at Moishe. "Stay out of here, Moishe," she yells. She points her gun back at Jena. Jena just stands and stares at her. Mary's need for revenge is far past just firing a gun at the woman who killed the love of her life; she wants too kickass. Mary throws the gun down, steps over Matt's body, and rushes toward Jena. She jumps on Jena, hitting her as hard as she can with her fist. The gun drops out of Jena's hand to floor. Jena punches her in the stomach. They both fight like two boxers in the ring. Jena punches Mary in the face. Mary hits back by punching her in the stomach. Jena grabs ahold of Mary and throws her down to the floor. She punches her several times in the face. Mary tries to hold her off and manages to flip Jena over. She grabs Jena's neck. Mary's face and eyes are red as fire as she chokes Jena. Jena's eyes roll back. Jena thinks back to the night Mr. McNeil shot her father. How she felt when she saw her mother on her knees with her father's blood on her hands, crying in total despair. She thinks back to the night she was raped, her face beaten, and her innocence taken. Her rage grows more and more as Mary grips her neck tightly. Jena manages to lift her hands and place them on Mary's face. She inches her fingers over to Mary's eyes, and she starts scratching Mary's eyes so deeply that blood begins to flow from them. She pushes Mary over, picks her up, and throws her up against the bookshelf. Several books fall, including Franklin's book, Cold Reda Jones. Jena stares down at the book and then drags Mary's exhausted body to the window and throws her out of it.

Mary lies on the ground, unable to move and bleeding from some of the window glass that pierced her skin. Mary's eyes are bleeding, her face and body battered and bruised. She stares up at Jena, still alive but barely conscious. She bats her eyes slowly, staring at Jena, begging through her eyes for her to stop. Jena sits on the windowsill, dress torn, staring at Mary's terrified face. The warm breeze runs through her hair and her red dress. Mary's breathing is shallow. She looks away from Jena's face in shame, sorrow, and pain from the loss of her love, Matt.

Moishe walks up behind Jena holding his gun in his hand. Jena stands up and continues to look down at Mary. The wind blowing with the sudden sense of calmness, Jena stares at Mary. She remembers that somber look of loneliness and hopelessness. It is the same look she saw on her mother's face when her father was killed. Mary lies on the ground like a child who is lost in the forest. Someone who had been abandoned by everyone, even the man she loved. Although he was killed by another, Mary still blamed him for his actions leading her down a road of regrets of ever being in love with him at all. Mary looks up at Jena, who is staring at her with a pitiful look on her face. The two of them lock eyes in the understanding that, although they bare different reasons for the pain caused in their lives, they knew that a life without the loves that kept them sane—Matt and Jake—would be a life of death.

Mary screams out loud as she cries, "Oh, Matt. Matthew, please come back." She digs her fingernails in the dirt and shouts. "Kill me! Kill me! Oh, Matt. He's gone. You took him away. He's gone."

Moishe points his gun at Mary. He can't take anymore of her self-pity, but he hesitates to shoot. Jena grabs Moishe's hand with his finger resting on the trigger, and she forces him to shoot Mary. She removes her hand before he can react to stop it. Moishe gives her a long stare.

Jena stares back at him without fear. "I took her life away. Matt's dead. So now, I just gave it back to her. When a person is that torn inside, the pain just grows until all that is left is a silent person. A person who will never view life the same again. Never speak to her daughter or see a husband smile at her." She walks away, leaving Moishe standing over Mary's body. Moishe watches as she walks away.

Jena walks back to the room. Jake is still sound asleep. She walks to the mirror and looks at her beaten, dirty face and her torn dress, an outward expression of her tortured soul. "Who am I?" she asks out loud. "The more I think I know, the less I understand." She looks at Jake. Questions run through her mind: What do I tell him when he awakes? Do I tell him I've committed more crimes? That I've vindicated our love by defending it? Will he understand, or will he finally see me as that creature in the night—the person I fear when I look in the mirror? She walks over to Jake and sits on the bedside next to him. "Why do you love me so much?" She caresses his wounded chest. "Don't you see me? Don't you see who I am?"

Jake slightly opens his eyes, reaches for her hand, and squeezes it. He looks into her eyes. "Yes. I know who you are, my beautiful Jena," he utters. "You are the woman I love very, very much." He struggles to sit up and then brushes his hand gently on her face and pulls her in closer to him. He whispers, "I'll never leave you." He rubs the back of her head. "Never." He lies back down, smiles at her, and places her hand on his heart. "Do you believe me?"

She tears up. "Yes. I do believe you. Why you do is a mystery to me, but I believe you." She chokes up. Jake shapes his hand like a cup, places it under her face to catch her teardrops, slowly takes the handkerchief out his costume's coat pocket, places her teardrops in it, folds it, and puts it back in his coat pocket. Jena burst in tears.

He rubs her arm. "I'll carry you as long as I can, my sweetheart. My love. I told you there's nothing else but you."

"Jake, everyone …" She wipes her face and continues, "C. A. T.'s dead, and Mary's dead too."

Jake is silent. "Call my brother. Tell him we're coming back to Maplesville, and we need his help." He reaches in his coat jacket, grabs his phone, and hands it to Jena.

Jena dials Jake's house phone. Ted answers. "Ted."

"Jena?"

"Yes, it's me. Can you talk?"

"Yes. Moms at the hospital."

"Jake's been hurt."

"What?"

"He's been stabbed, but he's all right." Ted is quiet. "We need your help. We're coming back to Maplesville, and we need somewhere to hide."

"Ask him about Dad," Jake says in the background.

"Jake wants to know how your father is doing."

Ted laughs. "He's recovered. He's awake."

Jena smiles and turns to Jake. "He's awake." Jake sighs in relief. "That's great news, Ted!"

"When are you guys coming?"

"We're leaving tonight. I will drive." She stops. "I will drive to my house."

Jena, that's dangerous. "I know, but I want to go home. I want to go to my house. See my Mother's and Father's pictures. I need to be home, Ted!" she screams. Jake sits up.

"It's okay," Ted says. "We'll find a way. Just meet me down the street from my house, and I'll take you to your house."

Jena starts crying. "I don't know, Ted."

"It's okay. Drive safely. Get my brother back home. I can't wait to see you two."

"Me too, Ted. Good-bye."

"Good-bye."

Jena hands Jake the phone. "I'll get washed up, and then we'll go." She kisses Jake on the forehead. "I …"

Jake listens with an eager look on his. Please say it, Jena, he thinks.

"I'll be back soon to pack up everything."

I know she will say it, he thinks. I know she feels the deep, unbreakable connection between us. I don't need her to say she loves me because I know she does. Jake grunts as he tries to sit up in the bed. The room door opens. Moishe is standing in the doorway with his gun in his hand. "Get out!" Jake shouts.

Moishe puts his gun away. "I'm not here to hurt you or her." He walks closer. "I'm here to help." He reaches to help Jake up. "What do you need me to do?"

"We need to get to Maplesville." Jake looks at the bathroom door. "Jena is in no condition to drive, and I'm not either. Can you drive us?"

"Yes. I will. First, let me help you get to the car. Then I will come back to help Jena pack. We'll pack everything we can take from this house—including the money that's in the living room."

"Money?"

"Yes, a bagful that Matt Ross brought."

"Matt Ross is here?"

"He was, but now he's dead."

Jake is confused. "Dead? How?"

"Jena killed him. She killed him, she and Mary fought, Mary killed C. A. T., and—well, I guess you can say I killed Mary." Moishe puts his arms around Jake's waist. "No need to be sad or upset. They were all crooks. Con men who robbed, cheated, and killed people. Many of them." He walks slowly with Jake. "So have

I." Moishe opens Ted's car door and eases Jake onto the backseat. He starts to close the car door, but Jake stops him, giving Moishe a look. "Don't worry—I won't hurt her. She's a lot like me. She doesn't want to do it, but something inside of her can't stop. We are simple people, kind in unimaginable ways," Moishe thinks back to Jena and him standing together over Mary's body. "But if we are pushed, whoever is doing the pushing will see a side of us that no men or women will ever recover from. Matt saw it tonight. Mary saw it too." Moishe looks down before closing the car door. "There will be many more who will see it." He smiles at Jake. "It is good she has you to bring balance into her life. I once had my balance, but they killed her." He closes the car door and walks back into the house.

Jena is just coming out of the shower. She panics when she sees that Jake is gone. "Jake!" she yells.

Moishe walks into the room. "It's okay. He's in the car waiting for us."

"For us?"

"Yes, us. He asked me to drive you to Maplesville, and I said yes."

"Why?"

"Because I believe that you have a destiny to fulfill." Moishe grabs Jake's and Jena's bags. "I'll take these out and come back for more things, including the money, which we will need." Moishe steps to the room doorway then stops. "I think you still have a chance to change …" his voice turns melancholy, "unlike me. I will go on this journey with you … because I may see that miracle that I wished so much would have happened for me and my Maria." His eyes tear up. "I see my Maria in you." He walks out of the room.

CHAPTER TWENTY-SEVEN

Moishe remains quiet for the first half of the drive. Jena is in the front seat, while Jake is lying down in the back. Jake wakes in severe pain. Jena can hear him moaning. She looks back. "Are you okay?" Jake doesn't speak. He moans again. "He's in pain. Did you bring anything?" Jena asks Moishe.

"Check the bag on the floor. I'm sure I put some medicine in it." Jena reaches in the bag. She flashes back to the doctor's medicine bag on the train. Moishe catches her drifting off. "It's on the side." Jena reaches in on the side of the bag, pulls out the pain pills, and hands one to Jake. Jake takes it and instantly falls back to sleep.

"He fell asleep quick. Was that medicine safe?"

"Yes. It is strong medicine, but it will not kill him. He will not feel any pain for quite a while." It's dark out. Moishe drives with caution. "You love him, don't you?" he asks.

Jena pauses. "Yes, I do. I love him very much, but I haven't told him."

"What are you waiting for?"

"I don't know. Every time I try, I just can't get the words out. It' like I feel like I don't deserve him … or his love."

"Don't you think that he should be the one to make that determination? You can't stop someone from loving you, no matter how much you wish they didn't."

"Where are you from, Moishe?"

"I'm from a place far away from here."

"Where?"

"A small village in a poor country."

"So, you don't want to tell me."

Moishe pause. "I don't tell people a lot about myself."

"Why are you helping us?"

"I told you, I want to see you change. I believe you can. Do you believe you can?"

"I don't know. There are times when I think this is all over— that Jake and I can live a normal life. But then tonight I realized that I'm never going to have a normal life. Now that this angry beast within me has been let out, I can't seem to find a way to stop it. He shouldn't be dragged down with me. He is too wonderful, kind … he's the only person in the world I'd die for."

Moishe opens up. "Her name was Maria … Maria Flotino, and I loved her very much." Jena listens. "She lived in an orphanage, just like me." Moishe flashes back to his life. "Her father beat her mother almost every day, and where we were from no one cared. Men were allowed to beat their wives. She watched her mother cry from the bruises her father left. Her body black and blue, face swollen, eyes bloody. Her mother had an emotional breakdown. Maria was fifteen. She came home from school and saw her father lying on the floor, facedown with a knife in his back. Her mother was in her room crying … afraid that they would take Maria away from her, and she'd be killed. Maria helped her mother hide the body. But as the day's past, people started to notice that her father was missing. Soon the police came and took her mother away, and that's when Maria was placed in an orphan home. I was already there. My mother had abandoned me when I was baby. I was sixteen when Maria arrived. I remember the first time I saw her. She looked afraid and alone. I love her the moment I saw her. Her beautiful smile. The way she moved, the smell of lavender in her hair. She didn't know the hidden secrets of the orphanage." Moishe voice hardens. "She didn't know that she had come from one hell to another. Girls were being raped … so were the boys. They barely fed us. Some of us didn't take baths for days, and the water was contaminated with dirt and filth. She and I would meet and pray together. Pray that we'd find a way out of that place—a way to be together. One night we saw an opportunity to escape, and we did. We both ran as fast as we could, but we didn't get far before a tall man caught us. He threatened to take us back, but he said he wouldn't if we'd come freely with him. We both agreed and went with him. He was the leader of an assassin unit. They train both me and Maria—gave us weapons, taught us how to defend ourselves."

He looked over at Jena. "They taught us how to be killers. Maria and I would be given assignments. We'd find ways to see each other … make love. Then she was given an assignment that she didn't want. The assignment was to kill her mother. Her mother had been released from jail, and over the years she'd become an activist against the government. Maria was being sent to kill her. I begged Romli to give me the assignment. He refused, said Maria had no family and it was her duty to kill her mother. Maria left, but she couldn't do it. Romli sent out another assassin to kill her and her mother—he sent me. He told me if I didn't do it, that he would kill all three of us. He sent another assassin with me just so he could witness that I'd done it. We tracked them both down, but I couldn't kill her or her mother. I knew that before I'd even left. I'd just agreed to take the job because I knew he'd find someone else to do it, and I wanted so badly to see Maria. Maria had escaped the town with her mother. With her skills, she managed to hide them both out in the jungle. I could not find them, but Romli had tricked us. He sent out more than one assassin with me. He sent many out to find her. By the time I found her, Maria and her mother had both been executed. Romli wanted me to find them. He wanted me to feel unbearable pain. I held her in my arms for hours, hoping that she'd awaken and just hold me one last time. Kiss me, touch my body, and make love to me one last time. I buried her out in the jungle while the other assassin hid and watched me, waiting to make his move to kill me. But I killed him. I was Romli's best man. He had taught me skills that he'd hidden from the other trainees. He taught me how to smell the scent of all of the other assassins. I trained like a dog. He told me he wanted at least one person to know this trade. He trusted me. It was his trust that saved my life and allowed me to track the other person down. I hung him from a tree so Romli and his men would find him easily. Then I escaped to here, to this town where no one knew me. C. A. T. offered me job. It was safe, and I never told him my true past."

Jena reminds silent. Moishe continued, "So you see, I understand the life you lead now, when circumstances lead you down the path of uncertainty. You and I both were calm and peaceful people until the darkness found us, and now we are trapped and trying to find a way back to that calm and peaceful place we once knew. For me, my life has been one hell after another—but finding Maria was my peace. It was my chance to live and love. Now she is gone forever, and I'm just a shell waiting for the sun to go down."

Jena feels sorrow for Moishe. "How many people have you killed?" she cautiously asks.

"I've killed hundreds. I've been on assignment since I was eighteen years old. I'm now fifty-five. I've killed many people—some who deserved it, and some who have not. Now tell me about you. How many people have you killed?"

"I've killed at least six, counting Mary and Matt."

"You didn't really kill Mary."

"I helped pull the trigger, so I killed her."

"You mentioned seeing the way she was. What did you mean?"

"I just knew that she wasn't ever going to be the same again. That's what happens when someone you love dies." Moishe doesn't push. "I know you want to ask me who I loved who died? Don't you?"

"I'm not that kind of person. I don't ask questions that don't want to be answered. If you want to tell me, then you can. If you don't, then you don't have too. I'm not here to judge you. I'm here because I want to be—because I can see the extension of me and Maria in you and Jake. You two still have the opportunity to see your horizon together."

"I hope so."

Moishe pulls into a gas station. "I need to get gas before we all are walking." He leaves his wallet in the car. Jena picks it up, opens it, and looks at his license. It doesn't say Moishe; it says Rick Patrick. Jena looked around in Moishe's wallet. She finds a card that has Officer Reyes's name and phone number on it. Jena looks back at Moishe as he pumps the gas. Is he lying? Who is Moishe? And who is Rick Patrick? She smiles at Moishe. Why is Moishe in contact with Officer Reyes? Moishe gets back into the car and drives back on the road.

Jena is suspicious. "Who are you?"

"What do you mean?"

She yells, "Who are you, and who is Rick Patrick?"

Moishe speeds up. "Why were you snooping in my wallet?"

"Because that's what I wanted to do. How do you know Officer Reyes?"

"You ask too many questions."

"Really? You sat here and spoon-fed me this unbelievably sad story about you and Maria, and now I find out that your name isn't Moishe, that you're someone named Rick Patrick."

Moishe drives faster. "Jena, you have to trust me. If you don't trust me, then I can't help you."

"Why should I trust you when you can't even tell me the truth."

"I told you the truth, but there are many truths. There is the truth that you want to hear, and the one that you don't."

"What is that supposed to mean?" Jena is angry.

"It means that I knew who you were when I first met you. It means that I was working with the police. But after I saw the love between you and Jake, I couldn't turn you in—not even with their threat of sending me back to my country. They found out who I am. I've been spying on C. A. T. in exchange for the police keeping their silence, but I don't care anymore. There's nothing left of me."

The cell phone rings. It's Ted. "Where are you?"

"We're close," Jena tells him.

"How close?"

"We are about twenty minutes from Maplesville."

"Okay. Meet me at the garage near my house."

"All right." Jena clicks off the cell phone and turns back to Moishe. "I'm sorry for not trusting you."

"I could have captured or killed you and Jake when I drove you to the party, but I looked at you two in the backseat—the way you looked at each other, the way Jake loves you—and I saw my Maria. I saw the beauty of love, passion, and the length that a man and a woman would go through to be with one other. I cannot bring Maria back, but I can help save you from self-destruction. Help you to understand and control the anger that rises when you are tested beyond your means. If I can somehow save the love between you and Jake, then when I leave to see my Maria we too will bask in the passion and glory of love."

Jena feels hopeful for the first time. "I want so much to put the past behind me. To give the man I love children. To feel his touch without fear bearing over my shoulders."

Moishe reaches for Jena's hand. "You can … and I will help you."

And like the calm right before a storm, they both feel like they're reaching the top of the mountain after a tough climb—that maybe there can be a light at the end of the tunnel. Moishe rolls down his window. The wind blows as he drives, while he and Jena talk and laugh along the way. Jena turns to look at Jake, the wind blowing through her hair. She reaches to touch him and smiles at him as he sleeps quietly and peacefully in the backseat.

CHAPTER TWENTY-EIGHT

Jena has her head down, reading a book.

"Is your name Jena Parker?"

She slowly looks up. "Yes," she says shyly.

He holds his hand out. "My name is Rick Johnson." Jena squints, trying to place the name. "We went to Maple High School together."

She nods her head. "Oh, okay." She starts reading again.

Rick sits down. Her eyes zoom up from the book. "I knew you didn't remember me." He laughs. "You may not remember me, because I was somewhat of a nerd—a loner. That's why you probably didn't see me when you came into the library." He grins. "I was in the back ... kind of hiding ... out of sight, you know." He looks at Jena's book. "Already studying, and it's just our first day of college." Jena is quiet; she's not sure how to react to Rick's friendliness. Rick feels her uneasiness. He stands up. "Well, I'll let you get back to what you were doing." Jena stares off at the library doorway. She sees a boy standing in the shadow of the door, wearing a hoodie. Rick turns around. "Something wrong?" Rick appears to be concerned. Jena stares at the library doorway, blinks, and the boy is gone. She stands up with fear in her eyes. Rick grabs her arm. "Do you need help?"

"No, I just thought I saw someone staring at me, but I'm tired so I'm sure I was just seeing things." Jena sits down.

Rick shrugs his shoulders, smiles, and walks off. "I'll see you around."

The librarian taps her on the shoulder …

She suddenly tunes back into Moishe as he talks about his life and Maria. Moishe notices the look of concern on Jena's face. "What's going on? Why do you look afraid?"

"I had flash of a memory that I'd forgotten." Jena pauses. "Someone I didn't even remember speaking to, but there he was … I guess I blocked it or something."

Moishe thinks hard, What is Jena hiding?

Jena leans back in her seat. The laughter and great moment she was sharing with Moishe instantly fades away. She is left in a state of solitude. Sometimes you try to run, but you can't move; sometimes you try to speak, but the words just won't come out; and sometimes you try to forget the painful truth, but it finds you no matter how hard you try to bury it with love and laughter. It won't let me forget, and now it's coming back to make me face it, to make me swallow its spoiled food, dirt, and filthy water.

"We're almost there." Moishe tries to bring her back.

"Okay. Thanks." Jena spots the garage. "Turn here. Park. I'm sure Ted will be here shortly."

Moishe parks the car in the garage. They both sit quietly waiting for Ted. Moishe finally says, "Something is bothering you, Jena. What is it? We all have a past. I've told you mine. I hope you know that you can trust me to tell me yours. I've seen it all, Jena, so there's nothing you can tell me that will frighten or surprise me."

Jena breaks her silence. "I was …" Moishe listens closely. "I was …" She begins to cry.

Ted knocks on the driver's window. Moishe rolls down the window. "Hello, my name is Ted." Ted shakes Moishe's hand. "Jena, are you all right?"

"Yes, Ted, I'm fine."

Ted opens the back door. He shakes Jake. "Hey there."

Jake slowly opens his eyes. He's happy to see Ted. "What's up, man?"

Ted helps sit Jake up. "Oh, man, it's good to see your ugly face." They both laugh.

"Yeah, I bet. It looks like you had a rough night."

Ted looks around the car. "It looks like you had a rough night. Ken called the house. He's worried about you guys. He told me about Carol and Chance—wow, can you believe that she'd do something so horrible?"

Jena looks away. "I can believe it," she answers abruptly. "Ted, I want to go to my house." She turns around. "So, what's the plan?"

"Well, I borrowed a friend of mine's car." He points. "It's parked right over there. I figure I'd drive you guys down the street, get close enough so you can walk, and hopefully none of us will get caught."

Jena gets out of the car. "Ted, no one's looking for you." Ted and Moishe help Jake walk to Ted's friend's car.

Jena stops Moishe from getting into the car. "Moishe, you don't have to come. I truly appreciate all of the help you've given us, but I don't want to drag you any further into this dreadful situation."

"You're not dragging me into anything. I want to be here, so let me." Moishe opens the back door for her. Jena sits next to Jake in the backseat.

He holds her hand. "I've been out for long time, huh?"

"Yeah, but I'm glad you're doing better."

He kisses her hand. "Me too."

Moishe hops in the front seat. Ted puts the car in reverse, backs out, and drives toward Jena's house.

Jake is cautious. "Are you sure you want to do this?"

"Yes, I'm sure, Jake. I want to go back. I believe this will help me face my fears—what I've been hiding from. I can't run anymore. The time has come for me to start from the beginning. I know this is the only way. Please trust me."

"I do, Jena." Jake kisses her hand. Ted peeks at them through the rearview mirror. His eyes blaze with curiosity of the love Jake and Jena share. Jake catches him. "You like to watch?" He laughs at Ted.

Ted is embarrassed. "No. I just think you two are very lucky to have each other."

"Thanks, bro. I'm sure one day you'll find someone you love just as much as I love Jena." Ted stares at Jena. She stares back at him.

Something strange about him today, she thinks. Maybe he's just lonely, worried about his mother and father.

Jake is happy. Ted stares back at Jake in the rearview mirror. Moishe watches as his eyes move back and forth. He makes conversation with Ted. "You are a strange one, huh?"

"No. I'm just quiet. I don't have many friends, except for my brother and one or two more." Ted drives slowly through Jena's neighborhood. The streets are empty, quiet, and dark. He stops the car. Jena gets out.

"Wait," Jake yells.

"Why?" She closes the door and walks around to his side. "Can you walk on your own?"

"Yes."

She reaches for his hand and peeks into Ted's window. "Ted, take Moishe to your house to eat and get cleaned up, and then bring him back." Ted nods his head.

Moishe holds his hands out and looks at them. "I guess I could use some cleaning up." He wipes the dirt from his hand onto his pants. He touches Jena's hand, waves to Jake, and then they drive away.

The car is quiet. Ted feels uncomfortable being with Moishe, but he trusts that Jena and Jake wouldn't allow him to be with a maniac. He makes conversation. "So, you helped my brother and Jena?"

"Yes."

"That's great, man. I really love my brother and, well, Jena's always been like a sister to us." Well, that is until my brother fell in love with her, so now I guess they are an item, Ted thinks to himself.

Moishe spies him from the corner of his eye. "Jena is a beautiful girl," Moishe says. "I could see anyone finding her attractive—would do anything for her."

Ted smiles. "Yes, she is. I once had a crush on her myself, but she never really found any interest in me. My brother seems to get all the girls."

"Does that bother you?" Moishe looks at Ted.

Ted shakes his head, playing it off. "No, of course not. I'm not jealous of my brother. He can't help being better looking than me."

Moishe is suspicious of Ted. "So, do you have a girlfriend? Someone you love?"

Ted flashes back to a girl standing out in the school yard. Her face is blurred out. She waves, and he waves back at her. "Yes, there was a time when I loved this girl so very much that I'd do anything to get her to notice me. When we were kids, I used to stare at her all the time. She caught me a few times, but I pretended I was looking at something else." He smiles to himself thinking of her. "I wish I could have been more to her, but I guess she didn't see in me what I saw in her."

Moishe listens. "Hmm … why didn't you tell her you loved her?"

Ted thinks, starts driving faster, and a mean look comes over his face. "I didn't tell her because it wouldn't have mattered anyway. I wasn't the popular guy. I wasn't a jock. I didn't know how to speak to girls." He raises his voice at Moishe, "Could we talk about something else? I mean, I barely know you—and I hardly want to expose my love life to a complete stranger." Ted pulls into his driveway, gets out the car, and leans in Moishe's window. "My mom's not home, so we should be able to get in and out without any problems. You're welcome to use our bathroom, and there's plenty of food in the fridge." Moishe gets out of the car. Ted walks up to him. "Look, I wasn't trying to be rude. My dad is in the hospital. My mom's been worried. Jake has been stabbed. So, I hope you understand I'm a little on edge."

Moishe just stares at Ted. He looks him in the eye. He can see the lies, feel Ted's uneasiness. He's hiding something. "Sure," Moishe says and starts walking. "Just take me inside and show me where things are."

Ted opens the house's front door. Moishe walks inside, checking out the house. Ted points to the bathroom. "There are some clean towels in there." Moishe walks into the bathroom without saying anything to Ted. Ted flops down on the living room couch. He leans over, rips his fingers through his hair, and stomps the floor. "Why was he asking so many questions? Who the hell does he think he is?" Ted talks to himself. "Let him ask me one more thing. I'll show him." He stands up and walks quickly back and forth around the room. "Piece of shit, question asking." He looks back at the bathroom door, continuing to pace back and forth and talk to himself. "It's none of his business." He goes into the kitchen, opens a drawer, and grabs a knife. "I'll stab him. He better not ask me anymore question, or I'll really stab him." He grips the knife tightly in his hand, walks toward the bathroom door, and puts his hand on the doorknob. There's a knock at the front door. He looks back, walks toward the door, and quickly places the knife underneath the couch pillow before opening it. He tries to turn on the porch light, but it won't work. He opens the door. There's a girl with a red jacket with the hood thrown over her head standing in the doorway. Ted tries to close the door quickly, but she pulls a gun on him.

CHAPTER TWENTY-NINE

Both of them stand in the doorway in the dark. The girl moves farther through the doorway. Her face is revealed: it's Chance. She holds the gun on Ted. He's frightened and starts to shake.

"What the hell are you doing, Chance?" She sticks the gun closer to his face. "What do you want?" Ted asks.

"I want you to come with me."

"What? Come with you where?"

Chance starts to slowly back up with the gun in one hand, pulling on Ted with the other. "To my car." She backs Ted all the way out the door into the dark driveway. Her car is parked behind his. "Now, turn around," she demands.

Ted pleads. "Come on, Chance. You don't want to do this."

"I said turn around." Ted slowly turns around. His face is sweating. "Now start walking to my car." Ted moves slow. Chance pushes him. "I said start walking, not crawling like a turtle."

Ted breathes hard. "Okay. Okay. Chance, please don't kill me like you killed Carol."

She screams, "Shut up and walk." She stops Ted when they reach the back of the car and hands him her keys. "Open the trunk!" She dangles the keys in front of Ted. "Take it! Open the trunk!" Ted grabs the keys and wiggles the first one in the trunk keyhole. His hands are sweaty and shaky. The keys drop to the ground. "Pick them up!" She points the gun down at him. Ted quickly picks up the car keys. He manages to open the trunk of the car. There's a still body lying in the trunk with a sheet over the head. The hands and feet are tied.

Ted starts crying. "Who the hell is this? Chance, please. Please. Don't do it!" Ted turns around. Tears of fear run down one cheek. "I'll do anything, but please don't kill me." He looks back down at the body and then turns back to plead with her. "What did I do to you? Huh? I've always been a good friend to you."

Chance pulls down the hood of her jacket from her head. "Shut up, turn around, and remove the sheet from the head of that body."

Ted stands with his hands in the air. He shakes with the rumbling thunder of Chance's voice. "I don't want to see. Please."

Chance rushes closer to him. "I said do it!" Ted carefully takes the sheet off the body in the trunk. It's dark, and he can't see the face. The person still isn't moving. Chance keeps the gun on Ted as she moves over to the end of the trunk. She shakes the person's feet. "Wake up, sleepy head." A male voice tries to talk through the mouth tie.

Ted moves in closer to the body. He leans down. "Ken? Man, is that you?" Ken tries to talk and wiggle out of the rope. Ted turns around. "Chance, why is Ken in the trunk of your car?"

Chance points the gun while she walks closer to Ted to make him back up a little. She reaches for the mouth tie, talking to Ken, "I'm going to take this tie off your mouth, and if you scream or so much as say one single word, I'll shoot you and I'll shoot Ted." Ken's eyes grow big. Even in the dark his eyes glow from fear. Chance removes the tie. Ken remains quiet. She grabs Ted by his shirt. "You want to know why he's in my trunk?" Ted nods his head. "He's in my trunk because I put him there and because he cheated on me in high school, he's a jerk, he's womanizer ..." She points the gun at

Ted. "Do you want me to go on?" Ted shakes his head and hands to signal no. "Okay then." She puts the tie back on Ken's mouth.

Ken tussles, trying to stop her from putting it back on. He quickly speaks, "Chance, no—please. Ted, help me. Help me, man. She's crazy."

Chance smacks Ken with her hand. "Shut up! Shut! Up!" She puts the tie back on, closes the trunk down, and then roughs Ted up some more. "You bring Jena and Jake to me, or I'll kill Ken and I'll track you down and kill you too." Ted is silent with fear. "Are you clear on what I am saying to you?"

Ted can barely speak. "Yes, I'm clear."

"Good. That's a good boy." She hands Ted a small piece of paper. "Take this and put it in your pocket." Ted snatches the paper, quickly putting it in his pocket. "On that paper is my cell phone number. You call me in an hour, and I'll let you know what to do next." Ted nods. "In the meantime, you get Jena and Jake. I don't care how you do it, but you get them and bring them to me." Chance puts her hood back on. "Don't make me look for you." She gets into the car and spins off.

Ted stares at the car as it spins off. He runs into the house, slamming the door behind him. "Oh shit. Oh shit," He mumbles walking around the room. "Oh shit. Oh shit. She's crazy. Chance has gone completely crazy." He picks up the house phone to dial his cell to warn Jake. The cell phone rings with no answer. His voice mail comes on, and he leaves a quick message. "Jake, Chance was here." His voice sounds scared. "She had a gun on me. She's got Ken tied up in the back of her trunk, man." He pauses. "She's gone crazy. Look, she wants me to bring you and Jena to her. She said if I don't, she'll kill Ken and find me and kill me! Call me back, man. I don't know what to do. We've got to find this maniac to rescue Ken. Man, he's lying in the trunk all tied up." He tries to calm himself. "Call me … Call me." He hangs up the phone. Pacing around the room, he looks for a weapon to use. He stops in front of the couch and remembers the knife he'd stuffed under the pillow. He grabs the knife just as Moishe opens the bathroom door.

Moishe pulls out his gun. "What are planning on doing with that?" Moishe walks slowly toward Ted, pointing his gun like an expert shooter.

Ted holds the knife loosely in his hand. "Umm …" He's in shock and doesn't know what to say. "Wait. You have no idea what just happened to me."

Moishe aims at him like a sniper ready to hit his target. "Really? What happened?"

Ted tries to explain, "Chance was here. She had a gun." Ted sits down on the couch. "She has Ken tied up in her car's trunk."

Moishe keeps the gun aimed, not sure if he should trust Ted. "Yeah, go on."

"She wants me to bring Jena and Jake to a location."

"What location?"

"She just gave me her cell number and told me to call her, and she'd tell me."

Moishe reaches out his hand. "Give me the number." Ted just stares at him. "You heard me. Give me the number." Ted reaches in his pocket, pulls out the crumpled piece of paper, and gets up to hand it to Moishe. Moishe opens the paper. "There's no number here. It's just letters." Moishe thinks back to his espionage days. "Ah, I see. She used letters instead of numbers." Moishe stares at the knife in Ted's hand. "And just what were you going to do with that?"

Ted looks at the knife, remembering it was originally to deal with Moishe. He lies. "I … I picked it up to take with me." He walks around the room. "I needed something to fight against Chance."

Moishe raises his chin. He doesn't believe Ted. "She had a gun?"

Ted stops, looks around the room being careful with his answer. "Yes, she did."

Umm, Moishe thinks. "So, you were going to take her out with a knife? While she has a gun."

Ted's eyes move quickly. He turns around. "Yeah. I don't have anything else."

Moishe eases his gun down, though he still doesn't trust Ted. "Well, I do, and we are going to go find her, rescue Ken, and I'll deal with Chance."

Ted grips the knife. "She said to bring Jena and Jake. If we go without them, she'll kill Ken, me, and you."

Moishe laughs. "She'll probably kill you, but she won't kill me. Now let's get out of here." Ted doesn't move. Moishe walks up to him. "What's wrong? Are you afraid?"

Ted just stands there. "I'm not afraid … I've just never been in this kind of situation."

"Really? You've never done anything you wish you hadn't?" Moishe stares Ted square in the eyes.

"What are you trying to say?"

"I'm not trying to say anything. I'm telling you. You've got a dark side. I can see it in your eyes. You can't hide it from me. I've seen too many men—or in your case, boys—who try to hide their monsters, but you can't hide a monster from a monster." Moishe walks to the door and opens it. "Let's go." He stands in the doorway. "I will deal with Chance." He stands with his back facing Ted and slightly turns around. "And then later, I will deal with you." Ted is angry. He rushes toward Moishe. Moishe quickly turns around, leans down, and has the gun pointed at Ted's stomach. Ted stands up, knife in one hand, with both hands in the air. "Don't push me. You don't have my skills."

Ted stands humiliated with his hands in the air. "You think you know me, but you don't."

Moishe leans up. "Oh, but I do—and there's a time and a place for everything. This isn't the time," he looks around the house, "or the place. If you are not who I think you are, then we will not have any more problems. But if you are …" Moishe walks out of the house without finishing his sentence, leaving Ted to ponder what his words would have been.

Ted doesn't want to push Moishe. He follows him out the door and gets in the car. Moishe sits in the backseat. Ted gets in the car and gives him a strange look. "Why are you sitting in the backseat?"

Moishe crosses his legs, one over the other. "Simply because I don't trust you."

Ted gets in the car, adjusting his rearview mirror so he can keep an eye on Moishe. "I have to say I'm uncomfortable with you sitting in the backseat."

"You should be. Now call the number."

"You have the paper." Moishe hands Ted the paper. He dials the letters. The phone rings.

Chance answers and speaks before Ted can say a word. "Meet at the old mill. Park, and I'll find you." She hangs up the phone.

"What did she say?"

"She said to meet her at the old mill, that she'd find me there."

"Okay then, let's go. As we get closer, I will get out, and then we will handle this situation so we may get back to Jake and Jena."

Ted doesn't reply. He drives until he gets to a dirt road littered with scattered rocks and tree branches. He stops, sighs. "How am I going to drive over this mess?"

Moishe opens the car door and gets out. He peeks in Ted's window. "I don't know but do it. I'll get out here." He taps on the back door to get Ted's attention. "Keep your eyes and ears open." Moishe disappears in the grass alongside the road. Ted continues to drive slowly and cautiously down the road.

CHAPTER THIRTY

Chance is standing in front of Ken. He's tied to a chair. She removes his mouth tie and laughs at him. "It's kind of funny seeing you tied to that chair, begging for your life. I wish I had a mirror right now to let you see your face as you beg, cry, and plead. You'd probably laugh at your own self."

Ken's face is red. "Untie me, Chance. Let me go."

"No. That is definitely something I'm not going to do. So, ask me to do something else."

"Like what?"

"Oh, I don't know—maybe ask me to take off my clothes."

Ken turns his face away. "Why would I want to see you naked?"

She grabs Ken's face really hard. "Because that's the kind of person you are. That's what you wanted from me before, so why not ask for it now?" Ken avoids looking in her eyes. "Look at me." She tries to force his face to look at her with her hands. She screams, "I said look at me! Look at my beauty. Ah—you see it now, don't you? My beautiful face, my eyes," she stands up and rubs her hand over her body, "my body. You like that, don't you?" She continues to caress her body all over.

Ken is angry, but he's also aroused. "I'm sorry I hurt you."

Chance takes off her shirt. "Are you?" She takes off her bra and starts to slowly caress her breasts, playing with herself. Ken tries to look away, but he can't. She slides down her pants, sits on his lap, and starts kissing him. He tries to resist, but he can't. "Oh, the passion between us. We had so much sex." She bites Ken's ear. He squirms. "Oh, why squirm? You used to like it when I'd bite you." She squeezes his balls. "Yeah—now that's a man's balls." She looks down at Ken. "You've got big balls, don't you?" She squeezes them really hard.

Ken yells. "Stop it!"

"Oh, am I hurting you?" She toys with him.

He squints his eyes. "You're crazy, Chance. You need help."

Chance stands up and slaps him. "I need help! Who are you to tell me that I need help? What I need is to kill you! That's my help." Ken's just stares at her with a crazed look. She gets back on his lap and starts playing with his hair. Ken feels helpless and trapped in her insane world. "Do you remember the first time you asked me out? We were in the ninth grade, and I was quite surprised because I really didn't think you liked me." She nibbles on his ear, smiles. "Even back then I thought you liked Carol. You always flirted with her and never paid me much attention, so I was quite shocked when you chose me." She sits back to look at Ken. "Why did you choose me?" She ponders her thought. "Well, Carol was somewhat of a slut back then—easy breezy—and I was the shy girl. The virgin. That's why you chose me, right? Because Carol was easy. She wasn't a challenge. Heck you could have gotten her anytime, so you prayed on me. You wanted to take away my control. Make me one of your stories you tell when you get around your friends—laugh about how you had me over and over again. In all those different positions. How I moaned and screamed as you took my virginity. Ruined me. Ripped my insides out, and then turned me into your slave. That was your whole, entire plan. To strip me down until I'm bare minded, simple, until I only function enough for you to play with my emotions without me even knowing it." She gets up and starts redressing. "All the while, you were screwing my best friend. The other girls at school, laughing while I was crying floods and floods of tears. Worthless tears over you ... You," she shouts out loud, "you're nothing. Look at you, sitting all tied up by a little bitty girl. Somehow, now you look small to me." She picks up the gun from the floor, holds it loosely in her hand, plays with it, looks at it. "It's not because of this gun that I feel power." She looks at Ken sitting in the chair trying to hold back his feelings of fear, regret, and pain. "It's not the gun. It's me. I feel powerful because of me. I took back the power you stole from me. I took it back from you, and now I have it. Now I have your power too. Now you know how it feels to have someone break you down." She looks over. Ken has his head down. "How does it feel?"

He raises his head up. "I feel like shit, Chance. I'm sorry I hurt you. I'm sorry that I'm a user, but you didn't ..." He starts to sob. "You didn't have to kill her ... You could have ..." He stops.

"I could have what!"

"You could have been free of me without killing her. Now she's dead."

Chance gets angry. "Wow!" She waves the gun around. "Wow! Wow! Wow! You're tied up in a chair, about the be killed, and you are worried about a girl who's already dead. And you call me insane. Wow!"

"Chance," Ken calls out her name.

She stops him. "Just shut up! Don't speak anymore! I don't want to hear anything else you have to say! You're weak, powerless—so shut up." She hears the mill door open. "Shush, be quiet. I hear something." She yells out, "Who's there?"

Ted comes walking out. "It's me. Ted."

Ken starts moving around in the chair, yelling, "Help me, man! Get me out of this damn chair!"

Chance points the gun back and forth between Ken and Ted. "Shut up!" she yells at Ken. Pointing the gun at Ted, she tells him, "Pick up that tie, and put it back on his mouth."

Ken panics, pleading as Ted walks over to do what she said, "Please, man, don't. Just grab her ... wrestle her down ... get the gun ... do something!"

"Man, I'm sorry," he tells Ken as he ties his mouth.

"Where's Jena? Jake? I told you that I wanted them here."

Ted holds up his hands. "I couldn't get ahold of them."

"Liar!" Chance screams. Ken starts moving around in his chair.

"Chance, I left a message. Jake has my cell, but we took them Jena's mother's."

"Her mother's? Why? That house is abandoned."

"I know, but that's where she wanted to go." Ted tries to talk his way out of being killed. "I'm sure he'll call me as soon as he checks the message, and when he does, I'll tell him to meet here."

Chance eyes him. "Yeah, I know you will." She shoots down at Ted's feet. Ken jumps up and down in his chair. Ted runs back. "Come on, don't shoot me. I did what you wanted. It's not my fault that he didn't answer the phone."

Chance turns the gun on Ken. "You're right. It's not your fault—it's his." Ken tries to yell through his mouth, but only a muffling sound comes out. Ted is terrified. Chance cocks the gun. She shoots Ken in one leg. Ted runs. Ken screams in pain. Two-gun fires are heard. Chance looks around, but she doesn't see anyone. She starts firing her gun aimlessly around the mill. "You want some?" she yells as she shoots around. "You want some of me? Well come get it." Moishe shoots down at her feet. Chance spies around the mill. "I'm not afraid of you, asshole."

"Put down the gun, little girl," Moishe voice echoes through the mill.

"I'm not a little girl," Chance says, "and I'm not putting down the gun." Moishe walks out of the shadows.

Chance is surprised. "Who are you?"

"That's not important right now." He looks over at Ken's bleeding leg. Ken pleads for help with his eyes.

"Yes, it is important, because I want to know the name of the man that I'm about to shoot."

"I do not exchange names with strangers. Now put it down!" Moishe tries to keep his temper cool.

"No. Why don't you go after your coward friend, Ted. This is my problem, not yours."

Moishe's eyes grow big. "If it deals with Jena, then it's my problem now."

"Ah, I see." Chance flexes. "I remember seeing you as you pulled up to the party. Yes, you were the driver. Hmm, well I guess Jena wins again. She manages to charm every man she meets, even old ones."

"I don't want to shoot you, but I will. So, I'm telling you again— put down the gun and walk away while you can." Hard stepping and then running is heard coming from the back of the mill. Ted is running fast to try to tackle Chance. When he gets halfway to her, she turns and shoots at him. She barely misses. Moishe is able to get close enough to her to take away her gun. Ted stands up. He's not hurt, suffering only a scuff to his knees.

Chance pushes Moishe; his gun drops. She grabs her gun back and points to fire at him. Ted sees the scuffle, gets up, and tackles her to stop her from shooting Moishe. She falls down, but then she manages to get back up and start running. Moishe is also knocked down to the floor. He quickly gets up, grabs his gun, but it's too late—she's gone.

Moishe is stunned at Chance's quick maneuver. He gives Ted a thankful look. He stands, breathing hard from the excitement. "Thank you." Moishe puts his hand out to Ted. Ted graciously accepts his handshake. His eyes gleam with a sense of pride and happiness that Moishe would want to shake his hand. The two of them lock eyes for a second, and then they race over to help Ken, who's bleeding from the leg pretty badly. "Left his leg," Moishe tells Ted. "We must stop the bleeding." Moishe rips off his shirt to use it as a tourniquet around Ken's leg. Ted holds Ken's leg firmly so

Moishe can tie it. "Now untie him so we can get him to a hospital." Ted stops. "Why are you stopping?"

"We can't take him to a hospital. It would raise too many questions. The police are looking for Jena. Ken's shooting would only raise the police's suspicion that Jena is possibly in Maplesville." Ted unties Ken. "We just can't risk her and my brother getting caught."

Moishe thinks. "Okay, we'll take him back to Jena's. We'll all hide. But we must stop by a drug store so I can get supplies to fix the wound. If we don't hurry, he could bleed out and die. We must go now."

Ted and Moishe carry Ken to the car. All of the tires are flat. "Damn it, Chance," Ted says. They drag Ken into the car. Ted pulls his fingers through his hair, looking at Moishe. "What are we going to do?"

Moishe gets in the driver's side. "Get in. We're going to drive this car on all rims." Ted hops into the car. Moishe puts the car in gear. "Hold on, because this is going to be a hell of a ride." Moishe drives the car as fast as he can without causing sparks from the rims.

Ted is frustrated. "We're not going to make it. Ken's going to die. Look at him, he's barely holding on."

Moishe drives. He keeps his cool. "I've seen men shot five and six times and make it. We will make it."

An old black truck is coming down the road. It's driven by a man in his sixties wearing a country straw hat, toothpick in his mouth, smoking a cigarette. Moishe stops and the man stops, looking at the flat tires and at Ken in the back. He takes his toothpick out, but leaves the cigarette in. "Looks like trouble," the man says.

Moishe opens the car door and walks up to the truck. "It is trouble. We need your truck."

The old man gripes, "My truck? Old Annie here? I can't do that."

Moishe opens the truck door. "You can, and you will old man." The man reaches for his shotgun. "I can use this thing."

Moishe puts his hand on his gun, which is tucked outside his shirt in clear view. "Not before I use this. Now get out of the truck. We need it. Our friend is shot."

The old man grabs his shotgun, gets out of the truck, and peeks in the car at Ken. "Oh, he's about to die." Ted picks up Ken, and Moishe helps get him onto the bed of the truck. Moishe gets in, backs up, turns around, sticks his head out the truck window, and says, "I'll get it back to you." He drives off, leaving a burst of dust in the old man's face.

He throws his shotgun down and then pulls a cell phone out of his dirty jeans. "Earl, come get me. 'Cause someone stole my truck. I don't know who, just come get me at the old mill. We got a car here—tires flat, but it looks new. Get down here now." The old man puts the cell phone back in his pocket, picks up the shotgun, and walks to the mill.

Chance comes out the woods and pulls a gun on him. "Who did you call?"

The old man drops the shotgun. He can't speak. "Ah ... I called ..."

Chance yells, "You called who?"

"I called Earl."

"Give me your cell." The old man reaches in his pocket, takes out the phone, and gives it to Chance. "Now, when Earl gets here, you're going to tell him that this is my car and you're helping me."

The old man has his dirty hands raised in the air. "Why would I do that?"

Chance brings the gun around to the front of him. "Because if you don't, I'll blow you and your dirty, dusty jeans away."

CHAPTER THIRTY-ONE

Moishe drives as fast as he can, dust misting from the truck as it spins down the dirt road onto the highway. Ted checks on Ken—pale face, chilly body. Ken passes out. Ted is afraid. He yells to Moishe, "Pull over!"

"What?"

"Pull over. I think he's dead."

Moishe pulls over. He jumps in the back of the truck and feels Ken's pulse. He sighs. "He's not dead, but he won't make it unless we get him to a hospital."

Ted holds his head down. "The hospital is five miles from here." Moishe jumps in the truck, quickly gets situated, and puts his foot all the way down on the petal. Minutes later, he pulls into the St. Mary's hospital emergency room entrance.

Ted goes inside and yells for help. Nurse Louis comes running out. "We need help." She runs to the truck, sees Ken, and then runs inside to get a stretcher, two more nurses, and a doctor. They all help get Ken into the bed, and then they race him the emergency room. Moishe and Ted rush in with them. Nurse Louis stands at the counter, letting the other two nurses and doctor take over. "What's his name?"

Ted looks at her. "Umm … Ken."

"Ken who, sir?"

Ted gets nervous. "I don't know his last name. Just his first. His name is Ken."

"Okay. Do you know his parents?"

"Umm. No, I don't."

"Sir, in order for us to properly treat this patient, we have to have more information."

Moishe walks to the counter. "If this is a matter of money, I'll pay for everything. He reaches in his pocket. In cash."

Nurse Louis starts typing. "Okay then, we list him as John Doe. Please go around the corner to arrange payment."

Moishe walks to the payment counter. "I'd like to pay for this emergency visit for … John Doe."

The clerk looks up the name John Doe. "Sir, he has just been admitted for five minutes. We have no idea how much this visit will be. I will need a copy of your driver's license and for you to fill out some papers so we may contact you when a bill is ready."

"I can't do that."

The clerk frowns. "And why not, sir?"

"Look, I'm not from this country. This is a friend of mine who I'm trying to help. I will come back tomorrow to check with you on the amount of this visit. Please take care of my friend." Moishe walks away.

Ted meets him outside. "What happened? Did they call the cops?"

"Not yet, but I'm sure that woman will. Let's go." Moishe walks to the truck. Ted follows. "We must get back to Jena and Jake before Chance finds them."

Ted looks over at Moishe. "What makes you think she'll find them?"

"Because I overheard you tell her that they were at Jena's house. If she is looking for them, then that's where she will go."

"I have to go home first."

"Why? We don't have time to stop by your house."

"We have too."

They get into the truck. It's quickly blocked by a police car. A police officer walks up to the truck. "Is this your truck, sir?"

Moishe answers, "Yes. Is there a problem, officer?"

The officer walks around the truck, writes down the license plates. He walks back to the window. "I'll be back." He goes to run the license plates.

Ted looks behind them. "Back out, man. He's going to find out this truck is stolen."

Moishe looks back. "If I back out, then we have cop problems."

Ted gets mad, but he lowers his voice down to a whisper. "We've got cop problems whether you back out or not. We've got to get the hell out of here, or we're going to be arrested."

"We will wait."

"What? I'm not going to jail." Ted reaches for the door to make a run for it.

The officer comes back. "Okay, your good. This truck isn't the truck we're looking for. We're looking for a truck that was stolen and is associated with the burning of a house and a murder."

Moishe tries to get more information. "A murder?"

"Yes, a murder. Possible suspect—Jena Parker. But this is your lucky day because this isn't the truck." The officer gets into his vehicle and drives off. Moishe follows him out.

Ted is relieved. "Man, you're one cool cat. My heart was about to pound out of my chest."

Moishe is quiet. He looks around as he drives to Ted's house. "Such a little town. Little towns are always filled with mysteries," he turns, "and murder. I want to apologize for what I said to you earlier. You know, about me not trusting you. You saved my life back there at the mill, so I owe you a lot of gratitude."

Ted smiles: he feels honored. "Thanks." Ted plays with the truck's glove box. "This is an old truck."

"Yes, but this old truck saved Ken's life." Moishe looks in the rearview mirror and notices someone is following him.

"What are you looking at?"

"Someone's following us. I'll turn here to make sure." Moishe turns into the gas station. The car follows him in. It's a woman driving a blue car with black tinted windows. Moishe pulls in and then out again. The car follows him. Ted looks out the back window. "Don't look back!" Moishe yells.

"Sorry. Do you think it's, Chance?"

"I don't know. Could be her. Could be a cop or could be a coincidence. We just don't know yet." Moishe turns down Ted's street. He parks in the driveway. The blue car follows him. They sit in the car. The blue car parks: no one gets out. Moishe reaches for his gun. "You wait here." He opens the door. "If they start shooting, you run." Moishe gets out and walks to the blue car. He stands glaring at himself in the shiny, tinted window. The window slowly moves down. He points his gun.

An old woman with gray hair wearing sunglasses stares back at him, a gun resting in her lap. "Who are you?" she asks Moishe.

"Who are you? And why are you following me?"

The old woman takes off her shades. "You're driving my old man's truck. I was following you because I thought you was him, heading over to another woman's house." Moishe puts his gun down. The woman puts her shades back on and returns her gun to the glove box. "I was about bust a cap in someone's ass, but he got lucky today." She starts pulling out of the driveway. "If you see him, you tell him I'm looking for him." Moishe is quite surprised.

Ted gets out of the truck. "Who was that?"

"Some gangster old lady looking for her old man. How long do you need?"

"Just an hour, maybe only a half hour. Come inside. Relax a little. I'm sure my brother will appreciate every free moment he has with Jena." Moishe walks inside with Ted. Both of them seem relaxed. Moishe flops down on the couch. He lies his head back and closes his eyes. "You got anything cold."

"You mean a beer?" Ted goes to the refrigerator. "Here you go. My dad keeps a few in the fridge."

Moishe pops open the beer. He takes a sip. "You don't drink?"

"Yeah, I do—but not like my dad. He drinks a lot." A sad feeling comes over Ted. "So does my mother. But Jake and I, we aren't big drinkers … although we did get drunk one night. It was his first day at college, and they had a party. So, I went up there to hang out." Ted sits down next to Moishe. "We had the time of our lives. Jake was a little bummed out that Jena didn't want to go to the party, but Ken and I cheered him up. Got him drunk." Moishe stares at Ted, takes a big gulp of the beer. Ted puts his hands behind his head as he remembers about that night.

Moishe takes another sip of beer. "So, you guys had a wild night, huh?"

"Yeah, it was wild. I mean, beer and alcohol and—oh man—the girls. I'm not very popular in high school, but I was popular that night." Ted laughs. "There were so many beautiful girls there, and my brother couldn't even enjoy his night." Ted stands up.

Moishe finishes his beer. "Why, because of Jena?"

"Yeah, because of Jena. He just couldn't get her off his mind. Every time a girl would approach him, he'd open his wallet to look at the photo of Jena." Ted puts his head down. "Every time he'd open his wallet, Ken and I would laugh our asses off." Ted just stops talking midstory.

Moishe gets a strange look on his face. "Ted?" Ted zones out. "Ted?"

Ted looks at Moishe. "You want another beer, man?"

"Sure." Ted gets Moishe another beer. "You want to talk about something? You seem strange all of a sudden."

"No, I'm just worn out from today. It's been a very wild and crazy day. I wonder where Chance is. Think she'll come here looking for us?"

Moishe drinks down the beer. "I don't think so. I think she's had enough for today. She's quite a disturbed young lady."

"She wasn't always like that. She was once a very sane person. Beautiful, nice, and kind. I used to talk to her every day at school. We'd eat lunch together. If you knew the Chance I knew, you would have never thought she was the same person you saw today. It's strange how you think you know someone, but you really don't." Ted walks off to his room. "I'll be back. You can help yourself to anything in the fridge or in my brother's bathroom in his room." Ted leaves the room.

Moishe goes to the refrigerator and pulls out the entire case of beer. He turns on the TV and drinks at least five more beers. He starts laughing at a funny show on TV. Moishe gets tired, but he fights sleep. He looks at his watch and realizes that at least two hours has passed since Ted left to go to his room. Moishe stumbles to the refrigerator to get more beer and then heads back to the couch. Ted is taking a long time in his room. Moishe's laugh fades as he tries to keep his eyes open. His head bobs back and forth as he drifts off to sleep. He shakes his head to try to wake himself up. He looks at his watch. He has spent three hours on the couch. He gets up and calls for Ted. "Ted." His vision is blurred, and the room is dark except for the light from the TV. "Ted. What are you doing?" He slides open Ted's room door. There's a small night lamp on, the bed's empty, and his room window is open. Moishe opens the door wider. "Ted?" He's barely able to stand, but he slowly looks around the room. Suddenly he feels a thump on his head. He falls on the bed. His hearing is limited, and he has double vision. He can feel his body being dragged across the floor. He tries to speak and see who's dragging him. It's someone wearing a hoodie, but their faced is a blur to him. "What's going on?" His voice drags. "What are doing?" Moishe feels another thump on his head and totally blacks out.

CHAPTER THIRTY-TWO

J ake holds Jena's hand as they walk in the dark to the rear entrance of her house. Jena stands back as he tries to push open the door. He presses his body as he hard as he can into the door. His wounded shoulder is injured further. Jena touches him. "Are you all right?" She touches him all over. "I'm sorry, I know you're in pain. Let me try."

Jake stands between her and the door. "No, I want to." Jena stands back while Jake pushes as hard as can he on the door. The door pops open. He stands back, holding his shoulder. Jena stands in the dark doorway. Her feet are frozen. Jake lightly runs his fingertips through her hair, rubs her shoulder. "It's all right," He comforts her. "I'm here with you."

She steps one foot inside the house. "It's dark and cold in here."

Jakes whispers, "Turn on the lights."

"We can't. If we do, someone will know we're here." Jena steps completely through the doorway. "My father has flashlights in the kitchen. We'll use them." Jake follows her inside. "Besides, the moon is bright tonight." She reaches for Jake's hand. "We'll pull back the curtains, let it shine through." Jake leads her into the kitchen. "That's funny."

"What?"

"You know my house better than I do."

He reaches for the flashlights under the kitchen cabinet. "Here." He hands her one, picks up another, and turns it on.

"Keep it low, Jake."

He places his flashlight on the living room floor. Jena flashes the other around the house, staring at the pictures on the wall, the furniture, the mantle where the antique vase her grandmother gave her mother sat. Everything looks the same to her, even in the dark. Jake sits down on the floor near the flashlight, holding his shoulder. Jena kneels down near him. "You're in pain? I'll find something to help you."

She begins to stand up; he grabs her arm. "No." He gently pulls her close to him. "Just come sit next to me."

Jena turns her flashlight off and cuddles next to Jake. "You're warm."

He grins. "Yeah, well I guess I'm just a hot-blooded person."

"Hot blooded, huh?"

"Yeah." They both laugh.

"Thank you for coming with me. I really wanted to be home."

Jake reaches over to touch her face. "I'd do anything for you."

"I know." Jena kisses him. "I'll do anything for you too." Words Jake has been waiting to hear. Jena rubs his chest, moves her hand down to his bulging pants, starts rubbing him. He leans his head back and breathes out softly.

"Jena, let me find the heater to turn it on."

"No. We can make our own heat." She starts kissing Jake's neck and face and then takes the tip of her tongue and lightly traces it over his lips. She moves over to sit on top of him. He breathes hard. "I'm not hurting you, am I?"

"Not at all—and even if you were, I could give a shit right now." Jena starts the motion of her body on his. He claws his fingers into her back, squeezing her as she plays with him. She unbuttons Jake's belt, zips down his jeans, and reaches for his jock.

"I'm so ready for you," she whispers.

"Show me," he whispers back. He unbuttons her blouse, pulls her bra halfway down, and licks her hard nipples. He pulls down on her as she braces herself on him. "Awe ..." They both moan. Jena digs her fingers into his good shoulder and leans back. She pants and moans in the delight. He clenches on to her harder. "Oh, Jena," he cries out. "Jena." He whispers, "I love you. I love you so much."

Jena leans forward bringing her face next to his. "Tell me again."

"I love you."

"Again, scream it."

"I love you, baby. Oh ... I love you," he says it over and over again.

She nibbles on his ear, whispers, "Please don't ever stop."

"I won't. I won't ever stop."

She lies still next to him. Both of their hearts beating together, creating one beat. "You are my hope," she whispers softly to him.

Jake holds her tightly, but then moans a little. Jena kisses his wounded shoulder. "I'm sorry. It's okay, really. I just have to man up."

She slides to the side of him. "I know my father had some pain medication. I'll get you some, turn on the heat, and find us some blankets.

Jake sits up. "Turn on the heat? Wasn't I hot enough for you?" He snuggles her face with his. "Didn't I light you on fire?" They both laugh.

"Yes, you did, but now I'm cold." She grabs a flashlight and puts it up to her face, giving her a creepy look, and says, "I'll be back."

Jena walks into the kitchen and searches through the drawers to find the pain medicines. She finds the bottle, walks to the thermostat, turns the heat on, and grabs a few blankets out of the downstairs closet. It's only been two weeks, but I feel like I have been gone forever, she thinks as she flashes the light through the house. Everything is the same, but it's not. Nothing is the same. She holds the blanket close to her chest and shines the flashlight up the stairs, capturing each stair, one by one, until the light reaches the top. She shines the light on the very spot where she would sit listening to her parents talk, laugh, and dance to their favorite song. Her father's whispers in her mother's ears. Her mother's high-pitched giggles. How they swayed together as he romanced her with his smooth dance moves.

"Kitty," her dad whispers. "You're my little Kitty." Her mother laughs. "Purr for me, Kitty."

"Stop it, John. You know I don't purr like a kitty cat." He picks her up.

She softly screams, "Put me down." He swings her around the room, Kitty smiling down at him, and then he'd slowly slides her down and kiss her.

Jena remembers when her father landed the most romantic kiss on her mother's lips, and then he picked her up again, like a princess, and carried her to the couch. Jena took that as her cue to leave them alone. *I always dreamed of having such a love as my parents had.* She stares at Jake as she walks toward him. *And now I do.* Laying the blanket on him, she says, "Here's a soft blanket for you."

"Thanks, my love."

She holds her hand out. "Here are some meds too."

Jake takes the bottle. "What is it?"

"Umm, not sure, but I do remember my dad taking them for his back." She sits down next to Jake. "They make you a little sleepy." She plays with his hair.

"I don't want to go to sleep. I want to sit up all night and stare at you," he jokes.

"Take them, Jake. It'll help you with your pain." She slides the blanket over them both. "And if it will make you feel better, I'll go to sleep with you." Jake takes two pills. They both cuddle close. Jena kisses him on the nose. "See, doesn't this feel great."

Jake starts getting drowsy. He's beginning to drift off, but he replies, "Yeah, it does feel really groovy."

"Groovy?" Jena laughs. "Oh, the pills are starting to take effect."

Jake slowly fades out. "Yeah."

"Yeah?" Jena plays with him. "So how many of me do you see?"

Jake slightly grins. "Just one." He pulls her close. "I don't care what drugs I take, there's only one Jena ever." Jake falls asleep.

Jena holds him. She whispers, "You're my king, and I'm your princess." Jena stares around the dark room, her eyes focusing in on every corner of the living room. She sees a light. A force pulls her. She tries to resist, but her body gets light like a feather. She can feel it floating away, and in moments she is looking down on herself and Jake. She turns and walks slowly toward the light. Her body movement feels robotic. An unseen force calls for her. She walks and walks toward the bright light and finds herself in an open field with twelve black doors—all open, waiting for her to walk through. She doesn't know which door to go to, so she walks to let her spiritual body guide her. She closes her eyes and walks to the door of its choice. She walks through it, and discovers little children playing. Parents walking around and talking. School buses. Jena stares at it until it's all out of sight. She walks barefooted in the cool, white sand. It's a playground with seesaws, swings, and a place to play in the sand. She sees a little girl on the swings, laughing as her father swings her back and forth. She walks toward them. The little girl has a bright red bow in her hair, a white dress, and blue shoes. The girl holds on tightly to the swing. Jena can see only the back of the head of her father, but she somehow knows he is smiling and talking to the little girl. Jena feels happiness. She feels like she knows where she is. It's me … That little girl is me. Jena smiles. The little girl's laughter gives her joy and a sense of comfort. If that's me, then that is Dad. That's Dad swinging me. She looks up and sees her mother standing next to the swing, bent down with her hands on her lap, smiling at the little girl and the father. "Mom," she utters as she reaches out for her. A gust of wind blows; Jena's hair swings back, her body pushed backward … The father runs to the little girl, picks her up, and holds her. Her mother is standing with one hand on her face with tears of joy seeping from her eyes. Jena wants to be a part of that moment. She walks slowly up to the father. Her mother stares at her with a dreadful face, the little girl screams, and then the father turns around, but his face is melting ...

Jena suddenly awakens. She looks around the room and then at Jake and realizes that it was just a horrible dream. "I hate him," she utters to herself. Why is he still here? Why is he still in my mind? She pulls the blanket off of her, slides up her pants and buttons them, picks up a flashlight, and walks toward the stairs. She shines the flashlight up the stairs. "Mom ...," she says as she walks slowly up the steps. The flashlights catch her shadow on the wall, the stairs make a cracking sound with every step she takes. At the top of the stairs, she flashes the light on every room door until it finally reaches her mother's room. She walks toward it. Opening the door, she shines the light on the dresser, the window, her mom's closest, and then the bed—where she last saw her.

CHAPTER THIRTY-THREE

What have I done? She closes her eyes as they begin to tear up. If there was ever a time, I regret my own doings, this would be it. My mother, my precious mother is gone. She slides her fingers over the covers and remembers her mother's face right before she drank the milk—her sunk-in eyes, her drooping face, the gray in her hair, and the bags under her eyes. It seemed that she aged overnight from a woman in her forties to an old woman. My mother's body was occupied by a stranger and kept alive so she could relive the death of my father every single day of her life. A woman whose spirit had left her behind to wander the earth in torment of why it had abandoned her without its beautiful presence. She stares at her mother's empty bed and flashes back to that night, walking up the stairs with the milk in hand. Just hours before, she had taken the life of a doctor on the train who merely asked her name.

"What's your name?"

"Jena Pa ... Jena Gray."

He, too, dead with a cold, stricken look on his face, as if he had seen something that scared his skin lily white. He didn't see a ghost. He saw a girl who had been broken in many pieces until her light had flickered out, blown away to the stars, hiding out somewhere in the universe.

I want so much for my light to return. She looks at her mother's pillow and stands up. But do I even deserve it? I've taken away my mother's darkness, hoping that would bring her light—but what if it didn't? What if she's just out there, afraid, crying, waiting for my father to come? Sitting in a dark room alone, staring at the door, waiting for him to come to dance with her. She could very well be no freer than I am.

Jena hears a noise. She flashes the light throughout the room and then walks toward the door. She shines the light down and sees shoes, shines it farther up and sees pants, and then shines it right into a face. Ted is standing, staring at her. She shines the light closely at his face. "What are you doing here?" He just stares. "What? Is something wrong with your father?"

Ted steps closer to her. "No, there's nothing wrong. I just wanted to come check on you and Jake."

Jena moves around the room, keeping the flashlight on Ted's face. "Jake is fine. He's asleep."

"I know. I saw him downstairs." Ted steps around the room in the dark. Jena follows him with the flashlight. "Jena, do you remember when we were kids playing at the playground, how I always put sand in your hair?" Jena listens. "You ever wonder why I did that?" Ted continues to walk around the room; Jena follows him. "You know when we were both in high school, I would wish we'd have every class together," he chuckles, "because I knew it would make Jake jealous. Ken too."

"What's wrong with you, Ted?"

He shouts, "Nothing's wrong with me. Why does something have to be wrong with me?" He walks closer to Jena.

"Because you're acting strange. You're here in the dark, telling stories. I ... I just don't understand."

He walks close to the light. His face sets off a dark shadow. "What don't you understand? You don't understand why I always put sand in your hair? Why I always wanted to play with you when your mom brought you over? Why I always watch you when you're not looking or when you're too busy smiling with my brother? Or … maybe it's something else you don't understand. Maybe you don't understand what happened to you that night."

"What night?" she shouts.

He grins. "Oh, that night. I know you remember … or maybe you don't want to remember." Ted turns around and steps toward the window. He's wearing a hooded jacket. His silhouette in the window sets off a memory for Jena. She flashes back to the library, when she thought she saw someone standing in the library window door wearing a similar jacket.

She slowly walks behind him. "Ted, do you know what happened to me that night?" The room is dark, but for Jena it gets darker as her anger grows. "I asked you a question," she says in a forceful voice. "Do you know what happened to me that night?" she yells.

Ted tells the story. "We were all at the party. You had just told Jake that you didn't want to go. I know this because I was watching you and him. I saw the angry, disappointed look on his face after you said you were going to the library. Jake, Ken, and I all met up at the party." Ted flashes back. "The music was awesome. Girls everywhere. We started drinking. I'm excited to be hanging out with the college kids, drinking with my bro, Ken, and all of the rest of the gang. Chance and Carol were there too. It was the party of all parties, but my brother wasn't in a party mood. That's because his beloved Jena wasn't there. Do you know every time a girl would come over and try to talk to him, he'd pull out his wallet to stare at your picture? Man, I'd never seen someone so in love with a girl … someone besides me. You see, Jena, I loved you too. But you …" he smirks, "but you didn't notice me. I was invisible to you. All of the signs I gave you from when we were kids, grade school, high school … nothing. You saw nothing!"

Jena's voice starts to shake. "What happened, Ted? What happened!"

Ted pauses. "Jake wanted to leave the party and, well, so did I. Ken didn't. He was having the time of his life. We were all pretty damn toasted, but we managed to walk out of the party. Jake was the drunkest of us. He was stumbling all over the place, but somehow, he remembered you were at the library. I knew it, but I was hoping he would just leave with another girl. But he just couldn't … He just couldn't let me have you. I left with a red cup full of alcohol—and yeah, I had some roofies in my jacket. I told Jake and Ken I'd go inside to get you, and I did, but you were chatting with some nerd. That made me so mad. You saw me, and I raised the cup up, signaling for you come. That's when the librarian tapped you on the shoulder, telling you it was time to go. You met me at the door with a smile—the most beautiful smile in the world. It was the first time you had smiled at me that way. You were like an angel that just came down from heaven. I knew that this was my only chance to be with you. Jake and Ken were so drunk. I knew that this was our time. Yours and mine, Jena. I showed you the red cup and told you to drink it, that it was good. You said no. No. I didn't want to talk, but I played with you. Made you laugh. You trusted me, so you took a sip. I could see the roofies taking effect right away. You leaned on me. That really turned me on, so I took you out back. Jake and Ken were out front, probably passed out. You were so zoned. You didn't know what was going on. It was dark out there, cold … cold as ice, but I never felt so much warmth as I did to be close to you. I started kissing you. I could tell you were still coming in and out from the drug, because you called me Jake and then you thought I was Ken … and then you saw me, and you started to scream. I couldn't have that, so I started hitting you in the face. I felt so horrible. I didn't want to hit you, but you were starting to get too loud. If Jake heard you, I knew he'd come running. Your voice faded once the drug took full effect, and I had my way with you. You were even willing at times. When I was finished, I looked down at you and realized what I had done. I was sorry, but … there was a part of me that was so happy I finally had gotten to be with you. That you finally saw me."

The flashlight is beaming on Ted's jacket. Jena is close to Ted's back. She whispers in his ear, "I'm going to fucking kill you." She throws the flashlight down and slams Ted up against the window. His face slams into it. She grabs him and slams his face against it again and again. Her strength is twice his. Ted tries to fight back, but Jena starts beating on him. Ted pulls the knife out from his pocket, nicks her with it. She stands back like a raging bull ready to charge him. He stands with the knife tightly gripped in his hand, nose and face bleeding, hood still on his head.

He shouts, "You wanted the truth. Well, now you've got it." They both circle each other. Jena's face glowing red, even in the dark. Ted wipes the blood from his nose, holding the knife in his hand. "I don't know why you're so damn mad. We could have had the best life together. Better than you and Jake, better than anything."

Jena breathes hard. "The only life you're going to have is a life six feet under." She charges Ted and pushes him up against the window. The glass break outs. Ted drops the knife as he slips out the window. Holding on to the sill with one hand, he begs Jena to pull him in. She just stands there and watches while his hand slips.

"Jena, please. You don't want to do this."

"Yes, I do. I want to watch you beg, watch your hand slowly slip, and then I'm gonna watch as you fall to your death. You're wrong. I do want you to die." Ted tries to pull himself up, but he slips.

"Jake—my brother—he'll never forgive you."

Jake walks out from the shadows and pushes Jena out of the way. "Yes, I will." He releases Ted's hand and watches as he screams, falling to his death. Jake stares at his brother lying on the ground, body crooked.

Jena walks up beside him. "What did you hear?" she asks in a concerned voice.

Jake puts one hand on his wounded shoulder, walks toward the door, and stops. "Everything." He walks out of the room.

CHAPTER THIRTY-FOUR

Jena stands in the window with her arms crossed. She looks down at Ted's dead body with a cold and uncaring expression. Destiny. Oh, how it will find you, even when you aren't looking for it. Somehow it knows when to rear its ugly little head. When you feel safe, secure, that's when it wants to reveal itself—claim itself as the winner. That's until it meets me.

She walks away from the window and goes down the stairs. Jake is sitting on the couch. He is in shock that his brother was responsible for hurting Jena and that he just killed him. Jena stands in front of him. "I know that was hard."

"He hurt you, Jena."

"He did, but he was still your brother."

He looks up at her. "Was he? He wasn't the brother I knew." He stands up and faces her. "Anyone who hurts you or tries to hurt you will not be a part of me." He walks to the back door of the house. "I have to bring Ted's body inside before someone finds him."

"I'll help you." Jena walks toward him.

"No. I'll do it alone. We'll have to put him somewhere until we can figure out what to do with him." Jake walks out and comes back dragging Ted's body inside and upstairs to the hall bathroom tub.

Jena stares off out the living room window to the McNeil's house across the street. The moon is shining bright on the roof of the house. She thinks back to when she saw Mr. McNeil hiding next to his house holding a shovel, his dark figure glaring over at her house. All the while plotting to kill his own wife and unknowingly becoming the man I grew to hate.

Jake slowly walks downstairs. "We should get some sleep." He lies down on the floor without saying another word to Jena.

Jena lies down next to him, facing the opposite way. It is the first time in a long time that Jena has felt Jake distance himself from her. She knows that he is hurting from Ted's death. But she also knows that if anyone deserved to die, it was Ted. She is not glad he is dead; she is glad he is among the likes of Mr. McNeil. Two undeserving souls trapped out there together with nothing and no one but themselves and other selfish yokes like them.

She closes her eyes and, just like magic, when she opens them the living room is lit up like a Christmas tree. The sun is blaring through the front window, casting sparkles off the dust that hangs in the air. Jena first thinks it is a dream, but she knows it isn't because of how she felt when her eyes opened. She leans over. Jake is lying shirtless under the blanket, sound asleep. The patch on his wounded shoulder is bloody. Jena touches it, his arm, and his chest. "You're my hero," she whispers as he sleeps. She looks around the living room as if she is seeing her own house for the first time. The antique vase her grandmother gave her mother shines like it never has before. Her parents' photo sits next to it on the mantle. Jena picks the photo up, wipes off the dust, and kisses it. She holds it close to her heart. She gently puts the photo down and walks to kitchen. She remembers when her mother cut her hand, how she helped her, and how her dad complained about having no meatloaf for dinner. She smiled. Her father's voice echoed in the kitchen. She remembers coming home from school when she was ten and discovering her father was in the kitchen trying to cook.

"Jena, honey, open the cabinet and hand your old man two cans of sweet peas." Jena opens the cabinet, reaches in for the cans, and hands them to her father, who is having a hard time keeping the pots on the stove from boiling over. She laughs at him. "Oh, you this is funny?" he says.

"Yes, Dad. You don't know how to cook."

"Well, your mother does all the cooking, but she is sick."

She goes over to give her dad a hug. "Do you want me to help?" He looks at her with desperate eyes. Jena starts helping him.

He kisses Jena on the forehead. "You're the best daughter ever."

"You're the best Dad ever." They both talk and laugh in the kitchen.

She walks back over to the living room, looks down at her bag, reaches in, and pulls out the letter her mother wrote her. Holding the letter in her hands, she walks upstairs to her mother's room. She sits on her bed. She could hear her mother's voice. "Jena … Jena, get up. It's time for school." She closes her eyes, and she smells breakfast coming from downstairs. How I miss you, Mom, she thinks. Her mom would get up every morning to cook her breakfast. Jena could feel the tears brewing up inside of her as she held the letter in her hand. Her mother's lovely face flashes in her head—the sound of her sweet voice. How much I took you for granted, Mom. I'm so sorry. She slowly tears open the letter and unfolds it. She closes her eyes, but she knows this is long overdue. It's time for her to read it.

My dearest Jena,

There is so much I want to say to you, my darling daughter. I'm so very proud of you. The day that your father and I have been waiting for has finally arrived. I want you to know that I'm very proud of you. You have grown up to be such a beautiful, caring young lady. I couldn't have asked for a better daughter, a more wonderful, smart, and understanding person than you.

I'm so sorry that I have been so distant, but the death of your father crushed me in an unimaginable way that can't be described in any words on the earth. His death ripped my heart out. I knew I was never going to be the same after that night when I saw your father lying there dead on the floor, killed in cold blood. I wanted to die with him.

I did die, Jena. My mind took me with him, and I'm so sorry that I left you alone to deal with your own pain. It is unbearable for me to be in this house without him—to lie in that bed without his warm body beside mine. I've wanted to kill myself so many times, but every time I'd try, I'd see your face—your little girl face, your eyes, your smile when you were a baby—and I couldn't do it. But, my sweetheart, the time has come for me to tell you the truth. A truth that may make you hate me in a way a daughter should never a hate a mother. There are things you don't know. Things that I've hidden from you. I now realize, though, that your obsession with Miles could lead you down a path of destruction and that I have to do everything in my power to stop that destruction from happening— even if it means I may lose you forever.

Your father and I fell in love in high school— but, my darling, he wasn't my first love. I was in love with Miles until he lied and cheated on me. That's when I broke off the relationship, and I started dating your father. Eventually your father and I got married. It was always our dream to have a beautiful daughter like you. We tried and tried, but it never happened. I felt so depressed, so lonely, and so desperate that one night I confided in Miles—a night that seems so long ago. Yet the blood on my hands from your father's death wasn't just from the bullet. It was my own doing … Jena, Miles is your father. Miles McNeil is your father.

I know you must hate me. I hated myself for so long, until I saw your beautiful face the day you were born and the happiness that it brought your father. You were everything to him. His world. He loved you so much. I could never have told him the truth. I didn't have too; he knew and had forgiven me. He held me like he'd always held me and loved me like he'd always loved me. The bond between your father and I was strong.

I had one weak moment that caused Miles to become obsessed with you—not because he was some dirty old man, but because he was your father. Miles wanted to build a relationship with you, but I had forbidden it. Your father hated when Miles was around you. He didn't want you to know the truth.

Please never doubt the love I feel for you. It is so painful for me to have to tell you this. You're everything to me. When you are much older, you'll find that life isn't always so simple. The choices we make can lead us down a path of darkness, but we must forgive ourselves so others can find us in the light. True love can guide you and bring you out of any storm. The love I shared with your father is beyond this universe. He and I are one. We are one with each other, and we are one with you. Please don't destroy your life.

One day, my sweetheart, you will find a love so intense, so far beyond what this world will ever reveal. You will be in this world, but with him you will feel like you're in heaven. Every time your father held me in his arms, I was in heaven. I know that I will see your father again. We will sing, dance, and laugh again, and he will hold me so tight as he whispers in my ear, "I love you, Kitty. You're my light."

I love you, my sweet daughter. You are my heart, and you're my light. Please find it in your heart to forgive me.

Love you always,
Mom

The tears run down Jena's face like never before. She huffs and tries to catch her breath, but she feels the room closing in on her. The sun has risen. She has been born again—born back into the world. She chokes up with tears. Her emotions are out of control. She stands up, looks around the room, and runs downstairs.

Jake is standing in the living room. She stops and looks at him. He can see the letter in her hand. She opens the front door and runs—runs so fast. Jake calls for her. He runs behind her. She runs and runs until she is standing in front of her mother's grave. Tears stream down her face. She falls to the ground. Her knees cave in the dirt. "Mom!" she yells. Jake reaches for her; she folds her hands. "Don't." She screams even louder, "Mom. Mommy!" She lies down near the grave. "Mommy, please. I'm so sorry. I'm so sorry, Mommy." Jake's heart is breaking for her. Her pain is his. Her tears drop from her eyes onto her mother's grave." Mom! I'd do anything—anything—to bring you back! To have you here! Now! I ... I ... I can't go on like this. I can't be this person ..." Jena stands. "I won't be this person anymore." The wind blows through her hair. She puts her hand on her mother's tombstone. "You are the most wonderful person I could have ever asked to have as a mother." She breaks down again. "I will not, Mother ... I will not be like this anymore!" She turns around and starts running. Jake grabs her. She screams, "Let me go! Leave me alone!"

"Jena, stop!"

"No! I won't be this person, Jake. Not anymore!" She runs … runs as fast as she can.

Jake follows her, calling her name behind her, "Jena! Jena!"

She doesn't stop until she gets to the police station's parking lot. Police officers are walking around. No one notices her. She breathes out and walks in the door. Officer Reyes is behind the counter. He looks up at her. Her face is red, her hair wild. She is breathing hard, with the letter gripped in her hand. He stands up.

"My name is Jena Parker, and I'm turning myself in."

Jake flings open the police door as Officer Reyes is handcuffing Jena. "You have the right to remain silent," Officer Reyes says.

Jake screams, "No! Stop!" Other officers grab hold of Jake. "Jena, don't!" She looks at him.

Officer Reyes holds Jena's arm. "Do you understand these rights?" Jena nods her head yes.

"No! It was me," Jake yells out.

Officer Reyes looks at him. "Were you there?"

Jake pauses. "Where?"

"When she was—"

Jena cuts off Officer Reyes. "No. He wasn't there. It was just me."

An officer comes running in the door. "We found a dead body in the tub at the Parker's house." He takes off his hat. "It has been identified at Ted Paterson."

Officer Reyes lets out an angry sigh. He grabs Jena's arm to take her away for booking. Jake fights to try to get loose from the officers. "Calm down or we are going to arrest you."

"Arrest me," he screams. "I don't care."

Officer Reyes is frustrated with Jake. "Lock him up until he cools down." Five police officers struggle to hold Jake down and take him to a jail cell. They push him in a cell, close the door behind him, and lock him in.

He braces on tightly to the jail bars and yells, "Don't arrest her! Jena!"

A criminal in the next cell yells back, "Give it up, man, she's done!"

He yells back, "Shut up!"

"Hey, I'm just trying to give you the real, hard facts."

Jake beats his hands on the bars, holds his head down, and tries to control his tears and anger. He sits on the bed to think what do next. He runs back to the bars and screams out. "I want my phone call! I want my phone call!"

A police officer walks up to him. "What are you screaming about?"

"I want my phone call. I'm supposed to get at least one phone call, and I want it."

The officer frowns. "If you attack me when I open the cell, I'm going to shoot you dead on the spot." He reaches in his pocket for the keys. "You got that son?"

"I got it. Now let me out."

He opens the door, handcuffs Jake, and walks him to a pay phone. "Here's a quarter. Now make your damn call." The police officer stands right next to him.

Jake gives him an angry look. "Is there such a thing as privacy?"

Officer Tuck gives Jake a dirty look, crosses his arm, and backs up just a little. Raising his eyebrows, he waits for Jake to proceed with his call.

CHAPTER THIRTY-FIVE

"Turn forward." Snap. "Turn to the left." Snap. "Now turn to the right." Jena turns to the right as Officer Smith takes her photo. She is escorted to a jail cell. Walking the jail hall, a few women recognize her and start screaming her name.

"Jena! Jena!" Soon that entire area of the jail is chanting her name. "Jena Parker! Jena Parker!"

Officer Smith yells at them, "Shut up!"

One of the women scream out, "You shut up. She's our hero! Jena! Jena!"

Jena looks at the women. Some were hookers. Others look like young girls like her, moms, and even a woman with a black eye and busted nose stares at her as she passes them. Officer Smith opens the cell door, takes off Jena's handcuffs, pushes Jena into the cell, and closes the door behind her. He whispers to her. "Now you're famous."

Jena backs away from the bars, turns, and faces the wall. The women continue to chant her name.

Jake calls his mother. She doesn't answer. "Mom, I'm jail." He hangs up the phone. The officers grabs his arm, takes him back to his cell, slams the door, and then walks away.

Jena and Jake both sit in their cells. Jena stares off thinking about her mother, her father, and the road that brought her to this lonely jail cell.

Jake's only thoughts are of Jena. What is happening to her? Are they hurting her? Is she all right? He can't think of anything else. The police guard brings him his food tray. He looked over. "I'm not hungry."

The guard sets the tray inside Jake's cell. "We don't care." He walks off, leaving the tray.

Jake looks at the tray, but he doesn't move. He stares at the ceiling, desperately hoping that he can find some way to help Jena get out of jail and avoid going to jail for the rest of her life. The thought of never seeing or touching her again is driving him insane. Jake begins to cry, breaking down in tears. Jena, damn it, I let you down. I'm so sorry, babe. I'll find a way to get you out of here. He lets the tears run down his face.

Jena sits in her cell with her head down. Her mind finally lands on Jake. She feels guilty for dragging him into her insane world—for letting him fall in love with her, knowing that she is trapped to live a life of revenge and despair. She lies on the bed, stares up at the top bunk, close her eyes, and asks the Lord to forgive her. "Forgive me, Father, for I have sinned." She puts the covers over her body and head to block out the light. The guard stands watches her, gives her a long stare, reaches for the covers, hesitates, sets the food tray down instead, and locks the cell. He stands outside the cell and watches her to see if she'll move if he can get a glimpse of the famous Jena Parker.

Jena doesn't move. She can hear the guard's heavy breathing. She waits until he leaves to remove the blankets from her head. She peeks over at the food, puts the blankets back on her face, and closes her eyes. I'm truly afraid of tomorrow, but even so it will come. And when it does, I'll have to embrace it. This is only way I will survive.

Jake doesn't sleep a wink. He watches the ceiling of the cell most of the night. At times he gets up, stands against the wall, and then lies down again. It is the most restless, loneliest night of his life.

The guard opens Jake's cell. "You're free to leave. Your mother has bailed you out."

Jake gets up. "I didn't know I was arrested."

"Well, now you do." He cuffs Jake and pushes him out of the cell.

Mrs. Paterson is waiting up front, depressed and sad. Her eyes are red, her face looks worn out from depression. She runs up to Jake after the handcuffs are removed. "Ted. He's gone."

Jake doesn't move. "Sorry, Mom."

"Jake, let's get out of here."

"Mom, I can't leave."

"What do you mean, 'you can't leave'?"

Jake can't bear to hurt his mother in the police station. He leaves with her and reluctantly gets in the car. Jake seems aggravated. He doesn't speak.

Mrs. Paterson is nervous. "Jena killed your brother, didn't she? She murdered him."

Jake tries to remain silent.

"She's a cold-hearted killer, and I hope she rots in jail." Jake gets angry, but he lets his mother vent. "What did poor Ted do to her to make her hate him so?" She starts crying. "He was such a nice, peaceful kid. And now he's dead. My son is dead!" she screams. "He didn't deserve it!"

Jake loses it. "Yes, he did!"

Mrs. Paterson is in shock. "What are you talking about?"

"Jena didn't kill Ted. I did."

"What!" she yells in shock.

"I killed him."

"Why would you kill your own brother! For that slut!"

"She's not a slut, and he deserved to die for what he did to her."

She slams on the brakes. "He did not deserve to die!"

"Mom, Ted raped Jena! He raped her and beat her!"

Mrs. Paterson stops and stares off into the distance. "Get out, Jake." Mrs. Paterson says in settled voice.

Jake sits for a moment. "Mom," he calls.

She yells, out of control, "Get out of my car now!" Jake gets out. He looks back at his mom. Her eyes are bulging out, her face as red as a beet. "Don't you ever speak to me or your father again." She spins out.

Jake watches as she spins away, the car wiggling out of control. Jake walks down the road. He has nowhere to go. No money. No family. No Jena. He's lonely and lost. A white car pulls up next to him. A girl sticks her head out. "Get in."

He looks. It's Chance. "I'm not getting into your car."

"Jake, you need help. You have nowhere to go. You may not like me, but let's face it—I'm all you've got right now."

Jake isn't thinking straight. If he has to use Chance to somehow free Jena, then that's what he is going to do. He gets in the car. Chance drives toward her home. "Just how are you going to explain to your parents why I'm in your house?"

Chance smiles. "My parent are away, so they'll never know."

"Where are they?"

Chance hesitates. "They're out of the country, like they always are. You can sleep in my older sister's room. It's a comfortable room—has a bathroom and everything." Chance reaches for Jake's hand. He pushes her away. "I'm just trying to be friendly. To comfort you," she says in a sly voice. "I know how hard this for you—to know Jena has been arrested ... that you may never see her again."

"Oh, I'll see her."

"Jake, you have to be realistic. Jena has killed multiple people. There's no doubt she's going to go to jail for life. Probably even the electric chair."

Jake gets angry with her. "Chance, you killed Carol—you should be in jail."

Chance is silent. "Well, I'm not. And those bastards don't know that I killed Carol." She looks over at Jake. "Are you going to tell them?"

"I'll do whatever it takes to get Jena out of jail, even if it means turning you in."

"Well, you can tell them I killed her, but they won't believe you. Jena is the one they want. They don't want me."

"Please, can we not talk about this anymore? I have to find a way to break her free."

Chance says in a rude voice, "Maybe she's already free. Have you ever thought about that?"

Jake snaps at her. "She loves me, Chance. I know she doesn't want to be apart from me. And right now, the way I feel, I'd kill for her freedom." He looks over at her. She remains quiet.

CHAPTER THIRTY-SIX

Jena sits in her jail cell. She doesn't want to eat. She doesn't want to think about the world outside.

The guard opens her cell door. There's a man standing next to him wearing a blue suit, a red tie, and carrying a briefcase. He walks up to Jena and stands in front of her. "I'm your lawyer." Jena is silent. "My name is Josh Pillars, and I'm a court-appointed attorney sent here to represent you."

"I don't want your representation."

"Oh, but you should think about it. I'm one of the best attorneys in this little town. I know I can get you back your freedom."

"I don't want to be free."

He sets his briefcase down, walks around the cell, stares out the tiny cell window. "So, you want to be locked in a hellhole cell like this for the rest of your life?"

"This is what I deserve."

He claps his hands, applauding her. "So, you deserve this?" He turns around. "What about the ones who you hurt you? What do they deserve?"

"They got what they deserved."

The lawyer tries to get into her head. "So, are you telling me that there is no one worth it for you to get out of here?" Jena thinks. "Ah, yes—there is someone, right? Someone you care deeply about."

She thinks of Jake. "That's none of your business."

"Maybe not, but you can let it be my business. Let me represent you."

Jena stares up at the lawyer. "I'm not innocent."

He laughs. "You're not guilty until the court says so, and even then, we can still fight it." He whispers to her, "Don't throw your life away. What's done is already done."

Jena smirks. "You're a slick lawyer. Why do you really want to represent me?"

"Because I believe I can get an innocence verdict from the jurors. I believe I can get them to set you free." He comes closer to her. "So, you can be free forever. You won't have to look over your shoulder or worry about the cops chasing you down. You'd be free to go out into the world as you please. Free to love … Jake."

She looks at the lawyer. "You don't know him."

"No, not personally, but I've heard you two are inseparable. That you have a love so passionate that you'd sacrifice yourself, claiming a murder he committed."

"What are you talking about?"

"I'm talking about his brother, Ted."

"Ted's death wasn't his fault."

"Really? I believe the district attorney will find otherwise. It's only a matter of time. They will go after him, and I know you don't want that."

"No … I don't."

"Jena, let me be your lawyer. Let's distract them with our case. Your case is indeed very, very enticing to this town. To the police department. To the world."

"No one cares about me."

"You see, that's where you're wrong. Your story is unlike any other. People in town crave more news about you. The press is going crazy trying to find out every detail about you. Heck, there are at least twenty lawyers lined up outside to come represent you." The lawyer holds his hand out. "You don't believe me? Come see. Come look out the window."

Jena walks slowly to the small window in her cell. Jena looks out the barred window. There are people everywhere. News reporters from all the television channels. Reporters from different states, fighting over who will stand in the closest spot near the jailhouse. Little children, families, people with signs supporting Jena: "Free Jena Parker," "Jena Parker is innocent," "Jena Parker was a victim herself, so why is she in jail?" There are hundreds of people outside the jailhouse. Jena stares in amazement. Her eyes scan the crowd. She sees a man holding a big sign: "Free Reda Jones." It's Franklin.

"See, I told you. Look, you're famous."

Jena walks away from the window. She thinks about Jake. The love they share. All of the sacrifices he's made for her. His beautiful eyes, his smile, and his hands as they wrap around her body, handling her gently like a precious jewel. "Why should I trust you instead of one of the other lawyers?"

"Because some of them were hired by the district attorney to convict you. Others have their own personal reasons for wanting this case—I guess you can say the eye of greed."

"What about you?"

"Well, I see a case that restarts my career."

"So, you have a motive too."

"Yes, I do, but my motive is no good if I lose. I want to win! In doing that, I not only get you back your freedom and give you back your love, but I also redeem myself. We have to give and take—that's the way of the world—but it doesn't have to be bad. We can take this extraordinary moment to tell your story in a way it will never been told if you don't let me help you."

Jena stares out the cell bars. "I will never see Jake again if I don't fight to get out of here. I know him. He won't rest until he gets me out, in turn, leading his life down a road of nothingness. And we still won't see other." She turns around. "I don't have any money."

The lawyer puts on a bright smile. "You don't need any. The court supplies me, and we'll use that to our advantage." The lawyer holds his hand out to Jena again. "This time, it's to seal the deal."

Jena shakes it. "Welcome to my world."

The lawyer calls for the guard and looks back at Jena. "Don't worry, we're going to win this. Our first hearing is tomorrow morning. Be ready." The lawyer leaves Jena's cell.

She walks back over to the window. The guard comes back in to bring her breakfast. He sits it down. "Looking out the window to find freedom?" he asks.

"No. I'm just looking out the window."

The guard comes closer. "Good, because freedom isn't outside this window. Freedom is in your heart, and that's only place you're going to find it." Jena's a bit surprised to hear those words come from a jail guard. He closes the cell door. "Don't hide from yourself. Face it. Understand why things are the way they are. Seek, and you shall find."

But what will she find? She thinks, When I pull back the curtains, will I find the Jena Parker ... or Jena Gray?

The day goes by quickly for her. The many, many people who crowd around the jailhouse keep Jena fascinated by their curiosity of her life. Franklin seems like her biggest advocate. She sees him talking to people and showing them his sign, chanting, and cheering with people, raising his hands up in the air. Jena can feel Franklin's emotions for her.

"Time to wake up, Jena Parker. You have a busy day ahead." The guard taps on the bars with his stick.

Her lawyer stands behind him. He walks in the cell with a smile on his face. "Are you ready?"

"Yes."

"Well, let's go." The guard handcuffs Jena and then walks her out of the cell, down the hall, into the courtroom. News reporters are all lined up in the hall, trying to talk to police officers, lawyers, anyone they can get information from. The court is packed, with people standing and fighting to get in the doorway.

The judge already seems frustrated. "Bailiff, get these people out of my courtroom!"

"Yes, Your Honor." The bailiff starts pushing people out. "Move people. We can't hold all of you." News reporters and lawyer attempt to hand him money. They'll try everything to remain in the courtroom. Bailiff Charles Thomas frowns at the money. "You take me for a fool? Get out of here!" He yells at the young reporter. "Hmm … twenty dollars. Man must be crazy."

The judge screams, "Order!" She slams down her gavel. "Order! I want order in my court!" Jena stands in the back doorway. Franklin peeks in the main doorway, sees her, and screams, "Jena! Hey, Jena!" Bailiff Thomas slams the door. Jena walks in the room behind her lawyer.

"State your case," the judge says.

"Your Honor, we are here today to set bail for Jena Parker," Jena's lawyer says. "This young lady hasn't been a threat to society. All the charges that the district attorney has submitted to the court can be debunked. No one has seen Jena Parker kill. Everything they have is just hearsay. Your Honor, we believe that Jena Parker is innocent, and she deserves a chance to prove her innocence in a court of jurors—not by the district attorney's office."

District Attorney Al Adams stands up. "Your Honor, how are you?"

"I'm just fine, Al. Now proceed."

"Your Honor, this young lady," he points at Jena, "may look innocent, but she has committed multiple crimes in Maplesville, New York, and other counties. We can't let her go free to roam around our nice town and to kill more people. You're an honorable judge, and I know you don't want to have a murderer running lose—"

Attorney Pillars interrupts. "Your Honor, there's is no evidence that Jena is a going to kill anyone."

Adams outshouts him. "Your Honor, I don't want to disgrace this court, but this young girl," he puts his head down, "well, she killed own mother."

Everyone in court starts talking among themselves. News reporters take notes. Everyone eyes Jena. Jena puts her head down.

Pillars touches Jena's shoulder. He walks up closer to the judge, turns around, and stares at Adams. "Your Honor, we all can see that the DA just wants a grand show, but the fact remains that they don't have any proof that Jena killed anyone. Do they have pictures? Do they have witnesses? The question is do they have the appropriate evidence to stop bail for this young girl?"

The judge stares around the room. Everyone sits in silence, waiting for her to make a decision. "Attorney Pillars, please go back to your seat. I have reviewed some of the information in the case. I can see that Jena Parker hasn't had any past conformations with the law or the court. But there are still some concerns about these murders that were committed coupled with the fact that she couldn't be accounted for. Even after she was accused, she still could not be accounted for. Therefore, I believe I have a duty to this court, to this town, and to the judicial law process to deny bail for Ms. Parker."

People stand up. Reporters start talking, and DA Adams smiles. The judge yells, "Order in the court." The judge looks at Jena. "Ms. Parker, you're denied bail, and you are to remain in jail until your court case. At that time, the DA and your attorney will provide me with more evidence so I may make an appropriate decision on whether you will be charged. Do you understand?"

Jena nods her head. "Yes, Your Honor, I do."

"Good. Court is adjourned."

"All rise," the bailiff says, releasing the court.

CHAPTER THIRTY-SEVEN

Attorney Pillars begins putting all of his paperwork back in his bag. The court guard comes to get Jena. "Jena, this isn't over." Jena nods her head and leaves with the guard.

Adams tugs up on his pants while walking over to Pillars. "You're taking a hefty case." He laughs. "You're in a little over your head, aren't you?"

"That's what you seem to think." Pillars grabs his briefcase and walks away out the courtroom.

Adams talks as he follows behind him, "Pillars, you don't have a chance. This girl is going down." Pillars keeps walking as Adams screams behind him, "Your career is already blown, why take another chance?" Pillars walks out of the courthouse building.

News reporters swamp him with questions. A reporter asks, "Is Jena Parker going to prison? Did she kill her mother, Mr. McNeil, and the man on train?"

Pillars stops. "I have no answers to give you right now."

A reporter gets angry and yells out, "Oh, yeah you do! So, tell us what we want to hear!"

"Yeah," another screams out. "We've been waiting out here all night! All day! We want answers."

Pillars muscles his way through the crowd. "Well, you aren't going to get any today." He gets into his car and drives off.

DA Adams comes out. The reporters all swamp him with questions as well.

"Is Jena Parker guilty?" one reporter asks.

Adams has no problem answering. "Yes, she is, and we're going to make sure she spends every day of her miserable life in jail."

Another yells out, "What if she's found not guilty."

Adams turns around and gets in the reporter's face. "She won't."

The reporter gets cocky. "Well, you don't know that for sure, do you? You're just trying to convict this young lady."

Adams pokes his finger in the reporter's face; suddenly, he becomes the news. "What I'm trying to do is make sure a killer is put behind bars. You got that!" Adams pushes his way through the news crowd. Adams leaves. The reporters scramble back around the jailhouse.

Jake wakes up. Chance is staring at him. "Are you hungry?" she asks.

"It's early, Chance."

"I know. That's why I'm up. I'd like to make you breakfast."

"You don't have to do that."

"Yes, I do. You're a guest in my house, and I want you to feel at home."

"This isn't home, Chance."

"It's home for now." She stands up and Jake realizes she is wearing nothing but G-string red lace panties.

He looks away. "I suppose you plan on making breakfast in your underwear?"

She snaps the string of the underwear. "Oh, this old thing. It is kind of sexy, don't you think?"

Jake removes the covers, keeping his eyes focused away from her. "I'd like to get up now so I can go see Jena."

Chance stands in the doorway. "Well, I don't think you're going to get to see her today."

"Why not?"

"Because I just heard that the DA managed to stop her bail, at least until the next court hearing."

Jake jumps out of bed. He's just wearing briefs. Chance glares at him. "Get out, Chance." She stares for moment and then walks out and closes the door. Jake walks to the window. Damn. I have to do something—but what? Jake moves the curtain back. There are nails in the window. He tries to open it, but he can't. He looks for something in the room to use to break the window, but there isn't anything. He runs to the door and tries to open it, but it's locked. "Chance!" he screams. "Open this door."

Chance is standing outside the door, smiling. "Not until you say you love me."

"Are you nuts?"

She plays with her hair. "Maybe."

"Open the damn door now!"

"No. Like I said, you have to tell me you love me."

"I'm never telling you that."

"Then I'm never opening this door. Oh, I hear my parents calling me."

"You said your parents were out of town."

"Got to go. I'll be back with breakfast, and hopefully you'll have some very nice words to say to me." She leaves him banging on the door.

"Open this door! Open it!" He puts on his clothes, muttering, "I'm going to kill that girl." Don't worry, Jena, I'll get out of here somehow.

Jena is led back to her cell. The guard walks behind her. "Not good, huh?"

"No. Not at all."

"Well, you shouldn't be down about it. Most people don't get bail. Some people get bail, but it's too high for them to make it, and they end up right back in this place called jail."

Jena turns around quickly. "What do you want from me? Why are you talking to me?"

"Calm down, little lady. I'm just a very sociable person."

"Really? Is that what it is? You're just being nice to me?"

"Turn around, and keep walking," the guard says.

Jena turns around and starts walking. "It must be something for you to have to see criminals come in here, day in and day out." She tries to get inside the guard's head. "You've probably seen it all. Killers, robbers … woman who have been raped, beaten, or both."

"I've certainly seen enough." He opens Jena's cell door, takes off the cuffs, and then steps out and closes the door. "My mother went to jail when she was seventeen. She was charged with murder." Jena stares at the guard. "You're not going to ask me who she murdered?"

Jena turns around. "No, I'm not."

"She murdered her father for raping her. She was sentenced to life in prison. But back then they were a little more sympathetic toward women, so she got released early for good behavior. That's when she met my father, Leroy. She and my father fell in love, had a baby—me."

Jena turns around. "Why are telling me this story?"

"Well, maybe I feel a little sympathetic toward you. I've heard the stories about what happened to you up at that college. Can't help but think about my own mother and what hell she went through being in jail just for killing an asshole. Young girls like you shouldn't have to go through such pain and humiliation. My mother died three years ago. She was a good mother. Gave me everything she could, despite her horrible past. The only way she got through it all is that she never gave in to this world's letdowns. She served her time. Forgave her Father. Regained her spirit—took it back from the darkness—allowed herself to love and be loved. Most woman probably wouldn't want to have a baby after what she went through, but she did everything she could to have me. So, I'm telling you, don't give in to the darkness. Fight it! That boy, Jake, he loves you, and I can tell you love him too. Life comes with the good and the bad. It's unfortunate that you've seen so much of the bad at such an early age, but those challenges you can overcome." The guard walks away, leaving Jena with a lot to think about.

Jena realizes that she isn't the only woman to face such challenges—to have done something that society deemed wicked. She walks back to her cell window. There are still hundreds of people standing outside with signs—some nice, some not so nice—all out there because of me, she thinks. I wasn't born to be this way.

Jena thinks back to when she was that simple girl living a simple life. She and Jake would walk down the halls of the school, talking and laughing. How they'd sit at the lake and talk for hours. How she'd always known that Jake loved her, but their friendship was so precious to her that she never wanted him to confess to it—because if he confessed, then she would have too as well. That's her fear: she doesn't want to lose the one person who she knows can give her a life of unconditional love—the same kind of love her parents shared.

She remembers the dance she and Jake shared. Looking into his eyes was like looking into the doors of all her inner desires. She could she them getting married. Her standing in a beautiful lace wedding dress. Him with a sky-blue tuxedo. Just them and the minister out in the middle of nowhere, standing on top of an ice mountain, blue skies, and beautiful white doves flying around them. She could see their house and children running around playing. Jumping up and down on the couches. Jake coming inside to play with them. A handsome boy and two beautiful little girls—twins. All that shined in Jake's eyes as they danced and laughed together. Why can't I have that? She thinks. Why can't I just live a simple life of eternal love with Jake?

The guard comes back with Jena's food tray. He walks inside, sets it down. "You might want to eat. Keep your strength up."

"Thank you."

The guard walks out. "Remember what I said earlier. Don't give up."

Jena eats for the first time since she was arrested. A sense of confidence comes over her. She wants to see Jake so badly, and she hopes tomorrow she will.

The night falls quickly. Jake is still trapped in the room. All day he refused to eat or say what Chance wanted him to say. Chance stands outside the door. "I know you're hungry." Jake is angry and doesn't respond to her. "I'm not a cruel person, Jake. I don't want to treat you this way."

He yells out, "Then don't! Let me go!"

"I can't do that."

"Why not? I don't love you, Chance, and I never will. I don't even understand why you're doing this. We barely spoke in high school, and now you want me to tell you I love you?"

Chance's voice is sad. "I just want someone to love me. Someone to just want me for me." Jake sighs. "Everyone wanted Carol or Jena, but what about me? Why doesn't anyone just want to hold me in their arms." She wraps her arms around herself.

"Chance, your parents can't be happy about you locking me in this room." Chance is silent. "Chance? Are you still there?"

"Jake, my parents are dead. I killed them both. They're upstairs lying-in bed, all dressed up like dolls. That's what they were to me—just dolls. They never spent any time with me. They were always out of town, going somewhere, seeing the world without me. Well, I guess now they're permanently out of town."

"You're better than this, Chance."

"Am I? You love Jena, and she's a murderer. Why can't you love me?"

"Because I can't, so let me go."

"No. I won't." Jake bangs on the door.

Chance screams, "Jake, you can bang all you want, but I ain't opening this door. I won't let her have you." She lowers her voice and says, "There are candy bars behind the stuffed animals. That's all you'll get until you love me. Until you make love to me."

Jake bangs on the door harder. She jumps. "You get this straight: I'll never love you, I'll never make love to you, and when I get out of this room—and I will get out of this room—I'm going to make you pay for every moment you kept me away from Jena." He kicks the door. "You got that!"

CHAPTER THIRTY-EIGHT

Several weeks have passed since Jena's arrest. Jake is still trapped at Chance's house, and Jena is still trapped in her cell.

Attorney Pillars pays Jena a visit. "Sorry I haven't been able to come as often as I hoped, but I have other clients." He sits down next to Jena. "We have court in a week, so we must prepare for it. Jena, I have some bad news. The DA has found some evidence. They have photos of you entering the hotel where Mr. McNeil was allegedly murdered—photos of you walking in with him and leaving with Jake. Now, I don't believe that their case is strong. However, they have you on camera, and that sends a strong opinion to the judge. The thing is, they don't have the murder weapon, and they can't prove without doubt that you murdered him. The other murders—the doctor on the train, the clerk, Ted," his speech slows, "and your mother—they can't be proven at this time. But the DA will still try to link you to all of those murders. I'm prepared to fight against any allegations they bring up in court. I want you to know that I'm on your side, and I will bring forth an innocent verdict."

Jena stands up. "I want to see Jake."

Attorney Pillars stands. "Jena, the police haven't been able to find Jake since you were arrested."

"What!"

"He's missing, Jena. They can't say for sure if he's dead or if he's alive. They just don't know. They have been searching for him to ask him questions, so have I, but we can't—"

Jena is hysterical. "What do you mean, you can't?" She grabs Attorney Pillars' suit jacket. "You look here—you better find him, or I'll be that creature in the night."

He gently removes Jena's hands. "I know you're upset, but you can't lose it now. We're too close. The DA is looking for every inch of doubt he can present to the judge. I'm sure Jake is all right, but if you get convicted, you'll never know!" He grabs his briefcase and calls for the guard. "I'll be back in four days, the day before our next hearing. We will win this, so pull yourself together." He walks away.

Jena's emotions come to a standstill. She feels frozen in time. All the magic she felt, her hopes, her dreams, they all lifted from her body the moment Pillars gave her the news about Jake. She falls to her knees and bursts out in a whirlwind of tears. Lying on the floor face up, her hands pinned to the floor, every fear she'd had, love, sadness, and anger all disappear from her. She feels lifeless, as if millions of people walked up to her and, one by one, each took a piece of her soul, leaving her alone to bare the truth of the madness she created—that the truth of her world is harsher than she had imagined, much more unbearable than her heart can withstand. She can see the horizon up ahead, feel the cool breeze of freedom, but the further she walks without her soul, the less she can feel the breeze and the further the horizon seems.

Then the darkness comes, and all of the people around her are gone. Her arms lift in the air, back to the wind as it strips her of every piece of clothing, leaving her bare naked for her self-shame to judge her and for her wickedness to laugh at her. Nowhere to run. Nowhere to hide. The ugly truth has found her, taken everything from her, and left her to live out the rest of life to never forget it. She'll walk the earth naked, shamed, and forever without love or even hate … nothing.

The tears run down her face to the floor. Jena has finally reached that breaking point, the end of her cold raindrops. "Jake," she utters as she lies in a pool of her own tears. She is exhausted from the emotional breakdown. Lying on the floor, she slips away to the only place that ever truly made sense to her. Her dreams.

A bus horn blows as people are crossing a crowded street. The bus driver yells, "Come on, people, get out of the street. Move it!" Jena can feel she's in her body, but she can't see herself. There's a tall man standing next to her. She sees him smiling at her. He's talking to her, but she can't see his face or remember what he's saying. He's wearing a black trench coat, dark sunglasses, and a scarf around his neck. He's carrying a briefcase and a gun. She walks next to him across the street. She is sharp and poised. People are walking around every corner. Jena and the man stand in front of a tall glass building. Her eyes follow his up to read the sign: Airport. The man opens the door for her, and they begin walking through the airport like secret agents. Jena can read his lips as he talks. "We have to check in now," he says. He speaks in code words that only she can understand. They walk through crowds of people at the airport. A little boy eating ice creams smiles as he passes with his mother. They all seem like they're in a rush to get somewhere. The man begins talking to one of the ticket attendants, who is standing around giving out information and directions. He taps Jena on the shoulder to signal it is time to go. They begin walking and then step on the airport escalator. There are mirrors on both sides. Jena looks at herself. She can finally see herself clearly. She isn't the young Jena anymore. Her hair is shorter and colored black, and she is wearing black shades, black boots, and a red leather trench coat with a gun at her side. She looks at herself quickly and smirks, and then she looks forward.

Jena is shocked to see herself. She wants the older Jena to look back at the mirror, but she never does. She sees the man and her walking, their backs facing her in the dream. They give the flight attendant their tickets. He gestures for her to walk in front of him. He follows her in as they board the plane. Jena can't see beyond this point, and she feels her body drifting away from the attendant, away from the crowded airport, and away from her dream.

She suddenly opens her eyes. The cell room is dark. She finds herself splattered in wet tears on the floor. She gets up, wipes herself off, and stands by the bars. Looking out down the hall, she sees it's empty. No guards. The other inmates asleep. She lies back on her cot, drapes the blankets around her body, and tries to recall the dream. The man, the airport, the mirror, me ... that was me. She ponders the dream until the morning sun shines in her window. The dream stimulated something inside her. She realizes that she isn't going to be a young girl forever, that she is going to become a woman one day—a woman like the guard's mother. Will I be free? she thinks. Days go by quickly, and soon the day comes for her to return back to court.

Jake is still trapped in Chance's house, surviving off of only candy bars, water from the bathroom sink, and his own anger.

Chance comes to the door. "Aren't you tired of being caged up like an animal?"

Jake is quiet. His anger has overcome him, and he's done speaking to Chance. His only reason for living is Jena, and now he knows the time has come; he has to break free from Chance's insane institution to rescue the woman he loves.

She yells, "So you're not going to speak to me? Well, you can just die in there!" She walks away, out of the house, gets in her car, and speeds off.

The guard opens Jena's cell. She leaves to conduct her daily hygiene and then returns to her cell to eat. She'll be left there until it's time for her to go to court. The guard comes to her cell. "You have a visitor."

"I thought I'm not supposed to get to see any visitors."

"Well, we're not supposed to allow it, but seeing as you are going to court today, I'm going to let you. She says she's your aunt Denise."

Jena stands up. "My aunt? Really?"

"Yeah. She looks kind of young to be an aunt, but she sure seems eager to see you before you go to court. Now, I'm going to sneak you in a room. You'll have five minutes—that's all." The guard walks Jena to the room, lets her in, and closes the door.

The chair turns around. "Hello, Jena," Chance says.

"So, I see you're not only trying to pass yourself off as me, but also as my aunt?"

"I just wanted to come by to say hello."

"Well, that's quiet odd—since the last time I saw you I wanted to rip you to pieces. You think if you can dress up like me, look like me, that you'll be me?"

Chance stands. "No, but I do understand why you love Jake. He's a handsome one, especially when he sleeps."

"Where is he?"

"Oh, in my bedroom."

Jena runs up to her. "You better be glad I'm still in these handcuffs, because I'd really be convicted for murder if I wasn't."

Chance laughs. "You're going to jail anyway, and I'm going to have Jake all to myself. He's a little reluctant right now, but when you're locked up and he's horny, I'm going to be the one to satisfy him." Jena and Chance continue to confront each other.

Jake tries to pull the door open. He walks around the room trying to figure out a way to get out. Throwing the bed over, he takes the bed frame and slams it up against the wall until it crumbles apart. He takes a piece of the wood and uses it to break the window out. He grabs his things and jumps out the window.

He sees a woman walking down the street on her cell. "Ma'am." The woman gives him a crazy look. "Ma'am, please—I need to call the police." She hands him the phone; he dials 911. An operator answers and asks for the reason for the call. "Yes, there's been a murder at 115 Lowtowers Road. Hurry. The Killer is Chance Middleton. She's killed her mother and father." Jake hands the phone back to the woman, who's in shock and instantly calls back to tell the person she'd been on the phone with that there's been another murder in town.

Jake hitches a ride to the courthouse. The traffic leading there is backed up. "What's going on, man?" he asks the driver.

"Where you been? That mass murderer Jena Parker's trial is today. Today we'll find out if she's going to jail for life or going to be set free to kill more people. We're only a few minutes away, but it looks like we're going to be here for hours." Jake gets out of the car and runs like he's never ran before. People stare at him as he passes.

Jake walks through the jailhouse doors. The office is empty, since all of the police officers are out manning the traffic, taking interviews from the press, and standing guard for possible riots at the courthouse. The jail guard walks out and discovers Jake.

"I know you."

"Sir … out of breath. I really need to see Jena before she goes to trial."

"You're the kid that loves her, right?"

"Yes, sir. I love her. Please help."

"Well, she's in with a relative right now." He looks around. "Come on."

Just then an APB comes over his walkie-talkie. "Ten-four, go head." He listens as he walks Jake to the room.

"There've been two more murders on Lowtowers Road. Everyone be on the lookout for a young lady about five feet five, red hair. She's Chance Middleton, possible suspect in the murder of her parents."

The guard and Jake walk quickly to the visitation room. "Man, what's going on in this town?" the guard says as he opens the door. They look in and see that Chance has pulled a knife on Jena and is about to stab her.

Jake yells out, "That's her! That's Chance."

The guard pulls out his gun. "Put the knife down!"

"Put it down, Chance!" Jake yells out. Jena just stares Chance in the eyes.

Two more cops walk in the room. They pull out their guns and circle Chance. "Put it down!" one yells out.

Chance is trapped. She surrenders, dropping the knife. The cops grab her. "Chance Middleton, you're under arrest for the murders of your parents and the attempted murder of an inmate."

The guard runs to Jena and holds her close to him. Chance gives Jena a dirty look. Jena smiles at her. "Well, you wanted to be my twin—now you are." The police officers walk Chance out.

Jake stares at Jena. The guard walks Jena to the door, but he feels bad for Jake. "Look, you two have ten seconds. Make it count." He steps outside the door.

Jake grabs her, holds her in his arms, and kisses her face all over. "I love you. I love you, Jena."

The guard grabs Jena's arm and takes her back to her cell.

CHAPTER THIRTY-NINE

Attorney Pillars is searching for his client. He goes to Jena's cell, sees she is missing, and yells for the guard. He sees the guard walking behind Jena down the hall. "Where have you been, guard? It's time for court. Please bring Ms. Parker along now." Pillars walks swiftly to the courtroom.

The circus has already begun. News reporters are everywhere, some fighting each other to get in the courtroom. Hundreds of people stand outside the courthouse waiting for the verdict. People scream Jena's name. "Jena! Jena! Jena!"

The DA walks into the courtroom with confidence, smiles at Pillars, and winks. Pillars is nervous.

"All rise. Here is the Honorable Judge Mary Cliffersom. You may be seated."

DA Adams begins. "Your Honor, I've provided supporting evidence that Jena Parker was on the hotel surveillance tape, which I believe puts her at the scene of the crime at the time of the murder. She was seen leaving a New York club with the victim as well. Ms. Parker was checked in at the hotel where the clerk was murdered. She also purchased a ticket for the train where the doctor was murdered. We also believe that she is responsible for the murders of her mother, Kathleen Parker; her neighbor's wife, Mrs. McNeil;

and Ted Paterson. Your Honor, the evidence is clear that this young lady," he points as he shouts, "killed all of these people. Do not let this murderer run free in our town! In our society! It is simply ludicrous! She's a dangerous individual, and she should be locked up behind bars."

"Okay, District Attorney Adams, thank you. Attorney Pillars, please state your case."

Pillars looks at Jena. "Your Honor, has the DA provided you the murder weapon? I believe that answer is no. Has the DA provided any other evidence beside hearsay that Jena Parker murdered these people in cold blood? I believe that answer is also no. Your Honor, how could this court convict a young girl for murders based on this evidence? It may put her or someone who looks like her at these scenes, but it doesn't mean she murdered these people. Your Honor, my heart truly goes out to the murder victims and their families, but to send a young girl to jail for these crimes when there is no murder weapon—well, I find that to be ludicrous."

The judge says, "I will review the case, and the jurors will make their decision. Court will adjourn for one hour."

The bailiff says, "All rise." Everyone leaves the courtroom.

Pillars feels confident about his plea to free Jena. Adams grabs his coat and walks out of the courthouse. Pillars smiles at Jena as the guard takes her back to her cell to wait for court to come back in session.

An hour has passed. Everyone is back in the courtroom. "All rise."

The judge sits down. All twelve jurors take their seats. "District Attorney Adams and Attorney Pillars, now would be the time for you to present your closing arguments."

Adams goes first. He walks up to the twelve jurors and smiles at them. "Do you see my smile? It's nice, right? I look like a nice guy—someone who would never, ever hurt any of you. But you know that I'm here in court today fighting for the safety of the great people of this town. You know that I'm smiling because I want to convict a murderer today, a murderer who smiles and whose face may appear innocent. But just like my motives to sway you to believe my case against Jena Parker," he turns around, "her attorney, Attorney Pillars, is here to smile at you to make you believe that an innocent, young girl couldn't have possibly committed these crimes. That somehow, she could be in all of these places where these people were murdered and not be the murderer—I find that to be the biggest smile of all. I would tell you jurors to ask yourselves this: if you knew that a person was at ten stores with ten murders," he stares them all in the face, "what's the possibility that this person didn't commit the crimes? Thank you." DA Adams looks over at Attorney Pillars and Jena, lifts his eyebrow, and sits down.

Attorney Pillars is concentrating in his chair. He looks over at Jena, back at the spectators and reporters in the room, and then he walks up to the jurors. "Good afternoon to you all. I know that you're all exhausted and ready to get home to your families, so I'm not going to keep you long. I'm going to keep you only long enough, in hopes that you leave this courtroom with a clear conscious that you didn't convict the wrong person. You see, I'm not smiling. I'm not smiling, because this is a serious situation." DA Adams frowns. "Yes, very serious. So, there's no need for smiling as the DA suggest. Jena Parker is just like your daughters or your granddaughters. She's just a teenage girl who had to witness her father being murdered and bare her mother's withdrawal from her. Yet this young lady managed to graduate high school and get accepted into college—just so she could have her innocence taken from her there. Now you ask yourself this, would you be disappointed? Would you be sad? Probably yes. I'd say twelve out of twelve of you would be. Having those emotions doesn't make her a murderer. That wouldn't make any of us murderers. And just because I am at the store, doesn't mean I stole the milk. The DA doesn't have any murder weapons to prove this young lady killed anyone. Therefore, her life is in your hands. I hope that you think about that when look at all of the evidence. Thank you." Pillars sits down.

"The court will adjourn until the jurors have made a decision," the judge says. She hammers down with her gavel.

"All rise." Everyone leaves the courtroom. Jena gives Pillars a proud smile.

He pats her on the shoulder. "See, I told you everything will be all right." He smiles at her as the guard takes her back to her cell.

The guard is happy, which makes Jena feel more confident. "I think you've got a shot at winning this."

Jena feels hopeful. "Maybe." He closes the cell door. "Thank you so much," she says just before he walks away. "Seeing Jake was all the hope I needed. No matter what happens today to me, knowing that he's alive is my victory."

The guard nods his head, his eyes gleam with glory that he could bring two people who love each other together. "I'm a sucker for love," he says as he walks away.

The twelve jurors weigh the information from the case: the photos of the victims; the video from when Jena walked into the hotel room with Mr. McNeil and out with Jake; the records showing that she was at the hotel the night the clerk was murdered; the train slip showing that she had purchased a ticket on the same train as the doctor.

One of the jurors, a doctor, reviews the medicine found in her mother's system after the autopsy. He says, "This medicine is rarely given to patients without a doctor's prescription." They all look over the evidence over and over again, trying to agree on a verdict.

"That doesn't mean she murdered the doctor," another juror yells out.

"Well, it could tie her to both murders, because how did the doctor's medication get into her mother's system?" another juror says. They all look at each other.

An angry juror stands up. "Look, I'm not convicting this young teenager of all these murders just because some of you want to play detective. We're not here for that. We're here to review all of the evidence to determine that there isn't a responsible doubt that she could commit these crimes—and right now I have reasonable doubts." He flops down in his chair.

They begin arguing over the evidence. Hours pass, and they still don't have a verdict. Two more hours pass. The bailiff alerts the judge that there's been a verdict reached. All the jurors are escorted back into the courtroom. The court is let back into session. DA Adams, Attorney Pillars, and Jena are back at their tables.

The bailiff takes a piece of paper from one of jurors and hands it to the judge. She opens it, reads it, and then looks at Jena and the court.

"Jena Parker, please stand," the judge says. "I'm about to read the verdict that the jurors have decided in this case. I want everyone in this courtroom to remain seated and maintain a sense of respect for this court once I read this decision."

Jena stands up slowly. DA Adams has an intense look on his face. He plays with his tie, jerking it back and forth. Attorney Pillars grips his briefcase, sweat pouring down his face. People in the courtroom are on the edge of their seats, eyes wide. The reporters are locked in on the judge, DA, Pillars, and Jena.

The judge hesitates before she speaks. She looks over at the jurors one last time. "Jurors, is this decision final?"

The juror on the end stands up. "Yes, Your Honor."

"Jena Parker, you have been found guilty of murder and are hereby sentenced to life in prison without parole." The court crowd gets rowdy.

"Order!" the bailiff yells out. "Order in the court."

The judge finishes. "You will serve out your sentence in the Luttonville County Penitentiary. Court is adjourned."

"All rise!" The courtroom crowd goes crazy. Some people start throwing chairs. News reporters are on their phones and in front of cameras reporting the verdict. Pillars loses it and starts arguing with DA Adams, accusing him of submitting false evidence. Jena begins to cry. The guard cries too as he escorts her back to her cell. Jake is outside the courthouse when he hears the news. He falls to his knees and starts crying, as people who were for Jena and against her begin to argue and fight.

CHAPTER FORTY

I had a dream once that I was lying naked in a mud puddle in the middle of the forest. I could hear birds flying above, small animals running around, and trees blowing swiftly with the wind. I lay in the mud as if I were sleeping in my bed, imagining warms blankets and soft pillows—all those things that comfort the mind. This mud didn't smell horrible or disgusting like most mud. It smelled of beautiful lavender and roses. The smell was so inviting that I began smoothing the mud all over my face and body, as if it was lotion. I covered my entire body and then walked through the forest, breathing in the beautiful, crisp air, touching the bark of the trees, watching the animals play. I allowed myself to absorb the wonders and mysteries of my surroundings—the beauty of nature when it's not corrupted by misfortunes or temptations. I felt as though I was a part of a hidden secret nestled in the forest. Forbidden to be found. A safe haven to protect my spirit … my soul.

I feel a rupture in the earth. The trees shake, and leaves fall everywhere. The animals scatter, trying to find a hiding place. Suddenly the forest grows dark, and the mud begins to ripen of an odor. People with their faces covered ride on horses down the road toward me. There is a black horse, a white, and a brown. With every step of the horses, the earth shakes harder. The men ride up to me, pointing at me with shame, and then they ride away. There's always a reason why secrets are hidden. They are hidden deep in our hearts, disguised as pleasant-smelling mud, only for us to discover they were just covered under layers of lies.

Jena stands near the door with her hands and feet shackled in chains. She stands with several women who have also been sentenced to prison. They all stand waiting to see the light from the outside, knowing the light that shines in when the doors open is only an illusion of freedom and the beginning of a life of pure hell. Outside the doors are hundreds of the same people waiting to see, waiting to judge, wanting to look into each of their eyes to see if they can capture a gasp of sorrow or laughter.

Jake is among those people, and Jena can't help but to look at him as she passes. One last look at my dying love. Of the love that once was, is, but never will be. Several police officers stand next to Jake. They fear he will run wild and attempt to free her, but the look in his eyes when she sees him is a still look of hope and love. He gently smiles at her with just a few teardrops falling. He's cried so much that his well feels dry, yet he couldn't have loved her more than he does at that moment. And even though she is leaving, he knows he is leaving with her—for wherever she is, he is, and that will always be their story.

Jena and the other women get on the bus. People cheer her name: "Jena! Jena!" But they are just voices in the distance to her because the only words she can hear are the words soaring from Jake's eyes. A glimmer blazes from them, circling her and shooting straight into her heart. All of her desires, fears, and love are embodied in his eyes. No words need to be spoken. The magic of the moment isn't the people cheering, the police walking around touting their might, or the dramatic view of her in chains and orange clothing. It is Jake and her. When he smiles and she smiles back. Two friends, lovers— unshaken by distance or by circumstances. They will weather it all, knowing that their love is beyond a life sentence. That the world can't hold it back when the passion two people share lives above the clouds, the world, deep in the universe. Those are the only words that matter to her.

They watch each other until the bus is out of sight. She knows that she will see him again, touch him, and make love to him, because love has no chains. Jena gazes out the bus window not knowing what might lie ahead, but knowing she is ready to face it.

Alongside the dusty road is a man holding up a sign: "Reda Jones Will Return!" It is definitely Franklin, and although the trial is over, his determination to keep his Reda alive is unstoppable.

Jena is placed in a cell with another woman. The woman is quiet when Jena enters. There are pieces of paper and pencil on the top bunk. Jena looks around and then climbs up top.

"I put that there for you," the woman says. "That paper and pencil. Use it to write down your feelings or to tell someone you love them." Jena is quiet as her cellmate speaks. "I know that being locked up can be lonely at first, so maybe writing will help you. It's helped me. By the way, my name is Paula Johnston. I've been in jail for five years. I have a daughter. Her name is Amy, and I hope to one day see her again."

Jena picks up the paper and pencil and writes down Jake's name. "My name is Jena Parker. Thank you for the stuff."

Weeks go by. Every day Jena tries to write down her feelings, but she can't put the right words together. Getting used to prison took some time for her, but after a while things became routine, and she became routine with it. Word comes down that Chance had been convicted of the murder of her parents and was also sent to the prison, but their paths haven't crossed yet.

Jena hears keys jingling. There's a guard standing in the door. "Jena Parker," A prison guard calls her name as he opens the cell door. "Come with me." Paula peeks open one eye. Jena jumps down from her bunk and walks with the prison guard. He puts her in an all-white room and sits her down in a chair. He nods at the other two prison guards in the room, who stand wearing black prison guard uniforms, black guns, and brown sticks by their sides. He closes the door. Jena sits and waits.

The door opens, and Warden Peters, Attorney Pillars, Detective Martin, and Officer Reyes all walk into the room. Attorney Pillars smiles at her. Officer Reyes stands behind her, and Detective Martin leans against the wall. Pillars says, "Jena, there's been a new discovery involving your case. We have someone who is asking to see you before any final decisions are made. Warden Peters has agreed to this meeting. Officer Reyes and Detective Martin are also in agreement." Jena has a confused look on her face. "This individual has asked to speak to you alone, without us sitting in and without us videotaping this meeting." Jena is quiet. "Do you understand?" Pillars asks.

"Yes," she replies.

"Bring him in," the warden yells to the guards. The guards go out and bring in a man. It's Moishe. Jena's eyes grow big. She'd thought Moishe had been killed or had abandoned her. Everyone begins to leave the room. Officer Reyes and Warden Peters stand in front of Moishe, giving him a dirty look. Moishe walks in between them and then sits down in front of Jena. Warden Peters and Officer Reyes's eyes follow Moishe. Officer Reyes is extremely angry. He puts his hand on his gun.

Warden Peters stops him. "Not here." Officer Reyes storms out of the room. Warden Peters follows.

Attorney Pillars is the last to leave. He pats Jena on the shoulder as he walks out. "You two have fifteen minutes," he says before the guard closes the door.

Jena has a surprised and happy look on her face. "Moishe, what are you doing here? What happened to you?"

Moishe just smiles. "A lot. It's good to see you, Jena." He looks around the room. "Not in here, but still, it's good to see you."

Jena blinks her eyes, stares at Moishe. "What's going on?"

He stares deeply into her eyes. "Jena Parker. What a magnificent person you are. You bit the bullet. Your courageous act to take responsibility for your life proves that you are worthy of your freedom."

Jena looks away. "I deserve to be here."

Moishe taps his fingers on the table. "Maybe. Even so, you have braved it all. It must be hard being in here knowing that you will never be able to touch the one you love again."

Jena lifts her chin up. "I will see him again."

Moishe leans back in his chair. "Yes, but you won't touch or feel the warmth of his hand, or he the softness of your skin."

"He's in my heart and mind forever."

"It's not the same, Jena." Moishe says as he leans forward, folding his hand. Jena is quiet. "So, Ted is dead?" Moishe asks as he smiles.

Jena gives him a mean look. "He deserved to die."

"I must agree with you. The creep knocked me out, obviously to get to you. Luckily, I have friends, friends in high places, whom I told that they must find me if they were without contact from me in twenty-four hours. And they did. Unfortunately, I was in the hospital and couldn't get to you until now." Moishe rubs his head. "Remember the assassin group I told you about?"

"Yes."

"Well, I still have friends from that group, and we have formed another group."

Jena gets a little nervous. "Moishe, they can hear us."

"They can't because I have a device to ensure they can't. Even though they said they wouldn't listen in, I don't believe them. So, I made sure that this conversation will remain strictly between you and me. I have a good friend named Pulue. He's helped me and called on many, many favors for me. Or should I say, for you."

"For me? What kind of favors?"

"Favors that you call in when you want to get a young girl free."

Jena doesn't believe Moishe. "That's impossible."

"Is it? Have you ever heard of corruption?"

"Yes."

"Well, there is a lot of corruption in this society. People who pretend to be something they're not. Now it's time for me to cash in on those corruptions, and Officer Reyes and Warden Peters have answered my call. Police brutality should be called criminal hospitality. Isn't it something when you can't distinguish between a man of the law and a man of crimes? Officer Reyes is a man of crime and a man of falsehood, as he imposes his law-binding attitude to lock up criminals who are innocent. Over half of the inmates in this jail are innocent of their crimes."

Jena looks in his eyes. "I'm not innocent."

"No, you're not, but neither is Reyes or Warden Peters. Those two men are vicious criminals who are paid out of the deep pockets of other free criminals and corrupt politicians. They are both involved in the cover-up of the murder of the mayor's wife and his two daughters—an investigation that is still ongoing, with no intentions of being solved."

Jena has a shocked look on her face. "How do you know this?" she asks.

Moishe looks at her and slightly smiles. "I know this because I was the man for hire." He has an ashamed look on his face. "I was supposed to turn you in the night of the party. But when you shot Kyler to protect the man you love, I saw something in you that reminded me of my Maria. I saw a powerful young girl and a courageous young man in Jake, two people willing to sacrifice it all—not only for love, but for the right to love. You two aren't in the world; the world is in you; in the love you share. I thought of my Maria and all of the promises that will be broken because our love was allowed to fade away in the wind when she was killed. You two don't have to fade away in the wind. Jena, you're free."

"What do you mean?"

"I mean after this conversation; you will be set free from this place."

"But the murders?" She shudders. "They have evidence."

"Yes, they do, but it doesn't point to you anymore." He stares at her. "All of the evidence now points to me."

"Moishe, you can't do this—"

"I can … and I have. All of the murders—the hotel clerk, the doctor on the train, Carol, Ted, Mr. McNeil, and … your mother—all now are my murders."

Jena has a shocked look on her face. "How?"

"Easy—I call in favors, and they deliver. The assassin group is much more powerful than you can imagine. I worked for an evil man years ago, but now they have reestablished the group, reorganized everything. We have high technologies, the best in the espionage business. We are located all over the world, even in places you have never heard of."

"How did you do all of this, Moishe. You weren't at these places."

"Yes, I was. My name is in the book at the hotel from the night you were there. The train system's records have my name as one of the passengers on the train the same day you traveled. I was at the party when Carol was murdered."

"And Mr. McNeil?" Jena asks curiously.

"The surveillance tapes? Yes, I'm on them. I'm on the tape, showing that I also entered Mr. McNeil's hotel room. I can be linked to Ted. I was seen with him. I have also arranged it that I was in Maplesville the night your mother died. Everything has been arranged. Everything leads back to me. I confessed to the murders, and I'm now going to take your place."

Jena gets out of her seat. "I won't let you do this."

Moishe stands up. "Jena, it's already done. They have the murder weapons with my prints on them: the knife that killed the doctor, the medicine that killed your mother, the gun that killed Mr. McNeil and I killed the hotel clerk. My prints are even on the window Ted was pushed out of. They will officially arrest me after this conversation is over. I told them that I would confess to all of it if they would let me talk to you first. Now you can see Jake, now you can be free again—or you can make another choice. You can come be a part of our group."

"An assassin?"

"Yes. We could train you. Enhance the skills you already possess."

"Is that why you're doing this? To make me an assassin?"

"No. I'm doing this to give you back your life, but you must think about your beginning. Why do you think you are different? You saw the dark side in yourself and how quickly you mastered the skills of being a killer. You have it in you. It's up to you to choose."

She closes her eyes. "But Jake?"

"You will see Jake after you have gained your skills. Do you think you can control your anger? Will you strike again if someone provokes you? Take the darkness that you have and transform it into the lighter darkness. One that kills people who steal from others, create crimes, take from the poor. People like Officer Reyes, Warden Peters, or the slimy creeps like Ted."

Jena quickly looks up at Moishe. "I will not see you, Moishe."

"Yes, you will."

"How? You will be in jail."

Moishe softly laughs. "A part of every deal is always another deal. I will not be in jail long. This is just a smoke screen to get you out. Officer Reyes and Warden Peters couldn't just let you walk out. There has to be some reason for you being released, and I'm your reason. Besides, my friends will rescue me in a few days with a little help with my escape from Officer Reyes. They will be looking for me, and not for you. Just like the mayor's family murder, the search for me will never be solved. So, go to Jake and be his Maria, and then come fulfill your destiny. They will be coming back in here to arrest me in a few seconds, so now we must pretend. Let them hear what they want to hear."

The room door opens, and Moishe begins to put on a show—mostly for the sake of the guards and Attorney Pillars. Everyone stands in the room, watching as Moishe starts his show.

"Jena Parker, I apologize for committing these crimes that you were unfortunately blamed for, and I appreciate Officer Reyes," Moishe says as he stares at him, "and Warden Peters allowing me to confess and personally apologize to you."

Jena is quiet but catches on quickly. "Thank you for coming forward to reveal the truth." The guards stand Jena up. She takes one last look at Moishe before they handcuff him and take him away. Jena stops to thank Attorney Pillars. He smiles at her.

"I'll be taking care of all the paperwork today, and you will be out of here by tomorrow." Jena nods her head as she takes one more look at Moishe and then stares over at Officer Reyes, who is eyeing her closely. The two lock eyes. Jena remembers the dream where he arrested her in the desert and the day, he handcuffed her when she turned herself in. She knew from the look in his eyes that they would see each other again, and the next time it would be all-out war.

The guard holds on to her arm as he leads her back to her cell. Walking the prison halls, Jena thinks of Jake and everything that has happened up until this very moment. She feels empowered as she passes all the other cells while the inmates yell and scream for freedom and for justice. The guard opens the door.

Paula is asleep. Jena tries to be quiet as she climbs back up to the top bunk. She picks up the paper and pencil Paula had given her and thinks back to when she was a child, a teenager walking the halls with Jake, the smiles, the tears, the laughter, the horrible night her father died, the night that changed everything—but did it? Was I always heading down this road? she thinks. She thinks about her father and her mother. She imagines her parents happy together, kissing and dancing high in the heavens, and then her father swinging her mother high in the air. She thinks about her mother—how she was always there for her, being the best mom, she could be. "I forgive you mom, and I love you. My father is Jonathan Parker," she utters.

She feels the compassion of the moment and the heat from the love that she knows awaits her when Jake will hold her in his arms.

But she also knows that Moishe is right; there is still a coldness in her—that ball of fire that brews when her anger strikes a passion inside of her that is beyond her control. She picked up the paper and pencil and then begins to write.

As a child, I used to dream of being someone famous …

Now I am.

The End

JENA PARKER
"THE FINAL RESOLUTION"

PROLOGUE

A spark of light can ignite desire, melt a cold heart, and bring hope to a burning world that yearns to connect to the warmth and mysteries of the universe. You can feel the brightness drawing you in, raging in your spirit, and howling at your soul, lifting you up to a Higher Being more powerful than the Earth's rumbles, shattering your nightmares: like a Mother draping you from the harsh reality of the unknown. Why does the beginning of your life often feel much like the end, where in an instant, everything you hope and dream changes, leaving you limp, as if your brain suddenly becomes paralyzed, crippled, and vulnerable?

One minute you're a young girl sitting next to your best friend on the school bus, laughing, joking, as he gazes into your eyes, hoping for a kiss, or maybe more, and the next minute you're pointing a gun at someone who soon will not see anything at all. How does life change so fast? It is almost as if the Earth stopped, but you kept going at full speed while trying to put the pieces back into place. But these pieces are tiny teardrops of blood spattered everywhere, like tracks you hope someone will find to rescue you—not from an evil villain, but from yourself.

When your father comes home from work and smiles at you, then you are forced back into the moment. Your father goes to the kitchen to laugh with Mom, while you hurry upstairs to do homework, to peak out the window and spy on the neighbor.

A man filled with intrigue: a human with the face of a jackal and the eyes of a monster.

Rapists, crooks, killers, con men, and murderers are like bees searching for their next hive filled with the nectar of the weak, wounded, and the innocent. They feed on others' hopes, fears, wishes, and desires to empower themselves with unlimited insanity.

How does this kind of thinking begin?

At birth? Does darkness—cold and imprecise—rise from the moment of conception? Does it begin when a young girl, her emotions conflicted, her dreams altered, is propelled into horrifying reality: Is that how she is enticed to that singular moment of murder? Is it caused by the boy's love—too much of it—obsession and desire, uncontrollable? … Or could it be because of the man who was killed by another man—the man who is revealed to be the real father, a devilish creature no longer among the living, who even in death attacks the mind like a plague devouring the body? Or does evil live in all of us, even calm, simpleminded people—dormant until unleashed by unforeseeable, unknowable, ungovernable circumstances?

Why is it that the Dark has so much power that can take over your mind?

One moment you're just a young girl on that school bus next to your best friend, who wants so badly to kiss you—maybe more—laughing and joking. The next moment, you're pointing a gun at a man you despise so much that you are consumed with the dream of putting a bullet into his head. The man is your estranged father.

How does life change so quickly? All you want is to put the broken pieces of your life back into one place. How is it that the beginning of your life feels so much like the end? You want to find your way back to that moment when your father came home from work and smiled at you; when you went upstairs to do your homework, when you were just ... that ... age. The phone would ring, and your best friend would try to put words to the words stuck in his heart. A strange man would come over, smile, and gaze at you; you didn't understand your discomfort. Was it all a nightmare?

Did I dream all this? Am I still asleep, lost in space, waiting for Jake to find me and wake me? Do I want to find something different or something familiar? Nothing seems real.

Why does the darkness have much power to take over your mind?

<hr />

It seems like only yesterday that I was that young girl on the school bus next to Jake. I can see his big, beautiful green eyes, lost in the sunbeam, smiling at me with his innocent charm, desperate to share the love in his big, bright-red heart.

I see his lips move. Words fall from his mouth. His eyes focus only on me.

So often I want to pull him close and hold him tight. One day, he would take me far into the universe, close to the heavens.

We'd dance, just like the night we danced at the party, and he made me feel like the most wanted person in the room. No moment in our lives had ever had more passion, love, and romance.

I hear my mother's voice: "Wake up, Jena, get ready for school."

CHAPTER ONE

A prison guard stands in the dark hall in front of Jena's cell. His hands are in his pockets. His breathing is shallow. He watches while Jena and Paula sleep. He leans forward to stare into the cell.

Jena opens her eyes, her body stiff in the bed as she listens for any sound from the prison guard. She can feel his eagerness. What does he want?

The guard steps back. Jena can hear his shoes on the concrete floor. He jiggles the keys, then walks away. Jena sits up a little and peeks down at Paula; she's sound asleep. Jena lies down, stares at the ceiling, and glances around the dark prison cell.

She thinks of Jake. Where is he, what he is doing? Is he worrying about her?

How is he going to bust me out of jail, then hold me and never let me go? We'd live in a Happily Ever After fairy tale, and he would be the prince who rescues me from this dungeon. He would wake me, and all of this, every single murder, would have been a nightmare that never happened.

But it isn't a nightmare. She really is in jail. Still, the countdown to her release started a few hours ago.

I will see Jake soon, but our freedom together will be no fairy tale, just a return to a life where bad shit happens to people for no reason. No reason at all.

Jena closes her eyes. She tries to imagine the last time she saw Jake's face: his sad, beautiful face as he watched her walk out the courtroom toward the prison bus, her hands and legs shackled in chains. But her heart and soul were free and belonged only to Jake, even though at that moment life seemed over. It wasn't that their love had grown. Jena had grown. She knew some things are meant to be, others are sheer coincidence or circumstance, nothing is permanent, even death has a plan.

She would see him soon, the love of her life. She would hold him without the fear of leaving him again. Or would her dark side erupt again and separate them? Could she control the dark? Or does she have only one path? Is there another path, like the one Moschi told her about? The world needed to be relieved of the likes of Reyes, Peters, Ted, McNeil, and all of the scumbags. But that path would surely take her away from Jake. *Is this the only path where I feel like I belong?*

The lights in the cell come on. Paula moves in the bunk below. "Jena, are you awake?"

Jena says nothing.

Paula continues to call out. "Jena?"

"Yes. I'm awake."

"I had a dream about my daughter last night," Paula says. "I was walking toward her wearing this awful orange jumpsuit. The closer I got to her, the further away she seemed. I reached out to her. I yelled for her, but she just stood and stared at me, as if she didn't recognize me.

"There were times when she even frowned at me. I was devastated. I felt lost and confused. I just kept reaching for her and calling her name until she ... just ... disappeared. Then, suddenly, I was behind bars again. Even now that I am awake, I can feel the sadness I felt in the dream. It's as if I'm still there."

Jena listens to Paula's haunting story and sits up in her cot. Paula is quiet. "I'm sorry, Paula."

Paula begins to cry, then she screams. "I failed her! I failed my little girl! Now I'll never see her again."

Jena listens to Paula's breakdown.

"I'll never see her grow up, get married, or see her kids. I'm a loser."

Jena crawls off her mattress. "You're not a loser, Paula. You had to defend yourself from that asshole. *He's* the loser."

A guard approaches the cell. "You two, be quiet. Get ready for breakfast." The guard shoots Jena a menacing look. "Just because you're leaving doesn't mean you don't follow the rules around here."

Jena stares as he walks away.

Paula sits up. "You're leaving," she says, wiping away tears.

Jena looks down, glances around the room. "Yes, I am."

"How? You just got here."

Jena walks to the sink. "It's a long story. You wouldn't understand." She turns the faucet. "I don't quite understand it myself."

Paula moves closer to Jena. Tears cascade down her face. She gently touches Jena's shoulders. "Please take me with you. There's got to be a way." Paula looks desperate. Jena stares at her, feels the sadness in her eyes, enough sadness to make a room full of people cry.

"There's nothing I can do for you, Paula—at least, not now, not until I'm free."

Paula moves away. "I know you can't. I'm stuck in this hell."

Jena turns around. "When the time is right, I will do what I can to help you get out of here. Until then, you have to be strong." Jena turns back to the sink, washes up, then sits beside Paula, who has drifted away.

The prison guard comes back. "I hope you two are ready for breakfast." He laughs. "I hear it's better than IHOP." He laughs louder as he walks away.

Paula finally gets up and takes her turn at the sink. "You'll see, Jena, when you leave you won't have to deal with assholes like him.

I'll still be here with this bullshit and all the other bullshit in this hellhole." Paula's anger rises. "The people in this place make you want to kill someone." Paula turns off the water. "You didn't get a real taste of this. You haven't been here very long. The way the guards treat you, the way the warden runs the place, not to mention the inmates. Some of them are ruthless." Paula pauses. "Some of them have even murdered their own children."

Jena looks away. She thought she knew everything about this place. Perhaps she hadn't been here long enough; she thought she had been here far too long.

Paula smirks. "You think hell lives in one place. No. Hell is in many places, especially here, in this prison. Demons seem to crawl from every cell."

The cell doors open. Guards begin guiding inmates to the dining hall.

This is it.

Paula moves. Jena watches.

This is it.

Paula turns to Jena.

It begins.

The guard signals to Jena and Paula to leave their cell and head to the dining hall.

"Hey, ladies," one guard calls out with a sneer, his hand lingering over his uniformed crotch. "Which one of you would like a nice big fat *sausage* with your breakfast?

The other guards laugh and slap each other on the back.

"Hey, Mike," the first guard chimes in again. "I bet most of these ladies would like to pack some tasty round meat right about now.

"What do you say, ladies," says one of the other guards. "My buddy here, Tim, he wants to know, who's up for sausage today?"

An inmate stares at the guard named Tim. "Stuff your sausage, pal."

"Oh, check his one out, Mike. She doesn't like a long, hot sausage."

Tim blocks the inmate's path, but he still talks loudly. "So, what do you like? Muffins? You like munchin' on muffins?" He pushes her back in line with the other women. "You, muffin-munchin', get back with the rest of you worthless whores."

Jena stares at the guard.

Tim walks up to Jena. "You haven't been here long, have you?"

Jena just stares ahead.

The guard, whose name badge reads Mike Fredmond, walks over. "She's off-limits, man."

Tim circles Jena. "And? Why is that?"

"She's Jena Parker."

"Oh, well, that explains it!" Tim laughs with vicious sarcasm. "The famous Jena Parker! I should've known."

Tim moves closer to Jena's face. "You think your hot shit because you're getting out of here. But lemme tell you somethin'. No one leaves here without tasting some of my sausage."

He grabs her hand and tries to pull it to his crotch.

Jena stares into Tim's eyes. "Really?" she asks. She's at least as strong as he is. Her arm doesn't move, if only because she's more determined than he is.

"Yeah. Really." He releases her wrist. "What? You don't like sausage, either?"

Tim looks over his shoulder at Mike. "What is it with your friends here—"

"They're not my friends, buddy."

"They're not anyone's friends if they don't like sausage."

"You're an asshole," Jena says.

Tim grabs her again, more forcefully.

Mike moves between them. "I told you she's off-limits. Go get breakfast, Parker."

"What's up with you?" Tim growls.

Mike moves within an inch of Tim's face. "You touch Jena Parker and Warden Peters will have both of our asses. Now, take your eyes off her."

Tim defiantly stares at Jena as she walks away.

Paula catches up with Jena in the breakfast line.

"Are you alright?" she whispers.

"I'm fine, Paula. I've dealt with worse."

Paula clings to Jena's side, still whispering. "Yeah, well, in this shithole, you don't know what's gonna happen. One day they might leave you in peace, and other days you have to deal with horny guards and prison wolves howling at you." Paula pauses. "They treat you like trash."

Paula glances around the dining hall. "Maybe I am trash. Maybe we all are."

Jena takes her tray and stares at the brown slop in disgust. A prison cook slams a spoon onto the counter. Jena looks up.

"Not good enough for you, princess?" The cook looks at Jena, up and down. "Too bad. This is your life. Eat up."

Jena and Paula look for seats among the criminals in this cage. Most of the tables are full, except for one, where a young woman sits alone with her back to them.

Jena and Paula slide onto the bench, and the girl looks up, then lowers her head.

"This is shit," Paula says, sliding her spoon through a mound of glop that has the color and consistency of actual shit. "I can't live like this anymore."

Jena stares at the girl and asks her name.

The girl keeps her head down, but Jena sees her eyes move, left and right, up, and down, trying to avoid looking at her seatmates.

"You got a name, girl?" Paula asks.

Jena shoots Paula a glance that says, "calm down," and to the girl, Jena says, "It's alright, we're not going to mess with you. We just want to know your name."

The girl mumbles: "Karen."

"Okay, now we're getting somewhere," Paula says.

Jena introduces herself, then: "She's Paula. She's harmless."

Karen eyes Paula, not so sure.

"Seriously, don't be afraid of her, she won't hurt you." Jena nudges Paula to ease up. "Nobody likes it here, Karen. It's shit."

"Yeah, it's shit," Paula says, too loudly, as if she's itching for a confrontation that will only make things worse.

Too late.

Some of the other women start chanting. "This place is shit! This place is shit!"

Guards gather.

Karen looks around and starts laughing.

Paula just stares at Karen, then looks back at Jena.

Jena looks back but says nothing.

Paula starts eating again. "What? I gotta eat." Paula is gripping her spoon so tight that her knuckles are white.

"So, Karen, what got you in here?" Jena asks.

Karen stops smiling.

Paula flinches.

Karen clears her throat.

Paula and Jena wait through a long, even bizarre, pause.

"I … I …" Karen can't seem to get her story out; maybe she can't get her story straight. "I got drunk at a party and got into my car." She stops, another long pause.

Jena studies Karen and can almost feel the pain in Karen's throat as she tries to speak.

"I killed a family." Her words are a whisper that falls like a hammer.

Jena and Paula trade stares.

"I was so drunk I didn't realize I'd killed anyone. The crash knocked me out, almost killed me. When I woke up, I didn't remember anything. It took a while, a few months, before I could talk or walk, before I could remember what happened, and even then …"

Her voice trails off, but her eyes are steady, as if she is in a place and time that she can remember but badly wants to forget. "When

I … finally, my mother told me I killed an entire family: a father, a pregnant mother, and their six-year-old daughter. I wanted to die."

Karen focuses again on Paula and Jena.

"As soon as I recovered, I went to trial. Guilty." She looks around the chattering hell. "Obviously." She drops her head in shame. "I deserve to be here. I deserve to die, too."

Paula and Jena say nothing.

Jena looks away, her thoughts drifting back to the night she was raped—by Ted, the brother of the love of her life, Jake.

She returns her gaze to Karen, then to Paula. "I bet neither of you has done anything as horrible as what I did."

She thinks again of that night, sees herself climbing the stairs in her house with a glass of milk. She gives the glass to her mother, who drinks. And her mother dies. Five people murdered. Maybe two of them who did not deserve it, Jena reminisces with teary eyes. Her mother, one of the innocents—when she thought she was setting her mother free.

Jena closes her eyes tightly. "Oh, I wish my mother were here," she whispers to herself.

She bolts up from the table to quiet her thoughts, hissing as she glares at Karen. "No. I believe there are people in here who have done much worse than either one of us."

She shifts her stare to Paula. "We *all* deserve to be here."

She walks away, toward the window where trays are left for dishwashing.

A woman purposely bumps her.

Jena's tray clatters to the floor, food spattering everywhere, splashing another inmate. Jena turns in rage at the woman who careened into her. "What the hell is wrong with you, Chance?" She feels her face flush and clenches her fists.

Chance just smiles. Her hair is shaved almost bald. She has a tattoo on her neck.

"If it ain't Jena Parker," Chance says. Her smile seems to be backed up by two inmates standing on either side of her. Both have shaved heads. "Fancy meeting you here."

Jena steps closer to Chance and stares at her. "You think this is a game?"

Chance moves in closer, too. "No. I don't. But since we're here, I'd say anything goes."

Jena clenches and unclenches her fists: one, then the other, then both.

"I see you haven't learned anything," Jena says, snarling. "Look at you? You still dress like me."

Jena shoves Chance, and Chance falls to the floor, stumbling over a third inmate. Meanwhile, Chance's buddies rush Jena.

"No!" Chance yells, picking herself up off the floor. "She's mine." Chance swings and lands a punch in Jena's stomach.

Jena is unfazed. "That's all you got?" she taunts. "I don't think that tough hairstyle of yours means shit!" Jena punches Chance in the face. Her nose gushes blood.

The two women jump at each other, but Jena quickly gets the advantage.

The dining room erupts with inmates jumping on top of tables and chanting, "Fight!" "Kick her ass! "Fight, fight, fight!" "Kill her!"

Fights break out everywhere as old rivalries and grudges explode.

Jena and Chance fight on, oblivious to the melee. Jena punches Chance's stomach, then her face, and pins Chance against the wall. "You had enough yet?" Jena's breathing is hard and hot. But her eyes are cold. She is angry and eager to kill Chance.

Chance pushes Jena back. "No!" She lands a hard smack to Jena's face.

When Jena closes her eyes, all she can see is Jake.

The room seems to move in slow motion. The riot of other inmates doesn't exist. Jena just visualizes Chance leaving the masquerade party bathroom, dressed as her after killing her own best friend, Carol Jones. She feels only black hate.

Her eyes fly open, and she flies at Chance, hitting her again and again, in the face, stomach, her head.

Fueled by hate, she picks up Chance as if she were a child.

Jena's head is spinning. And then she actually does spin, with Chance in the air. Everyone stops as Jena throws Chance to the ground.

Chance lies crumpled, her taut, compact frame looks fragile.

Jena bends over, out of breath, and holds her knees, watching Chance moan in pain.

Guards are rushing in through the cheering crowd. Now it's Jena's turn, as the guards slam her to the floor, next to Chance, and handcuff her. Jena doesn't resist, she just lies still, eyeing Chance as other guards pile on. The prison medical team swoops in to pull Chance out of the way.

The guard who had come to Jena's defense earlier, Mike Fredmond, gets to Jena and manages to lift her away from the rest of the staff and prisoners. "What were you thinking? You're about to get out of here."

Jena remains quiet.

Tim approaches Mike. "Warden Peters wants to see her now."

Mike squeezes Jena's arm as he leads her to Warden Phillip Peters' office.

The rest of the guards, meanwhile, try to control the other inmates. Most resist, screaming and fighting, as they are herded back to their cells. Tim shoves Karen and Paula. "Get moving, you two pieces of trash!"

Karen has tears in her eyes, but Paula's eyes are cold.

"You two think you're safe," Tim taunts. "You're not safe here. The moment you walked into this prison; you were both dead." Tim screams louder. "Dead!"

Paula spins around. From out of nowhere, Tim pulls a gun, unauthorized, on Paula and shoves the pistol toward Paula's face.

"Oh?" Tim says, itching for a fight. "What are you going to do? Huh?"

Paula just stares into his black eyes with a look that would terrify most people.

"Say something!" he screams.

Finally, tears form in Paula's eyes and her lips begin to quiver. She can barely speak. "You ... One day you're going to get yours."

Tim moves within an inch of her face. "Yeah, maybe. But it ain't today, and it ain't you. Now turn your ass around and get moving."

Paula sheds a single tear, then pulls herself together and walks into her cell.

The cell door closes behind her.

He stands on the other side of the bars, glaring at her. She doesn't turn around but feels his stare like a hot flash down her back. Tim pushes his face against the bars. "Like I said, you're not safe here," he whispers. "And don't you ever ... ever ... forget that."

Paula peeks at him as he walks away. She feels a sudden wave of panic.

"Jena will be gone soon. And I'll be here alone again. She's gotta find a way to get me out of here before Tim kills me."

She sits on her bed, and her eyes tear up again with a mix of fear and sadness as she pictures her daughter's angelic face and smiles—the way she looks when the sun makes her curly, blond hair sparkle. Little Kathleen, a three-year-old full of energy. Paula thinks about her daughter playing in the park, chasing other kids, playing tag.

Paula jerks herself up and storms to the cell bars, pressing her face hard against the metal as Tim struts away. "I will survive!" Tim turns around. "I will survive!" Her voice echoes down the prison halls.

Other inmates' voices chime in. "I will survive!"

She smiles and chants the chant she started. "We will survive!" The slogan sounds like waves running down the prison halls.

Finally, the guards have had enough. "Quiet, all inmates!" but the inmates' roar takes over the halls, all the way to Warden Peters' office.

Jena hears the chant, and she feels unity with her fellow inmates.

She feels that all things are destined, especially if there is a raging desire to fight for freedom. Freedom was taken from these women, even if for just cause. But a kind of dignity lives behind these walls of tragedy, in this pit of women who are paying their debt to society, though many were victimized themselves by rape, assault, humiliation, and even death.

Mike holds tightly to Jena as they walk toward Warden Peters' door. Two security guards, Jeff, and Benny, stand outside. Jeff opens the door to alert Warden Peters, and all five of them—Mike, Jena, and the two guards—walk into the office.

Warden Phillip Peters sits at his desk, wearing black-rimmed reading glasses and a frown as Jena enters the room. He gestures for Mike to place Jena into the chair in front of the desk.

Jena sits, never taking her eyes off Warden Peters.

As Mike and the two other guards turn to leave, Warden Peters looks into Jena's emotionless face. He stands.

"Wait." The guards stop. "Mike, you and Jeff stay. Benny, you can leave."

The warden continues staring at Jena.

"Mike, close the door." He and Jeff take their place behind Jena's chair.

The warden sits at the corner of his desk, like a bird of prey perched above Jena.

Jena's eyes are still locked on the warden.

The room is silent.

Warden Peters picks up a file, Jena's prison record, and flips through the pages. He clears his throat. His voice is deep, dry. "What happened in the cafeteria today?"

Jena is silent.

"Miss Parker," he says, "this doesn't look good, considering the recent decision that you be released from this prison. An explanation might shed a better light on the situation."

Silence, still.

Warden Peters loses his patience and slams her file onto his desk. "I'll ask you again. What happened in the cafeteria?"

Jena looks up at him. "Chance Middleton was looking for a fight." She smirks. "And she got one."

Warden Peters stares at Jena again. "Chance started this fight?"

"Yes," Jena answers defiantly and returns his stare. "Is that so hard to believe?"

Warden Peters smiles, almost to himself, as he rises slowly from the corner of his desk. He removes his glasses and twirls a stem in his fingers. "Well, yes," he says, sarcastically, as he leans slightly toward Jena. "I mean, with your track record, it's hard to believe that someone else started this fight."

Jena doesn't bother to disguise her feelings about the warden's comments. "It so happens that in most instances people get what they deserve."

Warden Peters moves even closer to Jena. "Really?" He says, hissing softly. "So, your mother got what she deserved?"

Jena quickly looks away. "Why am I here?" she asks abruptly.

Warden Peters is abrupt, too, but full of authority now.

"You're here because you were involved in a fight. A fight that put a young lady in the medical ward."

"And ..." Jena replies nonchalantly.

"And ... this behavior is not tolerated in this prison facility," Peters says, more loudly. "In any prison facility!"

Jena squirms a little in her chair.

The warden notices and backs away.

"Like I said, she wanted a fight and she got one. I didn't go to the cafeteria to fight, but I certainly wasn't going to let her get the best of me." Jena says, finally.

"That kind of attitude, Miss Parker, is what has landed you in prison in the first place." His voice is condescending. "Maybe, had you just walked away, you could have avoided these situations."

Jena smirks, unwilling to give up the battle of wills. "Sure. That would have made a big difference in a place like this."

The warden turns red, visibly angry again. "What does that mean? I run a highly professional prison facility."

Jena yells, now even angrier. "Really? Then how do you explain the rapes and beatings that go on in this place? Huh?" She yells louder yet. "Maybe you should give your staff members the memo because they sure know how to make everyone here feel right at home."

Warden Peters looks at the guards, Mike, and Jeff.

"You know, Jena, I've been a part of this town, this area, for a long, long time. I know just about everyone in this town and the town next to it and the town next to that one. And I certainly know a lot of people in Maplesville."

He stares more intently at Jena. "That's where you're from, right? Maplesville."

He touches his chin, as if for dramatic effect.

"I knew your father, Jena." On a roll now, he pauses and points his finger at Jena with a flourish. "And I'm not talking about Jonathan Parker."

Jena feels her face flush with anger.

"No," the warden continues, "I'm talking about Miles McNeil. You know—the man you killed."

Jena can't smother her response. "How do you know he's my father?"

"Well, you did leave your mother's letter behind at your house, and let's say a certain officer obtained that letter."

Warden Peters paces around the room, walking back and forth in front of Jena's chair.

"Now, don't worry, child, or should I say, young lady, now that you're nineteen years old. No one else knows about that letter or your secret, except for me, the officer, and, well"—Warden Peters looks at Mike and Jeff—"these two fine men. And I don't believe your big secret is of any concern to them."

Warden Peters walks back to his desk, condescending again.

"I understand that you've had a complicated life. Some awful things happened to you up at that college. But according to these files, you've done some pretty bad things yourself."

"Wait," the warden drawls sarcastically. "You've been cleared of those charges, and you'll be leaving us."

He clears his throat. "But until then, you will obey the rules of this prison. The rules are that there will be no fights, and all inmates involved in fights will be punished.

"So, Miss Parker, though you are destined to leave us"—he shakes his head—"in the meantime, you will spend some of your remaining time in solitary confinement. At least two days."

"What?" she asks, in sincere disbelief.

"You heard me. You will be sent to solitary confinement for two days." Warden Peters motions to the guards. "Take her away. Please."

Jena stands up. "You're trash, warden. I know what you did."

It's Warden Peters' turn to be angry, but he says nothing.

Mike grabs Jena's arm and steers her toward the door.

Jena manages to twist around to face the warden. "I know men like you, the ones who want to rule an insane world created to satisfy their wicked ways. Men like you have only one destiny." She stares at him. She pauses again and smiles, locking eyes with Warden Peters. "And, Warden, you are definitely headed toward that one, the one you deserve."

Mike finally manages to maneuver Jena out of the office and away from the warden's glaring eyes.

But Jena is still frustrated and not ready to give up the fight as Mike half-drags and half-pushes her down the prison hallways.

"Are you his lapdog?" Jena asks. Mike doesn't answer. "What, Mike you can't speak? Or are you afraid of me?"

Mike stops in front of Jena, whose arms are tightly cuffed. "I'm not afraid of you, and I'm not the Warden's lapdog. I'm doing my job."

Jena lets her head drop, then looks up again "Really? This is what you call doing your job? Women getting charged for crimes they didn't commit. The rapes! The killings! This prison is hell. You are part of it, or you've turned a blind eye. Either way, you're guilty."

"Jena, I know a lot of horrible things go on here."

Jena stops him. "Then do something!" stomping her foot, like a child.

"Don't you think I've tried? I've told the warden, several times."

"That crook?" Jena says, defiant again.

But Mike's having none of it. Hands on hips, eyebrows raised, lips pursed. "That crook happens to be my boss."

"That's no excuse, Mike. That's you, being a coward. Why don't you just call the feds, tell them everything."

Mike steps forward. "Oh, and lose my job, my pension, everything I've worked for? Never mind, that they would probably kill me. Really kill me."

Mike's eyes are filled with fear, but Jena has no mercy.

"Kill you, Mike? What about the women who get killed in this prison at the hands of guards—after they rape them, of course," she yells.

"You're worried about you? One singular person? You? You're weighing yourself against the hundreds of women who fall victim to this circus."

Mike melts inside as he looks into Jena's beautiful eyes. He's mesmerized by the set of her lips and face, her strong posture. To hide his emotions, he steps behind Jena again and walks her down the hall to solitary confinement, far from the rest of the prison cells.

Mike hesitates before opening the door. Jena watches him. His hands sweat and shake. But he opens the door, the door creaking a little as it springs open. They both stare at the dark room.

Mike asks Jena to step into the room, and as she complies, he removes the handcuffs. Her wrists are red from the handcuffs. She rubs them, still facing the dark, away from Mike.

Mike stares at her back. "Jena," he whispers.

"Just leave, Mike. I've been in far darker places, trust me."

With that, Mike backs slowly out of the room and closes the door. He can speak to Jena through the tiny, barred window in the door. "Jena you're here for two days. I'll be back to check on you, make sure you get food."

Jena just stares into the dark.

"Jena, despite what you think of me, I care."

Mike walks away. Jena hears the jangle of his keys as he puts them back into his pocket.

Jena can only pace around the dark room. She can't run. She can't hide. She leans against the wall and slides to the floor, hugging her knees to her chest. She closes her eyes and conjures up the one face that will bring her peace. Jake.

Meanwhile, Mike walks slowly down the prison hall. He feels close to this young woman whose strength is greater than the strength he had seen in much older women.

He hears his name through the static of the radio, secured tightly by his belt.

"Mike?" It's Tim. "Hey, we need you at the medical ward. This girl Chance is in bad shape. The doctor wants to talk to all of the guards who saw the fight."

Mike quickens his pace, arriving at the medical ward to find at least ten wounded women, inmates suffering from stabbings, beatings, rape, and illness.

The women eye Mike as he walks through the room. Their faces make Mike sad. He can't help but think of Jena and her harsh words, accusing him of being part of this, or at least, turning a blind eye to it.

Mike tries to avoid the eyes of the women, knowing that he might have been able to prevent some of their pain and suffering.

Tim beckons Mike to the bed where Chance Middleton lies moaning and crying. One of her eyes is black and swollen; her nose is bleeding; her body has scrapes and bruises. But she is far from quiet. In fact, she is screaming over and over that she wants to kill Jena.

Mike and Tim watch as the nurse tries to calm her.

"You need to be quiet. There are a lot of sick people in this ward, and you're disturbing them."

"Shut up!" Chance screams. "Just shut up! You have no idea how much pain I'm in." She moans, as if to prove her point. "I need meds! Give me something for this pain!"

"Where's your pain?" the nurse asks.

"Everywhere!" Chance screams.

The nurse rolls her eyes and gestures for the doctor. "Give her a shot of morphine," the doctor whispers. "That should relax her for a while."

The doctor turns his attention back to Chance as the nurse leaves to get the syringe of pain medication. "I know you're in pain, but can you tell these guards what happened?"

Chance looks at the doctor and the two guards in disbelief. "I got my ass kicked. That's what happened." She is yelling and moaning at the same time. "But I'm going to kill her. I'm going to kill that Jena Parker!" she screams, just as the nurse returns with the morphine.

The nurse wastes no time stabbing the syringe into Chance's arm, and she's rewarded with another scream. "What the hell did you give me!"

Chance is already fading as her caregivers and guards walk away. A patient in the room sighs. "Thank God she's shut up."

The doctor asks Mike and Tim to step into the hallway.

Once they are alone, the young, frail, perfunctory Dr. Walker folds his hands behind his back, still holding Chance's medical file. "What do you guards know about this fight?"

Dr. Walker carefully examines their plastic identification badges, with their names and pictures: Lead Guard Tim Manner and Mike Fredmond. He looks at one man, then the other, waiting for an answer.

"We don't know much. She was already on the floor by the time we got through the cafeteria," Tim answers.

Dr. Walker looks at Mike.

Mike looks at Tim.

"Exactly what he said, Doc," Mike says. "The room was full of out-of-control inmates. There were a bunch of fights going on all at once. It was chaos."

Dr. Walker isn't satisfied with either answer. "This girl is in severe pain. She may have suffered a concussion."

Tim appears unconcerned. "Doctor, you do realize that this a prison, and fights happen every single hour of every single day?" Tim pauses, more annoyed. "I mean, look at your ward—sick and injured women everywhere. We can't prevent every fight."

Dr. Walker's response surprises them. "That's because you guys are too busy causing violence," he spits, storming away.

Tim is still unmoved. "What a jerk." He turns to Mike. "Why does he even care about these losers."

Tim is taken aback when Mike's expression says he clearly doesn't agree.

"Don't you realize that these women committed crimes?" Tim asks. "They're not just in here for stealing candy from a candy store or ..." he stutters "... or ... or... littering. They're in here for murder, burglary, child abuse, and every other horrible crime imaginable."

Mike turns away to hide his anger, toward the wounded women, before looking at Tim again.

"I'd kill them all," Tim says, grinning. "Especially that Jena Parker."

Finally, having said everything on his mind, Tim darts away, pleased with himself.

Mike stands still, shocked.

Jena is right: He's partially responsible for Tim's madness and his violence.

"I'm part of the problem," Mike says to himself. "And now I have to do something."

He stares into the medical ward, shamed, as he thinks about how these women fight desperately for survival, lying in these beds with no hope, no way to redeem themselves in the eyes of those who judge them—inside and outside of the prison.

What about Jena? Mike panics as he remembers Tim threatening her.

He rushes through the halls to the solitary confinement area. He passes two cells before reaching Jena's. He tries to slow his breathing as he reaches her door. He peeks through the window but can't see or hear her.

But she sees Mike. "What are you doing here?" Jena's voice creeps from the corner of the room.

Mike is startled, but relieved. "I came back to check on you."

"Why?" she asks, defiant.

Mike takes a minute before answering. "Because it's my job."

Jena doesn't reply, so Mike attempts to make conversation. "Did any of the guards bring you lunch or dinner?"

No response.

"Jena, I'm not your enemy," he says quietly, laying his head on the cell window.

Jena finally walks to the cell door. "Yeah, but you're not my friend, either are you Mike?" she whispers.

Now Mike is quiet. He doesn't want to break the slight, almost imperceptible connection he has with Jena at this moment. He looks up, and Jena is staring into his eyes. He's caught off guard, looks down, then back at her. He gazes deeply into her eyes, then realizes that he is betraying too much of what he is feeling.

He steps back quickly.

But Jena can feel his desire to touch her, to reach beyond the cell door. And she wants him back. She calls his name, even as he is trying to compose himself. "Mike," she calls again.

He still doesn't answer and starts to walk away.

"Don't go," Jena begs.

Mike stops.

Jena puts her hands on the tiny bars of the window.

Mike stares at her fingers, her nails, her hands. He wants to touch her but can only stare.

"Mike, I know you're still out there."

She can hear him breathing, can sense his yearning. She knows that he cares for her, but—just as important to Jena—she knows that he understands that what goes on in this prison isn't right.

Mike leans against the opposite wall, fantasizing that he can wrap his arms around her.

Jena is thinking only of her cause. "Mike, you have a chance to make a difference, to stop the violence against these women, and to fight this corrupt system. I know you want to. Right?"

But Mike isn't thinking about the prison. He reaches for Jena's hand as she speaks. He'd never seen such beautiful hands.

"Mike," Jena implores.

Each time she says his name, he closes his eyes tightly.

"Jena," he says, just for the pleasure of speaking her name.

But she says nothing more.

"Jena," he says again.

But she is still quiet, and Mike walks away.

Jena can hear his footsteps. She takes a deep breath and raises her voice slightly. "You can't walk away from everything, Mike."

The footsteps stop.

"You can't," she says. "One day you'll have to come to terms with all of this."

Mike is deeply sad. He takes a long breath, then continues down the hall.

Jena listens until she can't hear his footsteps anymore. She moves her hands from the cell window, steps back into the dark, leans against the wall, and slowly slides to the floor, wrapping her arms around her knees again.

Jena's mind begins to wander as she stares into the dark. She opens and closes her eyes, and shadows seem to move around the room. The shadows dart back and forth, then seem to stop as they move closer. They leave a chill in the darkness, a chill that also seems to roam the room.

"What do you want?" she asks of the dark cell. "I'm not afraid of you."

To herself, she says: "I am not afraid of the dark because I was the dark, too—even when the days were light. So, if you've come for me, you'll have to wait until my work is done, and even then, you'll leave without my embrace."

CHAPTER TWO

Warden Peters sits at his desk staring at his office phone. The black phone sits on the desk near a photo of him and his wife, Ellen, and their children. He looks at the office door, then at the clock on the wall. He sighs impatiently and abruptly stands, turns, and moves to the window.

He mumbles to himself and folds his arms. "He thinks he can just make me wait. He's playing games. I won't be played with."

A hard knock at the door startles him. The warden doesn't respond. Another knock. This time harder. "Who is it?" Warden Peters asks impatiently.

"It's me, Reyes."

Warden Peters opens the door but only peeks out at the officer who was recently promoted to Maplesville's Chief of Police.

"What?" the warden asks.

Clark Reyes seems angry. "What, yourself?" he spits back.

"Lower your voice," Warden Peters demands. "I don't have time to play cops with you. I'm waiting for an important call."

The warden tries to close the door, but Reyes stops him.

"I need to talk to you."

Warden Peters still won't open the door more than a few inches. "About?" he asks, staring into Reyes' eyes.

Reyes moves closer. "About the plan. About our next move." Reyes seems nervous, even placing one hand on his gun.

Warden Peters looks down. "Really?" he asks sarcastically, staring at Reyes' hand on the gun.

The warden opens the door but walks back to his desk without saying a word to Reyes. Reyes follows, his hand still on his gun.

Peters walks around his desk to face Reyes. "Don't you ever touch that gun in my presence"—he pauses—"unless you plan on using it."

Reyes complies, but gives the warden his best tough guy look. "I'll use it if I have to."

"I don't like silence. I want to know everything," Reyes says, walking closer to the warden. "My ass is on the line, too. You think I want to lose twenty years of pension?"

Peters looks at Reyes coldly. "Your ass is going to be in even more trouble if you walk into this room with your hand on that trigger. You think that you, a cop, are running things?"

Reyes backs down. "Then what's the plan?"

Peters sighs and sits again. "I don't know yet." He looks up at the clock. "Like I said, I'm waiting on the call."

Reyes, like the warden, stares at the phone, then pushes back. "Why don't you call him?"

Peters explodes, slamming his hands on the desk and pointing at Reyes. "You don't call people like him!" Peters' yells. "You wait! That's what you do."

The warden's eyes are wide with rage. "Now, get your ass out of my office and take care of that other problem we have. The one you were supposed to handle a long time ago: that slut you were sleeping with."

The warden sits down, trying to project authority. "I'll call you when he calls me, and not before, so don't come back to my office until I send for you. You got that Reyes?"

Reyes frowns but walks out of the warden's office without answering, leaving the door wide open behind him.

Warden Peters picks up the phone and dials.

"Hey, I want you to watch every move Chief Clark Reyes makes. He's a time bomb waiting to explode."

Peters' slams down the phone. It rings just as he is about to go close the door. He looks at the clock again, tries to regain his composure, sits down slowly, and answers the phone.

"Warden Phillip Peters," he says into the phone, holding it tightly to his ear.

"Your line was busy," replies a man with a foreign accent.

The warden tries to breathe normally, "A call came in and, well, I thought it might be you." Peters' lie is greeted with silence.

"I want three," says the man on the other end of the call. "Three. Not one. Not two. Three. I want them here in two days. No later. No excuses."

The line goes dead with a click and the dial tone. Peters waits nervously, as if the conversation will continue somehow. He finally hangs up, thinks for a minute, then quickly picks up the receiver again and dials.

Someone answers. "Yes, sir?"

"Find Chief Reyes and send him here now."

As the warden stares out the window once again, Reyes walks the prison halls, unaware that the warden is looking for him, glaring at everyone he passes. He brushes against a prison guard.

"Hey!" the guard yells. Reyes just keeps walking.

No one is surprised to see him, but no one is happy to see him, either. His job, which now means he is also the Maplesville Police Department's prison liaison, allows him free rein.

Chief Reyes stops at the medical ward and peeks through the window where Chance is lying with her eyes closed in pain, bruised, and broken from the fight with Jena. Reyes looks around the room and notices that all of the inmates have been released except Chance.

He opens the door and stands like a tall, dark shadow over Chance's bed. He listens to her shallow breathing and remembers when he first met her, back in high school, back when she was a teenager, a witness to the fight between Ken Stewart and Jake Paterson in the biker bar. And he remembers how Chance Middleton and Carol Jones had lied to him and how Chance had showed up at his office at the police department, crying and scared.

Reyes recalls how it all started: "Officer, there's a really terrified young lady out here who wants to speak to you."

When Reyes motioned her into his office, Chance walked slowly, crying, and shaking, as if she feared for her life. He asked what she needed, and Chance tried to calm down. "I don't know if you remember me, but I was one of the kids at the bar fight," Chance said, still crying.

Yes, he remembered. Chance Middleton.

Hesitating, Chance had told him: "I know you're looking for Jena Parker. Well, I just saw her up at King's Diner near the college.

"She was there, and I heard gunfire, so me and Ken Stewart jumped out of a window that she blew open with one shot."

Chance started to ramble, but Reyes stopped her.

Reyes remembers that conversation like it was only the day before.

"Are you telling me that Jena Parker is at King's Diner with a gun?"

"Well, no, probably not now, but she was."

Reyes was skeptical.

He asked why Chance had been at the diner.

Stuttering and sniffing, she said she was hanging out with friends when Jena came in and started shooting.

Reyes asked why she hadn't called the police. The college is at least an hour away.

"In the time it took you to drive here, you could have called," Reyes said. "Maybe the police could have caught her."

As Reyes' voice got louder and louder, Chance jumped.

"I thought she'd kill me. ... I didn't think ... I just drove." Chance started to cry harder.

Reyes got angrier and stood to confront Chance again. "So, you drove all the way here just to tell me that Jena Parker ... a known criminal ... a murderer ... was at some diner?"

At that moment, Reyes remembers closing his office door. "Chance, why don't you tell me what you're really doing here."

"I told you," Chance insisted. "That's all I know." She tried to stand, but Reyes yelled at her to sit down again. She did.

"You're lying to an officer of the law, and people who lie to the police are considered criminals, just like murderers."

Finally, Chance relented. "Okay. Okay. Stop yelling," she said, shaking her head. "You're right, it never happened."

Reyes remembers teasing and threatening her. "Well, what can we do about this?"

Chance stopped crying.

"I know," he said, menacingly.

He asked Chance if she liked Jena Parker. "You don't do you?"

Chance tried to act innocent but failed. Reyes knew that Chance was guilty of something and told her so.

"Do you know who I am?" he asked her.

"You're Officer Reyes."

"*Chief* Clark Reyes now," he said, smirking. "I *was* Officer Reyes. I'm also the person you met in a dark alley one night when you were trying to buy a gun."

"No," Chance said. She was sincerely alarmed and confused. "I didn't see any officer in an alley."

"No. Maybe not. Maybe you didn't know he was an officer. But you did meet a tall man, wearing a hoodie, right? You told the man in a hoodie that you wanted to buy a gun, so you could kill someone."

Chance was shocked for real. "Then why act like you didn't know me when I walked in here?"

Reyes toyed with her. "Because I like it when people come into my office and act all innocent, so I can burst their bubble." He remembers laughing out loud and clapping his hands.

"If you haven't already figured it out, understand now that I can't let you leave this police station. I have to arrest you, which will probably land your ass in prison."

Chance started to beg.

"Please. Please. I can't go to jail. I can't." She whined. "I won't survive.

"Look, I didn't even use the gun. I threw it away. Please don't put me in jail. I'll do anything you want."

In the present, he laughs now, standing over Chance's bed, thinking of the way she squirmed back then.

"You'd do anything?" he asked. She nodded. "Okay," Reyes said. "I have something you can do. You may even enjoy doing it."

Reyes' musings come to a halt as he is startled back to the present, in the prison medical ward.

"What are you doing here?" Chance asks, awake now and afraid. She looks frantically around the ward for someone who might help her.

"I came to visit you," he says.

"Why?" she asks, suspiciously.

"Why?" He's taunting her. "Because you didn't keep up your side of the bargain."

He reaches for his gun.

"Please don't kill me," she pleads.

"Well, you're already half-dead, so it shouldn't hurt much," he snaps.

"I gave you a simple job. I told you to go to the masquerade party and help my friend capture Jena Parker. But you didn't do that. You were more worried about getting your revenge. So, you killed your best friend, Carol. Carol Jones."

Reyes bends even closer to Chase.

"And it wasn't just you who betrayed me. … Moschi …"

- 452 -

Reyes' voice trails off, and he shakes his head.

"Moschi helps Jena, of all people." Reyes spits out the words. "You two have severely disappointed me."

Chance tries to scream.

"Shut up," he hisses.

"Look at you, all beat up, shaking like you did the night you came to my office with that lying, pathetic story. I should have arrested you then," he shook his head again. "No matter, you ended up in prison anyway. ... Killing your parents. Killing your best friend."

Chance is angry, now. "She didn't act like a best friend!"

Reyes pulls out his gun. "I said shut up."

As the door to the medical ward opens, Reyes hastily re-holsters his weapon.

A nurse walks in and looks at him with suspicion.

Reyes nods at the nurse.

The nurse looks at Chance, whose face is red and whose eyes are pleading for help.

The nurse says nothing and walks to the office across from the room.

"You're lucky," Reyes whispers, glancing toward the office to make sure the nurse is still there.

Tears run down Chance's bruised face.

The door to the ward opens again. This time it's the guard, Tim.

"I've been looking for you," Tim says. "The warden wants you."

Tim looks at Chance without a hint of sympathy. "You made her cry," Tim says, smirking. "That's my job."

Turning his attention back to Reyes, "The boss wants you. Right now. I think he may have gotten the call."

Reyes smiles. He and Tim both turn toward the terrified subject of their cruelty, Chance. "We'll be back," Reyes says.

When they are gone, Chance lies still, paralyzed with fear and trying to catch her breath. "Nurse," she whispers. The nurse is on the phone and doesn't hear her. "Nurse," she tries to call out, a little louder. But the nurse still doesn't hear. "Nurse!" She screams, finally.

The nurse hangs up the phone, runs to Chance, and finds her trying to tear the IV needle from her arm.

"Calm down," the nurse says, trying to soothe her frantic patient. "Calm down," she says again, now a bit more firmly.

Finally, Chance stops trying to pull out the IV and pleads: "Please. I need to see Warden Peters."

The nurse looks at Chance. "What?" she asks incredulously.

"Please, they're going to kill me," Chance says.

The nurse tries to reassure her. "Look, no one is trying to kill you."

"You don't understand. … That officer … that officer who was here … he—"

"Okay, there was a policeman here. Chief Reyes," the nurse says, staring at Chance. "What are you trying to say?"

Chance suddenly stops talking. She's staring at someone behind the nurse.

The nurse turns and sees the guard, Tim, has returned. "I didn't hear you come in, Tim," the nurse says.

Tim smiles. "I'm a quiet one, you know."

The nurse turns back to Chance. "Tim, I don't have time to talk right now. I need to attend to this patient."

Chance stares at the nurse, then at Tim, but says nothing.

Finally, Chance says, "I'm in so much pain." Louder: "Morphine, please! Now, please!"

The nurse pulls a needle from her coat pocket and plunges its contents into the IV.

Almost immediately, Chance's eyes start to glaze over. Her eyes are still fixed on Tim as she falls asleep.

The nurse covers Chance with a blanket, checks the IV, and only then turns to address Tim. "She was frantic," the nurse explains, still confused.

"What did she say to you?" Tim demands.

"Why?" the nurse asks. "Tim, your job is to be a guard and my job is to be a nurse, so I suggest you do your job and let me do mine."

Tim is surprisingly cowed. "Sorry," he says, and leaves the room.

Checking on Chance one more time, Nurse Tonya May walks to her office and makes a telephone call.

"Hi, Patty, this is Tonya May, a nurse down at the medical ward. … Oh yes, I'm fine. … Patty, I just wanted to know what our policy is on prisoners getting a meeting with the warden."

Nurse May listens to the woman on the other end of the line and responds. "Oh, you know, I'm talking about prisoners who are ill or injured."

She listens again. "Okay, so as a nurse I can make a call for a prisoner?" Another pause as Nurse May gets more details. "Well, thank you, Patty."

Nurse May tries to hide her intent. "I'd love to have lunch. Maybe we can get together next week." She continues to try to change the subject. "No, no, you don't need to make a call or anything. I just wanted to get some clarification."

She listens again to her friend on the other end of the line. "I'll take care of it. Thanks, Patty. Talk to you soon. Goodbye."

Mike stands in the hallway near the warden's office with his head down. He feels guilty for not stepping forward and reporting the abuse these women endure.

He looks up to see Reyes and Tim walking toward him. They're talking but go silent as they get closer to Mike.

The three of them stand in the hallway, awkwardly.

Reyes glares at Mike.

Mike ignores Reyes but turns to Tim. "Where have you been, man?" he asks.

"Around," Tim answers with a chuckle.

"Around?" Mike echoes. "I've tried to call you three times on the radio."

Tim looks at Reyes. They both shrug and walk past Mike, dismissing him.

"Tim!" Mike yells.

Tim stops, impatiently, and turns around to face Mike. "I've got a very important job to do right now, Mike."

He hurries to catch up with Reyes. He yells at Mike, without turning. "I'll get with you later."

Mike knows Reyes and Tim are up to no good. He watches them walk down the hall until they are out of sight. Mike tries to let go of the sense of foreboding but remembers Jena. He again runs toward her cell as if a fire alarm has gone off.

He slows as he gets closer to Jena's cell. He sighs with relief when he sees that her door is closed and that no guard is nearby.

Mike peeks into her cell window and sees her staring into the dark.

"Jena?" He calls her name.

She looks up at him.

He unlocks her cell door, opens it, and stands in the shadow of the door with his keys in his hand.

"Jena, it's time for you to take a shower."

He walks toward her and kneels.

Jena looks at him.

"And you need to eat," he says.

Smiling and shaking her head, she stands with Mike's help.

"Oh, so now you care," she says, teasing him.

He hesitates as they stand closer to one another than they should.

"You know I have to cuff you."

She turns and puts her hands behind her back. Mike stares at her hands, resting just above her lower back. He slowly reaches for his cuffs and places them gently over her wrists. He leans close to her ear, gently brushing her shoulder.

"I'm going to walk you to the showers, uncuff you, then you'll have fifteen minutes to yourself. I won't be far away."

She stands still for a moment, then turns toward Mike and smiles.

"You won't be far," she repeats slyly.

Mike refuses to take the bait, grabs her arm, and walks her to the shower—not too slow, not too fast.

"Here we are," he says, removing the cuffs. "Fifteen minutes," he reminds her.

Jena looks at him and says, this time sincerely: "Thank you."

"I'll radio the kitchen to send your dinner down to your cell."

She turns again, saying nothing.

"I'll make sure it's someone I trust," he says.

Satisfied, she walks into the shower area, where there are five stalls. The concrete is stained with dirt and rust. The showerheads leak, so everything stays wet. The drains stink. She doesn't want to know what makes them smell so bad.

Shrugging, she looks down at her orange jumpsuit in disgust and grabs the zipper to pull it open. It's stuck. "Great," she says out loud. She yanks and tugs impatiently until the zipper breaks. She steps out of the offensive garment and throws it aside, walks into the stall, and turns on the water.

Jena is amazed that the water feels fresh and warm as it runs down her hair and body. She closes her eyes tightly as the steam fills the room.

Mike jumps at the sound of the water. He can't stop himself from imagining Jena's naked body. As the steam seeps out of the shower room, Mike feels as if it's swirling around him, tempting him to follow.

Jena rubs soap into her hair and onto her body. Her inner thoughts surface, too, as she loses herself in the warm water and the lather of the soap.

But Jena thinks not of Mike, but of Jake. She even whispers his name as she remembers showering at Jake's home. Jake's voice seemed so close as he spoke to her through the door. She knew he had pressed close to the door as he fought the urge to open it and take her into his arms.

"I miss you, Jake," she says out loud.

Mike is leaning against the outside door, too. His hands are tightly clenched. He swallows deeply as he tries to focus on anything besides Jena's naked body—just a few feet away under the stream of warm water.

"Mike!" a voice yells.

Mike hears only the running water.

"Mike!" again.

Mike, startled, looks around, feeling guilty and a bit panicked.

"Mike! Mike!" the calls continue. "Mike, pick up."

Finally, Mike looks at his radio.

He jumps a little as he picks it up. Trying to sound as nonchalant as possible, he says: "Yep?"

"Where the hell have you been?" It's Shawn, the head cook.

It's hard to know who is more annoyed: Shawn, who had to wait for his call to be answered, or Mike, whose fantasy was coldly interrupted.

"Hey, you said you wanted me to make sure that Parker girl gets a good plate," Shawn says. "I'm about to finish my shift, and, well, Nasty is coming on and you don't want Nasty serving up her food."

"Thanks, T-Bone," Mike says, using Shawn's nickname. "Bring the food in about ten minutes." He clicks off the radio.

"Jena," he calls.

Jena doesn't hear. She's laying her head against the shower stall, thinking of Jake.

"Jena," Mike calls again.

This time Mike's voice cuts through her thoughts. She stands still for a moment, savoring the memories. But she also has a problem. She walks to the shower room door, covering her breasts with one arm, and peeks around the corner where Mike stands.

He doesn't see her, so she takes a deep breath, tries her best to cover the rest of her nakedness, and walks a few more steps toward Mike.

This time when he calls her name and turns around, Jena says quietly, "I'm done."

Mike tries to speak but cannot, as he takes in the reality of Jena's naked, dripping wet body, right in front of him.

"I broke the zipper on my jumpsuit," she says simply.

Mike feels as if the air has been sucked out of his body, as if he is stuck in midair. He still can't speak—or move.

Her hair is dripping, and the water trickles down her soft almond-colored skin.

Mike is acutely conscious of being caught between two worlds: the world he wants to be in right this minute with Jena and the world of truth. And the truth is that they are in a broken-down prison, where women are abused, and where Jena has plenty of horrors yet to come.

Two male voices are loud as they approach Mike, who is still mesmerized by Jena's body. Quickly, he snaps into defense mode and jumps in front of Jena, daring either man to touch her.

"Well, well, what do we have here?" one of the guards says, as he smirks at Jena.

Mike turns around. "Go get dressed," he barks at Jena.

"No. No. She doesn't have to do that," the other guard says, eyeing Jena like she is prey.

Mike puffs himself up and raises his voice, pointing at the two guards. "Rick, Tyrone, get the hell out of here," he demands.

"This is my section!" he yells. "My prisoner!"

Jena finally tries to tiptoe away to get dressed.

"Sure, Mike," Tyrone says as he walks closer to Jena. He tries to bully his way past Mike.

Mike pushes him back. "Get the hell out of here."

"What Mike? You don't know the rules."

Both guards try to grab Mike.

"Yeah, the rules," Rick says. "The rules are that we do what we want in this prison."

"That's right," his friend echoes. "So, get out of my way, man, because I am taking what I want. And what I want is her."

As Mike and the guards shove one another, Jena walks out of the shower room in her jumpsuit, the zipper somehow rigged to stay mostly closed.

She watches as Mike tries to defend her.

But one guard, Rick, gets past Mike and close enough to Jena to touch her face. "There you are," he seethes, like a movie villain. "Why did you get dressed, sweet thing."

Jena glowers at him. "Fuck you."

"What did you say?" the guard yells, and he pushes Jena against the hard cement wall.

"You heard me," she says, defiant.

"Fuck you. Fuck you, Rick." She utters his name with as much disdain as she can muster, his name tag now biting into her skin, as he continues pushing her harder against the wall.

Alarmed, Mike tries to help, but can't. If he helps Jena, he'll lose control of the other guard.

"Who do you think you are!" Rick yells in Jena's face, as he tries to slap her.

Jena just stares at him. "Hit me," she says, without blinking.

Rick stops.

"Hit me," she yells.

That's exactly what Rick intends to do, but he pauses just long enough that Jena has time to brace against the wall, kick her leg up and out, and slam her foot into Rick's groin.

As he grabs himself against the pain, she wraps her arms around his neck, squeezes his neck as tight as she can, and jams her knee into his face.

Rick falls to the cold concrete floor and cradles his body in pain, moaning.

Mike finally pins Tyrone against the wall, turns around, and watches as Jena stares down at Rick. She is sneering at the man as he groans, then bends over and says, "I told you to hit me."

Mike is alarmed, frightened on Jena's behalf.

As he grabs her arm, she looks coldly into his eyes, and Mike suddenly realizes that he is falling in love with a woman who is cold, dark, and fearless. He'd never seen this side of her and realized that she was indeed capable of the killing that had sent her to this prison.

Jena doesn't flinch under Mike's gaze. "What?" she asks Mike, arrogantly.

Mike shakes his head and says nothing as he, too, watches Rick squirm on the floor. Unfortunately, Mike is so stunned by Jena's behavior that he's forgotten about Tyrone, who decides to jump back into the fray. Tyrone looks from Rick to Mike to Jena and pulls back his fist and aims it as Jena, as Mike steps between them.

"Get out of the way, Mike, I'm going to kill this freak," Tyrone threatens.

He stops, as they become aware that someone else is talking in the hallway.

It's the chef, T-Bone, bringing Jena's food tray. Now, it's T-Bone who stops in his tracks, trying to take in the scene in front of him, clearly deciding that it is best to say and do nothing at all.

Mike waves him forward. "Come on, T-Bone, this is a prison. You've seen this shit before."

T-Bone holds the tray tightly as he walks slowly toward Jena.

"T-Bone, you take Jena and the tray and get her back in the cell," Mike says. He looks at Rick and Tyrone. "I'll take care of these two."

Mike steps close to Jena. "I won't handcuff you, Jena, but if you try to run or hurt T-Bone …" Mike stops. "I'll take you down myself."

Jena practically hisses at Mike. "I save your ass and you want to take me down. You arrogant prick."

She walks off to her cell as if she's the one in charge.

Mike watches her and can't help but see her beauty—even after everything he'd just witnessed. He knew he could no more harm her than he could harm himself. But he had to act like he was in charge, even if she knew better.

Mike tosses T-Bone the keys to Jena's cell, and T-Bone catches them in one hand while holding the food tray high above his head—acting like a waiter in a five-star restaurant.

T-Bone says it all with one look, "Yeah, man, she's a badass," and follows Jena to her cell, leaving Mike and the guards behind.

Jena is still stewing as she waits in front of her cell, furious at Mike for not understanding that she's more than just a criminal. She has feelings, and she is a revolutionary—a woman who understands that battles aren't fought alone, that she must fight to keep what is hers, that she is willing to fight for freedom, even willing to fight for Mike.

T-Bone stands behind Jena, not quite sure what to do next.

Jena can hear him breathing. T-Bone decides to wait. Finally, she looks at him—less angry—steps aside, and gestures, inviting him forward. T-Bone fumbles with the keys and the hot tray and even considers setting the tray on the floor. Jena laughs a little at T-Bone's confusion. It eases the hostility she feels toward Mike. She reaches out to take the tray, as if accepting a peace offering. T-Bone plays along, unlocks the door and steps back with a flourish. But the cell is not her kingdom, and the spell is broken for them both as the door slams closed and the key clinks in the lock.

Jena looks at her prison tray and turns to see T-Bone staring at her through the small window in the door. He looks sympathetic, and his sympathy causes tears to well up in her eyes.

Just moments before, she had felt a powerful adrenaline rush. Now she is in prison again, not merely the prison of walls and doors and keys and solitude, but also the imprisonment of her heart and soul. Her love for Jake is trapped, too, locked away from her, along with all things beautiful. This is what happens when a person allows their freedom to be taken away.

T-Bone's face fades from the window. Jena is alone. The darkness of the room takes her back to where she was in the hours before Mike came. Jena puts the food tray on the floor. She sits next to it, takes off the top, and stares at the shockingly pretty plate of food. She looks back at the cell's window, and T-Bone is there again, smiling. He has given her the best meal anyone can get in prison, and his gentle smile lets her know that he's watching out for her.

T-Bone senses her calm and smiles even wider. Jena laughs out loud at the neatly folded napkin on her tray. She looks up and T-Bone is gone again, this time for good.

Jena picks up the food to unwrap it, and one single sweet pea falls out. She opens the packet and finds an entire handful.

She begins to cry in earnest. Sweet peas were her father's favorite food. The tears fall like gentle drops of rain, mixing with the peas. Jena thinks she has never seen anything so beautiful.

She remembers the last meal her mother made before her father was murdered. "Sweet peas," she whispers. "Dad ... oh, Dad ... I miss you." And the tears keep falling.

CHAPTER THREE

Tyron and T-Bone help lift Rick from the floor.

Rick stands slowly, still gripping his groin. He limps as his co-workers help him walk down the hall to the employees' first-aid room. Mike follows them but can't help glancing back toward Jena's cell. He stops.

Mike and T-Bone exchange a look, as Tyrone and T-Bone keep guiding Rick toward the medic. But Mike walks the other way. He takes a deep breath and decides to confront Warden Peters about the chaos in this prison. Sure, he is fired up about what almost happened to Jena. But he's heard rumors, too, and not just from Jena—rumors of abuse, even missing inmates, and murder. Rumors of women never seen again, taken in the night by mysterious men with foreign accents.

The more Mike thinks about it, the angrier he gets. His face is hot, and his fists are clenched.

But when he reaches the warden's door, he hears voices, and so he stops.

He can't quite figure out who's talking or what they're talking about. Mike checks the hall to make sure no one is watching him and tries to get close enough to hear the conversation.

Inside the office, Warden Peters is sitting at his desk, with Chief Clark Reyes and Tim Manner standing in front of him. Reyes is impatient; Tim is shifting his weight nervously; and the warden looks annoyed, as usual.

"So, what's the deal?" Reyes asks.

"Keep your voice down," the warden hisses.

"He wants three girls." Peters stands up. "And he wants them now. They need to be there in two days."

Tim and Reyes look at each other, then back at Peters.

Reyes smirks. "Well, just say the word, and we'll get 'em."

Peters is worried, and his face shows it. He turns around and looks out the window.

"Well?" Reyes is impatient and speaks louder.

Peters turns around. "Okay, you guys pick the girls." He eyes Tim and Reyes. "Do you have anyone in mind?" Now Peters speaks eagerly.

Reyes laughs. "I sure do. How about we nab that Jena Parker!"

Tim grins. "Yeah man, I'm down with that. That one, she's a real troublemaker.

"And if it wasn't for Chance being laid up in the medical ward, I'd gladly send her, too."

Peters walks back to his desk, no longer titillated. "Parker is off-limits." He sighs. "You guys know that."

The warden taps his fingers on his desk. "And we sure can't send a woman who is wounded."

Peters is angry now. "Are you two insane? Do you know how much money we're getting paid for this? We have to send women who are up to the standards of the kind of money we're getting."

Moving his hand toward his gun, Reyes is angry now. "You mean, what *you* are getting paid."

Reyes faces Peters as if he's in Wild West standoff.

"I say we send Parker!" Reyes says. "I mean, do you really think anyone is coming for her?" He chuckles. "And what if they do? If she's gone, she's gone. Nothing!"

Tim nods at Peters. He agrees with Reyes.

Peters isn't having any of their insubordination. He slams one fist on his desk.

"Damn it, I said Parker is off-limits. There are hundreds of women in this prison. Choose two."

Peters returns to his chair. "Find three women who rarely have visitors, family, or friends. Someone who can disappear without anyone noticing. Loners, too. We don't want the other prisoners noticing."

The warden points toward Reyes and Tim. "And by no means do you touch Jena Parker. I mean it."

The warden perks up. "I've got an idea. What about that nurse in the medical ward?"

Reyes shakes his head and rolls his eyes. "Now, why in the hell would we send our nurse to these guys?"

"Because ..." Peters pauses. "Because Patty Smith, my secretary, got a weird telephone call from her. Patty said the nurse, the one named Tonya May, was talking about something strange. She wanted to speak to me, maybe wanted to report something to me."

Peters gives the two men a hard look. "Do either of you know what that nurse might want to talk to me about?"

Reyes' face falls as he thinks of how he'd threatened Chance right before the nurse walked into the room. Reyes mumbles. "It might have something to do with Chance Middleton."

"What about her?" Peters asks, knowing that Reyes had been up to something.

"Well, I paid her a little visit just a while ago," Reyes said. "I was thinking about being her last visitor ... you know ... I was thinking about taking her out. But that nurse walked in, and I couldn't finish the job."

Reyes gives Peters a cocky look.

Tim folds his arms and chimes in. "You know, I went into the medical ward right after you left, Reyes. It seemed to me like Chance was trying to tell Nurse May something. But when Chance saw me, she stopped talking, started screaming for pain meds."

Reyes leans over Peters' desk. "Let's send Chance, broken down or not, we need to get rid of her.

"In due time," Peters answers. "For now, you two go talk to that nurse. Find out what she knows."

The warden looks serious and raises his voice. "Either way, find three women. Tonight. I want you to grab them up tonight."

Reyes and Tim both shake their heads. Reyes reaches for the doorknob but stops.

Outside, Mike steps back from the door as quickly and quietly as he can. He rushes down the hall and around the corner so he can pretend that he is just now walking to the warden's office.

Inside, Reyes is still obsessed with Jena. "I won't go after Parker now, but mark my words, I'll get her, and when I do, you won't be able to stop me."

Reyes opens the door, and Tim follows him out.

Tim closes the door behind him, and they see Mike turning the corner.

"What are you doing here?" Reyes asks.

Mike just stares at Reyes. "I'm here to speak to Warden Peters."

"Oh yeah?" Reyes moves closer to Mike, challenging him. "About what?"

Mike doesn't back down. "What's it to you?"

Reyes reaches for his gun. Tim grabs Reyes' arm, out of reflex, but Reyes jerks away from Tim and gives him a dirty look. "Don't touch me."

He turns back to Mike. "Let's have it, Mike, what do you want to talk to the warden about?"

Mike lies. "About my hours. I think I should take on some extra hours, keep an eye on things around here."

Reyes stares at Mike. "You want more hours? Keep an eye on things, huh?" he says, continuing his interrogation. "Well, the warden is busy right now."

Reyes turns to Tim for support.

"Yeah," Tim answers quickly. "We just came out of a meeting with him, and he's dealing with some pressing issues."

Tim puts his hand on Mike's shoulder. "Maybe you should come back tomorrow. He seems pretty pissed off."

Mike looks at Tim's hand on his shoulder. "Right," Mike says, as he walks away.

Reyes nods to Tim. "Good move man," he says. "I'd blow that one away and think nothing of it."

"Let's get to the medical ward," Tim says. Then he lowers his voice and whispers to Reyes. "Be careful with that renegade cop routine. You're gonna get both of us in trouble."

Neither man says anything more as they walk to the medical ward. Chance is still out cold from the morphine. And the ward has one other patient now.

Tim walks straight toward the nurse's office. Reyes recognizes the other sick inmate and walks to her bedside. The woman is immediately alarmed when she sees Reyes, looming like a dark shadow over her bed.

"I know you," Reyes says. "You're that prostitute. Hmm. What's that name of yours? Cake? Cookies?"

He enjoys tormenting her. "Oh, yeah, your name is Candy."

Candy stares at Reyes in fear and confusion.

"What are you doing in prison, Candy? I didn't put you here."

Candy is too afraid to say anything at all.

"You wanna open that pretty little mouth of yours?" Reyes laughs. "It sure wouldn't be the first time."

"I stabbed and killed my pimp," Candy answers slowly.

Reyes laughs even louder, loud enough, he thinks, to wake Chance, though she pretends to still be asleep.

"Really?" Reyes says as if Candy is telling a joke. "Are you serious?"

Candy just stares.

"So why are you here in the medical ward," Reyes asks.

Candy's lips quiver and she starts to cry silently. "Because I'm pregnant, and I'm having some complications."

"Is that right," Reyes says, pursing his lips.

He doesn't bother trying to appear sympathetic, and he isn't.

"Well in your line of work, good luck figuring out who the father is. You don't have a clue, do you," Reyes says.

Candy tries to keep from sobbing.

"But I do know," she says as her voice cracks. "And you know, too."

"Is that right?" Reyes spits back.

Candy starts to weep uncontrollably.

"It's yours," she says between sobs. "You know that you're the only man I've been with for months."

Reyes is immediately furious. "You shut up!"

Candy's lips tremble, and she tries to tell Reyes that she loves him.

Reyes is shocked silent. And so is Chance in the bed nearby.

Candy catches Chance listening to their conversation.

Reyes notices and turns around quickly, but Chance closes her eyes.

Reyes turns back to Candy. "You keep your damned mouth shut." He bends over so that his face is close to hers. "You got that? Never say that out loud again—to anyone."

Candy nods and swallows hard.

Reyes is shaking with anger as he leaves the woman and walks to Nurse May's office in the back of the ward. He finds Tim flirting with the nurse. He's annoyed, but maybe Tim is trying to get information.

Nurse May is surprised to see Reyes.

"Well, this is a special day. I get to see both of you twice," she says, closing the office door. "I know what Tim is doing here. It's part of his routine to come in here and flirt with me. But what about you, Chief Reyes?"

Reyes is still rattled by what Candy said. "What do you know about the new patient?" Reyes asks.

Nurse May glances through the glass window that divides her office from the rest of the ward.

"She's new," the nurse says.

"Anything else?" Reyes asks, trying to sound nonchalant.

Tonya stands and sits on the edge of her desk. "She's pregnant," the nurse says.

Reyes unconsciously runs his fingers over his gun.

"Who's the father?" Reyes asks abruptly.

Tonya doesn't hide her confusion. She looks at Tim and then at Reyes.

"Why in the world would you even care?" she asks incredulously. "And, besides, just because she's in prison doesn't mean she doesn't have a right to keep her medical history private. And you have no right to judge her—or to be asking questions that have nothing to do with you."

Reyes won't give up.

"So, you don't know who the father is?" Reyes asks in a gruff voice. "You don't know?"

The nurse folds her arms and stands firm. "No, I don't know, and I don't care. She is here for medical treatment, and that's my only concern."

Nurse May walks around her desk and sits down. She eyes both Reyes and Tim. "I don't care who fathered her child, who she slept with or who she killed. It's none of my business."

"What about Chance Middleton, that other inmate?" Reyes asks.

Tonya looks at Tim for help. "What is this? Why am I being interrogated? Tim, what's going on? Am I in trouble for something?"

Tim looks at Reyes and away from Tonya's confused eyes.

"I'm the one asking the questions, Nurse May," Reyes says, leaning on her desk with both hands. "Why don't you tell me why you called the warden's secretary?"

The nurse is shocked, and her expression shows it.

"Because I wanted to find out what the policy is when an inmate asks to speak to Warden Peters," she answers.

"What inmate," Reyes demands.

Nurse May refuses to answer. "That's between me and the warden, officer."

She stands up. "I don't work for you, Chief Reyes. I'm a state employee who works for the state prison. I come to work, and I do my job, which is to care for the medical needs of these inmates. I don't have to answer your questions, and I don't appreciate you and Tim trying to bully me."

She looks at Tim. "You come to my office and treat me like a criminal. If the warden wants to know something about me or this medical ward, then the warden needs to call and ask me those questions."

Tonya sits again and tries to calm herself.

"Now, if you two would please leave my office, I need to get back to work."

Reyes glowers at the nurse, as he and Tim start to walk out of the office. Reyes stops abruptly, lets Tim leave, and shuts the door behind him.

Alone with Nurse May, Reyes drops any pretense of professionalism. "You don't know who or what you're dealing with," he says forcefully.

Nurse May reaches for her phone.

"Put it down," Reyes demands.

She complies.

"Here's what you do, Nurse May." He speaks softly, but menacingly. "You keep your mouth shut. I mean, keep your mouth closed so tight you can barely breathe. Because, if you utter a single word about what went on in this office, or about me, you will find yourself in a very bad situation.

"Now, I know Tim's all sweet on you, but I'm not. I don't care about anyone. I'm a ruthless, angry cop who isn't afraid of you, the rules, or even the warden. You open your mouth, and I promise you that I will close it. Permanently."

Reyes opens the door, walks out, and glares at both Chance and Candy as he leaves the ward.

Tim looks at Tonya and starts to go back to her office, but she waves him away. He gives her one last sympathetic glance before following Reyes.

They both head back to the warden's office—Reyes walking quickly, Tim trying to catch up.

"Did you have to threaten her?" Tim asks breathlessly.

"Yes. Yes, I did," Reyes answers. "Do you want to go to jail just because you're chasing a pair of panties that you'll never get?"

Reyes stops suddenly.

"Now you get this straight," Reyes says. "We're taking her."

Tim leans against the cement wall. "No, man. No," he pleads.

"Yes. She's leaving. Period. Now we just need to find two more women," Reyes says, offering not an ounce of sympathy.

"The warden says we should take loners, inmates who no one would miss," he says. "And the warden also told us to take care of the problem back there. And Nurse May is a problem."

Reyes starts walking again, talking as he moves through the hallway.

"If only the warden would let us take Jena. We're going back to his office, and this time I'm demanding that Jena Parker is gonna be one of the women to leave tonight."

Tim is quiet, still hurt and upset that Tonya is one of the women who will be kidnapped and trafficked to another country.

Reyes walks into Warden Peters' office without knocking. Tim follows slowly, his eyes on the floor.

Reading a newspaper, Peters is startled when Reyes barges in.

"That nurse," Reyes says, furious. "She's one of them. She has to go."

"Why?" Peters asks.

"She knows too much. She'll blow us all out of the water.

The warden nods in agreement. "Fine with me."

Tim sits in the chair where Jena sat not long before. He shakes his head, his hands pressing on his temples.

Reyes isn't finished.

"Now I know you don't want this, but we gotta send Jena Parker."

The warden's patience is exhausted, and he slams the newspaper onto his desk.

Reyes cuts him off before Peters can say anything.

"Now hear me out," Reyes says. "Parker would be worth a lot of money. Look at the publicity she caused. She's strong, and they could use her. Why send a weakling when we can send Parker?"

The warden starts yelling and so does Reyes. They're yelling so loud that one can't hear the other. As for Tim, he doesn't care, still sulking over the decision about Tonya.

Not one of them notices that the office door is wide open and that their argument can be heard all the way down the hall.

"I'm getting Parker!" Reyes yells.

"Parker who?" A strong voice with a deep accent startles them.

Tim looks up slowly. Reyes turns to see a tall, tanned, muscular, and well-dressed man standing in the doorway.

The man stares back at Reyes and Warden Peters.

"You wouldn't be talking about Jena Parker, would you?" the man asks, stepping boldly into the office.

Reyes notices that the man is flanked by two other men, dressed similarly and just a step behind.

"Who are you?" Reyes asks.

The warden answers, "Pulue," and walks across the room to shake the obviously powerful man's hand.

Reyes takes a clue and backs away, but the man named Pulue follows. "I asked you once. I'll ask again. Are you referring to Jena Parker?"

Reyes nods that he was.

"Well, how can that be?" asks Pulue, his voice getting louder. "Aren't we all aware that Jena Parker isn't to be touched? Isn't that right, Warden Peters?"

Peters looks at Reyes. "We are aware, sir." Peters' shoots Reyes an I-told-you-so look.

Pulue turns his attention to the warden. "Since that is settled, where is Jena?"

Peters looks at Tim. Tim looks at Reyes. Reyes stares at the door, where Mike had suddenly appeared.

Pulue turns around and says hello to Mike, who simply stares straight ahead. Sensing that he's not going to get any information from the man, who hasn't even bothered to introduce himself, Pulue turns to Peters. "Is he one of your guys?" he asks.

"Yes," the warden answers. "This is Mike Fredmond, one of the prison guards."

"Okay, Mike. Can you tell me where Jena Parker is?"

Mike finally answers. "She's in solitary confinement."

Pulue turns to Peters again. "Why?"

"Well, sir," the warden says, deferring to the man who is clearly the most powerful person in the room.

"She got into a fight, and, well, even though we all know the deal, there are still prison rules … prison policies … and everyone has to follow those rules … those policies."

Peters just keeps talking nervously. "And besides, it would look suspicious if we didn't put her in solitary confinement."

Pulue lightly scratches chin with his thumb. "I suppose that's understandable, as long as she isn't harmed."

He clears his throat. "She belongs to me. The deal is the same as the deal you have with our compound command officer. The rules

I command are the same as the rules you have with Moschi. I speak for him. Obey me as you would obey him."

Everyone in the warden's office is quiet. Reyes and Tim have no idea what the man is talking about, and no one explains.

Pulue turns to address Mike again. "Mike, we will be taking Jena tonight. She can't see our faces or know where we are taking her."

He looks at Mike but sees no reaction, so he continues. "I need you to handcuff her, cover her eyes, then bring her to our van out back."

Pulue locks his hands behind his back as if he is a professor, offers no further explanation or farewell, and walks out the door, his associates in tow.

Mike knows that Jena is supposed to be leaving the prison, but he hadn't known when, and he certainly doesn't know what this man, Pulue, intends—whether good or evil or something in between.

And Mike certainly doesn't know how he feels about whatever is going on.

Peters tells Mike to get Jena. The warden's expression lets Mike know that he had best do it quickly.

Mike weaves his way through the hallways to Jena's cell. When he arrives, he looks through the window of her cell door to see that she is asleep on the cot. The food tray is on the floor next to her.

Mike opens the door, and Jena doesn't move. He's pleased that the tray is empty, except for a few sweet peas set neatly to the side. He just stands over Jena, staring at her. He is moved by her beauty. He kneels beside the bed and whispers her name.

Jena moves slowly to face him.

"Someone has come for you, Jena," Mike says gently. "It's time for you to go."

He touches her lightly on the shoulder. His voice is sad and strained.

Jena merely sighs, gets up, puts on her shoes. "I'm ready," she says, simply.

"Jena, I have to handcuff you and cover your head." Mike reaches for a pillowcase. "I think it might be for your protection, and their protection, too."

The young woman nods and puts her wrists behind her back so that Mike can put the handcuffs on. "I'm ready," she repeats.

Mike's hands shake a bit as he handcuffs Jena and gently places the pillowcase over her head. He turns her around, puts one hand on her wrists and one on her shoulder and walks her slowly down the hallways, and to the back of the prison where Pulue and his men are waiting.

Mike begins to take the handcuffs off, but Pulue stops him.

"Leave," Pulue tells Mike firmly. Mike stares at Jena, then back at Pulue.

"What's going here?" Mike says in a demanding voice. His stare bores into Jena's eyes.

Jena manages to raise one of her eyebrows. She winks at Mike.

Mike backs down, turns to walk away. But he stops.

"I said leave," Pulue says again, louder, and even more firmly.

And then Mike is gone.

Pulue walks to Jena and takes her arm.

"Jena, I am Pulue, a trusted friend and associate of Moschi's. You are with us now. I believe Moschi will explain all of this to you."

Pulue turns Jena toward him, even though she still can't see anything. "Do you understand?"

Jena nods yes.

"We have a long journey ahead," Pulue says. "Unfortunately, you will have to wear this prison jumpsuit—and the handcuffs and pillowcase—for a bit longer. But I assure you that you will be no prisoner where we are going. Do you understand?"

Jena nods again that she understands.

Pulue looks toward one of his associates, who pulls out a long needle.

"Jena, this may hurt a little."

The man with the needle sticks Jena, and she is instantly unconscious.

The other man catches her as she falls, picks her up like a child, and places her on a cot in the van.

Pulue removes the handcuffs and nods again to his associates.

Both men look out the van doors, one way and then the other, see no one, and they close the van's doors. One man gets behind the wheel as Pulue and the second man gets situated in the front of the van.

And so, Jena and the men leave the prison—into the night.

CHAPTER FOUR

Warden Peters is still so angry that his face looks like it is about to pop, and his anger is directed at Reyes. "Don't you say one single word!" Peters' yells. "Close the door, Tim."

Tim complies as Peters continues his tongue-lashing.

"Are you trying to get us killed? Do you see what would have happened if you'd gotten to Jena before Pulue got here?"

The warden pauses to catch his breath. "He would have killed us! All of us!"

Reyes' arrogance gets the best of him. "He wouldn't have killed us. I would have killed him." Reyes pats the gun on his hip.

The warden refuses to back down. He eyes Reyes, "How many times are you going to reach for that weapon? Huh? Just use it, for God's sake. Stop with the threats."

Reyes refuses to stand down.

"I'll use this gun when I'm damned ready to use it," he says. "Look at you, scared shitless. You might as well have a nameplate on that desk that says 'Coward'. If Miles were still here, you wouldn't even have the chance to boss us around."

Reyes draws closer to the warden. "Would you?"

Peters backs away a bit. "Miles isn't the warden of this prison anymore. I am!"

Reyes is still angry. "Jena Parker is the reason Miles isn't running things. That crazy chick is supposed to his daughter killed her own father. Miles ran a smooth operation. We were raking in the dough. He would have dealt with that pushy bastard the way a real boss would."

Peters points a finger at Reyes. "Miles McNeil was a hothead just like you. He nearly blew this whole operation because he couldn't keep it in his pants. Slept with the mayor's wife, for God's sake, got her pregnant and even killed Jonathan Parker, who'd been his friend for years!"

Peters takes a deep breath. "Miles McNeil killed Jonathan Parker; the man Jena knew as her father. McNeil caused this whole mess."

The warden shakes his head at the tangled miasma of small-town crime.

"To make matters worse, the mayor found out about his wife's affair, and when he confronted her, she threatened to reveal everything she knew about Miles McNeil and his shady deals. Of course, she never would have known anything if McNeil had just kept his mouth shut."

Peters walks to his desk, furious.

"McNeil's own wife found out about the affair, so he killed her," he goes on.

"Then I have no choice but to ask Moschi to kill the mayor's whole family—just to keep him from having us all arrested. McNeil was reckless. Your hero was the only thorn in this operation."

He's yelling now. "Hell, I'm glad Jena killed Miles McNeil—whatever her reasons."

Reyes is beyond enraged and pulls his gun from its holster, even points the gun directly at the warden.

"McNeil was my friend," Reyes says, out of control. "He made us a lot of money! A lot! And we'd be rolling in it right now if it weren't for Jena Parker. He was even in New York City, making even bigger deals. We could have built an unstoppable empire."

Peters is too shocked to say or do anything at all, especially since Reyes is still pointing the gun at him.

Reyes suddenly remembers Tim, who is standing close to the door. Reyes turns and points the gun at Tim, too, for good measure.

Everyone is quiet, waiting to see what Reyes will do next.

Finally, Reyes' fever of violence seems to break.

He lowers his gun and shakes his head.

"Let's go, Tim. We have a nurse to prepare for a long trip."

Tim is still upset about kidnapping Tonya. "Can we please just find someone else?"

Reyes' temper flares again. He walks to Tim and puts his pistol directly against Tim's forehead.

"She's going," Reyes says, seething with anger and impatience. "Either you're with us or you're not. And if you're not, I'm gonna kill you right here, right now.

"We're taking Nurse May, and I've got someone special in mind to keep her company."

Reyes eases the gun away from Tim.

The warden jumps back into the surreal situation.

"Who would that be?" he asks.

Reyes smiles as he turns around, putting the gun back in its holster.

"Well, if I can't have Jena Parker, then I'll take her cellmate, Paula," Reyes says. "She's quiet, and she doesn't have any family that comes to visit. She's perfect. Just like you wanted, warden—or should I say, boss," Reyes says, sarcastically.

Peters is still furious. "Get out of my office. Both of you get the hell out of my office. And get this job done tonight before you get us all killed. These people aren't going to accept late deliveries."

Reyes turns and bumps into Tim on his way out the door. Tim follows reluctantly, knowing full well that he'd best keep his mouth shut.

Jena is still out cold from the injection, still on the cot in the back of the van, her head still covered with the pillowcase.

The destination for the three men and the unconscious woman is an airport where a private jet is waiting. Pulue and his two associates get out of the van and see that the stairs have been let down from the jet to the runway. Two attendants, a man and woman, walk down the steps to greet Pulue and the others.

"Welcome, sir," the man says to Pulue. "We are here to serve you and your team."

Pulue directs the attendants to help get Jena out of the van. "Be gentle with her," Pulue says. "When she wakes up, give her the best food and drink you have. Let her bathe and give her the clothes we've brought for her."

"I want Miss Parker to feel our warm hospitality," Pulue says.

The attendants nod. "Is there anything we can get you, sir," the male attendant asks.

Pulue looks with suspicion down the dark, quiet runway. "No, just take care of Miss Parker. I will call for you if we need anything."

The two attendants and Pulue's associates slide Jena onto a stretcher and pull her out of the van and up the stairs to the jet.

Pulue's men come back to take their usual place next to their boss.

"Keep your eyes open. We can't trust that Romli hasn't sent our enemies—someone from his team—to follow us," Pulue instructs.

He stops suddenly as they make their way to the jet. "And keep an eye on the airplane attendants, too."

"What about the pilot?" one of the men asks.

"He's my brother," Pulue says.

Inside, the plane looks more like a ballroom than a jet: black leather chairs, deep red carpet, even small crystal chandeliers. Each seat has its own television, telephone, and minibar. A thick glass wall separates the pilot from his passengers. It protects the pilot but also allows the boss to keep an eye on the man flying the plane.

Pulue walks into the cabin where his half-brother, Telo, is preparing the jet for takeoff.

The two men hug and exchange warm greetings. "Hello, dear brother," Pulue says with a smile. "We are glad to be here. It was a long drive."

"I'm sorry we're running a bit late," the Telo, who's the pilot says. "It won't be long now."

Pulue walks away but looks back over his shoulder. "Just get us home," he says.

Attentive to every detail, Pulue glances toward the back of the plane and sees the attendants preparing a meal for Jena. He finally sits and unbuttons his suit jacket. His associates are quiet but seem to be focused on the pilot.

Pulue startles them: "Strange that the people we trust most will always be the ones who betray us first."

The plane finally takes flight, and Pulue allows himself to doze off as his associates keep watch.

The attendants in the back are chatting while they wait for Jena to wake.

Jena's eyes flutter a little—she's still sound asleep under fresh soft blankets.

She dreams as if she is in a fog with the breeze gently caressing her cheek. She walks in the dark dream, lost, and confused and afraid.

The three-inch heels of her red boots click against the stones of a sidewalk; the black leather coat keeps her warm as she digs into the pockets for something—she isn't sure what.

She is afraid but keeps walking, as if daring someone or something to come out of the dark. There are no houses or cars— just the sidewalk leading her into empty space.

Only her footsteps fill the silent void. As the wind picks up, Jena begins to walk faster toward the unknown. When the wind howls, she walks even faster, drawn into the darkness.

The farther she walks, the darker it seems. And then she stops and stares at her feet. The sidewalk has come to an end. There is no place to walk.

Gradually, she sees that she is standing on a sandy cliff. There are no more steps unless she steps to her death. She breathes deeply and stares into the black cavern, then, curious, she eases one food off the edge of the cliff—teasing the edge, daring it to pull her in.

The breeze whispers in her ear. All that is left for Jena is the truth and the end. She falls like a bird without wings into the silent black cavern. She knows that no one can save her, so she embraces the fall, lifts her arms, and rides the wind. She feels free, no longer fearing the darkness because the darkness was never the threat.

The heavens might save her, but her sins swirl around her like a carousel. As she falls, she sees a light flicker across her vision and hears a voice far away. The voice becomes louder until she can hear it clearly. She looks toward the light, and of course, the light is Jake. The sound is Jake.

Jake is standing on top of the cliff, reaching out to her, calling her name. But she is too far gone now. She has fallen too far. The wind takes her, as the pit of earth swallows her.

Jena wants to be with Jake and feels his pain, and her tears stream upward to him in slow motion. As her tears reach Jake and touch his face, he screams, knowing that his love is lost. Her tears surround him, until the dark rain falls, taking away even her tears.

Jake falls to his knees, calling Jena's name.

The Earth spins past Jena, her life passes by—her parents, her friends, and then Jake. Her body disintegrates, as if into dust. She begins to struggle under her blankets, trying to release herself from the dream.

She wakes with tears streaming down her cheeks and gasps for breath. She tries to calm herself. But the dream haunts her.

Jena lies still, but the tears will not stop. The tears are from a deeper place, from her past, from her present and from the uncertainty of her future.

In her mind, she sees a flash of Jake. Her heart aches from missing him so deeply.

At that moment, one of the attendants walks to her bed and sees Jena crying.

"Jena, I'm Elma," the woman says. "What can I do for you?"

Jena just stares. The woman is wearing a black and white maid's uniform. Her dark hair is pulled away from her face—a striking face with black eyes and golden-brown skin.

"Nothing," Jena says, sobbing now. "I don't need anything."

Elma backs away to give Jena privacy.

But Jena changes her mind and stops her.

"Wait," Jena says. "Yes, you can do something."

Jena speaks tentatively. She doesn't know the rules. "I need a phone. Please. I need a phone," she asks, pleading.

Elma glances around the room. "I'm not sure if we are allowed." She hesitates.

Jena decides to try being more forceful. "I want a phone, now."

Elma leaves the room and comes back with a cellphone that she hands to Jena.

"Take it," Elma insists quietly. "Take it. This cellphone belongs to you, but only for this flight. Once the plane lands, you will not be able to use this phone ever again."

Jena takes the phone and stares at it, clenched in her hand.

She punches in a number.

On the other end of the call, the phone rings, and rings. A woman answers. A calm voice.

Jena can't say anything.

"Hello," the woman says again.

Jena quickly cuts off the call.

"It's Mrs. Paterson," she says to herself. She can't ask Jake's mother to put Jake on the phone. Mrs. Paterson would know Jena's voice.

Elma steps back to Jena's side. "Is something wrong?"

Jena nods, thinking quickly: "I need you to do me a favor."

"I'm here to serve you," Elma answers.

"I need you to take this phone and call the number I just called and ask for Jake Paterson," Jena tries to explain.

"Jake Pat-er-son." Elma has trouble saying Jake's last name.

"Yes. Jake Paterson," Jena says. "A woman will pick up the phone, and you need to ask her to let you speak to Jake Paterson. And if he's not there, get the woman to tell you where he is."

Jena hands Elma the phone. Elma takes the phone but just stares at Jena. Clearly, Jena's request is difficult for Elma to process.

"Alright, I will try. Give me the number, please."

"Just use the last number I called," Jena explains.

Elma nods obediently. She finds the number and presses the button to make the call. The phone rings and rings again.

Finally, Mrs. Paterson answers. Elma is silent, going over the task in her mind.

Jena is beginning to worry that her ruse won't work when Elma speaks up.

"Yes," Elma responds clearly and professionally, as if this is what Elma is trained to do—and maybe she is.

"My name is Trisha McGrines from Shelby Corporation and I'm trying to reach Mr. Jake Paterson."

Jena is shocked that Elma, seemingly, went from barely speaking English to speaking English like it was her native language. Jena sits on the bed and listens intently.

"This is in reference to a job," Elma lies.

Mrs. Paterson says Jake is not home.

Elma pauses to think about what to say next. "Oh, that is too bad. Do you know where I might reach him?"

Mrs. Paterson hesitates. "Well, I guess it's okay for me to tell you that he's at work—a minimum-wage job at Café Crew. I know he has been looking for something better.

"You can call back … hmmm … around 7. He'll be here then."

Elma smiles at Jena and breathes a sigh of relief. "Thank you, I'll do that," she tells Mrs. Paterson.

Mrs. Paterson sounds excited. "I'll tell Jake that you called."

"Perfect, goodbye."

Elma clicks off the cellphone and practically tosses it to Jena.

Jena can only stare at Elma, who transformed herself into a completely different person in a matter of seconds. Who is this woman? Jena asks herself, still holding the phone.

Elma starts to leave, her mission complete. She seems pleased with herself. She stops to give Jena some advice.

"You're about to enter into a completely different world, Miss Parker. A world you never knew existed. I'm here to serve you while you are on this flight and until Pulue tells me that my job is complete."

Elma sounds almost stern—yet another change from the manner of an obedient maid—or the professional-sounding woman on the telephone.

"Pulue has a schedule. You have about five minutes before I return to take you to your bath, then you will eat dinner and relax until the flight is over. From that point on, Pulue will provide you with instructions."

Elma walks away, leaving Jena confused. But she is grateful for the woman's help, and she doesn't have time to waste thinking about the strangeness of things.

Jena quickly calls directory assistance and asks for the number for Café Crew in Maplesville. The operator finds the number and offers to connect Jena directly to the café. Jena readily agrees. She doesn't have much time.

But Jena's plan seems to come to an unlucky end when the operator tells her that the line is busy.

"Please, please try again. I can't call back."

"Yes, ma'am," the operator replies, helpfully.

"Ma'am, the line is still busy. Please call back later. Thank you," and the operator hangs up quickly.

Jena is devastated but looks at the time and knows she has one minute left.

She dials directory assistance again. "Yes, operator, please connect me to Café Crew in Maplesville." The call goes through and the phone rings!

Jena is so excited that she can barely speak.

A young girl answers the café phone. "Yes, please, I'd like to speak to Jake Paterson," Jena says quickly.

Jena waits, frantically watching the clock count down.

"Ma'am, Jake is on another line," the girl says.

"I'm sorry, but it's an emergency. Please hurry. Can you please tell Jake that he has another call?"

"Sure," the girl says, putting Jena on hold.

Jake is talking to his mother; Jena and Elma's plan worked a little too well.

"Jake, you got a call from a lady about a job. She said she's from some corporation. It sounds like it could be a really good opportunity." Mrs. Paterson is excited for her son.

Jake is silent. "Jake, just because I'm mad at you doesn't mean I don't want the best for you."

"Mom, I have to go."

"Jake, wait. I know you didn't kill Ted. I know it was that awful Jena Parker."

"Mom," Jake tries to make her stop talking.

"Jake, I know you couldn't have possibly killed your own brother. I know you, son."

"Mom."

The young receptionist interrupts, and Jake is grateful. "Jake, there's some woman on the other line. She needs to talk to you, and she says it's an emergency," the girl says.

"Mom, I gotta go." And Jake hangs up without explanation to his mother.

Jena is nearly hysterical when she hears Jake pick up the phone and say hello. She's hearing his voice for the first time in forever.

"Hello," Jena says, suddenly losing her nerve—and her voice. She tries to say Jake's name, but it's as if the J is broken. She can't speak.

"Jena?" Jake asks, tentative and confused.

Then, nothing. Only the dial tone. Jake's boss, Harold, has his big fat finger on the off button.

"You're on the clock, Paterson," Harold says, snatching the phone away from Jake and slamming down the receiver. "That means you're getting paid to wash dishes, not talk on the phone."

His nasty rebuke means nothing to Jake. Jake's mind is miles away, as he wonders whether Jena had really been on the other end of the line.

"You got that Paterson?" Harold asks, still yelling.

But Jake races past his boss toward Tina, the teenage girl at the front desk.

Jake peppers her with questions. Who was on the phone? What did she sound like? What did she say? He grabs Tina's arm, but Tina looks at him like he's an alien.

Tina shrugs. "I don't know. Just some girl asking for you. She said it was an emergency."

Jake is frantic. "Was her voice soft or hard? Was she loud? … What the hell. … Was she Jena Parker?"

Tina is oblivious, probably the only person in town who doesn't recognize Jena's name. "Who's that?"

Jake takes off his hat and runs his hands through his hair in frustration. Then, he throws the hat down and runs to the locker room to grab his bag.

Harold follows, but Jake ignores his presence and his threats. "Just where do you think you're going?"

Jake doesn't answer, doesn't even listen.

"Paterson, if you walk out of here, you're fired, you get that?"

Jake finally decides to deal with Harold. "Mr. Riggs," Jake says. "It's my mom. She's sick. I've gotta go."

Harold clearly isn't buying this cockamamie story.

"She got sick, what, like five seconds ago?" Harold asks sharply.

"Yes, five seconds ago," Jake answers. "She got ill quite quickly, and I have to go home and take her to the doctor."

Harold scowls. "What about your dad?"

"What about him?" Jake asks, having lost his patience sometime before.

"My dad can't take her. He can't drive. He just got released from the hospital."

Harold relents. "Paterson, this is your last chance. If I find out you lied, you're outta here for good."

"I got that," Jake says, backing out the door. "Yes, Mr. Riggs, it won't happen again."

Jake runs out the door without looking back, jumps in his car, digs his cellphone out of his bag, and calls his best friend, Ken Stewart.

Jake gets Ken's voice mail and curses.

He leaves a message: "Hey, man, I'm on my way. I hope you're there."

Jake races out of the parking lot and down the street to Ken's apartment. Ken's car is out front.

He runs up the steps, two at a time, shoves open the door and quickly turns on the television. Ken is out cold on the couch but wakes up in a panic when he hears Jake come in.

As he tries to wipe the sleep out of his eyes, he complains, "Can't a man who just got out of the hospital—after getting shot—get some sleep around here?"

"Be quiet," Jake commands, as he grabs the remote control and searches the news channels. "I'm sorry I haven't seen you since you got shot by that freak, but there's something you got to watch."

Ken sits up slowly. His shoulder is still heavily bandaged from the gunshot wound that Chance had inflicted.

"What's up, man?" Ken asks.

"I'm not sure," Jake says, still frantically looking for something on the television. "I just have this feeling."

"Huh?" Ken asks.

Jake mumbles Jena's name.

Ken is still shaking his head about Jake's strange behavior when one of the stations broadcasts breaking news.

A woman TV reporter is standing in front of the prison.

"There is breaking news tonight," the reporter says. "Warden Phillip Peters has announced that Jena Parker has been released from prison, and all charges against her have been dropped."

The reporter pauses for dramatic effect. "Maplesville police are telling us that there is a new suspect in the recent murders, including the murder of Jena Parker's mother, Catherine." The reporter, maintaining the drama, walks closer to the camera. She sighs before speaking again. "Jena Parker is now a free woman."

The screen flashes images of Jena and her mother. Jakes' heart jumps.

The reporter continues: "Officials from the prison, the police department, and the District Attorney's office are not releasing the name of the new person of interest."

This is an important news story for the young reporter, and she is making the most of it. Viewers will be fascinated, she knows, maybe even angry.

"However, our sources, who have requested anonymity, tell us that the suspect's name will not be announced. The case is still under investigation, but what we do know is that Jena Parker is not the killer we thought her to be."

"We have also been unable to determine the current location of Jena Parker, but we will continue to bring you details on this important story as they develop."

Jake can't move. He's gripping the remote control as if it's the most important thing in the world.

Ken can't move or speak.

"Holy shit, man," is the only comment Ken can manage.

"I knew it," Jake says finally. "I knew it!"

Jake is yelling, loud enough to wake people in nearby apartments. "Jena's out of jail, and she tried to call me tonight."

Ken tries to shush Jake. "Come on, man, we got neighbors. If we get kicked out of here, we're screwed, with me laid up and all."

"Dude," Jake says, as he paces back and forth in front of the television. "You don't get it. Jena really did try to call me tonight. I know it was her."

Jake can't calm down. He walks around the room, picking up random objects, then putting them back in places they don't belong.

Ken, still in pain, limps around the room trying to understand. But Jake seems to be in another world.

"Where could she be?" Jake says, mostly to himself.

Desperate to help his friend, Ken puts his hand on Jake's shoulder. "We'll find her. Wherever she is, we'll find her."

———

Jena, of course, is far away, though her mind is most definitely on Jake, who is frantic, in another world.

Elma returns to Jena's room, with Nash, the other attendant.

They treat Jena like royalty, leading her to the bath and presenting her with a satin robe and slippers.

The food is delicious, and though Jena's worries are many, she can't help but savor the special treats, after suffering prison food.

The helpful attendants leave Jena to her own thoughts and to enjoy the feast.

"We are only a buzz away," Peter says, as he prepares to close the door to her room. "Call us if you need anything at all."

She stops him, just before he leaves.

"Who are you two?" she asks. "You remind me of two people I knew before. One was a woman named Mary, and I killed her. The other was someone named Moschi, who claimed to be a driver, but I know he isn't a driver at all."

Nash smiles.

"Who are you?" Jena asks again.

Nash seems faintly amused, but not shocked, by Jena's audacity. "We work for the same man you'll be working for."

With that, Nash closes the door and leaves the room.

CHAPTER FIVE

Chief Reyes walks swiftly down the prison hallway. Tim walks beside him keeping his eye on Reyes' gun. Reyes catches him staring at the gun and pulls it out and points it at Tim for the second time that night.

"You're asking for it, man," Reyes says, eyeing Tim. "So, are you scheming to take my gun away?"

Reyes waves the weapon at Tim, daring him to make a move.

"What? You think you're going to save your sweet Nurse May?" Reyes asks, squinting to look even eviler. "You'd better hope this job goes off well."

Reyes body-slams Tim. "Because if it doesn't, you'll be the one shipped to an unknown country in a body bag."

Reyes turns and strides toward the medical ward. Tim walks beside him, ashamed of what they're doing, sad about Tonya, but too afraid to confront Reyes.

Reyes peeks through the door, looking for Nurse May. He sees Candy and Chance, both asleep in their beds. But the nurse is nowhere to be seen."

"She's got to be here," Reyes says. "She must be in the back."

Reyes reaches for his gun again.

"Wait a minute," Tim says. "You're not going shoot her, are you?"

Reyes smirks. "Maybe," he says.

"Here's what's going to happen," Reyes says, laying out his devious plan. "You're going to go talk to Nurse May and make her feel good—you know, with your phony sweet talk."

Tim shudders.

"Then, you're going to ask her to go outside with you for a little lovers' stroll. When you both get outside, I'll nab her, and we'll tie her up and throw her in the van."

Tim seems like he is someplace else.

"You got that?" Reyes demands.

Tim stares at Reyes. Tim's eyes are darting back and forth.

"I said, you got that?" Reyes growls.

Finally, Tim says, "Yes, I got it."

"Good," Reyes says. "No slip-ups because slip-ups will get you *and* Nurse May killed."

Tim slowly walks into the medical ward. He closes the door quietly. The room is dark. Candy and Chance are quiet.

He stops and stares at Tonya, in her office, finishing reports.

He slowly walks toward her office, but his heart is beating like a racehorse on its final lap.

Finally, Tim stands in the doorway of Tonya's office, staring at a woman he cared about, admired, even dreamt he might have a future with. Now he knows the dream is turning to a nightmare with every step he takes.

Tonya looks up and sees Tim. She's still angry about his earlier visit to her office with Reyes.

"Yes?" she asks, abruptly. "What do you want now?"

Tim tries to think of something to break the ice. He steps into her office. "Listen, I wanted to come and apologize for that awful interrogation you got earlier from Reyes."

Tonya shakes her head, dismissing him. "I'm busy."

Tim sighs and stares at her. "I'm sorry, Tonya. Please forgive me."

Tonya looks at Tim and melts visibly. She adores him, too, and can't stay mad for long.

Tim sees his opening. He knows he must seize this moment to earn her trust. So, he does something he's never done. He walks closer to her, reaches down, and gathers her into a hug. He holds Tonya tightly and releases his fear into the embrace.

"I love you, Tonya," he says, looking deeply into her eyes. He moves to kiss her. "Can I kiss you, or should I say, *May* I kiss you." He grins, and she is both moved and surprised by his sweetness. Before Tonya can answer, Tim kisses.

Their lips connect perfectly, softly, becoming a long, slow kiss that morphs into a tidal wave that carries them both away, if only for a moment.

"Let's go for a walk," Tim whispers into Tonya's ear. "You know, like we use to do in high school."

Tonya demurs. "I have a lot of work to do."

"The work will wait."

Tonya smiles. "Tim, this is a prison. There's a guard everywhere." She tries to escape Tim's embrace. "This place isn't exactly romantic."

Tim pulls her back. "Don't ruin this moment."

He thinks fast. "Remember, I'm the head guard. I know all of the spots around this prison," he says, trying to be funny.

Tonya laughs quietly, and he has won her over. "Okay. But just for a little while. I have to get finished up here and get home to Sam."

Tim is stumped. "Sam?"

"My dog," she explains and laughs a real laugh.

Tim blushes.

Meanwhile, Reyes has not left. He peaks through the window of the medical ward until he sees shadows moving toward the door.

Reyes darts into a corner and watches Nurse May and Tim walk out holding hands.

Tim turns his head to nod at Reyes, signaling that everything is going as planned.

Reyes can't resist tiptoeing into the medical ward so that he can inflict a little more fear.

First, he walks to Candy's bed and stares down at her and her belly. He is disgusted that his child is growing inside this horrible person.

A light flickers somewhere in the room and distracts Reyes temporarily. He turns toward Chance, who is startled awake.

Reyes leans down close to her face. "Feeling better?"

He looks like a snake to her. "No," she says. "No, I'm not."

Reyes leans back. "That's too bad because it looks like you may be leaving."

Chance blinks. "What?" she asks, alarmed.

"I said, you may just be getting out of here." Reyes smiles.

"What are you talking about?"

Reyes shakes his head and chuckles. "Oh, you'll see."

Candy wakes up and yawns. "Chance, are you okay?"

When Candy opens her eyes and focuses, she sees Reyes staring at them.

"Look at you two girls," he smiles and rubs his gun. "All laid up in bed. Both of you useless—at least for now."

Reyes sucks his teeth. He looks back and forth at Chance and Candy, then focuses on Candy. He walks over and sits on the edge of her bed.

"You've got something of mine, and I want it," he tells Candy. "Yeah, I want it. And you will never see it. Ever!"

Candy begins to whimper.

Chance lies in her bed, feeling too helpless and too scared to help Candy.

Reyes rises, walks to the door, and turns to stare at the women one more time. He licks his lips.

"I will be back, and I bet you girls will be right here waiting for me."

When Reyes leaves, Candy begins to cry. "Oh, my God," she calls out loud.

Chance sits up, still trying to get over her terror.

Candy is sobbing uncontrollably. "My baby. My poor baby."

Chance's eyes get wide. "You're pregnant?" she asks.

Candy keeps crying and screaming, over and over, "My baby, my baby."

Chance remembers hearing Reyes say, "You'll never see it."

"Please don't let him take my baby," Candy weeps. "Chance, please don't let him take my baby."

Chance swallows hard, moved, but afraid to say anything.

"Is Chief Reyes the father of your baby?" Chance asks.

Candy manages to nod.

Chance is shocked. "How in the hell did that happen?"

Candy tries to talk through her tears. "I'm a whore," she says, crying harder. "Chief Reyes arrested me once and after my pimp found out about me being arrested, he beat me so bad that I couldn't open my eyes for a week." She tries to wipe away her tears. "When Chief Reyes caught me the next time, I begged him not to arrest me and told him I would do anything to keep my pimp from beating me again. So, Reyes forced me to sleep with him. He wouldn't let me turn tricks anymore. I couldn't have sex with anyone but him." She then says she had to tell her pimp. "I told him I didn't want to be a whore anymore, that I just wanted to live a normal life. We argued, and he was pulling and jerking me around." She confesses she was terrified her pimp would kill her, but then, after a long pause and from out of nowhere, she says, "A girl came around the corner with a gun. She asked me my name, and I told her." She takes a deep breath. "She said, 'Candy, get the hell out of here.' So, I ran and never looked back. But I heard a gunshot. I knew she'd killed my pimp."

She continues with her story. Reyes rented a room in a rundown hotel, and he'd come to have sex with her whenever he wanted.

"In a weird way, I felt like a normal person. You know, like he was my man, and I was his girl." She says she believed Reyes had feelings for her. "He brought me flowers once. Nice flowers."

She stops mid-memory to collect herself.

Chance studies her, with a look at that encourages Candy to go on.

"My life was going good," Candy says. But that didn't last long. Soon, the police knocked at her door and arrested her and charged her with murdering her pimp. She couldn't reach Reyes, and no one believed her story or believed that she even knew Reyes. Reyes never stepped up to help her.

She was convicted and ended up in jail. "It was a nightmare," she weeps. To make matters worse, she figured out during the trial that she was pregnant, and that Reyes had to be the father. "I was only a little over a month along. It's not fair. I didn't kill my pimp. It was probably that crazy girl in the hallway. Now I'm in jail with a baby on the way."

Candy rubs her red eyes.

Chance looks at her with something like compassion.

"Then, Reyes turns up here, acting crazy, and says he's going to take the baby away," Candy says. "This is the first time in my life that I've ever loved anything. I love my baby." She stops talking and stares into space, tears flowing down her cheeks. "Maybe I should kill myself and the baby to save us both."

Chance manages to get out of bed and limp across the room with her IV stand. She sits next to Candy and strokes her hair.

"No, Candy," Chance says. "Killing yourself and that innocent baby is not the answer." Chance suddenly turns from uncharacteristically gentle and sympathetic to angry and threatening. "The answer is killing that motherfucker Reyes. That's the answer." She stares into Candy's red, teary eyes. "You got that? You are done taking the blame. It's time to fight."

Candy wipes away the tears.

"You need to fight for yourself," Chance says, laying a hand on Candy's stomach. "And you need to fight for this baby."

Candy is overcome and hugs Chance as hard as she can. "Thank you, Chance. Will you help me?"

Chance moves away from Candy's embrace and stares into space. "You're damned right I will. Now get some rest." Chance walks back to her bed and turns around with a hard gaze at Candy. "That girl who shot your pimp, what did she look like?"

Candy shakes her head. "I don't know. It happened too fast, and I was scared to death. She might have had red hair. She was pretty." She says she was high, too, but that when she was hiding, she heard a man calling for the girl with the gun. "That girl's name might have been Jen, or Janet, or Julie. I just cannot remember."

Chance grimaces.

"The guy seemed pretty desperate to find that girl, but I don't know if he was looking for the same girl as the one who shot my pimp," she explains. "Really, anyone could have killed him. He pissed off a lot of people."

Suddenly, the light comes on and Mike appears. "What are doing out of bed, Miss Middleton?"

Chance crawls back into bed. "I was just getting some water," she lies. "The nurse isn't around, so I had to fend for myself."

"What do you mean the nurse isn't here?" Mike asks. "Isn't Nurse May on duty?"

Chance nods that Nurse May had been on duty.

Candy stays as still as she can, trying not to attract any attention.

Mike shakes his head, confused. "You two stay in bed where you belong and go back to sleep."

Before leaving, he looks toward Nurse May's office, doesn't see her, then turns off the light and leaves the room. He sets out to find the nurse. He calls into the women's restroom but hears nothing. He walks from hall to hall and doesn't see or hear a thing.

But Reyes sees Mike.

He walks up behind Mike, startling him. "She's outside."

Mike whirls around.

"You're looking for Nurse May, right?" Reyes asks. "She's outside fooling around with her boyfriend, Tim."

Mike shakes his head and walks away, not sure what to think.

Once Mike is gone, Reyes glances into the medical ward and sees Chance and Candy resting quietly, then he heads out of the prison to find Tim and the nurse.

It's dark, except for two beaming lights. A guard is standing nearby.

"Have you seen Tim?" Reyes asks.

"Yeah, he and that nurse walked around that corner," the guard says, pointing.

"Thanks," Reyes says, as he walks away. He stops. "Oh, by the way, I ran into Mike, and he told me that you should take a break."

"I'm at this post for thirty minutes," the guard responds.

"No, it's okay," Reyes says. "I'm here, and so is Tim." He chuckles, trying to be clever. "I don't think anyone is going to try to escape in the next thirty minutes. Go ahead and take a break. I'll tell Tim."

The guard finally leaves, and Reyes smiles as he walks up to Tim and Nurse May. They're cuddling and whispering to each other, and Tim is leaning in for another kiss.

"There you are," Reyes teases them.

Tonya is unfazed. "What do you want, Reyes?" she asks. "Wait. I don't care."

Tonya jerks away from Tim and starts to walk away, but Tim grabs her arm.

"Wait," he begs.

"Tim, let me go. I don't want to be anywhere near Reyes."

Reyes pulls out his gun, and Nurse May is startled. She looks to Tim for help but finds none.

Reyes points the weapon at the nurse. "Whether you hate me or not, it won't be an issue for you much longer."

"What are you talking about?" Tonya asks frantically.

"You think you're just out here smooching with your man? No. No. No. It was all just a ruse to get you outside," Reyes says in a devilish tone.

Tonya understands she's in trouble. She tries to yell for help, Tim grabs her and puts a hand over her mouth.

He whispers, "I'm sorry," in her ear, as she continues to struggle. Reyes pulls out a syringe and pokes it into her arm.

Her body goes limp.

Tim holds Tonya, staring at her, knowing he has betrayed her in the worst way.

"That wasn't so hard, now was it, Tim?" Reyes taunts him.

"Okay," Reyes says. "I can count, so that's one down and two more to go."

"Take this one to the van, tie her up good, and stuff something in her mouth so she can't scream," Reyes orders.

Tim stands still, holding Tonya. "I can't do this!" he blurts out.

Reyes points his gun at Tim's head. "You can do this," he says, moving the gun to Tonya's head, then back at Tim. "It's up to you. Either way, it's going to get done." He shakes his head. "You need to wise up. You signed up for this a long time ago, Tim, and it's no use getting a conscience now, just because you're sweet on this one. We get paid a lot of money, and these are ruthless people. If we don't deliver, we get delivered. All of us! Everybody in this whole prison will go down." He's on a roll now. "And it isn't just this prison. Think of all the people out there who are involved in this. Your family's store and their name would get dragged through the mud."

Tim starts to tear up, still holding Tonya.

Reyes glowers at him. "No one is going to show you any mercy when you've been involved in all of these so-called missing-persons cases since the beginning." Reyes backs away. "Get your shit together because there is no turning back. Pull this crap again, and I will put a bullet in you and bury you where no one will ever find you. I might even take out your family, too." He stops. "Get her in the damned van and help me get two more. We've got a deadline. Now get moving."

By now, Reyes' face is beet red, and his eyes look like pure evil.

"I'll meet you inside," Tim says.

Tim becomes irrational in his grief, holding Tonya tightly. "What about Sam?"

Reyes turns around quickly. "Who the hell is Sam?"

"Her dog. I can't just leave the dog out there with no home."

Reyes is losing his patience. "Tim, I will shoot you, this nurse, and the damned dog."

Tim searches Reyes' face for pity, but Reyes' cold eyes don't melt.

"The van," Reyes growls, "put her in the van. Now, I said."

He hears the guard returning to his post and rushes to the door to stop the guard from seeing them. He grabs the door as the guard is walking out.

"What the heck, Reyes?" the guard asks. He tries to push past Reyes.

Reyes won't move. "Tim told me you should take the night off."

The guard isn't having any part of it. "I'd rather get my orders from Tim."

"What's wrong with my orders?" Reyes asks.

"For one thing, you don't work here," the guard says. "We all know your friends with the warden, but that doesn't mean we take orders from you. Tim is my supervisor, so I'll take my orders from him."

Reyes has had enough. He pulls out his gun, sticks it into the guard's stomach, and pulls the trigger. The guard tries to grab the gun as he goes down. Reyes puts the gun to the guard's head and shoots him again. "Now you don't have to take orders from nobody."

Tim stares at Reyes and the dead guard.

Reyes doesn't even look at Tim. "Call a couple of your guys to clean this up."

Tim makes a call on his cellphone.

"Did you take care of Nurse May like I told you?" Reyes asks.

Tim nods silently.

Two guards appear quickly to clean up the blood and try to do something, anything, with the body. They don't say a word.

Reyes and Tim walk inside.

The shock of the shooting seems to have distracted Tim from the fact that he had just kidnapped a woman that he loves.

"Here's the deal, we need two more women to ship out tonight, and I know who they are going to be: Karen Fuller and Paula Turner. No one will even miss them."

"Paula does have a daughter," Tim says.

Reyes looks at Tim. "What good is a momma who's in jail?"

"I'm saying that maybe one day the daughter or somebody else will come looking for Paula," Tim explains.

"We'll cross that bridge when we get to it," Reyes says. "For now, those two are the easiest targets." He tells Tim to find a guard named Francis to help him nab Karen. "I'll get Billy, and we'll go to Paula's cell. Tell the women that we're doing a random drug test." He pauses. "Got it?"

Tim nods.

"How about something more than a nod," Reyes says, frustrated. "This is a million-dollar deal. I don't want a nod. I want words. So, I'm asking again. You got all that?"

Tim looks at Reyes and rolls his eyes. "Yes. I got this."

"Then grab Francis, and let's go get those girls." Reyes smiles. "Let's make some money."

Reyes quickly finds Billy, who was expecting him, and they head to Paula's cell. They stare silently at her for a while, then Billy opens the cell.

Paula is startled and sits up quickly. "What's going on?"

"We're picking women at random and searching them and their cells. Then we're running a drug test."

Paula grabs her blanket. "I don't have anything, and I haven't used any drugs."

"Then you don't have anything to worry about, do you?" Reyes says. "Now, put on your shoes, and let's get going."

Paula is scared. Nothing good can come from this. "Can I talk to the warden first?"

Billy laughs and so does Reyes.

"What the hell are you talking about?" Billy asks derisively. "No. The answer is no. Besides, we're acting on the warden's orders."

"So, like I said, put on your shoes, and let's get going," Reyes says. "The sooner we get this done, the sooner you'll be back in your cell."

Paula reluctantly gets out of bed, puts on her shoes, and rinses her face and mouth. She steps out of the cell.

Billy sneaks up behind her with handcuffs and a pillowcase. "You'll have to be handcuffed, of course," Billy says. He quickly slips the pillowcase over her head.

Paula panics.

"Stay calm, now," Reyes says. "We're taking you to an undisclosed place. It's nothing to worry about."

Paula is terrified. She thinks about her little girl and starts to cry. *What if I never see my little girl again?* she thinks. She knows this isn't any routine drug test. She'd heard the rumors of women being beaten and raped. She'd heard the rumors about women who go missing, never to be seen or spoken about again.

She cries as they guide her down the hallways, blind and helpless, the guards on either side of her.

It seems like they walk forever. A door opens, and she feels a blast of fresh air.

They push her through the door and walk a few more steps. Guards tell Paula to take a big step up into a vehicle.

She almost screams when someone's head flops onto her shoulder.

When Paula starts to cry even harder, she feels the prick of a needle in her arm, and everything goes black.

Tim and Francis appear in the doorway with Karen, who is wiggling and crying and yelling. The four men lift her roughly into the van.

Reyes injects her with the same drug that knocked out Paula and Nurse May, then turns to the three guards. "We only have twenty-four hours to get these three women on the plane, out of the country, and delivered. We can't have any more delays or mistakes."

Reyes suddenly pulls out his gun and points it at Tim. "You're the weak link in an operation we all built from scratch."

Tim tries to object.

"First, Miles McNeil has an affair with the mayor's wife. Somehow McNeil's daughter, Jena, gets involved and almost blows this sweet operation all to hell," Reyes says. "Now, Tim, it's you, trying to bring us all down just because you have a weakness for that nurse."

Reyes waves his gun at Tim and orders him into the van.

All three men looked shocked, but Tim is equal parts afraid and confused. "What? What the hell?" he half-asks, half-yells at Reyes.

"I said, I want you to turn around, Tim, and get in that van," Reyes says sternly. He looks at Billy and Francis, and they draw their guns, too.

"You heard me," Reyes says. "Get in the van."

Tim backs away from the three men. "That ain't happening," he says, continuing to move away from them.

"Yes, it is," Reyes says calmly—and then shoots Tim in the arm.

"Your presence has been requested for rehabilitation," Reyes says, laughing as his former friend moans and tries to stanch the bleeding, writhing in agony.

"Don't be such a whiny person. You're not going to die," he says, further taunting Tim. "We think it will do you some good to get more training about the importance of this business. Because it seems like you've forgotten!"

With only one good arm, Tim tries to struggle away from Reyes and the two guards.

Another needle appears from Reyes' pocket. In a moment, Tim crumples to the ground.

"Get him into the van," Reyes orders Billy and Francis. "Patch him up, and make sure he doesn't bleed to death along the way."

"Yes, boss," they say, almost in unison.

Billy steps aside and Francis gets into the driver's seat.

"Get all of them on the plane, and out of here. Now," Reyes orders.

And with that, the van, and its prisoners—Paula, Karen, Tonya, and Tim—disappear into the darkness.

CHAPTER SIX

J ake has stayed awake all night, sitting on the sofa near the house phone thinking about Jena. He fidgets nervously, stares at the phone, picks it up to listen for the dial tone, just to make sure that the phone is working. He stares at the television. But there is no news program, only some long-forgotten movie. He hopes in vain for another news update about Jena. His eyes are red. He is heartbroken—and worried.

Ken walks slowly out of his bedroom, turns off the television, and sits on the other end of the couch. "What are doing, man?" Ken asks. "You're acting like a zombie."

"I *am* a zombie," Jake says slowly. He continues to stare into space. "Where is she? ... She's out of jail. ... I know she tried to call me at work. ... So, where is she now?"

Jake lets his head fall onto the couch.

Ken just stares at him.

Jake runs his fingers through his soft black hair. "I love her. I miss her so much." He looks up at Ken. "I need her. And I know she needs me, too." He jumps up, turns to look at Ken with desperation in his eyes. "I've got to find her. Tomorrow, I'm going to start searching for her, and I'm not going to stop until I find her." He opens the apartment door and stares into the darkness. "She's out there, and nothing in this damned world is going to stop me from finding her."

Ken gets up and walks slowly to Jake. He puts a hand on Jake's shoulder. "It's gonna be okay, buddy."

Jake can barely hold back his tears.

Ken squeezes Jake's shoulder. "Whatever you need me to do, I'm here," he promises.

Jake just keeps staring into the dark. He closes his eyes tightly, and memories of Jena flash through his mind.

"We'll find her," Ken says softly. "I promise you."

Jake starts down the steps.

Ken closes the door behind his grieving friend.

Beyond the stars, he can picture Jena smiling and laughing, back when they rode the school bus together. The sunlight is shining through her hair. He can hear her beautiful, soft laugh. He sits on a step and stares into the sky.

"Please let me find her," he prays, silently. "It is our destiny to be together. … Our destiny."

———

Far away, up in the sky somewhere, far from Jake, Jena wakes and stares out the airplane's window. But it's black, and she can't see anything.

Jena gets up and goes to a door that separates her from the rest of the cabin. She turns the handle, but the door won't open. She jerks at the handle again.

"What's going on?" she says loudly.

She hears a click, and the door swings open. Elma is standing in the doorway.

"We're about to land," she tells Jena. "You need to dress. Pulue wants you to be prepared before we land," Elma says, emphasizing the word *prepared*.

Jena is baffled. "What do you mean, '*prepared*?'"

Elma stares at Jena and walks toward her until she is standing very close. "I mean you need to get ready because your life is about to change in ways you can never imagine." Her voice sounds cold, and Jena stares at her as she backs away. "Behind you," Elma says, pointing at a rear door, "you'll find a shower." Then she points to an open closet, arrayed with nice clothes.

Jena shudders. She quickly showers and dresses.

Elma returns with a breakfast tray but is silent.

A knock at the door surprises Jena.

It's Pulue. He calls Jena's name.

"It's very nice to meet in a manner that is more cordial," he says, walking into the cabin. "This is so much better than how we brought you onto the plane—in handcuffs and a prison uniform." He pauses. "Moschi cares very much about you. I've known him for many, many years, and I've never seen him make a sacrifice like this for anyone." He looks at the ceiling, briefly lost in his thoughts. "There was one other person—"

"Maria?" Jena asks.

Pulue stares at the young woman. "Yes, Moschi's love, Maria. He told you about her?"

Jena nods. "He told me all about her. How they met. How he loved her."

He stares at the young woman.

"Romli," Jena says.

His face puffs up, and he shakes his head. "Don't say that name in my presence again," he says in a quiet voice that belies his anger. "You'll soon find that his name is never to be used among us. Among our team. Our family. And you, Jena, are now family. Your life in Maplesville, your life in prison, is over. You are now a member of one of the most powerful underground teams in the world." He explains that the group has special weapons, special skills, special knowledge. "We will teach you everything. You will know everything. You will understand everything we fight for."

He shakes his head and looks through Jena, not at her, then continues. "I'm sure Moschi would never have brought you to us if he hadn't believed you were ready."

He turns to leave, but as he walks through the door, he stops and looks over his shoulder at Jena. "I apologize for getting angry when you said that name. I know you don't understand, but you will learn. You, too, will hate."

Then he's gone, the door shut behind him.

Jena sits. She is stunned by Pulue's entrance and his exit—and everything in between.

Elma knocks and enters quickly. "It's time. Please buckle your seatbelt and prepare for landing."

When Elma leaves, Jena closes her eyes and remembers a dream about another plane trip. That plane was full of men, who were all staring at her as she walked down the aisle. She felt in control, powerful, unstoppable.

Now, she isn't sure who is in control.

She hears the landing gear as the aircraft descends. She peeks through the darkened window and it seems that she can see tall trees, but no houses, nothing she can identify.

She braces when the plane shudders as it hits the tarmac.

Elma walks in and motions for Jena to get up. "Come," she says with eyes that appear cold.

Jena stands slowly and walks out of the cabin.

Pulue and his two associates are waiting. He stands and eyes Jena up and down, checking out the white suit Jena selected from the wardrobe in the closet. He adjusts the lapels of the jacket and smiles.

"Jena," he says, "welcome home." His smile becomes more of a smirk, and he turns to his associates. "Please stay here with Miss Parker while I go speak to my brother in the cockpit."

Pulue is still smiling as he walks into the cockpit and takes his half-brother's hand and pulls him into a hug. "Brother, thank you for getting us home safely." He kisses his brother's head. "You are by far the best pilot on our team." Abruptly, his smile turns inexplicably into a frown. "And that's why I am so saddened that you arrived late, delaying our departure."

Telo speaks, beads of nervous sweat beginning to form on his forehead. "I'm so sorry, brother. I just couldn't leave for your destination in time. But I did get there, I did you get you here—to our home."

"Yes, you did get us home," Pulue says, pulling a gun from his waistband in the small of his back. "But you have not told the truth about leaving late." He points the gun at his brother. "We have this plane under full surveillance. You must know that brother. We know where you were, and we know why you were late. My brother, you are a traitor to our team."

Telo tries to defend himself. "No. No. I'm not."

Pulue waves the gun coolly at his half-brother in the cockpit, obviously not convinced.

Telo begins to plead. "I had to. They said they would kill Mother. Brother, you must believe me. I was just late. That is all. You wouldn't want them to kill Mother, would you?"

"Of course not, brother, but you are still lying," Pulue counters.

Telo continues to beg. "No. No," he cries futilely.

Pulue pulls the trigger, shooting his brother in the head.

Jena jumps with fright and alarm. She looks at Elma, who is smiling.

Pulue watches his half-brother fall over in his seat, blood spilling everywhere, then without batting an eye, he turns and walks back to Jena and the others.

"Now," he says, a huge grin on his face, "let's go meet the rest of the family."

Jena says nothing and wouldn't know what to say, anyway.

"Oh, Jena you're going to fit right in. You'll be among the best in the world. A renegade. A fighter with new technology that the rest of the world has never seen."

Jena looks at Pulue: so dignified, but so ruthless that he killed his own brother and then smiled at her as if nothing at all had happened.

Jena lifts her chin and maintains her composure as she follows Pulue and the rest of the crew toward the stairway leading off the plane. All the while, she keeps her eyes on Pulue's gun.

Elma and Nash the two bodyguards disembark and stand to wait for Pulue, who puts his arm around Jena's shoulder.

"Come see your new home," he says, and they leave the plane together.

Jena is puzzled as she looks at what appears to be a forest.

Pulue catches her eye. "I know what you're thinking: What home?" he says. "All you see is the forest. No land. No people, except us."

She looks at Pulue. "Yes. That is exactly what I'm thinking."

He is amused. "Oh, but you are wrong, Jena."

He and Jena stop while his four comrades walk ahead, then disappear into the trees—as if into a different dimension. Jena feels it's almost magical, with something unimaginable on the other side of the trees.

Pulue looks at Jena's expression and laughs.

"It looks like an illusion, doesn't it," he says. "Well, it is."

Jena's eyes show her confusion. "How is this possible?" Jena asks.

Pulue grins, thrilled at Jena's response—his dead brother clearly forgotten. "Come, it's our turn." He reaches for Jena's hand.

Jena hesitates.

"Don't be afraid," he says gently. "The world you've been waiting for lies behind those trees."

"But what is it? What kind of power makes something like this, something so strange?" Jena asks.

"This is not magic, Jena." He stops, then: "We are the top espionage team in the world. We have technology that can do almost anything. This is just a small deception that keeps people from discovering where we are. Do not fear what's behind these trees. You belong here."

The two-walk side by side toward the trees.

Jena closes her eyes and braces herself for whatever lies behind the trees, the illusion of a forest. She opens her eyes as she and Pulue disappear through the trees.

Pulue watches her expression. Jena stands with her mouth slightly open. She closes her eyes again thinking this can't be true.

Pulue stops, stares at Jena. He says, "Open your eyes, Jena."

Jena slowly opens her eyes. Her face freezes at what she sees.

"Welcome," Pulue says.

Jena stands in amazement.

The outside of the compound appears like a huge warehouse. Jena seemed impressed by the size of her enormous, new home, a capsulated place of the unknown,

As they walk into the large home, it looks like a castle. The marble floor sparkles almost like it has diamonds. The huge chandeliers shine above her, dripping with what appear to be rubies and sapphires. The room is full of expensive furniture. Leather couches. Brocade chairs. Artwork. Paintings everywhere.

Puluc walks around to face Jena and breaks the spell. "Jena," he says, smiling. "I can see this is all a shock. But think of this house, this room, as one of many illusions. We have many tricks." He takes her shoulders, which alarms Jena slightly. "Let's say someone lands on that strip we just came from, makes it through those trees, into this house and then to this room. All of this beauty that is so inviting—it is also deadly."

He startles Jena when he yells, "Mona!"

Instead of seeing a person, as she expected, Jena watches as the paintings on the wall slide open, and in their place, firearms with lasers point at her.

Jena steps back, involuntarily.

"Don't move," he says, reaching for her. "You may get shot."

He yells again. "Lisa!"

The paintings move again, this time, to conceal a deadly arsenal.

"Now, you try," Pulue tells Jena.

"What?" she asks.

"You call the weapons," Pulue says.

Jena looks around the room. "Mona," she says.

Nothing happens.

He stares at her.

"Mona," Jena says, louder.

Again, nothing moves.

"You see, Jena, only certain people within our team can control our weaponry. We can't allow everyone to have access to everything. We'd be setting ourselves up for failure." He looks into her eyes, trying to decide whether she understands. "The codes are programmed to our voices. Maybe you noticed that the weapons pointed only at you? The system recognizes the fabric of my clothing, and the clothing of the others, to protect us from our own weapons. The system recognizes the actual fibers."

He taps the floor with the tip of his shoe.

The parts of the floor that sparkle like diamonds become red lasers.

"My shoes are made of special materials that identify me. When I tap the floor, I am signaling that I need help."

She realizes that the room she thought was so beautiful is a room filled with killing machines.

"Now! The truth!" Pulue says, loud enough to scare Jena.

"Truth," he says again.

The room grows dark for a moment, and when the lights come on, the paintings, the marble floor, the furniture are gone.

Jena sees only doors.

Through one of the doors, Elma walks toward them, dressed in a leather dress that clings to every curve of her body. She wears black heels and carries a briefcase in one hand and a purse in the other. Her hair is down, black, wavy, and long enough to reach her shoulders.

He claps with excitement when he sees Elma. "Bravo," he exclaims, then walks to her and kisses her cheek. "You look fabulous, my dear."

Elma smiles and nods but says nothing. She turns to Jena. "You see. Just like that, things change."

Jena stares at the beautiful woman. "Where are you going?" she can't help but ask.

"Oh, no," Pulue interrupts. "We never reveal our missions."

"Mission?" Jena repeats.

"Yes," he answers. "Just like you will have a mission one day."

His two associates from the plane enter the room, both dressed in dark suits with rich leather jackets, pointy-toed shoes, and sunglasses—though there is no sun. They nod at Pulue as they pass him and take their places next to Elma.

Elma's expression says she is ready for whatever lies ahead. She looks nothing like the subservient woman from the plane.

Pulue and Jena, still overwhelmed by all she has seen, watch as Elma and the men leave.

"Now, Jena," Pulue says. "Follow me."

They walk to the door where Elma had entered, and Pulue waves Jena ahead.

Jena finds a room that is bizarre in a different way. The large space has two staircases, one on each side of her. She can't tell for certain, but it appears that a dungeon-like area may be at the bottom of the staircases.

Pulue takes a step down the right stairwell, and Jena starts to follow him.

"No," he says, stopping her. "You must walk down the left side of the stairs. No two people on our team ever walk down the stairs together. We all walk down alone. I will walk down the right. You will walk down the left," Pulue explains. "Understand?"

Jena nods.

"When you reach the bottom, stay there until someone comes to get you." He asks again, "Understand?"

Jena nods, though she understands little of what is happening to her. Still, she begins walking down the long stairway.

Pulue descends on the right, but as he does, he watches Jena to make sure she is doing as he has instructed.

Jena stands alone at the bottom of the stairs, waiting to find out what she should do next.

A man approaches Pulue and whispers in his ear. Jena can't see much about the new man in the room because the room is dimly lit. She looks at her surroundings. It seems as if the room stretches at least three-quarters of a mile. She sees people here and there. They are all standing still, all anonymous. She can't see anyone's face, can't even see whether they are men or women.

She hears footsteps approaching. She looks to the other stairwell and sees Pulue and the man who whispered in Pulue's ear. She doesn't move, and neither do they.

"Jena Parker," says a male voice.

"Yes," she replies, trying to get a glimpse of him out of the corner of her eye.

"Turn toward me," the voice says.

Jena does and sees a rather short man, shorter than she is, about five-foot-one. She's surprised to see that he is dressed in blue jeans, a T-shirt, and a cap. She can't see his eyes, between the dim lighting and the fact that he doesn't look directly at her.

"My name is Luis, and I will take you to your room." His voice is surprisingly deep, and he speaks quietly.

He walks ahead, and Jena follows.

Pulue, the man who spoke to Pulue, and the shadowed figures in the rest of the room are quiet and still.

Luis slows his gait to allow Jena to walk beside him. He tells her she will stay in this room while she receives training. Side by side, they enter yet another secret location.

He opens the door, and they walk into a well-lighted and very wide hallway that looks like the first room she had entered. Paintings decorate the walls, expensive furniture lines up under the paintings, and marble floors are beneath their feet.

She feels like they are robots walking down the hall.

Luis doesn't say a word.

"Where are we?" she asks, finally.

Luis looks straight ahead and doesn't reply.

"Turn right," he finally instructs.

Jena isn't ready to give in to the silence. "I asked you a question," she says. "Where are we?" She raises her voice a little. "What are we doing here?"

Luis seems to pay no attention.

They walk into another wide hallway that has many doors with numbers on them, like an apartment or hotel hallway.

Luis stops at number 201.

He turns to Jena. "This is your place of peace," he says, pulling a key from his pocket. He hands the key to her. "This is yours."

Jena takes the key, slides it into the lock, and opens the door halfway.

She peeks around the door with curiosity and apprehension. She can make out a kitchen with stainless steel appliances.

Luis smiles a bit as he watches her. "It's okay, Jena, This is your place."

For the umpteenth time this day, Jena is speechless at the palatial surroundings. She feels like an actual princess.

She spins around to face Luis. "What is this?" she asks. "Why is this so lavish?"

Luis tries to back away without answering, but Jena grabs his shirt, pulls him into the room, and quickly closes the door.

She pushes him up against the pretty blue wall. "Tell me where I am, and why the hell I'm here."

Luis is unfazed. He stares passively at Jena. "Let go of me. I don't want to hurt you."

"Hurt me?" she spits, pushing him harder. "Just how are you going to do that?"

"Jena," he replies calmly. "I have skills you have not learned yet. And, besides, I would get in trouble if I hurt you. So, please, again, let go of me, and I will tell you what you want to know."

Jena lets go of her grip on Luis' shirt. "Who are you?" she asks.

Luis takes off his hat, and Jena is shocked when his blond hair falls loose to his shoulders.

Luis is not a man at all.

"You're a girl?" Jena asks in amazement. "But ... you looked and sounded just like a guy."

"My real name is Luis. I was born a girl, but I live my life as a boy."

"Where did you come from?" Jena asks.

Luis shrugs and tells his story.

"My name is Luis Fargo, and I was born in San Diego. Two years ago, two friends and I passed through a town called Maplesville during a road trip to Florida." He explains the girls stopped for gas and a man walked up to them and asked for help. The man said his car wouldn't start. "We were young, and he seemed harmless. My friend, Darlene, was actually a mechanic, so we all—me, Darlene, and Sharon—we said we would go with him and see if we could help."

He says they walked around the corner with the man, and his hood was up, so everything seemed legitimate. "But then this guy just stood there looking at us, with this weird expression."

He explains that the man, in his mid-fifties, tried to make conversation with the girls, asked where they were from, where they were going. "Sharon just started telling him everything. I looked at him and knew that she ought to shut up. Darlene was still looking at his car but couldn't find anything wrong. The next thing you know, a cop car pulls up. The cop talks to that man, and all of a sudden the cop comes over to us and tells us we're under arrest for solicitation ... prostitution ... and trying to steal a car."

He says the girls were terrified, and all three talked frantically at the same time, trying to explain that they weren't doing anything besides passing through town.

Jena is beside herself. "Who was it? Did one of those guys give you a name?"

"Miles," Luis says.

Jena's face turns red. "Did you say Miles?"

"Yes," Luis says with certainty. "I remember like it was yesterday. One of the names was Miles."

"So, how did you end up here? And what happened to your friends?"

Luis tells Jena that all three were taken to jail, tried in court, and sentenced to five years in prison.

"It was ridiculous," Luis explains. "None of our families knew where we were. We weren't allowed to make phone calls. This one cop, Reyes, was so horrible. He was around the prison all the time. We never knew what he was doing there."

Jena's emotions are so heady that she feels nauseated. She sits down on one of the fancy chairs.

"All I know is that one night, I woke up in this van with a pillowcase over my head. They must have drugged me. I didn't know where I was or where I was being taken. But I could hear other people, other women in the van."

"Where did they take you?" Jena asks with increasing urgency.

"We were taken to a horrible place that Pulue will tell you more about. When we got there, the guys in charge put us through tests," Luis says. "Some of us became pawns in their war games, like animals to be hunted. Others … others were made to be …"

"To be what?" Jena asks.

"You'll find out, Jena."

Jena has no intention of making this any easier for Luis. "I'm going to find out because you're going to tell me."

"To be killers, Jena," Luis says. "To be killers on this team, to help them fight their missions. You'll live lavishly, Jena. They'll give you anything you want. You'll live an independent life. You'll have money and a lifestyle you never dreamed about. But, in return, you will kill for them. You will kill anyone they tell you to kill."

Jena looks around her apartment. It is certainly lavish. She turns to Luis again. "What happened to your friends, Sharon and Darlene?"

The tough young fighter struggles to hold back tears. "They were taken at the same time they took me. We went through the tests. Sharon and Darlene both failed. Sharon managed to redeem herself."

Luis swallows hard, and a tear falls from one eye.

"I never saw Darlene again. I assume she is dead."

Luis puts his head down. "There was a time when Moschi and Pulue were a part of a different team. A more ruthless team. When Moschi made the decision to leave, he recruited Pulue and many others like myself. Somehow Moschi found a way to rescue me and a few others, and we helped build this place." Luis says. "To test our loyalty, we are given a test, but it is different than the test given at the other place. I can't describe how awful it was. I still think about Sharon and wonder what happened to Darlene. Yet, I'm grateful that Moschi rescued me and some of the others. We were brought here. The ground here was mainly an empty area with few tents. I was given a new assignment to be a part of Moschi's team. Our assignments are to take down the other team. And me and the others help build this place."

Jena is still fixated on the test Luis describe as awful. "What was the test?" she asks.

Luis stands tall. "I can't tell you about either of them. It is a code within our team not to reveal the test to new recruits. You must face the test alone, without knowing what's to come. Just know that the team you were chosen for is the better of the two. Moschi wants freedom for all of us. However, in order to do this, we must take down a greater evil. Moschi offered all of us freedom. But knowing what I know, I choose to be a part of his team."

Luis stares into Jena's eyes. "I'm sure you were given a choice as well," he continues. "All of us here have chosen to stay to fight against a horrible force. The test is more than the test of the physical body. It is the will of the spirit." Luis stops, then says: "I will tell you this much. You will die."

"What?" Jena asks with dismay.

Luis stares Jena in the eye. "You will die. You must die in order to survive."

Jena is silent, finally.

"I must go. I'm sure I'm being watched, what with you being a new recruit."

Both are silent, taking in all that has been said between them.

"The word is that you were handpicked by Moschi," Luis says. "Moschi only picks the best fighters."

Luis turns to leave.

"Wait," Jena says. "Won't you be in trouble for everything you told me?"

"No," Luis replies. "I have a device that scrambles our conversation. I've been here long enough to learn how to play their game. You will learn, too."

Jena watches Luis walk down the hall.

Now Luis is gone.

Jena closes the door and begins looking around the apartment in earnest. The lamps and tables and décor are luxurious. The mantle is decorated with small novelty items, knickknacks. Jena picks up a small ceramic dog with a bone in its mouth. The homey touch makes Jena think about her house where she grew up. She remembers the antique quilt her grandmother had given to her mother.

The memories don't stop there.

She thinks of the awful night she killed her mother, the day she read her mother's sad and shocking letter, and she learned that Miles McNeil was her biological father. She remembers being sentenced to prison.

And, finally, as always … Jake … the beautiful smile, the beautiful face, the beautiful man she misses so much.

She knows she must get home to Jake, but she doesn't know when, and she doesn't know how.

She thinks back to Luis' words: She would die trying.

CHAPTER SEVEN

Chance wakes, opens her eyes halfway, then closes them again, remembering everything that had happened the day before? Reyes' threats. Candy's baby. Candy's story. She opens her eyes again. The room is still dim. She props herself up with one arm and looks toward Nurse May's office, then she looks at Candy, who is still asleep, and squints at the clock on the wall. Six o'clock in the morning.

"Candy," she calls softly to her new friend. "Candy," she says again, a bit louder. But Candy just rolls over in the other direction. "Candy."

Candy finally turns over. "What?" she snaps back.

"Look over there," Chance says. "Nurse May's office light is still on, and I'm pretty sure her purse is still there. And I don't see her anywhere."

"So?" Candy says, hoping to go back to sleep.

"So?" Chance says, frustrated. "So … she's never here this late—I mean, this early. Anyway, she's never here now. She comes in at eight o'clock. She has a dog, so she goes home every night."

Candy sits up in bed and wiggles around to get a good look at the nurse's office. "She probably just changed her schedule."

"No," Chance says adamantly. "Something is up. Her purse is right where she left it, and besides, she always wakes me up for my last dose of medicine before she leaves. She didn't wake me up last night." She shakes her head. "Like I said, something is wrong. I can feel it."

Chance pulls back the blankets, swings her legs around, and grabs her IV pole so she can go get a good look at Nurse May's office. She makes it exactly one step before the door to the medical ward opens and she sees Chief Reyes staring at her.

"Where do you think you're going, Chance?" Reyes asks.

Her eyes dart around the room as she tries to come up with a good excuse.

Candy slides back into the bed and pulls the sheets over her head.

"Well, umm," Chance stutters, "umm … I had to use the bathroom, and since the nurse's light is on, I thought I'd ask her for some help."

Reyes practically snarls at Chance. "Let me get this straight. You needed help getting to the bathroom, but somehow you managed to get out of bed." He continues taunting her, patting his gun in its holster. "I think maybe you're trying to escape."

"No. No. I wasn't," Chance pleads. "Here's the truth. Really. I was just checking to make sure that Nurse May is okay. She's never here this early. … And. And. … Isn't that her purse on her desk?"

Reyes flushes red as he realizes he has left evidence no one will be able to explain. The officer looks at Chance. "She's in the bathroom. I just saw her going that way. Now get back in bed, close your eyes, and go back to sleep. And mind your own business!"

Chance obeys.

Reyes walks into the nurse's office, turns off her light, and grabs the purse. He glances back at Chance again, then at Candy, who's under her blankets.

"I'll make sure Nurse May gets her purse back," he says. "You two ladies have other things to worry about. So, keep your mouths shut, and like I said, mind your own damned business."

Chance is worried. When she is certain that Reyes is gone, she calls out to Candy. "Why would Reyes take the nurse's purse with him? He doesn't really know her. I don't think she even likes him. I mean, who does, when it comes right down to it?"

Candy mumbles in agreement.

"I need to find out what's going on," Chance says.

"We're prisoners, Chance," Candy says, stating the obvious. "How are we going to figure out anything, and if we did, what could we possibly do about it?"

Chance looks at Candy, then around the room. "I don't know yet."

"What you're going to do is get yourself killed by that maniac, who is also the father of my child," Candy says, too loudly.

She starts shaking when she remembers that her secret is out. After the talk with Chance the night before and the confrontation with Reyes, she could be in real trouble.

Candy tears up. "Chance, I'm already in so much trouble, I can't … I just can't … help you do whatever you're thinking about doing."

Candy pulls herself together for a moment. "But I'll kill that man if he tries to take my baby away from me."

Chance turns cynical again. "Really? And just how are you going to do that? We're in prison. Isn't that what you said?"

Chance is angry.

Candy is sad and starts to cry again.

Chance melts a little. She can't help feeling sympathy for Candy. She knows what it's like to be hurt. She thinks back to the night she was at Ken's party, the night she figured out that Carol—her best friend—had been screwing around with Ken Stewart. Chance remembers how devastated she'd been. In fact, she was so hurt she became enraged enough to kill Carol, the girl who'd been her friend for many years. She listens and remembers as Candy sobs in pain, humiliation and, most of all, terror from the tyrant who thinks he's king of the world—at least, this world. She vows to herself to defeat Reyes in whatever game he's playing. But she'll need Candy's help. If they defeat Reyes, Candy will be safe.

When Chance thinks about revenge, she involuntarily speaks Jena Parker's name out loud. Jena needs to die, too. But revenge on Jena will have to wait.

Right now, Candy needs Chance—one woman to another, one victim to another.

Chance struggles to get out of bed again and walks to Candy's bed, where Candy is sobbing uncontrollably. She sits near the vulnerable girl, and then reaches for her.

Blinded by tears, Candy dives into Chance's arms.

"It's okay," Chance croons, as if comforting a child. She strokes Candy's hair. "I know how you feel. I know what it feels like to be betrayed and broken inside."

Chance thinks back to the night she overheard Ken hitting on Jena at his high school house party. She can feel the rage in her throat as she also remembers Carol admitting to her love affair with Ken. The thought of the two incites her anger.

She pushes Candy away abruptly, leaving the girl bewildered. Chance can't control herself. The rage keeps rearing its head. It has taken away all the good in her.

She jumps up from the bed, looks at the ceiling, and gets even angrier when she thinks about the night of the masquerade party when she dressed as Jena so she could kill Carol, making the police believe that Jena did it.

A grin makes its way across Chance's face. She looks at Candy's puffy face and then glares at Candy's stomach, where the helpless child is growing.

All empathy drains from Chance's body and soul. But she is still determined.

"Your baby doesn't deserve to be born in this hellhole, and no matter what our sins are, we don't belong here, either." She paces as she speaks—mostly to herself but also to Candy. "No, we don't belong here at all."

Candy thinks Chance is beginning to sound a bit unhinged.

Chance keeps up her tirade. "That demon Chief Reyes belongs here. So, does that worthless Ken Stewart, along with that murderous mother-killing Jena Parker. They all deserve each other. They all deserve to live in this shithole. Forever."

Chance turns to Candy. Chance's eyes are blazing with tears and hate.

"I'm going to get us out of here," she yells, not caring who might hear. "I'm going to get us out of here no matter who I have to kill."

Candy wipes her tears away as Chance gets more and more wound up.

Even Chance doesn't realize how loud she's yelling. "I'm going to get you, Reyes. I'm gonna get them all. Reyes. Jena. Jake. Ken. And the warden!"

The door to the medical ward swings open.

Chance jumps and nearly chokes on her words when she sees Mike standing at the door.

"I bet you're wondering whether I overheard your plan," Mike says slyly.

Chance's eyes are wide open, but she keeps her lips sealed.

Mike moves closer to Chance. "I'm here to tell you that you can make all the plans you want, but you're an inmate, and the only place you're going is back to your cell." He relaxes a bit and clears his throat. "Now, some of the people on that list might deserve exactly what you're suggesting. But not Jena Parker. She's okay." He looks around the ward. "Where's Nurse May? She should be here by now."

Chance doesn't move. Candy keeps her mouth shut.

Mike walks around the room as if he expects to find the nurse hiding behind a curtain. He makes his way to the office.

The lights are off, and there's no sign of the nurse, but the computer is still on, and it's hot enough that he knows it has been on all night.

Chance and Candy exchange nervous but knowing looks.

He demands, "Where is she?"

"We don't know," says Chance.

Mike knows she's lying. "When did the nurse leave? And why has her computer been on all night? You two need to spill your guts or else I'm going to go tell the warden that the nurse is missing and that you both have something to do with it."

Chance and Candy exchange another furtive glance.

"When we woke up this morning, she wasn't here," Chance says, truthfully.

"Her light was on, and her purse was still on her desk. I was worried about her," she says.

Mike looks over his shoulder at the office. "Well, I was just back there, and the light was off, and her purse was gone. So, what, you two went back there and lifted her purse? That's pretty low." He glares at Chance and Candy, who are now sitting next to each other on Candy's bed.

Chance mumbles Reyes' name.

"Say what? What did you say about Reyes?" Mike demands. "Speak up, Chance. You didn't have any trouble yelling for all the world to hear when I walked in a few minutes ago."

"Okay. Okay, already," Chance yells at the guard. "Chief Reyes was in here really early this morning, and he was bullying us and carrying on the way he always does. He caught me out of bed and wanted to know what I was doing." She takes a deep breath. "I told him I was going back to the office to figure out what was up with Nurse May. Her light was on, and her purse was on her desk. ... When I said that, Reyes went back there and turned off the light and took her purse. He said Nurse May was in the bathroom and that he'd make sure she got the purse." She takes another deep breath. "And that's the truth."

Mike is skeptical. "He took the purse?"

"Hey, you asked for the truth, and that's the truth," Chance insists.

Mike stares at Candy. "When are you due?"

Candy starts to cry again, as if on cue. "I'm not sure of my due date," she sniffs.

"And that sleazebag, Reyes, is the father," Candy tells him.

Chance is more surprised than Mike. She's surprised that Candy would tell Mike her secret.

Mike is confused but just shakes his head and sighs. He's not sure that he can be shocked by anything that goes on in this dirty, violent, corrupt prison.

Chance notices the change in Mike's expression and thinks he might be vulnerable.

"Mike," she says. "Chief Reyes is the most horrible person in here."

Chance pretends to cry. "He tries to touch us," she says as she manages to shed a tear. "He threatened to take Candy's baby and then kill us. That's why you heard what you heard when you walked in here. We're afraid he's going to hurt us." Chance dissolves into a pool of fake tears.

She slowly gets up from Candy's bed and stands close to Mike. "She's about to have a baby," she cries, pointing at Candy. "In prison for God's sake. … That cop deserves to be in prison way more than any of us."

Mike shuffles, clearly uncomfortable.

"Please, Mike, please," she begs. "I know you think we all deserve to be here, but not all of us are guilty. Some of us were framed by Reyes and that sneaky warden." She knows she may not be a convincing liar, but she can cry on cue—now she's crying on the outside and grinning on the inside. "Please help that unborn child," she says dramatically. "We can't let Chief Reyes take her baby."

Mike feels guilty and sad as he looks at Candy and her little baby bump. This horror is what Jena was trying to tell him about. But he's not about to give in to Chance, either.

"Get back in bed, inmate," he orders. He just stares at Chance as she does as she's told. "I don't know just yet what I'm going to do, but I assure you I'm going to do something. First, Nurse May could be missing, and I have to find out where she is." He starts to leave but turns around. "I never thought I'd say this to an inmate."

He looks at Candy with sympathy.

Chance smiles inside.

"I'm going to help. My mother was a single mom, so I understand what you're going through, Candy," Mike says. "I'm going to take this place down. This prison has no honor, and the man who runs it has no honor."

Mike leaves, and as soon as he does, Chance slides down in her bed barely able to contain her excitement.

Candy feels hope for her baby for the first time since she found out she was pregnant. Maybe, she thinks to herself, she can still have a normal life and rear her baby the right way. She stares at Chance, who looks like she just won tickets to Disneyland.

"Are you alright?" Candy asks.

Chance ignores Candy and smiles into thin air. "I'm fine, Candy. I'm just fine," she gloats, continuing to smile even as she dozes off.

Mike heads down the hallway wondering what to do next. Should he help Candy and Chance escape, or should he confront Reyes and expose his secret to Warden Peters? Reyes is no man of the law. He's a coward and a cheat. Mike walks faster as thoughts race through his mind. He thinks of resigning, even fantasizes about killing Reyes.

He quickly comes within a few doors of the warden's office. He steps forward, his fist balled up, his face red, his eyes on fire. He stops at the office—and just like the last time—he hears voices inside the office.

He listens.

He can hear the warden, who sounds angry.

"How clumsy can you be?" Warden Peters yells. "Who knows you took that purse from the nurse's office?"

Reyes stares at the warden and refuses to answer.

The warden stands suddenly. "Tell me what's going on. Tell me who knows what," Peters demands. "Tell me!"

Reyes draws his gun, as he usually does when he feels cornered, and moves closer to the warden.

Peters shows no fear or shock. In fact, he reaches into his top desk drawer and pulls out his gun. "I'm tired of your shit," he says.

Reyes points his gun at the warden's forehead.

Mike listens quietly outside the door.

"I asked you to tell me who saw you take the nurse's purse," the warden says.

Reyes cocks his gun.

The two men just stare at one another, not moving, not speaking.

Reyes almost dares the warden to shoot him.

Peters' blinks first and lays his gun down on the desk. "Do you think this is a sick game? You stand there holding your gun like you're some kind of cowboy. Don't you know that we're dealing with the most ruthless people on this planet? Romli and his people will destroy anyone—women, children, family, friends. He won't think twice about getting rid of you and me. We're nothing to him. Just a couple of small-town gamblers selling their souls for cash. He'll keep the cash and eat our souls." Peters is practically roaring with rage. "You won't survive, and neither will I—after he's done with our families and friends."

Reyes can't manage to sneak in a word.

"Now, put that gun down," the warden says quietly. "And tell me which women saw you take that purse."

Reyes slowly lowers his gun and places it back in his holster. "Don't worry about the women who saw me."

"Why?" Peters asks.

Reyes chuckles and says casually, "Because they're two dead women. I'll take care of it personally. It will be a pleasure." He pauses as he remembers that Candy is pregnant with his child.

Peters sits down and relaxes again. "What's the plan?" he asks.

Reyes chooses his words carefully. He can't reveal that Candy is having his baby, but he must convince the warden that he'll do what needs to be done. "I'll figure out a way to rid of them both."

Peters' presses for details. "Tell me how you're going to do it."

Reyes crosses his arms. "I'll get a few of the men. We'll wait until dark, then we'll get the two women from the medical ward. We'll take 'em someplace quiet, then silence them."

Peters' nods, approving Reyes' plan. "Just do it and get rid of that damned purse. We don't need any loose ends." The warden wants to make sure Reyes is taking him seriously. "Any loose ends can be deadly for you and for me."

Reyes rebels, as always. "I think I've been doing this long enough to know how to handle two nosey chicks." He starts to walk away when he remembers one more surprise for the warden, then he says nonchalantly, "By the way, I shot Tim and shipped him off with the women."

Peters is truly shocked. "What the hell! Why would you shoot Tim?"

Reyes shrugs. "He was in love with that nurse, and he was giving me a hard time. I knew he would betray us sooner or later. So, I got rid of him."

Reyes fiddles with his fingernails. "Now he's with her."

Peters is so angry he can barely speak. "He was the head guard here. He was in this with us since the beginning. Do you know what they're going to do with Tim?"

Reyes bangs his fist on the warden's desk. "You just told me that we can't afford any loose ends! Didn't you say that?"

"They're going to kill him," Peters yells.

"Tim was a loose end, and I don't really care what happens to him. He can't interfere with our plans anymore." Reyes spins around to leave, but now it's his turn for a surprise.

On the other side of the door stands Mike, his fists clenched, his eyes twitching, his face full of anger. He's blocking Reyes' way out.

"What the hell do you want, Mike?" Reyes asks.

Mike doesn't move an inch and points an angry finger at Reyes and then at the warden. "I want to talk to you and Peters right now! Or would you rather that I call the real cops?"

Reyes reaches for his gun, but Mike gets to his own gun—hidden in the small of his back.

"Back up!" he yells.

Reyes just stands in the doorway.

"I said back the hell up!"

Peters stands up, stunned—even in this day of surprises—and lifts his gun. "Reyes, stand aside. Let him in."

Reyes backs up but keeps his eyes on Mike's gun. "Man, you're fooling with wrong people." Reyes turns and looks at Peters as if this is his fault.

Mike slams the door closed. The three of them are alone together.

"Look at you two," Mike scolds. "Supposedly, men of the law. You two sleazebags, treating the women in this prison like they are less than nothing."

"Now, Mike," the warden begins.

But Mike's having none of it. "Shut up! Just shut up, warden. You don't even deserve to hold that title." He waves his gun at Reyes and the warden. "Forget that. I want to know what has happened to Nurse May. And, from what I heard just now, where is Tim? Even better, where are all of the women who have disappeared from his place?" He looks down at the floor and spies the nurse's purse. "What is that? That's Nurse May's purse, isn't it?"

Peters and Reyes look at each other. Neither has a plan for getting out of this unexpected mess.

"I'm asking again, why is her purse here?" Mike reaches down to pick it up, and the keys fall out. "And her keys are still here."

Reyes doesn't say a word. He stares at Mike, watching for a chance to take Mike's gun and shoot him.

"We don't owe you shit, Mike," Reyes says. "We aren't telling you a damned thing, so if you're going to shoot us, just go ahead and do it."

Peters has his gun trained on Mike, as Reyes continues to taunt him.

"Because if you don't kill us, we're sure as shit going to shoot you," Reyes says.

Peters and Mike keep their eyes and their guns aimed at each other, but Mike has managed to maneuver Reyes over to Peters' side of the room.

Mike says nothing and refuses to react to Reyes' threats. Still holding his gun with one hand, he backs toward the door, Nurse May's purse clenched in the other hand.

"You two, and anybody else involved in whatever this is, are not going to get away with it. I'm not going to let you," Mike says, finally out the door.

He slams the door shut and takes off running down the hall.

Reyes takes off after Mike.

Meanwhile, Peters grabs the phone and alerts the other guards that Mike is armed and dangerous. "He's gone off his rocker, all of the sudden. You guys need to get him before he gets away or hurts someone."

Mike runs as fast as he can toward the medical ward.

Reyes fires and the shot catches Mike's arm.

Mike doesn't slow down and tries to fire back at Reyes. He thinks he may have hit Reyes in the shoulder but doesn't waste time turning around to find out.

Mike's bullet has done some harm, and Reyes is forced to stop running.

Clenching the purse and his gun and bleeding, breathing hard, and running like a mad man, Mike flings open the door to the medical ward.

"Let's go!" Mike yells at Candy and Chance through panicked breaths. "Come on, ladies, let's go. Now!"

Candy and Chance are stunned. Mike looks like a lunatic or a prisoner trying to escape from prison—which, in a way, he is.

It takes Chance a minute to process Mike's sweating face, the blood gushing from his shoulder.

Chance knows an opportunity when she sees one. She yanks the IV out of her arm and yells at Candy to get up.

Chance grabs Candy's arm and half-drags her out of bed.

They jump into their shoes and take off running after Mike.

They follow Mike down the hall and into a storage room.

"Mike, what the hell," Chance yells. "We can't hide in a storage room."

"Shut up," Mike hisses. "This isn't just a storage room. This is a back way out."

The women's hearts are racing.

Mike's heart is about to explode out of his chest. "This is an emergency exit for the guards in case of a prison riot," he says with labored breath. "Just follow me!"

They follow Mike to a prison sub-basement.

Meanwhile, the rest of the prison is pandemonium.

Reyes is reeling from his wound.

Peters is running down the hall with his gun, He finds Reyes struggling.

Five other guards show up, but no one is quite sure what to do next.

"Where is he?" Peters demands.

"I don't know," Reyes spits, jerking away from one of the guards trying to help him. "I'm pretty sure he got to the medical ward and took those two chicks with him."

"What the hell?" Peters asks, yelling in unison with the other guards.

"Sound the alarms," Peters says. "Somebody call the police and tell them we have a prison break over here."

The guards scatter.

Reyes grabs a towel from one of the guards and tries to stanch the bleeding.

"We should have killed that bastard when we had the chance," Reyes says.

Peters helps Reyes up. They run as quickly as they can to the medical ward.

Any guards near them dash off in the same direction.

Reyes hits the door hard and finds exactly what he expected.

The room is empty.

Peters turns around and around, to prove to himself that it's true.

Reyes and Peters don't exchange a word.

Peters is crazy with the thought of what will happen to him if Mike blows their operation wide open. Romli will make sure that none of them are left standing.

"Find them," Peters yells at the guards. "Check the emergency exit in the storage room. That's where he'd go."

Half of the guards go to the storage room, the other half goes to the other end of the passage to try to block Mike, Chance, and Candy from escaping.

The three escapees are still running.

Candy gets tired. "I can't. I can't go any farther," she says as she grabs her stomach.

Mike and Chance stop to help her.

"Candy, we've got to get out of here," Mike pleads. "You and your baby will not survive in this prison. Reyes is going to kill you! And, Chance, he's going to kill you, too."

Chance stares at Mike.

"I overheard Reyes and the warden. So, going back is not an option for you anymore. Candy, you've got to get up and fight for your baby." He grabs Candy's arm.

Chance and Candy both nod that they understand.

"Fight," he yells again.

"They'll be waiting for us on the other end," Chance says. "By now they'll have us surrounded."

He shakes his head as he keeps urging Candy on. "No, there's another way. Me and one other person are the only ones who know about it."

Chance asks who the other person is.

"Tim."

Candy and Chance look at Mike like he is insane.

"Tim's gone. He's as good as dead. No time to explain the rest," he says.

All three are breathing hard, but Mike continues to lead Candy and Chance through the secret passage. They come to the end, and he peeks out a door to see if the path to their freedom is clear.

"Come on, I don't see anyone," he says.

He walks out first, then helps Candy and Chance to step up and out of their getaway tunnel.

They find themselves in a wooded area, with just a little light filtering through the trees.

"Oh, my God, thank goodness. Thank you, Mike," Candy says, as she begins to cry.

He urges them forward. All three drop to the ground when they hear a gunshot. The sound seems to come from behind them, and Mike aims his gun, but he has nothing to aim at.

He doesn't see a thing, but then he hears a voice.

Reyes.

"Nowhere to run now, Mike," Reyes says.

Mike swivels around and yells at Chance and Candy to run. "Now! Get the hell out of here."

They run, but can't see where they were going, and run right into Reyes.

Reyes grabs Candy's arm. "Where do you think you're going with my baby!"

Mike jumps on top of Reyes, who is holding onto Candy.

Chance tries to pull Candy's arm away from Reyes. She manages to get the frantic girl away from Reyes.

Mike punches Reyes.

Candy is so dazed she just stands still.

"Candy, run!" Chance yells.

Mike manages to knock Reyes' gun away and points his own gun at Reyes' temple.

Candy disappears into the forest.

"Put it down, Mike."

Another voice.

Mike turns and sees the warden pointing his gun at Chance.

Mike and Chance stand perfectly still.

Reyes and Peters are breathing hard, sweat dripping down their faces.

Mike figures he and Chance look even worse. Chance's hospital gown is ripped, and her feet are filthy.

"It's over, Mike," Warden Peters says, pointing his gun now at Mike. His hands are sweaty, and the one holding his weapon starts to shake.

Reyes is furious and impatient. "Shoot him!"

In the dim light, Peters' breaths are even more labored. "We don't have to kill them. We can take them back to the prison and hold them there."

"Are you crazy?" Reyes yells. "Just kill them."

Reyes roots around on the ground for his gun, and when he finds it, he immediately fires a round into Mike's upper shoulder.

Mike runs but Reyes shoots his leg. Mike hops, then staggers to the ground. Feeling his evil power, Reyes laughs. Peters stands, looking like a wild man watching Reyes and Mike.

Chance sees the chaos and figures that she doesn't have much chance of getting out of this alive. She takes off running.

Peters chases her, shouting, "You stop running, girl, or I'm going to shoot you."

Chance keeps running. She loses a shoe, so she kicks off the other and runs barefoot through the weeds, brambles, and rocks. Her prison medical gown flaps in the wind as she runs and runs.

Peters fires a shot, and Chance finally stops, too frightened to turn around and look at the warden.

"Please," she pleads, coughing, and struggling to catch a breath. "Please don't kill me."

She hears the leaves crackle under the warden's feet as he gets closer to her.

"Please," she begs again. "Please don't kill me. I'll do anything you want."

"Turn around," the warden orders.

Chance is bent over, still breathing hard and trying hard not to cry.

"Turn around," the warden demands.

Chance just can't make her body move.

"I'm not going to say it again," Peters says.

Chance slowly turns. Her leg buckles as she tries to move, and her body shakes from exhaustion and fear. She has no more fight. She looks into Peters' cruel eyes.

"So, you say you'll do anything," the warden says without a trace of pity or even humanity. "That's good."

CHAPTER EIGHT

A faint ray of light shows the terror on Chance's face as she nods her consent to Warden Peters.

Peters takes a step toward Chance, and she involuntarily takes a step back.

"I want to hear you say it," Peters says. "Say it out loud."

Chance sniffles. "I'll do anything," she whispers.

"Say it louder!" Peters' yells.

"I'll do anything you want. Okay? Anything you want!" Chance says louder, weeping.

"Let me tell you what you're going to do. You're going back to the prison, back to the medical ward," Peters says.

"You're going to do a really, really good job of pretending that nothing happened," Peters says, as Chance struggles to breathe. "You'll stay there until we move you to a cell. Talk to no one. Say nothing. And if the cops or anyone else comes snooping around about Nurse May or that Candy girl, you will keep your mouth shut."

Peters gets so close to Chance that he can whisper in her ear. "You just remember. You are a convict. No one is going to believe you over me."

The warden shoves Chance so that she's in front of him. "Now don't you worry. You won't be at the prison very long. The time will come that I will use you in a different way. But as long as you're in my prison, you will do what I say. You got that?"

Chance sniffles. "Yes," she says, quietly.

"You'd better," he warns. "Because if you cross me, you'll die in that medical ward, and not a soul will miss you. Now, start walking."

Trapped and alone, Chance slowly walks back to the prison. Peters is behind her, watching every step.

"Stop!" Peters' yells to Chance. "Turn around and start walking back. I want to make sure Reyes finishes the job."

Suddenly, they hear Reyes shouting. Reyes is a dark shadow, leaning down as Mike lays on the ground bleeding.

"Look at you!" Reyes yells. "Look at you helpless on the ground. You think you can shoot me and get away with it? You think you can run away from me? Who's the smart guy now?"

Mike breathlessly speaks. "Just shut up and do it."

Reyes repeatedly kicks Mike in the stomach. Chance and the warden keep their distance.

"Speed it up!" Peters' yells at Chance. "You've wasted enough of my time." Peters' shoves Chance as they get closer to Reyes and Mike. Peters' patience with Reyes has run out. "Oh, get it over already," he says.

Reyes turns to Peters. "I got this." He says while turning back to Mike.

Reyes points his gun down at Mike. "I've already shot you twice. Why are you still alive?" Reyes says, menacing. "But that's okay. I feel like shooting you again."

Reyes fires his gun again. He shoots Mike in the stomach.

Chance screams.

Reyes turns to Peters. "Shut her up. Why is she even still alive?"

"Now that is a brilliant question from a so-called genius," Peters taunts. "She's alive, you idiot, because she's going to be useful. Now do your job."

Peters' grabs Chance's arms and starts walking her back to the prison.

Mike is lying motionless on the ground.

"Leave him," Peters says, over his shoulder. "He'll bleed to death."

Reyes seethes. He wants to kill Mike once and for all. "What about this purse?" Reyes asks the warden.

"Leave it. Whoever finds his dead body will find the purse next to him and think he did something to Nurse May," Peters says, is thinking a few steps ahead of the enraged Reyes. "We'll just say we don't know anything. They'll find Mike dead, and they'll never find the nurse."

Chance listens to their evil plans and fears for her life.

Reyes spits on the ground next to the bleeding and unconscious Mike and then walks over to Chance and the warden. He's holding his wounded shoulder, which is still bleeding.

Chance can barely think. *This must be my punishment for killing Carol*, she thinks to herself.

"What about that girl, Candy?" the warden asks Reyes on their way to the prison.

Reyes laughs. "She won't talk."

"And how do you know that?" Peters asks.

"I know," Reyes says. "She knows I'll find her and kill her if she says a word to anyone."

As he hears the others getting farther and farther away, Mike opens his eyes, lying on the ground. He looks up at the rising moon. He can feel his life slipping away, his eyes growing heavy. He grips Nurse May's purse with his bloody hands, holding it as tight as he can. He doesn't even have the conscious thought to know why at this point. He watches as the moon rises higher in the sky and stars start to sparkle. He thinks, inexplicably, of Jena—of waiting outside the prison shower while he imagined what she looked like and what she would feel like with the warm water running over her. He remembers Jena walking out, wrapped only in a towel, her hair still dripping, her skin still damp and even more beautiful than usual. He feels the way he felt back then, and the love begins to fill his heart as his eyes begin to close, probably for the last time.

And he sinks peacefully into those feelings.

And he hears a voice, a hallucination?

"Mike." He hears a soft whisper, and he shivers. He wants to go back into the feeling of peacefulness.

"Mike," he hears again. "Mike, please don't die."

Mike struggles, almost against his own will, to open his eyes slightly.

He calls out for Jena.

"No, Mike, listen to me."

He moans and closes his eyes again.

"Mike, it's me, Candy. … Mike, where is your phone?"

His eyes don't open, but Candy frantically searches Mike's pockets for his cellphone.

"Mike don't die! I found your phone! I'm going to get us out of this."

She dials 911. "Please help," she pleads to the dispatcher. "My friend is dying, please help us!"

"Ma'am, where are you?" the dispatcher asks.

"We're in the woods near the prison," Candy whispers. "Please help."

"Ma'am just keep your phone on so we can find you," the dispatcher says.

Candy stares at the phone, making sure it stays on. She looks at Mike, who is struggling to stay alive, and she is grateful. Because of Mike, her baby won't be born in prison. She lays the cellphone on Mike's chest and then slowly walks away. She's crying so hard she can barely walk, much less see where she's going. But she can hear ambulance sirens getting close.

She turns and looks toward Mike one more time, then scurries through the woods as fast as she can.

———

Chief Clark Reyes opens the blinds in his office to a beautiful sunny day. He stares out the window and thinks about the evening before. He feels great about killing Mike. He grins at the memory but clenches his fists when he thinks about Candy getting away. He knows he will track her down sooner or later. Maybe he can hurry things along.

He picks up his phone and dials. "Yeah, it's me," he says to the person on the other end. "I've got a job for you. I need you to find someone. Fast." He listens for a moment. "Her name is Candy. Candy Pindle. She may change her name. She's a whore … and she's pregnant. Maybe four months, but she's skinny so you won't be able to tell. Brunette. Five-foot-seven."

Reyes listens, then: "Her family lives over there in Perryville, the bad side of town." He waits to make sure the other person has the information he needs. "No, I don't want her dead. Find her and bring her to me. … Yeah, that's right. … I'll owe you one."

Satisfied, he sits down, puts his feet on the desk and turns on the television with the remote. He waits for the local news to report that Mike is dead. "Mike Fredmond, a longtime guard at Luttonville County Prison, has been found dead": That's the way the news will report it.

Reyes fiddles with the bandage on his arm. The wound is still sore. His eyes are glued to the television. "Any minute now," he says aloud to no one. The office is dimly lighted, a bit of sunshine coming through the blinds and the television providing most of the light. "Yeah," Reyes muses with high expectations, "they'll announce that Michael Fredmond is dead and suspected of killing prison Nurse Tonya May."

Reyes leans back in his chair, folds his arms, and grows increasingly annoyed.

Finally, he stands up in a huff. "What the hell is going on?" He changes channels, then starts to flip through the local news programs.

His grin changes to a grim frown, until ... he stamps his foot.

"Breaking news" flashes across the bottom of the television screen. He can't contain his excitement. "Yep, this is it."

"This is KBYS in Maplesville bringing you local news, and I'm Anna Simpson standing in for Todd White."

Reyes gets impatient. "Get to it, lady."

"We have breaking news," the news anchor says. "Michael Fredmond, a local prison guard, was brought to the Maplesville Hospital late last night." The hospital has the area's largest ICU, 45 miles away. "Breaking News" flashes in a chyron along the bottom of the screen. "We just got a report that the medevac helicopter has arrived at Maplesville Hospital, and Mike Fredmond has been taken into surgery.

"What!" Reyes yells. He turns the volume as high as it goes.

"Fredmond, age thirty, was brought in with multiple gunshot wounds. He is in critical condition and unconscious. He has not been able to speak to the police or medical personnel," the newswoman reports. "We are waiting for Dr. Ralph Carter to make a public statement about Fredmond's condition."

Reyes is livid.

From the studio, anchorman Marshall Watson asks the reporter, "Anna, what are the local police telling us?"

Reyes is as confused as he is angry. "What's she talking about? I *am* the local police," he screams at the TV.

"Police are telling us that they suspect foul play," she replies. "Not only was the victim shot multiple times, but a purse was found with him. Police are still trying to determine the owner of the purse."

Watson cuts in: "I assume the police will be interviewing the warden at the prison where Mr. Fredmond works."

"That's right," Anna, says. "We have the only trauma center in the area, and Mr. Fredmond was flown here because of the serious nature of his wounds."

"Our team has done some investigative reporting at the prison, isn't that correct, Anna?" Watson asks.

"That's correct. Our sources have told us that a nurse who works at the prison is missing. Her family confirms that she has not been home," she reports.

Watson asks, "What else can you—"

"Police are also looking into the whereabouts of Jena Parker," Anna says. "No one is saying that her disappearance is connected to this shooting or the possible disappearance of the nurse. We do know, of course, that Ms. Parker was exonerated of charges that she murdered her mother." Anna signs off. "That's all for now, Marshall. We'll continue gathering as much information here as we can."

Reyes turns the television off in disgust and throws the remote across the room. He stomps to the door, flings it open, and starts yelling at the rank-and-file officers. "Who in the hell out there gave information to the TV station without talking to me first!"

None of the officers makes a peep.

"You all look like dumbasses," Reyes yells. "I want to know who has been investigating this case about the prison guard without involving me."

As if on cue, a man wearing a long trench coat over a dark blue suit walks in.

Reyes can barely compose himself in time to process the arrival of the newcomer.

"Detective Martin, what are you doing here?" he asks, looking truly puzzled.

Detective Martin approaches Reyes, and two other men dressed the same way walk in just after Martin.

"Let's step into your office, Chief Reyes," the detective says.

Reyes heads straight for his desk chair.

"Don't sit down. This won't take long," Martin orders. "Listen, Reyes, we've worked a lot of cases together—like when we teamed up to capture Jena Parker. That was challenging."

Reyes shuffles his feet nervously. "Get to the point."

"This case of Mike Fredmond, the guard who was shot … and now with this nurse possibly missing—all at the same prison where Jena Parker was held before she was released." He pauses. "The District Attorney assigned me and my team to take over this case."

Reyes grimaces but tries to cover his anger with something like a smile. "You're taking a case in my jurisdiction without even consulting me?"

Reyes is clearly upset. And Martin clearly is not interested in debating the issue.

"I'm consulting," Martin says.

Martin gives Reyes a hard look. "The bullets removed from Mike Fredmond's body during surgery are being analyzed. It looks like it might be a professional hit. Bullets may have even come from a cop's gun." He stares at Reyes. "I'll let you know if I need you." He walks out of the office.

Reyes isn't the only one watching the news broadcast.

Jake is back at Ken's apartment in time to hear Anna Simpson's report. He barges into Ken's bedroom and shakes him awake.

"Get up, man," Jake says.

"What? What do you want?" Ken asks as he wakes up slowly.

"Ken, you're not going to believe what's going on. The news says one of the guards over at the prison has been shot and is in bad shape, and a nurse who works over there is missing."

Ken sits up, wide awake now.

"And they talked about Jena," Jake says breathlessly. "They said again that she's out of prison, but they still don't know where she is."

Ken makes his way slowly out of bed, still nursing his injury.

"Well, you thought Jena tried to call you at work last night," Ken recalls.

"So now all of this bad shit is going down at the same prison," Jake says as he walks into the living room. "I've got a sick feeling that it's all connected. This guard getting shot, this nurse missing, Jena out of jail, except no one knows where she is—including me!"

Ken shakes his head. It's too much to process.

"Jake, are you trying to say that you think Jena shot this guard and maybe that nurse, too?" Ken asks.

Jake won't answer, or perhaps doesn't hear the question.

"Do you?" Ken asks again.

"No," Jake says in earnest. "I just don't know what the hell to think."

Jake plops down on the couch and covers his eyes. "I just want to see her. I want to tell her I love her. I want to kiss her. And I don't know how to make any of that happen." He sighs hopelessly. "I may never see her again."

"Hey, you can't give up." He grabs Jake's hands away from his eyes and sits on the coffee table. "We know all about not giving up, right? … I mean, Chance had me tied up in the back of her car. She terrorized me. She took me to that warehouse … and, man, she shot me! I thought it was over for me. Done!" Ken cradles his shoulder. "But here I am and despite it all, I've healed up good." He pushes Jake's legs off the couch and sits beside him. "Don't you feel that strength?" Ken says in a joking voice. "I told you before, and I'll tell you again, we're going to find her. You're going to see her again. You two love each other way too much to never see each other again."

Jake looks utterly hopeless, then gets up and starts pacing again. "There's one person who might know where I can find Jena—that asshole who put her in jail in the first place: Chief Reyes. I'm going to the police department."

Ken stands. "I'm not sure that's a good idea."

"I have to go," Jake says. "He knows something. He must know something. And I'm going to find out what, even if I have to beat it out of him."

Ken shakes his head. "Bad idea, man. You'll end up in jail, just when Jena has gotten out."

Jake gives Ken a forlorn look. "I have to do something," he says, as he grabs Ken's keys and races out the door.

Ken tries to follow but can't move as fast. He opens the door and yells at Jake to wait. "I'm going with you."

Ken is surprised when Jake turns off the car to wait for his friend to get dressed.

Jake turns on the radio and it's playing Jena's parents' favorite song. He starts to sing along: "*If I can't have you ... I don't want nobody, baby ...*" He closes his eyes, thinking of how much he misses Jena.

Ken opens the passenger-side door and startles Jake.

Jake turns down the radio.

"Where were you?" Ken asks. "I called your name, like, five times."

Jake, putting the car in Drive, doesn't respond, but his thoughts are still with Jena.

Ken sits quietly, staring out the car window. He knows Jake is worried and doesn't want to talk. He tries to change the subject, at least a little. "Listen, remember when we were ten, and we were playing in that pond after school, trying to catch frogs?" Ken smiles to himself, but Jake stares straight ahead. "You remember? You said you wanted to catch one of those frogs for Jena? You said she'd like a frog hopping around the house because it would remind her of you."

Jake finally cracks a smile.

"You chased frogs all around that pond like you were trying to catch a fish in the ocean," Ken says, trying to keep Jake engaged. "And finally, you fell face down in the mud."

Ken laughs uproariously, and finally Jake joins in.

"Damn frogs," Jake says, still laughing. "You know, Ken, I went back to that pond the next day and tried all over again, trying to catch a frog for Jena. I tried until it was dark." After a long silence, he says, "I finally caught one."

Ken is surprised. "I never knew that."

"It slipped and jumped around in my hands. It was gross, but I was set on making Jena happy, making her laugh," Jake says. "But that frog just wouldn't keep still. Finally, I just leaned over the pond and let it back into the water."

Ken smiles, and Jake laughs.

"I figured Jena being the way she was—the way she is—that she probably wouldn't want that frog. She's a free spirit. She wouldn't want me to capture a free creature—even if it was a frog." Jake looks sad again. "She's a free spirit. A sweet, gentle, free spirit."

Ken nods in agreement and smiles. "I know you love her, man. But, you know, I bet she'd love you even more if she saw you face-first in that mud."

They laugh hard together—at the memory. Jena would laugh, too, Jake imagines.

They laugh all the way to the police precinct.

Little do they know; Reyes is already in a rage. After the detective leaves, he slams the door as hard as he's ever slammed it. Then he picks up the edge of his desk, just to see the paper, coffee cup, telephone, and pens slide to the floor.

"Damn," he says out loud. "Damn!"

He walks to the file cabinet and pulls out a file, holding it tightly in his fist. He watches through the window as the detectives walk to their car.

"*Damn!*" he yells again and throws the file back into the drawer.

He opens his office door again, and out of frustration, starts yelling at the junior police officers.

"I want all of you out of this office!" he screams. "Get out there on the streets where you belong. Write some tickets, make some arrests, anything instead of sitting in this office eating donuts and drinking coffee."

The officers look stunned and start to move quietly toward the door.

One man stays behind to sit at the front desk. Reyes gives him a nasty look.

"Officer Pine," Reyes yells.

Pine turns slowly to face Reyes. "Yes, sir," he says respectfully.

"I need you to run out and get us some breakfast," Reyes says. "It's going to be a long-damned day."

Officer Pine grabs his keys, a little confused. But he knows better than to cross Reyes. "Yes, sir," he replies again.

With an empty precinct, Reyes goes back to his office. He looks at the mess he made, picks the phone up from the floor, and dials it.

Warden Peters answers.

"If you haven't heard, Mike's alive. How many times did I shoot him? And he's still alive," Reyes says, furious.

Peters is silent. Then, "I heard."

"It gets even better," Reyes continues to rant. "I'm not on the damned case. The DA assigned Detective Martin and his crew to investigate. That means we're fucked."

Peters tries to sound calm. "Well, then, you'd better do something quick because I'm not going down. You've made too many damned fool mistakes. Shooting Mike … I told you we should just bring him back here and lock him up. But, no, you have to act like a lunatic and shoot him. Now what?" Peters is so frustrated that he stands up and walks back and forth behind his desk. "Hey, Reyes, I asked you, what in the hell are we going to do now?"

Reyes is breathing hard. "I don't know, but it could get worse. Mike could wake up anytime. And Candy is still out there somewhere, and she knows everything. What if Martin finds her before we do?"

Peters blows up. "I'm the one who had to deal with Miles McNeil and his cocky attitude. Now I have you and your self-righteous, wanna-shoot-everybody attitude. I'm done. I'm done being terrorized by you."

Reyes doesn't respond.

"You shut Mike up permanently. You find Candy, and you throw Martin off the trail—or I'll kill you and bury this whole thing," Peters threatens.

"Don't you threaten me," Reyes fires back. "I've already got someone on Candy's trail." Reyes takes a deep breath and lets his words fly at the warden. "Get this straight, Warden, I run this operation. Every minute. Every day. Every night. I'm running the show. You aren't the boss, you got that?"

He doesn't give Peters a chance to respond. "You want to kill me? I could get rid of you any time and shut this thing down. But I want my money. I sweated for that money. I worked damned hard for that money. So, don't you threaten me! I'll find Candy, and I'll deal with Detective Martin, and I'll make sure Mike is dead, if he isn't already."

He stops to take a breath. "But know this, Warden. After I get paid, I'm going to kill you! So, you'd better take your cut and run without looking back—because my bullet will be waiting for you."

Reyes slams down the phone and throws it against the wall. He slams both hands down on his desk, breathing so hard that he nearly passes out.

Reyes sits down to pull himself together.

It's just then that he raises his head and sees Jake and Ken staring at him.

Reyes reaches for his gun, but Ken and Jake have the advantage of surprise and pounce on the weapon, pinning it to the desk.

"You dirty bastard," Jake says, struggling to speak and keep control of the gun at the same time. "Where's Jena Parker?"

"I'm not telling you shit, and you two wimps are going to regret this in a big way," Reyes says.

"We heard everything," Ken says. "You were talking to the warden at the prison, weren't you?"

Reyes is startled.

"I heard what you said about some girl named Candy and that guard. I'm going to call the FBI and blow this whole thing to hell!" Jake screams.

Reyes turns his full attention to wrestling the gun away from Jake and Ken. They struggle, but the weapon is still pinned to the desk.

"So, you love Jena Parker, you poor boy," Reyes says, taunting Jake. "A little Romeo trying to find his Juliet."

Reyes' cruel comments distract Jake long enough that Reyes is able to grab Jake's arms.

The scuffle also gives Ken a chance to grab the gun. Ken is startled by his success, but quickly backs up, out of the way of Reyes' dangerous hands.

Reyes smiles an ugly smile. "Jena is far, far away. And you'll never find her unless I tell you where she is. So, you'd better come to your senses, both of you, and back off!"

Jake tries as hard as he can to get loose of Reyes' stronghold. He kicks, jabs, and pulls at Reyes, but nothing works.

"Did you hurt her?" Jake demands.

"You're insane, kid," Reyes says. "You don't have a clue what the hell is going on in this town."

"What we do know is that you're a crooked cop," Ken chimes in.

Jake and Reyes look at Ken—and the gun—as if they've forgotten he was there.

Ken cocks the weapon, stopping Jake and Reyes in their tracks.

"I'll tell you what, guys," Reyes says. "We'll all go on with our day like this never happened, and you come back tomorrow, and I'll tell you everything you want to know about Jena."

Ken knows he won't have the advantage long, and he knows that Reyes isn't going to tell Jake what's happened to Jena. Ken empties the gun, putting the bullets in his pocket. He tosses the weapon gun into the opposite corner.

"Come on, Jake, let's get out of here," Ken says.

Jake notices the bandage on Reyes' arm and punches him there as hard as he can. He backtracks to the door with Ken.

They hear a gun cocked behind them.

"You two are under arrest," Officer Pine says. "Put your hands on your heads."

Ken and Jake do as they are ordered, and they prepare themselves for the worst.

Officer Pine, Jake, and Ken are all shocked at what comes next.

"Stop!" Reyes yells, firmly.

Jake and Ken exchange confused expressions.

"It's okay. Let 'em go," Reyes says.

Pine backs up but keeps his eyes and his gun trained on Ken and Jake.

Jake and Ken just keep backing slowly toward the door.

Ken drops the bullets, and they make a loud clang in the quiet room.

Despite what can only be considered good luck, Jake is still enraged. "Get this, I will be back tomorrow, and you will tell me where Jena is, and if you don't, I will kill you—and I don't care who is holding a gun on me."

Ken grabs the back of Jake's shirt and continues backing out of the squad room.

Officer Pine runs to pick up Reyes' gun.

"Sir, he threatened to kill you," Pine says. "I can still go arrest them right now."

"No," Reyes says again.

He looks around his trashed office. "Pine just clean up this damned office. We'll deal with those two idiots later."

CHAPTER NINE

Paula and Karen are blindfolded, handcuffed, and their mouths taped as they sit quietly on the airplane. Two armed men sit in the back of the small plane with a gun pointed straight at them. Tim is bleeding, slumped in the corner of a seat. It appears he is barely alive. He opens his eyes from time to time.

"Help me," Tim whispers to the two-armed men.

But the men don't move or even respond, though they do give him sips of water from time to time—just enough to keep him quiet.

Tim feels the life leaving his body with every breath and every spurt of blood. "I'm dying," he whispers again. "Help me."

Then, he is no longer breathing. One of the armed men sighs and gets up to check Tim's pulse. He looks at his partner and waves his hand in front of his one neck to signify that Tim is dead.

Paula and Karen notice, and they are terrified. Karen begins to cry. Paula nudges Karen to be quiet, but Karen's emotions are out of control. She tries to scream through the tape that covers her mouth tightly.

The armed men are annoyed, as Paula had feared.

One of the men walks up to Karen and shakes her, yelling at her to stay quiet.

Karen doesn't. She can't.

The man shakes Karen more violently.

Paula fears for her own life, feeling helpless.

Fortunately, before the guards can get more violent, the plane lands with a loud screech and bump.

The two men grab Paula and Karen, and Karen tries to resist, to no avail. She is overpowered and forced off the plane.

The two women are led through what seems like an underground tunnel, with water in it that comes up to their knees. A door opens at one end, and the men shove the two women through the door.

Unbelievably, Karen tries again to resist, but is pushed through anyway.

Finally, their blindfolds are removed, and the brightness of the room stings their eyes. Karen's eyes are red from crying, and her face is flushed from struggling with the guards.

"Clean her up," a voice instructs the men.

A man comes over and roughly wipes Karen's face with a wet towel.

Karen starts to cry again, and the voice tells the man to remove the tape from her mouth.

"Let me go!" Karen screams over and over, louder, and louder every time.

"You must calm down, young lady," the voice says.

"No," Karen screams again. "I will not calm down! You kidnapped us! Let us go!"

The man with the calm voice, who so far has been patient with Karen, points to one of the armed men, and then at Karen.

The man points his gun and shoots Karen in the stomach. Karen drops to the floor, and blood flies everywhere.

Paula fights to stifle her scream. She can't believe that Karen has been shot, right in front of her.

"Clean it up," the voice instructs.

The armed men pick up Karen's limp, bloody body.

Paula can't take her eyes off of Karen. She tries not to cry, but tears roll down her cheeks. She hangs her head, fearing that she will be shot next.

The man with the calm voice gets out of his chair and walks over to Paula.

"Are you afraid?" he asks. "Look around the room. What do you see?"

Paula looks around the room for the first time. The walls are lined with women, all dressed in fighting gear and armed with weapons.

One woman catches her eye. A young woman almost the same age as she is. The woman's face looks familiar. In fact, Paula thinks a lot of the women look familiar. Slowly, she realizes that she recognizes the women from the prison—women she'd seen, eaten with, even showered with. Women who just disappeared and were never seen again.

Paula looks back at the man with the calm voice.

She stares at him, trying to appear brave and strong.

"Do you want to leave us, too, just like your friend?" the man asks, looking over his shoulder as Karen's body is dragged out of the room.

Paula shakes her head, no.

"Good," he says. "Cut her loose."

One of the guard's cuts through the ties on Paula's arms and rips the tape from her mouth.

The calm man, obviously the one in charge, walks back to his seat, sits down, and stares at Paula.

"Now run," he says unexpectedly.

Paula is utterly confused. She looks around the room, hoping for help, or at least direction, from the women. But no one budges. They all share the same blank expression.

"I am Romli. I own you, and I am telling you to run!"

One of the guards opens the door, and Paula can see only wilderness. The women in the room turn to Paula and point their weapons at her.

Paula is terrified. She is breathing hard as she looks around the room, then at the man who calls himself Romli, then back at the door.

Fear takes over, and she runs toward the door. But she stops, trying to figure out where she is going. She finds no answers, so she just starts running through the forest—stepping through branches, brambles, grass, mud, and anything else in her path.

Paula runs like a crazy person. In the back of her mind, she realizes she has no sturdy shoes, no food, no water, nothing to help her survive whatever is happening to her.

But she knows she has the courage to live to see her little girl again.

Back in the room with the other women, Romli makes an ugly smile.

"Give her a day, then hunt her," he instructs. "If she survives, then she becomes a part of the team. If she is hurt or wounded, kill her. We can't tolerate weak teammates."

The women stare at Romli as he speaks.

They are forced to do what they do and have become accustomed to it. Practically in unison, the women nod at Romli, signifying that they agree and understand.

But they do not agree. They despise Romli and have been trying to find a way to retaliate and escape.

Later, the women whisper among themselves.

"I know that girl," says a woman named Matty, who was kidnapped a year before. "Her name is Paula. She has a little girl."

"We can't worry about Paula," says another woman, Suzanne. "Paula has to survive on her own. If she doesn't, we'll keep trying to figure out a way to save ourselves.

Suzanne has a masculine way about her. She leaves Matty wondering whether Paula will survive the traps waiting for her or if they will find her dead, eaten by wolves.

⁓

Jena may be worried, but she is certainly not worried about being eaten by wolves.

She has never seen such luxury, as she looks at the white leather couch in her living room. The dark wood coffee table and end tables have glass tops. But the tables are sunken into the floor, which seems odd. Jena steps on top of the coffee table and looks through the glass. She's worried about falling through, but she sees nothing unusual. She picks up the remote control lying on the couch and looks at all the buttons. The remote has a button for everything. Each button has a name: kitchen table, refrigerator, couch, every object in the room. Jena steps back from the glass-topped table and presses the corresponding button.

She watches in amazement as the table begins to rise from the floor. She pushes the button for the refrigerator, and it turns to face the other way. She smiles and plays with the remote like a toy.

She stops suddenly and remembers the first room Pulue had shown her, the room where paintings move to reveal machine guns.

Intimidated, but curious, she tries speaking to the remote.

"Move."

"Show weapons."

Nothing happens.

"Jena," she says.

Nothing.

She takes the remote and walks toward the closed blinds. She knows she is underground, so what is behind the blinds? A wall? Another illusion?

She presses the button labeled "Blinds."

The blinds don't move. But "outside," or what appears to be outdoors, appears. She can't believe what she sees. A lovely forest, trees, rabbits, squirrels, birds. She presses the button labeled "Sun," and the sun shines. She presses the label, "Moonlight," and the scene is bathed in the softness of night.

She realizes it's a simulation—but a calming and serene simulation. She feels hope, the hope of freedom, the hope of finding Jake, the hope of finding her life as a young woman.

Jena feels as if she's discovered some secret of the universe, right in this room.

The lights in her room dim.

She backs away, puzzled, and presses the buttons on the remote. But the blinds will not open again.

She hears a man's voice behind her. "Fascinating, isn't it?"

She jumps and turns to see her door wide open and Pulue smiling at her with his arms crossed.

Pulue walks closer to Jena. "You must be wondering about all of this," he says.

Jena puts the remote down and stares at Pulue. She glares at the floor, the blinds and at Pulue. "Yes, I was wondering. Why the forest? Why the animals?" she asks.

Pulue smiles and walks toward the closed blinds. "It was for you. It was to calm you with its mystery. You were mesmerized. You forgot where you were, how you got here, and why you're here." He pauses into a smile. "This peace is for you, Jena, as you prepare for war. Your mission here is essential. So, we offer you the finest. The most luxurious. The best technology. The best teaching. The best food, clothes. The best of everything." His smile seems to disappear, just like the pretty view of the forest. "It's because we expect the best from you."

Pulue stands eye to eye with Jena. "You're part of this team now. Enjoy. And be ready for the challenge that lies ahead. I'm sure Moschi wouldn't have sent you to us if he didn't think you would exceed our expectations. I believe he saw something in you that he knew would bring us much success."

Jena doesn't know what to say.

"By the way," Pulue says. "You don't have to use the remote control. Everything can be activated by your voice. However, you will need a code name."

Jena stares at Pulue, not comprehending all that awaits her.

"What about my life?" she asks.

Pulue laughs lightly and turns around as he is leaving her apartment.

"The only life you have now, Jena, is this life. And this life has begun," he says, closing closes the door behind him and leaving Jena to stare into space with no more answers than when she left the prison.

But she knows that time is running out.

The time for strength has come—not just for her own survival, but for everyone whose life she touched or, even, destroyed.

Paula runs through the woods, looking behind her from time to time while trying not to fall. Her heart is racing like the hearts of ten black horses. Tears stream down her cheeks—from emotion, but also from the wind stinging her eyes.

She can hear voices in distance behind her. She tries to stay ahead of them and prays that someone can rescue her from this horrible nightmare.

She sees her daughter's tiny face, and the tears fall uncontrollably.

Paula stops and hides behind a tree.

Voices get closer, and one of the women calls out her name.

"Paula!" she screams. "We can smell your fear."

She tries to catch her breath, but her hope is fading. She can hear her child's laughter in the misty air. She catches her breath and starts running again. She is running as fast as she can, but it is not fast enough.

One of the women catches up to her and pushes Paula to the ground.

"Where do you think you're going, girl?" the woman says.

"Please," Paula begs, unable to catch her breath.

"Please what!" the woman asks. "Please let you go? You're not supposed to get caught." The woman laughs out loud.

"Get off of her, Pam," says another woman, with a Southern accent. "You're not supposed to catch her yet."

"Shut up, Sharon," Pam says. "Let's have some fun."

Pam pulls a knife from her back pocket and sticks it in Paula's face.

"You're a cute one, aren't you?" Pam says.

"Romli is going to kill you," Sharon warns.

"Shut up, you snitch," Pam yells, turning to threaten Sharon with her knife. "You were a snitch in jail, and you're a snitch out here."

Paula sees her chance to break free. She gets up and starts running again.

Pam starts to follow but changes her mind. "We'll get our chance to kill her tomorrow," she says.

Pam smirks. "She can only run so far. These grounds are rigged. Damned girl has no idea what's ahead." She turns around to face Sharon. "Let's go, snitch."

They walk back to the main camp.

"We didn't know what we were getting into either," Sharon says, in her Southern drawl. "But we're here, so maybe she'll make it, too. We're all just a bunch of prison convicts kidnapped to do someone else's dirty deeds."

"Oh, screw you, shut up," Pam says, and they leave Paula to carry on with her "test" alone.

Paula can feel her body slowing from sheer exhaustion. Her throat is dry, and her lips are brittle. Her stomach is cramping from the lack of food and water; she stops to bend over in pain.

She looks up and sees Matty, who is pointing a gun at her.

"Please, no," Paula begs.

Matty stares at Paula. "Do you remember me?" she asks.

Paula looks up, sweat and tears dripping from her face. She squints at Matty, trying to recognize her.

Paula blinks twice. "Matty," she whispers.

"Yeah, it's me, Matty."

"Please let me go," Paula pleads.

"I can't do that," Matty says. "If you don't finish the test, Romli will kill you anyway, and you'll never see your daughter again."

"My daughter," Paula leans into the pain.

Matty just watches as Paula suffers. "You have to get up and be strong or you'll never survive this place. This is nothing compared to the challenges later on."

"I can't." Paula cries and collapses into despair. "I can't do it."

Matty grabs Paula's shirt and pulls her close. "You can and you will," Matty says, glaring into Paula's eyes. "Crying isn't going to save you."

That's the last thing Paula remembers because Matty punches her and knocks her unconscious. Then, she drags Paula to a cave that only a few other women know about. She pulls Paula by the arms, Paula's feet dragging dirt, weeds, and leaves from the forest. With her gun holstered, Matty uses all of her strength to pull Paula. She leaves Paula on the ground, along with a plastic bag that holds a sandwich, a canteen of water, and a cigarette lighter.

Matty heads back to camp.

After being unconscious for more than an hour, Paula wakes in the darkness of the cave; night has come. She has no idea how she got there. She is afraid.

She rubs her head, and as she tries to get her bearings, she squashes the sandwich. She picks it up and then finds the canteen and the lighter. She gradually understands that someone has brought her to safety.

She flicks the lighter and looks around the cave. It's scary, but now she is not as frightened, knowing that someone is looking out for her.

She closes her eyes, trying to gather her wits, and Matty's face appears in her mind. She remembers Matty swinging her fist—and then nothing. Matty must have brought her here and left the water and sandwich.

Paula tears open the sandwich and eats it in almost a single bite. She drinks the water in nearly a single gulp. She feels a bit better and lies down, holding the lighter up so she can see the top of the cave.

As her pain and fear ease, she becomes angry at the thought of being kidnapped and left alone out here, possibly to die without ever seeing her daughter again.

She thinks of Chief Reyes and Warden Peters, who are responsible for sending all of these women to be used as targets.

Paula stays awake for hours, her anger festering. But exhaustion gives way to deep sleep.

The warden may be responsible for the pain he has inflicted on these women but sitting alone in his office he feels only anger—at Reyes, for the moment.

"Damned loser. Jerk," he says aloud.

He walks to a window and decides that he wants Reyes dead.

"He's nothing but a screwup," the warden mumbles. "He's messed up all of my hard work."

Warden Peters thinks back to the first conversation he had about kidnapping the women prisoners and sending them to Romli's team. It was ten years ago. They met at a remote spot off a dirt road. The man he met smoked a cigar and wore a black cap and black trench coat. He was younger than the warden.

It was Miles McNeil.

"How are you, Phillip?" McNeil asked. "It's been a while."

"Why are we here?" the warden asked after they exchanged a few more pleasantries.

McNeil sighed. "Well, Phillip, you know I've been traveling lately, to several foreign countries. I've got a proposition for you," he said, "seeing as you are the new warden. Warden Phillip Peters."

"Not interested," Peters said bluntly.

Peters began to walk back to his car, but McNeil called to him with an angry voice.

"Now, how do you know that you're not interested if you don't even know what I'm going to say?" McNeil said.

"If I know you, Miles, it's something unethical. I don't need to hear what you have to say," Peters said.

"Then why did you come?" McNeil wanted to know.

"I came because you are my half-brother, and you said you needed to talk to me. I guess I was hoping you'd changed," Peters said, starting to walk away again.

"I'll tell Ellen," McNeil yelled. "I'll tell Ellen that you slept with that girl, got her pregnant, took her to get an abortion, and she died." He laughed. "It'll break poor Ellen's heart. And your son and daughter, what will they think? Plus, you'll ruin your fancy new career as warden."

Peters' face turned red with anger. "How can you, as my brother, even half-brother, be so damned cruel?"

McNeil laughed again.

"We're not that different. We're talking about a lot of money—and all of it from foreign sources. I need this money. I need it for my daughter. She doesn't know me now, but she will one day. I'll tell her the truth and give Jena everything she will need in life."

Peters couldn't help but consider what the extra money could do for him and his family.

"You know Jonathan and Kitty Parker don't have much, but I'm going to give Jena the life that she deserves. A beautiful life," McNeil said of his biological daughter.

He walked quickly after Peters. He was eager to close the deal.

"Listen to me. I know this man who runs a … well … call it … an operation. And he's looking for new recruits. He's having a hard time finding the people he needs, and I thought of a brilliant idea." McNeil looked at Peters, clearly pleased with himself. "Can you guess what my idea is, brother?"

That all may have been ten years ago, but the warden remembers the conversation as if it had taken place the day before.

He shakes his head and sits down at his desk. The memories keep flooding back—to the day he met Clark Reyes, long before Reyes became Chief of Police.

"Welcome to my prison, Officer Reyes," Peters said as he stood to shake Reyes' hand.

The young officer was humble and sat down in a chair in front of the warden's desk.

"The police chief, Bob Carr, told me that you were the best officer on his team. He said you'd make a great liaison between the police department and the prison," the warden had said. Reyes had a sharp record. "I couldn't agree with him more. Reyes, you are an outstanding officer of the law."

Reyes had blushed with pride. But he had an arrogant side, too.

"You're too kind," Reyes said. It seemed that Reyes had spoken with more than a little sarcasm. "But I did graduate at the top of my class at the academy."

Reyes continued to list his accomplishments.

Warden Peters, younger then, listened patiently.

"I just believe in giving my all to the force," Reyes said. "Being an officer of the law is something to be proud of, and I will uphold the law to the fullest, and I'll punish anyone who breaks that law."

Peters welcomed Reyes to the prison's team.

"Damn. Damn. Damn," Peters says, thinking back. He slams his fist on his desk when he remembers the conversation with Reyes. He wishes he had never become involved in this mess at all.

It was a year after that first meeting that the warden had called Reyes in for another talk. The warden had taken a stern tone with the officer.

"Sit down, Officer Reyes," he said. "When I first met you, I had high hopes, but some of the guards tell me that you've been flirting with the female inmates."

Peters walked around his desk so that he was closer to Reyes. "One of the guards said he caught you in the closet with one of the women prisoners. And he says he has it on tape."

Reyes just looked away and frowned. "Well, Warden, I don't like your tone," Reyes said.

His manner was much different from the deferential attitude he showed when he joined the prison team. "I mean you asked me to come here, and now I feel like I'm being intimidated."

Peters is angry. "If you feel like you're being intimidated, then it's probably because you're being intimidated. I'm running a prison, not a whore house."

That's when Peters proposed a deal with Reyes, a deal he now wishes he had never made.

As much as he wishes he could take back the conversations he had with Miles and Reyes, he knows it's too late.

"This is a damned mess," he says aloud to no one.

His phone rings, and he figures that it is Reyes. He lets his voicemail pick up the call.

He listens to the message being left.

A calm voice says, "One down. We need you to send another."

The warden rushes to grab the phone receiver, but it's too late.

Romli had already hung up.

Just what he needs, the warden thinks. Another problem. He starts to pick up the phone to call Reyes but can't. He's too angry.

Peters calls one of his guards, Carl, on the radio and asks him to come to the office.

"I want you to bring one of the inmates to my office," the warden says when Carl arrives. "I need you to go to the medical ward and bring Chance Middleton to me."

Peters uses a grave tone with the guard and looks at him sternly.

Carl asks no questions and goes straight away to the medical ward, where Chance is lying in bed watching television.

Carl appears at the door like a giant. "Middleton!" Carl calls out. "Come with me."

Chance is afraid. She's still shaken from the ordeal in the forest. Mike shot. Candy gone. She gets out of bed slowly. What could be happening now?

"Where are taking me?" she asks slowly.

Carl looks at Chance with a grim expression. "The warden wants to see you. Now stop asking questions. Let's go."

Chance takes a deep breath and hesitates, then walks toward Carl like a doe being fed to hungry tigers.

Carl pushes her ahead, and when he comes to the warden's door, he knocks and enters.

Chance walks into the office and stands in front of the warden's desk, with Carl standing behind her. She looks down, peeking up at the warden, without a clue of what is coming.

Warden Peters stands next to Chance. "Remember how you said you'd do anything?"

The warden smiles at Carl and nods. Carl jumps into action, grabs Chance's arms and handcuffs them. The warden hands Carl duct tape, which immediately goes across Chance's mouth.

"Here's your chance to make good on that promise." The warden speaks to Chance in an ugly tone.

Chance snaps out of her shock. She kicks and tries to scream as Carl drags her out of the office.

CHAPTER TEN

S herry Paterson stands, looking down at her husband, Gary, as he sits in a chair with a blanket wrapped around his legs. Gary stares out the living room window.

Her mind drifts back to the morning she had heard that her son, Ted, was dead. Cruelly, she heard about his death on the television news.

She was in a hospital room, waiting for her husband to return from a lab test. She turned on the television to kill time, only to hear that a young man had been found dead lying face down on the front lawn at the home of the late Catherine "Kitty" Parker and Jonathan Parker.

She jumped up, guessing that her son, Jake, had been killed and that Jena Parker had killed him.

Before Sherry Paterson could even process what she'd heard on television, a police officer walked into her husband's hospital room.

"Mrs. Paterson?" The officer spoke slowly and held his hat in his hands, as a gesture of respect.

Sherry Paterson gripped the television remote and stared at the officer as he walked toward her.

"No," she begged, tears already rolling from her eyes to her cheeks. She was shaking now. "No. Not my Jake! Not my Jake, please." She became more hysterical.

"Mrs. Paterson, I am Officer Jacobs, and I am sorry to tell you that your son is dead."

The woman collapsed into the chair next to her husband's empty bed, still holding the television remote. She buried her head in the blankets.

She turned toward Officer Jacobs. "Who killed my Jake?" she asked.

He looked at the grieving mother, looked away, and then looked back at Mrs. Paterson. "Mrs. Paterson, ma'am, I'm sorry to tell you that your son, Ted, is dead. Not Jake." He repeated the name, quietly, for emphasis. "Ted."

"No!" Sherry Paterson screamed, holding her stomach as if she'd been stabbed. It seemed that her grieving started all over again. The remote fell to the floor, and pieces broke off.

She tried to stand, but Officer Jacobs caught her as she started to fall.

"No, not Ted! Not Ted, please," she cried as she bent over in Officer Jacobs' arms.

The officer did his best to console her, but her grief could not be assuaged. Sherry could no longer stand, and the officer helped her into the chair.

"Who did it?" she demanded.

Officer Jacobs looked at the crying mother without saying a word.

"Who did it!" she screamed again.

"Ma'am, Mrs. Paterson, we are just starting to investigate this horrible crime," the officer said.

Ted's mother became angry. "It was Jena Parker," she insisted. "That murderous evil girl killed my baby."

"Mrs. Paterson, we do not know yet who killed your son," he attempted to explain.

Sherry stood, though Officer Jacobs feared she would faint again.

"What are you talking about? She's already murdered her own mother, and at least three other people! You say you don't know? What do you mean, you don't know who killed my child? She did. She killed my Teddy, and she's going to pay."

"Mrs. Peterson, Jena Parker is not a suspect at this time."

Sherry looked up at him with a mix of horror and rage. "What?" she asked.

"Ma'am, it's really too early for us to give out information or make any conclusion. Neighbors said that Jake and Jena both left the house, so we aren't sure what happened."

Mrs. Paterson stared at him as if he was a crazy person.

"Ronald," she says, pointing her finger at the officer. "Are you trying to say that Jake could have killed his own brother?"

She tried unsuccessfully to pounce at Officer Jacobs. "You're crazy. You're as crazy as you were in high school. Get the hell out of here before they bring my husband back. God only knows how I'm going to tell him that his youngest son is dead."

Mrs. Paterson screamed so loud that orderlies came to attend to her. They quietly suggested that the officer should leave, for everyone's sake.

A nurse entered and asked Officer Jacobs if everything was okay.

"No," he said. "But I'm leaving."

The orderlies and nurse hesitated, but finally left the room.

Officer Jacobs walked toward Ted and Jake's mother.

"Sherry … Mrs. Paterson … you must know that this is as difficult for me as it is for you." He looked around the room and even into the hall to make sure no one was nearby. He whispered, "Sherry, you know this hurts me as much as it hurts you. You know it does. Ted was my son, too. Our son."

The officer tried to touch Sherry, but she jerked away. "Get the hell out of here!" she screamed. "Don't you ever say anything like that again! My husband can never hear you say anything like that. How dare you come to his hospital room and say such a thing!"

Sherry frowned deeply. "You're no dad. You're no father. My husband is the father of our two boys. We never even had a paternity test, so we don't know, and no one ever needs to know."

She stood and ordered him out of the room.

"I love you, Sherry," Jacobs had said as his eyes teared up and he gripped his hat.

"I don't love you," she said definitively. "Now get out before I call the nurse back in."

Officer Jacobs bowed a bit, from the weight of the crime, from embarrassment and sadness. And he left the hospital room.

Sherry hastily washed her eyes and face before her husband was returned to his room. She was facing away from the door as the nurse wheeled Gary Paterson into the room and helped him get settled into bed. She greeted her husband, pasting on a fake smile.

Gary's head was bobbing, as he tried to stay awake and focus on his wife. He didn't say anything. His medication kept him from being alert; he went in and out of a fog.

Sherry, feeling utterly alone, began to cry, but she hid the tears when Gary opened his eyes. Even with his sick eyes, he knew that something bad had happened to his wife.

Sherry started to cry hard enough that she could no longer look at her husband, and she walked out of the room.

Gary tried to call after his wife, but all he could manage was a pitiful moan. He shook, knowing that something was very wrong and that he very much wanted to comfort his wife.

Sherry noticed but was so distraught that she could not help her husband. She asked a nurse to check on him, but the nurse couldn't calm the sick man, who became more and more frantic.

The nurse called two attendants to help. In the end, Mr. Paterson was sedated so that he wouldn't hurt himself.

Months later, little has changed for Sherry and Gary Paterson.

Gary is out of the hospital, but she has yet to tell him about his son's death. Her husband is still very ill. Mostly, he just moves from the bed to the chair and back again.

Sherry pulls a chair close to her husband's chair, and they both look out the window.

She closes her eyes, trying not to think of Ted. She tries to stay composed and present a cheery face to her husband.

"Look at you, you handsome man," Sherry says.

Gary looks into his wife's big brown eyes. "Brown eyes": that's his pet name for Sherry.

"When are the kids coming home? Ted and Jake? Where are they?" he asks.

Sherry's smile droops a little. "They're grown now," she says. "They're big boys, so they don't come home as often as we'd like." She touches Gary's cheek.

"Why?" Gary asks sadly. "Why don't they come home to visit us anymore?"

Sherry looks away, trying not to cry as she keeps her sad secret. She stands, faces the window, puts her hands on her hips. She slightly turns to look at Gary.

"That's just the way boys are," she says, trying to comfort her husband while maintaining her composure. She becomes quiet as she remembers Ted and Jake as children, jumping up and down on the couches. "They grow up," she whispers. "Sometimes, they go away." She runs her hand across his forehead. "You're tired. Come on, I'll help you to bed."

She walks slowly with him to the bedroom, helps him to sit on the edge of the bed, and he lays down. She pulls a blanket over him and kisses his lips.

"Get some rest," she says.

She walks out of the room, heavy with a deep sadness. She hasn't seen her son, Jake, since she yelled at him to get out of the car—after he confessed to killing his own brother.

But Sherry wasn't convinced that Jake had killed his brother, not then and not now.

"I know it was Jena Parker who killed him," Sherry says to herself, thoughts racing race through her head.

She gets up, walks to the kitchen, and picks up a piece of paper with Ken Stewart's cell number on it. She picks up the phone and calls the number. The call goes to Ken's voicemail.

"Yeah, it's Ken. I'm the man, and, no, Chance didn't kill me, so leave a message."

Sherry leaves a message asking Ken to have Jake call home.

She hangs up and walks into the living room and opens a drawer in the bookcase. She pulls out a gun and holds it tightly, cocks it, and pretends that she is pointing it at Jena Parker. She imagines Jena being afraid, and she imagines telling Jena that she is going to kill her.

"You killed my son, you horrible being," Sherry imagines telling Jena.

Sherry stares at the gun she's holding.

The front door opens suddenly, startling Sherry. She's even more startled to see Ken and Jake walk in.

She quickly tries to put the gun away, but Jake sees her.

"Mom, what are you doing?" Jake asks in an angry voice.

Ken doesn't want any part of whatever is going on and tries to slowly back out of the house.

Sherry puts the gun back in the drawer, and Jake moves quickly toward his mother.

Instead of saying anything, Sherry reaches out to Jake and hugs him tightly. Then, she begins to cry.

"Oh, Jake, I am so happy to see you. I've missed you so much," his mother says, crying and pleading. "Jake, please." Her mother looks directly into her son's eyes. "I know you didn't do it, son." She tries to sound calm. "I know you didn't kill your own brother."

Jake just stares at his mother. "Mom …" he starts to say.

Sherry stops him. "Don't say it, Jake. Don't say that you killed your brother because I know you didn't. "Jena did it," she says definitively, squeezing Jake's arm and looking into his eyes.

She turns quickly hysterical. "I know you didn't do it," she screams. "I know it was Jena Parker! I know it was her! You would never kill your brother. It was her, and she's going to pay."

Jake backs away from his mother, but he is emotional, as well. "Mom, you have to stop this! You have to stop is now!" he yells.

"Lower your voice," his mother demands. "Father is resting."

Jake turns around to leave, but his mother grabs his arm. "Don't go, Jake," she begs.

Jake turns to look at his mother's sad, drained eyes. His heart swells to think of the pain he'd caused her. She must be so disappointed in him. And no matter what he does or says, he can't bring his brother back—as much as he would like to.

Jake breaks away from his mother's grasp and backs away from her.

"Mama, I can't do this with you. I can't let you blame Jena for something you know I did!"

Sherry Paterson just stares at Jake. "Don't you say that!" she yells.

Jake's heart breaks to see her denial. "Mom," he says as he turns to leave the house.

She calls after him as he walks through the door. "Jacob! Jacob!"

But Jake is gone.

Ken is waiting outside. "Hey, man, your mom has a gun. I can't believe that."

Jake ignores his friend, gets into the car, cranks it up, and holds the steering wheel tightly. Ken jumps in, and before he can even slam the door, Jake is spinning out of the driveway.

"Hey, calm down," Ken says. "What's wrong with you?"

Jake just keeps driving.

Ken takes his cue from his friend, and they are both silent.

Jake is thinking about his mother holding that gun, of his brother falling out of the window, and he thinks of Jena and wants to know where she is now.

Jake goes crazy thinking that Reyes might know where Jena has been taken. He turns to Ken and looks angry.

"Man, are you okay?" Ken asks.

Jake turns away and doesn't answer.

"I know you're worried about Jena," Ken says. "And I know you have to be worried about your mom having that gun. Man, if I saw my mom with a gun, I'd be wondering what's up. I'd be wondering, why does my mom have a gun?"

Ken shakes his head. "I can only think of one reason why your mom has that gun," Ken says. "I know you don't want to hear this, but she got that gun to kill Jena. She hates Jena. You know that."

Jake starts to speed up again.

He definitely does not want to hear what Ken has to say. "I killed my brother," Jake says.

Ken is quiet.

"I killed my brother so she would be mad at me and not Jena."

Ken is shocked.

"Did you just say that you killed your own brother? You killed Ted?" Ken asks, alarmed.

"That's exactly what you heard me say," Jake replies.

Ken lowers the car window to get some air. "I can't believe it was you and not Jena," Ken says. "Dude, how could you kill your own brother? I mean … what's up with that?"

Jake pulls the car to the side of the road.

They quietly sit in the car.

Ken wants answers, but Jake just stares into the distance as he grips the steering wheel.

"Ken?" Jakes asks. "Do you have any idea what he did to Jena? Do you know what he put her through?"

Jake looks away. "You have no idea what it was like to overhear my own brother admit to that nightmare. I was enraged. I could have killed anyone. Ted deserved to die for what he did."

Jake's voice is shaky. "I never thought I could harm anyone, let alone my own brother."

Ken looks back at his friend, still shocked at Jake's confession. But he doesn't say anything.

"After what he did to Jena, I just couldn't just walk away," Jake says.

He and Ken lock eyes.

"So, your brother is the one who raped Jena? That's why you killed Ted?" Ken asks, suddenly putting the whole story together. He shakes his head at the memory. "I can't believe that Ted would do something like that."

Jake turns the car lights back on and pulls into the road.

"I don't want to talk about it anymore, Ken. I don't want to talk about anything except finding Jena," he says, his voice cracking. "She's all I want. She's all I need, and I have to find her now."

They drive in silence for a while.

"I'm not asking you to forget what I told you," Jake says. "I can't take it back. I can't go back and get my brother. I can't go back and stop myself."

Ken looks at Jake. "I get it, man," he says sympathetically. "I gotta be honest with you, I can't say that I feel bad about Ted being gone. I'm here for you. I'm going to help you find Jena. I'm going to help you bring her home. I'm your friend."

Ken's words make Jake feel calmer. Just thinking about bringing Jena home again makes him remember her beautiful smile. He imagines her hair blowing like feathers in the wind. He can see her glistening eyes as if she were sitting right next to him.

"Did you hear what I said, Jake?" Ken asks. "I said I'm with you all the way."

All Jake can see is Jena, calling his name and reaching for him. Jena's exquisite smile flashes in front of him; she glows like an angel.

Jake realizes that he'd better pull himself together and turns into a convenience store parking lot.

He looks at Ken, gives him a grim look. "You're right, man. We'll get her back. And the first thing we need to do is go back and confront that prick Reyes. He holds the key to finding Jena."

Jake thinks about the phone call they overheard Reyes making, back at his office.

"First, I think we need to find this woman named Candy, the one he was talking about on the phone. And that prison guard who was shot? We need to see if he's awake and talk to him," Jake says. "Maybe one of them can confirm that Reyes had something to do with Jena's disappearance."

Jake shakes his head. "You heard Reyes. He's trying to find this Candy for a reason, and we need to find her first."

Jake takes a deep breath. He'd been talking so fast that he'd forgotten to breathe. And he'd also forgotten about the effect of the bombshell he just dropped on his best friend.

"Ken, I need you to understand that I never wanted to hurt my brother. But what he did to Jena was ruthless."

Jake tears up thinking about what Ted did to Jena. He drops his head onto the steering wheel, and Ken reaches over to put his hand on Jake's shoulder.

"I can't imagine what you're dealing with emotionally—knowing that you're responsible for your brother's death," Ken says. "But I'm your friend. I've known you since we were kids." He squeezes Jake's shoulder and then moves his hand away. "I'm here for you."

"Thanks. I really needed to hear that. Right now, I just need you to trust me," Jake responds.

He pulls back onto the road, and he's grateful to have Ken by his side as they head back to town to find the prison guard Reyes was talking about, the one in the hospital.

Mike is still not awake. He lies silent and unknowing, attached to IV tubes and a ventilator.

Two nurses enter the ICU. One nurse checks the machine and records Mike's blood pressure and temperature while the other nurse rearranges his pillows and blankets.

"Do you know what happened to him?" one nurse, Marlene Nelson, asks the other.

"Not sure," replies her co-worker, Colleen Megan. "I just know he was shot multiple times, someplace near the prison, and police think there's some kind of foul play involved. But I'm no detective. And neither are you, so just do your job."

Marlene rolls her eyes as Colleen leaves. She stays behind and stares at Mike.

"What's your story?" she whispers. She decides to check his vital signs one more time, but when she turns to leave, she sees a man standing in the doorway of the hospital room.

"Who's there?" she asks with the authority that tells him non-medical personnel are not supposed to be in the Intensive Care Unit.

"Hello, ma'am. I'm Chief Clark Reyes of the Maplesville Police Department."

He walks farther into the room, and Nurse Nelson just looks at him.

Reyes looks at Mike and then back at the nurse.

"I am investigating how this man got shot, and I just wanted to come and see how he was doing," Reyes said.

Nurse Nelson does not reply.

"So how *is* the man doing?" Reyes asks, trying to sound sincerely concerned.

Nurse Nelson signs off of the computer.

"Well, he's not responding right now, though he has opened his eyes from time to time. We are all expecting that he will regain consciousness eventually," the nurse says.

Reyes nods earnestly. "So, it was some kind of accident?" he asks, trying to find out how much she knows.

"We don't know," Nurse Nelson replies. "But it's one of the most serious cases we've ever had. We don't have many patients who have been shot like this, so many times." She catches Reyes looking at Mike intently. "Do you know him?" she asks.

Reyes shakes his head. "Like I said, I'm part of the team investigating this. I promise you that we'll find whoever is responsible." He looks around the room and out into the hall. "So, how is security around here?"

Nurse Nelson looks puzzled.

"I mean, whoever did this might be lurking around the hospital," Reyes says. "Maybe he wants to finish the job."

Nurse Nelson opens her mouth, but nothing comes out. She is shocked at the notion that a criminal could be someplace in the hospital.

As soon as Reyes' words sink in, she says, "Are you saying that someone could come in here and start shooting at all of us?"

"Calm down. Calm down," Reyes says. "I'm just saying that we, down at the police department, we want to make sure that the patient and staff are safe."

Nurse Nelson gets a sinking feeling. "Well, you're the first police officer we've seen since this patient came in. But we did get a call from a detective. I can't recall his name." She looks down, trying to remember the name. "Detective Martin, that's it. He left a message that he would be here tomorrow to check on our patient."

Nurse Nelson says she won't be working the next day, but that Nurse Colleen Megan would be. "We have a small staff, you know, so sometimes we're here in this unit by ourselves." She steps away from Mike's bed. "That's all I can really tell you. I need to get back to work, and I can't leave you here with the patient. If you like, I can have Nurse Megan call you tomorrow or have Detective Martin call you if he comes in."

Reyes doesn't want that to happen. "No," he says quickly. "No but thank you. I'm sure the detective will be in touch with me." He nods. "You have a good night, nurse." He looks at her name tag. "You have a good night, Nurse Marlene Nelson."

They walk out of the room together. "And don't you worry. We at the police department are here to keep this hospital and this town safe." He looks into her eyes a little too directly. "We can't afford to lose any of our hardworking, dedicated nurses."

She shivers at the officer's odd talk. "We appreciate your service, officer."

Marlene stares at Reyes as he walks away. Her colleague, Colleen, notices and asks what Reyes wanted.

"He's a strange man, but he's law enforcement, so I guess there's nothing to worry about," Marlene says. "You do know that you'll be the only nurse on staff tomorrow, right? Please make sure you keep a good eye on this patient, okay?"

"I don't need you to tell me how to do my job," Nurse Megan says in a huff, and she walks away.

CHAPTER ELEVEN

Carl has no problem dragging Chance out of the warden's office.

"Stop fighting, Chance, or I'll kill you right here," he threatens her.

Chance does as she is told, but she is afraid.

Carl forces her out the back of the prison to the waiting van. Two men are standing by to take her.

"You know what to do," Carl says.

One man pushes Chance into the van, jumps in behind her, and closes the doors behind him.

Chance is struggling on the floor, and the man lifts her onto the bench.

She is trying to stay calm, but her heart is pounding. The man smells bad, and he is staring at her.

Her captor removes the duct tape from her mouth, looks her up and down, and smiles. He puts his hand on her knee, and Chance tries to squirm away, but the man just smiles at her with an evil grin.

"Do you know where you're going?" he asks in a deep foreign voice.

Chance shakes her head, no.

"No, of course, you don't know where you're going. You don't know what you've gotten yourself into. But you now belong to someone who is going to put you to very good use. You're going to be better than you ever thought you could be," he says.

Chance is confused and frightened.

"You're afraid, as you should be. But you look different than the others. I see something besides fear. I see the desire for vengeance and violence. I think you're going to find it," the man says, as if he is reciting some kind of riddle.

The man stares at Chance. "I think you have a fire burning inside of you. I think that you are searching for something that will put out that fire."

Chance suddenly feels calm. It seems as if the man can see inside of her.

"Talk to me," the man orders her.

Chance swallows hard. "Who are you?"

The man looks at her as if she has asked a foolish question. "I'm taking you to your new home, to your new life." He moves to the bench across from Chance and crosses his legs. "Now, you tell me everything about yourself. Tell me about your fears. Tell me about the revenge you seek. Tell me who you really are."

Chance wonders what she should say, what the consequences will be. She works up her confidence. "I need to know your name first," she says firmly.

The man just smiles. "You want to know my name. You want to get personal, so that I will have sympathy for you. That will never happen."

He settles into his seat, as if it is the most comfortable place he has ever been.

"You can call me Black Thunder," the man says. "Now tell me your story. Tell me everything."

Chance looks away from the man's gaze. She feels the heat rising in her body as she thinks about the past.

"My name is Chance Middleton, and it was only a few years ago that I was leading a normal, everyday, teenage life. I grew up in the small town of Maplesville, which is where my parents lived—but they're dead now." She looks into her captor's eyes. "I have no brothers or sisters, and as an only child, I was given the best life could offer. I lived in a beautiful home and had expensive clothes. And"—she pauses—"I thought I had loyal friends. But I know now that I have no friends."

The man grins and leans forward, looking into Chance's eyes. "Why wouldn't a young girl like you have friends?"

Chance thinks back to the night of the masquerade ball when she dressed as Jena and plotted her revenge on Carol for betraying their friendship by having sex with Ken. The more she thinks about it, the more vindicated she feels about killing Carol.

Chance stares at the man guarding her and leans forward, just the way he'd leaned forward and looked into her eyes.

"I don't have a friend because I killed her, and I killed my parents, and when I'm free, I'm going to kill Jena Parker. I'm going to kill Ken. I'm going to kill Jake." Chance pauses. "And I'm going to kill you."

The man responds by laughing so hard and so loudly that the driver stops the van to make sure everything is okay.

"Everything's fine. Don't worry," the man yells to the driver. "In fact, everything is wonderful back here. We have a winner on our hands. She's strong. She's tough. She's going to do quite well on our team.

"She says she's going to kill me," and then he starts laughing louder and clapping.

"Chance, I love your spirit. You are just what we need."

His voice grows deep and stern, and his eyes grow dark.

"Rule One is, don't threaten your teammate. Let me tell you, I grew up in a poor country. I had no clothes. I had no house. I had no family. I had no food. I had nothing except hate, and then I became part of this team at the young age of ten. I learned to handle a weapon. I learned to survive. I learned how to hold a big knife and to kill for my food. I learned to kill people."

The man adjusts his posture again. "So, you take this into account, you strong-willed woman. You grew up with everything, and you killed. I grew up with nothing, and I killed." He leans closer to Chance. "Who do you think is a better killer?"

Chance swallows hard and feels the fear rushing through her body again.

She doesn't see his hand reach out and grab her neck. He squeezes. "I'll tell you that if it wasn't for my boss—your boss, our boss— I'd kill you right now. I'd take out my knife and gut you like I'd gut an animal."

Chance is now straining for breath.

"Your story is interesting. Your spunk is appealing. But do not ever threaten me again."

Chance's face is starting to burn from lack of oxygen. She wonders how long it would take for him to strangle her to death.

But he turns her loose and sits back on the bench of the van and crosses his legs. He pauses for emphasis.

"Now that we have an understanding, sit back and enjoy the ride. When we get to where you're going, your new home, you can use that passion to kill and multiply it. We are better than anyone at finding recruits like you who will carry out our mission. All you need to do is stay in line and obey. Remember, my name is Black Thunder."

He becomes quiet and seems to go to a different zone. He does not speak again for the rest of the ride.

The van pulls up to a secluded place where a small airplane waits.

Chance's captor puts duct tape over her mouth again and places a black sack over her head. He takes her arm and guides her into the plane, and she feels the plane take off—destination unknown.

Back at the training camp, Romli is as impatient as ever.

"Bring in the next girl," he orders one of his men.

The guard leaves the room and comes back with Nurse May. Her hands are tied, and she is blindfolded.

"Remove the blindfold," Romli orders.

The guard does so and pushes the new prisoner closer to Romli, who is now sitting.

Nurse May looks around the room in terror. Like Paula before her, she sees women lined up along every wall. She recognizes half of them. She feels even sicker than she already was. She tears up as she locks eyes with some of the women.

She looks back at Romli, who is not happy.

"What's your name?" he asks.

She clenches her jaw, trying to hold back her tears.

"What is your name?" Romli asks, impatiently.

"My name is Tonya May," she whispers.

Romli demands that she speak up. "I've already had my patience tested today."

Nurse May clears her throat and answers again, a bit louder. "My name is Tonya May."

"Good," Romli says. "Now, Tonya, look around the room again."

She does. Her heart sinks looking at the women she recognizes from the prison. She looks at the guards, all with weapons in their hands. She looks up at the ceiling, down at the floor, then back at Romli.

"What is this?" she asks in a shaky voice. "Where am I?"

Romli doesn't answer. He gets up from his chair and walks closer to May.

"I think you know," Romli answers. "I think you can pretty much figure out where you are and what you're doing here."

He stares at her, then sits back down.

"Unfortunately, one of the young ladies who traveled with you is dead."

Tonya gasps.

"The young lady who is still alive, for now, has begun the first phase of being a part of our team. And yes, you, Tonya, will now enter that phase, as well."

"Please let me go," Tonya pleads.

Romli sighs. "That's not possible," he says, his voice grim. "You can either stand here and whine or you can embrace this moment as an opportunity to become a more disciplined and powerful person. I'd say the choice is up to you, but it is not. The choice is up to me, and you will obey."

The nurse is speechless. She looks around the room once more. The women look like robots. They are all holding guns, and they're dressed like terrorists.

She turns back to Romli. "I can't." She starts to cry. "What do you want from me?"

Romli just stares at her. "Right now, I want you to prepare yourself to run, to run as fast as you can and as far as you can. Do not let fear take over. Conquer your fears. That's all you can do now."

Romli orders one of the guards to untie her.

Tonya's arms are limp and weak from being restrained for so long. She tries to rub them back to life. Her wrists are red and bruised. She can't help herself and starts to cry again.

Matty watches in disgust and sorrow, thinking of her own initiation.

Tonya starts to breathe hard and feels as if she might faint. "Please. Please, don't do this," she continues to plead. "I have a home. I have a family. I have a dog," she says, grasping for something that might help her survive.

"Take her to the door," Romli orders. "I'd kill her right now, but I can't afford to lose another one."

The guard grabs Tonya's sore arms. She tries to fight back, but he is too strong. The guard drags Tonya to the door, where she can see the forest.

"I can't!" she screams.

Everyone in the room points their weapons at her. Romli points his weapon, as well, and he stands and walks to Tonya. He places the barrel on Tonya's forehead.

Her eyes grow large, and tears flow uncontrollably. She shakes, and the flush of fear takes over her body.

The gun still pressed against her forehead, Romli leans over to whisper in her ear.

"You can and you will." Then he screams, "Now run!"

She begins to breathe harder and looks around the room one more time as panic races through her veins. She backs out of the door and into the wilderness, still looking at everyone with eyes that plead for help.

No one flinches or reaches out to help her.

She begins to run, but immediately falls and hurts her knee. It's bleeding, but the pumping adrenaline keeps her from feeling the pain.

"Oh, my God! Oh, my God!" she cries, running for her life.

She just keeps running. She stops to look for an escape route as terror overwhelms her. But she sees no safety. She feels trapped, lost, and her emotions are out of control.

She stops running.

She looks at the sky, looking for an answer.

Sweat pours from her forehead. She is hungry, tired, and nearly delusional.

She looks down at her filthy nursing uniform. She takes off her shirt, rips off the bottom of it, and uses the strip to bandage her knee. She looks around to make sure no one is hunting her. The pain from her knee is worse as she becomes calmer.

Tonya May, the former prison nurse, starts walking slowly through the forest, looking for something she can eat. She finds nothing.

"I'm going to die out here," she says out loud to herself. "No, you're not." She thinks she is hallucinating.

She turns to see Paula standing behind her. Her eyes grow wide with excitement, but she is still afraid.

"Nurse May," Paula says as she walks closer to the other woman. "I see they kidnapped you, too."

Tonya just stares at Paula. "Who are you?"

"You don't remember me?" Paula asks. "I was one of the inmates. I came to the medical ward about a year ago after I got beaten up by another inmate."

The nurse leans over in pain. "I … I … I don't know. I don't know anything."

"It's okay. You don't remember me. But I remember you," Paula says.

Tonya looks at Paula with desperation.

"Do you have anything to eat?" Tonya asks.

"No," Paula responds. "I ate the one bit of food I had. I'm hungry, too."

Paula steps closer to the nurse, who still seems afraid of her.

"It looks like we're both meant to stay out here and starve to death or fight for our survival," she says. "I don't know about you, Nurse May, but I'm not ready to die."

Paula begins to be hysterical, too. She tries to take deep breaths to get some semblance of control.

Tonya isn't ready to calm down yet. "Where in the hell are, we, and who the hell are these people? Why are we here? What do they expect from us? How could the prison be involved in a hideous crime like this kidnapping?"

"I'm sorry, but there is no doubt that the prison is involved," Paula says. "Otherwise, how do you explain us being here? That damned crooked warden."

Paula is feeling more and more desperate. "I recognized several of those women inside. I think one of them—I don't know who—helped me yesterday. I woke up last night with water and a sandwich. If I hadn't had those, I'd be dead right now." She looks around and all she sees are trees, in every direction. "I don't know what this game is. But I'm going to fight my way back home to my daughter. I won't die out here!"

Paula's scream echoes through the forest.

"You'd better get a grip on yourself," Tonya says. "Yelling is only going to lead them to us."

Paula is annoyed. "Like they can't come get us anytime they want."

"We just have to be smart," Tonya says, suddenly more composed. "We need to move now before it gets dark. But all I can see is trees."

"Just follow me," Paula says. She starts walking back toward the cave.

"What about food?" Tonya asks.

"I don't know. Maybe the fairy from last night will come again," Paula says, hoping it might be true. "Let's just get out sight for now and pray that someone has mercy on us."

The one-time nurse follows her onetime patient to the cave. They sit on the cold ground, doing the only thing they can do—waiting for a miracle.

Both women are physically, emotionally, and mentally exhausted. Neither wants to speak, hoping that silence will save them.

Paula looks up to see Nurse May staring at her.

"How did you get here," Tonya asks.

Paula swallows. Her mouth is dry from dehydration. "I was kidnapped, just like you."

"I know," Tonya says. "But how?"

"I was in my cell when they came to get me." Paula tries to remember. "I knew the minute I saw that corrupt officer… Reyes … that I might never see my daughter again."

"You mean Chief Reyes?" Tonya confirms.

"Yes," Paula says.

"That crook, that fraud. He took me, too," Tonya says. "And from the look of things, this has been going on for a long time. Some of the women I saw back there … I was told they'd been released. Some of them have been gone for a few years now." She sighs deeply.

"Now I know where they've been." She looks around the cave. "We're going to die."

"No," Paula insists. "We're not. If they wanted us dead, they'd just kill us." She thinks about everything she had heard since coming here, remembers the women back at the camp in their fatigues, holding their guns. "They want us to survive so that we can fight for them. Fight whatever cowardly mission they have. We're supposed to find the strength to live and fight."

"Really?" Nurse May asks. "How? Without food or water?"

"By any means," Paula responds. "Now, we need to stop this pity party and think. We have to find something to eat, something to drink. They must have hidden something for us. We just have to find it before it's too late."

Paula tries to bolster Nurse May's spirits. "Think," she says. "Was there something out there that we missed? Something that we were supposed to see or find?"

Tonya's hunger and exhaustion get the best of her. She begins to weep. "I don't know," she cries. "I don't know."

Paula decides she needs to get tough. "Look, I know they'll be looking for me. They said they'd give me twenty-four hours to try to survive, and then they'd come hunting for me. Well, it's been twenty-four hours, and if they come and take me away, you'll be alone. I can't let you die. So, stop your damned whining and think."

Tonya tries to dry her tears and thinks back to the place where she'd fallen and hurt her knee.

"The ground," Tonya says. "I fell and hurt my knee, and when I fell there wasn't any grass. Just dirt—and a log that I fell on. It seemed odd, but I didn't think about it at the time." She pauses. "Why would there be a bare patch of dirt in a forest like this? Maybe they put food or water there. Maybe we have to dig for it."

Paula is deep in thought.

Both women think they might be delusional.

Suddenly, Paula gets up. "I'll go back," she says.

"You don't know where I fell. I have to go with you," Tonya says.

"Nurse May …" Paula begins.

"Listen, considering the mess we're in, call me Tonya."

Paula goes to peek out of the cave. She signals to Tonya that the area looks clear.

Tonya limps while Paula walks through the forest, looking for the spot Tonya remembers.

"There," Tonya says, excited. "That's the spot. Look, it's the only place that doesn't have any grass."

They look around to make sure they are alone.

They drop to their knees and start digging with their hands.

Paula stops. "Are you okay?" she asks, looking at Tonya's knee.

"Food and water trump pain," Tonya responds. "Look, it's not dirt, and it's not real sand either."

"Just keep digging," Paula says.

They dig until they find a metal box tied with rope and several knots.

Both were wondering how they could possibly get it open.

Tonya starts yanking on the rope. Paula helps.

"We've got to get this box open," Tonya says, frustrated.

Both women try everything they can think of, but nothing works.

Tonya collapses onto her back, weak from exhaustion, thirst, and exertion.

Paula kneels over her. "Please don't die. Not now."

Tonya's eyes open and close.

"Just keep trying," Paula begs. But Tonya looks bad.

Paula looks around, trying to find something that can open the box. She falls to the ground, too—weak and mentally exhausted.

She thinks back to the last time she saw her daughter's radiant face, her smile lighting up the room and Paula's heart. Next, she sees Reyes grinning at her as he stands in her cell, ready to take her farther away from her beloved child. She thinks of Karen getting shot, right in front of her, and how helpless she had felt.

Fear crawls through her body like a million ants. Tears form in the corners of Paula's eyes. She feels like she had the night before when she had flicked the lighter on and off.

"The lighter," Paula screams, her eyes flying open.

She reaches into her pocket and pulls out the lighter that Matty left for her. She grabs the box and holds the flame over several of the knots. Quickly, the flame burns through the rope in several places.

Paula peeks at Tonya, whose eyes are watching the rope come apart.

Paula opens the box and begins to sob.

Tonya can barely speak. "What's wrong?" she asks.

Paula turns to the other woman with despair in her eyes. "It's nothing," Paula says, her voice cracking. "There's nothing in the box. No food. No water. Nothing."

She throws the box down, and inexplicably, pieces of something fly out.

Paula crawls to the box and sees that the pieces are a few crackers. She stares at the crackers and takes them to Tonya. She breaks a piece off and puts it in Tonya's mouth.

Tonya's eyes express gratitude and confusion.

"The box must have had a false bottom or something," Paula says, shrugging.

Paula continues putting pieces of a cracker into Tonya's mouth until she looks more alert. Paula thinks about slipping a cracker into her own mouth but can't bear to deny Tonya the tiny bit of nutrition.

"There was no water," Paula says.

Soon, the crackers are eaten.

"Bravo!" comes a loud voice. Matty is standing over the women. She's standing in the shade, as the sun is setting.

Tonya and Paula look at her like she might be a mirage.

Matty pulls a canteen from her side, leans down, lifts Tonya's head, and pours a bit of water down her throat. Tonya begins coughing violently. But she is grateful.

"Thank you," she whispers in a raspy voice. "Thank you."

Paula takes the canteen and enjoys a long, delightful swallow of clean water.

"Matty, I don't know what to say," Paula says.

Matty cuts her off. "They're looking for you," she says. "Your time is up, and you have to go through Phase Two now."

Paula stands.

"We can't leave her like this," Paula says, looking at Tonya. "Look at her." Paula shakes her head. "I was able to survive, with your help, but I don't think she will." She kneels next to Tonya. "I think fear will be her worst enemy."

Matty lays Tonya's head gently on the ground. "She will survive," Matty says in a strong voice. "And you have to get out of here. Start heading back. They'll find you. If I were you, I wouldn't resist. Your life is about to get very complicated."

Paula shrugs off Matty's serious and stern advice. "I don't care how complicated my life is about to get. I care about not letting this woman die. You helped me. I don't know why. I'm grateful. But now you have a choice to help Tonya survive this hell."

Neither Paula nor Matty knows what to say.

"She's not even an inmate. She's a nurse," Paula says.

Matty looks puzzled. "Then why is she here?"

"I don't know," Paula says. "I don't even know why I'm here. All I know is that I want to see my daughter again."

Matty points her gun at Paula. "Well, if that's what you really want, I suggest you start walking in that direction." She swings her gun toward the camp.

Paula looks at Matty, and then at Tonya. Paula is angry but understands and begins walking toward the camp. She stops and turns around. "Help her. Please," she says to Matty. Then she walks and doesn't look back.

The crackers and sips of water have helped Tonya. She is able to sit up. Matty starts to walk away.

"Please don't leave me here," Tonya pleads.

"Just because I helped her doesn't mean I'm going to help you," Matty says.

"I gave you water. Be thankful," Matty barks.

Tonya tries to stand. Her knee has started bleeding again.

Matty watches her.

"What do you get from this?" Tonya asks. "I know you! You were one of the girls who got beaten up during a gang fight. Your face was so injured that you were unrecognizable. I was your nurse. You must remember me. I don't belong here!" Tonya wobbles, trying to stand. "I don't know why you're here, either. I don't know why any of these women are here. But surely you want to leave this place?"

Matty scowls at Tonya. "Leave and do what?" she asks. "Leave and go back to prison? Look at me? At least I'm holding the gun instead of some prison guard pointing a gun at me. Tell me which prison is better. This one? Or the one I left behind?"

Tonya frowns. She doesn't know what to say.

Matty reaches into her side bag and pulls out a wrapped sandwich. She gives it to Tonya.

"Take this. Think of this as a thank you for being nice to me when I was beaten up. I do remember you. You had red hair then, and it was longer. You were nice. But this is all I can offer," Matty says. "The rest of your life here won't be about giving—or receiving, for that matter. It will be about killing."

Tonya takes the sandwich.

Matty gives Nurse Tonya May one last look and then turns to walk back to camp, in the same direction Paula has gone.

Matty quickly catches up with Paula, who isn't moving very fast.

Tears are running down Paula's cheeks. "We can't leave her," she says.

Matty shoves the gun in Paula's direction and leans close. "We are leaving. Now walk, or I'll fucking shoot you."

Paula looks over her shoulder, but she can no longer see Nurse Tonya May.

CHAPTER TWELVE

C andy hitches a ride to the home of a friend, a woman she used to work with on the streets. Standing on the porch, she can hear screaming inside.

"You whore, you'd better have all my money—or else," she hears a man yell.

The door flings open, and a man wearing a wrinkled black suit and white T-shirt stomps out. He stares at Candy.

"Who the hell are you?" he asks without bothering to take the cigar out of his mouth.

A woman's voice booms from inside the apartment. "Ray, just because you're my pimp doesn't give you the right to question my friends."

Candy is nervous as Ray looks at her, up and down her body.

The woman inside comes to the door, tying the belt on a blue robe.

"Look who has decided to grace me with her presence—Candy Pindle, short for Candace, of course." The woman laughs loudly and doesn't stop.

Candy stands on the porch, looking dejected and holding her stomach.

The woman stops laughing and takes a long look at Candy. "What's wrong, honey?" she asks and takes Candy's arm. "Ray, get the hell out of her. Come inside, Candy."

Candy slowly walks into the broken-down apartment. The woman shuts the door behind her.

"I know it's been a long time," Candy says to her childhood friend, Micky Newton. "I need a place to stay."

"What are you talking about?" Micky replies. "Why don't you sit down? You don't look too good."

Candy brushes a television remote, a telephone, and a hairbrush off the couch and plops down.

Micky sits in a chair next to the couch.

"Candy, why? I don't live in the greatest place, and besides, I heard you stopped sex work. So why come here?" she asks.

"Micky, I'm in a lot of trouble," Candy confesses. "I'm pregnant, and on top of that, I'm hiding from the father—who's a maniac cop. Do you remember that cop named Reyes who used to hang around hassling us?"

Micky jumps up out of her chair. "Cop? Reyes? Oh, hell no. I can't have you here with a cop—Reyes!—looking for you. You've gotta leave. Like, now."

"I know. I'm sorry, Micky. I have nowhere else to go. This cop knows where my family lives, and I know he'll look for me there," she says, pleading her case. "He doesn't know you. You're my best friend. We've known each other since the third grade, and I really need you." She pats her stomach. "*We* need you."

"Damn it, Candy. With Ray hanging around here all of the time, it going to be almost impossible," Micky says.

She looks at Candy and remembers back to when she was thirteen years old and standing next to their lockers at middle school. She was crying because her boyfriend had just dumped her, and Candy was consoling her. Back then, Candy Pindle told Micky Newton that everything was going to be okay and that her boyfriend had been a jerk anyway. Candy told Micky that she deserved a better guy. Micky refused to be consoled until Candy said that the boy was too short for Micky. They both laughed so hard that Micky forgot for a while about her young broken heart.

Micky sits down on the couch next to Candy.

"So, is it a boy or a girl?" Micky asks.

"I don't know. I'm not that far along," Candy says. "I haven't had good medical care." She looks away from Micky and starts to cry. "I'm so sorry. I have to tell you something else."

"What now?" Micky asks.

"I just escaped from prison."

Micky starts jumping up and down, waving her arms wildly. "Oh, my God, girl! What the hell are you getting me into? What are you even doing in my house?" Micky doesn't stop for a breath before launching into another tirade. "Let me get this straight. Not only are you pregnant, but you're pregnant by a cop, and to top it all off, you just escaped prison?" She exhausts herself and has to sit down. "Did I miss anything?"

"No," Candy says sheepishly. "Look I know this is really hard, but where am I supposed to go? We were inseparable as kids, before we got caught up in all of this crap—drugs, prostitution, pimps, crazy people."

Micky looks down and bites her fingernails. "I know, Candy. I really do want out of this shit. I can't take Ray anymore." She gets up and walks into the small kitchen. She pours a small glass of booze. "But I can't get out. Ray, that asshole … if I even hinted that I wanted out … I don't know what he'd do." She takes a sip and sits down. "He beats me, he rapes me, and then beats me again. He makes me have sex with the grossest guys, and they beat me up, too. I don't know what to do."

Micky starts crying, and Candy moves to put her arm around her friend, just like she used to do in high school. "It's okay, Micky. He's a jerk, and he's way too short for you."

Candy starts laughing, and Micky starts laughing and crying at the same time.

"I'll never forget you saying that" Micky says. She looks at Candy for a long time. "Candy, we have to leave here. You're not safe"—she puts her hand on Candy's belly—"and my little niece or nephew is not safe."

The sweet sentiment brings tears to Candy's eyes.

"I have money saved—money that Ray doesn't know about," Micky says. "We're going to pack up this place right now. I'll call a friend of mine. He says he loves me, but he's really just a john. But he'll do anything for me." She stands up and pulls Candy up, too. "We'll leave tonight, and we'll go far enough away that you can have this baby in peace. No one will find us. I swear."

She quickly picks up the phone. "What are you waiting for, girl? Start packing up my stuff."

Micky starts talking to her friend on the other end of the line.

"Hello, my love. It's Micky. Micky Newton," she says in a seductive voice, rolling her eyes at Candy. "I need a favor, baby. Can you do me a favor?" Micky listens for a bit. No doubt, her friend is voicing his undying love. "Me and a friend need a place to hide." She listens again. "No, we have to go really far away, really soon. Like, tonight."

Micky giggles like a little girl—totally faking. "Well, you know you told me that if I ever wanted to stop this line of work … well … you said you'd take me away. Did you mean that baby?" She listens for a long time. "It would be me and my best friend, you understand?"

She listens again. She wants to push but not too hard. "Oh, sweetie. I love you so much. I'll be your baby forever and ever. You are the best."

Micky puts down the phone and starts jumping up and down. "He says he'll be right over," she squeals.

"Let's get on it. We're on a mission." She throws a garbage bag at Candy. "Start throwing my clothes in here."

They pack as much as they can, as quickly as they can—emptying drawers, closets, cabinets, and shelves, shoving everything into a few boxes and a whole box's worth of garbage bags.

Micky looks embarrassed. "I'm sorry. I'm a deadbeat whore, and all I've got is plastic bags."

Candy wipes the sweat from her forehead. "It's okay with me," she says. "I don't have any stuff at all. I'm lucky to have you! Now we just gotta get out of this place."

A tall man in a tan suit knocks at the screen door. Micky and Candy stop still.

"It's him," Micky whispers. "Let me run into the bathroom and clean up a little. Open the door and introduce yourself."

"Why me? I don't even know him," Candy says.

Micky snickers at her friend. "Geez, you sound like a teenage girl. Okay, I'll get the door."

"How do I look?" Micky asks. "Now who sounds like a teenage girl?"

She goes to the door and puts on her best sexy voice. "Come in, sweetie. Just let me run to the little girl's room and pretty up a bit."

Candy backs up, trying unsuccessfully to fade into the dirty walls.

He's a good-looking man, about 40 years old. He acts casual, with one hand in his jacket pocket and a big smile on his face. He's wearing a hat, and when he takes it off, he twirls it around in his fingers.

Candy just stands near the corner and stares at him. His mannerisms are so unusual that she's speechless.

The man walks around the apartment like it's a grand hotel room, then stops and winks at Candy.

"Well, I guess we might as well sit down and get acquainted, right?" he asks in a cheery voice.

Candy sits on the chair, while Micky's man takes the couch.

"My name is Franklin. Franklin Bosler, and I'm an author. So, tell me your name."

"I'm Candace. Candy for short."

"Pretty name," Franklin says with a smile. "I have a character by that name in my third book, *It's Finally Over*. The character's name is spelled with an 'ie' instead of a 'y.'"

Candy smiles a little. "Well, I'm Candy with a 'y.'"

Franklin chuckles. He gets up and paces around the room again, impatiently staring down the short hallway, waiting for Micky. He eyes the garbage bags that Micky and Candy had been packing.

"I take it you didn't have boxes?" he asks.

The question doesn't seem to need an answer, so she doesn't give one.

He walks into the kitchen and back to the living room. He steps carefully around the bags and looks at Candy.

"I'm thinking that we might need some help packing up." He glances down at the black plastic bags. "I don't think garbage bags are going to hold everything in this apartment."

He suddenly senses something tragic about Candy. "What's wrong?"

That's all it takes to make Candy tear up again. Soon, she's sobbing loudly—and embarrassed.

"What is wrong?" he asks again.

Candy cries even harder and spills her whole story about the pregnancy. *The cop is the father. No money. No place to go. Her desperation.*

"I'm scared," she says, finally.

He has stepped away from her. His eyes dart around the room. "This cop? Is he here?"

"No. No," Candy says. "That's why I have to hide."

"I mean, is he nearby? In this neighborhood?" he asks.

"No, he's not around here," she replies.

Franklin sighs with relief. He steps close to Candy.

"I'll get you out of here. You and my love. And where is my love?" he asks impatiently. "What's taking so long?"

"She just wants to look pretty for you," Candy says, smiling finally.

"Okay, then," he says, smiling, too. "Well, I might as well take this opportunity to call some friends."

As Franklin makes his call, Candy can hear a man on the other end of the cellphone. "You bag 'em. We send 'em," the man says.

Franklin starts talking. "It's me. I need a favor," he says. "We don't have a lot of time, so get your team over here ASAP."

Franklin snaps off the call.

Candy grows suspicious and afraid. "Who was that? Who did you call?"

"Just a few friends who can get the job done," he says.

The bathroom door creaks open and catches Franklin's attention immediately.

Micky steps into the room with full makeup, bright red lips, and a tight blue dress that squeezes her busted-up thigh. She's even wearing heels and a scarf around her neck. She smiles seductively at Franklin, and he melts.

Candy is pretty impressed at the turnaround, too.

Micky spins around like she's in a pageant, and Franklin grabs her into his arms, and the two dance around the room—like they're part of a fairy tale.

"You're an angel, and I am your servant," he says softly.

Micky gives him a big kiss on the lips, and they keep sashaying and whispering, in their own world.

Candy, meanwhile, is so nervous she's ready to jump out of her skin.

When she can't stand it anymore, she interrupts them. "Okay, I know this is a special moment and all, but there are at least two maniacs out there—a pimp named Ray and a cop named Reyes. And they're not going to be happy about us taking off."

"So, you told him everything?" Micky asks, incredulously.

"Everything," Candy and Franklin say in unison.

"Well, then," Micky says and flips her scarf dramatically. "I guess we'd better get out of here. "But my darling Franklin is going to take care of us both."

Franklin kisses Micky's hand like she is a queen. "She's right, Candy, don't worry about a thing. I have this all under control."

He twirls Micky again like she is a ballerina, and they start dancing around the room again.

Candy watches until her fear comes roaring back. "Please. Please stop it," she yells. "You don't know what I had to go through to get here, to this point. I can't. … We can't blow it now." She starts sobbing. "I'm sorry. I'm sorry. I'm happy for both of you, but I'm just so scared."

Micky stops dancing and walks over to comfort Candy, who is shaking.

Franklin looks on with an expression neither of them can read. He hears a noise and peeks out the window, further terrifying Candy.

"It's okay, it's my friends," he says.

A hard knock on the rickety door announces his friends' arrival.

Candy is still afraid that Franklin may have betrayed them— that Reyes might be on the other side of the door. She crouches down instinctively, as if she can hide. She and Micky hold each other tightly. Franklin just shakes his head in wonder and opens the door.

He points out to the street. "Like I said, I called some friends to help us."

Sure enough, when the women cautiously look between the blinds, they see a truck with *You bag 'em. We send 'em."* painted on the side.

Through the door, shocking the women, walk three little people. Micky's and Candy's mouths open, but no sound comes out.

The three moving men pay no attention.

The man in charge, Allen, rushes past Franklin and starts surveying the apartment. The other two, Bobby and Steve, follow.

Allen looks into the kitchen and living room, walks down the hallway and into each room. When he returns, his brothers are waiting.

"This won't be a problem at all," Allen says in an animated voice.

"Bobby, you get the kitchen. Steve, you get the bathrooms, and I'll do everything else. We'll all pitch in—including you three," he says looking at Franklin, Micky, and Candy. "We'll all start carrying these plastic bags out to the truck."

Bobby and Steve start moving quickly around the apartment pushing furniture and checking the closets and cabinets.

Allen looks at Candy holding one of the black trash bags. "Lady, that's not exactly how we usually do things."

"Umm, we're kind of in a rush," she says sheepishly.

Allen grumbles as he goes on about his business.

Candy gets frustrated. "I'm sorry, this is an emergency, and we couldn't wait for you guys to show up to get started." Micky stares at the movers, turns and frowns at Franklin.

"How is a bunch of midgets going to pack up this entire apartment and get us out of here quickly?" Mickey says in a sharp, dissatisfied voice.

Candy and Micky, both with their hands on their hips, stare at Franklin, who has started twirling his hat again.

"You look here, lady!" Allen gets angry, but Franklin steps between them.

"Listen, all of you, we don't have time for fighting," Franklin says. "Like this lady says, we really do need to do this as quickly as possible."

Allen gives Franklin a tight-lip stare. "Really? Just like you helped me lose two grand on that bet?"

Franklin swallows hard. "Okay," he says looking around the room at all of the people looking at him. "We don't need to bring up the past. We both lost money. I've got cold, hard cash for you today. Let's get back to packing."

The three midget brothers look at each other and nod in agreement.

"I got just one more thing to say, lady. We might be small, but we know what we're doing," Allen says. "And don't call us midgets. It ain't right. We're little people. Actually, we're just people."

"I'm really sorry," she says in earnest, her voice cracking. "I'm pregnant and not exactly in my right mind, I guess. But I swear, there are really scary people who could be after us right now."

The three brothers look at each other. They're touched by Candy's fear. "Brothers, we better get busy so we can get this lady to someplace safe."

They all hear a sound and fear they've jinxed themselves.

But before anyone can process what's going on, the front door bursts open.

Ray, his pistol pointed straight at Candy, is standing in the doorway.

"Don't you move. Where's Micky?" Ray demands.

Everyone stops, dead still.

Franklin moves toward Ray, but Ray pushes the gun closer to Candy's face.

"I said, where's Micky?" Ray yells.

"She's in the back—with the packer," Candy answers.

"In the back with *who*?" Ray yells. "Micky, get your ass out here!"

Micky peeks into the room from the hallway, with Allen peeking alongside her.

"Who the hell is that" Ray yells. "Is that a damned midget?"

Ray grabs Candy around the neck and points the gun at everyone in the living room.

Micky and Allen walk slowly into the living room. Ray stares down Allen as he points the gun from Micky to Allen and back again.

"Well. Well. Well. What the hell is going on here?" Ray asks. "It looks to me like you're trying to skip out on me, Micky. Am I right?"

Micky shakes her head, no.

"You think I'm some kind of fool, Micky? You think maybe my brain is as tiny as these damned midgets running around here?" Ray taunts.

Allen loses his temper. "Quit calling us midgets!"

Ray points his gun at Allen. "What else am I supposed to call you? You're a damned midget, and that's what I'm calling you. Did you sleep with this midget, Micky?"

Franklin looks at Micky, then Allen, then Ray. "Hell no, she didn't," he yells.

Ray still has a tight grip on Candy's neck.

"Hey, let her go, she's pregnant," Bobby chimes in.

"I don't give a shit," Ray says, rage in his eyes.

"What do you think, Micky?" Ray says, taunting her.

"She's my lady," Franklin says, with an air of superiority.

Ray starts laughing. "Lady?" he spits, choking on his own laughter. "Did you say she's your lady? She ain't your lady. She's mine. She works for me. She belongs to me."

Ray waves his gun around the room dangerously. "I have enough bullets in this gun to shoot every last one of you. And I'd be happy to do just that. So, if I were you, I'd get the hell out of here, unless you want to eat my bullets."

No one moves.

Allen looks at his brothers. They're used to communicating—and acting—without saying a word.

Candy starts to struggle against Ray's hand, which is squeezing her neck tighter.

"You're hurting me," she screams.

Bobby makes his move and jumps, with surprising agility, at Ray. Steve and Allen join in quickly.

Micky screams as a shot rattles the whole apartment.

No one realizes what's happened until they see blood spilling from Bobby's shoulder.

Ray doesn't stand down. "Now who else wants some bullets?" he says, pointing his gun at Franklin. "Is this weird-looking dude your lover, huh?"

Ray stomps toward Franklin, dragging Candy with him.

"Let's all calm down," Franklin says. "Put the gun down, and let Candy go. We need to get Bobby to the hospital."

Ray throws Candy to the floor and sticks his gun in Franklin's face. "You're giving orders, now? I don't think so." He shakes his head and the gun in tandem. "You think you're the first guy to fall in love with a whore."

Ray scowls at Franklin, pushing the gun deep into his jaw.

"No!" Micky screams. "Ray, stop!"

Allen and Steve are on the ground, holding towels to their brother's shoulder.

"Hey, tough guy with a gun, put that gun down and come fight like a man," Allen says.

Ray starts laughing. "There's only two men in this room—and I'm the only one with a gun—and three damned midgets."

The sound of a gun cocking cuts through the noisy room.

A man, well above six feet tall, stands behind Ray and is pointing a gun right at his head.

"I'll take that gun," he tells Ray.

Ray knows when he's beat. He holds the pistol up high over his head, and the mystery man takes the gun and grabs Ray by the back of his coat jacket. Then he uses his full weight to fling Ray against the opposite wall, knocking over two chairs.

"Now, who's a tough guy?" Allen asks as Ray tries to pick himself up. "Everyone, meet our *little brother*, Sam Jr."

Franklin and Ray and the women all stare at Sam.

They're too embarrassed to ask how the big, tall, Sam Jr. could be related to these three small men. The shock lasts for only seconds.

Then, everyone springs into action.

Micky flings herself to the floor to comfort Candy and finds out whether she's hurt.

Franklin immediately runs to Micky, trying to shelter her from whatever comes next.

The brothers all tend to Bobby.

"Steve, help Bobby get to Sam's car," Allen says.

"What do you want me to do with that guy?" Sam asks, pointing at Ray.

"Shoot him," Allen yells.

Ray tries to get off the floor, but his hand slips, and he falls again. Ray, not going down easy, pulls another hidden gun from his jacket. He shoots at Sam but misses.

Sam shoots Ray in the chest before Ray, or anyone else, can move a muscle.

Allen smiles. "Nice job."

Candy, Franklin, and Micky are too shocked to say anything.

Allen takes charge again. "Sam and Steve, get Bobby to the hospital before he bleeds to death."

Sam nods, and he and Steve carry Bobby away as fast as they can.

"The rest of us are going to pack up this apartment and get the hell out of here before another asshole tries to shoot us," Allen says.

Allen turns to Micky. "You're free."

Micky is too stunned to say anything.

"So, like Candy said before all of this mess started, let's stop wasting time and get going," Allen says. "We gotta get her baby out of here."

"What about the body?" Micky asks.

"What about it?" Allen says calmly. Then he walks back to Micky's bedroom to finish packing.

CHAPTER THIRTEEN

Chief Reyes is talking to himself, sitting in his squad car outside of the hospital. "I bet you're awake," he says aloud, thinking about the prison guard, Mike.

Nurse Marlene Nelson and Nurse Colleen Megan chat on the sidewalk as they change shifts. He's certain that they are talking about Mike.

Just then, Nurse Nelson takes the keys out of her purse and waves goodbye to her coworker.

It's night, and the wind is blowing fiercely. He leans back in his seat so that Nurse Nelson doesn't see him as she walks to her car. The wind blows Nurse Nelson's jacket open as she juggles her purse, keys, and coffee mug.

Reyes opens his car door quietly. He doesn't close it so that he can be as quiet as possible when he walks up behind Nurse Nelson. She senses him behind her and reflexively screams, but she stops when she sees the man behind her is a police officer.

"Well, hello. Windy night, isn't it?" Reyes says, staring at Nurse Nelson.

Nurse Nelson smiles. "I'm surprised to see you. I didn't know we were going to have police protection out here in the dark parking lot."

Reyes continues to smile. "I imagine that a woman would be scared, walking to her car in the dark. But I'm here, the best officer in the county. I've got you covered."

Nurse Nelson drops her keys, and Reyes reaches to pick them up for her.

"I'd best be getting home to my husband. He's waiting on me to cook dinner," she laughs. "Even after a twelve-hour shift, my David expects me to come home and cook a nice meal. But I don't mind. I was only seventeen years old, and he was nineteen when we got married. He's a good man."

"Why, that's very nice of you, Nurse Nelson," Reyes says.

She puts the key in the door lock and gets an uneasy feeling as she looks up at Reyes.

"If you don't mind, I have just one question, Nurse Nelson," he says.

Her hands shake a little as she tries to make the key work in the lock.

"Sure," she says.

"That detective you were talking about, Detective Martin, the one who called about the prison guard? Can you tell me what questions he asked you?"

Nurse Nelson is uncomfortable. She looks around the parking lot, hoping that someone will walk by. But she sees no one. She glances up at the window, the room where Nurse Megan will be tending to Mike. But she knows Colleen can't see her.

Nurse Nelson looks back at Reyes. "Officer, it's been a long day. Could I call you tomorrow or I could come by the station? I really do need to go now."

Reyes leans in close to Nurse Nelson.

"No, I want you to answer me right now," he says, in a voice that makes his request sound more like a threat.

Nurse Nelson is provoked to anger. "You're overreaching, sir. You can't detain me any longer." She speaks loudly, hoping that someone will hear, and starts digging in her purse for her phone.

"I'm going to have to call my husband. I feel very uncomfortable staying here any longer!"

Reyes grabs her and yanks her close. "You need to shut up," he growls. "I'm not someone you want to mess around with. You got that?"

Marlene Nelson starts to scream loudly, but Reyes puts his hand over her mouth, easily drags her back to his squad car, and throws her into the back.

He pulls out his gun, and Nurse Nelson stays quiet.

"Give me that number," he demands.

"What number?" she asks, confused and afraid.

"The number," Reyes says impatiently, "for Detective Martin. The number he gave you to call in case anything changed with Mike Fredmond."

It takes Nurse Nelson a moment to figure out what Reyes is talking about, and then she stutters, trying to form an answer.

"Umm, well, umm," she says, trying to remember. "I believe I gave it to Nurse Colleen Megan. Yes, I gave it to her, just in case Mike wakes up and she needed to call Detective Martin."

Reyes is angry and barely lets Nurse Nelson finish her sentence.

"Call that detective," Reyes says, even angrier. "Never mind, you're under arrest."

"For what?" Marlene asks, terrorized.

"For lying to a police officer," he says.

Reyes pulls out his handcuffs, cuffs her, and slams the rear door. He grabs her purse and cellphone, and he gets into the front of the car. He points his gun at her through the mesh wire that separates the officer from the prisoner in a squad car.

Still holding the gun, he looks around the parking lot to make sure no one's watching. He stares up at Mike's window—the same window Nurse Nelson had looked at—knowing no one there could help her. He needs to get upstairs, but he can't leave the hysterical Nurse Nelson in the backseat while he's gone.

He steps out of the car and pulls his phone from his pocket.

"Listen," he says to the person on the other end of the call. "There's a car in the hospital parking lot." He gives the license plate number. "I need it to disappear. Tonight. Get over here, now."

He clicks off his phone and walks back to the car and gets in. He adjusts the rearview mirror. "Are you afraid?" he asks the nurse flippantly.

Marlene starts to cry and manages a weak, "Yes."

"You should be," he yells as loudly as he can and then laughs.

Reyes turns the key in the ignition, just as another police car pulls into the hospital parking lot. It's one of his police officers—and not one of the crooked guys.

The car pulls up next to Reyes' car. Reyes turns his car off and gets out to speak to the deputy.

"Well, look who's here," the officer says, rolling down his window. "It's the boss. What are you doing here, boss? This is my territory."

Reyes hopes that Officer Fred Pike won't look into the back of his car.

But Pike does.

"Got another one, huh?" Pike jokes.

"Yeah," Reyes says. "Yeah, I do. I'm headed back to the station. I'll see you there."

Reyes gets back in the car, turns the key in the ignition again, and puts the car in drive.

Before he can pull away, Nurse Nelson stares at the other police officer, crying, and mouthing, "Help."

Reyes spins away. He picks up his cellphone and calls the same number.

"We've got another problem. Officer Fred Pike. He saw something he shouldn't. Take care of him, too. … Yes, tonight."

Marlene is still sobbing in the backseat. "Where are taking me?" she asks through her tears.

Reyes ignores her.

"Please tell me where we're going," she begs again.

Reyes looks at her in the rearview mirror. "You want to know where you're going?" he asks. "You're going away to a new life." He laughs, without a hint of sympathy.

"I want my old life," she cries.

"Oh, well," Reyes says, caring nothing for her fear or pain. "Actually, we're heading to the airport because I need to get rid of you quick. They weren't expecting you, but they'll make good use of you."

Marlene cries for miles and miles as they drive down the highway. But Reyes is oblivious.

He gets to the airport and pulls up to the ubiquitous private plane waiting there.

Reyes gets out, just as the pilot walks down the stairs to confront him.

"What the hell is going on?" the pilot asks. "We don't have anything scheduled for tonight."

Reyes explains his predicament.

"That's a lot of fuel and time for one damned person," the pilot says.

"Stop whining and do your job," Reyes says. "This was unexpected. I could just kill her, but we'll both make money off her if we get her to Romli."

The pilot finally nods in agreement.

Reyes opens the rear car door, grabs Nurse Nelson by the handcuffs, and hands her off roughly to the pilot.

Two men walk off of the plane and pick her up and she kicks and screams all the way up the stairs and into the plane.

"You'll get your money when you make the delivery," Reyes says, grinning.

Reyes turns his back on the pilot and the plane, gets back in his car, and starts to pull away.

His cellphone rings almost immediately. "Yeah?" he answers.

His partner in crime—and murder and kidnapping—is on the other end of the line.

"We got the car," the caller says. "It went flying off a cliff about forty miles away from the hospital. There's no way they'll figure out whose car it is."

Reyes asks about Officer Pike.

"Don't worry. We'll take care of him tonight," the caller says. "He's still on patrol. He's an easy target."

"Easy or not, I want it done," Reyes commands.

As soon as Reyes clicks off the phone, it rings again. He answers. It's Warden Peters.

"Get your ass over to my office now," Peters screams.

Reyes doesn't respond.

"I know you heard me," Peters yells.

"I heard you," Reyes says.

Reyes hangs up and watches the plane take off in his rearview window.

Hungry, Jake and Ken are at a burger joint getting takeout and giving some more thought to their situation.

"My mother has lost her damned mind," Jake says.

"I sure can't argue with that. She really hates Jena." Ken looks over at Jake, chomping on his burger. "I can't imagine how she feels about Ted's death … with your dad on his last leg."

Jake puts down his soda and looks at Ken.

Ken stares back with regret. "I mean, he's in pretty bad shape. And let's face it, you're not there for her."

Jake pulls the car up to a trash bin and angrily pitches in his burger, fries, and drink.

"How can I be there for her? I killed my brother, but my mom thinks that the love of my life, Jena, killed him," Jake explains. He tries to calm himself. "We need to get back to figuring out how to find Jena." He wonders out loud: "How can we get that dirtbag Reyes to talk?"

Ken leans back in his seat, finishing off his burger, and handing the whole mess to Jake to throw away. "I think we need to find that Candy chick."

"That makes sense," Jake agrees. "We've got to find her and that Mike guy, the guard. He has to be in the big hospital, the one in Maplesville."

"But Reyes is after that guard, too. Remember what Reyes said?" Ken reminds his friend. "Do you really think this is going to be easy?"

Jake slams his fists on the steering wheel. "This asshole is a cop, and he's responsible for a whole string of criminal activities. Who knows what he could do?"

Both shake their heads, just thinking about the path they've set for themselves.

"We have no idea what the hell we're up against," Jake says. "We just graduated high school."

Ken stares into space. "Man, we're in our first miserable year in college, and I've been shot. Carol is dead. Chance is a criminal. And Jena …." Ken's words trail off.

"It's okay," Jake says. "I know what you were going to say. Jena's a murderer. Right?"

Ken shakes his head. "Until we find her, we don't really know. So, let's find her." He absentmindedly rubs his wounded shoulder. He laughs. "I just hope I don't ever run into Chance again."

"She's in jail. What are you so damned worried about?" Jake replies.

"Jena was in jail, too," Ken points out.

"You've got a point," Jake concedes. He cranks up the car and pulls out of the parking lot.

———————

Candy is in the back seat of Franklin's car, wedged between bags of clothes and other items from Micky's apartment. She's trying to be grateful and patient as she listens to Micky and Franklin sweet-talk each other in the front.

Franklin leans over to kiss Micky on the cheek. She smiles and kisses his lips. Then, Franklin tries to return her kiss with a longer one—and looks up just in time to keep from hitting an oncoming car.

"Hey, cool it, you guys," Candy fusses. "You've got a pregnant lady in the back."

Micky stares at Franklin and smiles. Then she smiles at Candy, in the back. "Sorry sweets. My man loves me."

Franklin grins. "Sorry, Candy. I just can't take my eyes off of this beautiful lady. She's the sexiest, most wonderful woman in the world."

Franklin starts blowing his car horn foolishly in celebration of his love for Micky.

Micky grabs one of his hands. "Stop, sweetie. You're gonna get us arrested."

He seems to be in another world, smiling, and swaying to the music, and thoughts in his head.

"You must be having some sweet thoughts, Franklin," Micky says.

Franklin just laughs. "You're right, my sweet Micky. I'm thinking about what we did last week." He lifts his eyebrows twice. "You know, when I was pretending to be the safari hunter and—"

Micky cuts him off but giggles.

Candy makes a nasty face. "Could you two save the sex talk for your private time?"

Franklin looks at Candy in the rearview mirror.

"Sure, we could," he says smiling. Then he looks at Micky. "But what would be the fun in that?"

Franklin and Micky start laughing.

Micky turns to look at Candy. "Did I tell you that Franklin is going to make me one of the characters in his next book?"

"No, no you didn't," Candy replies.

"You know Franklin is a writer? He's going to be one of the best authors ever," Micky says. She gets excited. "His next book, *It's Finally Over: Life is Filled with Mysteries and Then There's Death,* is going to put my man's name in lights!"

Micky gets quiet, daydreaming of the life she hopes to build with Franklin.

Candy relishes the quiet. She's thrilled for Micky and her newfound love and happiness. But Candy is also terrified for her own unborn child. She is afraid that Reyes will find her, take the baby, and kill her after the baby is born.

Candy thinks back to the night she, Chance, and Mike tried to escape the prison. She was so scared when she saw Reyes shoot Mike, and she was so helpless when she saw him bleeding, maybe dying, on the ground. She felt so helpless.

"I hope you're okay, Mike," she mumbles to herself.

Micky turns her head around to look at Candy. "What did you say?"

Candy shakes her head and tears up. "Nothing. It's nothing," she says.

Micky reaches back to comfort Candy.

"You know you're going to be okay, now that we're with Franklin, right? He's not going to let anyone hurt us, are you baby?"

Franklin squeezes one of Micky's legs. "If anyone ever tries to harm you"—he looks at Micky—"or even you, Candy, I'll kill them."

Micky is stunned. "Baby, I never heard you talk like that." She plants a kiss on his cheek. "I'm so turned on right now that if Candy wasn't in the backseat, we'd be pulling off to the side of the road right now!"

Franklin flushes like he just might pull over right then.

Candy looks behind them, trying to figure out how to stop this crazy train.

She doesn't see Allen with the moving truck.

"Franklin, where are the guys with our stuff?" Candy asks.

"Don't worry," Franklin says. "They know where to go. They're taking your stuff to my place out in the country."

Micky smiles. But the smile suddenly turns to a moan. She doubles over in her seat.

"What's wrong?" Franklin asks, alarmed.

Candy unhooks her seatbelt and takes Micky's shoulder. "What is it, honey?"

"I don't know," Micky says with fear in her eyes. "I just started feeling this sharp pain in my stomach. Oh, Franklin, it hurts so bad."

He pulls the car over to the side of the road. He and Candy try to console Micky.

"No, Franklin, you're gonna have to take me to the hospital," she says, yelling now.

Franklin doesn't need to be told twice. He pulls back into the road and heads back toward Maplesville, to the nearest hospital.

As Franklin races toward the hospital, Nurse Megan is tending to Mike.

She's standing beside the unconscious man's bed, checking his vital signs when another nurse walks into the room.

"You have an important call at the nurse's station," says Megan's coworker, Nurse Connors.

But when Nurse Megan leaves Mike's room to answer the phone, no one is on the line.

Colleen calls Nurse Connors over. "No one was there. Are you sure someone was asking for me? Did they say who they were?"

"I'm sure," Connors says. "It was a man, and he asked specifically to speak to you. I just assumed it was your husband, Chris."

Nurse Connors shrugs. "I'm sure he'll call back."

Colleen agrees. "Yeah, the kids were probably bugging him, and he had to hang up."

Nurse Connors heads back down the hall to tend other patients, and Nurse Megan sits down to catch up on Mike's chart. But as soon as she signs onto the computer, the machines in Mike's room start blinking and making alarm noises.

Nurse Megan immediately rushes to Mike's room. She isn't sure what's wrong; Mike's eyes are darting back and forth, and he's shaking like he's having a seizure.

The nurse calls for help, and Nurse Connors and Dr. Charter come running immediately. They all set about checking the machine's readings, Mike's IV, and the ventilator. Nurse Megan tries to soothe the patient by talking to him and massaging his shoulder.

Eventually, Mike calms down, and Dr. Charter takes out a light and a stethoscope to check Mike's eyes, heart, and lungs. The nurses reset the machines and make sure that Mike's vital signs are back to normal.

Then, as suddenly as the machines had gone off, Mike's eyes open.

Dr. Charter gets closer to his patient. "Welcome back," the doctor says. "If you can hear me, Mike, will you blink your eyes one time."

Mike does.

"Try to move your hands and legs a little bit," the doctor instructs.

Mike doesn't move.

"Okay, blink one time if you cannot move your arms and legs," Dr. Charter says.

Mike blinks and looks frightened.

"It's okay," Dr. Charter says. "You're fine. We're here for you. You've been in a coma, so your body's just getting used to being awake. This machine over here has been helping you breathe. Once we know you can breathe on your own, we'll take that tube out for you."

Mike looks at each nurse and then the doctor.

"You're awake, and that's a good sign. We'll have more good signs in the next day or two," Dr. Charter says.

"Why don't you just try to relax and get some rest," Nurse Megan tells Mike. "One of us will be close by, and we'll check on you often."

The doctor and nurses go into the hallway to talk.

"It's good that he's awake. But we need to keep a close eye on him," Dr. Charter says. "He should be a little better each day. Make sure to look for signs of movement, keep checking his vital signs, and I'll order some blood work to make sure we're not missing something."

The doctor makes a note of the tests he wants done.

"Does he have any family?" Dr. Charter asks Colleen.

"No family that I know about," Megan says. "Nurse Nelson has spent more time with him, but she's gone for the night. I can give her a call and find out if she knows anything more."

"He came in alone by ambulance, and we haven't been given any official information. And, of course, he couldn't tell us anything himself. We've all just been trying to keep him alive," adds Nurse Connors.

The doctor nods. "Understood. But we need to find out if he has any family that should be notified."

"I'll get right on it," Nurse Megan says.

Colleen returns to the nursing station, but the phone rings before she can call Nurse Nelson.

"Maplesville Intensive Care Unit," Nurse Megan announces into the phone. "How can I help you?"

A man begins speaking on the other end of the call. "This is David Nelson," he says. "I'd like to speak to my wife, Marlene Nelson."

"Hi, David. This is Colleen Megan."

"How are you, Colleen? It's nice to hear your voice."

"David, Marlene isn't here. She left about an hour ago," Nurse Megan tells him.

"She should be home by now, unless she stopped somewhere," David says.

"I think she was going straight home, David. I'm sure she'll be there soon. Let us know if you don't hear from her, okay?"

They say their goodbyes, and Nurse Connors walks up looking confused. "Is something wrong?" she asks Nurse Megan.

"That was Marlene Nelson's husband. She isn't home yet, and she should be there by now. He's getting pretty worried," Nurse Megan says.

"That's strange." Nurse Connors says with a puzzling look on her face.

"I know. It's just not like Marlene."

"I hope everything's okay," Nurse Connors says just as the nurse's station phone rings again.

Nurse Connors quickly picks up the phone. It is the emergency room ER supervisor, Justin Harris. She tells Nurse Connors they are short-staffed and asks if Nurse Megan could please come down to help.

"Well, this is going to be a busy night," Nurse Connors says. "That was the Emergency Room Supervisor, Nurse Harris."

"She said they have an overload of sick patients. They want you to come down to help—"

"I guess we don't really have a choice," Nurse Megan says. "I had better go see what's going on. Hopefully, it won't be anything too bad, and I'll be able to come back soon."

"Good luck," Nurse Connors says.

"Good luck to you. Make sure you keep an eye on our patient, Mike. I hope we hear good news about Marlene, too," Nurse Megan says.

The police officer on duty at the hospital sees the nurses talking and walks over to see if he can help. "Is everything okay?" he asks.

"I'm not sure," Nurse Megan replies. "The good news is that our patient who has been unconscious woke up a little while ago."

"That *is* good news," says Officer Cann.

"It is, but we have a couple of issues," Nurse Megan tells him. "We don't have any contact information for the patient, Mike, and we need to see if we can get in touch with a wife or family or someone."

"Well, I'll let Detective Martin know that our patient is awake and find out if he has any more information about the man."

Nurse Megan nods again but still looks worried.

"Is something else wrong?" the officer asks.

"Yes, my friend, Nurse Marlene Nelson, was working with Mike, and she left over an hour ago. Her husband just called for her, and she isn't home yet. And with everything that's going on, I'm getting really worried."

"We have an officer who patrols the parking lot, and he was around not too long ago," Officer Cann says. "I'll see if I can reach him and find out if he saw anything out of the ordinary."

"Let me know what you find out, please. If you hear anything, I'll be down in the Emergency Room. Nurse Connors will handle things up here," Nurse Megan says. "Thank you, I really appreciate your help."

"Absolutely," he says. "That's my job."

Officer Cann walks down the hall to the visitor's lounge, pulls out his cellphone, and calls the precinct to get in touch with Officer Fred Pike. The police department dispatcher says Officer Pike has been off duty for about an hour but did check the hospital parking lot before he left.

Officer Cann decides to call Reyes instead. The dispatcher told him Reyes was on his way to the prison.

Reyes answers his cellphone right away.

"Sir, I hate to bother you, but we may have a situation here at the hospital. Nurse Marlene Nelson left here over an hour ago, and she hasn't gotten home. Her husband and the nurses here are pretty upset. Fred was the last officer to patrol the parking lot, but I can't reach him, either."

Reyes doesn't respond directly, just hemming and hawing, trying to get off of the phone. "Keep me informed, officer. They'll probably both turn up soon."

"Oh, and sir, not to keep you, but I thought you might want to know that the patient who came in with multiple gunshot wounds?

He's awake," Cann says. "The nurse who is missing? Well, they were hoping she would have some contact information about him."

"Hmm," Reyes mumbles, immediately turning his car around to speed back to the hospital. "Maybe I'd better come check things out over there after all."

"Yes, sir," Cann replies.

"You keep trying to reach Officer Pike," Reyes says. "I'll be there in less than fifteen minutes to see what I can find out about Nurse Nelson. I'm sure she'll turn up somewhere."

Reyes hangs up without waiting for Cann to respond.

As Reyes speeds down Highway 61, going nearly ninety miles per hour, Ken, and Jake spot Reyes' police car.

"Wasn't that Reyes?" Jake asks.

"Pretty sure it was," Ken responds. "And I think we need to be going where he's going—because he's driving like a bat out of hell."

Jake pulls a quick U-turn, and takes off after Reyes, keeping some distance between them.

"I wonder where he's going," Jake wonders out loud. "Wherever it is, it might be our best chance of finding out where Jena is."

CHAPTER FOURTEEN

Starlight. When Jena's eyes linger on the stars, her heart begins to beat like ten horses galloping in the wind. She is hungry for the Earth's magic to whisk her away from the madness that surrounds her—some, if not all, because of her own choices.

She can feel Jake's hands slowly sliding down her body, his soft fingertips gently exploring. He pulls her closer, gripping her so tightly that she can barely breathe.

She doesn't want to breathe.

She just wants to be with Jake.

Every inch of him is connected to every inch of her.

Jake's face appears, but when she reaches for him, he seems to move farther away. The farther she reaches, the farther he slips away.

Pained, she watches as his face fade into the bright stars of the night.

The stars light up the sky, almost like a rocket launching into space.

Jena is curious about the meaning of her life. She takes a soft breath and wonders where Jake is and whether he's thinking about her, too.

"Jake," she whispers. "There is so much I'd like to say to you right now. My heart weakens at the thought of your touch. I'd gladly drift into the universe with you, make love at zero gravity, our bodies woven together like stars and planets."

Jena imagines making love to Jake endlessly. No interruptions. No people. Nowhere else to be. They would float among the stars, her hair floating backward, Jake staring down at her. He would whisper in her ear and tell her how much he loves her.

The illusion slips away as gently as it began.

Jena looks around at the beautiful things created to make her room elegant and majestic. All of this, she thinks, is to groom her into becoming a ruthless killer.

She walks toward her bedroom and stands in the doorway. She looks at the plush red carpet, bright gold drapes. She gazes upward to the sparkling diamond chandelier, then walks to her bed, made with white silk sheets, cashmere blankets, and puffy silk pillows. She slides her hand across the blanket, then walks toward a huge closet.

She stands in front of the closet, opens it, and her gaze hardens.

The closet is filled with weapons, camouflage clothing, grenades, and other fighting gear and equipment. She eyes every weapon and piece of clothing, all neatly arranged.

Sadness overcomes her.

Her heart slows as she remembers how she had beaten the hotel clerk to death and how she was soaked in his blood. That's when it began for her, right after her father's death and her brutal rape.

She was so calm when she killed the doctor on the train—an innocent man who boarded the train one day only to encounter a girl who had shed her skin of hope and changed into a skin of leather.

Jena closes her eyes tighter to battle her pain, trying not to think of the night she freed her mother. Tears begin to fill her eyes. She steps back from the closet, but the tears won't stop. It is too late. All she can see is her mother's face.

Jena slams shut the closet doors.

"Bastard," she screams out loud.

She curses Miles McNeil for starting a war.

She falls to her knees, tears streaming down her face and neck onto the ruby red carpet.

All she can see is blood, so much blood.

She remembers her mother's silence after her father's death, her mother on her knees, crying, her father's blood soaking her hands.

Pain shoots through Jena's heart. She bends over with the sick feeling of unbearable pain.

"Why?" she yells. "Why couldn't I have opened the door and found extravagant gowns, dainty shoes? Why did I have to be reminded of my guilt?"

Jena remembers her mother's funeral.

She remembers reading the letter her mother left, the letter with the confounding truth that Miles McNeil was her biological father.

Jena tries to console herself. The tears slow, and she lies on the carpet, staring at the ceiling. She allows her mind to slip into a happier place, the enchanted night when Jake made her feel like a woman. She felt so loved, so safe.

She lets a small smile escape as she thinks about the masquerade party. She danced in a lovely red gown, and Jake took her into his arms, twirled her around, and swept her off her feet.

Thinking of that night, she doesn't feel like a murderer anymore, just a teenage girl with feelings that live beyond the words of love—a mix of insanity, reality, and something she can't describe.

She felt like a princess in the arms of a man who not only stole her heart but stole every molecule of her body. All of it belonged to him, even her dark side belonged to him—and he saw the dark side and loved her in spite of it.

She remembers Jake's smile, his kindness, and his tender heart. In their private moment, there was no purpose, no world outside. They were lost in each other's existence.

Jena sheds a tear. She tries hard not to cry. She tries not to be weak. But another tear falls and slides down her cheek. But it doesn't fall onto the carpet. The tear dries on her face.

The pain had been a release. She felt more at ease.

Lying on the floor, she thinks of happier times with her parents. She sees her mother's radiant smile. She remembers standing at the top of the stairs, listening to her father tell her mother how much he loved her.

He could never live without his wife, and he wouldn't want to live without her. They would dance slowly and quietly, absorbing each other's emotions, usually without speaking a word, just sharing an unforgettable moment in each other's arms.

Then Miles' face flashes into her mind. She sits up, stares at the closet doors, then stands. Thinking of her parents' love, she realizes that they were whole only when they were together. Apart they were only half a person.

"How can one half live without the other?" she asks herself.

Her parents could no more live without each other than she could live without Jake.

Resolutely, she walks to the closet and opens it again. She picks up a gun.

A voice surprises her. "Your code name, please?"

Jena looks around the room.

The automated voice continues. "This weapon belongs to you. This conclusion is based on your unique body heat. Your code name is needed."

Jena is befuddled. She holds the gun and peeks into every corner. She decides to ignore the voice and squeezes the trigger. Nothing happens.

She puts the gun back in the closet and picks up a grenade.

The voice resumes: "This weapon belongs to you. This conclusion is based on your unique body heat. Your code name is needed."

Jena holds the grenade and decides to toy with the voice. "I don't have a code name."

"This weapon belongs to you. This conclusion is based on your unique body heat. Your code name is needed."

At first, the voice sounds like a woman's voice. But then it becomes Moschi's voice.

Jena quickly puts the grenade back into the closet.

The voice is quiet.

"I don't think I'll be making a code name today," Jena says, into the nothingness.

She is surprised when the voice responds, as a woman. "Your choice. Understand that the past is not your future."

Jena closes the closet door and stares at the closet. She looks around her bedroom and feels trapped. She rushes back, through the living room and to the front door. She yanks on the handle, and the door opens.

She steps out into the hallway and stops at the door next to her door.

A young woman opens the door. She has long, straight red hair, and pale blue eyes. She's wearing a skimpy T-shirt, jeans, and a bandana over her forehead.

She's also standing in a battle position, ready to challenge Jena. She steps closer to Jena, crosses her arms, and stares.

"Get ready for battle," she says.

Jena stares back fearlessly.

Another door opens down the hall, then four more doors open.

Jena steps away and begins walking down the hall.

The girl walks behind her.

Jena passes another door. A young man, about Jena's age or a bit older, steps out of his doorway. He is muscular and tan, with green eyes and sandy-brown hair. He blows on his fingers, smiling.

"Get ready to fight," he says.

Every time Jena passes another door, someone whispers the same thing.

One door opens, and she faces a young boy, barely a teenager. He has dark skin and shiny hair. He says nothing, but he stares at Jena as she passes.

Luis, the young woman living as a man, steps out. She says, "Get ready for the truth."

Another woman steps out. "Get ready for war," she says.

Next, a much older woman with dark, long hair that hides her face stands in the hallway, almost blocking Jena's way. Bright light shines from her room. Jena stops. The light is blinding.

The woman steps back into her room. Her necklace blazes in the bright light. Jena follows the woman into her apartment. They stand in the shadow in the center of the room. They are silent for a moment. Jena can only see the woman's dark silhouette.

The woman finally whispers, "Get ready for death."

Jena pushes the woman hard into the wall behind her. The blinding light shines on the woman's face, obscuring her again.

"Who are you?" Jena demands.

The woman laughs. "I am the reason." She laughs louder.

Jena grips the woman's shoulder and notices that she is wearing a beautiful diamond necklace.

The woman laughs again, taunting Jena. "Tough girl."

Jena is angry and takes the woman by both shoulders and pushes her to the floor. The woman struggles.

"I am the one you seek," the woman says. "I am you, and I am the one who will kill you."

Jena is frustrated and angry. "What are you talking about?" Jena yells.

They struggle, pushing one another around the room in the blinding sunlight.

The woman punches Jena twice in the stomach and once in the face. Then she grabs Jena by the hair. "I told you. I am the reason."

Jena is breathing hard. "You're the reason for what?" she asks.

The woman smiles and lets Jena go.

The women stand face to face in the room, the sunlight still beaming on them.

Jena clenches her jaw and raises her fist, ready to go another round with the woman. Jena lets a punch fly into the woman's face, leaving her mouth bleeding.

The woman grunts. "You're such a tenacious fighter."

She kicks up into Jena's face, but Jena moves away quickly and grabs the woman's leg, wrestling her to the floor.

"Don't make me kill you," Jena threatens.

But the woman just laughs and somehow releases her legs and grabs Jena's neck with one of her legs. She twists Jena to the ground, stands up, and jams the tip of her foot against Jena's throat.

She stands over Jena, her hair blowing in the nonexistent wind, the light shining through her long, thick black hair.

Jena grips the woman's foot but can't move it. Jena struggles to breathe.

"Feeling a little overwhelmed, are we?" the woman continues to taunt Jena. She woman takes her foot off of Jena's throat and walks to the doorway. "Little girl, you have not learned the way yet."

Jena gets up and rubs her neck. "Who are you?" she asks again.

The woman begins to walk backward, past Jena back into her apartment, into the bright light.

"As I told you, I am the reason," the woman says as she backs up, and she vanishes into the light.

Jena struggles to breathe and bends over to compose herself. She straightens up and looks around the room. All of the people she had passed, including Luis, are surrounding her in a circle.

They are all chanting the words they had said to her earlier.

The tall, muscular man shoves Jena hard and says, "Get ready to fight."

Jena stumbles.

A blond girl grabs Jena by the shirt. "Get ready for battle," she says.

The other woman steps in front of Jena and looks angry. "Get ready for war," she says.

Luis walks closer to Jena, pulls out a gun, and points it at Jena's face. "Get ready for everything you've ever feared."

Jena closes her eyes at the instant Luis fires the gun.

When she opens her eyes again, Jena is on a train. She is confused. People walk past her and pass as if they don't see her. She wanders through the train, coming to a place that has rooms with seating. She peeks into one of the rooms and sees a doctor's satchel on the floor.

She sees her former self looking out the window of the train while the doctor asks her questions.

"What's your name?" he asked.

"Jena." She isn't sure she should say her name. "Jena Gray."

Jena watches while her former self kills the doctor. She closes her eyes, ashamed of her treacherous crime.

She rushes to find an exit. She passes people who are, again, chanting: "Get ready to fight. Get ready for battle. Get ready for war."

Jena turns frantically to face her old self. Her old self is smiling. "Get ready for death." The old Jena punches today's Jena hard in the stomach. Jena falls and lands hard on what seems like the ground, and it seems to be nighttime.

There are broken trees around her, and the mysterious forest sounds pique her curiosity about this place—a place the old Jena had pushed her into.

She lifts her sore body from the ground, and a dark crow zooms past her. Jena ducks to avoid the bird. As she slowly looks around, she sees a plane in the willows to the left. It's obvious that the plane is far off course and has crashed, falling from the sky.

The plane seems familiar somehow.

She remembers all of the flights she had taken, all of the encounters that had led her down a dangerous path. And predicted each move she made in her old world. The world where she was born. The world where her parents danced. The world where her beloved Jake is waiting for her.

Swallowing her fear, she slowly inches toward the plane. She walks through the swampy mud, and her feet sink so deep that it seems like she won't be able to pull her feet out again.

As she gets closer to the plane wreckage, she realizes that people are lying on the ground. Dead people, or so they seem.

She stops at one body and looks down to see a tall, slender man. She stands quietly and then bends over to look at him more closely. The man she thought was dead opens his eyes and speaks to her.

"You don't remember me, do you?" the man says, and he grabs Jena's hand. "I'm the delivery man. I came to your house and helped your mother back out the driveway. Remember?"

Jena jumps and yells, "What?"

"I was never going to harm you," he says. "I just wanted you to know that."

Jena backs away, terrified, and stumbles over another body.

He's the clerk she killed at the hotel. He stands up and is wearing the same clothes he was wearing when she killed him. His shirt is stained with mustard.

"Yeah, it's me," the man says. "I know you don't have sympathy for me. After all, I tried to seduce a teenage girl. I'm a slob. A creep. I'm a nasty person, and I just want to thank you for killing me because I'd already raped and killed twelve teenage girls and one boy. The boy was the exception. He looked like a girl, and I just couldn't stop myself. I was going to rape and kill you, too. You would have been my thirteenth victim. I was looking forward to it. The moment you checked in; I knew I was going to make you mine. But you got me, didn't you?" He screams at Jena. "Didn't you?"

Jena walks quickly but carefully away from the hotel clerk. He was angry, and she is deeply shaken.

When she reaches the plane's entryway, she finds another body in front of the broken stairs. The man stands. He is the doctor, holding his satchel. "You know who I am."

Jena drops her head in shame. "Please, don't," she begs.

"Why?" the doctor asks. "Look at me."

Jena's face flushes with shame.

"I was dying," the doctor says. "I had leukemia. I was months away from dying."

Jena doesn't know what to say, if anything.

"That's no excuse for you killing me in such a brutal way, but I was in so much pain. My body ached. I was so tired. I wanted to heal and help people, but the truth is that I had no fight left in me," the doctor explains. "I was going to kill myself. That train ride was going to be my last, but I chickened out. I couldn't do it. Then you came along. The moment I saw you, I knew. I felt death coming for me. And you cut me. You cut me very badly."

Jena runs away from the doctor, but he grabs her arm.

"Thank you," he says.

Jena yanks her arm away and steps into the plane.

Miles McNeil is waiting for her there. "Well. Well," he says. "Look who's here. Now the show can begin." He grins. "Wow, you look sensational, daughter, and by that, I mean … you look like shit."

Jena flinches.

"It looks like you've been in another fight." He tries to touch Jena's face. But she moves away.

"Don't touch me, you fucking maniac," she tells him.

"I do bring out the worst in you, don't I?" Miles taunts her, grinning still. He starts to dance to music that only he can hear. "Jena, do you remember New York City. Do you remember dancing, quite provocatively, with your dear old dad?"

"I didn't know you were my father," she spits back. "And I was never going to sleep with you. I was only there to kill you."

Miles smiles from ear to ear. "And kill me you did."

Jena grows angrier and angrier as Miles laughs loudly at her. She is about to jump at him when her mother steps between them.

"Mom?" Jena asks. "Mom, what is happening to me?"

Jena's mother caresses her daughter's face. "It's all coming full circle, baby. You're going to face far more than you have faced tonight." Her mother looks sad. "The feelings of hate, fear, and love—they're all coming for you."

Jena doesn't understand. She looks at her mother, who is now the only person on the plane.

"When you were a little girl," Catherine Parker tells her daughter, "you were afraid of the dark. Maybe that fear grew something dark inside of you, making you fight the same darkness you once feared. But now you will face something much bigger than you can imagine." Jena's mother is calm, and she steps very close to her daughter. "There's no turning back for you, Jena."

Catherine Parker sighs. "There are no gentle moments ahead. No white sand. No blue skies. No doves flying over the clear blue ocean." She is quiet. It seems she wants to make certain that Jena understands. "What you have to do now is get ready. Get ready for the evil—it will try to drag you down. The evil will try to confuse you, just like this dream is confusing you with complex emotions of love, hate, and anger.

"The evil will try to make you weak," Jena's mother explains. "Instead of running in fear, why don't you stand and fight? Why don't you face all of it?"

She cocks her head to see if Jena understands and points outside the airplane. "You must conquer not only the external world, but also your internal world."

Jena stands still, absorbing her mother's words. She begins to feel strong again.

"Mom, I'm so sorry," Jena says sincerely.

Catherine Parker smiles. "Jena, the time for feeling sorry is over." Stroking her head and embracing her daughter, she says. "The time for resolution is here."

CHAPTER FIFTEEN

When Jena opens her eyes, she's lying face-up on the floor, back in her apartment. She sees the chandelier above her and watches the light bounce off the crystals. She hears a knock at the door and what sounds like paper sliding under her door.

She stands up and walks to the door and finds a thin, folded, white paper on the floor. Jena stares at the paper before picking it up. She unfolds the paper, which in elegant writing says that she is cordially invited to dine at 1800 hours. The letter instructs her to wear the military gear and boots now in the closet.

"Please leave your weapons behind, as they will not be needed," the letter says.

It also says that women should wear their hair in a neat bun and wear makeup and a diamond necklace that Jena would find in the jewelry drawer of her dresser. Men were to be well-groomed with a fresh haircut and no facial hair. The letter tells them to wear their platinum watches.

Jena is stunned by the invitation and rolls her eyes. "All of this, just so I can become a killer."

She casually walks to the bathroom and finds a huge gold-plated shower. She stops at the doorway and stares at herself in the mirror.

She remembers when Mike took her to the shower at the prison—not as glamorous, to say the least.

Jena smiles when she thinks about how she knew he was standing outside fantasizing about her. Yes, she admits to herself, she cared for Mike. They had a connection.

It is nothing like the love she feels for Jake. But Mike would fight for her love if she gave him the chance.

Unfortunately, thinking back to that time also means that images of Warden Peters and Chief Reyes flash into her mind, and thoughts of Mike fade into the background. She grows hard inside and visualizes killing Reyes and Peters.

She shrugs. There's nothing she can do about that now.

She removes her clothes, showers, and dresses as instructed. Standing at the mirror, she touches the red tips of her long dark hair. The red is the only reminder of the moment she dyed her hair red. It was the day Jena Gray was born.

Jena lets her hair fall and picks up pins to twist her hair into a bun. She grabs her uniform and boots from the closet and dresses as the invitation instructs. She opens a small jewelry drawer and finds a sparkling diamond necklace.

She touches it gently and then puts it on.

Strangely, the necklace looks good with her killing attire.

She reaches for her makeup brush, applies foundation, and begins applying mascara. Her hand slips, and some of it smears. It's impossible to wipe off, so she stares into the mirror and grabs a container of cream that will remove the mascara.

As she works quickly in front of the mirror, the sparkling diamonds catch her eye and remind her of the woman in her dream, the woman who kicked her ass and vanished into the light. Was it a dream? A hallucination? One of Moschi's illusions? Her own mind?

The woman kept saying that she was "the reason."

"What reason?" Jena asks herself. Or was it all nonsense? Whatever the woman was, whatever she meant, Jena certainly doesn't understand.

She throws the mascara brush onto the dresser. "I'm not doing this," she says out loud. She takes off her sparkling necklace and lays it on the dresser, too.

She hears another tiny noise at her door. Another note has been slipped under her door.

"It's time," the note reads.

Jena lets the paper drop to the floor.

She opens her door and looks outside, hoping to get a glimpse of whoever brought the note. But the hallway is empty. Nothing like her dream, where there were people everywhere, taunting her with instructions she didn't understand.

She goes back into her apartment, into the bedroom, and puts the necklace back on. She looks at herself in the mirror and thinks she will pass muster.

And she walks out of the apartment, into the hallway, and braces herself with every step for whatever will come next.

When she reaches the end of the hall, a butler greets her. He doesn't speak, but he smiles and waves her to into another hallway with his white-gloved hand and indicates that she will walk in front of him.

Jena hesitates, but returns the man's smile and begins walking. She tries to catch glimpses of the man behind her. When she reaches the end of the hallway, she stops at a door.

The butler steps in front of her, smiles again and opens the door to a lovely dining room. A long, elegant dining table is flanked by chairs that look like antiques. A large painting of Moschi hangs on one wall, near the table. As in the other rooms, magnificent works of art fill the walls, and tables and cupboards are scattered around the room.

The table has eight chairs.

The seats along the sides of the table are occupied. She knows these people will soon become her rivals.

Pulue sits at one end of the table. The chair at the head of the table and the one next to it are empty.

The dashing butler extends his arm to usher Jena into the room, and then he steps back. As he moves, his coat briefly slips open, and Jena sees a gun tucked in his inside coat pocket. He continues to back up and closes the door gently behind him, leaving Jena to stand in the dining room, waiting for someone to tell her what she should do next.

Jena calmly eyes the people in the room. Her colleagues seem to have devious smiles on their posed faces. She stands tall and looks directly at each person.

Pulue stands. "Welcome," he says with a huge smile.

Jena nods her head to acknowledge his greeting.

"Please sit," he tells her.

She walks to the empty chair, not the chair at the head of the table. She pulls out her chair, but Pulue stops her.

"No, not there," he says.

Everyone abruptly turns toward Pulue and then toward Jena. They look surprised and angry.

"Please, Jena, sit at the head of the table. You are our new member, and we want you to feel welcome," Pulue says. "Normally, the chair would belong to Moschi, but" Pulue smiles as he speaks, "obviously Moschi is not here. He would want you to sit there in his absence."

Jena can feel the rage directed at her by the other diners.

Some stare at her with an evil look. Some move in their chairs, obviously uneasy. She looks away from them, pulls the chair out, and sits at the head of the table. Uncomfortable, she puts her hands on the table, but that doesn't feel right, so she puts them in her lap.

"What is the problem here?" Pulue asks.

Some of the diners grumble audibly.

"I will have order!" Pulue yells. "Do you understand? What I say is law!" He looks around the table at each unhappy team member. "The law is for all of you. Is that clear?"

Jena is uncomfortable enough to become bold. "I say, if anyone has a problem with me, that person should address me," she says.

Pulue looks at Jena. He admires her gumption.

Everyone looks at Jena, and she stares back at each person.

"You heard me," she says as she sits tall in Moschi's chair. "Let your issues be known."

The woman named Tammy stares at Jena. Jena had seen her in the hallway. She's the woman with pale blue eyes and hair as red as fire.

"You must think you're important," she declares, in a voice that is both sarcastic and vicious.

Tammy looks at Pulue as if asking him for permission to continue.

Pulue raises his eyebrows, folds his hands and nods at Tammy, indicating that she may proceed.

Tammy is still in a rage. "Here's a news flash. All of us crawled out of dark places. We've all done things." She smirks while fiddling with the tip of her fork. Suddenly, she slams the fork onto the table. Everyone else turns to Tammy. But they don't get up or change their expressions. "I guess that's why people say we are evil. So, you are the new evil force in town, and you're going to show us all how tough you are." Tammy stands and begins to shout. "You're not the only person in this room who has killed for sport. You're not the only badass in this room."

Tammy, clearly making a sport of taunting Jena, goes on: "Look around this table. Everyone at this table is a badass. Soon, you'll find out how much of a badass you are. It will be a revelation. You will feel born again. But trust me, it hasn't even begun.

"Remember yourself as you are right now. When it all begins, you will want to remember who you are right now. You won't feel like this when the darkness wraps its arms around you." Tammy leans over the table to emphasize her angry words. "In your mind, you are the ultimate badass. You've done things you thought you would never do. You feel powerful. At times you feel immortal. You've hated people. You've killed. You've hated yourself. Well … hold off on that thought."

She laughs loudly and continues. "Hold off, dear, and remember my words. Breathe in everything you have done, then multiply it by one hundred million. That's how much anger you will feel by the time this shit is over."

Tammy sits back down.

The young muscular man, Andy, looks at Tammy with his green eyes. He raises his glass and says very loudly, "Cheers. Now that excited me."

Luis, Patricia, and Veronica sit quietly.

Pulue is quiet, too. He is observing Jena, whose eyes are locked on Tammy.

He knows Jena is angry. He watches for her to react. Her actions now will give him a sense of who Jena is. He has much knowledge of killers and fighters, but he thinks that Jena comes from a different kind of darkness. She is calculating, calm.

Pulue thinks that he and Moschi may soon regret their decision to bring Jena Parker here.

He is becoming impatient.

Jena stands.

Pulue's eyes glow with curiosity.

Everyone at the table stares at Jena.

Jena looks directly into Tammy's eyes.

"I assume you think that you made a fine speech. But I found it quite boring," Jena says. "You thought it would make me afraid, make me feel inferior to you, make me question my motives."

The tension between them grows.

"My name is Jena Parker. I come from a small town called Maplesville, where I had two loving parents." Jena steps away from her chair as she continues her speech. "I had friends that became enemies. I met many people along my journey. I've killed. Others, I wish I had killed."

She pauses and thinks of Jake. "My best friend and the love of my life is out there somewhere, waiting for us to be together again, to hold each other again, to make love again."

Jena circles the table. She passes the sandy-haired Andy. He turns to follow her with his eyes.

"I witnessed death at the hands of a coward named Miles McNeil. I killed him. She stops at Pulue's chair. "I would kill him over and over if I could."

Jena walks to Tammy's chair and stops again.

"My biggest regret is the death of my mother. I take full responsibility for her death. I couldn't bear to see her fall deeper and deeper into depression. She was dying, living in a shell." Jena's face grows red, and her eyes turn dark. She leans closer to Tammy. "I do feel remorse for my mother's death, though I also believe my mother died the night my father was killed. I just released her."

Jena is eye to eye with Tammy. "So, let me tell you something ..."

Pulue stands up and moves out of the way—in case there's a fight.

Everyone at the table stands and moves their chairs.

"I'm going to set you free, just like I set her free. I'm going to watch you as you die, as your eyes lose their light," Jena whispers to Tammy.

Jena stands up straight, calmer. But she jumps when ... Pulue starts clapping!

"Welcome Jena to our team." He claps hard and cheers.

Everyone at the table follows suit, clapping and cheering.

Tammy is the last to join in. But she does join in. She welcomes Jena with a smile and a new attitude.

"Welcome to our team, Jena," she says. Tammy stops clapping, and everyone else does, too. Tammy smirks. "I will take that challenge. So, get ready for battle."

"Get ready to fight," says Andy.

"Get ready for truth," says Luis.

Veronica takes an eager step toward Jena. "Get ready for war."

Jena looks at Patricia. Patricia just stares at Jena.

Jena wonders if Patricia would bring death.

Patricia just stares at Jena, then says the words Jena heard in her dream. "Get ready for death. Get ready for everything you've feared." Patricia's gaze softens. "I do believe that you'll find your new life most rewarding."

Jena looks at Tammy one last time, then looks around the table. She confidently walks back to her chair and sits down. Everyone else sits down, as well. They all begin chatting informally as if nothing out of the ordinary had occurred.

The servants bring out the first course, a small bowl of broth, bread, and water. Everyone dips lightly into their soup bowls, as if they were dining at the most elegant of occasions.

Like their exquisite jewelry, the meal seems to camouflage the military attire. It seems as if they are celebrating the killing, that the lavish lifestyle in this hidden location is life itself. No love. No desire for sun. No remorse or true emotion.

Killers.

Jena watches them eat.

She is silent as she remembers the time her father tried to cook dinner, and it ended in a colossal mess. She remembers, as she did in the prison, her father's favorite food, sweet peas. Jena closes her eyes and dreams of sweet peas. Her father loved to eat them on a bed of white rice.

The servants bring each course. All of the courses are small portions.

The soup. Salad. The main course: potatoes, broccoli, and corn. For dessert, a small, delightful, chocolate cake drizzled with strawberry sauce.

Jena stays out of the conversation. She eats small bites of each course and watches every person's gestures and facial expressions as they talk and dine.

She can discern that Andy is attracted to Tammy.

Luis is constantly staring at Veronica.

Veronica would return Luis' gaze, then look away.

Patricia seems to have no interest in anyone, but Jena catches her giving Pulue a very unpleasant look when he isn't watching. Jena is the only one who notices.

Patricia glances at Jena and realizes that Jena may have seen her disrespecting Pulue.

Jena winks at Patricia, and Patricia turns away quickly and pretends to join the conversation.

Jena knows that she does not need to look far to find her enemies. They are all sitting at this table.

But they are right about one thing. This is her new life.

Moschi had given up his life temporarily to give Jena her freedom—freedom to live a different life, a life that Moschi thought would better suit her redemption to rid the world of people who destroy others for their own wicked satisfaction. She knows it is a darkness she has tried to deny, yet her darkness is to combat the larger darkness that doesn't destroy one life, it destroys the world.

Jena thinks back to the day she pointed her gun at Miles McNeil. She felt such hatred for him. She felt such a need to avenge her father's death.

She realizes that if she embraces her new life, she will be giving up her old life—a life that included her beloved Jake.

She has no desire to pull Jake further down the rabbit hole she now lives in. She loves him too much. Jena knows she will pay for her sins by forever losing a love that is unmeasurable and unforgettable. But she also knows that not even death would be the end of their love.

The meal is over, and Jena has been so deep in thought she hasn't realized everyone has left the dining room, except Pulue, who is staring at her with his hands folded.

The dining room is quiet, and the lights are dimmer.

Jena can feel Pulue's burning stare.

She returns his gaze.

"How was dinner?" Pulue asks.

Jena pauses. "It was great," she says finally.

"Wonderful," Pulue says. He begins to get up from his chair. "You may return to your room."

Jena stays seated. "When will I be given my first assignment?" she asks eagerly.

Pulue turns. "This was your first assignment. Reacting to the attack from Tammy was your first assignment."

Jena is frustrated. "So, this all about games?" she asks.

Pulue frowns at her. "I assure you, Miss Parker, this is no game." He looks at her to see if she understands. "You see, we have a different way of training recruits than our adversary."

Jena is more confused than ever. "Adversary?"

"Yes," Pulue says definitively. "There is another team. And the leader of that team is not as ... well ... compassionate ... as we are. We care for you. We give you lavish gifts and an elegant living space." He looks at Jena again to see if she is beginning to understand. "You are fed well. You are paid and will have a large bank account. We don't think of you as a slave. Our adversary gets his recruits a different way than we do. Everything is different there. We bid for the same assignments. Our recruits are skilled. Their recruits are savages. We try not to battle each other."

Pulue takes a sip of water, then goes on: "The bad blood between Moschi and Romli has gotten worse over the years. Moschi once worked for Romli. Their relationship ended badly, and Moschi decided to create his own elite team. Each one of you, me included, was handpicked by Moschi. He is highly skilled in every kind of espionage and espionage training. We don't throw our recruits into the world to kill for us. We make sure you fully understand our mission."

Things are beginning to make sense to Jena, and she nods.

"We want you to have the tools a prestigious killer needs: skills, battle techniques, how to harness the power of the mind, physical strength. You must understand the structure of our team. You must understand that loyalty and trust must be earned and must come first, even before self."

Pulue pauses again so that Jena can absorb the weight of what he is saying. "We have to ensure that you stand for the same things we stand for. You must prove yourself in many challenging ways. Tonight's dinner was just one way. One of hundreds of drills and tests."

Jena is laser-focused on Pulue now, no longer daydreaming about the good days or the bad days.

"Moschi obviously saw something in you that makes him think that you can develop these qualities. I'm sure he did, otherwise he would never have agreed to let you come here. We expect our people to achieve their greatest potential." Pulue relaxes his shoulders and takes a deep breath. "I hope that provides you with some insight into why you are here. If you have no other questions, I recommend that you return to your room and get as much rest as possible."

Pulue turns and begins to walk away.

Jena stands, too. "Who will we be asked to kill?" she asks as Pulue is leaving.

He turns toward her, patiently. "Our assignments come from all countries, all around the world. We help people who want to rid themselves of those who get in their way. We don't ask questions. We get paid, and we kill."

Jena steps away from her chair. "What about my freedom?"

Pulue turns around once again. "What freedom? Freedom is for birds. Life is about doing or dying." He walks toward the door and tells her, without facing her, "And please ensure that you create a code name. The name 'Jena Parker' will no longer exist after tonight."

Pulue leaves, the door closing behind him.

Jena understands a great deal more than she did a few hours before, but she is still puzzled. She wonders whether Moschi made a mistake in choosing her.

Yes, she has killed. But she has killed out of necessity and to satisfy her own needs for justice and peace. Now she is being asked to kill for others—and the reason might be peace, but it could also be greed. She doesn't think she feels comfortable with that idea.

The maid and butler enter the dining room. They stand in silence, waiting for Jena to leave. Jena walks toward them. The butler extends his gloved hand toward the door and opens it, as he did before dinner. As before, he escorts her through the hallways and back to her apartment.

He waits as she opens her apartment door, then walks away.

Jena calls to him when he's halfway down the hall. "Why are you here?"

The butler turns around. No one had asked him that in a long time. He doesn't know what to say.

Jena walks quickly toward him as he stands still, surprised by what she asked.

"Why are you here," she asks again when she reaches him. "What is your name?"

"My name is Sir James," he answers.

"What is your *real* name?" she asks again in the sincerest tone she can manage.

"We don't speak of our real names here."

Jena looks deeply into the man's eyes, as if to seduce him. He is, in fact, curious about her, even mesmerized.

"My name is James McArthur."

"Why are you here, James?" she probes.

They stare at one another intently.

He speaks slowly. "I was captured."

"Captured by who?" she asks, not letting up.

Now she has pushed him too far. He is angry. But he answers. "I was captured by Romli and rescued by Moschi." Then he abruptly turns and walks away without another word.

Jena walks to her room and opens the door with her key. The mess she'd made before leaving had been cleaned up. Her bed was refreshed, her closet was organized, her makeup was put away, and the shower stall had been polished. Casual clothes had been laid out for her, a gray cotton shirt and gray pants.

She begins to understand the nuances of the game. Pampered to become killers. Treated like royalty to become comfortable with the idea of being an assassin on Moschi's team.

Jena had never needed all this extravagance when she was on her venture to clear evil, but she knows she's a part of something much larger now.

She undresses and showers after the ordeal of the banquet.

She changes into her new clothes and, with wet hair, lies flat on her expensive silky bed. Her hair soaks the pillowcase while she lays staring at the ceiling.

Time seems to slip away.

Eventually, she finds herself in darkness but sees a closed door with light shining under it.

Jena walks slowly to the door and opens it.

She's nearly blinded by the sight of a bright blue sky, shimmering white sand, and a clear turquoise ocean.

She looks behind her at her room and steps onto the white sand. The sand is warm on her bare feet. She sees that her toenails are painted red. Then she realizes that she is naked. Her hair is different; it is longer, brighter, and flows free in the warm breeze.

But she feels different inside, too. She feels peace. She walks slowly, almost in slow motion, toward the vast expanse of ocean. She basks in the light and the warm breeze.

And then her spirit takes off, above where the white birds serenade her. She smiles as she watches them play, swooping and diving in the sky.

Mountains gleam in the distance. She takes a deep breath as she floats back to the ocean. Everything is perfect, beautiful.

She understands that this is not her real life, but at this moment, it is the life she desires. Pure. Free. She looks at the water, thinking that she would go for a swim. She looks at her nakedness and smiles. She is dressed for the occasion.

She reaches down, runs her fingers through the clear water. She stands up and gets ready to dive in—then feels hands around her waist, squeezing her tightly.

Tears come to her eyes as she remembers his smell.

"Hush," she hears, "Don't say anything." He kisses her neck from behind. "I thought I'd never see you again," he says.

Jena leans back, breathing deeply. Her tears dry.

"I missed you so much. Every moment we were apart felt like thousands of years," she says.

He squeezes her tighter.

"Jake, I don't want to leave this place," she says. "I want to stay right here forever."

He kisses the top of Jena's head, turns her around to face him. He's smiling at her, and he is crying. Tears are running down his face. He is overwhelmed with joy. He picks up Jena, and she wraps her legs and arms around him as he spins her around and around. They smile and laugh and play in the sunshine.

They fall into the sand, and Jake lies next to her, staring into Jena's eyes. He leans over and gives her a long, soft, passionate kiss. He stretches out her arms gently so that he can admire her bare body.

He leans over and kisses her lips, her neck, then her breasts. He softly licks her nipples.

Jena moans with desire and squirms a little in the sand as Jake caresses her body with his tongue. He sweeps one of his hands slowly down to her stomach, pressing firmly. Jena's body moves, anticipating his touch in the most delicate places.

He relishes her, fondling her in the most sensuous way, giving her a taste of what's to come.

Jena is overwhelmed by the heat of her longing. She can't wait any longer and crawls on top of Jake. She looks down at him.

But Jake has no expression. He rubs Jena's shoulders gently and looks at her with eyes that seem hopeless. He slowly moves from beneath her, stands, and picks up clothing that has appeared suddenly nearby.

Jena is puzzled. "Jake?" she asks quietly as he dresses.

He doesn't answer but reaches down and finds the gray clothing she had been wearing earlier. He tosses the clothes to her.

Jake gazes down at her. "Get ready to fight," he says as he backs away.

She gets dressed quickly. "Wait," she begs.

He stops for a moment and turns to look at her again. "Get ready for battle."

Jena runs to him and grabs his arm. "Why are you saying those things?"

Jake takes hold of her shoulders forcefully. "Get ready for war!"

She wiggles out of his grasp—and slaps him.

"No," she pleads. "Don't say that. This is our moment. This is our place of peace. We can stay here."

Jena starts to cry. "We can make love. Jake, don't go."

But Jake turns around again and walks to the door that she had come from. He cocks his head slightly. "Get ready for death."

And he disappears.

Jena falls to the ground in despair.

When she finally opens her eyes, Luis is standing beside her bed, barefoot, wearing the same clothes that had been left for Jena, except Luis' are red.

Jena jumps up.

"Are you ready?" Luis asks.

"Luis, why are you in my room?" Jena asks, alarmed.

"I've been trying to wake you," Luis says calmly. "I've been asking you if you are ready."

"Ready for what?" Jena asks.

"Ready for truth," Luis says, walking into the next room.

Jena is wide awake now. She dresses quickly. She follows Luis, and they both walk out of the apartment. They walk down several hallways, to a large open room.

The room is dark, and people stand around the edge of the room. Light shines only on their faces. Each person stands still, disciplined. All are dressed in the same plain garb, but all in different colors.

Jena remembers the room. This is where Pulue brought her when she first arrived.

"Truth will soon begin," Luis says. "Follow me."

Luis and Jena walk farther into the room. Andy walks past them and then takes his place.

He locks eyes with Jena. "Are you ready? This is just the beginning. I heard life is a mystery, Jena."

Jena looks at the floor, preparing for her destiny. She looks at Luis, then back at Andy. To prove her fearlessness, she says in a soft, firm voice, "And then you die."

Andy walks away.

Luis leads Jena to the center of the large room. Jena notices that the floor is concrete, as Luis leaves to take his place in the line of people at the edge of the room.

A bright light shines down on Jena.

The people at the edge of the room remain in place but begin a roar of chanting.

"Get ready for battle."

"Get ready to fight."

"Get ready for truth."

"Get ready for war."

Jena stands still, but the circle of floor begins to rise.

Feeling almost as if she's on a surfboard, she tries to keep her balance.

The chanting stops when the circle of floor stops rising.

From out of nowhere, someone swings toward Jena and lands in the center of the circle. She has not seen this person before. Everyone below looks up at them. She can see only their faces.

The person in the circle is a young woman, about Jena's age. She is wearing the same clothing, but the color is light blue. She has short black hair and a scar on her right cheek. She is holding a pole that must have helped her swing onto the platform.

The girl moves around the circle, drops the pole to the cement platform, then charges Jena.

Jena fights back, and they get very close to the edge of the circle. They exchange hard blows, kicks, and chokeholds.

Jena doesn't know all the techniques that her opponent uses. So, she fights the only way she knows how—just as she had kicked Chance's ass in jail. Street fighting.

Jena manages to get on top of the young woman and starts pelting her with punches. Jena lands a few in the woman's face and stomach.

But with a quick maneuver, the young woman manages to get back on top of Jena. Jena's head and body lie close to the edge of the circle platform. She begins choking Jena.

Jena feels her body go limp, and darkness starts to fall over her eyes.

Memories flash through Jena's oxygen-deprived mind. She sees herself as a child. She sees her parents laughing and dancing. She sees Jake's precious smile and feels the dazzling dance when he swept her off her feet. She sees Ted's fall to his death. She sees the death of the clerk and the doctor.

Lastly, she thinks of Jake. The thought of never hearing his laughter or seeing his face gives her a sudden burst of strength.

She uses every bit of her strength and reaches for the pole, grips it tightly, and uses it to pry her opponent off of her.

The two women lose their balance and fly off the edge of the platform—Jena holding the edge and her opponent dangling, holding onto Jena at her knees.

Jena grabs the platform and stares down at her opponent. Jena can see the fear in the woman's eyes.

Her face screams what her lips cannot: "Please don't let me die."

But it is too late. The darkness has overcome Jena. She stares down and sees only Miles McNeil's face, the clerk's face, and Mary's face when she unleashed her wrath, saving Moschi's life.

Jena knew nothing could stop this moment. She glares at the woman.

"You go and tell them I'm coming for them," Jena says before swinging her legs hard enough to send the woman flying into the cement floor below.

Jena gathers her strength and pulls herself back up to the high center platform while trying to catch her breath. She sees the bleeding body below.

The circle of people begins to move toward the woman.

Jena sits on the platform trying to catch her breath and gather her wits.

As she stands, Luis jumps onto the platform and kicks Jena in the face. Blood spurts from Jena's mouth.

"What are doing?" Jena says, trying to speak through her bloody mouth.

"Showing you truth," Luis says, while managing two kicks to Jena's stomach.

Jena falls to her knees.

Andy enters the platform.

He's yelling, "Get ready to fight," while he kicks Jena again and again.

Jena tries to stand, to repel Andy, but she is too weak. Again, anger fuels her. She kicks Andy in the face, knocking out one of his teeth.

Andy begins to pound her face, but soon Veronica enters the circle.

"Get ready for war," Veronica shouts.

One of Jena's eyes is swollen shut. Her lips are bleeding and swollen. She can't feel the other side of her face. She thinks that one of her arms and probably some of her ribs are broken. She can barely breathe.

People around her are a blur. A man walks up to her as she lies on the floor.

"Stop," he says faintly.

He moves closer to Jena and leans down to her.

Moschi.

Jena has little energy to speak. But she must. "You lied to me. You said this was my destiny."

Moschi has a gun and points it at Jena. He leans even lower to whisper in her ear: "This is your destiny. You have to die in order to live."

Bloody tears stream from Jena's eyes. She is in pain—pain in her body and pain in her spirit. She manages a few last words. "I'll kill you, Moschi. I'll kill …."

Moschi rises and shoots Jena before she can finish her words. "I hope so Jena. I hope so," Moschi says as Jena fades away.

Moschi looms over Jena's body, along with Luis, Veronica, and Andy—plus Tammy and Patricia.

Moschi orders everyone to leave the room, except Veronica and Patricia. He tells them to undress Jena, then drag her into the woods.

"Phase Two begins," Moschi says.

Moschi leaves the room.

The women undress Jena and carry her out of the room. She's wearing only her bra and underwear, and blood is dripping from multiple bullet wounds.

The woods are almost dark. Tammy, Andy, and Luis follow them. They slowly drag Jena's limp body farther and farther away. Jena is barely alive. Through one eye, she can see the three team members walking behind them.

Tammy, clearly angry she didn't get the chance to fight Jena, pulls out a gun. Luis and Andy struggle to get the weapon away from Tammy, as Veronica and Patricia keep dragging Jena through the mud.

Jena has no feeling in her body as she is pulled through the woods. She can make out the blur of Luis and Andy still wrestling Tammy—trying to keep her from shooting Jena.

The gun fires into the air as they continue to struggle.

Jena blinks, and then she sees, feels, and hears nothing at all.

CHAPTER SIXTEEN

The siren screams and the lights flash as Reyes' police car speeds down the road, as if it were racing the wind. The tires slide on the pavement, splashes of rainwater shooting from the wheels. Reyes concentrates on keeping the car on the road while driving as fast he can now that he knows, from Officer Cann, that prison guard Mike Fredmond is awake.

Reyes cuts through the lanes, passing cars, and running stoplights.

Following fast behind him, Jake, driving, and Ken, riding shotgun, try to keep up with Reyes without being noticed.

As Reyes speeds down the road, his cellphone rings. Warden Peters' name flashes on the display. Reyes ignores the phone and keeps his eyes on the road.

"Asshole," Reyes yells at the phone. "Like I have the time to deal with his shit."

Reyes waits for the phone to stop ringing, then he picks it up and dials. When the man on the other end answers, Reyes tells him to get rid of the "cargo."

"You want to kill her?" the man on the other end asks. "Even after you took her all the way out to the airport, you want to kill that nurse— Nurse Nelson, is that her name?"

"You heard me!" Reyes yells back. "Get a message to the pilot and tell him to get rid of her. That jackass, Peters, is on my back." He clicks off his phone and throws it down on the seat next to him.

He peeks at the rearview mirror before pulling into the hospital parking lot.

Jake tries to be patient and keep his distance but stays on Reyes' tail.

"Why is he going to the hospital?" Jake asks Ken.

"Maybe he's sick," Ken replies.

"We couldn't get that lucky," Jake says. "But he's sick, all right, he's a psychopath."

Jake looks at Ken, "Keep it together, buddy. I know you're tired."

"Don't worry about me. I'm here for you. I'm all in," Ken says.

Reyes drives to the back of the hospital, where he can hide his police cruiser in the dark.

Jake watches as he pulls into the other side of the hospital.

"I hope we can see where Reyes is going from here," Ken says.

"We can't afford to let him see *us*," Jake responds, smirking. "I mean, the hospital is only two stories tall. How far can he get?"

Reyes sits parked in a dark spot behind the hospital. He catches a glimpse of himself in the rearview mirror—his eyes make him look like a crazy person. He'll need to turn on the charm once he's inside.

He looks around the dark parking lot, grabs his phone, and gets out of the car. He checks the area again before walking into the hospital.

"We're gonna have to go inside. Obviously, he's not coming around to the front," Ken says.

Jake agrees, and—like Reyes—they take a good look around the main hospital parking lot, then get out of the car, and head into the hospital.

Nurse Colleen Megan arrives in the Emergency Department to find only a few people waiting, but she's immediately called into the room where Micky is crying in excruciating pain.

"Please, please help me," Micky cries. "I don't know what's wrong."

Meanwhile, Franklin and Candy are pacing in the waiting room. Franklin is impatient and keeps demanding that the receptionist tell him something about Micky.

The receptionist is watching the news on the overhead television.

"Excuse me," Franklin says tersely.

The clerk doesn't look at him.

"Excuse me, Miss," Franklin asks again.

"Mrs. Samuel," the receptionist corrects him with a dismissive stare, until she finally says, unhelpful at best, "Can I help you?"

"My lady is back there in severe pain," Franklin says, pointing toward the patient rooms. "I need to see her." He starts to choke up and even sheds a tear. "She's hurting."

Candy lays a hand on Franklin's arm and tries to console him. She decides to see if she can make headway with the receptionist.

"Ma'am, the woman back there, she's my best friend. We're both very concerned about her," Candy says.

Mrs. Samuel frowns. "Sir, is she your wife?"

Franklin looks at Candy, unsure what to say. "No, she's not my wife, but she's going to be."

Mrs. Samuel purses her lips and raises her eyebrows.

"Well, 'going to be' is not the same as actually being married," she replies curtly. "We can only give information to a relative or spouse—and neither of you falls into that category."

Franklin is about to lose his temper. He paces back and forth more frantically.

The receptionist does her best to ignore him.

He stomps to the desk again. "Are you insane, lady? I mean, you saw us bring her in. You heard her call me 'baby.' I filled out the paperwork. And I made the payment! Why can't we see her?"

The receptionist stands up. Her appearance surprises them. She is at least six feet tall and stout. Franklin's eyes follow her as she stands.

"I'll tell you why you can't see her—because … you're … not … her husband," she says, squinting at him with suspicion. "For all I know, you could be the one who hurt her."

Franklin's face turns red. "Oh, for sure, that makes sense." He looks at Candy. "She calls me 'baby.' I pay her bills. And maybe I'm the one that hurt her?" He gets more and more wound up, even threatening. "I'm putting this in my next book. There's going to be a damned receptionist at the damned hospital who won't let an upstanding man, such as myself, see his true love." He points at the receptionist and shakes it. "You are going to fit that part very well."

Candy tries again to make some headway with the receptionist. "Ma'am, I'm pregnant."

Mrs. Samuel looks at Franklin. "I hope not by him."

"No, ma'am," Candy says, ignoring the rude remark. "Micky is my best and only friend in the world. We really just want to know how she's doing. She's in a lot of pain, and we just want to make sure she's okay."

The receptionist looks at Candy sympathetically but says nothing.

"Franklin is wonderful to her," Candy says, still trying to curry favor. "I know he's showing his temper, but have you ever had a man who loved you so much that he'd do anything for you?"

Franklin looks apologetic, and a tear falls from his eye again.

Mrs. Samuel appears to soften up a bit.

"Can you believe he's paid the hospital bill?" Candy continues. "Those bills are expensive."

"That's no lie," the reception says, finally. "I work here, and I can't pay my hospital bills."

She begins telling Candy her story. Candy nods. She knows that people open up to strangers sometimes, and she hopes it might help their case.

"You know, I had a man once who I thought loved me. I did everything for him. I worked two jobs, cooked him dinner every night," she shakes her head. "I even let his grumpy old mother move in with us."

The receptionist chokes up a little, and Candy nods sympathetically.

"I changed her bed—you know what I mean?—four or five times a day while he just sat and played video games. But I didn't complain. I loved him, and I thought he loved me."

Franklin and Candy exchange a look but keep listening.

"But one day I came home from work early, to surprise him. I opened the door and there was a woman cooking in my kitchen, acting like all those pots and pans and such belonged to her!" She shakes her head. "I couldn't believe it. Of all the places she could be, she was in my kitchen. And him? He was on the couch, with his shirt and pants off, covered with nothing but my mother's old afghan.

"I slammed the door so hard it might have broken the hinges," she goes on. "He jumps up, grabs the afghan to cover his privates, and starts going on about how she was his friend, but that girl was no older than twenty, maybe twenty-five years old."

She slams her hands on the counter. "I asked him if he took me for a fool. Well, I saw him trying to come up with another lie, but I wasn't having it. Not a bit. So, I ask him why he's naked. He says he's just *relaxing* while he waits for me to come home."

Franklin and Candy look at each other, wondering how long this story is going to go on.

"My heart was broken," she says. "I went into the kitchen and shoved that slut into the living room. Then, I went into the kitchen and picked up every pan and dish of food and started throwing it at them."

Candy thinks this really will make a great chapter in Franklin's next book.

"I grabbed a long spoon from the kitchen, and I went crazy. I just started beating them with that spoon until I beat them completely out of the house."

With sympathetic sighs, Candy nods.

"Then his mother started calling for help. I was so mad. I went into her room, put her into a wheelchair, and wheeled her right out the door after them." Mrs. Samuel shakes her head and zones out, remembering how she had been betrayed.

Finally, she looks at Franklin with more sympathy. "I guess you are a good man."

She pats Candy's hand. "I'll go check on your friend."

Candy stares at Franklin. "That *was* a terrible story." She sighs, relieved. "I just hope Micky is okay." She rubs her belly. "I could tell my own sad story about this crazy cop who gets me pregnant. Now, that's a story you should write about."

Franklin sighs and hugs Candy. "It'll be okay. You, me, and Micky. As soon as we get Micky fixed up, we'll help you get through this … crazy cop situation."

"Thank you, Franklin," Candy says. "Micky really is lucky to have you."

He and Candy are quiet as they wait for the receptionist to return.

The Emergency Department door swings open. Two police officers bring in a barefoot, dirty man wearing torn, bloody jeans. The man is handcuffed, drunk, and, probably, homeless. He is struggling and cussing and making things even worse for himself.

"Let go of me, you goons!" he yells. "A man has a few drinks, and all of a sudden, he's some kind of outlaw."

"Yeah," one of the officers says. "A few drinks, then you stand on top of the bar and try to kiss the bartender, who is definitely not interested."

"Sir, you have the right to remain silent, and I suggest you do so," says the other officer, whose name badge says he is Officer Richter.

The other police officer, Officer Lee, seems to know the belligerent man. "Ernie, just let us get you fixed up, we'll throw you in the drunk tank, and we'll let you out tomorrow when you're sober."

"You know, if I didn't know better, I'd say you set me up because you found out that I was doing it with Sandy," the drunk man says. "Yeah, that's right. I'm keeping time with your girlfriend."

Officer Lee grits his teeth and tightens the handcuffs. "No decent woman is ever going to sleep with your drunk, homeless ass."

Ernie keeps carrying on while Franklin and Candy stare in amazement, and the two police officers try to ignore him.

"You want to know why she wants me?" Ernie asks, slurring. "I am more of a man than you could ever be. You've got a big gun and a big hat, but I've got a big manhood. That's right. I said I've got a big manhood."

Office Lee yanks the drunken prisoner by his handcuffs and pushes him into a chair in the waiting room.

He leans down to Ernie's face. "Let me tell you something, Ernie. You may be my cousin, but if I ever catch you near Sandy again, you won't have to worry about your manhood because you'll be dead."

Ernie keeps kicking and squirming and mumbling in his chair, and Officer Lee leans back like he's going to throw a punch, but Officer Richter steps in to stop him.

Officer Richter looks at Candy and Franklin and smiles, as if he's embarrassed by the whole situation.

Candy feels a sudden panic working through her body. "We have to get out of here," she whispers urgently, grabbing at Franklin's arm.

Franklin just stares back at Candy. "What are you talking about? Micky's still in there, and we don't know a thing yet. Micky is the only reason we're here."

"There's cops all over this place," Candy says urgently. "One of them is going to recognize me for sure. I think that officer over there might have arrested me once."

Sure enough, when Franklin looks at the two officers and their offensive prisoner, it seems like Officer Richter is staring at Candy.

"Franklin, we have to go now," Candy insists. "Besides, Reyes is bound to show up here sooner or later with all of this going on."

Officer Richter watches Candy whispering to Franklin and approaches them.

"Where's the receptionist?" Richter asks. "Who's in charge here?"

As best she can, Candy tries to stand behind Franklin.

"The receptionist is back checking on a patient," Franklin explains.

Richter tries to get a good look at Candy. "Do I know you, miss?" he asks.

Candy starts shaking and can't seem to catch her breath. Now she remembers him. He didn't arrest her. He was a client, back when she was working the streets and strung out on drugs. Her hair was dyed blue back then, and she was ten years younger, in her early twenties. Richter was thinner then. He picked her up several times, and she had sex with him in exchange for him not locking her up. She remembers that he was kind of rough and left bruises on her arms. That was when Candy still had a pimp before Reyes took her in and got her pregnant before he accused her of killing her pimp because he wanted to have something to hold over her.

"No, officer, I've never seen you before," she stammers.

Richter keeps staring at the woman. He feels sure he knows her but can't remember for certain.

Richter won't let up. "What's your name?"

Candy lies. "Samantha. My name is Samantha." She turns to Franklin and smiles. "Samantha Bosler."

Franklin's eyes grow large.

"This is my husband, Franklin. My sister is sick, so we brought her here."

Richter eases up. "I feel like I've seen you somewhere, but I'm sorry to bother you."

Candy looks at Franklin and squeezes his hand. "That's okay. It's a small town."

Franklin eyes Candy, then looks at Richter.

Officer Richter stares down the hall to the area where patients are being treated. "I guess I'm going to have to go find this receptionist before Ernie bleeds to death."

Richter walks toward the back, and Franklin yanks his hand away from Candy. He peeks down the hall to make sure the officer can't hear. He looks to the waiting room, and Officer Lee is still arguing with his drunken cousin.

"What the hell is wrong with you?" Franklin whispers to Candy.

He watches Officer Richter walk to the back, He's jealous that he can't just saunter back to Micky's room and find out what's going on. He is fed up and angry with the whole situation, including the way the drunk man is being treated in the waiting room.

Foolishly or not, Franklin decides to say something about it. "Officer, why can't you just leave this homeless man in peace? He clearly needs medical care."

Officer Lee stands up. "And what's it to you?"

"I am a citizen—and a published author," Franklin announces arrogantly. "You're an officer of the law, but right now you are acting like a criminal."

Officer Lee stares at Franklin in disbelief and anger. "I am an officer of the law, and this man broke the law."

As if on cue, Ernie chimes in, "I ain't broke shit."

"Shut up, Ernie," the officer hisses.

Lee turns back toward Franklin. He is so mad his face is puffy.

"Now you understand, Mr. Published Author, this man got shot in the leg because he didn't obey the law." Lee stands up tall, asserting his authority. "Now, I suggest you mind your own business, or I'll put handcuffs on you, too."

Franklin raises his arms dramatically. "I surrender."

Officer Lee isn't interested in any more banter. "Just get the hell out of here, mister."

Franklin, reluctantly, but much to Candy's relief, walks back to the counter.

The receptionist, Mrs. Samuel, meets Officer Richter in the hall before he gets to the patients' rooms.

"Hey, my partner and I brought in a man who has a gunshot. We need someone to see him right away," Officer Richter says.

Mrs. Samuel walks past Officer Richter and sees Ernie snoring in his chair.

"I understand, officer," she tells Richter. "But I need you to fill out some paperwork before the patient can be treated."

Officer Richter stares at Mrs. Samuel. "I don't think you heard me."

The receptionist interrupts him. "Sir, I heard you just fine, but before this patient can be seen, we need paperwork completed. Now, I might be able to expedite the paperwork, but it has to be filled out first." The receptionist looks at Richter's name badge. "It's obvious your man can't fill out these papers himself, Officer Richter. Maybe you can reach a family member—or maybe you'll accept responsibility for him yourself."

"No, I am not taking responsibility for this patient," Richter says. "But my partner over there is his cousin, and I'm sure he can round up a family member to take care of the final paperwork. In the meantime, we need to get him treated."

Franklin is impatiently watching this exchange, until he finally interrupts. "I'm sorry, officer. But I was really hoping that Mrs. Samuel could give me some information about Miss Micky Newton."

"Oh, yes, your girlfriend," the receptionist says.

Officer Richter looks at Franklin, puzzled.

Candy, standing back at the counter, is practically jumping up and down with nervousness because her ruse is about to be discovered.

Franklin realizes the problem and tries to cover it. "Mrs. Samuel, well, I'm sorry, I must have misspoken earlier. Micky is my sister-in-law."

The receptionist shakes her head. "Huh?"

Officer Richter looks back at Candy, who is pacing in circles and holding her belly. His suspicions are renewed.

Just then, the radio on Officer Richter's hip starts going off. "Officer Richter. Officer Richter, please pick up."

He does, and the dispatcher proceeds to tell him he's needed at home urgently.

"Your wife, Judy, called," the dispatcher. "She called 911 and said she was afraid that someone was trying to break into your house. She's been trying to call your cellphone, but she couldn't reach you."

Richter reaches into his pocket and realizes that he left his phone in the squad car.

"We've dispatched a car to check things out," the operator says.

"Copy," Richter says. "I'm on my way."

Richter takes one last look at Candy, then starts walking toward the exit and yells to his partner that he has to leave. "There's an emergency at my house. I've got to go. I'll let you know what's going on."

Officer Lee looks annoyed but shrugs and goes back to killing time in the waiting room.

Mrs. Samuel gives Franklin a dirty look. "You said that young woman was your lady friend."

"She is my woman," Franklin says. "But these cops got me all nervous … well … I can't really explain. There's a lot going on."

Mrs. Samuel frowns.

"Please just tell me how she's doing," Franklin begs.

The receptionist sighs. "The doctor is examining her, so I couldn't see her. I'll know more in about fifteen minutes."

Mrs. Samuel walks back to the counter to prepare paperwork for the homeless man, not relishing the idea of arguing about it with the other officer.

Franklin stares down the hallway, worried about Micky.

Upstairs, Dr. Charter is examining Mike again.

Mike's eyes are open, and he can hear and see and breathe on his own, but he still can't move or talk—even though the breathing tube had been removed.

"Just continue to blink once for yes and two for no," Dr. Charter says.

Nurse Connors is watching the examination. "Mike, we're trying to locate your family. Is there someone we can call for you?"

Dr. Charter and Nurse Conner wait for Mike to respond, but he doesn't blink.

Mike is thinking about how Chief Reyes shot him several times. He remembers Candy running. He remembers that the warden caught Chance, so she is probably locked up or dead. No, Mike thinks, as he thinks of Jena, too. No, he doesn't want any of his family to be involved in this violent mess. He stares into the distance.

"Mike," Dr. Charter says. "Michael, right? Do you know who shot you?"

Mike doesn't respond.

"Nurse Nelson, the nurse who took care of you for a couple of days," the doctor says, watching for a reaction and getting none, "she spoke to Detective Martin about your case. And one of the officers here contacted Detective Martin to tell him that you are awake." The doctor appears confused about why Mike is not responding. "Detective Martin, or someone from his team, may come to question you. Is that okay?"

Mike just stares at Dr. Charter, not blinking a yes or a no.

"Well, we'll just leave you to rest and come back to talk to you another time," the doctor says, shrugging and looking toward Nurse Connors.

She nods that she will join the doctor in the hallway shortly. She checks Mike's vital signs, tucks his blanket around him, and squeezes Mike's hand in a gesture of comfort.

Outside the room, Dr. Charter tells Nurse Connors to contact Detective Martin.

"He's already been contacted," Nurse Connors replies. "Officer Cann told Nurse Megan than he would do it."

Dr. Charter nods. "Start trying to feed our patient. But make sure he can tolerate it before you give him much."

"Yes, Dr. Charter." Nurse Connors replies.

"I will back within an hour." Dr. Charter's says.

He walks away with his head down, reading the notes for his next patient.

Chief Reyes is watching and listening, too, as he walks around the first floor. He passes some staff and a security guard, but no one paid him any attention. Reyes moves swiftly, briefing staring back to ensure they notice him. He walks by the first-floor nurse's station, and a nurse asks if she can help him.

"I'm fine," he says. "I'm just here to check on a patient."

"Did you pass one of the security guards on your way in?" the nurse asks. "They're supposed to be making sure the media doesn't get wind of that patient, Mike, the prison guard who just woke up."

"I didn't really pay attention," Reyes says, trying to sound nonchalant.

"Well, it's a good thing we have all of these cameras to keep an eye on things," she says.

Reyes looks around to locate the various cameras.

"Are you sure I can't do anything for you?" the nurse asks again.

"No ma'am. You have a good night."

Reyes slips into a stairwell to make his way to the second floor.

He makes his way to the Intensive Care Unit and peers through one of the small windows on the doors. The nurse isn't at the nurse's station. He scans the room and sees the doctor entering a part of the room filled with family members, near the end of the unit.

He pushes the door open into the ICU. He walks quickly past the space where Dr. Charter is working. The doctor doesn't see him. A woman does, but she's crying too hard to pay Reyes any attention. He walks slowly past Mike's room. He stands to the side of the door and looks in to make sure Mike is awake—but Mike has fallen asleep.

Reyes steps up to the nurse's station just as Nurse Connors is returning. She is occupied on her cellphone and doesn't notice him.

Chief Reyes doesn't want to be noticed.

"Which door should we go through?" Ken asks Jake as they approach the front of the hospital.

Jake looks around. "There's the Emergency Department. I've been there," he says.

"Watch out, Ken, a cop is coming out now," he says, pulling his friend into the shadows.

They wait for Officer Richter to leave before walking around to another entrance. At a side entrance, they don't see a security guard. Jake opens the door, and Ken follows him inside. The two friends walk softly through the hallways like they're trained detectives.

"Keep an eye out, man. Reyes is somewhere in this hospital," Jake says. "That sneaky bastard is up to something."

A nurse walking the halls approaches them. "Can I help you?" she asks, somewhat suspicious.

They pretend to look lost.

"You sure can. We're … umm," Jake can't spit out a lie.

"You two aren't with the media, are you?" the nurse inquires, a bit more harshly.

Ken steps up, in more ways than one. "I'm sorry, ma'am. No, we're definitely not with the media. Please excuse my brother. We're from out of town, and we've had a long car ride, and he's a little daffy."

The nurse's expression softens. "It's okay. Don't worry about it. It's just that the local media has been driving us a little crazy," she says. "They're trying to get information about a patient we have, a patient who was in a coma."

Jake and Ken sneak a quick look at each other. Wisely, they say nothing. The nurse who had been suspicious is now downright chatty.

"You know a local man was shot, right? I guess you might not if you're from out of town. He was shot several times. We weren't sure he was going to make it, but he's awake now. He was found somewhere near the prison," the talkative nurse continues.

Jake and Ken look at each other and can't believe their good luck.

Jake pastes on a sad face. "Ma'am, he's our older brother. That's why we're here."

The nurse looks distressed and grabs Jake's hand. "I'm so sorry."

"It's okay. There's no way you could have known," Jake says solemnly. "You can help us. We don't have a clue where we're going."

"Your brother is in the Intensive Care Unit," the nurse says with a sympathetic and worried look on her face. "I don't work on that floor, but my good friend Nurse Megan does. She's downstairs helping in the Emergency Department, but I'm sure Nurse Connors or someone else is up there." She pauses. "I could take you up there if you like. My name is Nurse Foster."

Nurse Foster guides them to the elevator and gets into the elevator with them. The nurse presses the button for the second floor.

———

Nurse Connors jumps when she looks up and sees Chief Reyes glaring down at her.

"My goodness, officer, you frightened me," she says.

Reyes tries his best to look harmless. "I'm sorry to startle you. You seem busy," he says.

"How can I help you?" the nurse asks.

"I was coming to check on our patient, Mike Fredmond," Reyes says.

The nurse is excited. "Are you working with Detective Martin?" she asks.

Reyes nods. "Of course. The entire police department is working hard to track down whoever is responsible."

Nurse Connors frowns a little. "I hope they find the person who did it. It was heartless—what someone did to that man."

Reyes, eager to get closer to Mike, is becoming impatient with the nurse's chitchat.

"May I see him?" Reyes asks carefully.

"I'm not sure. He's not awake and can't answer questions," Nurse Connors hesitates. "I don't think it's a good idea."

Reyes leans over the counter. "He's a colleague and a friend. I just want to say hello, even if he can't talk back." He puts his head in his hands and pretends to look sad.

Connors is moved. After all, Mike and this officer are part of the law enforcement community. "Sure, officer, I understand. You go right on in. Just don't stay too long."

Reyes starts to walk into Mike's room, but he can't resist turning around to see the smiling Nurse Connors.

"This won't take long," he assures the nurse.

Reyes opens the glass door to Mike's room and strides over to his bed with one hand on his gun.

That same moment, Jake, Ken, and Nurse Foster get off the elevator near the Intensive Care Unit.

"You have to be very quiet in this area. These patients are very, very ill. Some of them won't even make it. So, we have to make sure they're as comfortable as possible," she explains.

Jake and Ken nod in unison.

"Of course," Jake whispers.

They approach the nurses' station, but Nurse Connors is gone, assisting Dr. Charter with another patient.

Nurse Foster sighs. "She can't be far. I'll go look for her."

She turns to Ken and Jake. "In the meantime, that's your brother's room," she says.

Jake looks into the room, and his face flushes red with anxiety and anger. Ken sees what Jake is upset about. Chief Reyes is in the room, standing over Mike's bed.

"We'll take it from here, Nurse Foster. I'm sure the ICU nurse will come back soon. We'll be fine," Jake says quickly.

"Okay, then. Good luck with your brother. I hear there's a Detective Martin who's working on the case," she says before heading toward the stairs.

Reyes is consumed with rage as he looks down at Mike.

Jake opens the glass door to Mike's room as quietly as he cans. He motions to Ken to follow him.

Adrenaline pumping, they are able to creep up behind Reyes.

Mike opens his eyes slowly. His eyes become huge when he sees Reyes standing beside him. He can't fight back or even scream. He just watches Reyes with hate and fear.

Reyes hears a sound and quickly turns around just as Jake grabs Reyes' gun. Ken struggles to grab Reyes' hand and arm. They hold onto Reyes with all their might, every bit of their combined strength.

Jake manages to get control of Reyes' gun, but neither he nor Ken is foolish enough to think they're in the clear.

Reyes has experience on his side, and quickly jerks away from Ken's grasp.

Mike watches the standoff—Reyes staring down the two young men and Jake pointing Reyes' own gun at him.

"Mike. Mike," Jake calls. "Are you okay?"

Mike blinks several times.

"I'm Jena Parker's boyfriend," Jake says. "You know Jena, right?"

Mike's eyes grow wider.

"Where is she, Mike?" Jake begs.

But Mike can only stare and cry inside at his own incapacity.

"This asshole knows everything!" Mike screams silently in his mind.

Jake turns his attention to Reyes. "Where is she, Reyes? What did you do to her? I know you shot this poor guy, didn't you? Tell me!"

"Keep it down, man," Ken shushes at his friend.

"Let's go, Reyes," Jake says, continuing to wave the weapon at Reyes. "Do what we say, or we'll call your police station and get them out here. We'll tell them what we overheard you say in your office."

"What was it that Nurse Foster just said?" Ken asks. "Detective Martin. We'll call Detective Martin. Somebody will know where he is."

Reyes looks down at Mike, seething. "I'll be back—after I finish with these two idiots."

"Time to go," Jake says, keeping Reyes' gun trained on the police chief. "Ken, open the door."

Ken opens the glass door slowly, never taking his eyes off Jake and Reyes.

Jake motions Reyes forward He walks just far enough behind Reyes to stay out of his reach. Reyes starts walking toward the elevator.

"Nah, we're taking the stairs," Jake says.

Jake gets in front of Reyes, still holding the gun on him, but walking backward to keep an eye on Reyes. Ken stands behind him.

"We're going to take this nice and slow," Jake says, backtracking slowly down the stairs.

Reyes follows along with Jake's plan, but he manages to show Jake just how angry he is, and how violent he can be.

"You know I'm going to kill you, right?" Reyes laughs, hoping to catch the young men off-balance. "What exactly do you two think you're going to do?"

"I just want to know where Jena is," Jake says.

They make their way closer to the first-floor landing.

Reyes tries to get closer to Jake. "Go ahead and shoot me," he seethes. "Shoot me if you've got the balls. Go ahead. Shoot me, I said."

Reyes keeps ranting, and Ken sees what Reyes has undoubtedly noticed: Jake is starting to shake a little under the strain of emotion and anger.

"Shut up, you bastard," Ken says as menacingly as he can.

Ken knows that Jake would rather just shoot Reyes, consequences be damned. But he also knows Jake wants answers about Jena.

Now, Ken has gotten a little too close to Reyes.

Reyes shoves Ken hard enough that Ken loses his balance on the stairs, and Reyes rams Jake like a linebacker.

Reyes slams through the stairwell's first-floor door and takes off running through the hallways.

"You okay man?" Jake asks Ken. "Yeah."

"My adrenaline is a lot higher than any pain I had."

"Let's get this jerk."

Jake and Ken gather their wits and start chasing Reyes.

Reyes sees a set of double doors and a red Exit sign. He runs straight through and takes a quick right to ditch Jake and Ken. He ends up in the middle of the patient care area of the Emergency Department. A few nurses and attendants and a doctor are moving around, treating patients. Reyes zooms past them, not certain where he's going. A nurse has to jump out of his way to keep from being run over.

Jake and Ken run through the door after Reyes.

Reyes keeps running and quickly ends up in the waiting area of the Emergency Department. He runs right past Candy and Franklin and directly into Officer Lee.

Reyes bends over trying to catch his breath, while a confounded Officer Lee looks on. Reyes' zigzagging gives Jake and Ken time to catch up.

Jake points the gun at Reyes out of reflex, and Lee hastily pulls out his and points it at Jake.

"Put down the weapon," Lee orders.

Franklin and Candy see the commotion, but only Candy recognizes Reyes. She hides behind Franklin again while Franklin stares at Jake.

"I said put the weapon down, or I *will* shoot you," Lee threatens again. He takes his eyes off Jake just long enough to look at Reyes. "Chief Reyes, what's going on here?"

Reyes is distracted, though. He has seen and recognized Candy, who is hiding behind a man he doesn't know.

Lee still doesn't have any idea what's going on—except that a young man has a gun that he clearly shouldn't be pointing at anyone, least of all Reyes.

Candy is whimpering and whispering at the same time, trying to get Franklin's attention. "That's him. Franklin, that's him, the man I've been hiding from."

Jake looks in the same direction that Reyes is looking—at Franklin—and asks, "Franklin, what the hell are you doing here?"

CHAPTER SEVENTEEN

J ake looks at Franklin in amazement.

"Tell me what's going on," Franklin says, alarmed at the sight of Jake pointing a gun at a police officer.

Candy is standing as close to Franklin as she can.

Reyes sees her and pretends to ignore her. He doesn't want the whole Emergency Department to know that he is the father of Candy's child.

Officer Lee, who appears to be more confused than anyone, keeps his gun trained on Jake and Ken while he tries to make sense of this crazy scene.

"Put down your weapon!" Lee yells at them again.

Mrs. Samuel, the receptionist, is too afraid to move, but when she can't stand the tension anymore, she panics.

"This is an emergency room, you crazy people! Stop all of this, everyone, and stop right now!" she screams.

Reyes turns to Mrs. Samuel. "Get out of here, if you know what's good for you."

Jake keeps his gun pointed at Reyes.

Officer Lee yells again. "I don't know what more you two need to hear. Put that gun down now!"

"You're going to jail, man," Jake threatens Reyes. "The only person in here who deserves to go to jail is this crooked cop, Reyes!" He yells to the entire room.

Officer Lee steps back, trying to determine whether he can gain control over everyone in the room, and trips over Ernie's foot.

His gun goes off. The bullet hits Mrs. Samuel, who's still behind the counter.

She falls to the floor, and Candy and Franklin drop behind the counter to hide and to see if they can help her.

Mrs. Samuel is breathing hard. Franklin tries to console her, and Candy cradles the woman's head, urging her to keep her eyes open. The receptionist is losing blood quickly, but she looks up at Franklin.

"Mister, I'm sorry I gave you a hard time about your woman," she says, struggling for breath.

Franklin realizes that he should try to get to Micky, who is still in the back of the Emergency Department. He leaves Candy crying behind the counter while an attendant futilely tries to revive Mrs. Samuel.

By the time help arrives, Mrs. Samuel is dead.

Before Franklin can get to Micky, a nurse stops him, and the scene in the Emergency Department has become even more chaotic.

Officer Lee has called for reinforcements. Police officers start streaming through every entrance and hallway. Patients are cowering in their rooms and have no idea what is going on.

Even though Franklin easily brushes past the nurse, a police officer is standing behind her, and he points a gun directly at Franklin.

A doctor walks over to find out what's going on.

"Look, I'm sorry, but I just wanted to get back here to find out how my girlfriend has been doing. I've been waiting forever," Franklin explains desperately. He turns to the doctor. "Her name is Micky Newton. Can you please just let me see her?"

The doctor looks away, while the confused police officer keeps his gun pointed at Franklin.

"Sir," the doctor says.

Franklin wonders why the doctor looks so upset.

"With everything going on in here …" the doctor says, his words trailing off into sympathy. "I'm sorry. I'm very sorry. But Miss Newton passed away ten minutes ago. We were on our way to tell you when we heard the gunshot."

Franklin looks like he's going to crumple.

"We have to wait right here until the police officers get things under control," the doctor says.

Franklin is stunned with shock, but he can't contain himself for long. He tries to run past the officer and the doctor, but they easily hold him back. The nurse he had nearly bumped into tries to comfort Franklin, but he doesn't hear a thing.

An irrational Franklin breaks free and runs back to the lobby, with the police officer on his heels. Franklin drops to the ground next to the terrified Candy and the receptionist's dead body.

He stares straight ahead, but his protective instincts kick in and he scoots to a safer location, pulling Candy with him.

Jake manages to get his arms around the distracted Reyes and puts the gun against his head.

Ken sees what Jake has done and grabs Reyes, too. "Two guys are better than one," Ken says to Jake.

Jake and Ken, with Reyes, back slowly away from Officer Lee, the wall to their back.

Two more officers train their guns on the three men.

"Son, I'm Officer Bailey," one of them says. "We can sort this all out. You just have to put that gun down and release Chief Reyes."

Jake and Ken refuse to answer.

"Don't do this, son," Bailey says. "Whatever's going on isn't worth throwing your life away."

Jake is overly cocky. "I'll tell you what's not worth it," he says, shoving the gun harder against Reyes' head. "It's not worth it for you to defend this scumbag of a cop."

Ken isn't confident of Jake's strategy, but he's all in.

"Now, Reyes, you tell them to back off or I will start talking about Warden Peters and Mike," Jake warns.

Reyes is silent, and Jake twists the gun even harder into Reyes' head.

"Tell them!" Jake yells.

"Back off, men. No one else needs to get hurt here," Reyes says.

Lee, Bailey, and another officer, Officer Rice, aren't about to obey—they can't abide one of their own being held hostage.

"I said put the guns down! Now!" Reyes yells. "That's an order. Back off!"

The officers slowly lower their weapons.

"Now, one of you throw your handcuffs over here," Jake says.

"Do it," Reyes instructs them.

Jake keeps a grip, and the gun, on Reyes, while Ken handcuffs Reyes. Reyes is clearly furious, but silent.

Ken grabs Reyes' handcuffed wrists, and they slowly back out the doors to Emergency Department parking lot

Jake sees Franklin and a young woman hiding in a corner and gestures for them to come along. He watches Franklin help Candy get up from the floor. Ken runs toward the young woman so they can all make their escape together.

Franklin is breathing hard and holding Candy's arm tightly. Candy finally snaps out of her paralyzed fear. She stops abruptly and looks at Franklin.

"What about Micky?" she asks, and she notices the grief-stricken look on Franklin's face.

Franklin can't bear to tell her the news that even he hasn't processed yet.

But Candy can tell something is wrong. "What about Micky?"

Franklin looks at Candy solemnly, but calmly. "Micky's dead. I couldn't get the details." His voice cracks and he doesn't think he can go on. "The cops didn't … they wouldn't even let me see her. I don't know what happened."

He tries to get past his loss for a moment, for the sake of Candy and the baby. Candy starts to sob.

"Candy," Franklin says gently. "We have to go."

Franklin takes one hand, and Ken grabs the other.

"Let's go. Now!" Ken yells.

Franklin, Ken, and Candy reach Jake, who's still holding Reyes and staring down the other three police officers.

"What's the game plan, man? We can't take this cop with us," Franklin says.

"Where's your car?" Jake asks.

Franklin wants to know why it matters.

"My car is too small for all of us," Jake explains.

"What do you mean, all of us?" Franklin asks.

"Listen, we don't have time to debate this. We have to stay together. I've got my reasons, and I'll explain. We've got to get out of here before we have the whole police squad surrounding us," Jake says. "Now go get your car and pull it around, so we can get the hell out of here."

Franklin takes off running. It isn't long before he pulls up.

They all pile in. Franklin speeds out of the parking lot and onto the back roads to try to avoid the police.

"Where do we go?" Franklin asks.

"Anywhere," Jake responds unhelpfully.

Candy is in the front of the car, with Jake and Ken in the back and Reyes squeezed between them.

Candy peeks at Reyes over her shoulder. His eyes are as dark and mean as ever, and she quickly looks away.

Jake notices. "What's the deal with you two? Franklin, who is this chick?"

Reyes snarls into the dark.

"This is Candy," Franklin says without explanation. "She is, I mean she was, I mean … She's a friend of Micky's. My girlfriend."

Jake and Ken exchange a long look. They recognize Candy's name, but they have no idea what she's doing with Franklin.

Reyes lurches, as if to attack Candy, but Jake and Ken yank him back.

"Don't even look at her," Jake threatens.

Reyes snarls.

"I'm going to my place, way outside of town. They won't find us," Franklin says.

Everyone in the car is silent as Franklin drives on.

Candy stares out the passenger window and cries silently for Micky. She's afraid for herself and her baby, especially with Reyes so close.

Franklin finally says he needs to get gas and pulls off the road and into an old filling station. It's dark, with no other cars in sight. The gas station has only two old pumps and a small convenience store. An older man walks out, wearing a cap and dirty overalls, a wad of dip lumped in his left cheek. The old man walks up to the car and stares at each person.

Franklin jumps out of the car before the gas station owner can get more curious.

"Can I help you?" the old man asks as he spits tobacco juice on the ground.

Franklin says he needs gas. He uses his best Southern drawl.

"Well, you'll have to pay me first," the station owner says. "And I only take cash. You got cash?"

Franklin nods and shows him a twenty-dollar bill out of his wallet.

As he starts pumping, the station owner takes the twenty.

"Yeah, you gotta pay in advance 'cause I've already had two cars drive off without paying. My wife says if it happens again, I'd best not come home."

Franklin nods again and mumbles something to indicate that he's listening.

"And I can only take cash 'cause the wife says it costs too much to run the credit card machine."

"It's fine, really," Franklin says, wishing that the gas would pump more quickly.

Finally, the gas tank is full.

The man takes the bill and says, "Let me go inside and get your change."

"Don't worry about it. Keep the change," Franklin says.

The old man is staring at the car, and Franklin wants to get back on the road before the guy sees the cop in the back seat.

Reyes turns toward Jake and smiles an ugly smile.

"You'd better not say a word," Jake threatens.

"I have to go to the bathroom," Reyes says.

"It'll wait," Jake pops back. "We'll stop on the side of the road."

"I'm a police officer, and I like to have some dignity."

"You will never earn the right to use the word dignity," Jake says. "We'll dump you out here in the middle of nowhere. You can make your way back to town." He pauses. "Now tell me where Jena is. Tell me because that's the only way you're getting out of this."

Reyes refuses to say anything.

"You're going to tell me where she is," Jake repeats.

The nosy old man is starting to circle the car, but Franklin jumps in and pulls away before he can discern any more.

"How much longer?" Jake asks.

"Yeah, we need food and a bathroom break," Ken says. "I'm sure the pregnant lady wants to eat, too."

"Give me ten minutes," Franklin says. "I'm going to turn here. We'll be on a very secluded road, and my house is just five minutes farther in an even more secluded area. You'll have everything you need once we get there." He looks back at Jake. "What are we going to do with this cop? It's not like I have a jail at my house."

Jake smirks. "Don't worry. Ken and I have this under control. We'll take turns watching him."

Ken gives Jake a dirty look in the dark.

"We'll tie him up. He's not going anywhere until he tells me where to find Jena," Jake says.

"Jena's in jail, right?" Franklin asks.

"She was the last time I saw her," Candy says quietly.

"Well, she's not in jail now," Jake says. "And this loser of a cop knows where she is, and he's going to help me find her."

"Jake, I need to know what's going on," Franklin says.

"We'll talk later," Jake says. "I promise. Let's just get to your place."

Franklin speeds up and looks over at Candy, who is still crying. He reaches for her hand to comfort her.

As terrifying as all of this chaos has been, it distracts him from the pain of losing Micky. It seems impossible that she died so suddenly. He decides that he will find a way to get answers as soon as they get past whatever mess Jake has gotten them into.

Candy and Franklin look at each other. They hear snoring from the back seat. Candy looks back, and Ken is passed out, his head against the window.

"Wake up," Jake yells.

Ken jumps. "What? What's going on?"

"Stay awake," Jake commands.

"It won't be much farther," Franklin says as he turns down a gravel road.

Soon, he pulls up to a large, elegant home. There are two cars in the driveway, and the house lights come on as Franklin approaches.

Everyone in the car is surprised at the extravagance of the home.

A man, apparently a servant, comes out to greet the car.

"Welcome back, Mr. Bosler. Very good to see you."

The man peeks into the car when Franklin opens his door. "You brought friends," he says, surprised.

"Good to see you, Mr. Tindale. How is your wife?" Franklin asks.

"Very well, sir. Thank you," the servant says.

Jake is shocked. He never thought Franklin was anything more than a two-bit writer.

Everyone is speechless, even Reyes.

"Mr. Tindale," Franklin says in an authoritative voice.

"Yes, sir?" Mr. Tindale asks, with deference.

"My guests are in need of food, bathrooms, and showers," Franklin instructs. He leans close to Mr. Tindale's ear and whispers. "And we have a cop who needs to be guarded, but those two guys in the back say they have things under control."

Mr. Tindale nods. "Very good, sir."

Jake gets out of the car, keeping the gun low, and points at Reyes to get out.

Ken gets out on the other side, and Mr. Tindale opens the door for Candy and escorts her inside.

Jake and Ken walk beside Reyes, keeping a close eye on him.

Mr. Tindale, who is wary of guns, leads Candy to the largest and prettiest room, then he takes Jake and Ken to the second biggest guest room. Franklin follows to make sure they can handle Reyes.

Jake is blown away by the luxurious room and Franklin's elegant lifestyle.

He lets Reyes walk in first. Jake and Ken follow Reyes. Franklin follows them all. Franklin nods at Mr. Tindale, to let him know that he can leave.

Mr. Tindale stops Franklin before he leaves. "Sir, there's been a moving van here, and some unusual looking men were looking for you … um, small people. They said they will be back early in the morning."

"Thank you. I'll take care of it tomorrow," Franklin says, and Mr. Tindale leaves.

Jake lowers his gun when Franklin enters the room.

"Where's the bathroom?" Jake asks.

"This room has one adjoining it," Franklin says and points to the door.

"What about windows?" Jake asks.

"There are no windows in the bathrooms," Franklin answers.

"Okay, the bathroom is all yours, Reyes," Jake says.

"About time," Reyes snaps back. "You're going to have to take off these handcuffs."

Jake complies reluctantly.

Ken announces that he needs to use the facilities, too, and Franklin points him to another bathroom.

Reyes walks toward the bathroom.

"Reyes?" Jake calls out.

Reyes turns around.

"If you have a phone, I want it. I want your watch, and I want your belt, too," Jake says.

"I don't have a phone. It's back where you kidnapped me." He starts removing his belt and throws it and his watch to Jake.

"Wait a minute," Jake says, shaking his head. "I need to pat you down." He looks at Franklin. "I'm sorry, man, will you take this gun and cover me while I check this guy out? I promise it'll only take a minute."

Franklin reluctantly takes the gun while Jake makes sure that Reyes doesn't have a phone, another gun, a knife, or any other weapon. Jake declares Reyes unarmed and lets him go into the bathroom.

He takes the gun from Franklin, and the two of them stare at each other.

"Jake, I need to go pull myself together," Franklin says. "I need a shower, clean clothes, and I need to grieve for Micky. But if you want—and if Ken can keep that cop in line—you can meet me in my den in about an hour. Mr. Tindale will come to get you."

Jake nods. "That's fine. I understand."

"I want to know why you're holding this police officer captive. And I need to know what it has to do with Jena," Franklin says.

Jake nods.

Franklin opens the door, and Mr. Tindale is there with a serving cart and an array of food. He pushes it into the room, and Jake and Franklin smile.

"Thank you, Mr. Tindale," Jake says. "Thank you, Franklin."

Franklin leaves, and Jake starts rummaging through the cart. He finds utensils and gives them back to Mr. Tindale. "I'm afraid we can't have any of these because of ... our friend."

Mr. Tindale nods. "But what will you eat with?" he asks.

"Our hands," Jake replies.

Mr. Tindale gives him a disapproving look.

"Better that than getting stabbed in the back," Jake explains.

"I see," Mr. Tindale says. "There is plenty here to eat and drink and I hope you enjoy it."

Mr. Tindale leaves, and Ken strolls in wearing a fresh white robe, showered, and cleaned up.

He is excited to see the food cart. "Now, this is living!" he says, popping a handful of grapes into his mouth.

"I'm headed to the bathroom, Ken," Jake says. "Keep a close eye on Reyes. He's slick, so be prepared for anything."

"I got this, Jake."

Ken continues eating while Jake walks away.

Even Reyes looks refreshed when he walks out of the bathroom, still wearing his uniform but, without a belt, trying to hold his pants up.

Ken chews slowly and stares at Reyes.

"There is a bathrobe in there, isn't there?" Ken asks sarcastically.

"I'm a cop," Reyes says arrogantly. "And I'm still on duty, even though I've been kidnapped by two dumbass punks."

Ken reaches into his robe pocket for the gun. He holds it in one hand while grabbing food with the other.

"Well, then, you can just take off your pants," Ken says. "You're wearing something under them, aren't you?"

"Why don't you just give me back my belt—or are you afraid that I'm going to beat you with it?"

Ken laughs.

"So, Jake is the boss of you two, huh?" Reyes says.

"Oh, you think you're going to use some cop psychology on me?" Ken asks, laughing. "It ain't gonna work. Jake's the boss, and

I'm just fine with that. Quit trying to get under my skin and get something to eat."

Reyes lifts the lid on one of the food trays. Steak, mashed potatoes, broccoli.

"Where's the silverware?" Reyes snarls. "What kind of richy-rich place doesn't have silverware?"

"I got rid of it," Jake says as he walks out of the bathroom with his shirt off and drying his face. "We can't exactly give you access to weapons. Use your hands."

Jake grabs a piece of steak, takes a big bite, and chews hard. "See how easy that is?"

Reyes takes a plate, sits down, and eats with the others.

Jake takes the gun from Ken and sits across from Reyes.

"Tell me where Jena is," Jake says.

Reyes ignores Jake and scoops his fingers into the mashed potatoes and jams them into his mouth, then licks his fingers.

"These are some delicious," Reyes says, trying to get a rise out of Jake. "You should try some. Really tasty. Buttery and fluffy."

Jake loses his temper, cocks the gun, and points it at Reyes' head.

"I didn't think I could ever murder someone again, but you … well … you might be an exception. Now tell me where I can find Jena," Jake says.

"If I tell you, what happens to me then?" Reyes asks.

Jake just stares at Reyes. "I set you free. I don't want to harm you. But I will kill you if you don't tell me where she is."

"I'll think about it," Reyes says as he keeps eating.

Jake scowls at Reyes, but also knows that Reyes is trying to get a rise out of him.

He walks over to Ken and hands him the gun. "I need you to keep an eye on him, a close eye. I have to go see Franklin. We have things to discuss."

"Shouldn't we tie him up?" Ken asks.

Jake stares at Reyes.

He'll probably pull something with Ken, Jake thinks.

Jake grabs a chair. "Sit over there," Jake orders Reyes.

Reyes glares at Jake.

"Sit!" Jake orders, and Reyes throws down his plate and complies.

Jake puts the handcuffs back on, then they use the extra sheets in the closet to tie Reyes to the chair.

"We still need to keep an eye on him," Jake tells Ken as he walks out the door.

Mr. Tindale is waiting. "I will take you to Mr. Bosler."

Jake thanks the man and follows him down a long hall, until they reach an elevator.

Mr. Tindale stands to the side and pushes the button. The elevator door opens. They enter.

Before Jake can make polite conversation, the elevator door opens to Franklin's den.

Jake steps out. Mr. Tindale takes the elevator back downstairs.

"Come in, Jake, have a seat," Franklin says.

Jake looks at the shelves and shelves of books, the deep leather furniture, the expensive rugs—and Franklin dressed more like the lord of a manor than the guy he just picked up at the hospital.

"Are you the same Franklin Bosler who worked as a clerk in a rundown hotel?" Jake asks.

"Yep, same guy," Franklin says. "Have a seat." He pours himself a glass of bourbon. "I inherited all of this from my father. He started out selling vacuums and died a millionaire." He takes a sip and stares at a photo of Micky on the table in front of him. "Success comes with loss," He says. His eyes are wet with tears—he can't hide his sadness.

"I never wanted to have anything to do with my father's money. My mom and dad divorced when I was twelve. I went to live with my mom, and that's when I started creating my own reality."

Jake listens with sympathy.

"I wrote this quirky kid's book for a school assignment and called it *The Mystery of a Lonely Boy*. It was about a boy whose parents split up, and the boy becomes a detective who helps lonely kids find lost toys that help them cope with their lives."

Franklin says that's when he decided he wanted to write stories for the rest of his life. Franklin's mother remarried his father, but a year later, his mother fell ill and died. Franklin was sixteen.

"My father was a proud man, but he showed real emotion at my mother's funeral," He says.

A few years later, Franklin went to college and studied journalism and creative writing. "But I didn't want to write average stories. I found journalism boring. I love the unknown, the unexpected. I found that I was fascinated with making up stories: murder mysteries." He looks at Micky's photo. "Maybe I'll stop writing mysteries and write about a love story that will never be lived."

Franklin stands and puts his glass on the fireplace mantle. "Anyway, I never came back here. I traveled the world, dressed in tacky clothes—beach shirts, shorts, and a hat."

Franklin says he wore a hat, because to him, a hat meant mystery. He felt like a detective. His father asked Franklin to come work for him, but he had no interest.

"I was a writer searching for a story. I ended up in a little town in South America. I met a woman named Reda. Reda Jones."

Like Franklin, she was traveling the world. He asked her out to dinner, and she accepted, but Reda never showed up.

"I thought she stood me up, but the next morning I learned that she had been murdered in her hotel room," Franklin says.

Apparently, she was killed while Franklin was at the restaurant waiting for her.

"So, I took her name, and she became my character, Reda Jones," Franklin explains. "When I met Jena, at the hotel while traveling, she reminded me of Reda. Tough and forceful," he says, making Jake quiver a little. "And I met you and Ken at the diner… the shootout. What a wild and crazy day that was and now here we are on another venture." He pauses, sips his bourbon, then: "It's your turn. Tell me your story. Why are you holding this police officer captive? And where is Jena?"

Jake gets up and paces in anxiety and frustration.

"Honestly, I don't know very much," Jake says, sighing deeply. "You know that Jena went to jail, right? Then one night, out of the blue, I hear on the local news that her conviction has been overturned, but they didn't have any information on where she was. Or why.

"Speaking of mysteries," he goes on, "I got a phone call at work that night, and whoever it was hung up, but I just know it was Jena. Who knows where she was calling from?"

Jake says he had always heard stories about the corruption at the Luttonville prison and the Maplesville Police Department. He heard even more rumors when Jena was arrested and tried, and most of those stories involved the warden at the prison in Luttonville, as well as Reyes.

"We also heard on the news that a prison guard was at the hospital, unconscious, with multiple gunshots and that a nurse from the prison was missing," he says. "Like I said, a mystery—just like your mysteries."

He tells Franklin that he and Ken decided to go to the police department, hoping the police could tell them something about Jena and whether the wounded guard had anything to do with Jena's disappearance.

"Well, we accidentally heard Reyes say that he shot this prison guard and that he was looking for a girl named Candy," Jake explains. "Reyes was obviously talking to the warden at the prison in Luttonville County, where Jena was sent, and Reyes was saying all kinds of crazy things—threatening to kill this person and that person and cussing and carrying on."

Jake explains how he and Ken had miraculously gotten the drop on Reyes, and though they didn't get any more information, Reyes told them they would never find Jena.

"I know he knows where she is. He practically told me so," Jake says, shaking his head. "I know Reyes is working with that shady warden." He shakes his head, overwhelmed with his own story.

"Then there's that poor prison guard," he goes on. "Turns out his name is Mike Redmond. Now he's only partly conscious at the hospital, where all that crazy shit just went down. We found Mike's room, and Reyes was there, standing right over his bed."

"And that's when you decided to kidnap him?" Franklin says.

"Right," Jake says. "Then we end up in the middle of a shootout, and we find you—and that girl, Candy." He stops long enough for Franklin to process the details. "So, how did you and Candy end up at the hospital? Do you even know her?"

Franklin turns away to hide his emotion. "It all started with Micky. She's been my girlfriend on and off for a while. It's a long story, and I just don't have it in me to tell you now. But the short version is that we took her to the hospital with a bad stomachache, and she ended up dying."

Jake nods and doesn't know what to say. "I'm sorry for your loss, Franklin."

"Micky wanted to run away from her life and needed me to take her and Candy away to hide. Candy was there when Mike, the guard, got shot, and she's pregnant—by Reyes. She's scared to death. Apparently, Reyes threatened to take the baby and kill Candy."

Franklin and Jake are solemn while they take in the weight of their situation and how they both got to this point.

"Reyes is a monster," Jake says, finally. "Franklin, I need your help. We have to get Reyes to talk, and I have to find Jena. I'm sure that crooked warden and the cops are looking for us, and they're all part of the corruption." He pauses reflectively. "And somehow, Jena must have gotten caught up in it."

Franklin sighs. "Jake, we're in deep. Do you get that? We have no choice but to turn Reyes in—to the FBI, maybe. Someone has to be on the up-and-up."

"A nurse we met at the hospital mentioned something about a Detective Martin investigating the case," Jake says.

"Reyes tried to kill that prison guard you mentioned. He'll vouch for us, then we'll get Reyes into prison where he belongs," Franklin says.

"But what about Jena?" Jake protests. "Turning Reyes in won't tell us where Jena is. In fact, they'll probably all clam up about all their schemes and crimes."

"How are we going to get him to tell you what he knows about Jena?" Franklin ponders out loud. "I write murder mysteries, but I'm not going to commit murder."

"Nobody wants to kill anyone—well, I guess we don't," Jake says sheepishly. "We just want him to talk."

"Look, Jake, I want to help, but no matter how awful this man is, he's still a cop. And we kidnapped him."

"We're all in deep now, but Candy is afraid of Reyes."

"Why?" Franklin asks.

Jake pauses. "You're going to need to sit for this one."

"I'd rather stand."

"Reyes is the father of her baby. We've been looking for Candy and we found her. She can also help us stay out of jail because she can identify Reyes and be a witness to his crimes."

They stare at each other in silence for a good while. Then Franklin gets unnaturally excited.

"I've got a book idea. *Reda Jones: The Only Resolution She Has Left*. What do you think?" Franklin asks.

"I think I have no idea what you're talking about," Jake says. "And I think I need your help."

Franklin smiles for the first time all night and hugs Jake. "You got it, man. You got it."

———

Warden Peters is sitting in his office when he gets a call from the new mayor, Cannon Russ.

"We've got a new problem to deal with," the mayor tells Peters. "Believe it or not, your guy Reyes was kidnapped at the hospital by two punk kids, and a man and a woman were with them."

"What are you talking about?" Peters demands.

"You heard me right. Two guys kidnapped Reyes. All the men involved with you and Reyes are now in jeopardy, so you'd better do something," the mayor says. "I didn't get elected to go to prison. I've got the whole police department out looking for him. And you, Warden Peters, need to do your part. I don't know who over there can help, but you'd better do something."

The mayor doesn't give the warden a chance to react. "What's the status with your man, Mike?" Russ asks.

"I've got a nurse there telling me that an officer and two young guys were in his room at some point," Peters says. "I don't think that nurse is on duty now, but the last report I got is that Mike has fallen back into a coma and—"

"What?" Russ asks roughly.

"Reyes told me—I guess before he got kidnapped—that the District Attorney has appointed a Detective Martin to investigate Mike's shooting," the warden says.

"You see how things get out of control when a bunch of hotheads takes charge?" the mayor shouts into the phone. "Find Reyes before Martin does, and you'd better pray that Mike doesn't wake up."

The warden hears the mayor slam the phone down loudly.

CHAPTER EIGHTEEN

Sherry Paterson stares into the dark room. The table next to her has a small lamp, a glass of red wine and a half-full bottle of liquor.

Her husband, Gary, is sleeping in the next room.

Sherry glances at a photo of Ted and Jake, brothers, standing on the football field, just after Ted's team won a game. Jake's arm is draped around his brother's shoulder as other team members cheer and laugh in the background.

Tears run down the mother's cheeks. She wipes them away, but they won't stop. She picks up the glass of wine and drinks all of it. It's not her first.

She looks at the liquor bottle and can't help herself. She takes a long swallow out of the bottle, holding onto it as she stumbles toward the photo of the boys. She snatches up the photo, and the bottle slips from her hand, spilling liquor onto the carpet.

Sherry falls to her knees in agonizing pain, emotionally and physically drained from the grief of losing her son and the strain of caring for her sick husband.

"No. No. Not my baby. Not Teddy."

Sherry lets her body go limp, falling to the floor and still gripping the photo. She lets her soul empty.

Staring into nothingness, she feels hate. "I will kill you, Jena Parker. I'll kill you." Then she slips into a drunken sleep.

Jena's aunt, Denise Parker, steps off the plane and into the airport in the small town of Maplesville. She's wearing dark sunglasses, jeans, and a light jacket and carries an expensive purse close to her body.

"Have a nice stay in Maplesville," an airline attendant tells her.

Denise looks at the woman. "Thanks, but I've been here before." She picks up her bags. "I'm here to visit my niece. Can you call me a taxi?"

"Sure. My brother, Ferguson, is right out front in his cab," the attendant says. "He'll be happy to take you to wherever you need to go." The airline attendant says with a bright smile showing all her teeth.

As she walks out of the airport, she spies a middle-aged man in a white T-shirt, slouched in the driver's seat of a cab. His hat is over his face, apparently napping.

Denise knocks on the passenger-side window and startles the man, who adjusts his hat. He jumps out of the car and greets her.

"Hello there, ma'am, I'm Ferguson," he says, picking up her bags and putting them in the trunk. "Maplesville's best cab driver. I can take you anywhere you want to go."

The animated driver opens the door for Denise.

Denise gets into the back seat, and the driver closes the door behind her and hops back behind the wheel.

He looks at Denise in the rearview mirror. "So where are we going, pretty lady?"

Denise hesitates, but finally answers. "The prison, please."

Ferguson looks up and smiles.

"The prison is over in Luttonville County. I can take you there, but it'll be about forty dollars," he says.

Denise Parker smiles. "Of course, and how much extra for you to wait for me—I'd say about thirty minutes—and bring me back again?"

"Hmm," Ferguson says, calculating. "How about forty dollars there, fifteen dollars for waiting, and forty dollars for the ride back?"

"That sounds fair," Denise says. "I'll give you a big tip, too."

He cranks the ignition, but the cab stalls. He smiles at Denise, hoping that he doesn't lose the woman's confidence. He keeps trying. "Don't worry, ma'am, my Pearl here never lets me down."

Denise smiles politely.

Finally, the car starts, and Ferguson turns around again. "See? My Pearl, she's a good girl."

Ferguson, blessedly, drives in silence as they travel the forty-five miles to Luttonville Prison. He screeches to a halt in front of the prison.

Denise Parker looks at the dim, dark prison, with its electric fences and gates. She opens the cab door and addresses Ferguson. "I'll be back soon," she says.

"I'll be here, pretty lady," the driver says.

Denise walks to the prison check-in window. A woman greets her, wearing flashy attire and sparkling earrings.

"Welcome to Luttonville Prison. My name is Blossom. How may I help you?"

Denise Parker struggles to retain her composure as she thinks about Jena being trapped in this dreadful place.

"I'm here to see my niece," she says.

"What's her name, ma'am?"

Denise pauses and remembers that Jena is considered to be a notorious killer. She swallows hard. "Her name is Jena Parker," Denise says finally.

Blossom doesn't react. She types Jena's name into her computer.

"Hmm, well …" she says. "It looks like Jena Parker is no longer here—at least, not in this prison."

Blossom tilts her head and smiles.

Denise is confused and a little alarmed. "Where is she?"

Blossom shrugs. "I don't know, but she isn't here anymore. The computer says she's been released. It doesn't say where she went. It just says she was released."

Denise Parker's mild voice changes. "Who's in charge here?" she asks.

Blossom's forehead wrinkles. "Well, Warden Phillip Peters is in charge, but he's a busy man. We have more than a thousand inmates here."

Blossom tilts her head again. "I'd suggest you try to contact Miss Parker."

Denise glares at the clerk. "How am I supposed to contact her? That's why I came here? I want to see the warden. I'm her next of kin; that should be listed in the records there. I should have been contacted when she was released." Denise slams her fist on the counter. "I want to speak to the warden. Now!"

Blossom's eyes widen. "Sure," she says, shaken. "I'll call him right now."

She dials, then whispers into the receiver, hangs up, and turns back to Denise Parker.

"The warden says he can speak to you tomorrow."

Denise is furious. "You tell that warden ... did you say Warden Phillip Peters? You tell him that he'd better find time to speak to me unless he wants the media here by the end of the day." She pauses. "I came a long way to see my niece, and I want to know where she is."

Blossom picks up the phone again and turns away from Denise so that Denise can't hear what she's saying. After hanging up, she says, "The warden says a guard will come to escort you to his office."

She smiles a weak smile at Denise and then pretends to ignore her while she types away on her computer.

A tall guard finally enters the lobby and approaches Denise. The guard glares at Denise, but she ignores him. He reaches out and shakes her hand.

"I'm Victor," he says in a deep voice. "I'll escort you to Warden Peters' office.

She follows Victor through the prison halls. The walls are covered with old white paint. The smell of disinfectant fills the air. Victor's heels click on the shiny floors.

Finally, Victor stops at a door and knocks, then walks in.

Warden Peters adjusts his suit coat, clears his throat. "Come in," he says, waving them in. He rushes to Denise, trying to make a good impression.

Peters stands face to face with Denise. She notices that his face is sweaty and that his eyes are twitching. But he has a big smile on his face.

"Welcome, I'm Warden Peters." He grabs her hand and squeezes it between both of his. "Please take a seat."

Denise smiles a small smile and sits down. She doesn't wait for the warden to speak or even to sit down. His back is still to her when she asks, "Where is my niece, Jena Parker?"

Peters says nothing but turns and sits down. He stares at Denise Parker.

"The clerk out front says she's been released," Denise says, "But I have not been notified, and I'm her official contact and next of kin. Why can't I get any information?"

Peters tries to keep his expression still. "Your niece did turn nineteen. She is not a minor," he says.

Denise isn't going to play games, and she's not going to waste time. "Where in the hell is my niece?"

Peters poses in his chair and puts on an innocent air. "Your niece escaped from the prison one month ago, and we have not been able to capture her," the warden lies boldly.

Denise is shocked. "Escaped?" she says with disbelief.

"If you know your niece, and I'm sure you do. … You know that she is a smart and resourceful girl and fully capable of pulling this off."

Denise is heartbroken, but she isn't finished. "That certainly does not explain why you did not contact me. I would think you'd want to ask me whether I had heard from my niece. And I haven't heard a single media report about this."

Peters manages another lie. "The media hasn't reported it because the prison is working with an undercover team to find her because … well …" Peters pauses. "Your niece is violent and has committed many murders. That makes her dangerous, and we don't want to frighten the public." Peters clears his throat. "Let us handle the investigation. I apologize that you weren't contacted. Unfortunately, a prison is not a perfect place. I assure you that I will contact you immediately if we have information about your niece."

Denise nods. She can't think of anything else to say or do. She is overwhelmed by her emotions and disappointment, and she is afraid for Jena—out there all alone.

She stands. "I'll leave my number, and I will expect you to stay in contact with me." She opens the warden's door and then decides to drop one more threat. "If you don't, every media outlet within one hundred miles will know about this."

Denise leaves the office, and Victor is waiting for her. They walk through the halls and out the lobby, past Blossom, without conversation.

Outside, Denise's knees are weak as she approaches the cab, where Ferguson is sleeping again. She opens the door and startles him. His hat falls to the side as he tries to gather his wits.

"Please take me to a hotel in Maplesville," she says, "a decent hotel if there is one. I'll be staying in town for a while."

Ferguson can tell something is wrong, and he adjusts his mirror so that he can keep one eye on her. He drives back to Maplesville in silence.

Denise sits in the back of the cab, trying to hold back her tears. She had already lost her brother, Jonathan, and sister-in-law, Kitty. Now Jena is missing.

She remembers when Jonathan introduced Kitty to his family. Kitty was beautiful—young and pretty and full of life. She and Kitty had quickly become as close as sisters. Denise remembered when her boyfriend, Lincoln, had broken her heart, and Kitty brought over bottles of wine. They both got so drunk that they slept on the back lawn.

Tears escape from Denise's eyes. She remembers Jena's sweet baby face when she was born, how the family gathered at the hospital with flowers, well-wishes, and baby gifts. It was when Denise first held her niece that Denise fell in love. Jena was sound asleep in her arms, then Jena opened her eyes. Aunt and niece locked eyes. Denise knew then that Jena was special. The baby seemed so strong; her eyes sparkled; her smile lit up Denise's heart.

Denise is lost in memories when she begins to cry hard. Ferguson is concerned and pulls over to the side of the road. The cab driver turns to look at his passenger.

"Are you okay," he asks.

"I'm okay," she mumbles through her tears. "Just get me to the hotel."

Ferguson gives her a caring smile, and pulls back onto the road, making his way to Maplesville.

———

Warden Peters is also upset. He stares at the chair where Denise had been sitting. He stands, folds his arms, and looks out his office window. Then he breaks into a malicious grin, a smile that shows his polished teeth. As he stands, congratulating himself, an alarm blasts throughout the prison. He quickly looks around the room and grabs his radio. He hears Victor shouting.

"Warden, we have a prison riot!" Victor yells.

"What exactly is going on?" the warden asks.

"Two inmates have already been shot, sir," Victor says. "It started when an inmate confronted one of the guards about the whereabouts of missing inmates, one being her best friend, Becky, two years ago."

All Peters can hear is static for a moment.

"Then another inmate joined in and started saying that the guards are killing inmates," Victor continues. "One of them attacked the guard, and he shot both inmates." Victor sounds panicked. "Now, all of the inmates are out of control, sir. Several of them have shanks. Hold on, warden." Victor pauses. "I'm getting word from another guard. Sir, one of the guards is down. A mob of inmates took his gun and shot him."

The warden hears more static—and more noise.

"Sir, we need to call the police department for help," Victor says with fear in his voice.

"No, we're not calling anyone in," the warden says. He thinks about all of the questions this could cause, from the media, even from Jena Parker's aunt. Besides, too many questions are floating around about Mike Fredmond, Nurse May, the new mayor, and now Reyes. "We'll get too many questions. You men get things under control out there. Use tear gas. Use your guns if you need to. Then, get them back into their cells." Peters' yells. "You got that?"

"Yes, sir," Victor replies in a shaky voice.

Peters is still reeling from the latest crisis when his phone rings.

"Now what?" he says silently, trying to calm his voice. He picks up the receiver. "Warden Peters."

A man with a familiar, deep voice and an accent answers him.

"We need two," the man says abruptly.

Peters' swallows hard. He's never said no before.

"We have a prison riot going on right now," Peters says, stumbling over his words. "Can I get back to you about this?" The warden is starting to panic.

"No, you may not get back to us," the man says. "Send them now, or we'll send for you."

The man hangs up. The warden hears only the dial tone. He puts down the phone and slowly sits down. He rubs his hands across his face and covers his head.

"What in the hell have I gotten myself into?" he yells, alone in his office. He gets up and paces around the room in sheer terror.

The radio beeps loudly and nearly sends the warden into a true meltdown.

"Warden? Warden? Come in," Victor calls.

Peters picks up the radio. "What's the damage?" he asks.

"Everything is under control. I repeat, everything is under control."

"What is the situation?" he asks.

"Ten down: one guard injured, two inmates killed, seven inmates injured," Victor reports.

Peters is sick with disbelief. "I want an update in thirty minutes." He clicks off the radio. With a disgusted look of disbelief on his face, he says, "Contact the Maplesville's police stations and ask for help with handling the media and anyone nosing around."

"Yes, sir."

Peters put down the radio.

Warden Phillip Peters opens his desk drawer and stares at his loaded weapon.

Chance is silent throughout her plane ride. When the plane lands, a tall, masked man dressed in black grabs her and blindfolds her. He escorts her off the plane.

The man leans close and whispers in Chance's ear. "Are you ready to meet the man?" he says mysteriously.

Chance tries to stay calm, but she has trouble controlling her nerves. "What man?" she asks.

"Don't worry about it," he whispers again. "You'll find out soon enough."

Chance becomes bold. "I'm not afraid. You hear me? I'm not afraid."

The man isn't moved by Chance's bluster. He shoves Chance forward. "Good for you," he says and then laughs loudly. "Now walk, you pathetic creature."

Chance stops walking, out of anger. "You know, it's easy to talk shit to a person who's blindfolded and whose hands are tied behind their back. I may not be able to see your face, but I won't forget your voice."

"I hope not," he teases seductively, and he runs his fingers up and down her body. "I love a woman with spunk." He slaps her hard on her rear end.

Chance is so humiliated that she gasps for air and feels her face turning red. "I hope you feel that way when I come to kill you," she says with a clenched jaw.

Her captor just shoves her forward.

They come to a door, and the man leads her into a building, down the halls, and into a room.

She remains blindfolded, hands tied behind her back.

The man can't resist one final taunt. "My name is Romeo," he says. "Remember that when you come to kill me. I'll be waiting patiently."

He laughs again and says nothing more.

"Take off her blindfold," Romli tells Romeo.

Chance looks around the room. She recognizes Matty, Gypsy, Sharon, Suzanne, Paula, and other women. All of them are heavily armed. Chance remembers Paula from the fight with Jena at the prison. Then, she sees Romeo for the first time. He winks and licks his lips. She turns back to Romli, who wears a grim look and is tapping his fingers on the arms of his chair.

He smiles. "You know, one of the last young ladies who stood in that spot was shot to death," he says.

Chance is quiet, trying to tamp down her fear.

"Do you think I'm going to shoot you?" he asks.

"No," she replies.

"Why do you think that?" Romli asks again.

"Because you wouldn't bring me all this way to shoot me," she says, hoping she's right.

"Possibly," he replies. To Romeo, he says, "Untie her."

Chance tries to stretch her arms without attracting attention. One of her wrists has a blood-red ring around it. She puts her arms at her sides.

Romli stands and takes about two steps forward. "I guess you're wondering why you're here. Everyone who comes here wonders why they're here." He walks around the room, staring at the armed women, who will or have become secret killers. "I am Romli, and I want you to know that I've been in this business since before you were born."

He is handed a glass of dark brown liquor, takes a sip, and then hands it back to a servant.

He walks closer to Chance until they are face to face.

Romli sniffs dramatically. "I smell a person who has no loyalty. I can sniff them out. You … well … you seem to have revenge in your eyes. You have hate in your soul. I like that. You will be an outstanding servant for me."

"What?" she seethes. "Peters sends me all this way to be a damned servant? No. I came here to kill."

Romli quickly grabs Chance's neck and squeezes it hard. "You came here because I sent for you. I paid for you. You belong to me, and you'll do whatever I tell you … or …"

He stops. Everyone in the room, including Paula cocks their weapons and points them at Chance.

Romli goes on, "Or you'll be just like all the others who are shot and killed right in this very spot." Romli removes his hands from Chance's neck.

She coughs and gasps for air. When she gets a deep breath, she rushes to attack Romli.

Romeo grabs her and puts a gun to her head.

Romli laughs out loud. "Can you believe that she just tried to attack me in a room full of armed people?" he asks looking around the room. He laughs louder.

Romeo keeps his gun pointed at Chance's head.

Chance's eyes bulge with anger, and she struggles to remain still.

"Let her go," Romli tells Romeo. "Let her loose."

Romeo hesitates.

"Stand down," he orders Romeo.

The women in the room move closer, their weapons pointed at Chance.

Romli holds up his hand to stop them.

"You want me to be someone, someone specific. Who is it? Who do you want to kill?" he asks.

Chance is so angry that she is near tears.

"Who do you want me to be?" Romli yells in her face.

"I want you to be Jena Parker because I want to kill her." Chance looks around the room. "In fact, everyone in here is Jena Parker to me."

Chance bends over from the release of saying Jena's name and from the fear and frustration she feels with her situation.

"Do you want me to kill this crazy woman?" Romeo asks.

Romli looks back at Romeo, considering his question. "No. I don't. She's useful. She doesn't fear death," he says, with something of a chuckle. "Kind of takes the fun out of killing her. I'm going to make use of her anger." He points at Chance. "Know that you're alive only because I want you to be alive. Today, you don't fear death. By the time I'm done with you, you'll beg for my mercy. Trust me, I'll get my pleasure then."

He looks over Chance's shoulder, to one of the women. "Take her. Show her the ways."

Matty walks up to Chance. "Let's go." Matty points her weapon in Chance's face. "Move. Now!"

Chance starts walking. She is surrounded by all of the women, including Paula.

She singles out Paula. "What are you now—some brainwashed expert?"

Matty shoves Chance against the wall. "Do you know her?" Matty demands.

Chance refuses to answer.

"Do you know her?" Matty demands again.

"Of course, I know her. I know many of you, and I guess you were brought here the same way I was," Chance says.

Matty lets go of Chance. "How we got here is irrelevant now."

"Okay, so why are we here?" Chance asks brusquely.

Matty puts her weapon on her shoulder. "You'll soon find out. I suggest you go to your room and take comfort."

"Take comfort in what?" Chance asks, gritting her teeth.

Matty walks between them to confront Chance. "Take comfort that you are alive because tomorrow you will become one of us or you will be killed. Either way, I don't care. So, I suggest you keep your questions to yourself, because I assure you, they will become a distant memory. Your survival will become your top priority."

Matty opens Chance's room, which is more like a cell. "Enjoy tonight. Everything you need is in your room."

In a quick movement, Chance tries to grab Matty's gun.

They tussle, and the other women surround them and watch.

Matty slams Chance to the floor and starts to punch her.

The weapon slips from Matty's hands and slides to the other side of the room.

Chance kicks Matty off of her.

They struggle to stand and begin trading punches. Matty strikes a hard blow at Chance, but she doesn't fall. Chance eyes the dropped weapon and runs to it.

Matty catches up to her and struggles to get the weapon away from Chance. But Chance manages to turn the gun on Matty.

"Oh, yeah, now look who's sweating," Chance gloats.

Matty starts to laugh, which distracts Chance. Matty grabs the gun and pulls the trigger. Nothing happens.

"No ammo," Matty says as Chance flinches.

"They're just here to instill fear," Matty says.

Chance catches her breath. "What?"

The other women apparently have not been let in on the secret. They all check their weapons, and all are would they not be loaded?

"Our weapons are never loaded when we are inside the compound's walls," Matty tells the women.

Matty steps back. "Do you really believe that Romli would let us walk around with loaded weapons?"

Paula throws her gun down. "Then why the hell are we here?" Paula demands.

"Romli is the leader of a notorious killing organization. The men do the killing. We are here to serve—and service—the men," Matty explains, seething with resentment.

"Service them?" Paula responds angrily. "So, we're just prisoners?"

"Would you rather be a prisoner back there or a free prisoner here?" Matty asks.

"I'd rather be with my daughter," Paula says, her voice cracking.

"You know that's never going to happen. He'd kill you before letting you leave," Matty says.

"So, we're prisoners and whores?" Paula yells.

Matty gets tougher. "We're trained here to fight Romli's enemies." Matty's eyes stare into all of theirs. "We do what we have to do until all of us are free. Like I said, which prison would you prefer? Do you want what Peters, and the guards were doing to us back there? At least, now you have some freedom."

Suzanne and Sharon throw down their guns, too.

"You call this freedom?" Suzanne blurts out. "I've had more glares and unwanted attention since I've been here. They're dirty, and they beat us. And you call this freedom?" She is furious. "What difference does it make? Peters, Reyes, Romli—they're all assholes. We're just cattle being shuffled from one wicked hand to another."

Sharon tries to calm Suzanne.

Matty stands firm. "Then kill yourself, Suzanne, because that's the only way you're getting out of here." She glares at Suzanne. "I don't feel sorry for you. I was only eighteen when I came here. I was forced to have sex over and over. I was thrown into that prison by that loathsome Reyes. Then they sent me here to this ... prison."

"All this time, you've known these guns don't have ammunition?" Suzanne asks, still incredulous.

Matty shrugs. "Ammunition or no ammunition, Romli will kill you, or you'll die in the woods. One way or another, you'll die. And I can't say I care."

She looks around the room at the angry and disappointed faces. Then, she picks up her weapon, and she leaves.

CHAPTER NINETEEN

*T*hey say your life flashes before your eyes when you're dying. *Between worlds, Jena's body floats as if she is weightless, drifting upward, out of her natural state, into the air—soaring through moments of her life. Memories race through her mind as she lay covered in blood, limp and lifeless, waiting for death to hold her accountable for her deeds.*

Jena remembers when she was a child playing in the yard. Her mother was inside cooking, while father and daughter ran around the yard pretending to be choo-choo trains. Her father would act like the conductor, and Jena would be the lady traveler. He'd ask, "Is everything okay, ma'am?" Jena would laugh her laugh and scream, "Yes, daddy!" They would laugh so loud that neighbors would peek through their curtains to look at them.

She was six, but she was still discovering life's wonders. She never wanted to leave Neverland. She enjoyed her innocence, while her father got to be a kid again, picking Jena up and swinging her around and around.

But one instant, during each swing, would turn dark. She thought she could see a dark face staring at her. The dark man watched through the window in a house across the street. He seemed like a desolate soul, tormented by Jena's happiness, a predator waiting for his chance to strike.

Jena remembers telling her father to look at the man across the street. Her father would look, smile, and wave. Then he'd reach for Jena's hand to take her into the house. Her father said something she would never forget. He kneeled, touched her cheek, and whispered, "Jena, don't ever be afraid." She wondered why he would say such a thing.

Now that Jena's darkest hour has come, she can hear her father's voice echo in her fading mind. "Jena don't be afraid. Don't be afraid."

But Jena is afraid. She remembers the first time she experienced fear. It surrounded her, trapped her within herself. She was a prisoner, crying and begging to be released.

Jena became suspicious. She concealed her identity. Just like when she was a child, the dark toyed with her, swirled around her like a black ghost taunting her soul.

She struggled to scream, but the darkness kept her from calling to her parents for help. She fought the darkness so many nights as a child, even when she was a young teen.

Jena remembers praying for peace.

She also wanted to be famous, so important that she could escape her fear. She wouldn't have to run and hide.

She wanted to dance in the sunlight, but the darkness wouldn't let her. She ran, but the darkness followed.

Jena wants to run from the man in the window. Each time he looks at her, she dissolves in fear. She trembles. She wants to kill him. She wants him to stop looking at her. She wants to see him bleed.

Jena sees herself. Out of her mind. Killing a man. Following him down a dark dirt road. It seems that she walks behind him for hours, and when he turns, she points her gun at him and says, "You'll never look at me again." Then Jena shoots him.

Jake appears and smiles at her and her fears fade away. She melts into his existence. She visualizes his soft, sweet lips pressed against her own. He makes the darkness go away.

But the light is only temporary. She is slipping away.

She sees the dark face. This time, he is not the window across the street. He is wearing a black trench coat, his murderous hands in his pockets with the blood of her beloved father dripping onto his coat.

Jena is fading. But her unconscious is fighting death. She remembers something she wanted, with the passionate and caring part of herself. And she has a memory of dark deeds.

She's slipping further and further away, but she won't let her go. She is sitting on the school bus next to her handsome Jake. He's talking, and Jena is smiling.

Her eyes are nearly blinded by the sun, sunlight from Jake's eyes. For all of the darkness, Jake only saw sunlight in her.

Jake guides her to the top of the highest mountain. They can almost touch the clouds. They are standing on the edge of a cliff but aren't afraid. Even with death at the edge, he will hold her. He will lift her in his strong arms, stare deeply into her eyes, lean in, and kiss her for hours. Afterward, they would lie naked on the plush ground at the edge of the cliff.

Jake wants her. He is eager, but he wants to touch her gently. Showing his unfathomable love, he begins to make love to Jena.

But she knows it is not real. His hands go right through her. She can't feel him anymore.

Jena drifts into darkness, grasping for something to hold onto. She can't find her way. She thinks of Jake. She can feel her light rising. She feels only peace and love. She smells the grass, sees the animals as they run past. She feels no pain, no sorrow.

Jena walks into her childhood home, walks straight through it, and finds herself lying on a bed. People are standing around her. An old man and an old woman. They look tired and weary.

The old woman puts a cloth on her head, and the old man watches over her. Jena realizes that it is time to live again, to regain all she has lost, and to take revenge on those who deserve it.

Jena opens her eyes.

Two people stand over her wearing white medical coats. The man is tall and wears glasses. The woman is short and Hispanic and has dark cropped hair.

Both step back. They watch her wake up.

Jena leans forward, looks around the room, and then back at the man and the woman. She feels determined. She swings her legs around the side of the bed. Like a baby, she puts one foot on the floor, and then the other.

"Be careful," the male doctor says.

The female doctor takes Jena's hand.

Jena holds her hand for a moment, then pushes her away. "No," Jena says forcefully. She takes a step, stands straight, and faces the doctors. "How long have I been here?"

The man adjusts his glasses and walks toward Jena. "My name is Dr. Hannah, and this is my assistant, Dr. Lindsey," he says, extending his hand.

Jena stares at him and won't take his hand. "How long have I been here?" she asks again.

"You've been here for more than six months."

Jena closes her eyes tightly. "Six months," she repeats. "What have I been doing all of that time?"

"Surviving," Dr. Lindsay says.

"Who are you?" Jena asks.

"We all work for the same man," Dr. Lindsey says. "We are here to ensure that young recruits recover and adjust to their new assignments."

"You were severely beaten and bleeding from a gunshot wound," Dr. Hannah says.

Dr. Lindsey says her co-worker removed the bullet and helped her recuperate.

"I died," Jena says.

The doctors stare at one another. Dr. Hannah steps toward Jena.

"Several times you stopped breathing, but we were able to revive you and bring you back," he explains.

Jena takes another step. "Why?" she asks.

"Because you are now a part of the team, and this is what we do. We save the lives of our teammates," Dr. Lindsay says. "We do it so our teammates can move forward to their next phase of recruitment. We are caretakers of the wounded."

Dr. Lindsey stares at the wall behind Jena. Jena turns around. The wall is plastered with photos. Some photos show Jena entering the compound, and others show what she looked like when she was beaten.

Jena's anger grows as she stares at the photos. She remembers the battle between her and her teammates. She remembers that they nearly beat her to death.

Dr. Hannah and Dr. Lindsay stand on each side of her.

"Why are these here?" Jena asks.

"They are to remind you of your life and your pain," Dr. Lindsey says. She walks toward a closet in the examining room. She gestures for Jena to follow her.

Jena looks at the photos again and sees one of Moschi standing over her, firing his gun, nearly killing her. She walks toward Dr. Lindsey. The doctor steps aside, allowing Jena to stand in the doorway of the closet.

"This is your gear, your supplies, your food, your water, weapons, ammunition, and clothes—everything that you will need to survive your next task," Dr. Lindsey says.

"And when am I leaving?" Jena asks.

"Today," the doctor replies and then walks away.

Jena stares into the closet while Dr. Lindsey and Dr. Hannah talk to one another. They are looking through paperwork that she assumes is about her. She dresses, gathers her gear, water— everything she will need. She carries a weapon and slings another over her shoulder.

She steps out of the closet and stares at the doctors. "I'm ready," she says.

The doctors nod.

Jena stops. "You two have been doing this for a long time, haven't you?" Jena asks.

"Yes," Dr. Hannah replies. "Moschi and Pulue are both good bosses. We all have a mission. Ours is to keep new recruits like you alive." He steps toward Jena. "And your job is to kill for them. We do our job, and it's time for you to do yours."

Jena takes one last look at the photos on the wall. She thinks about the women back at the prison—those who were kidnapped and enslaved—many to become killers for a group of assassins. Who knows what happened to others? How many were ripped away from their families and children? She feels so betrayed that Moschi had lied to her and then shot her in cold blood—just as an initiation into the team.

Jena reaches for her weapon and points it at Dr. Hannah and Dr. Lindsey. She eyes them sharply. "Too many innocent women have suffered, and I'm here to end this."

She fires her weapon, first at Dr. Lindsey, then at Dr. Hannah. Both fall to the floor.

Jena steps toward them. They are both still alive.

She stands directly over Dr. Lindsey and fires twice.

Dr. Hannah moans, begging for his life. She swiftly fires one shot into his head.

Blood from her carnage stains the photos of her on the wall. Jena watches as the blood drips down the photos.

She stares at the bodies, grabs her bag, hoists it onto her back, and walks out the door of the medical unit.

Immediately, a shot is fired at her, then two more. She ducks and the bullets miss her. She runs into the woods and hides behind a large tree while she readies her weapon.

More shots are fired, and she doesn't know who's firing them or where they're coming from. She moves slightly away from the tree and fires twice into the distance before taking cover again.

At least three minutes of silence follow.

Jena walks out into the open, stares around the forest, runs to another tree, hides. And another shot comes toward her. This time, the shot is closer.

Jena pinpoints where the gunshots are coming from and runs toward them. The bullets keep coming but miss her.

She runs until she finds a gun lying on the ground. But there is no shooter. She turns each way. She sees no one. She examines the gun to see if it has been fired recently. Then she hears a gun cock behind her.

"Don't move," says a woman with a strong foreign accent.

Jena doesn't move. "What do you want?" she asks.

"Turn around," she tells Jena.

"Just shoot me and get it over with," Jena says.

"I said, turn around," the woman demands.

Jena slowly turns.

The woman is wearing a black mask, a black hat, and black clothing.

"Who are you?" Jena asks.

"That's not important right now," the woman replies. "My identity is not the question. The question is, what team do you work for?"

"What do you mean?" Jena asks.

The woman sighs, tiring of this game. She points her gun at Jena. "I mean, do you work for Romli or do you work for Moschi? It's a simple question."

"I don't work for anyone," Jena replies. "I'm on my own."

The woman eases her shooting stance slightly and pulls off her hat and mask.

She has long, wavy, black hair and darkly tanned skin. She removes a scarf from her neck to reveal a sparkling diamond necklace.

Jena remembers her dream about battling a woman with a diamond necklace.

The woman's eyes shine like black marbles. "What is your name?" she asks.

Jena tells her.

"How did you get here, Jena Parker?" the woman asks.

"I was in a prison in the United States and Moschi rescued me. He made me believe that he could offer me a better life, a life more suited to who I am, or who I thought I was."

"I understand," the woman says. "Come with me, Jena Parker."

She waves Jena ahead. The woman keeps her weapon pointed and ready, but she makes it clear she poses no threat to Jena.

CHAPTER TWENTY

Jena, walking ahead of M.I. A, stops but doesn't turn around. "Where are you taking me?" she asks.

M.I. A jabs the gun into Jena's back. "Keep walking," she says.

Eventually, Jena sees a camp ahead. Tents are set up. Men, women, and children walk around. Guards surround the entire area.

"Is everything alright?" one of the guards asks M.I. A.

"Take her gear," she orders the guard, then addresses Jena. "You'll be given a place to sleep. Once we look through your bags and weapons, we will return them to you."

M.I. A asks that her associate, Alo, be brought to her. When he arrives, M.I. A introduces the two. "Alo will escort you to your tent and be your guide while you're here."

"How long will I be here?" Jena asks, confused.

"As longs as it takes for me to find out who you really are," M.I. A says.

Alo points his weapon at Jena and guides her to her tent.

When she walks inside, two women have a bath ready.

Alo stands outside the tent.

Finally, one woman asks Jena if she needs anything and whether she wants them to stay.

Jena says no, politely.

As they leave, Alo peeks at Jena, as if to let her know that escape is not an option.

Jena looks at the steam rising from the bath, and it looks too lovely to resist. She takes off her battle clothes and immerses herself in the tiny tub of deliciously hot water. She splashes her face and tips her head back to wash her hair. But when water drips from her hair onto her shoulders, she imagines it is blood and flashes back to the prison.

She is disappointed that she feels like she is still in a prison cell and fears that she is destined to stay in a prison, one way or another.

She tries to relax. She sees herself in her childhood bedroom, staring into the mirror. She is glad to see the young Jena, who is getting ready for school—high school, before her nightmare began.

Young Jena could not have guessed what deeds she would commit.

Jena falls asleep in the steaming water.

She sees herself when she was young, back in her bedroom. She hears a woman crying. Young Jena walks out of her room and opens the door of the room next to her own. She sees a woman lying on a bed crying. When Jena moves the blankets, she sees that the woman is her mother. Her mother smiles when she sees Jena, and she sits up and reaches for Jena's hand. They sit side by side.

"Where have you been, sweet darling?" her mother asks. "I've been so sad and worried. I lost your father, so long ago now, and then you left, and I've been alone so long."

Her mother smiles again. "Tell me that you are okay. Has someone hurt you, child?"

Jena, still in her sleep, begins to cry. She knows her mother is not alive. Jena knows it's not real, yet the moment is emotional for her. She squeezes her mother's hand tightly.

"I'm okay. I'm okay, Mom," she says and smiles.

Jena's mother kisses her daughter's hand and pulls Jena toward her. Their tears run together.

Relieved, her mother says, "I'm so happy to hear that no one has harmed you. I would be so sad if you were hurt."

Jena stares at her mother. Why doesn't her mother know that Jena is responsible for her death and that Jena is trapped in a prison of guilt? Yet, Jena believed that she was freeing her mother from her pain, but she knows now she will carry her mother's pain for the rest of her life.

Jena stands slowly and pulls her hand away from her mother. Her mother, Kitty, stares at her daughter, her eyes begging Jena not to go.

Kitty doesn't say a word as Jena backs toward the door.

Jena sobs as she watches her mother's desperate eyes.

"I have to go," she tells her mother. "I have to go back and finish what I started, no matter how hard it is. I have a mission to fulfill."

"Where will you go, Jena?" her mother asks as Jena fades away.

"Mom, I have to go. I'm sorry that you have to live in my nightmares, even after I thought I was giving you peace. I hope you can be free if I am able to end all of this," Jena says.

"What are you talking about?" Kitty asks.

"I'm talking about justice for you and me and my father," Jena says.

She looks at her mother one last time.

Jena wakes.

She's lying on a cot in the tent. A candle is burning. She stares at the flame as it flickers with the breeze.

The tent is pitch black, but bright light is shining through the slit in the door flap. It's morning. She'd slept through the night.

She leans over the tub of water, cool now, and splashes her face. She pulls clean clothing from her bag and gets dressed. As she leans to tie her shoes, she sees she isn't alone. There is a shadow, a woman whose long hair is blowing slightly.

"Time to go." It's the woman who brought her here, M.I. A says.

"Where?" Jena asks.

"We have to hunt," she says. "You want to eat tonight, don't you?"

M.I. A leaves, and Jena grabs her gear and follows.

The bright light blinds her as she leaves the tent.

M.I. A is wearing dark sunglasses and camouflage. She hands a pair of shades to Jena, too.

Alo hands Jena a hunting spear. "Don't get any ideas," he says, smirking.

Jena looks around the camp and the woods, searching for a possible escape route. She notices another woman, who seems to be a captive. M.I. A wipes sweat from her face. She looks tired and overworked. Jena can see her desperation.

Jena wonders: Does she want freedom? Or has she given up? The woman's eyes seem to be screaming, *Help me.* Jena wants to free her, and everyone at the camp.

"Let's move out," M.I. A tells Jena and Alo.

"You're the leader of this prison," Jena says, boldly. "But who are you? And why are you keeping me here?"

The mysterious woman steps slowly toward Jena, takes off her sunglasses, and stares into Jena's eyes.

"You will know soon enough," she says. "You will know who I am, what I am, and what I want. For now, you'll do what I say." She puts her sunglasses back on. "Let's move out."

Jena refuses to move.

"Alo, take out your weapon," M.I. A says, threatening Jena.

Jena stares at Alo, then back at M.I. A. "His gun doesn't scare me," she says. "I'll move, but only because I want to move, not because you're telling me to move."

Jena begins walking, smiles to herself, and swings her weapon over her shoulder.

M.I. A turns to Alo, as Jena walks ahead. "I thought I told you to take out your weapon," she says.

"It wasn't necessary," Alo says.

M.I. A pulls out a knife and points it at Alo. "I'll tell you what's necessary. The next time you disobey me, I'll use your own weapon to get rid of you." She touches his face with the tip of her knife. "Is that clear?"

"It's clear," Alo replies.

Jena walks ahead.

"Slow down, we're not running a race here," M.I. A yells at Jena.

Jena is actually enjoying the sunshine, the trees, the sounds of birds and animals.

She remembers her dream of walking through the forest. Even with her flaws, she knows that she is God's creation. She has no idea where this part of her "mission" will take her, but she feels at peace. She feels, little by little, that she is finding her way through the forest of her life. That her recklessness and anger led her to the path she is walking now. It is a journey she knows she will have to complete.

Throughout the day, Jena does as M.I. A tells her, and after they catch some game, the two women begin to talk.

"You're a natural at this," M.I. A says, "just like I was when I started."

Jena hesitates. She doesn't want to pretend they're friends but decides to speak. "Were you a young girl when you came to this life?"

"Yes," M.I. A says. "I was young and eager to learn. I was tough, but a man broke me."

"Well, that may explain your anger. I have a man who loves me, and I love him." Jena thinks of Jake, who had been so gentle and kind to her.

"Did this man love you?" Jena asks.

"I wish you hadn't asked me that question," M.I. A replies.

Jena laughs a little. "Oh, so you're in love?"

M.I. A laughs, too, and walks away from Jena and toward Alo.

Alo throws the sack of their catch over his back and starts walking back to camp.

M.I. A wipes her bloody knife on her pants and walks back to Jena.

Jena watches as Alo walks away.

"Where's he going with our catch?" Jena asks.

"He's taking it back to cook, to feed the workers." M.I. A surprises Jena by throwing her bag down and beginning to set up her tent.

"What are you doing?" Jena asks.

"We're staying here tonight. It will give us a chance to get to know one another."

M.I. A pulls out a container of water. "Help me set up this tent and start a fire. We'll cook, eat, wash up, and, hopefully, you won't try to escape because I really don't want to kill you. I've grown quite fond of you, Jena. You remind me of me when I was younger."

M.I. A and Jena busy themselves with organizing a small camp.

"I believed in love until I was betrayed," M.I. A says, finally answering Jena's question. "Back then, I thought I was ready for the world, and the world was ready for me. I was wrong. You'll see, too."

Jena feels a connection to the mysterious woman. She doesn't necessarily trust her, but she feels a bond. She doesn't resist the feeling.

M.I. A pulls from the sack one of the dead animals and begins to skin it. She hands Jena a knife. "Help me," she says.

When they are done, they cook their catch and feast on their meal like savages, both famished after the long day of hunting.

They heat water and bathe as best as they can.

When Jena is done, she finds M.I. A staring into the crackling campfire with a bottle of whiskey next to her. She picks up the bottle and waves it toward Jena.

"Let's talk," she says.

"About what?" Jena asks.

"I'm not looking for a confrontation, Jena," she says. "The day has gone so well."

Jena slowly sits next to M.I. A. She picks up the bottle and takes a swig.

M.I. A takes the bottle from Jena and does the same. She wipes her mouth.

"You're a mirror image of me," she tells Jena.

"Tell me who you are," Jena says firmly, but without rancor.

"I'm a friend, and I'm an enemy," she tells Jena. "You will find out everything in due time." Then she asks, "Tell me about the man you love."

Jena turns away. "Why?"

"I know there is someone out there you love. I just thought you could use a friend right now," M.I. A explains.

"I didn't know we were friends," Jena replies. "But, yeah, there is someone. His name is Jake, and I do love him." She takes another drink. "But I'm bad for him. He's better off without me." She pauses. "Last he knew, I was in prison. He has no idea where I am. Hell, *I* don't know where I am." She looks around. "Someplace in South America, I suspect."

"Where did you meet this man?" M.I. A asks.

Jena sighs and begins to open up. "We've known each other since we were kids. He's my best friend, and I love him with everything I have." Sadness washes over her. She tries to hide her tears. "I never thought I could love someone so much."

Jena turns to M.I. A "Have you ever loved someone like that?"

M.I. A smirks. "Yes," she replies. "Actually, I've loved two men that way. Both were so dear to me for such different reasons."

The two women sit in silence for a long time.

Finally, M.I. A says, "Love can be satisfying and confusing and even deadly. I want to be your friend, Jena. I want to teach the true ways of this world. I want to teach you how to survive cruelty and overcome your fears."

"I don't have fears," Jena says defensively.

"We all have fears," M.I. A responds. "There is always a deep part that we hide from the world, from the people we love. It's like a volcano ready to explode. We hold onto it because it is ours. No matter how horrible or how good, we can't release it because it is ours, and we want to keep it sealed.

"But we must release it. It is the only way we can be truly free."

Jena thinks about the feverish dream of her mother. The dream seemed to say that she needed to free herself and her mother.

"You're right," Jena concedes. "I need to free myself, and there is someone else who is very precious who needs me to be free."

M.I. A looks at Jena with sympathy.

"Your love?" she asks.

"No," Jena replies. "My mother."

M.I. A and Jena take turns tipping the bottle until it's emptied.

"We must rest now," M.I. A says. "We'll have to leave early to get back to camp." But she has one more thing to say before they rest. "Join me, Jena. You and I together will be unstoppable. We can take down those who have kept us captive."

They lie down on opposite sides of the tent.

Both are asleep instantly.

Jena dreams again. She is in Jake's car. They are silent. The car is not running, but the headlights are on. She is in the passenger seat, but Jake isn't with her. She stares down the long highway and sees a shadow walking toward the car.

The shadow becomes a person, standing in the middle of the highway, in front of the bright headlight. A man. He's wearing a black button-down shirt and black pants. He has a pure white cross in the middle of his shirt collar.

He opens the driver's side door and gets into the car.

"Do you know who I am?" he asks.

She doesn't.

The man looks at Jena and smiles. "I am you. I am your conscience, your better side."

"Then why are you dressed in black?" Jena asks.

"Because you are in a dark place. When you become brighter, I will appear brighter to you."

Jena starts to cry. "I've done terrible things."

The man's shirt turns pure white. Jena is awed.

The man smiles. "You are beginning to realize that you can change your destiny. You can be brighter. It's up to you."

Then he disappears.

Jena wakes up a little. She knows she was dreaming but still feels shaky.

She knows she has been visited by an angel.

"I have to free my dark side," she murmurs. "It is the only path to true freedom. Then, I can finally love Jake. And my mother and father will be free."

She falls back into a light sleep. She is standing in the road, looking for the angel.

Instead, she finds Mike McNeil.

"Happy to see me?" he asks with a grin.

Jena becomes enraged and starts swinging at him. But her fist goes right through his body.

"You'll never get rid of me, Jena. I'll be with you forever," he tells her.

In the dream, she drops to her knees and begs the angel to return.

She sees a sparkling light. Maybe the angel is letting her know that she is not alone.

Jena opens her eyes and sees the sunlight, for real.

She hears movement and realizes that the mysterious woman is already gathering her things.

Jena jumps up, dresses, and begins packing. She says nothing.

"Good morning, Jena."

Jena smiles. "Good morning," she offers in return.

Suddenly, M.I. A begins to tell her story.

"Jena Parker, I say again that you remind me so much of my young self."

Jena stops and listens.

"Do you want to know who I am?" M.I. A looks around. The morning sun is making the forest shine. "I was a young girl trapped in a world of hunger. My parents were poor, and my father tried to provide for us, but he was cruel. My mother was the dutiful wife. She did everything she was told, but she hated my father because he beat her." M.I. A shakes her head. "I watched my mother beg my father for mercy, but he wouldn't stop. He hit her over and over … until … one day … she fought back. She killed him."

"What happened then?" Jena asks.

"I was sent away to what I was told would be a new home. But it was really a new hell. It was a camp ruled by a ruthless man."

Jena gasps a little at the mention of a camp ruled by a cruel man.

"Some of the men and women who were part of his empire became killers, and they killed who he wanted them to kill," M.I. A explains. Some are taken as lovers or wives. Yet all will serve him." M.I. A is silent for moment, then speaks. "I and others, some younger, were trained to be killers. I was ignorant about what lay in front of me, but I caught on quickly. I learned fast, and I met a handsome boy."

M.I. A. turns around to hide her rising emotions. "I loved him very much, and we spent much time together. We even planned our escape, but they caught us and brought us back. They watched us to keep us apart, but we still found ways to be together.

"Do you remember the ruthless leader I mentioned? He found out that we were sneaking away to be together, so he made me come work for him in his home. I saw less and less of my love, but I thought of him every day."

M.I. A pauses for a long time. "The leader was named Romli, and one night he made me his lover. He took me to his bed and made me his. I was his woman—at least, one of his women. I was his lover, his servant, and I killed for him."

Jena can barely contain herself; she has so many questions. But she doesn't want to stop M.I. A from talking.

"Once I earned his trust, I could sneak away and see my old love. We were so happy in those moments, until I had to leave. He would beg me to stay, but I could not. The strangest thing is that, even as ruthless as Romli was, I began to have feelings for him, feelings I had not expected. I loved two men."

M.I. A looks down in shame.

"My mother became an activist working against Romli, and Romli assigned me to kill her. My own mother. I could not. But I knew Romli would kill me without a second thought if I disobeyed. So, I snuck away and asked my first love to kill her for me. I asked my love, Moschi, to kill my mother."

Jena's face grows red with emotions and questions when she hears Moschi's name.

"Moschi agreed that he would do what I asked, what Romli ordered me to do, if I would leave Romli for good. He wanted to start a family, have a fresh start."

Jena can no longer contain herself. "You call yourself M.I. A. Short for Maria?" she stutters. "You're Moschi's Maria."

"Yes," she says. "I am Maria. M.I. A, that's who they all think I am."

"Moschi also told me that you were murdered by Romli."

"But I am alive. Obviously," Maria says. "And you want to know how that can be."

Maria turns her back to Jena. Clearly, her story is not an easy one to tell. Jena wonders how often she has told it. Probably not often.

Maria looks into the distance. "I allowed myself to be injected with a potion that made me appear dead. I let Moschi believe that Romli had killed me because I had not fulfilled my assignment."

Jena gasped audibly.

"I betrayed Moschi," Maria says. "He even buried me, but I dug my way out as soon as he left. Yes, it was an extreme act. But I couldn't bear to tell him that I was also in love with Romli. … I couldn't leave with Moschi, and I couldn't kill my own mother."

Jena is surprised that she feels anger on Moschi's behalf. "Do you know what he has been through for you? Do you know what he has done for me because of his love for you—the woman he loved but thought was dead," Jena says with great emotion. "He set me free from prison in my hometown because he knew that I was separated from the man I love. He understood my pain because he had shared a great love with you. He pitied me, and he helped me because he thought you had been killed," she tries to explain.

"You don't know the whole truth, Jena," Maria says.

"Oh, don't I?" Jena says with anger. "Do tell me."

"I know who you are, Jena Parker. You come from a small town called Maplesville. Your parents are both dead because of you, one way or another. And your biological father is Miles McNeil, a ruthless liar, killer, and kidnapper. And I know that you killed him, too." Maria is as angry as Jena. "Yes, my life is a lie, but your entire world has been a lie. Your father, Jonathan Parker, was once in cahoots with Miles McNeil and Warden Peters, but your father got out of the business when you were born."

"What business?" Jena asks.

"The business that you are part of right now," Maria says. "Women, then and now, are taken from American prisons and brought here to be whores, servants, assassins, whatever these criminal men want them to be. Most of the women have no family, and no one ever noticed that they were missing. They were easy targets because no one cared about them."

"You are lying about my father. He would never do anything like that," Jena says, defending the man she has loved her entire life.

"You are naïve, Jena. Most of the older women in Romli's camp were sent by your father. But, yes, there came a time when Jonathan Parker couldn't stomach the trafficking of women anymore," Maria acknowledges. "Miles McNeil, on the other hand, couldn't get enough. And that wasn't all. McNeil had an affair with the mayor's wife, and the mayor was involved in the kidnapping plot, too. When his partners in crime turned on him, the mayor and his wife were both murdered."

Jena had guessed the depths of the warden's lust for power and money, but she didn't know the details.

"It was all about money. They all worked for Romli. I know because I am Romli's woman, and he told me everything—probably to torment me. Moschi never knew I was alive. He left for the United States when he thought I was killed."

"You are ruthless," Jena spits at Maria. "You knew who I was all along, but I didn't know your story until now. You have to be coldblooded to let a man who loved you believe you were killed by his boss—only because you were that boss' lover. Moschi has lived with that lie and carried the weight of the guilt with him all of these years."

Jena moves closer to Maria. "You are despicable … but what about the parts of the story you left out?" She pauses, trying to put the pieces of the puzzle together, then: "Moschi went on to build his own killing empire, didn't he? And he may have had sympathy for you back in Maplesville—and, yes, perhaps, it was because he had once known love himself."

Jena goes on: "But he also let his recruits beat you nearly to death. Why are you defending him? Why do you think that one man is so much better than the other? Why do you think you are so much better than I am?"

Maria stops Jena. "I know what I have done. I accept my foul deeds. Your righteousness does not pain me more than the pain I feel every day," she says.

"But how can you defend, to me, a man who almost succeeded in killing you, who kidnapped you—albeit a bit more gently than the women here."

"I have told you the truth," Maria says. "Now you must accept your truth."

Jena starts gathering her things. "I'm leaving!" Jena yells in fury.

Maria pulls out her knife. "No, you are not. You will work for me and do what I say, or you will die."

"So, you are no better than the ruthless Romli and others." Jena turns to face Maria. "Then, I choose to die."

Both women take a battle stance and begin circling each other.

Maria jabs her knife at Jena, but Jena moves back.

They are like boxers dancing in the ring.

Maria runs toward Jena, but Jena flips her over and gets a grip on Maria's wrist, just inches from the knife's handle. Jena squeezes Maria's hand and keeps fighting.

Finally, Maria opens her hand, and the knife falls.

Maria kicks Jena in the stomach hard and runs for her gun.

Jena runs behind the more experienced woman and trips her, then flips her over.

Maria's bag flops over, and the diamond necklace falls out. It sparkles in the dazzling sun. Jena throws herself onto Maria's bag to keep her from reaching the gun.

Then the kicks, punches, and jabs begin again, both women landing blow after blow.

Maria finally lands a hard punch to Jena's face. Jena is stunned long enough that Maria has time to reach her gun.

Jena twists Maria's arm, and they both fall to the ground, with Jena fighting to keep Maria from pointing the gun at her.

Both women are exhausted, but at last, Jena wrestles the gun away from Maria and manages to point it at her as she lies on the ground.

Jena tries to catch her breath and steady her hands, when they hear a man yell from behind them.

"No, Jena. Please stop. It's Moschi." He begs, "Don't kill her."

It would be hard to say who is more startled.

Jena's face is red. She doesn't know how to stop. She keeps the gun trained on Maria.

Moschi walks closer. He has no words to express his shock at seeing Maria alive.

All three are silent.

Maria tries to stand, while simultaneously watching Jena and Moschi.

"You're alive," Moschi says in disbelief.

Maria is silent.

"You have no idea what she has done, Moschi," Jena says.

"Shut up," Maria spits. "I will tell him myself."

"So, you can tell him another lie?" Jena asks. "Moschi, she deceived you. She faked her death because she was in love with Romli," she says angrily.

Tears form in Moschi's eyes. He still loves her. "Say something!" he screams at Maria.

"Yes, it's true," she acknowledges.

"I was in love with both of you. He took me to his bed when I was just a girl. Somehow, I developed feelings for him. I couldn't run away with you. I loved you, Moschi, but I loved him, too." Maria is fighting tears, too. "The only way to free you was to let you believe I was dead."

Moschi lowers his head and cries. He turns to walk away.

Maria calls after him. "Moschi, please."

Moschi turns, slowly.

He fires his weapon directly into her stomach.

She falls to the ground. Moschi walks to her and stands over her.

Jena is in shock, but she is also angry. She walks to Moschi and stands beside him, as Maria appears to fade away.

Jena throws down her gun and turns away.

She begins packing her things, as Moschi continues to stare at the dying Maria. Just as Jena reaches for her jacket, she hears a single shot.

Jena turns and runs toward the gunshot. The barely conscious Maria had managed to get her shaking hand on the trigger of the gun just long enough to shoot Moschi in the chest.

Jena watches as Moschi falls to the ground, a bullet hole straight to his heart.

Maria's eyes close, and she is gone.

Jena, confused by her mixed feelings, rushes to Moschi's side.

Jena stares into Moschi's dying eyes. "You said this was my destiny." Jena yells.

"It is," Moschi says with his last fainted breath.

His eyes close as he lies mere inches from the love of his life.

And he is gone.

CHAPTER TWENTY-ONE

Jake leaves Franklin's cozy den. He's happy for the first time in weeks. They finally have a plan.

Once he reaches the bedroom where he and Ken are staying, and where Reyes is tied up with his own handcuffs and several bedsheets, Jake opens the door and calls Ken into the hall.

Jake is practically shaking with excitement.

"What is up with you, man?" Ken asks.

"Franklin and I came up with a plan. We just need a lot of luck to make it work," Jake says.

Franklin walks into the hallway, almost on cue.

"Well, the truth is that Franklin wants to turn Reyes in, to the police or the FBI," Jake explains.

Ken makes a face. "We came all this way just to turn him over to his crooked cop friends?"

"Believe me, I agree," Jake says. "You know how I feel about Reyes."

"But he is an officer of the law, and I don't feel like going to prison for kidnapping, which is exactly what would happen, regardless of what Reyes did," Franklin explains.

"Forget all that. We've got it worked out," Jake says, excited again. "We're all going to go in there after I fill you in on what's going to happen. Reyes already thinks he can drive a wedge between us, Ken, so we're going to use that."

Ken nods. He's curious.

Slowly, Franklin and Jake explain their plan to Ken, making sure that all three of them understand. They have to pull off some good acting, or they'll never get Reyes to step into their trap.

The men muss their hair. Franklin makes a tear in his shirt, and so does Jake. Ken pulls his robe askew as if it has been grabbed violently. Then, they jump up and down a few times to get flushed and sweaty.

Next, Ken and Jake go back into the room and slam the door loudly behind them. Reyes had nodded off, and the bang of the door wakes him.

Then the theatre begins.

"Franklin is right, man. We have to turn this cop over to his cop friends or the District Attorney, or, hell, maybe the FBI. In fact, the FBI sounds really good to me," Ken says, speaking loudly, pretending to be furious with Jake.

"Jake, you're acting like a crazy man. You can't treat me like you did out there in the hall. Me and Franklin, we're the ones who know what's what. You, my friend—maybe my former friend—are going to get us all killed or put in jail for the rest of our lives."

The two friends take a peek at Reyes, whose eyes are getting bigger and bigger.

"Calm down and stop being such a wuss, Ken. We got into this to find Jena, and that's what we're going to do—at any cost," Jake says.

Franklin walks in just as Jake and Ken are looking at each other like a pair of fighting bulls.

"Hey, you two. This is my home. Let's take it down a notch," Franklin says.

"Well, maybe you can talk some sense into him," Ken says, walking out of the room and slamming the door behind him.

"Jake, you are my friend. Jena is my friend. But we're committing more felonies than I can count. We need to take Officer Slime Ball here and turn him over to the authorities. Like I said, when Mike wakes up, he can vouch for everything we say," Franklin says.

"I can't do it, Franklin. I respect you, but I just can't do it. I can't just abandon Jena, wherever she is," Jake says. "And Officer Slime Ball, as you call him, is the only way we can possibly find her."

"We can't turn on each other, like what happened just now out in the hall," Franklin says. "Come back to my den. I could use a drink."

They leave to let Reyes contemplate his future.

He'd been so hung up on outsmarting these stupid punks—and, if he's honest, how much it hurts his ego—that he hadn't really thought about what was waiting for him back in Maplesville.

Warden Peters sure isn't going to stand up for him. That coward will probably pin the whole trafficking ring on him, Reyes thinks. And Romli? He'd happily kill them all at the first hint of trouble. He'd end up dead, just like the former mayor and his wife, not to mention McNeil, his old partner—even if it was Jena's gun that killed McNeil.

Reyes starts to sweat, tied up in a stupid chair with bedsheets, of all things. And the FBI? Reyes hasn't even considered that possibility. They aren't going to believe a small-town cop, no matter how powerful that cop is.

Honestly, Reyes had figured he could get the drop on Jake and Ken, shoot them, and leave them on the side of some dark road. Now this guy, Franklin, is involved, and it's pretty obvious that the man has a crap-ton of money.

Jake, Ken, and Franklin wait for what they hope is an appropriate amount of time—enough time for Reyes to decide that he'd better watch out for his own neck, but not enough time for him to come up with a way out on his own.

The three walk back into the bedroom, as if they are united on a plan.

Jake and Franklin approach Reyes.

"Tell me right now where Jena is," Jake says. "Because if you don't, I'm going to let my friends here turn you in to the authorities. You'll never see the light of day when people find out everything you've done."

Franklin threatens, "And, in case you hadn't noticed, I've got enough money to hire some really good lawyers."

Reyes just sits there, tied up, pondering his fate for a little while longer. He just can't come up with any good alternatives.

"Okay. Okay," Reyes finally stutters. "I'll take you to Jena. But it's not going to be easy, and I mean that."

"Just untie me, and give me back my belt," Reyes says.

"Where do we have to go?" Franklin asks. "I need to know what kind of plans to make."

Reyes takes another minute to think. This plan seems like his only real alternative. He looks at Franklin.

"We're going to need an airplane, weapons, plenty of ammunition, nonperishable food, a lot of water, and camping supplies. We're going outside the country," Reyes says. "You guys think you can handle all of that? I never said this was going to be easy."

"Don't worry about us," Ken says sarcastically.

"I'm serious. We could all end up dead," Reyes says.

Franklin feels excitement fluttering in his gut. He has always felt that he was destined for travel and adventure.

Jake feels relief. Finally, he thinks, there is hope that he will find Jena.

Ken, as ever, is ready for whatever comes—anything to help his friends.

Reyes keeps talking while Ken and Jake unwind the sheets that are binding him.

"We're going to be dealing with dangerous people. You guys aren't prepared for what's ahead, but if you want to know where Jena is, you'd better get it together. We're going south, way south, and, like I said, we might not come back. That's all I'm going to say for now. I'll give you the details when we're on the plane, in the air, and on our way," Reyes says. "Do we have a deal?"

Franklin asks Ken to stay in the room and watch Reyes, while Franklin pulls Jake back into the hall.

Franklin leads Jake toward the main living room. He and Jake are so relieved that they burst into laughter. Jake grabs Franklin and hugs him hard.

"I can't tell you how much I appreciate this," Jake says, his eyes glimmering with excitement.

Someone is waiting for them.

"Jake, this is my friend, Lander T. Curtis," Franklin trails off. "Lander is going to help us get the airplane, weapons, and everything we need." Franklin smiles. "Lander is also my go-to person when I want information that only a good investigator who has been in the business for over thirty years can get."

Jake turns to Lander and gives him a hearty handshake.

Franklin produces yet another hat.

It must be his detective hat, Jake thinks, shaking his head.

Franklin walks to his desk and pulls out a map.

"Jena must be somewhere in South America. I can smell the corruption. I can smell the collusion. Reyes is afraid. Did you see the sweat pouring off of his forehead?" Franklin asks.

"We were right. Reyes is on the run now. They're onto him back home," Jake says.

Franklin buzzes for Mr. Tindale, who arrives quickly.

"Yes, sir?" Mr. Tindale asks.

Franklin explains the situation and then tells him the plan. "I need you to arrange for my private plane to be readied. We need every supply you can pack into it. Weapons, ammunition, survival gear. We think we're headed for the jungle, so we need to be prepared for any contingency. And we don't know how long we'll be gone."

Mr. Tindale looks surprised.

"Oh—and you're going with us," Franklin says.

"Me, sir?" Mr. Tindale appears to be very uncomfortable.

Franklin puts his hands on Mr. Tindale's shoulders. "I need your help. What do you say? Are you ready for an adventure?"

Unexpectedly, Mr. Tindale's face lights up. "Yes, sir. I'd best go speak to Mrs. Tindale and start making arrangements. It will take some time. We need to be prepared."

Franklin turns to his friend, Lander. "How about you, my old friend? Are you in for an adventure?"

"Count me out this time, buddy," Lander says. "But I'll be here on the ground. You're going to need me when you return, and I'll be ready."

"Now, I need to go talk to Candy," Franklin says. "She needs to know what's going on, and we need to make sure she has the care she needs. We can't abandon her, and we can't take her with us."

Franklin stops Mr. Tindale as he walks away to start preparations. "Mr. Tindale, please make sure that Mrs. Tindale looks in on Candy and that your staff gets her anything she wants or needs." Franklin turns to Jake. "I also need to talk to her about Micky. Micky was my love, but she was Candy's best friend."

He peers into Jake's eyes. "Jake, are you ready for this?"

"How can you even ask?" Jake replies.

"Okay, then. You'd probably better get back up to Ken. You two should try to get some sleep," Franklin says.

The house begins to buzz with activity.

Jake and Ken pack their belongings, and the three of them, including Reyes, are eager to get going. Reyes watches every move Jake and Ken make.

"When are we getting out of here?" Reyes asks.

"Soon," Jake says. "There's a lot to do before we take off. Franklin and his staff are taking care of that." Jake turns to Ken: "Franklin suggests we get a little rest." He waves the gun toward Reyes. "Why don't you take the first shift, while I watch this guy?"

Reyes grumbles, but he and Ken are asleep in minutes on the two twin beds.

Franklin walks through his home. Yes, he'd always said he didn't want any part of his father's wealth. But he is full of gratitude now. What his father built has allowed him to live the life he wanted, and now it is helping Franklin help his friends. He goes into the study and makes a few notes for his next book.

He's pleased as he passes Mr. Tindale and his staff. Everyone is moving quickly, but efficiently.

Franklin goes to Candy's room and knocks. He's worried about this conversation.

"Come in," she replies.

Franklin opens the door to see Candy in a lovely robe and nightgown. Her skin glows, and so does her hair. He can see her baby belly through the gown.

He's also pleased to see that she has a cart of delicious food in her room. She smiles.

"Hello, Franklin," Candy says softly. "Thank you for all of this." It seems that she is finally calm and feels safe.

Franklin walks over to Candy and gives her an unexpected hug. He can tell she is pleased.

Franklin looks deeply into Candy's eyes and speaks plainly. "Candy, I'm going away for a while. And Ken and Jake and Mr. Tindale are going, too."

Candy is alarmed.

"It's going to be okay," Franklin assures her.

"When?" she asks.

"Soon," Franklin says bluntly. "We've finally gotten Reyes to promise that he'll tell us where we can find Jena. We're taking him and my plane, and we're going to go get her and bring her home."

Candy stands and paces around the room. Franklin's eyes follow her.

"It helps me to know that you guys are here," Candy says. "And Mr. Tindale and his staff have been so nice."

"And the staff will continue to take care of you," Franklin says, trying to make her feel better. "I've left specific instructions that from this moment on, you are the lady of the house."

"What?" she asks.

"You will run this house in my absence," he explains, smiling at her confusion.

"I don't know how to do anything like that," Candy stutters.

Franklin smiles again. "You don't have to know anything. My staff will take care of you. Mrs. Tindale and other members of the staff will be here." He squeezes her arm to reassure her. "We will be back in time for the birth of this beautiful baby. My personal doctor and his nurse will be at your beck and call. I've known him for years. You don't have to worry about anything." He pauses and continues smiling. "Besides, the guys—Bobby, Steve, Allen, and Sam—will be a phone call away. If you ever feel afraid, call them, and they'll be right here."

Despite his assurances, Candy's lips are quivering a little.

"After everything you've already been through …" He doesn't finish. "You're in good hands, Candy. And you're a strong woman."

"I miss Micky," Candy says quietly. She doesn't want to upset Franklin. "She's the whole reason I'm here."

"I miss her, too. You know how much I loved her. I promise that when I get back, we'll get to the bottom of what happened to her in that hospital," Franklin says. "I'd be looking into it already, but we won't have another opportunity to get out of this mess with Chief Reyes—and find Jena. You understand, don't you?"

Candy nods that she does.

"I've had Bobby make arrangements. He and his brothers finally twisted enough arms to get Micky's body released to the funeral home. She'll be cremated. When I get back, we'll have a ceremony and find a nice place for her ashes—some place she'd like."

Candy begins to cry quietly.

"I feel the same way, Candy. But she'd want us to try to put an end to Reyes' madness and whatever is happening to women over in the prison. You want that, too, right?"

"You're right," Candy agrees readily. "Now I know why she loved you so much."

"She loved you, too," he reminds her.

"I know," Candy says weakly.

"I will never let Reyes or anyone else hurt you. Micky would want me to take care of you. I want to take care of you," Franklin says sincerely.

Candy jumps up and gives Franklin a long hug.

She steps back.

"Please be safe. And tell Jake and Ken and Mr. Tindale the same thing," she says.

"Of course," he says, bowing a little and waving his hat dramatically.

Franklin backs out the door and shuts it quietly. He says a little blessing for Candy before walking away.

He jumps up the steps to Jake and Ken's room.

Jake opens the door, looks at Franklin, and he's speechless.

Franklin has on dark sunglasses and is dressed like he's on the set of *Indiana Jones*. He struts into the room, clearly comfortable.

Jake and Ken are still staring at him, and Reyes stares at him, too.

Reyes is even doubting his decision to go along with his plan.

"Look at this wannabe writer," Reyes grunts. "Can we stop the cowboy shenanigans and get this show on the road?"

Franklin calls for Mr. Tindale, who walks into the room and dressed just like Franklin.

Ken and Jake look away to suppress a giggle.

Franklin's ready to go. "Is the van here?" he asks.

"Yes, sir," Mr. Tindale responds.

"Then, let's do this," Franklin says, and they all troop downstairs and out the front door to the waiting van.

The door of the van opens, and a small man dressed all in black steps out. Before anyone can register surprise, another door opens, and another small man steps out.

Franklin makes the introductions. "These two men are friends of mine, they're brothers, Bobby and Steve. Candy might have mentioned that they helped us move out of …"—a wave of emotion hits Franklin—"helped us move out of Micky's apartment."

Ken and Jake nod.

Jake walks behind the shackled and handcuffed Reyes, who moves awkwardly toward the van.

Bobby and Steve open the van's rear doors. The van lights come on and reveal the best-looking van any of them have seen. Plenty of space for their gear, plush leather seats, and video monitors, and headphones at each seat.

"We're not just a moving service," Bob says proudly, as they all pile in.

"This van is badass," Ken says, voicing what everyone is thinking.

Bobby and Steve look proud, and when everyone is settled inside, they close the doors, high-five each other, and jump in.

As the van moves through the mist, everyone is quiet. Each person watches the others for a sign of what everyone else is thinking, but the fancy gadgets in the van give them all space to ponder their own thoughts, fears, and expectations.

The van pulls into a private airport. A pilot set up by Franklin's friend, Lander T. Curtis, awaits them boarding. The location is very remote.

Everyone jumps out, but Ken looks worried and pulls Jake aside.

"Hey, I've got something I need to do," Ken says.

Jake looks worried, now, too. "Are you pulling out?"

"No, it's my mom. I haven't talked to her in forever, and I'm sure she's worried sick," Ken says.

"Go ahead, step aside, and do what you need to do," Jake says. "I'll talk to Franklin."

Jake feels sick with guilt, and Franklin notices that something is going on. He walks over to Jake, while Steve and Bobby stand on either side of Reyes.

"What's going on?" Franklin asks.

"Ken's calling his mom," Jake says, his face crestfallen.

"And?" Franklin asks.

"It just reminded me that I haven't called my mom," Jake explains. "I've been so obsessed with Jena that I haven't even thought about my parents. The last time I saw her, my mother was half-crazy, and my dad was in bad shape."

"Call her," Franklin advises. "We don't need to carry any regrets with us, where we're going."

Jake reaches into his bag for the cellphone he hasn't used in days. When he turns it on, he sees several missed calls and a message. He listens to the voice mail from the day before; it's from his mother.

"Jake, your father went back into the hospital today," she says tearfully. "He's fallen into a coma. It doesn't look good. I need you to come here to the hospital. I've been calling you. Where are you, son? Your mother needs you."

Jake looks alarmed, which alarms Franklin.

"What?" Franklin asks.

"My father is in a coma. My mother has been trying to reach me. I need to go to the hospital," Jake says, shaking his head. "I know it's a bad time, but I need to go to the hospital."

"Give me a minute to make some calls. I've got a friend who works in air traffic control in Maplesville. Let me see if we can get clearance to land there," Franklin says.

He steps to the side as Jake puts his bag back into the plane.

Franklin comes back to Jake with good news.

"We can take off from here and land in Maplesville. The flight won't last any time at all," Franklin says. "You can grab a cab and get to the hospital. But you'll only have an hour."

Franklin gives Jake a knowing look. "Jake, I said you have an hour. Do what you need to do in that time, or we turn around and go back home. Do you understand?"

"We're not turning back now," Jake says. "But I have to see my father."

"Let's go, then," Franklin says, patting Jake on the back. "I understand. I never told my father how much he meant to me. You don't need to make the same mistake."

Mr. Tindale, Bobby, and Steve make sure all the gear is still stowed properly, then get Reyes back into the plane and round up Franklin, Ken, and Jake.

They close the hatch and wave goodbye to Bobby and Steve as the plane slowly moves down the short runway and takes off smoothly.

Franklin explains the new plan to the rest of the team, and they settle in for the short flight to Maplesville.

———

Gary Paterson is hooked up to a breathing machine in the Intensive Care Unit. His wife, Sherry, is sitting beside him, crying, and holding his hand tightly. She looks older and more run-down—even to herself.

A nurse comes to check on Mr. Paterson, and Sherry looks up, hoping for good news. The nurse looks at the machines that show the patient's vital signs. She smiles at the desperate woman, but she shakes her head to indicate that nothing has changed.

"Can I get you anything, Mrs. Paterson?" the nurse asks.

"No, thank you," Sherry says, swallowing deeply.

The nurse leaves as Sherry retreats to her memories, to her boys.

Once upon a time, Gary could play in the yard with his sons—in the summer, running through the yard, splashing in the sprinklers. They laughed and played in the summer heat. Sherry remembers that she would stand at the screen door watching them. She always wore dresses with flowery prints. Gary liked them. She would giggle when Gary saw her watching them. She'd blow him a kiss, and they'd both watch the boy's wrestle. Gary believed in letting the boys get a little rough with each other. Sherry's motherly instincts would kick in, but Gary would wave her away, wordlessly telling her to leave them alone. Sherry would quietly go back to making dinner.

The memories float away like the smell of her cooking.

The endless beeping of the machines in the hospital room brings her back to the unfathomable reality that she is about to lose her husband, just weeks after losing her youngest son, Ted.

A nurse steps back into the room. "Mrs. Paterson," she says quietly.

Sherry doesn't answer at first, so the nurse puts her hand on Sherry's shoulder.

"I'm sorry to bother you, ma'am, but there's someone in the lobby who wants to see you and your husband."

"Who is it?" Sherry asks.

"I'm sorry. I don't know," the nurse says.

Sherry drops her head. She doesn't want to leave her husband, but she pats his hand and follows the nurse to the waiting room.

Standing in the waiting room is a woman wearing a crisp skirt and blouse and holding a brown purse strap over her shoulder.

Denise Parker—Jonathan Parker's sister and Jena's aunt—moves to Sherry and puts her arms around her.

Sherry quickly steps out of the embrace. Her tear-streaked face becomes cold.

"Don't you recognize me? I know it's been a long time. I'm Denise Parker, Kitty's sister-in-law."

"I know who you are," Sherry says.

"Sherry, I heard that you are going through a terrible time," Denise says.

Mrs. Paterson cuts the other woman off. "You've got a lot of nerve showing up here."

The nurse scurries away, sensing family drama.

Denise is confused. "When I heard about Gary, I wanted to stop by and pay my respects. It's been a long time, but we were all such good friends when we were young. I'm sorry if I'm intruding."

Sherry is silent, but only because she's too angry to form words. Denise stands silently. She has no idea what has provoked Sherry's anger.

"You need to get the hell out of here," Sherry says, quietly but with as much fury as she can muster. "I never want to see you or yours again as long as I live."

"I don't understand," Denise says, thinking that perhaps the woman is crazed with grief. "I'm staying in Maplesville for a while, and ... well ... I thought you might like to see a friend."

"You're no friend of mine," Sherry seethes. "Your murderous niece killed my youngest boy, Teddy, and seduced away my sweet Jake. And now I'm going to lose my husband."

Denise is taken aback. She has no idea what Sherry's accusations are about. "I'm sorry I came. I had no idea you felt that way about Jena."

"Well, now you do, and I hope she rots in prison," Sherry says.

"She's not *in* prison," Denise says, and she instantly regrets telling Sherry.

Sherry's heart drops, and she loses all control. She's screaming, "*What!?*" when Jake rushes into the waiting room.

"Mom," Jake says softly as he takes his mother by her shoulders protectively.

Sherry can't process that her son is in front of her, no more than she can process the news that Jena is no longer in prison.

Jake shakes his mother a little to get her attention, and she finally looks into his eyes and falls into his arms sobbing.

Jake looks over his mother's shoulder at Ken, who would come with him.

"Ken, this is Miss Denise Parker, Jena's aunt. I don't know what's going on here, but can you take Miss Denise to the other waiting room?" Jake asks.

Ken doesn't look too happy to get involved in this sad and disturbing scene.

Sherry is furious at the sound of Denise's and Jena's names.

"Jake don't talk to that woman. My god don't even say her name, son," Sherry says between sobs. She won't let go of Jake long enough for her son to find out what's going on.

Denise and Ken are speechless.

"Mom. Mom," Jake pleads. "I'm here. I came to see you and Dad." He looks around his mother again and catches Ken's eyes. "Ken, please take Miss Denise somewhere and introduce yourself. I'll be back as soon as I can."

"We don't have much time," Ken says quietly.

Sherry is alarmed again. "Not much time? Where are you going? Your father is right over here. He needs us with him."

Jake puts his arm around his mother and walks with her to his father's room.

"Ken, you can tell her everything," Jake manages to say. "Find out if she knows anything more than we do."

Ken nods and taps his wristwatch, reminding Jake, again, about the time.

Jake is torn but knows his duty is with his wounded mother who desperately needs her son. Sherry holds onto her son tightly and walks toward his father's room.

"Thank you for coming," she cries. "Where have you been?" She doesn't know whether to be grateful or angry, or both.

Sherry pulls herself together long enough to warn her only living son about his father's condition. "He's in a coma. We don't know whether he knows we're here or not."

Jake walks slowly into the Intensive Care Unit. He is so crushed to see his father in this lifeless-looking state that he can't speak.

Sherry hugs Jake. "I don't want to lose your father. You and your father are all I have," she says.

"I know, Mom, but he's a fighter. He's gotten through this before, and he'll get through it again," Jake says, trying to sound confident.

Jake walks to his father's bed and leans close. "Hey, Dad, it's me. Jake." He pauses, trying to hold back his tears.

"I know you can hear me, Dad, and I want you to know I love you."

Sherry starts to sob loudly when she hears Jake talking to his father.

Jake kisses his father on the forehead and then turns around to take his mother into his arms. They are both crying, both trying to console one another.

The son takes a deep breath, knowing that he needs to say something to his mother that will cut her to the quick.

"Mom," he whispers. "I can't stay."

Sherry nearly screams at his words. "You can't leave me," she cries forlornly. "I need you. Your father is dying."

"Mom, I only have a few minutes," Jake says as kindly as he can. "Dad's going to make it through this, I know he is. And you're going to make it through this, too."

"You don't know that" Sherry says. "Even the doctors don't know whether he'll make it. What is so important that you can't stay here with me and your father?"

Jake looks at his mother sympathetically but can't think of any words to comfort her or to explain why he must go.

His mother straightens up, angry again. "Does this have something to do with that Jena Parker?" Sherry asks loudly.

"Mom don't do this. Not in front of Dad," Jake says patiently.

"You are choosing her over your own mother—and your own father," Sherry accuses Jake, crying and shouting at the same time.

"Stop, Mom. You know that isn't true. I love you, Mom. And I love Dad. More than you can know."

"And your brother," Sherry asks. "You love Teddy, too. Right?"

Jake stares at his mother. "Of course. Of course, I loved Teddy."

He holds his mother as he begins to cry, too. He knows he has to leave, but he is devastated to be abandoning his parents.

Sherry grabs Jake's arm.

"I mean, you love Teddy even though he's not here. He's still your brother, and you love him, right?" she asks pitifully.

"Of course, Mom," Jake says gently. But he can't help thinking back to the night he overheard Ted say that he'd raped Jena—right before he watched Ted fall to his death.

Jake and his mother are startled when they hear his father make a grunting sound. It seems like he's struggling against the breathing tube and trying to say something.

Sherry lets go of Jake and yells at him to get the nurse.

Jake rushes out of the room, and Sherry moves to her husband's side.

"What is it, honey? I'm here with you. Don't leave me. Jake is here, too." Sherry tries to comfort Gary and tries in vain to understand what he's saying.

Jake rushes back in with the doctor and nurse.

Sherry hesitates but moves away so the doctor and nurse can check on Gary.

Mr. Paterson seems to still be trying to say something, while the doctor and nurse check his vital signs and the readings on the machines.

"Mr. Paterson. Mr. Paterson," the doctor says loudly to his patient. "We have a tube in your throat that is helping you breathe. Please try to relax. You can't talk right now."

It doesn't seem like Gary Paterson understands the doctor's words.

The doctor shines a light into Gary's eyes.

"Mr. Paterson, if you can understand me, can you raise your hand or give me a sign?"

Everyone in the room is quiet while they wait for any kind of response.

"Mr. Paterson, can you understand me?" the doctor says again. "You're in the Intensive Care Unit at the hospital. Your wife and son are here, and we're all taking good care of you."

There's only silence.

Suddenly, Mr. Paterson moans loudly and tries to raise one of his arms.

Everyone in the room sighs in relief.

The doctor moves closer. "That was good," he says. "Now try again." .

Everyone waits in expectation.

But Mr. Paterson doesn't make another sound.

The machines start beeping and squealing loudly. It looks to Jake like the machine that monitors his father's heartbeat is a straight line.

Everyone panics, but the medical professionals spring into action. The nurse calls "Code Blue" into the intercom, and other nurses run into the room. One of them pulls Jake and a hysterical Sherry out of the room.

Sherry just keeps screaming "No!" over and over.

Jake is in shock and can't say anything.

He grabs his mother to keep her from running back into the room.

Unable to calm her, he takes her back to the waiting room, so that their noise doesn't upset other patients.

Sherry buries her face in Jake's chest. Ken has returned to the waiting room and stands close by, feeling helpless as his best friend and his best friend's mother cry inconsolably.

The doctors and two of the nurses leave Mr. Paterson's room and look toward Jake and his mother.

"We're deeply sorry, Mrs. Paterson. We did everything we could. We were not able to revive him," the doctor says. "He was just too weak."

The doctor puts his hand on Jake's arm, but Jake can only look at him in horror.

The nurse's fuss over Sherry and try to get her to sit down, but she doesn't seem to hear them.

Finally, they walk away to give Jake and Sherry time to process the news. One of the nurses looks at Ken and asks him to let her know if she can do anything to help.

Jake and his mother have no words, crying and holding each other. Sherry suddenly let's go of Jake and glares at him. Then her face goes blank again.

She slowly walks toward her husband's room.

Ken approaches Jake. "I'm so sorry. I don't know what to say or do. I feel helpless. What can I do?"

Jake tries to wipe away his tears. He's still staring at the doors leading to the Intensive Care Unit.

They stand in silence for a few moments.

"Let's go," Jake tells Ken.

"What?" Ken asks, shocked.

"I said, let's go."

"Your father just died, Jake. You can't leave right now. Your mom needs you," Ken says.

"My mom doesn't want me around," Jake says.

"You know that's not true," Ken says.

"Did you see the look she just gave me?"

"That's shock, man. That's just shock," Ken says, trying to be the voice of reason.

"I can't help my dad anymore, and, truthfully, I can't help my mom," Jake says.

Ken just shakes his head at his insensitive friend.

"I can't help them, but I might be able to help Jena," Jake says, trying to make Ken understand. "I love my family. I love my dad, and I love my mom, but I love Jena, too, and I have to find her."

"This is just wrong, Jake, and you know it," Ken says.

"This is the way things have to be," Jake says. "It's too hot here. We've got Reyes. All of Maplesville is searching for us. This isn't an easy choice. But I choose to find Jena. She needs me."

Jake walks uncomfortably close to Ken. "Are you with me or not?" He turns quickly starts walking away.

Jake is halfway down the hall before Ken starts running to catch up.

"I'm coming. We started this together, and we'll end this together," Ken says, secretly aching over his best friend's decision.

They walk out of the hospital.

"If we're doing this, then you're probably going to want to talk to Jena's aunt. I told her what we knew and that we were off to try to find Jena. Denise knows Jena is out of prison, but she doesn't know anything more than we do," Ken tells Jake, after his conversation with Denise Parker.

"Here's her card, but we'd better stay out of sight," Ken says. "I'll call a cab. Let's get away from the main entrance."

Jake calls Denise, and she picks up immediately. "Jake, how's your father?"

Jake pauses. "He's gone. He died just a few minutes ago."

"Oh, I'm so sorry."

"Ken told me that you know that Jena's not in prison," Jake says, changing the subject back to Jena.

"That's right. I tried to visit her, but they told me she was gone. I talked to that Warden Peters. He told me Jena had escaped," Denise says.

"Your friend, Ken, told me that you think you know where she is," Denise says. "Where is she? Tell me."

"It's too much to explain over the phone. But Ken and I and some friends are headed out of the country, and please don't tell anyone that I told you," Jake says. "Tell people that I'm on the run. We could all be in a lot of trouble."

"I'm coming with you," Denise insists.

"No, you're not," Jake replies. "This is going to be tough. This is no place for you."

Jake and Ken turn a corner as Jake continues talking, and they run right into Denise.

Clearly, she'd been waiting for them to come out of the hospital. All three stare at one another.

Jake and Denise click off their phones.

"Let me decide what's right for me. Jena is my only niece. She's my only connection to my brother. I want to help, and I'm going with you."

She just stares at Jake.

Ken interrupts. "Listen, people. Our cab is here, and we don't have time to argue about this. Get into the cab."

They do, but the question is still not answered.

"You're going to need clothes," Jake says, finally.

"Then we'll stop at the hotel. I haven't even unpacked," Denise says firmly.

Ken and Jake look at each other. Ken shrugs. It's Jake's decision.

"You're not going to let anything happen to Jena, right?" Denise asks Jake.

He nods.

"Then nothing will happen to me," she says.

Jake sighs and gives the driver directions, and after a quick stop at the hotel, the cab driver is speeding back to the private airport where Franklin and the others are waiting.

Jake and Ken climb the stairs to the plane, followed by Denise.

Franklin stands up. "Hold up, now. Who is this?"

Jake hesitates. "This is Denise Parker, Jena's aunt. It's a long story. Can we just go? I'll explain everything."

Franklin is clearly uneasy with the situation.

"Do you trust me?" Jake asks.

"Yes, I do," Franklin replies.

"Then let's go."

Like Ken, Franklin just shrugs. Then he gallantly leads Denise to the empty seat next to the pilot and makes sure she's buckled in.

"Sounds like we all have a lot to talk about," Franklin says.

"Thank you," Denise replies in earnest.

They all settle into their seats and buckle up. Franklin makes sure that he's sitting next to Jake.

Franklin gives the go-ahead to the pilot, and soon they are slowly moving down the runway again, then swiftly rising.

For a moment, everyone sits in silence.

Franklin finally speaks quietly to Jake. "Tell me about your father and your mother."

"My father is gone. He died right in front of me," Jake says, shaking.

"And your mother?" Franklin asks.

Jake doesn't want to answer.

"Jake?" Franklin asks again.

"She doesn't know I left," Jake says, tearing up. "She was hysterical. She was scared. She was angry. There was nothing I could do for her."

Franklin looks incredulous. He and Ken exchange a look, and Jake sees them.

"I know. I know. I didn't do the right thing," Jake says. "But I did the only thing I could."

Everyone in the plane is looking at Jake and feeling the weight of his sadness.

Jake looks around the plane, a bit defiantly. "I'm not talking about it anymore," he says. "Right now, I just want to find Jena." He looks out the window and refuses to say another word.

CHAPTER TWENTY-TWO

After the fight between Matty and Paula and their onetime prison-mate Chance, plus the revelation that they were being trained with weapons but no ammunition, Paula tosses and turns in her cot that night. She feels guilty about the thought of Nurse May out in the wilderness on her own. She wonders if she would have done something different then, if she'd known what she knows now.

She remembers Nurse Tonya May trying to stand, blood dripping from her injured knee. She could see Tonya was afraid and desperate, as Matty forced Paula to leave Tonya behind. She could picture Tonya looking into the forest and wondered how she would survive on a sandwich and a bit of water. Matty had given her the sandwich and water but refused any other help.

At the time, Paula kept stopping to look back at Tonya, in spite of Matty using her weapon to try to herd Paula back to camp. Ultimately, Tonya faded from their sight.

Tonya was hopeless as she watched Matty, and Paula get farther and farther away. Finally, in a moment of absolute helplessness, she dropped to her knees and prayed that God would give her the strength to make it through the test. Tonya tried to pull herself together, gripping her sandwich. She hobbled back to the cave that Paula had shown her, back when they were still together.

Paula walked defiantly as Matty prodded her along at gunpoint.

"You're cruel," Paula told Matty. "How can you leave a woman with no survival skills out there?"

Matty stared at Paula. "You made it through the test, right?"

Paula begged Matty to leave her in the forest one more night so that she could help Tonya. "They wouldn't notice.

Matty refused. "They notice everything."

"Then just shoot me," Paula challenged her tormentor. "What would your boss say if you killed one of his women, someone he paid for?"

"I'd just tell him you were trying to escape," Matty said. "Now put on your big-girl panties and get moving."

Paula broke down and told Matty that she had nothing to lose. Her only hope was to see her daughter again one day, but her daughter had been taken away when she went to prison. She said that hope grew dimmer every day.

Matty surprised Paula. "There's always hope."

Just as she had earlier that night, Matty told Paula that Romli's camp was no worse than the hellhole of prison they'd come from.

"Take the love for your daughter and your anger and make yourself into a person of steel," Matty advised Paula.

Paula called Matty heartless.

"I'm not heartless. I'm strong," Matty snapped back.

Matty said women are already seen as having less value than a man. "In prison, we have no value at all." She asked Paula how many times she'd been sexually assaulted in prison. "You're their property, and they can do with you whatever you please."

Paula asked how that abuse was different from this time, brought here to the middle of nowhere, to service men, to be their servants, and perhaps to kill for them.

That's when Matty told Paula that she had seen a picture of Paula's daughter.

"How?" she begged Matty in utter disbelief.

Matty told her that new recruits are researched so that Romli could find a woman's strengths and weaknesses. She told Paula that the prison guards looked for women who were lonely.

Once the guards send the women, Romli's people gather as much information as they can about them to see how a woman can be best used.

"I've been here long enough that I know where the research is kept," Matty told her. "There is a recent photo of your sweet little girl in your file." She said she could help Paula get the photo.

"Why would you help me, Matty?" Paula asked.

"Because I lost my son, too. I don't have any photos of him," Matty said.

Paula asked how Matty ended up in prison.

"I had a fight with my son's father, so I went out to this biker bar to get drunk. I went straight to the bar and started pounding drinks," Matty explained.

When the bartender cut her off, Matty got into her car to drive home, even though people tried to stop her.

"I don't know how fast I was going. I was so drunk. I don't know how I made it to my neighborhood, but I did."

Her house was at the end of the street, and as Matty got angrier and angrier, she floored the accelerator even harder.

"There was another car coming toward me, but I was driving so fast that I couldn't stop. I slammed head-on into the car. It should have killed me. I was unconscious for a day or two in the hospital."

When Matty regained consciousness, there were police officers in her room.

"I caused the death of two people," Matty said, unable to hold back her emotions. "It was my boyfriend and my son. Apparently, he was coming to look for me, and he had to pack up my little boy and put him in the car, too."

She got a long prison sentence. "I felt like I deserved it."

When she was kidnapped and recruited, Matty said she didn't resist.

"I didn't ask any questions or put up much of a fight. And I've been here for years now. It feels like where I belong. But I miss my boy. He would be six years old now. I can't have my boy back," she said.

She paused briefly, then: "But maybe I can help you by getting you that picture of your little girl. The opportunity you have is much more than just a photo. You'll meet people. People who might help you. Don't worry about that Tonya woman—and close the door on the chance to see your daughter again." She then went on to say Tonya May had to be tested, as they all were tested. "She'll either make it, or she won't."

Paula thought of the frightening night ahead for Tonya. It pained her.

"I want my daughter," Paula told Matty firmly. "I love her so much."

"Then, let's go. Romli is expecting us," Matty said.

Tonight, after arguing with Chance and Matty and learning that they were "training" with no ammunition and that they were more likely to be whores than hunters, Paula wonders whether she had done the right thing those first few days at the camp. Matty was right about one thing: Paula would eventually die, one way or another. What she did that day with Tonya probably didn't matter at all.

———

Sherry Paterson sits in her dark living room with a half-finished bottle of liquor and a bottle of sleep pills. She begins to sob.

"Why did they leave me?" she cries into the dark. "First Teddy, then Gary, and now Jake. Oh, Jake, why did you abandon me?"

She opens the bottle of pills.

There is a knock at the door. Sherry tries to ignore it. But the knock gets louder.

A drunk and stumbling Sherry heads to the door while she screams, "Who in the hell is it? Go away!"

A voice comes from the other side of the door. "It's your sister, Jesse."

Sherry opens the door. Her face is sweaty and wet with tears. She wipes her face and glares at her sister.

"What you want?" she demands.

Jesse ignores her sister and strolls into the house.

Five-foot-eight and wearing tight jeans and black leather jacket, Jesse carries a backpack and has a deep Southern accent.

"I'm here to be with my sister, of course," Jesse says, "throwing her bag on the couch. "You just lost your husband. I cared about Gary, too. He was my brother-in-law." She lights a cigarette and eyes the bottles and pills. "Looks to me like you're ready to join Gary." She takes a drag on her cigarette.

Sherry closes the front door while Jesse snatches up the bottle of pills.

"Why don't you mind your own business? Just be happy I let you walk through the door," Sherry spits back. She eyes Jesse's cigarette. "Give me one of those."

Jesse smirks. "Oh, you smoke now?"

"I just lost my husband and my baby boy, so yeah, I smoke."

"It's a stinky habit," Jesse says.

"Just give me a cigarette," Sherry demands.

Jesse flops on the couch and puts her feet up.

Sherry sits in a chair across from Jesse.

"Where's Jake?" Jesse asks, flipping her hair and taking another puff of her cigarette.

"He's not here," Sherry replies in a nasty voice.

"So, where is he?" Jesse presses. "He just lost his dad. He should be here."

Sherry stands abruptly. "Look, I don't want to talk about Jake. I don't want to talk about anything. I don't think I even want you here. So, shut up and stop asking me questions."

Jesse is confused.

Sherry walks toward her bedroom.

"Just one more question," Jesse says loudly, stopping her sister. "Where can I sleep?"

Sherry shakes her head.

"Outside, for all I care," Sherry says and slams her bedroom door behind her.

Nurse Connors enters Mike's hospital room for her hourly check. Dr. Charter walks in a few minutes later.

"How is he today?" the doctor asks.

"No change," answers Nurse Connors.

"Have we had any luck finding family or friends?" Dr. Charter asks.

"No," the nurse says, sighing. "Those two young guys came by and the police officer and Detective Martin from the District Attorney's office, but that's all." She pauses for a minute. "Those young guys were supposed to be relatives, I heard, but we never saw them again. That was the night that turned this whole hospital into complete chaos."

"I'll be by before I leave tonight," the doctor says.

As the nurse checks the drip on Mike's IV fluid, she sees Mike's eyes flicker.

She runs into the hallway and calls out to Dr. Charter. "Something is happening!"

The doctor walks back quickly.

When they return, Mike is shaking and breathing erratically.

"Help me hold the patient down," Dr. Charter asks the nurse.

Mike stops shaking and starts to breathe normally.

Then he opens his eyes again.

Dr. Charter stares into Mike's eyes. "Hello, Mike. I am Dr. Charter. Can you hear me?" If you can, blink."

Mike blinks.

"Can you speak?" the doctor asks.

Mike tries to speak but can't.

"That's okay, just relax," Dr. Charter says.

The doctor begins checking Mike's reflexes and vital signs. He looks into Mike's eyes and listens to his heart.

Nurse Connors takes a deep breath. "This is a good sign, right?"

"It is," the doctor replies. "We need to have two nurses watching over this patient at all times. When is Nurse Nelson due in?"

Nurse Connors looks sad. "No one has seen her since that first night she went missing, including her husband. That's the same night that poor woman was shot in the Emergency Department. I haven't heard a thing about her since then."

Nurse Connors gestures for the doctor to join her in the hallway. "Her husband called the police and reported her missing."

"Why haven't I heard about this?" Dr. Charter asks.

"I guess the hospital administration doesn't want people freaking out. We're already short-staffed. I'll have to make some calls to see who can work tonight. I'm already working a double."

"Let me know," the doctor says. "Make sure no one goes into this room unless they're family. We don't want another setback."

As Dr. Charter starts to walk away, Detective Dean Martin and another member of his team walk toward Mike's room.

The doctor stops them. "May I help you?"

The detective flashes his badge. "I'm Detective Dean Martin, and this is Detective Amar Smith."

"We're here to check on the patient, Michael Fredmond. What is his status?"

"I'm afraid we can't continue to release information about this patient until we can find a family member to consent," the doctor replies.

Martin looks at Smith and back at the doctor.

"Listen," Martin says impatiently, reading Dr. Charter's name on his lab coat, "we've been checking on this patient from the start. And there's never been an issue before. This is now a federal investigation."

"Oh, is that right?" the doctor replies.

"Yes, the District Attorney, who assigned us to the case, has asked us to report directly to the FBI," Martin says. "Doctor, I'm sure you would agree that we need to find out who shot and nearly killed this man."

"Yes, of course," the doctor concedes. "Mr. Fredmond opened his eyes a few minutes ago. He's resting now, so I'd prefer he not be disturbed for at least twenty-four hours. I'd like to make sure that he is in recovery. We don't want him to relapse."

"I understand," Detective Martin says, walking away with Detective Smith.

Martin looks over his shoulder at the doctor. "We'll be back in exactly twenty-four hours."

Martin and Smith walk back to the squad car.

"Hey, did you hear that Gary Paterson died yesterday?" Smith asks Martin.

Martin replies that he did not. "I knew he'd been really ill. That's terrible, I've known Gary and Sherry Paterson for a long time. Do you mind if we swing by her house?"

At the Paterson house, Jesse is awake and making coffee when Sherry walks in wearing an ugly old robe.

"Coffee?" Jesse asks.

"Sure," her sister says, walking slowly to the table.

Jesse brings Sherry a cup and takes a sip. "You still make crappy coffee."

Both of them try to avoid conversation.

Jesse takes another sip, sighs, and asks, "So, how are you paying for the funeral?"

Sherry takes a quick breath. "Why?"

"I'm just curious. I know funerals cost a lot."

"Did you come to help pay for the funeral?" Sherry asks in a testy voice.

Jesse acts insulted. "You don't have to be so surly."

"Gary and I have an insurance policy," Sherry says. "But I'm not having a funeral."

Jesse chokes on her coffee a little. She coughs. "What? Why?"

Sherry gets up and puts her coffee cup in the kitchen sink. "Because I don't want one. I'm going to have him cremated. Gary doesn't have any family, and you are my only family—except Jake." Her voice cracks. "What's the point of a big funeral? Who would come?"

"If that's what you want," Jesse says, getting up, leaving her cup on the table. She walks over to Sherry. "That's fine. I'm here for you, sis." Jesse reaches out to hug her sister, and Sherry hesitates but allows the gesture. "I mean … if you think it would help … I don't have a job right now, or any money, so maybe I could stay here for a while and keep you company."

Sherry quickly pulls away. "You just came here because you thought Gary had some big insurance policy. How could you!" Sherry says, very angry.

Jesse sulks. "I'm your little sister. You just said I was your only family." She sits back down, ungracefully. "Okay, okay. I do need your help."

Sherry starts pacing around the room. "I knew it," she says. "Coming in here, pretending to be helpful. You just want money. You haven't changed a bit."

Jesse hangs her head a little. "You were the one who cut me out of your life," she says, with real emotion. "After momma passed away, you stopped speaking to me. Why? Because she gave me the house."

"That's right. She gave you the house, and you let it go into foreclosure. You've never taken anything seriously," Sherry responds. She turns her back on Jesse. "Now, at the lowest point in my life—my baby is gone, my husband is gone, my oldest son has abandoned me—here you come, thinking only of yourself."

"Sherry, it isn't like that," Jesse says.

"Pick up that bag you threw on the couch last night and get out of here," Sherry says.

Jesse tears up. "I know I've been a spoiled brat. I know momma put a lot on you, and I got it easy. I know me coming here now might look shady."

Sherry rolls her eyes.

"But, truly, I need my sister. I need you, probably more than you need me right now. I stopped doing drugs and drinking. I've even been to church a few times," Jesse pleads.

Sherry smirks. "You went to church?"

"Yeah, I did. It hasn't been easy for me." Jesse sounds sincere. "I know this is bad timing. But the truth is that I've wanting to see you for a while." She starts to cry. "Last year, I was diagnosed with cervical cancer and had to have a hysterectomy. I can't have children."

Sherry gasps and puts a hand over her mouth.

"I'm <u>thirty</u>, and I'll never have kids. I wanted to call you a year ago, but I just couldn't talk about it. Now, with your losses—Teddy and Gary—I thought it was time," she explains, still crying.

Sherry begins to cry, too.

"I just need my sister," Jesse says.

Sherry sighs sharply, then walks over to Jesse and embraces her.

"Poor Jess," Sherry says, stroking her sister's hair.

"You haven't called me that in years," Jesse says, smiling.

The two women are standing still, silent, absorbing the emotion of the moment, when the doorbell rings.

"I'll get it," Jesse says, wiping her eyes.

"Hello, miss," the detective says. "I'm Detective Martin, and I'm here to pay my respects to Mrs. Paterson."

Sherry peeks around the corner, clutching her robe.

"Well, hello, old friend," she greets him. "It's good to see you."

"I'd ask to come in, but I know it's early," he says politely. "I just wanted to offer my condolences on Gary's death. We've all known each other for a long time."

"Oh, come on in," Sherry says.

Jesse is more than a little amused at the glimmer she notices in Sherry's eye.

"I wish I had on something nicer to receive you," Sherry says with a lilt in her voice. "But I guess you've seen me in less."

CHAPTER TWENTY-THREE

Romli lights a cigar and leans back in his chair, which is gilded as if it were made for a king. Lero, head of the entire team of fighters, sits across from him. Smoke billows toward Lero, and Romli offers him a cigar. Lero declines.

"Then, let's get down to business," Romli says. "What's going on with the girls? Who's next on our list of enemies? And what's the status of things in the U.S."

"Everything is under control with the women. The ones who are ready for action can get new assignments," Lero says.

"We have another enemy," Lero says. The Mummel team is on the rise. I've sent a couple of teams to see if we can get more information," he says.

"The Mummels are weak," Romli's says. We've taken them down every time."

Lero continues his report. "In the United States, the warden has lost control. Reyes is missing. And it appears that the whole operation is in jeopardy."

"And" he goes on, "most interestingly, Moschi is missing."

"What?" Romli snaps.

"Moschi is missing. I had a team following him," Lero says. "They tracked him into the woods, and then they lost him. There haven't been any reports of him returning."

Romli puts his cigar down. "That's interesting. Send more teams after Moschi. I want to know where he is. Do you understand?"

"I do," Lero says.

"You should know Paula made it through the test, but the nurse has a disadvantage of a bleeding wound. She has no survival skills and probably won't make it through the evening. Do you want to me take her out?" Lero asks.

Romli smirks and blows a billow of smoke from his cigar. "No, leave her. I find that the ones who appear to be the weakest turn out to be the strongest."

"What shall we do with the new woman, Chance?" Lero asks.

"The feisty one," Romli says.

They both laugh.

"We found something interesting in her background. She has some kind of feud with a woman taken to Moschi's camp—a woman by the name of Jena Parker," Romli says.

"And we discovered that Jena Parker was taken in by Maria," Lero says.

"What?" Romli asks, sitting up straight.

"Yes, a team found out a few days ago, when they were following Moschi," Lero says. "That's before we lost Moschi's trail."

"And what about Maria?" Romli asks.

"I don't know," Lero answers. He gives Romli some time to ponder this information; he knows Moschi, and Maria are touchy subjects. After a brief silence, he adds, "This Jena Parker seems to be a challenge for Pulue and Moschi."

Romli clears his throat. "Find Maria, Moschi, and Parker. Bring Maria to me."

"And the others?" Lero asks.

"Kill Parker and Moschi, if you have the opportunity," Romli says. "Take Chance with you and the team."

"She hasn't been tested yet," Lero replies.

"Let the mission be her test," the boss says.

Lero stands, grabs his hat, and leaves Romli to his own thoughts.

Still sitting, smoking his cigar, Romli stares into space, reminiscing about the young Maria. Her silky black hair looked stunning against her blue silk gown.

"Beautiful," Romli says out loud.

He remembers standing behind her, his breath moving her soft hair ever so slightly. He gently slid her hair to the side, placed a sparkling diamond necklace around her neck, and kissed her slender shoulder.

Looking into a mirror, Maria admired the beautiful jewelry.

Romli walked up behind her. "Moschi could never have given you such an extravagant gift," he bragged.

Maria was quiet. She missed Moschi. But she had chosen Romli. She smiled gently at Romli. "It is lovely. Thank you."

He asked her to wear it that night. "I want to make love to you while you're wearing it," he had said.

She hesitated, but then agreed. "Of course."

His passion for Maria turned dark, as it often did when she was with him.

He grabbed her by the neck and slapped her face.

"You were thinking of him, weren't you?" he accused her.

Maria touched her face and began to cry.

Romli didn't flinch until he calmed down.

He tried to placate her with another gift. He reached for her hand and slipped on a diamond ring.

Maria looked at him, still crying, but trying to hold back the pain.

Romli's dark eyes glowed, pleased with himself and her beauty.

He smiled slightly. "You think I'm a bad person?"

Maria just stared at him, and then said, quietly, "No."

Romli laughed. "I know you're lying. I know you're afraid of me. You're afraid of this kind of love. This love is strong," he said sternly.

"This is the strongest love you'll ever have. Moschi could never give you what I can give you. Moschi is weak, and I am strong. Soon you will grow to love me deeply, Maria. Deeper than you now believe you love him. I will show you a new world. I will train you to be a strong woman, a woman of power."

Romli pulled Maria close and tried to kiss her, but she spurned him.

"I'm sorry I hit you. I won't do it again," Romli said passionately.

Maria turned and looked at him, and he knew that she was attracted to him.

Romli kissed Maria's sore cheek. "I will fix everything," he whispered in her ear.

Lero unexpectedly walked back into the room and sees Romli staring into space. He calls out. "Sir, can we finish our conversation?"

"I thought we were done," Romli responds.

"I just wanted to say that I won't let you down. I will bring back Moschi, Maria, and Parker. I will bring them back so you can have justice."

Romli shakes Lero's hand. "Thank you, my friend. I know you will hunt them down and bring them to me. Don't bother bringing Parker. Just kill her on sight. That would be fine with me." He pauses and smiles. "Safe travels."

Lero nods and leaves the room.

Romli walks back to his desk, picks up the phone, and requests an outside line. He dials Warden Peters.

"Warden," Romli says in greeting. "I want to know why you are allowing my entire operation to be exposed."

The warden doesn't answer.

"Answer me," Romli insists.

"I'm doing my best to contain this situation," Peters says in a shaky voice. "Things have just gotten ... well ... a bit chaotic."

"You mean out of control," Romli corrects him. "I think we are far from things being merely a bit chaotic. Things are slipping, and that's dangerous."

Peters stays silent.

"So, I'm going to get dangerous," Romli says before abruptly hanging up.

The warden is filled with fear as the dial tone echoes in his ear. He lets the receiver drop as he stares at his closed office door. He is still trying to calm down after the prison riot, earlier, and his encounter with Jena's aunt, Denise.

"Where are you, Reyes?" Peters utters under his breath. "You're going to get us all killed."

Peters dials the police department.

"Maplesville Police Department," an officer answers.

"Yes, this is Warden Phillip Peters, over at the prison, I need to talk to someone about whether you have any leads in the disappearance of Chief Reyes?"

Detective Martin is standing nearby when the officer picks up the phone.

"Unfortunately, sir, we've found nothing. It's like Chief Reyes disappeared into thin air."

Detective Martin grabs the phone from the police officer.

"Well, hello, warden," Martin says.

"Who is this?" Peters asks.

"This is Detective Dean Martin. Call it a coincidence that I just happen to be standing here in the police department when you call to check on your buddy."

"He's not my buddy," Warden Peters replies quickly. "I'm just a concerned citizen, like everyone else."

"Right," Detective Martin says sarcastically. "Well, buddy or not, I'll be making a visit to your office soon."

"When?" the warden asks.

"Like I said, soon," Detective Martin says. He hands the phone back to the officer and walks away just as his cellphone rings.

A woman with a sexy voice speaks. "Hi there, dear. This is Sherry Paterson."

"Sherry, is something wrong?" Martin asks.

"I really appreciate you coming by this morning, and ... well ... I just wanted to know if you were interested in having a little dinner tonight?"

Detective Martin doesn't know what to say.

"I mean ... I just lost my husband, and I could use your company tonight. I'd feel a lot better if I had someone to talk to, and ... well ... it would be nice if that person were you."

"Sherry, I'm in the middle of an important case. I came by today to give you my condolences, but can I get a rain check on dinner?" Martin asks.

Sherry pauses, disappointed. "Sure."

"I'll call you tomorrow to see how you're doing. Take care of yourself, Sherry."

They say their goodbyes, and Martin clicks off his cellphone and puts it back in his pocket. He takes a good look around the precinct, sees no one and nothing that can help him.

His cellphone rings again. "Detective Martin," he answers.

"Are you still looking for Chief Reyes?" asks a voice he doesn't recognize.

"Who is this?" Martin asks. "And how did you get my cellphone number?"

"Don't be concerned about who I am," the low crisp voice says. "The point of my call is that I know where you can find Chief Reyes and those two guys who kidnapped him."

"Where are they?" Martin asks impatiently.

"Now you're listening," the caller says. "Let's just say that they are far, far up in the air and on their way to a deep forest."

"I don't have time for riddles," Martin says. "Tell me where they are and save the Sherlock Holmes routine for some other sucker."

"I can't tell you anything more. I just wanted to help with what I know, and I know that Reyes is a bird, flying far, far away."

Then, the caller is gone. Martin looks at his cellphone. It says, "Caller Unknown."

He walks back into the precinct and approaches the officer who answered the phone when the warden called.

"I want you to find every local and private airport in this state," Martin tells him. "And, while you're at it, I want a manifest of every commercial or private flight that has come in or out of those airports in the last forty-eight hours—especially flights with a destination outside of the United States."

"Sure thing, Detective. I'll get right on it."

"Thank you," Martin says. "And, by the way, consider this information top secret—in other words, not to be shared with anyone, including Warden Peters."

"Understood, sir," the young officer says.

Martin writes down his cellphone number. "Call me when you have all the information."

Then he walks out of the police station, this time a bit more hopeful.

<hr />

Everyone on the plane sits in silence, listening to the steady hum of the engines.

Jake dreams that he is falling and wakes up shaking and sweating. He looks around the plane. Reyes is slumped over, sleeping next to Ken. Franklin has left his seat next to Jake and moved to the back of the plane. He's writing in a journal, no doubt making notes for his next novel. Jake stands and looks at Franklin. He clears his throat to get Franklin's attention. Franklin, his reading glasses barely balanced on his nose, looks at Jake and slides down the aisle and back to his seat next to Jake.

"Hey, how you feeling? I'm sorry, that's a dumb question," Franklin says. "I know it's hard for you right now."

"Yeah," Jake says. "It's heartbreaking. I should be there for my mother, but I just had to leave. I have to find Jena. I know she needs me."

Jake looks at Franklin, to make sure he understands.

But Franklin is looking at his notes. He hesitates, then writes down what Jake just said.

"What are doing, man?" Jake asks, offended.

"I'm sorry," Franklin says. "I just had to record this moment. Jena Parker is my character or … I mean … she's like my character, Reda Jones. And Reda has found a love like you and Jena have."

Jake smiles. "Come on, your book is fantasy. Jena and I, we're no fantasy."

"Saying that tells me that you're not much of a reader. Books are just as real as anything else in this world. Books manifest reality … or maybe the other way around. My point is that the stories in books are very real."

Jake shrugs. He's not really interested in plumbing the depths of Franklin's creative process.

"How far is it to our destination?" Jake asks.

"I'll check with the pilot," Franklin offers.

"By the way, what do we know about this pilot?" Jake asks suspiciously.

"He's been my private pilot for years," Franklin says. "He's my friend." He pats Jake's shoulder. "I'll be back."

Franklin stands next to the pilot, between him and Denise, who is sleeping. The jet's so small there's no separation between the pilot and the passengers.

"Hello, my friend," Franklin says. "How long until we land?"

"Five hours," the pilot says.

"Excellent," Franklin replies.

"Do you need anything?"

"No, just get us there safely," Franklin says. "You're doing a great job."

Franklin sees a cellphone on the floor of the plane and picks it up. "Is this yours?" he asks.

The pilot hesitates. "I must have dropped it," he says.

Franklin looks at the phone more closely. He sees a number flashing.

"Right," Franklin replies. "I'll be back to check on you again, buddy."

Franklin stops and turns around again. "Hey, I may need to make a call later. Can I use your phone?" he asks.

The pilot's face goes blank, and there is a brief moment of silence.

"Sure, sure," the pilot says. "I'll make sure it's charged so you can use it."

"Thanks," Franklin says and returns to his seat next to Jake with a puzzled look on his face.

"What's up?" Jake asks.

"He says it'll be about five more hours," Franklin says. "But that's not what's bothering me. My pilot has a cellphone."

"We all have cellphones," Jake says.

"I know. But he used the phone recently. I could see the number he called. The question is, who did he call and why?"

"He's your friend," Jake says.

"Friends can be enemies," Franklin says. "I asked to use his phone later. I memorized the last number he called. Let me see your cellphone."

Jake pulls out his phone.

"I want you to put your phone on private mode. I'm going to call that number. I want to know who he called."

Jake does, and Franklin calls.

"Detective Martin," the owner of the other cellphone answers. Franklin is silent. "Do you have another tip for me?" Martin asks.

Franklin clicks off quickly. He sighs deeply.

Jake looks upset. He heard the same thing Franklin heard.

"Why is your pilot calling Detective Martin?" Jake asks.

They both stare at the pilot's back.

"That's a good question, Jake. And I'm going to find out the answer. But I'm going to wait until we hit the ground," Franklin says.

"Good idea. We don't want him crashing or steering us off course," Jake replies.

"I'll deal with this," Franklin assures his friend, then looks at the sleeping Aunt Denise Parker and back at Jake. "So, why don't you tell me who Denise is and how she ended up on this plane?"

Lero enters Chance's room. "Get your stuff," he says, roughly.

Chance sits on her cot and doesn't move.

"I said get your stuff."

"Where am I going?" Chance asks.

"You don't need to know where you are going. All that matters is that you need to get up and get your stuff."

Lero gives Chance a threatening stare.

Chance does as she is told, gathering her hunting gear. She gets dressed, without bothering to cover herself.

"Are you just going to stand there and stare at me?" she asks.

Lero smirks. "It's not like I've never seen a naked body." He sighs. "I'll be outside. Don't make me wait."

Chance comes out dressed like the rest of the team, with spikes on the front and back of her jacket. Her pants have spikes down the sides, and her black boots are spiked, too. She carries a big pack and holds a spear in one hand.

Chance's head is shaved, like it was when she was in prison.

"You look ready for battle," Lero says, approvingly.

She just looks at him.

"You'll be happy to know that we'll be hunting for Jena Parker today," Lero says.

Chance's eyes grow from dim to glowing. And she smiles.

"That's certainly a good reason to get dressed," she says.

"Just so you understand, you take orders from me," Lero says. "Step out of line, and I'll kill you."

The rest of the team is standing behind him. They're all watching Chance.

"I got that," she replies. "Now can we leave?"

"We leave when I say we leave," Lero shouts. He glares at her for at least fifteen seconds, then looks around at the group. "Let's go."

Everyone falls in line behind Lero and gets into an armored jeep with heavily tinted windows. The jeep bumps over dusty roads and heads into the woods.

There are camouflaged gates along the way. Guards open the gates to let them pass. The driver stops the jeep at each gate and asks questions about whether the guards have seen anyone in the woods, and he plans his route accordingly.

Lero and his team end up at a small village where Maria is said to be camped and leading her own team. Village women walk with water vessels on their heads. They are essentially slaves. One woman stops as the jeep pulls so close that it almost hits her. She doesn't move.

Lero and his team get out of the jeep.

The woman stands in front of them fearlessly.

"Greetings," Lero says to her as he looks around the village.

The woman nods.

"Do you speak?" Lero asks.

The woman just stares at him, then: "Yes."

"Good," Lero says. "Who leads this village?"

"M.I. A," the woman replies.

Lero mulls that over. "M.I. A," he repeats.

"Yes," she said.

"Where is she?" Lero asks.

The woman looks down. "We don't know. She left yesterday and has not returned."

"Where did she go?" Lero asks.

She points far out into the woods. "She went out there."

"Who did she go with?" Lero asks.

"She went with my brother, Alo, and a girl I didn't know. Alo returned with some fresh game last night, but M.I. A and the girl did not."

"A girl," Lero asks inquisitively.

"Yes, a girl who is new to the village. Her name is Jena."

Lero immediately heads back to the jeep, and the team follows.

Chance stops to stare at the woman.

The jeep starts back up quickly and swerves into the woods, faster than before.

"Stop here," Lero shouts. He hops out and looks around. He sniffs the air, like a hunting dog. He looks into the sky and sees scavenging birds.

"There are dead bodies, fresh bodies, nearby," he says. "Check this entire area."

Chance jumps out with the rest of the team.

"Look for freshly dug graves," Lero shouts.

Team members walk through the area, moving debris, kicking the dirt. One of the men shouts that he has found something.

Lero rushes to the site. The team is digging in some dirt that has been disturbed. As everyone suspects, it is a shallow grave. A woman's arm emerges.

Lero stops them while he stares at the arm. "Keep digging," he instructs.

The team members, including Chance, dig deeper.

The body is Maria's. Lero knows it is her.

Once she is unearthed, the entire team stares at her.

Lero breathes out hard. He turns to the driver. Use the radio to call for a larger vehicle.

"We must take her back to Romli," he says.

Chance sees what looks like another grave, next to Maria's body.

She and the team begin digging again.

When some of the body is uncovered, Lero knows that it is Moschi. He turns his head away. "Here they are. Two old lovers, next to each other, both gone from this world."

Chance doesn't understand the significance of their find, but most of the other team members seem to know.

"Get them both out and clean the dirt off of their bodies," Lero says.

He tells them to get the tarpaulins out of the jeep and use them to wrap the bodies. He walks away, into the forest, which is getting dark. One of the men approaches Lero.

"The second vehicle is on its way," the man says. "It should be here within the hour."

"Good. We must get back before dark. We also need to find whoever is responsible for this," Lero says.

Chance walks up as Lero is speaking. "I know who is responsible," she says, arrogantly.

"Who?"

"Jena Parker. She's responsible for these deaths. She's ruthless," Chance says.

"You don't think that maybe you just *want* the killer to be Jena Parker?" Lero asks.

"She tried to kill me, too," Chance smirks. "Now I'm going to kill her. Looks like she's given us plenty of reason to take her out. Isn't that why Romli put me on the mission? He knows how much I hate Jena and that I would do anything to make her pay. She takes things from people. She took my boyfriend. She made me take my parents. She even took Teddy—and her own mother and father."

The team members are looking at the new recruit like she's crazy.

"We're not going to listen to this nutcase, are we?" one of the men says.

Chance looks embarrassed but defiant.

Lero addresses Chance quietly. "You have Jena Parker's story all written, don't you?" he says. "What about your story?" He glares at Chance. "We are one team."

"I am a team, all by myself. I work for Romli. I take orders from Romli, but I'm a one-woman operation," Chance says, cocky.

"You're in my world now," Lero says. "This is a mission. When we are done, we go back to our quarters. You're not even on this team. I'm in charge. Do you understand that?"

Chance refuses to back down but stays silent.

"Now go back over there and help get the bodies ready for travel," he tells Chance.

She gives him a nasty look and goes back to help the others.

Jena walks through the dimming forest with a large pack and a spear on her shoulder. She is alert to her surroundings—she walks with confidence. She has no destination in mind. She looks at the sky. The stars are beginning to come out. The moon is already high in the sky.

She goes to the happiest place in her heart, that time Jake flashed a smile at her as they rode the school bus together. He looked at her in a way that made her believe they shared a special love. A warm breeze blows across Jena's face, brushing her hair back and making her feel calm. She closes her eyes and thinks of Jake's smile, then she thinks of Moschi, her mentor and also her tormentor. She remembers watching him die. She doesn't know whether to laugh or cry. Both emotions consume her, and she finds herself trembling as the forest becomes cooler. She reaches into her bag for a flashlight and blanket, then searches for a safe spot to camp. She's exhausted and knows not much light is left.

She throws down her duffle bag, lies down, and places her head on it. Her eyes are tired, her body is weary, and all she wants is sleep.

She has barely shut her eyes when she opens them to sunny skies. She feels the warmth and comfort of a warm breeze. She can smell seawater and hear ocean waves. She stands, lifts her arms into the sky, and leans back as far as she can. She looks down at her tan and toned body. She's wearing a sheer white gown. She looks at her arms and sees a beautiful ring shining on her finger. She admires it, twists it, and looks around to see if she is alone. Where could the ring have come from?

Then she hears a voice. "Do you like it?" It's Jake's voice.

Jena turns around. Jake is wearing beach shorts, and his hair is wet. When he sees her, he runs to Jena and hugs her tight.

"I hope you like it," he says as he kisses her ring finger. "It took me a long time to find the right one."

Jena is stunned by the sight of Jake. She is as quiet as a schoolgirl on her first date.

"You're never this quiet," Jake says.

"It's been so long," she replies.

Jake laughs. "It was only yesterday."

She doesn't understand.

Jake picks up Jena and swings her around and around.

Jena is overwhelmed with joy.

They laugh as Jake swings her high into the air.

Jake gently lets Jena slide back to the ground. He kisses her on the lips. They stare into each other's eyes.

"I'm so glad you said yes," he says.

Jena isn't sure what he means, but she's in love with the moment.

"I love you," she tells him.

His face lights up, then he puts his head down, teary with emotion.

"What's wrong?" she asks.

"It gives me goosebumps to hear you say that you love me," Jake says. "I've been telling you that I love you, but I've been waiting to hear you say it back to me."

"I do love you, and I always will," she assures him.

Jena's eyes glimmer with fire for Jake. She allows herself to bask in the moment.

Jake kisses her and doesn't stop. He grips Jena's body tightly and lays her on the sand. He runs his hands under the diaphanous gown.

They caress one another passionately, pleasing one another, waiting to consummate their moment of love.

But Jena feels distracted. She hears something.

"Don't worry," Jake whispers. "No one is here."

"Can't you hear them talking?" she asks.

"Relax baby," he says as he moans with pleasure. "You're beautiful."

Jena hears the voice getting louder. "No, Jake. We have to stop."

"Please, babe, I've waited so long to be with you," Jake says.

But he is drifting away.

She calls his name over and over.

Jena opens her eyes again and hears the sound of a plane. She sits up in the dark and realizes she had been dreaming. She shakes her head, but she hears a plane in the distance.

Then she hears voices. She stands up and picks up her spear and flashlight. She leaves her duffle bag and walks quietly but quickly toward the noise of the plane.

She starts to breathe heavily as she thinks she hears Jake's voice. She shakes her head hard, wondering if she is dreaming again.

She gets as close to the sound of the plane as she thinks is safe and hides in the bushes. Straining her eyes as the sun starts to rise, she watches in amazement, and a bit of alarm, as she sees people getting out of the plane. She shakes herself, wondering whether she is dreaming again.

Unbelievably, she recognizes Jake, Franklin, Ken, her Aunt Denise, a man she doesn't know, someone who appears to be the pilot, and Reyes—in shackles.

She hears Jake ask Ken to keep an eye on Reyes. Jake and Denise stand close to each other, and Franklin is speaking to the pilot. She sees Franklin, animated, moving his arms. She doesn't know what to do. She wants to call out to Jake, but she stays still for a moment. Breathing hard, she stares so intensely that she barely blinks.

Then she sets herself free.

She doesn't even stop to look where she's going. She runs through the bushes and stops a few feet from Jake, who has his back turned, talking to Denise.

She says his name quietly, then louder and louder.

Jake stops talking. Denise sees Jena first, and her face freezes. Jake turns around, stunned, thinking he's hallucinating, looking to Denise in confusion.

Jena whispers Jake's name again and stands absolutely still.

Jake finally understands what he is seeing and runs to Jena.

Everyone stops, wondering what is happening.

Jake runs like the wind and doesn't stop until he reaches her, still in disbelief. Standing in front of her, he just stares.

Jena flashes a huge grin, and Jake's face lights up with his smile. He grabs her tightly, then kisses her face, her neck, anyplace his lips can reach. And then he picks Jena up and swings her around and around in the dark.

Denise, Franklin, and Mr. Tindale walk, amazed, in the dark toward Jake and Jena. They stand silently, watching the lovers meet again.

CHAPTER TWENTY-FOUR

Tonya had been out in the forest for so long that she couldn't even keep track of the time anymore. She is alone and struggling and doesn't know how much longer she can hold on. "Why had no one come to get her or even kill her?" she wonders.

Night creeps in. How many nights have there been?

Her bleeding knee has become infected, making it even harder to move. She finds a good strong stick and uses it as a crutch and makes her way back to the cave, where she had spent each night. Bless Paula for showing it to her—before Paula was taken away.

Tonya has one cracker left. She'd been fortunate to find tiny amounts of food stashed around the forest—she remembers the "Easter eggs" in the video games her nieces and nephews played. She reaches into her pocket for the crumbled cracker and devours it. She sips a little water that she found in a creek that looked clean. While she hopes it doesn't have unseen bacteria or pollution, she knows she doesn't have the luxury of being careful.

She can't stop herself from crying. She cries so hard that she bends over with the pain. She screams into the cold, dark woods—louder, she thinks, than she has ever screamed before.

"Why! Why me?" she screams as her knee begins to throb again.

Finally giving up on trying to help herself, she lies flat on her back. She thinks back to her first day in nursing school. She was straight out of high school, eager to learn and help others. She always sat in the front row, wearing her pink uniform, while the nurse in charge, Mrs. Adams, taught the class.

The day came that they were supposed to learn to perform CPR. The nurses-in-training walked across the hall to the lab, where practice dummies were on the floor. Tonya stayed seated, waiting to speak to Nurse Adams, who stared at Tonya as the rest of the class left.

"What's wrong, Tonya? You're usually so enthusiastic," Nurse Adams had said.

"I don't know if I can learn CPR," Tonya told her instructor.

"That's why we're training," Nurse Adams explained, then asked again patiently. "What's wrong?"

"My little brother and I were having a pillow fight. All of a sudden, he started breathing hard. I didn't know what to do. I yelled for my parents. I didn't know if I was supposed to do CPR or mouth-to-mouth resuscitation, and I didn't know how. I just froze. It was awful watching him gasp for air. Finally, my father came rushing in and gave him his asthma medicine while my mom called 911." She started to cry, right there in the classroom. "I felt so guilty because I couldn't help him."

Nurse Adams consoled her. "We're all afraid sometimes. We learn what we have to learn to take care of ourselves and other people. Next time you'll be ready."

Tonya joined the rest of the class, learned CPR, and used it many times in her career.

Thinking of that moment eases the pain in Tonya's heart as she lies on the hard floor of the cave. It gives her hope that she can do more than she thinks—after all, she had survived out here far longer than she would have ever thought.

Maybe Romli's people would come to take her back to the camp. Maybe they would come to kill her. Maybe she had enough strength to make it through this night, perhaps even the night after.

She is startled by a bright light at the front of the cave. Perhaps her hope had been false.

"Who's there?" she yells. "Who's there?"

"Tonya. Tonya. It's me, Paula. I'm here to save you." Paula crawls into the cave.

"Paula," Tonya says. "Is it you? Is it really you? I thought I'd die out here. I thought everyone had forgotten me."

"Someone got word to Matty that you were still alive out here," Paula says.

"Matty? What? I don't understand."

"Listen, Tonya, we don't have time to talk. We need to move quickly. How bad is your knee?"

"I don't think I can walk very far," Tonya confesses.

"You won't have to walk far. There are four of us. Matty, Sharon, Suzanne, and me. We have a stretcher. We'll carry you."

Tonya starts to cry quietly in the dark.

Matty appears. "Can we hurry up," she asks in a tough voice. "If we stay out here any longer, we're going to get caught and killed."

"She's right, Tonya, we have to go," Paula says. She puts her arm around Tonya's waist and helps her to the stretcher.

The three other women hoist the stretcher and move in silence through the woods to the compound.

As they get close to the camp, Matty motions to set the stretcher down. She whispers and points to each woman, indicating they should watch the perimeter in case Romli's guards come by.

The women quietly scatter to walk around the compound.

Suzanne sees the men taking a break, with only one man pacing at the main gate. She reports back to Matty.

"Maybe we can take the underground tunnel," Matty says. "It will be a challenge. We won't be able to carry Tonya. She'll have to walk."

Matty gathers the women around.

"There's one guard in the front and one in the back, but we'll be surrounded soon," Matty says. "Paula you'll have to help Tonya walk. It's too risky to carry her. It would slow us down." She looks around to everyone else. "Everyone, make sure your weapons are armed and ready."

Matty had snuck ammunition to them before they'd gone into the forest.

"Romli's men are ruthless, and tonight won't be an exception," she instructs.

Matty silently directs the women to move ahead. Paula helps Tonya. One woman watches the front, one watches the back. Matty leads the way to the tunnel entrance.

Just as they're about to enter, Lero and his team enter the compound, returning from their search for Maria and Moschi.

The lights of two jeeps are getting close to the women.

"Hurry up," Matty whispers to the others.

They all get into the tunnel's entrance. Matty waits outside, staring toward the jeeps and watching them park. She keeps her eyes trained on Lero, Chance, and the rest of the team. The men are clearly carrying two bodies.

A light swings toward Matty. Chance looks in Matty's direction. Matty tries to hide, but Chance walks toward her.

"Where are you going?" Lero asks Chance.

"I thought I saw someone over by the tunnel," Chance replies.

"Stay here," Lero orders. "I'll send a guard to check."

"Why can't I go?" Chance asks.

"Go, but report back to me and me only," Lero says. "And be quick about it."

Matty sees that the other women are way ahead of her. She sees Chance walking her way and runs to try to get ahead of her.

Chance turns and sees footprints entering the tunnel and starts to go inside, but Matty makes a huffing sound to distract her.

Chance hears the noise, readies her weapon, and walks toward the sound. She turns but quickly sees nothing. Standing still, she looks around, then walks toward the compound.

Lero is waiting for her. "Did you find anything?" he asks.

She shakes her head.

"We're finished for the night. I will report to Romli. You return to your quarters," he says.

Chance nods and heads to her quarters.

She enters the kitchen, and the women are standing around like they're waiting for something.

Matty stares at Chance. "Where were you today?"

Chance returns Matty's stare. "I went out with the team. It was okay. I learned a lot." She pauses. "Why is everyone still awake?"

Chance hears a moan from down the hall.

Matty knows that Chance heard Tonya in the bathroom, where Paula is caring for Tonya's knee.

"Who's making that noise?" Chance demands.

"Another warrior, not that it's any of your damned business," Matty responds.

"Sounds like a wounded warrior to me," Chance says.

"Like I said, mind your own business. Just because you went out on a mission doesn't make you any better than the rest of us."

"Why don't you stop being a hag?" Chance replies, shrugging her shoulders.

Matty watches Chance grab a bottle of water.

Chance stops to listen at the bathroom door on the way to her cot.

Matty walks up behind Chance. "Need to use the bathroom?"

"No," Chance mumbles, opening the door to her cot area.

Paula and Tonya can hear Matty and Chance in the hallway and stop talking.

Matty sticks her head into the bathroom and motions for Tonya and Paula to be quiet.

They nod. Matty looks down at Tonya's infected knee, then closes the bathroom door.

Chance peeks around her door and watches as Matty tells the two women to be quiet. Chance lies down and realizes whose voice she heard coming from the bathroom.

Franklin, Denise, and Mr. Tindale stand in awe of Jena and Jake's reunion—right in the middle of an open field and in front of a small crowd.

Ken smiles as he stands behind the others, holding onto Reyes' handcuffs.

The two long-separated lovers embrace and kiss. It's hard to know whether the affection or the astonishment is stronger. Jake and Jena can't believe their eyes, and they also can't keep their hands off each other.

Denise has tears in her eyes, and Franklin is frantically writing in his notebook, trying to capture the moment. He forgets about his errant pilot for the moment and is the first to approach Jena and Jake. They don't even notice Franklin.

"Ahem," he clears his throat as they turn to him, startled. "I just want to say that I'm grateful to be here to see you two reunited."

Jake puts his forehead on Jena's. "It would be a more passionate reunion if we had a little privacy."

Everyone laughs.

"We're in no position to give you a private room," Ken yells. "We are literally in the middle of nowhere."

Jake and Jena laugh.

Jena yells toward Ken, who let's go of Reyes' handcuffs for a moment. "You would have to ruin a romantic moment." She hugs Ken tightly.

Ken picks her up and swings her around. "You see, Jake isn't the only one who can swing you around, I can, too!"

"You're silly, put me down!" Jena yells playfully.

"Easy with her, Ken," Jake says, "I just got her back."

Jena kisses Ken on the cheek, turns to Franklin, and hugs him, too. "Nice to finally meet you."

That breaks the spell. Franklin ducks in and hugs Jena tightly. "I'm so glad we found you—or that you found us."

Mr. Tindale nods at Jena. "It's nice to meet you, miss. We've come a long way."

"This is my friend, Mr. Tindale. He was a huge help in getting us here," Franklin says.

Jena hears a woman sobbing loudly and turns to see her Aunt Denise. The women rush into each other's arms. "Aunt Denise, what are doing here?"

"It's a long story, Jena. But I'm just happy to see you. I'm happy to see that you're safe," Denise says.

Denise can't stop crying, and she and Jena hold each other for a long time. "I wish there was more light so I could see your beautiful eyes," Denise says.

Jena smiles. "It'll be morning soon."

"My people," Franklin says, "it looks like our mission here is complete. Let's get back to the plane and get ourselves home."

Jena turns to Franklin. "We can't leave now!"

"Excuse me?" Franklin asks, astonished.

"We can't leave now because there's a war that needs to be settled," Jena says. "There's more going on here than just me. There's a whole world of corruption here, and it's all connected to Maplesville and the prison."

"What's going on, Jena?" Jake asks.

"It's a long story, Jake. But trust me when I say that we can't leave now."

The group lets out a collective groan. This is a contingency they did not expect.

"We have to stay and fight!" Jena says passionately.

"Fight?" Mr. Tindale asks, clearly frightened now. "Fight who?"

"We need to fight the people who tried to kill me!" she yells.

"Let's everyone calm down," Franklin says. "I think we all need to talk." He looks around at the group, and everyone nods.

"Jena clearly has a story to tell," Jake says.

Franklin looks at Ken, who is still holding onto Reyes. Now that the sun is beginning to come up, Jena is shocked to see her old nemesis.

"And we have a story to tell, too—and, it appears, a plan to make," Jake says.

"Let's get back to the plane, so we have a little cover. We can get some water and a little food from our supplies, and then we can sit down and talk," Franklin says.

Jena and Jake lead the way, arm in arm, while Mr. Tindale walks ahead quickly to gather up "breakfast" for his fellow travelers, who—it appears—will now be Jena Parker's team.

Franklin and Ken wrangle Reyes to the opposite side of the plane and make sure that he is secured. Mr. Tindale throws down a bottle of water for Reyes—the only one here, besides Jena, who knows what they are about to face out there someplace in the brush.

"Jena, we can get back on that plane and go home right now. We can turn Reyes into the police or District Attorney and leave this fight to the professionals. You and Jake, not to mention the rest of us, can, in fact, live happily ever after," Franklin suggests.

Jake and Jena are holding hands and exchange a long glance.

"I can't count the number of people out there who have tried to kill me," Jena tells Jake. She turns to face the group, looking hard at each person. "There is a war. It is time to battle."

Fervently, she explains that Reyes and the warden, in addition to other men who came before them, have been kidnapping women from the prison and bringing them to this desolate place.

"They're being bought and paid for like slaves. They *are* slaves," Jena says. "The evil operation is so deep that some of the women aren't guilty of any crimes at all. The police make up charges, just so they can throw women into prison and ship them away later."

Jena stops for a moment to think of the story she heard from Luis, back at Moschi's headquarters. "And while they are in prison they're mistreated and beaten and abused by people like that guy," she says, pointing at Reyes.

Jena becomes angrier. "They're shipped to this hellhole to serve organizations that are beyond evil by any standard, competing groups that will kill anyone for any reason—as long as they can get a good price."

Jena's rescuers look confused, and Jena remembers how confused she was when she first came to this place with Pulue.

"There are two main operations, one that was led by Moschi and Pulue and one led by Romli," she explains. "But there are probably even more crime organizations like these, killing organizations, out there." She pauses. "Sure, Moschi and Pulue seduce the women with luxury, while Romli beats them into submission with violence and fear. I ended up with Moschi, and I also ended up seeing him die, but in the end, I was beaten and even shot as they trained me to become an assassin.

"I escaped, but I'm only here because Moschi was killed."

Jake and the others try to absorb this information.

"We heard on the local news that your murder conviction was overturned and that you had been released. But no one knew where you were," Jake says.

"That's right," Aunt Denise chimes in.

"I went to the prison to visit you, Jena, and they told me you weren't there. I demanded to see the warden. And that sweaty, guilty-looking son-of-a-gun told me you'd escaped. And he wouldn't give me any more information."

Jena looks at her aunt with affection and admiration.

"Fortunately, I ran into Jake and Ken by sheer accident, and that's the only way I'm seeing you here today," she says.

"That's just it," Jena says. "These women are ripped away from their families and friends. If anyone comes looking for them, they're told that the woman died in jail. There are hundreds of empty graves behind the prison for women who aren't even dead."

Franklin looks up from his notebook, where he'd been writing down everything Jena says. "So, who in Maplesville is in on this thing? Who's making this happen?" he asks.

"Everyone is in on it," Jena says, trying to hold back her tears. "This man"—she points furiously as Reyes—"and the warden are the main ones. And they're raking in a fortune for their efforts. But it goes further. I just heard that my own father—I mean the father who raised me—was in on it at one time. He stopped when I was born."

Denise Parker gasps, and Jena looks at her with sympathy. "I know. I didn't want to believe it either."

She gets back to her story. "Mike McNeil was in on it when he was warden. The mayor … the one who was killed along with his wife … was in on it. Probably most of the guards at the prison are involved. Who knows how many police officers? That's just Maplesville. What about other mayors and police departments around Maplesville?"

Jake turns to Jena and squeezes her hand. "How do you know all of this?"

"You said you heard that I was released from prison?" Jena asks, pausing to gaze into Jake's eyes. "Moschi's people rescued me from prison. Moschi said he was going to help me. But he really meant that I would work for him. Because I had already killed and because he could see the hate in my heart."

She pauses and looks at her aunt with a sense of profound guilt, "Moschi thought he could train me to be a hardened assassin."

Franklin folds his arms and takes a deep breath. He looks over to where the pilot should be and doesn't see him.

"Jena," Franklin says, "if you're right, and I believe you are, how can we possibly wage war against these ruthless people?" He looks around their circle dramatically. "I'm a writer of fiction, and we have two guys who are barely out of their teens and might have a super-hero complex; we've got your determined and lovely aunt; we've got a loser of a cop; and we've got my butler, Mr. Tindale, who has never handled anything worse than a burned soufflé."

Mr. Tindale gives Franklin a dirty look.

"And my shady pilot seems to have disappeared," Franklin says. "No offense, Jena, you have more experience with a weapon than any of the rest of us."

Franklin shakes his head and begins to pace. "Jena we're outnumbered. We're in over our heads."

Jena approaches Franklin and looks straight into his eyes. "What you have would Reda Jones do?"

"What?"

"You heard me," Jena says. "What would Reda Jones do?"

The writer and the warrior study one another.

"You said I reminded you of your character, Reda Jones. So, when you write about her, what would she do now?" Jena asks.

Franklin studies his shoes while he thinks about what Jena has said. He reaches into a jacket pocket and pulls out more notes. He stares at them, then back at Jena.

"She'd fight," he says.

Jena nods. "You've got that right."

Franklin grins, beaten at his own game. Then he gets excited. "She'd track down every man who has ever kidnapped, killed, or raped a woman—only to line his own pockets or advance his own agenda. And she'd make them all pay." He sounds more amped up with every word.

"She would fight for justice." Jena finishes Franklin's thought.

"Yes, she'd fight for justice. I'm with you Jena," he says, then glances around at the worried faces of his cohorts. "First, I'd better go find my pilot. Then we'll make a plan."

Meanwhile, the others walk off their anxiety and stretch their legs.

Jake moves up behind Jena and squeezes her tightly. "I guess we have a lot to do," he says.

Jena turns around, embraces Jake, and kisses him on lips. "Yes, we do. Then we can go home, be together, and finally be free from all of this."

"I would fight a hundred armies just to be able to finally live a life in peace with you," Jake agrees.

Franklin enters the airplane. He walks with heavy steps toward the pilot. He reaches the pilot's seat to find his friend sleeping.

"Hey!" he yells.

The pilot is startled awake. He jumps up with wild eyes but calms down when he sees Franklin.

"Sorry." The pilot stretches and yawns. "I was out cold."

Franklin stares at the pilot as he wakes up fully.

"What's up?" the pilot asks.

Franklin keeps staring. The pilot is confused.

"Who did you call?" Franklin finally asks.

The pilot is still puzzled. "What are you talking about, Franklin? I didn't make any phone call."

Franklin demands to see the cellphone, and the pilot reaches for it and hands it to the boss.

"Here you go," the pilot says. "That's right. You wanted to make a call."

Franklin stares at the cellphone. The phone number he'd seen before is gone.

"There was a recent number on this phone when I looked at it before. Now it's been erased," Franklin says forcefully. "I'm asking you again. Who did you call?"

"I don't know what you're talking about. Who would I call and why would I call anyone?" the pilot responds.

Franklin loses his temper. "Okay, I'm tired of playing games. You called Detective Dean Martin, and I want to know why."

The pilot's face turns red, and he starts to stutter. "I don't even know a Detective—"

"Stop lying. It's time to come clean."

The pilot lowers his voice to a whisper and looks out the window of the plane. "Is that guy, Chief Reyes, out there?"

"What about him?" Franklin asks.

"I was standing next to him while we were waiting for Jake and Ken to come back, before we got back on the plane and took off," the pilot says. "Reyes told me that he knows he isn't going to make it back from our little journey, and he told me he wanted to say goodbye to his daughter. I believed him. He had tears in his eyes."

"And the fact that he was in handcuffs didn't tell you that maybe you shouldn't trust him?" Franklin demands.

"Looking back, it wasn't too smart," the pilot agrees. "But, anyway, I dialed the number that he gave me and stood by while he talked. He was whispering, so I didn't hear. I figured it was personal. Pretty soon, he handed the cellphone back to me."

Franklin looks at the phone. "Why did you erase the number?"

"I saw you looking at it earlier," the pilot says. "I was embarrassed. I figured if there was no number, there'd be nothing to talk about."

Franklin is still angry at the betrayal, no matter how innocent.

"I'm sorry," the pilot says. "I know it was dumb. Please forgive me. I was just trying to help the guy."

Franklin eases up. "Okay. I doubt it did much damage. But … this Detective Martin … he is probably looking for us by now."

Franklin doesn't know anything about Martin, but he wonders why Reyes didn't call the warden or one of his other cronies. Maybe he thinks the warden wouldn't bother looking for him.

"Thanks for telling the truth," Franklin says to the pilot. "Just so you know, Reyes is an evil man. He's done unthinkable things, and his day of reckoning will come."

Franklin tells the pilot to camouflage the plane as best he can and to get things ready for a quick escape when the time comes. "We have some dangerous things to accomplish here before we go home," he says. "Can I count on you?"

"Of course," the pilot says. "I will keep the plane safe and be ready to leave when you're ready."

"We have preparations to make before we leave, but I don't know when we'll be back," Franklin says. "There's a weapon in the back, so you can keep yourself safe. I'd keep it locked and loaded."

"I guess you're not going to tell me what's going on," the pilot says.

"No, I'm not. But it's nothing personal," Franklin explains. "Even we don't really know what danger is out there."

The pilot nods.

Franklin gives the cellphone back to its owner. "You're going to need to keep in touch with us. The rest of us have cellphones. We'll let you know where we are."

He walks out of the plane and back to the others.

Jake, Ken, and Mr. Tindale are gathering gear and supplies.

Jena is talking to Denise, trying to explain everything that happened to her in prison—and how Reyes, Peters, McNeil, and even her father had a role in what's going on.

Denise is stunned.

Jake approaches them and nods at both women. "I know it's hard to believe," he says.

The sun is high in the morning sky now, and they move swiftly. Jena and Denise help, too.

Jena looks around the forest.

"What is it?" her aunt asks.

"I don't know," Jena says. "I just feel something in the air. Something evil."

Denise says she feels it, too. "I trust you, Jena. I know that you want to rescue the women you told us about."

"You're right," Jena says. "But it goes beyond those women." She pauses. "It's knowing that the entire town where I grew up is corrupt and has been corrupt for many, many years.

"For years, women have been treated like slaves. Some did commit crimes. Others were framed. Either way, they were never allowed to pay their debt to society and have the chance to turn their lives around. They never had the chance to tell the world about the lies they were told." Jena goes on, even more fervently. "It is my duty to hold accountable everyone who is involved, and I won't leave here until it's done."

But Jena's plan goes further.

"Then, we'll take that truth back to our town and to every elected official, every cop, the warden, and every guard who took part in this—or looked the other way. And we will see that they are punished."

Jena reminds Jake and Denise of the children and husbands who think their mothers and wives abandoned them.

Now the whole group is listening to Jena intently.

"It is time to fight. It is time to battle for truth and justice—and for our freedom, too," she Jena says. "These women must be freed. Are we ready?"

"Yes," Jake replies. "I'm ready."

"I've been in on this from the start," Ken says, looking at Jake and then at Jena. "I'm still in."

Franklin struts forward. "I was born ready."

"Mr. Tindale?" Jake asks.

Mr. Tindale shudders a little under everyone's gaze. "I'm ready."

They all turn toward Denise. Jena takes her aunt's hand.

"Don't you worry about me," Denise says, smiling broadly. "I've got your back. I'm tougher than you think. I came to find you, Jena, and now I'm ready to finish the job."

"Well, are we geared up?" Jena asks. "We'd better get moving."

"We have all of the supplies and weapons ready," Franklin says. "But do we have to walk?"

"How else are we going to travel?" Jena asks.

Mr. Tindale and Franklin smile knowingly.

"It might be easier to get around in the fully loaded jeep we loaded in the back of the plane," Franklin says, cackling to himself.

"Hey, I'm not a rich guy for nothing," he says, smiling at the surprised faces of his friends. "Ken, get the keys from the pilot, and let's get this baby unloaded."

CHAPTER TWENTY-FIVE

Detective Martin walks into the District Attorney's office and finds Detective Smith.

"I got a tip," Martin tells his teammate. "I got a phone call from somebody who told me that those two young guys at the hospital are taking Reyes out of the country."

"Any idea who the tipster was?" Smith asks.

"No, but he seemed credible," Martin responds. "I can't imagine why anyone would be taking Reyes out of the country, but it seems like this case is getting bigger."

Detective Martin tells Smith about the officer who is busy tracking down commercial and private flights that left the area during the last forty-eight hours.

His cellphone rings. "Wait, this could be him." After hanging up, he tells Smith, "Let's head out. The officer over in Maplesville has the list ready."

When Smith and Martin arrive at the precinct, several police officers are on their way out.

"What's up?" Martin asks them.

"We've got a grid search organized to look for Reyes. We still haven't found him," one officer explains, and another says, "We're just all doing our part to find the boss. It's about teamwork."

Martin sees some of the officers eyeing him and Smith with suspicion.

"We're looking for your boss, too," he tells them. "Unfortunately, we think he might also be part of some criminal activities. But you men keep doing your job, and we'll do ours."

Some of the officers seem confused, while others seem defiant. Martin and Smith pay no attention.

"Keep the peace, officers," Martin says, and the two detectives walk into the precinct and stop at the front clerk's desk.

"Can I have that flight list, officer?" Martin asks.

When the clerk hands it over, Martin quickly scans the list. He stares up at Smith and shakes his head. He looks down again and goes through the flight manifest more thoroughly. "Here's a flight that doesn't have the pilot's name listed. This has to be it."

"What are you thinking?" Smith asks.

"This private flight here," Martin shows Smith what he found. "The flight plan doesn't even say where the flight originated. But they did check in with the tower."

"Do we know where it was going?" Smith asks.

"No, but it's something. We need to get to the airport and see if they can track down this plane," Martin says. "Can you head over there?"

"Sure, I'll jump right on it," Smith replies eagerly.

Martin's cellphone rings again.

The caller is Dr. Charter at the hospital.

"Detective Martin," the doctor says. "I wanted to let you know that Michael Fredmond has regained consciousness. He is asking to speak to authorities."

"I'll be right there," Martin says, stunned and looking at Smith. "The prison guard, Mike, is awake and wants to talk."

"Wow. I didn't have high hopes for that poor guy," Smith says.

Martin asks Smith to go to the airport while he heads to the hospital.

"Meet me at the hospital when you're done," Martin says as they both head out of the precinct.

In his car, Martin calls Warden Peters at the prison. Peters picks up, but Martin doesn't give the warden a chance to speak.

"Hello, warden, I just want to let you know that your days of being a warden of crimes may almost be over. I've got a pretty good idea of what you've been doing, and if I have my way, everything is going to crumble—with you and your buddies buried under it."

"What are you talking about, Martin?" the warden asks.

"You and Reyes thought that poor guard was as good as dead. But you were wrong," Martin says, clicking off the cellphone before the warden can continue.

Peters hangs up his office phone and quickly picks it up again to call the mayor's cellphone. "It's me, Peters," he says.

The mayor is far from pleasant. "I know who you are. What do you want?"

"I just got a call from Detective Martin. This whole … umm … situation is falling apart. All of us are going down. I think my guard is awake, and I'm afraid he's going to talk."

"Anybody found Reyes yet?" the mayor asks.

"No. No leads," Peters says.

The mayor is silent. "I'll send someone over to the hospital to end this situation with Mike."

Peters once again can't get a word in edgewise.

The mayor says, "I'm going to take care of the doctor, the nurse, and anyone else around. Then I'm going to take care of you and Reyes."

The mayor slams his cellphone onto the desk, then picks it up again and makes a call.

The voice on the other end asks, "Who's next?"

"Mike Fredmond, the guard from the prison, and anybody who's around him," Mayor Cannon Russ says. "After it's over, I'll be in touch." He clicks off.

The man on the other end of the mayor's call slides his phone into the pocket of his leather jacket, checks his gun, puts on the silencer, and tucks the weapon into his waistband. He takes the elevator of his apartment complex to the ground floor, walks out the back door, and jumps on his motorcycle. He easily makes good time weaving through traffic to the hospital.

When Detective Martin pulls into the hospital parking lot, it's mostly empty, but he looks around carefully. The detective sprints into the hospital and up the back stairwell to the Intensive Care Unit.

Dr. Charter is waiting in the hallway. He greets Detective Martin enthusiastically and guides him past the nurse's station, where Nurse Connors and two other nurses are on staff. Nurse Connors follows the doctor and the detective into Mike's room. Dr. Charter opens the door, and the detective is shocked to see Mike sitting up watching television.

Mike brightens when they walk in.

Dr. Charter walks to Mike's bedside. "Are you still feeling well enough to talk?"

Mike nods. "I feel great actually."

"Good. Detective Martin is here to speak to you. He's on your case at the request of the District Attorney's office," Dr. Charter explains.

Martin walks over and shakes Mike's hand.

"I'm glad to see you awake," Martin says.

"And alive," Mike jokes.

The detective asks Dr. Charter and Nurse Connors to leave them alone.

"The doctor tells me that you're ready to talk about the attack you suffered," Martin says.

Mike nods again.

"Well, let's get straight to the point. Who shot you?" Martin asks.

"It was Chief Clark Reyes. He shot me, and Warden Phillip Peters was there when it happened. Peters is running that prison like an organized-crime operation," Mike says. "A lot of the guards and plenty of the police officers are in on it."

Martin stares at Mike. "What exactly are they doing, Mike?"

Mike is quiet for a moment. He thinks back to the things that happened to the women prisoners. He thinks about Jena and how he felt about her and wonders where she is right now. He thinks about the things he'd seen and, even worse, the rumors that he'd heard.

"It's all about the women prisoners," Mike says. "They're being threatened and abused. I've heard, and I think it's true, that some of them are being abducted and sent away."

"What are we talking about?" Martin asks.

"I don't know, exactly. I wish I did. I know that women are constantly disappearing without any reasonable explanation," Mike explains.

"You have no idea where they're being taken?" Martin asks.

"No," Mike says.

Martin asks Mike to explain why he was shot.

Mike explains that an inmate named Candy Pindle was pregnant with Reyes' child and that Reyes had threatened to take the baby and kill Candy.

"She was scared for her life, and another inmate, Chance Middleton, told me she'd received threats, too," Mike tells the detective. "And just that day, a prison nurse up and disappeared without any explanation. I grabbed the two women prisoners and tried to escape with them, to keep them safe."

Mike looks at Martin, but he can't tell what the detective is thinking.

"Look, I know it all sounds crazy," Mike says earnestly. He clears his throat. "We were trying to get away when Reyes shot me, then left me for dead. The warden saw the whole thing. I thought I was dead. I don't have any idea how I ended up here."

Martin takes notes and shakes his head while Mike tries to tell his complicated story.

"Have you found Candy? Do you know where she is?" Mike asks.

"We didn't find anyone by that name," the detective says.

"I hope they didn't kill her," Mike says. Thinking of the frightened and frail young woman, he frowns. "You'll look for her, won't you?"

"We'll do our best," Martin says. "This case gets bigger and bigger all the time." He sighs. "I really need you to make a positive identification of Reyes in a lineup."

"Take me in. I'm ready," Mike says quickly.

"That's great, but we don't know where to find Reyes," the detective says.

"What?" Mike asks.

"It's a long story—just like the rest of this," Martin says. "Reyes has been kidnapped. We don't know where he is, but we've thought all along that he was responsible for multiple crimes, including yours."

"We have to get Peters, too," Mike says.

Just then, Smith opens the door.

"Pardon me," Smith says. "Can I speak to you in the hallway, detective?"

Martin excuses himself and walks into the hall with Smith.

"The airplane signal was picked up," Smith says. "They think it was headed toward South America."

"South America?" Martin says with surprise. "Why would they be headed to South America?"

"No way to tell," Smith replies. "The control tower doesn't have a read on them. They only picked up the one signal by chance. The air traffic controller thinks they may be using a scrambler to stay off radar."

"Why would someone kidnap Reyes and take him to South America?" Martin asks rhetorically.

Smith shakes his head. "What is Mike saying?"

"He says Reyes definitely shot him. He also says Reyes and Warden Peters and who-knows-who-else is running some kind of operation with the women in the prison," Martin explains. "Mike says women just disappear with no explanation. The women are the key. But if they're being taken somewhere, Mike doesn't know where it would be or for what purpose."

Martin turns toward Mike's room. "Let's go see if he can tell us anything else."

The two detectives walk into Mike's room, thanking him again for his help.

"Is there anything you can tell us about Warden Peters?" Martin asks.

"Only that he and Reyes are in on this is together—whatever this is. I walked up on them talking about the women at least twice. And I know the warden was there when Reyes shot me," Mike says. "That's all I know."

Martin continues taking notes.

"I don't know how high up this goes or how long it's been going on. I do know that if you don't get Reyes, I will. He tried to kill me. It's only right that I return the favor," Mike says.

"I think you should let us handle this, Mike," Smith says. "You don't need any more trouble. You just focus on recovering, and we'll handle Reyes, Peters, and anyone else involved."

Mike nods as Martin and Smith step out of the room.

The assassin sent by Mayor Russ is coming up the same stairwell that Martin had used and is making his way to Mike's room. He ducks out of the way just as Detectives Martin and Smith are leaving.

The killer is bold. He shoots one of the nurses walking down the hall, and Martin and Smith draw their weapons and yell for everyone to get down and take cover.

The detectives use a column near Mike's room for cover and begin shooting in the direction of the bullet.

"Who is this guy?" Smith yells.

"I don't know, but we need to take him down," Martin says.

The nurse lying on the floor is bleeding badly. Dr. Charter quickly closes the door to the room his patient is in. And Martin and Smith take cover with Nurse Connors and another nurse behind the nurse's station.

The assassin is standing fearlessly in the hallway.

"We are detectives with the District Attorney's office!" Martin yells. "Put down your weapon!"

The assassin fires at Martin in response, but the nurse's station protects him.

Smith gets on the radio and calls for backup while Martin darts in and out of the nurse's station, taking shots at the killer.

He hits the shooter in one shoulder, but it doesn't seem to slow the man down.

Police respond to Smith's call almost immediately and start flooding the hospital through all of the entrances and stairwells. Two of them have managed to get through the stairwell door behind the assassin and fire twice but miss.

The shooter turns on his heels and manages to wound both officers badly.

Everyone in the hospital can hear the gunfire, including Mike, and he's pretty sure that he's the target. He tries to disconnect his IV, but it takes too long, so he knocks the IV over and hides on the floor beside his bed.

Outside, more police officers move in, but can't get past the relentless gunfire of the assassin, who is now moving closer to Mike's door.

Detective Martin, still taking cover behind the nurse's station, can hear the assassin's boots on the slick hospital floor. As he hears the shooter turn the handle to Mike's door, Martin stands up, takes aim, and shoots at the assassin.

The assassin falls at the entrance to Mike's room.

Unable to reach his weapon, the assassin struggles to stand.

Martin, Smith, and other officers surround the man, who lies bleeding from several gunshot wounds.

Nurse Connors calls for help on the intercom.

Nurses and Dr. Charter manage to get the assassin and the wounded nurse to the Emergency Room, while the police officers help their own wounded. The nurse is alive, and everyone is working on the assassin.

Detective Martin quickly goes to Mike's room and helps him get back into bed.

"What's going on?" Mike asks frantically.

"It seems that someone was sent here to kill you. I hate to sound arrogant, but they might have succeeded if Smith and I hadn't been here. By the time it was all over, we had half of the police department here," Martin says. "He hurt a lot of people, and he could have hurt more. It didn't seem like he really cared who got caught in the crossfire." He sighs. "I've never seen anything like it."

Mike is relieved but angry. "They just won't stop."

"They took a big risk today. I called Warden Peters before I came here. I'm sorry to say that I must have tipped him off that you were awake," Martin says, looking downtrodden. "I never thought they would send an assassin to kill you—never mind someone who would try to kill everyone else on the floor."

Shaking his head, he tells Mike that one nurse and at least two officers were shot. "I'll be making a visit to the warden today. I'll see if the hospital can keep all of this quiet until I can get more answers."

Neither he nor Mike says a word as the detective leaves the room.

Dr. Charter and the hospital staff are quickly working to stanch the flow of blood as they work on the wounded shooter.

Detectives Martin and Smith wait in the Emergency Room for news, but it isn't long before Dr. Charter walks toward them.

His expression says it all.

"He didn't make it," Dr. Charter says. "He lost too much blood."

Martin looks at Smith and then at Dr. Charter.

"We need something more from you, Dr. Charter," he says. "I need you to keep this story from getting out to the public until we get more answers. I've already instructed the staff to contact the families of the wounded, and I can't guarantee how long this story will stay out of the press. I've heard that Nurse Connors has had some trouble reaching next of kin, so that may buy you some time."

"How are the nurse and the wounded officers?" Smith asks.

"They're okay."

"I need to get back to my patients," Dr. Charter says. "Good luck to you. And ... you saved lives today. Thank you."

After they all shake hands, Martin turns to Smith. "I think it's time to pay Warden Peters a visit."

"Agreed," Smith says.

As they head to their car, Warden Peters, on the other end of town, is hearing a knock on his office door.

"Come in," the warden says.

It's a new guard, Joe Preston.

"What can I do for you, Joe?" the warden asks.

"Sir, with all due respect, I wanted to talk to you about some things going on in the prison," Officer Preston says tentatively.

Peters looks blankly at the new guard. "Have a seat," the warden says, finally.

"I'd rather stand, sir," the guard says.

"Fine," the warden responds impatiently. "What's going on?"

"Warden Peters, sir, I appreciate being given the responsibility of guarding individuals who have broken the law," Officer Preston says. "I took this job because I believe in the law. I take this job seriously." He stops and clears his throat. "There have been rumors, sir."

"What rumors?" the warden asks.

"Well, sir, some of the inmates and a few of the guards say that there are inmates who are missing," the guard says. "Some of the women have been asking what's happened to their friends. We checked solitary confinement, but there are only two prisoners there now, and they aren't the ones the inmates were looking for." He stops and waits for an explanation. "So, I wanted to speak to you about it."

"I see," Peters replies. He stands. "I can assure you that the rumors are not true." Peters moves up close to Preston. "No women are missing."

Peters' glares at the guard, trying to intimidate the young man.

Then, walking away from Officer Preston, he says, "Prison is tough, especially for women. Many of these women are abandoned by their families and friends. Their children don't want anything to do with them. Their spouses don't visit. Some women make up stories—fantasies. It makes them feel better." He studies the guard. "They're trying to get attention because they don't think anyone cares about them."

Peters plays with a pencil on his desk, rolling it back and forth on his blotter. "Prison life is hard on all of us, not just the inmates. Your part is to guard the women and make sure they are treated properly. It's also your job to separate the truth from fiction and the difference between sad stories and reality," the warden says. He puffs himself up. "My job, as warden, is to run this entire place, with the help of the staff, of course."

Officer Preston stands silently, trying to absorb everything Peters has told him.

"Warden, I know one of the women who is missing. She's my biological mother, Matty Ellen Carson. She was sentenced to this prison nineteen years ago when I six years old. I couldn't get any information from the Maplesville Police Department or anywhere else because someone expunged all the information that I was her son." He grows angrier. "I've been getting the runaround for over a year now, so I got a job here."

The warden is stunned.

The guard continues. "I haven't seen her since I've worked here, so I started my own investigation, which leads me here to you warden."

The warden starts to sweat but tries to conceal his nervousness.

"I was raised by a foster mother, and she told me that my biological mother was sent to prison. This prison," Preston says. "I never came to visit her because I didn't want anything to do with her. I wanted a career in law enforcement. Ultimately, I decided to leave the police force and become a prison guard. My mother should be here. And she isn't. She wasn't transferred to another prison. She didn't die."

Preston stops talking and pulls out his gun.

The warden nearly faints.

Keeping his weapon trained on the warden, the guard, "So, tell me, where is my mother? And where are the rest of the missing women? You see, my mother doesn't know I'm alive. They told her that I died in the car crash that landed her in this jail. But I didn't die. And now I'm looking for her."

The warden can't speak.

"Some cop named Reyes made the arrest and filed the paperwork," Officer Preston says. "You think I'm stupid enough to believe that pretty story you just told me? I took this job so I could find out the truth. And all roads lead to this office. So, you're going to tell me the truth. Where is my mother and what did you do to her?"

Officer Preston shakes the gun at Peters' head.

"Son, the only answer you're going to get is a prison sentence of your own. Do you want that kind of life?" Peters says, trying to reason with the young man.

Preston doesn't flinch. In fact, he yells so loud that the warden almost falls out of his chair. "I want to know where my mother is. I want to know where the missing inmates are!"

Detectives Martin and Smith, standing in the doorway of Peters' office, hear the screaming.

Martin pulls out his gun and charges through the door.

"Put down your weapon, guard," Martin orders.

Preston turns his gun on the detective. "I'm not here for you, sir. But I need answers from this man," he says, turning and again pointing his weapon at the warden. "I'm here to find out what happened to my mother—my biological mother, who thinks I'm dead."

Martin tries to reason with the guard. "I know. We heard most of your story. We have a pretty good idea of what's going on in this prison, and that's why we're here. But think about this rationally. … So, I'll say again, put down your weapon."

Martin and Smith are quiet, hoping their silence will give Preston a chance to think about his options.

"Detective Smith, here, will take care of you," Detective Martin says calmly, "He'll get all of the details about your story and the other stories you've heard. You can file a formal complaint." Martin looks deeply into Preston's eyes. "You're not going to help us find your mother if you end up in jail."

Preston's shoulders slump, as he still faces the warden. He raises one arm above his head and gently places his gun on the chair with the other hand.

Detective Smith picks up Preston's handgun. He doesn't handcuff the guard but escorts him out of the office.

Detective Martin closes the warden's office door. "I think you and I have something to discuss."

Peters is still shaken and doesn't respond. "Thank you for taking care of that situation, Martin. That boy—"

"Quite an amazing story. You know, it's ironic, but his story is exactly the link that I needed to make my case. It all makes sense now." He leans onto Peters' desk. "Reyes is on your payroll, and everything I hear wherever I go leads straight back to this prison—the women and you." Martin glares at the warden. "You are the king of a shady operation that scoops up women and makes them disappear into thin air. And anyone who gets in your way gets dead—or almost dead."

Peters' snarls at Martin. "Me? King?" Peters keeps smirking. "You have no idea, Detective Martin, what you are getting involved in. You think I could run such an elaborate operation by myself?"

"Do, tell, warden," Martin says. "Tell me who else is involved."

"You'd like that, wouldn't you?" Peters says, standing up. "Wouldn't that be ironic that me, the warden of this prison, would spill the beans about what goes on in my facility?"

Detective Martin is not swayed. "Warden, your operation is falling apart. Mike is awake, and he's already told me that Reyes shot him and that you were there, too. It's only a matter of time before all of the pieces fit together." He leans farther across the desk in their game of one-upmanship. "You're going to prison. You, Reyes, and anyone else involved in this tragic scheme."

"Shouldn't you be arresting Joe Preston?" Peters says arrogantly. "You heard him threatening me. You saw him pointing a firearm at me. I'm an innocent man until a court of law proves otherwise."

"Warden, you sent an assassin to the hospital to kill Mike Fredmond—and probably me and my partner and a bunch of innocent people. And I tipped you off! I called you, then someone just happens to show up with a gun outside of Mike's hospital room," Martin says, furious.

"I have no idea what you're talking about, detective," the warden says.

"Oh, you know exactly what I'm talking about. And if you didn't send him with your own hands, you had your dirty fingerprints all over it," Martin says. "Now tell me who else is involved. How high does it go?"

The warden shrugs defiantly.

"Let's talk about something else, then," Martin says. "Where is Joe Preston's mother, Matty?"

The warden keeps his mouth shut.

"Nothing to say?" Martin says. "I'll tell you what's going to happen. I'm going to ensure that there is a full investigation into the records of every female inmate for the past twenty years—since you've been warden and since Reyes has been a so-called cop."

Martin informs Peters that he is an official suspect in the attempted murder of Mike Fredmond and that more charges would be on the way. He says he will obtain records for the warden's phone—his cellphone and his office phone.

"So, don't bother scrubbing your phone because we're going to find everything. I'll also be speaking to Mayor Cannon Russ to tell him about our investigation into these missing women," Martin says.

"Am I under arrest, detective?" Peters asks.

"Not now," Martin says. "Soon."

Peters turns away from the detective. "Well, if I'm not under arrest, then I have work to do."

"Don't make any vacation plans," Martin says. "You'll be apprehended for questioning very soon."

Smith opens the door to the warden's office. "Everything okay in here?" he asks.

"I think the warden and I have a clear understanding, don't we, warden?" Martin says.

Peters' smiles. "As a prison warden, I am well aware of the importance of the rule of law. Of course, I will cooperate with your investigation."

Martin glowers at the warden one more time, then he and Smith leave Warden Peters' office and close the door behind them.

Out in the hall, Martin lets out a long, slow breath. "He's a crook."

"You won't get any argument from me," Smith replies.

Martin asks Smith to get records for all inmates for the last twenty years. "I want to know the status of every woman. Were they released? Did they die? Are they still in prison?"

"The county should have all the records," Smith says. "I'll get right on it."

Martin and Smith start walking down the hall toward the prison exit. But four guards, their arms folded stop them. One of the guards walks toward them.

"May I see your identification, sir?" the guard asks.

Both detectives show their badges.

"We were just having a talk with your warden," Martin says.

The guard looks back at the three others. Two guards grab Martin, and two grab Smith.

"You are both unlawfully on the premises of a correctional institution," the first guard says.

"We have jurisdiction here," Martin protests.

The second guard ignores him. "We will have to keep you both in custody until the proper authorities arrive."

Martin struggles to get loose. "What are talking about? We *are* the proper authorities."

But the guards out-man them, take their weapons, and escort them to solitary confinement cells.

"You two stay put until we get this all sorted out," the lead guard says with a smirk.

"You have unlawfully detained two officers of the District Attorney's office," Martin says, grabbing the bars on the cell door. "The only thing that's going to get sorted out here is that you're going down with your boss."

One younger guard stays behind. "I'm just doing what I was told. They threatened to hurt my wife and kids." Looking around to make sure nobody sees him; he surreptitiously hands the detectives their weapons. "I'll just tell them that I locked the guns up somewhere. If you can get out, at least you'll have your weapons." The guard starts to leave, then turns around again. "Please don't let me go to prison. It's the warden and the mayor."

"Mayor Russ?" Martin asks.

"That's right," the guard confirms. "They have us all doing their dirty work. They found out I cheated on my wife, and they say they'll tell my wife—or worse—if I don't stay here." He looks more defeated than the two detectives who are now behind bars. "We're trapped in prison along with everyone else."

"Let us out," Martin demands. "We'll take care of you but let us out."

"I can't," the guard says. "I gave you back your guns. If you get out, just remember that a lot of guards here are innocent, too."

The guard hurries away.

Warden Peters, back in his office, is on his phone with Mayor Russ.

"I had to make a decision," he says. "It's not pretty. Martin and Smith are locked up here in the prison, for now. You just tell me what you want me to do next."

CHAPTER TWENTY-SIX

Lero directs his team to carry the bodies of Maria and Moschi upstairs to the living quarters. He asks them to wash their remains and dress them in royal gold clothing.

As his team carries the bodies upstairs, Lero bows his head and reluctantly walks into Romli's luxurious private office.

The door is open, and Romli is sitting inside with his legs crossed casually and holding a glass of wine. Three beautiful women stand near him. They are dressed in stately attire. The women are silent and still, waiting for instructions. Romli looks up and nods, signaling that Lero may enter the room. He snaps his fingers to signal to the women to leave.

"Come. Sit, Lero," Romli says. "Tell me what you've found."

"I should stand. I have not washed yet," Lero says.

"No bother, Lero. The women will clean after you leave. Please sit next to me," Romli says, sipping his wine. "Would you like a glass?"

"No, thank you," Lero says. "I have news for you. Disturbing news."

Romli puts down his wine. "Go on."

"I've found Maria. She is gone ... dead. She was buried in a shallow grave in the woods, near the village where she ruled."

Romli is quiet. He slowly closes his eyes in a moment of silence and takes a deep breath. "Where is her body?"

"I've asked that their bodies be taken upstairs to be washed and clothed," Lero says.

"Bodies?" Romli asks.

"Yes. We found Moschi. He was buried next to her," Lero says.

Romli stares at Lero for a long time. "What?" he asks, as if his ears have betrayed him.

"My team found them. First, Maria, then Moschi."

Romli appears sad and disappointed. He pulls out an old photo of Maria, sets it on his desk, and stares at it.

"Not my Maria. No," he says. He looks up at Lero. "This is the woman you are talking about?"

"Yes, Romli. It is. She is gone, and her body is upstairs in the living quarters," Lero says.

"I shall go to her now," Romli insists.

"Sir, she is not ready," Lero says.

"I must see her now. Come with me."

They walk upstairs to where the bodies are being prepared. They pass several guards along the way. The guards bow slightly as Romli and Lero pass.

There is a guard in front of the room where the bodies are being kept. He moves to the side when Romli approaches.

"Open the door," Romli orders the guard.

Romli walks slowly into the room.

Two women are carrying garments. Other men and women are arranging, cleaning, and preparing for a ceremony. One of the women greets Romli.

"Where is she?" he asks.

The woman guides Romli to a sacred room, lavishly decorated. A large window has breezy white silk curtains.

Romli sees Maria's still corpse.

She is lying on a high cement bed, sculpted with flowers and angels. Her body has been washed, the woman says, but she is not dressed. Her flowing black hair is brushed out beautifully.

Romli slowly walks toward her and tries to stay composed. He almost breaks down when he sees her.

"Shall I leave?" Lero asks.

"Yes, please give me a moment with her. I'll call for you."

Lero leaves the room with a heavy heart on behalf of his leader. He stands close to the door in case he is needed.

Romli stares at Maria. He tries to hold back his tears as he gently grasps her hand and kisses it, then he gently puts her hand back at her side.

"My Maria," he utters softly. "My beautiful Maria. Who did this to you? I will find them, and I will kill them." He touches Maria's hair, sliding his fingers through the strands. "Such beautiful hair. You always had beautiful hair."

He stops as his voice cracks. "I will avenge your death. I will ensure they pay." Then he leans down and kisses Maria's cheek.

Romli leaves the room quickly, and Lero is waiting for him.

"Moschi. Where is he?" Romli asks.

A woman leads Romli down the hall to the room where Moschi is laying. Romli enters the room. Moschi is dressed in royal gold. Romli stands near Moschi's cement resting place.

"Well, my old friend, someone got to you before I could," Romli says. "Or maybe I was never going to get you. Did you find the game enjoyable? Regardless, someone has ended it. I shall avenge your death as I shall avenge Maria's. Sleep well, my old friend."

Romli walks out of the room. "Lero, accompany me to my chambers."

Back at his office, Romli goes straight to his desk and puts the photo of Maria back where he'd kept it.

"She is gone now. I must not dwell on sentimentality," he says. "I will avenge her death, as I promised her. Tell me what you know."

"We don't know. Chance seems to think it was Jena Parker. But, as you know, Chance would use any opportunity to blame Jena Parker for anything." Lero explains that they examined the gunshot wounds. "It appears that Maria was shot with Moschi's gun and that Moschi was shot with her gun."

Lero pauses so that his leader can absorb this information. "But someone had to have buried them. The village people wouldn't have done it. They are too afraid to even leave their huts and tents."

Romli slams his hand down onto his desk. "Your observations about Chance are correct, but you still must find this Jena Parker. I want her to stand in front of me. I want you to kill her right before my eyes. Find her now!"

"Romli, the men are tired. It is dark. We must begin in the morning. I promise you, my brother, we will find her, and I will bring her to you."

Romli stares at Lero. He tries to calm himself. "I know you will. Double up your team. Take as many people as you can, as many as are fit. Track down Jena Parker and anyone she is associated with. I want her."

Lero had not heard Romli sound this determined in some time. "Do you understand?" Romli asks.

"Yes, I understand. I will not let you down. She will be found." Lero turns to leave. "I will report to you tomorrow. Goodnight."

"Wait," Romli says. "Invade Moschi's compound. Burn it to the ground if you need to. They must pay for Maria's death, as well."

Lero nods.

When Lero is gone, Romli stares into nothingness.

———

Lero stops at the women's quarters on his way to his room. Matty is in front of the entry.

"Why are you still awake?" he asks.

Matty looks away from him. "Because I'm not tired."

"Will you come to my room?" Lero asks.

Matty smirks. "Not unless you make me. I'm not interested."

"You're still angry with me?" Lero asks.

"What do you want, Lero?" she asks disrespectfully. "As you can see, I'm busy doing nothing."

"Matty, it has been a long day. Maria is dead and so is Moschi. Both killed and buried in a shallow grave. I had to carry them back here and then tell Romli."

Matty pauses. "Maria is gone? How is Romli taking the news?" Her tone is without sympathy and full of sarcasm.

Lero has no patience for it. "He is not happy." He takes on a business-like stance. "You and the girls will join me tomorrow on the mission to find Jena Parker. We are going to invade Moschi's compound."

"Is this what Romli instructed?" Matty asks, bordering on insubordination.

"Yes. We have an opportunity to destroy the compound now that Moschi is gone," Lero says. "Moschi was a great fighter and leader, but he's dead. We no longer need to battle him, and we can take down his operation." Lero stands up straighter. "We will be able to build one team. You will be in charge of the women from both compounds. Think of the power you will have."

He reaches out to touch Matty's face.

She pushes his hand away. "Romli will have the power, not me. You know that" Matty says forcefully. "We mean nothing to each other any longer, Lero—you and me. My team is ready, except for Tonya. She is wounded and will do us no good."

Matty begins walking to her room.

Lero watches her, then heads to his room.

He showers and visualizes Matty showering with him, kissing him, laughing with him. He would ask her to sing him to sleep, and she would.

Lero opens his eyes. Matty is not beside him.

He turns off the water and towels off, then falls into his bed.

<hr />

Matty is walking to her room. Chance is still up, too. She walks across the hall to the bathroom. She passes Matty, and the two glare at each other.

"What is it with you, Matty?" Chance says. "Why do you hate me?"

"I don't hate you," Matty says. "I just don't like you. Something about you gives me the heebie-jeebies."

"Maybe we're too much alike," Chance says.

Matty walks past Chance, knocking into her shoulder. "You're not like me," Matty says and walks to her room.

<hr />

Franklin is making final preparations, darting around like a tour guide, repeating his instructions to the pilot, making sure that those who have cellphones have everyone else's numbers, and checking that all of the gear is packed into the jeep.

Mr. Tindale is unsure of what to do. He follows Franklin around and finally clears his throat to get the boss' attention. "Sir, maybe it would be better if I stayed here to keep an eye on the pilot," he suggests.

Franklin turns to Mr. Tindale and looks concerned. "Are you afraid of the woods?"

Mr. Tindale sighs. "Sir, I am no warrior. I am a servant who has gotten his hands dirty a couple of times in his career. It's possible that I won't be of any use."

"Mr. Tindale, you've been my chief servant for many years. I know there is a fighter as tough as Rambo in you. Maybe it's time for you to let that person surface. You may stay here if you like, but I think we should all stay together."

Mr. Tindale nods.

Between talking, planning, and loading gear, it's taken all day to get ready. The sun will set soon.

Franklin turns to Jena. "Maybe we should wait and head out at dawn. It'll be dark soon. Everyone has flashlights. But I'm afraid that if we use them, we'll be easier to spot. What do you think?"

Jena looks toward Jake. "I think you're right. Let's leave at first light," she says.

"Where are we going first, and do you know how to get there?" Jake asks.

"I know my way back to Moschi's compound—or, I should say, the compound that Moschi once led," Jena says.

"You told us that Moschi is dead. How did he die?" Jake asks.

"Let's talk about it in the morning," Jena says.

Jake and Jena head off to find a good place to sleep.

Denise stands alone. She doesn't know what to do.

Franklin takes her by the arm. "You and I, Mr. Tindale, and Ken can sleep in the airplane until morning," he says. "Then we'll all head out."

Denise agrees.

Ken passes Jake and Jena on the way to get Reyes and take him to the plane.

"Shacking up together, we'll make a party out of it, y'know?" Ken says, teasing the couple.

"We're looking for space for two, and only two," Jake says a bit too harshly.

"Dude, I was kidding," Ken says. "But I see how it is. You get your girl back, and the best friend gets the ax."

Jake wears a blank expression. He owes Ken a lot. He never could have gotten this far without his best friend.

"Jake, Jena," Ken says, "I'm happy for you. I'm totally kidding. If I had just gotten my girl back, I'd dump me, too."

"I'm not dumping you, man," Jake says.

"I know. I know. I just don't want to get back on that plane," Ken says.

"Seriously, you can camp with us," Jena says. "I'm exhausted. We're in the middle of nowhere. We're not going to be doing anything sexy."

"What?" Jake asks abruptly.

"I'll just get on the plane," Ken says.

"No, you're staying with us," Jena says. "Let's set up and get some sleep. There's a pond nearby, and we can wash up in the morning. Am I right, Jake?"

"Sure," Jake says, albeit reluctantly.

"Great!" Ken says. He sounds like a kid.

Jena smiles in the dimming light and starts rolling out the sleeping bags.

Franklin walks over and asks Ken whether he's joining them in the airplane.

"No, we're making camp out here," Jena says.

"Right, that's what we're doing," Jake says sarcastically.

"Will you do something with Reyes?" Ken asks. "To be honest, I'm a little tired of hanging out with that guy!"

Franklin laughs. "I can understand that. Sure, I'll bring him onto the plane and handcuff him to something."

"You three be safe," Franklin says. "See you in the morning."

Ken is suddenly overwhelmed with affection for Jena. He gives her a big, tight hug.

"Let me help you with your sleeping bag," Jena says.

Ken thanks her. "You're such a strong, capable chick now," he says.

Jena smiles. "Thanks, my friend."

"Give it a break," Jake complains.

They all flop into their sleeping bags. Jake and Jena curl up together, with Ken only a few inches away.

"Don't you guys feel like we're all back in high school," Ken says.

Jena giggles. "I don't remember camping back in high school." Jake readily agrees with Jena.

"I thought we did. Maybe it was with Chance," Ken says without thinking and getting no response from Jena and Jake. "I guess that's a name I shouldn't have brought up." He sighs and turns over so that he's not facing Jake and Jena. "Oh, well, goodnight guys."

Jake pulls Jena closer to him. "You know I just wanted to be alone with you."

"I know, but we all need each other right now."

"He's just being a butthead," Jake says.

"I can hear you," his best friend protests.

They all giggle again. Maybe it is a little like high school, after all, Jake thinks, then as softy as he can, he whispers to Jena, "I love you. Good night, beautiful."

Jena kisses Jake's lips lightly. "I love you, too," she whispers back. She lays her cheek on his shoulder and quickly falls asleep.

Ken is already snoring, and Jake falls asleep shortly after Jena nods off.

Dawn wakes Jake in what seems like an instant. Jena is still sleeping. He watches her sleep and then peeks over at Ken, whose sleeping bag remains zipped over his head.

Jake closes his eyes. He doesn't want to wake Jena, he wants to savor the moment, but Jena's eyes open immediately. They smile at one another, basking in the joy of finally being together.

"Let's go to the pond, it's about a half-mile from here," she says. "I want to wash up."

"Fine with me," Jake says, grabbing a bar of soap and two towels.

They walk side by side, saying nothing. Jena grabs a toothbrush and throws one to Jake. With the toothbrush still in her mouth, she undresses. Jake can't take his eyes off of her. Jena laughs when she sees him with his toothbrush hanging foolishly from his mouth, too, but she stops giggling when she sees his gaze of love and commitment.

She slowly walks into the cool water, and Jake undresses and follows her. They swim and stare at each other while they swim.

"You're beautiful," Jake says breathlessly. He moves to kiss her gently on the lips.

"You're beautiful, Jake," Jena says. "You don't know how often I've thought of your beautiful eyes, your beautiful smile, your soft hair."

They kiss passionately. Jake wraps his hands around Jena in the cool, clean water. He slowly caresses her whole body. Jena arches her back as Jack kisses her neck. He holds her tightly and wraps one of her legs around his back.

"I've been imagining this moment for such a long time," Jake whispers.

"So, have I," Jena murmurs.

A fire ignites between them. Intimacy engulfs them. Jake and Jena bob up and down and sway with the water. They kiss and touch as he enters her.

Their pleasure is serene and passionate. They feel as if they are in another dimension—not conscious and not dreaming. They release together and embrace tightly.

Jake kisses Jena over and over. He doesn't want to let her go. They proclaim their love for one another again and again. He smiles and slowly swirls Jena around in the lake, making intertwined circles in the water, then lifts her and carries her to land, gently placing her on the ground. They hold each other again.

"It's a little chilly now," she says.

Jake reaches for clothes in Jena's bag and finds a wool shawl to wrap around her shoulders. He kisses her again, and she smiles.

"How's that?" he asks.

"Perfect."

"We'd better get dressed. Everyone will be awake soon and heading down here for a morning bath." He reluctantly pulls on a shirt. "I'm just so happy we got here first."

Her glowing expression says everything that's in her heart.

Jake hears footsteps and grabs Jena in alarm.

Soon they see Ken walking toward them.

"Don't sneak up on us like that," Jake says. "You could have gotten yourself hurt."

Ken leans over, grabbing things out of his bag, and smiles at Jena. "This girl is the only one out here who could hurt me. We both know she's a badass."

"Thanks, Ken," she says, pleased. "Let's leave Ken to his bath. We'll head back and tell everyone where to find the pond." She looks around. "We need to get moving. We have a long journey."

"How long?" Ken asks.

"About ten miles," she says.

Jena and Jake walk back to the plane, where Franklin is just stepping off.

Jena remembers that they have a jeep. Ken will be thrilled; she laughs to herself.

"Good morning, Franklin," Jena says.

"Today's the day. Let's get going," Franklin says.

"There's a nice, clean pond less than a half-mile down the path. Ken's washing up there."

"Super," Franklin replies. "I'll get Mr. Tindale and Denise."

When he returns with them, along with the pilot, Denise seems a bit shy, but they all take off down the path together.

Jena looks at Jake. "I'm going to go help my aunt," she tells him and skips down the path toward Denise.

"Are you okay?" Jena asks Denise gently.

"I know that you're safe, so I'm just fine," Denise says.

Jena promises her aunt that she'll find a private place for her to bathe—away from the guys.

"You know me so well," Denise says. "Thank you."

Jena and Denise giggle together. Denise asks Jena how she feels now that she is with Jake again.

"It feels like a dream," Jena replies as they walk along, "but he is the absolute love of my life." She tears up. "I love him very much, but I also feel responsible for turning his life upside down."

Denise nods.

"So much has happened. I just want to settle down, get married, have kids," Jena laughs. "Doesn't that sound lame?"

"Not in the least," her aunt says.

"Thank you, Aunt Denise," Jena says. "You've always been there for me."

"And I always will be." Denise smiles at Jena and kisses her forehead.

Jena shows Denise a good spot, quiet and private to bathe. Denise looks around to make sure.

"I'll be close by, in case you need me," Jena promises.

Hiding behind a boulder, Denise takes off her clothes and jumps into the pond.

In a few minutes, she dresses and returns to Jena and the others back at the plane.

Franklin takes the lead. "The time has come for us to join our precious and long-lost Jena on a journey for what she describes as justice." Everyone nods and looks toward Jena. "We are also going to battle for the town that we all know and love—Maplesville. I trust Jena, and I know how strongly she feels about our mission. Does everyone feel the same way?"

One by one, they nod.

"You will all have weapons. We hope not to use them, but they are for our protection," Franklin says, motioning Jena to the front of their little circle.

Jena steps forward, and the circle surrounds her. She is moved beyond measure. They look at her, recognizing Jena Parker as their leader.

"I know how much I'm asking of you—after you've come all this way to find me," she says, pausing to compose herself. "Now I'm asking you to fight a battle you never asked for, a fight you probably never imagined, a fight for justice." She looks intensely at each person. "I know what I'm asking of you because I know more than you do. I know what we will face.

"But I also know that innocent women are being kept against their will. Many are from Maplesville. They were whisked from the prison in the dark of night and brought here against their will to serve men and to kill for them."

Jena goes on to tell them she was brought to Moschi's compound to train as an assassin but that she escaped and now she wants to help as many of the other women as she can.

"You must know first that these are ruthless people. They will kill you without a second thought." She pauses. "I want to reach Moschi's compound. Pulue is in charge there now," she says, knowing these names mean nothing to most of them.

"I believe that Romli will attack Moschi's compound if he knows that Moschi is dead. And I believe Pulue will help us once he knows that a battle is imminent. I believe he will listen to me." Jena tells them that there is no guarantee of success. "We will go to battle against Romli, and Romli is Pulue's oldest enemy. He was Moschi's oldest enemy. If we are able to fight together, we will defeat Romli and bring some of the women home."

Nothing is certain, not even at Moschi's compound, she explains. "These are the same people who nearly killed me."

Everyone flinches.

"Anyone who has doubts should stay here with the pilot. We will not judge you," she says, looking to Franklin.

Franklin shares a glance with Mr. Tindale, whose face shows fear.

Jena takes a moment to look into every pair of eyes circling her. No one says a word.

"I want to say thank you," Jena says. "Now, let's go get them."

Although she knows Franklin brought the big, beautiful jeep, she says, "I believe we can move through the woods more quietly on foot. We'll leave the jeep here and loaded with the extra supplies in case we need to send someone back to rescue us."

"I understand," Franklin says.

The others groan.

Jena picks up her bag and her weapon and swings them over her shoulders. The others follow her lead and then follow her as she picks a path through the forest.

Jake stays close. Franklin, Denise, and Ken follow. Mr. Tindale lingers for a moment, then picks up his gear and heads into the woods.

When Jena stops, everyone else does, too.

She hears something.

"What is it?" Franklin whispers.

"It is the sound of the forest. The forest will communicate with us if we listen," Jena says.

Mr. Tindale stares at Denise, unsure of their decision to follow Jena.

"What is the forest saying?" Franklin whispers again.

Jena turns to look at everyone. "The forest is saying that we should move forward."

Everyone sighs with relief, and they begin walking again—with Jena as their undisputed leader.

———

The team members at Moschi's compound are beginning to ask questions about their leader.

Pulue, Andy, Veronica, Luis, and Tammy are in the dining room waiting for Sir James and his staff to serve breakfast. They are eager to discuss the business of the day.

Pulue stares at everyone sitting around the table, then stands. "Moschi left on a secret mission. He asked me not to tell anyone about it unless absolutely necessary." He pauses. "I've lost contact with him. I haven't gotten a message from him for several days."

Pulue pauses again, and everyone at the table starts to feel anxious. "I believe something has happened to him. He left strict instructions that we are not to look for him if he failed to return."

Pulue lowers his head a bit, then, standing taller, he shows only the slightest hint of emotion. "I always follow Moschi's instructions. He has built an astounding compound for us. He created one of the largest, most efficient, most high-tech espionage organizations in the world. He has trained us to be the best, and he deserves that we honor his orders."

Pulue looks at each individual at the table, and each nod in agreement.

"However, I don't think I should wait any longer," he says. "I've never had this much time pass without hearing from him."

If the team members are surprised, they don't show it.

"I believe I should put together a team, with me as the leader, to find Moschi," Pulue says. "I dreamed last night that I saw him falling, and I couldn't reach him before he fell. I could see him falling deeper and deeper into nothingness."

Pulue turns to Andy. "Choose two strong members from the East Wing Team to accompany me in the search for Moschi." He turns back to the group, once again looking at each person. "I know that he went to search for Jena Parker, so we will have to check all of the villages and all of the forest."

Veronica speaks up. "What about Romli's compound?"

Pulue frowns and nods. "Yes, it is possible that Moschi has been captured by one of Romli's teams. But Moschi never attacked Romli or other organizations. Moschi believes that our missions, and building our team, are more important than engaging in conflicts with other teams."

Pulue sits down as their meal is served.

"First we search for Moschi," he says with determination. "If we do not find him, then we will talk about moving against Romli's compound."

They eat in silence, and as soon as he is finished, Andy excuses himself.

Pulue leaves, as well, to begin preparing for his journey.

Andy walks the halls, looking into each room, observing the team members as they carry out their daily routines. He is greeted by the leader of the East Wing Team, Hero. They exchange pleasantries, and then Andy tells Hero that he needs two people to accompany Pulue on an important mission.

"I will go," Hero says, not unexpectedly.

"I respect that," Andy says, "but I prefer that you stay here."

With Pulue and Moschi gone, Andy knows he may need Hero if the compound is attacked.

Andy scans the room looking at the team members. "Who is your best?" he asks Hero.

"Rightpoint is very skilled, as is Finnsel," Hero says. "They would be my choices."

"How are their hunting and tracking skills?" Andy asks.

"Both are good," Hero responds. He stops to think about his roster of team members. "Terrus and Bonquet are my best hunter-trackers."

Andy is pleased. "That's great. We'll send Terrus and Bonquet with Pulue."

Hero calls them over. They nod to Andy and Hero, out of respect.

Andy tells them that their team leader has recommended them for a special mission. The two men smile.

"We have chosen you to accompany Pulue to search the villages and forests," Andy says.

Both men stand taller. They know Pulue has the highest status in the compound, other than Moschi.

"We are honored," Terrus says enthusiastically.

"Yes, sir, we are pleased to serve," Bonquet says.

"Pulue will explain the exact nature of the mission. But you will leave immediately," Andy tells the men sternly. "You may be gone a long time, so make certain you are well-prepared."

The men take off to gather their gear and soon return to meet Andy, who leads them to Pulue. Pulue is wearing armor and looks prepared for a long journey.

His gaze seems noble to Terrus and Bonquet, who carry their hunting spears. They are honored to be in his presence, and even prouder to be accompanying him on a mission.

CHAPTER TWENTY-SEVEN

Jena and the team reach the outer limits of Moschi's compound. She warns her friends that there are traps along the way, and she remembers some of them. She also remembers how to avoid some of the surveillance cameras and sensors.

She stops to survey the area.

"Is something wrong?" Jake asks.

"I'm not sure I can get into the compound without setting off the alarms," Jena says. She turns to speak to the whole group. "I believe I must go alone. If we go as a group, they will kill us. I will go first and tell them what I know about Moschi and explain our mission."

Jake speaks up. "Yesterday, you started to tell me how Moschi died."

"I saw it with my own eyes. He killed a woman he loved but who had left him for Romli, but she also managed to fatally wound Moschi," Jena says. "I doubt anyone in this compound knows about it yet."

Half the group looks slightly confused and the others completely baffled.

"It's a long story," Jena explains. "And it's not important to you right now. But everyone in this compound will be devastated."

Jake looks worried.

"I hope the news will motivate them to join us in our mission," Jena says.

"What about the women who were kidnapped?" Franklin asks. "Did Moschi have women from the prison in his compound?"

Jena thinks about Luis and his, or her, story. "I believe there are some, but everyone here is treated much better than those at Romli's compound."

She knows the story is incomprehensible. She remembers how confused she was when she was at the compound.

"It was Moschi who saved me from the prison. He told the authorities that he was responsible for my crimes. I was immensely grateful," Jena explains. "He told me he was going to take the fall for the crimes, but then he later shot me. I awoke in this place where there were doctors who saved my life. However, I realized they weren't really saviors. They were a part of this evil scheme."

She remembers the pictures of her battered body on the wall of the small hospital, and she remembers shooting both doctors—in what was, probably, her false hope of stopping the cycle of violence and healing, violence, and healing.

"It is a web of lies," she says. "It would take days to explain everything. But I will say that I am lucky that I didn't end up with Romli. I would surely be dead now."

She stares at Jake. So much has happened since she was taken from Maplesville. She looks at the others. They don't know half of what happened to her—and what she did herself—while she was still *in* Maplesville.

"I need you to trust me," Jena says. "I know I'm asking a lot, but we are doing the right thing."

Jake moves nearer to Jena. He sees the passion in her eyes.

"I just got you back," he says.

"I just got *you* back," she says. "But this is the best way."

"I trust you," Jake says. "But if you're not back in an hour, we're coming in after you."

Jake embraces and kisses his love.

"All of you, try to find some cover, and then try not to move around. There are traps everywhere," Jena says as she carefully steps over a wire.

They watch, worried, until she is out of sight.

Jena tries to reconnoiter a hidden entrance to the compound. She finds it and places her hand on the fingerprint sensor. The technology asks for her code name.

Moschi ordered her to choose a code name, but he never knew that she did.

The computerized voice asks for her code name again. "You have five seconds," the voice says and begins a countdown. "Five … Four … Three …."

Jena speaks. "Code name: Graybluebird."

"Code name accepted," the voice says.

Jena sighs with relief.

The first entryway opens, but it sets off a silent, second alarm, alerting the compound that someone has entered.

Veronica orders her team to get their weapons. "Everyone spread out," she yells. "We have a visitor."

Jena moves through the compound like a phantom. She remembers the way to the main dining room. She hears voices and hides behind a wall. She waits until the small group passes, then continues moving to the dining room.

As she turns the next corner, she comes face to face with Veronica.

"Hello, Jena," Veronica says.

Veronica holds a weapon. Jena stares at it but doesn't reach for her own.

"I need to talk to you, Veronica," Jena says. "I need to talk to all of you."

Lero waits for his team to arrive to load the jeeps and for Matty's team to arrive. He stares into the sunrise. A light breeze moves the air.

When his team arrives, he watches closely as they load the jeeps.

He sees Matty and her team. It pleases him to see her. He loves her but can't express it. He can't take his eyes off of her.

She greets him.

He turns to her, trying not to show emotion. "Good morning, Matty," he instructs her without looking at her. "First, we must call a meeting. Everyone must be united in the mission."

"And what is the mission?" she asks.

"The mission is to invade Moschi's compound, capture the new leader, and conscript their team," he says. "We are to kill anyone in our path. And we are to capture Jena Parker and bring her back to Romli." He ponders the task ahead. "All of this is on Romli's orders."

He walks away, not waiting for Matty to answer, as Matty walks toward her team.

Paula watches Lero watch Matty. She sees that he is trying to hide that he is following her with his eyes.

Matty is armed. Like all of the women, she is dressed in green camouflage. Some women add hats or scarves. They all know they are embarking on something important.

"Be ready for battle," Matty says. "Lero will speak to us before we leave. Paula and Chance, make sure our jeeps are ready and stocked, then meet us back here with Lero."

"Sharon and Suzanne, follow me," Matty says.

Chance gives Paula a dirty look. They walk together to the jeeps while the others move toward Lero and his team.

Matty walks between two of Lero's men. They gawk at her. She moves her team into the center of the circle surrounding Lero. Soon, Paula and Chance join them.

Lero tries to make eye contact with each individual.

"We are about to engage in a very important mission, ordered personally by our leader, Romli." He glances around to make sure everyone is paying attention. "Listen carefully. If you do not already know, Moschi has been killed."

Those who don't know are surprised and exchange puzzled looks.

"We are to invade his camp and capture the leaders. Those who challenge us will be considered the enemy. Protect yourselves and protect the mission," he says. "Am I clear?"

The men and women respond simultaneously. "Yes, sir!"

Lero raises his eyes to see Romli standing at the window in his quarters. Lero nods at Romli, who nods back.

"Let's move out!" Lero yells to rile up the teams.

Everyone rushes to the jeeps. Sharon drives Matty's jeep. Suzanne drives the jeep with Chance and Paula. Lero gets into his jeep, driven by Aeo. The others follow their lead.

The convoy moves onto the forest trail that leads to Moschi's compound. Aeo and Lero lead the way.

Veronica points her weapon at Jena. "I should kill you, right here and now."

Jena stands still.

"What do you need to tell me?" Veronica asks.

Andy, Tammy, and Luis catch up to Veronica, only to find her pointing a weapon at Jena Parker.

Luis steps forward. "Put the weapon down, Veronica."

Veronica challenges Luis. "Why should I?"

"Because she's not an enemy," Luis says. "She is a member of our team. Moschi brought her here. She is initiated, and she has made it back to us, and we need to listen to what she has to say."

Veronica keeps her weapon pointed at Jena. She and Jena glare at each other. Neither will blink.

Finally, Andy inserts himself between the women and says, "Veronica, put your weapon down unless you plan to shoot me, too."

She sighs and reluctantly lowers her weapon and takes a few steps backward.

Andy turns to Jena. "It's good to see you. We didn't know if you were alive."

"Good to see you, too," Jena replies.

Luis and Tammy walk forward to greet Jena, and then Andy leads them all into the main dining room.

The table is set for dinner. The butler, Sir James, and two servants are waiting for them.

Sir James nods to all of the team members as they enter, and he smiles at Jena, remembering the respect she had shown him. He pulls out her chair.

Andy and Luis sit on either side of Jena. Tammy and Veronica sit across the table from them. Sir James begins to serve the meal.

Veronica locks eyes with Jena, but Andy doesn't want the tension to build again, so he starts the discussion.

"So, Jena, you told Veronica that you have information for us," he says. "We all want to hear, but first we want to know where you've been."

Jena turns to Andy. "I lived through the initiation, but I woke to find myself in the medical unit. I killed two of the doctors, then made my way through the forest until I got here."

Veronica stands, reaches for her weapon, and points it at Jena. "Do you agree now that we should kill her?"

Andy stands. "Veronica, put down your weapon."

Veronica and Andy sit down again. Veronica eases back in her chair but keeps her eyes trained on Jena.

Andy looks at Jena. "Why did you kill them?"

Jena looks away. "I felt it was the right thing. I had been beaten and then shot. I woke up to two strangers who clearly helped this madness to continue. I did it to try to end this prison that we are all in."

"That's not for you to judge, Jena Parker," Veronica says.

"Maybe not, but I was brought here to be trained to kill," Jena responds.

"You were already a killer," Veronica says, taunting Jena.

Jena controls her temper and continues with the story she came to tell.

"I agreed to come here initially because I felt indebted to Moschi. He made a sacrifice to get me released from prison. I thought that I belonged among assassins, that I was born to be a killer, just like him. But I was wrong," Jena says. Jena barely takes a breath; she doesn't want to be prevented from telling her story. "As a part of the initiation, Moschi and all of you nearly killed me. I felt betrayed. I was angry when I woke up from a coma. But I deserved my pain because of the deeds I had committed in the past."

Jena breathes deeply but continues. "At that moment, I understood that the reign of bloodshed needed to end, that the practice of kidnapping women and forcing them to become killers must end—and the same for men who want another life."

She looks around the table, avoiding Veronica's stare. "Women from my town—and maybe other towns—are being kidnapped and forced to kill and serve and prostitute themselves. Most of them are not here. Most are in Romli's camp." She stops, then: "I have killed, but I do not want to kill anymore."

Veronica smirks. "Too late for that," she snaps.

"It may be too late for you, Veronica," Jena says. "But it is not too late for me." She looks around the table. "It's not too late for any of you. Or perhaps I should say, it's not too late for you to make your own choices."

Jena pauses for just a moment. She isn't sure of the reaction to her next statement:

"Moschi is dead."

Everyone stands and asks questions at the same time. They are all very emotional.

"What?" Andy asks.

"How?" Tammy asks.

"Maria killed him," Jena says.

"Liar!" Veronica shouts.

"I'm telling the truth," Jena insists.

Andy gasps. In shock, everyone slowly sits back down.

Luis is trying to hold back tears. "What happened to him?"

Jena is distraught about Mochi's death, too. "I loved Moschi, too," she says. "He saved me. He taught me so much. I would probably be dead, if not for him."

"Tell us the rest," Andy says.

"I was captured by Maria. Yes, I know that she was supposed to be long dead. Pulue told me that Romli's people had killed her. Yet there she was. She was not dead. She was alive," Jena tries to explain the unbelievable story. "She wanted to recruit me. She was the leader of a village in the forest. She took me hunting, and we camped for the night. We talked and Maria eventually told me that she loved Moschi, but that she also loved Romli, who had taken her to his bed when she was little more than a child."

After a long pause, she says, "She faked her death."

Everyone at the table gasps, almost at the same time.

Jena goes on. "The bottom line, as far as I am concerned, is that she planned to force me to serve her team. When we woke, I was determined to be free, not a slave, and we fought. That is when Moschi arrived. He was looking for me, maybe because he found the doctors I had killed. I don't know. And it didn't matter in the end. Moschi saw Maria and didn't believe his own eyes. He was heartbroken. He sobbed.

"Moschi and I thought she was dead. We stood over her body together. But when I turned my back, she was able to fire a final shot at Moschi. I ran to him, but it was too late. I held him in my arms as he died. And then I buried them in the forest," Jena says.

The room is quiet. Andy quickly stands. "We must find Moschi's body and bring it here for a proper burial."

Everyone stands.

"Wait." She looks around the table. "I have one more thing to say. I have others with me. Not warriors. Friends," she says, just as alarms are triggered throughout the compound.

Jena grabs her weapons. Andy, Luis, and Tammy all prepare to protect themselves and the compound.

Veronica becomes fierce and takes command.

"She's a traitor!" Veronica yells. "She brought others here to this secret compound! Kill her! Kill all of them!"

"No!" Jena screams. "It is not like that! They are my friends and family. They came all the way from Maplesville to rescue me. Please don't harm them." She speaks as quickly and loudly as she can. "I begged my friends to stay. I am certain that Romli's people will attack this compound when they learn of Moschi's death."

"Why should we believe you?" Veronica shouts. "We don't know you. Moschi brought you here. Now he's dead—at least, you claim he is—and you're responsible."

"No, I am not responsible for Moschi's death. I didn't even know about this place until Moschi brought me here. He and Maria both … they brought about their own destinies. We should all do the same. We should each decide our own destiny," Jena begs.

She turns to Andy. "Please, Andy. Believe me. My friends are here to help us. We need each other. Romli is ruthless, and he won't stop until he kills us all. I want to free the innocent women in Romli's camp who were being held against their will."

The alarms continue to blare throughout the compound. They can't think, much less talk.

Sir James opens the doors of the dining room. He is armed.

"We are ready to defend the compound," he says.

Andy stares at the loyal servant and then back at Jena. In an instant, he takes charge.

"Thank you, but stand down, Sir James. Please find someone to turn off that alarm," Andy says, as he walks toward Veronica. "Join us in defeating Romli, or you will be charged with treason. I want you to fight with us, but you must let go of your hatred of Jena. Decide now." He glares forcefully into Veronica's eyes.

Veronica cannot let go of her anger. She looks around the room to see if the others will join her.

"I'm with Andy," Luis says.

"So am I," echoes Tammy.

"While we're all standing here, we're being fooled by Jena Parker," Veronica says, pointing at Jena. "An army is entering our compound. Who are you people? You believe her over me? You are bewitched by her."

Suddenly, they notice that the alarms are quiet. They hear footsteps nearby.

Andy, Luis, Tammy, and Veronica draw their weapons. Standing in the doorway are Jake, Ken, Franklin, Denise, and Mr. Tindale. Sir James walks behind them, pushing them along with his weapon.

Jake runs toward Jena—his movement too quick. All the guns are quickly pointed at him. He immediately raises his arms above his head.

"Jena, I was worried. I had to come," Jake says.

He looks at Jena, then looks around the room and backtracks to stand beside Ken. His eyes are still darting around the room.

"My name is Jake. I'm Jena's ... umm ... I love Jena. We don't mean any harm," he says. "We came a very long way to find Jena."

Veronica's eyes seem to soften.

"Jena told us about what's going on with the women at the prison in Maplesville," Jake says. "We ... umm ...." He looks around again. "Maybe I should just shut up."

Jena smiles.

No one seems to know what to say next.

Sir James and the other servants are still armed and ready to fight, standing at the doorway.

The other members of Jena's crew look like their lips are glued shut.

Sir James looks at Andy, the anointed leader—at least, where the servants are concerned.

Andy steps forward. "Everyone! Stand down!" he commands.

"Yes, Sir Andy," the servants say in unison.

With that, their teammate Andy is now their leader—at least, until Pulue returns if he returns.

Andy nods at Sir James. He walks toward Jake and shakes his hand. "I am Andy. Welcome to our home. You are very brave—and perhaps not very bright."

Both men smile slightly. He introduces the others: Luis smiles, Tammy nods, and Veronica raises her eyebrows as she looks at Jake.

Jake nods at each one and smiles back at them.

Andy continues. "These are our servants. The head butler, Sir James, and the staff that works for him, Juliet, Henry, and Caesar."

Andy clears his throat. "Let me take that back—our chief of staff has gone by the name of Sir James while he has been with us; his given name is really Mr. James McArthur."

He winks at James discretely.

"There are many others who live here. They are not allowed in this room," Andy explains. "This is where the decisions are made."

Jake takes over the introductions. "I am Jake Paterson. This is Jena's aunt, Denise Parker; our good friend, Franklin Bosler, who got us here; this is my best friend, Ken Stewart; and this gentleman is Franklin's assistant, Mr. Willard Tindale."

Mr. Tindale turns to Sir James and bows.

Everyone exchanges handshakes, hellos, and smiles.

Sir James steps forward with a suggestion. "Our guests look tired and hungry. Why don't we serve them a meal?"

Jena's friends' eyes light up.

Andy turns to Sir James. "Yes, please." Then he turns back to the group. "We have much work to accomplish."

He pulls out his chair for Denise.

"Thank you," she says sincerely.

Sir James shows the others to their seats and directs his staff to bring more chairs.

Everyone takes a seat.

Franklin sits next to Veronica, who gives him a skeptical look. Franklin just smiles and shakes her stiff hand.

"I'm an author, you know," he says, ignoring Veronica's disinterest.

Ken sits between Luis and Tammy, who are both smitten with his good looks. They flirt shamelessly—simply for the fun of it.

The servants bring food and drinks to make everyone feel welcome and comfortable.

Jake sits next to Jena. They are both glowing in their success and their love.

Uncomfortable, Mr. Tindale stands.

Sir James smiles at him. "Sir Tindale, you are a guest in our home. Please let us serve you today," he says.

Mr. Tindale sits, lays a napkin over his lap, picks up his utensils, and attacks his meal as if he hadn't eaten in years.

Veronica stares at Andy. She stands, though everyone is still eating. She walks toward Andy and whispers in his ear. "This is ridiculous. For all we know, they are setting us up to be attacked."

Andy frowns. "Do these people look like killers to you?"

"No, but that doesn't mean they're not. We do know that Jena Parker is a killer. She claims she's not responsible for Moschi's murder, but how do we know?"

Jena notices Veronica whispering to Andy.

She walks away from Jake, who is eating and chatting with the group.

Veronica and Andy stop whispering as Jena approaches.

"Let me guess, you're still trying to convince Andy that we're traitors?" Jena says.

Veronica smirks. "Now you're a mind reader?"

"No," Jena replies. "It's obvious."

Jena turns to Andy and bows her head, subtly and briefly.

"Andy, we must prepare to battle Romli's team. By now, he likely knows that Maria and Moschi are dead," Jena says. "We should have gone immediately to his compound to have the advantage of surprise. We could have defeated those loyal to Romli and freed the women who are captives, taken from Maplesville and elsewhere."

Veronica rolls her eyes. "You keep telling us about these women. Do you have proof?"

"You are the proof," Jena says. "Where are you from? As much admiration as we have for Moschi, he, too, has been part of the kidnapping." She turns to Andy. "Romli, like Moschi, trains men and women to be killers. But Romli also is part of a trafficking ring where women are kidnapped, with the help of police, the prison warden, and others in positions of authority. Romli kidnaps these women to become slaves, to be killers who serve killers, and to prostitute themselves."

Jena glances at Luis and Tammy. "Here, at Moschi's compound, women—and men—are treated harshly. But they are also fed and housed." Jena ignores Veronica and addresses Andy. "My friends and I brought weapons, and we are ready to join you so that we may defeat Romli. This is what Moschi would want."

Veronica says, "You speak of what Moschi would want, even though you accuse him of being part of a kidnapping scheme."

Jena sighs. "Moschi was trying to help us grow. We now can fire weapons, use sophisticated fighting techniques, and know the ways of the assassin."

After a long pause, she goes on: "I am saying—perhaps Moschi would have agreed and perhaps he would not—that each of us is free to find our place in this world. We can fight for justice and righteousness and not for evil if we choose. We can take down Romli and his ruthless empire."

Lero and Matty stand beside their jeeps, parked about five miles from Moschi's compound. They can't be seen by guards inside the compound, and Romli's people use this spot to regularly spy on the movements of the operation.

Everyone is quiet, and the teams stay in their jeeps.

"Well, we made it this far," Matty whispers to Lero.

Lero turns to her, still feeling affection for Matty that he wants to hide.

"We must get in closer," he says. "We've trained for this moment many times, and the right moment is now. I hope your team is ready."

Matty smirks. "My team is always ready. We are not the weak link. Maybe you should look at your own team."

Lero ignores her. "We are going to move in soon. Get your team ready to meet."

Matty gives her team the signal to get out of the jeeps and points at a place for everyone to gather.

Paula is first out of the jeep. Chance, Suzanne, and Sharon follow. They follow Matty to join Lero and his teams. The team members all take the stance of warriors.

Lero stands in a circle of his teammates with a stern expression. He looks at each person to silently communicate the gravity of their mission. He keeps his voice quiet.

"We must perform our duties perfectly and prove our loyalty to Romli. Our mission is to invade Pulue's compound and capture or kill everyone inside. We must determine who the leaders are and whether Pulue is inside the building," Lero says. "A second part of the mission is to find whoever is responsible for the murders of Moschi and Maria. We believe the killer is a woman named Jena Parker."

Lero, staring at Chance, who is trying to conceal her grin, says, "Romli has ordered that Jena Parker is to be captured alive. He wants her returned to our headquarters. You will be punished if she is killed." When he looks at Chance again, her smile has faded. "If you harm Jena Parker, you will be deemed Romli's enemy and suffer the consequences."

No one notices the shock on Paula's face. She wonders what her former cellmate had done to incur the wrath of these people, thousands of miles away from Maplesville.

Lero continues explaining the battle plan. The teams will enter the south end of Romli's compound.

"We've found a weakness there," he says. "There are not many guards because the lake is a natural barrier."

They will use an inflated boat to cross the lake, Lero says, but the teams' two best swimmers will go first to scout out the area.

"Two team members have been specially trained for water missions," he says, and he asks the two swimmers to step forward.

Everyone looks around. The identities of the swimmers had been kept secret for security reasons.

Sharon steps forward, as does Aeo, who is Lero's driver.

The women are surprised. Sharon had always been afraid of the water. During her initiation, her fear was discovered. Whether for deception or torment, Romli chose her to join Aeo as a secret swimmer. Having completed their training, the swimmers are considered to be elite members of the team. Only Matty and Lero knew their identities.

Lero approaches them with pride.

Suzanne looks at Matty; she is angry. Matty knows that Suzanne had been captain of her high school swimming team and assumed she would have been chosen. Suzanne feels betrayed by Matty and Lero.

Matty ignores Suzanne's hostility and turns away from her. The decision had been made long ago. It couldn't be changed now.

Lero continues. "You two have been trained, and now we will put your training to the test."

Suzanne is still visibly angry, and Paula gives her a cross look.

"The water is not deep," Lero says. "The swimmers will put on protective gear but must exchange their large weapons for small ones."

Aeo hands his weapon to Lero, and Sharon hands hers to Matty. Then the team leaders give each swimmer the small weapons.

Matty smiles at Sharon and nods.

Sharon glances at Suzanne, who quickly looks away.

CHAPTER TWENTY-EIGHT

eo and Suzanne are proud that their secret has been revealed. Their compatriots seem pleased for them.

Lero sends Aeo to retrieve the swim gear from the jeep. He brings a case back quickly and opens it to reveal two wetsuits, one for a woman and one for a man. The suits are equipped with knives and all the gear they could need.

"Take your suits and change clothes," Lero says, taking his place again in the center of the team members' circle. "Now we must choose alternate leaders. Romli, our leader, in his absolute authority, has chosen Matty and me as team leaders. We are grateful to prove ourselves worthy. Although we work in teams, we are one family."

He stops and looks at Matty. "This mission is very dangerous. It is possible that Matty or I, or both of us, could be killed or incapacitated during the battle. So, we have chosen individuals to take over if we are not able to lead."

Lero is quiet while the gravity of his statement sinks in. "Matty will take full command of all teams if I cannot fight. I will take command of all teams if she cannot fight. You are all expected to willingly and enthusiastically follow the lead of either one of us." He pauses, then demands, "No insubordination will be tolerated. Is that understood?"

"Yes, sir," they reply in unison.

"However, a second-in-command will be named for each team in the event that either of us is not able to fulfill our duties," Nero says.

All are quiet as they wait for the names.

"The team member selected as second to Matty for the women's team is …"—Nero hesitates—"is Paula."

Paula is stunned because she is new to the team, but her eyes light up.

Suzanne is even more visibly furious than she was after the announcement of Susan as the chosen swimmer.

Chance is pouting, certain that she would have been a better choice.

"Paula, please step forward," Lero says.

Paula is slow at first, but then walks with authority to face Lero and Matty. Paula tries hard not to display nervousness.

"Paula, you are second-in-command to Matty," Lero says.

She nods in respect and, looking at Matty, still tries to guess why she was chosen.

"You are released. Return to the ranks," Lero orders.

Paula turns and tries not to make eye contact with anyone on the team. Still, she can't help but notice Suzanne's and Chance's expressions. Paula tries to project confidence so that the women understand she is ready for her new responsibilities if she is needed. Inwardly, Paula remembers her struggles and fear during her initiations. She thinks of her daughter and knows, now as then, that she would do anything to see her again.

Lero stares intensely at the team members, turns to Matty, then back to the team, and says, "It is now time for me to choose my own second-in-command." He pauses. "I choose … Chance."

There is a murmur of discontent among the men.

Lero grips his weapon and raises his arm to regain control.

Everyone is quiet again.

Chance is caught completely off-guard. She stares at the men who are staring at her with disdain. The women look surprised, too.

Lero calls Chance forward. She strides to the front of the group and stands in front of Lero and Matty.

"Chance, you will be second-in-command of the men's team and take over if I am unable to fulfill my duties," Lero says.

Chance tries to hide a smug look. She locks eyes with Matty, who clearly is not thrilled at the announcement. Chance and Matty glare at one another long enough that Lero notices the hatred between the two women. He might have made a different decision if he had known that, so he breaks the tension.

"Chance, you may return to your spot in the group," Lero says.

Chance smiles at Lero in appreciation and moves back to her place.

Lero turns to look at Matty, who turns away from him. Matty is hurt; she thinks Lero should have sought her opinion before making this decision.

Lero tells the teams to prepare for the mission. The team members walk to their gear to get ready. All of them are upset, and they already show a lack of confidence in the new leadership. Lero can sense the hostility and is eager to make amends with Matty. She has walked away to be alone, but Lero follows her. She can hear him behind her and turns to face him.

"How could you?" she utters.

Lero doesn't reply.

"How could you choose her?" Matty asks again.

"She showed strength on our last mission," Lero explains. "I can feel her determination to fight strongly for us."

Matty turns away. "Oh, I bet …" she says sarcastically over her shoulder. She spins around. "Did you sleep with her?"

"No. I did not," Lero says firmly.

From a distance, while everyone is busy with preparations, Chance watches Lero and Matty. It appears they are having a disagreement, and she senses it's about her. And that makes her happy.

Lero asks Matty, "Why would you ask if I slept with her? I thought you didn't care about me."

"I don't," Matty replies.

Lero smiles. "Matty, you know how I feel about you."

Matty struggles to steel herself. She doesn't want the teams to see her upset.

She glares at Lero. "Before Romli gave you full command, you were everything to me. Now you're as ruthless as he is. You sicken me." She starts to walk away.

"I love you, Matty," Lero says.

Matty turns back toward him, stunned. Trying hard to rein in her emotions, she says with her eyes full of love and rage, "Don't say those words to me. Don't ever say that again."

And she walks away.

Lero is stricken with hurt, and he says nothing more.

Chance sees Matty approaching and pretends she wasn't watching the confrontation. As Matty walks straight to her, Chance stops preparing her weapon and stands as a show of respect. But Chance doesn't have respect; she can only pretend. She raises her chin slightly in defiance. Still, Matty enjoys that Chance must at least pretend deference. She wants Chance to know that she is in charge. Chance doesn't give Matty a reason to strip away her status as second-in-command. She stretches out a smile to Matty. Matty doesn't smile back. Matty stays composed.

"Are you ready?" Matty asks boldly.

Chance keeps smiling. "Yes, Matty. I'm good."

Matty walks away without another word and heads toward Paula.

"Paula, come here," she calls.

Paula is preparing and praying at the same time but gives Matty her full attention.

"Do you have any questions?" Matty asks.

Paula swallows hard and tries not to betray any sign of weakness. She speaks slowly. "Why do you choose me?"

"That is not important," Matty replies.

Paula doesn't let it go. "You know that I'm inexperienced for leadership. I could barely get through the initiation. I'm new, and others are in line ahead of me."

Matty is quiet for a moment, then: "Paula, leadership is not about who has been here the longest. I considered many things. You and I share something in common. We both lost a child. I wasn't ready to take leadership either. Romli chose me." Matty gets emotional. "Of course, he used me before he gave me leadership. He only cares about money and power."

Paula is sad for Matty.

"I was kidnapped, just like you, and brought here as a young woman, lost and confused," Matty says. "I was taught to fire a weapon. I hated it. I hated everything about this place and the people. I hated Romli."

Matty catches Paula's gaze. "Maybe there's a way out for us. I chose you because you remind me of myself. I know if I don't make it through this mission, you are the best choice to replace me."

Matty watches Suzanne talk to Chance.

Suzanne turns and sees Matty. Suzanne looks away without smiling.

Matty turns back to Paula. "Suzanne is angry. She's aligning herself with Chance. Watch her closely. Don't trust so easily. She betrayed me once with Romli. I haven't trusted her since, and now she feels betrayed."

Paula is worried.

"I chose you because I know there is a leader within you," Matty says.

Paula smiles slightly. She feels relieved and, even, empowered by Matty's words.

"Thank you," Paula says. "I will not let you down."

That's the response Matty wanted. She nods her approval and strides away.

———

Tensions ease at the table in the dining room that Moschi had built, and people are paired off in conversations.

Andy stands. Everyone stops talking and looks at him.

"I'm happy that everyone has gotten a chance to meet and that we are all acting in a civil manner," Andy says. "However, if what Jena says is true, our enemies are sure to be here soon. The news of Moschi's death will empower them. We must make a strategy to protect the compound that Moschi created and to protect ourselves."

Andy turns to Sir James, who is standing in the doorway with two of his staff. "Sir James, will you and your staff clear the table and show our guests to their rooms? I ask that all of you return to this room within the hour to discuss our mission."

Mr. Tindale stands to help. But Sir James puts his hand on Mr. Tindale's shoulder.

"You are a guest here," Sir James reiterates. "I know you understand the work we do. Our commitment makes us great employees. But these people are our families. We trust them, and they trust us." He whispers, "My friend," then pauses and asks, "Can I call you my friend?"

Mr. Tindale nods, listening to Sir James' elegant tone.

"My staff and I will take care of everything. There is no need to feel guilty," Sir James says. "It appears you may have a larger mission to attend to at this time."

Mr. Tindale smiles brightly.

Sir James smiles back, then gets to work.

Mr. Tindale turns his attention to the conversation between Jake and Jena.

"Jena, we're about to take on something that is big and dangerous," Jake says.

"I know," Jena says. "But I can't walk away. I know that terrible things are happening, and I can't just walk away." She pauses. "I've done awful things, Jake."

Jake stops her. He doesn't want her to talk about the past.

Mr. Tindale continues to listen in.

"Jake, I can't ignore the things I've done in the past." She stares deeply into his eyes. "And you shouldn't forget them, either."

Jake tries to interrupt again.

"I can turn my life around. But I was convicted of actual crimes. I was sent to prison," Jena says.

Mr. Tindale's eyes grow large.

"I deserved to be sent to prison," Jena says.

Jake lowers his head. He doesn't want to remember.

Jena starts ticking off her crimes: "the clerk at the hotel, the doctor on the train, my mother …."

Mr. Tindale is wishing he had known this before he left home.

"Mike McNeil," Jena says, spitting out McNeil's name and continuing her list of crimes. "I'm responsible. I must redeem myself for my past bad deeds. All of them"

Jake hugs Jena.

Jena looks up at him. "And that's just what I did before I came here," she says mysteriously.

Jake notices that Mr. Tindale is close enough to hear them. Mr. Tindale quickly looks away, pretending to look for Franklin. He sees Franklin talking to Veronica and walks away to join their conversation.

Jake kisses Jena. "I don't care about the past. I love you."

Jena breaks the spell. "We have work to do, Jake. We have to put our feelings on hold for a little while."

"I'm not going to stop loving you," Jake says forcefully.

"I know," she concedes. "And I won't stop loving you, but I've got to make this right."

"I will take on your sins. We are one, Jena," Jake says.

Jena smiles at Jake. She wonders if he has any idea what she's getting him into.

She leaves Jake and moves toward Andy. Her thoughts have turned to her personal mission of releasing the kidnapped women who have been forced to become killers and slaves.

Andy is confirming details of the mission with Tammy and Luis.

"Andy," Jena says, interrupting. "I think we'd better start gathering everyone together. There is no time to waste."

Andy looks toward Luis and Tammy. "You're right, Jena. Sir James will show you to your rooms so that you can settle in, and then we'll get started."

Jena butts in abruptly. "We don't need to settle in. Let's just start."

Franklin overhears, and he and Denise approach Andy and Jena.

"I do need a moment to catch my breath," Franklin says.

Jena gives him a dirty look. But she looks at Denise, and Denise nods in agreement with Franklin.

"Okay," Jena says. "Andy is our leader, and we will follow his guidance."

Jena walks back to Jake. She passes Veronica, who glares at her.

Andy calls for Sir James and asks him to escort Jena's group to their quarters. "When they're ready, please bring them back here quickly."

Sir James nods and wastes no time rounding up the guests and finding their quarters.

Franklin and Mr. Tindale share a room. Denise has a room to herself, as does Ken. Jake and Jena are escorted to Jena's old room. Jena steps in first. She remembers when Luis escorted her into this room for the first time.

Jake waves at one of the servants as he closes the door. He watches Jena's eyes scan the room. She breaks her trance and turns to Jake.

"We should be discussing our strategy for fighting Romli's army. They are going to attack this compound to destroy everything Moschi built," Jena says.

Jake tries to calm Jena. "Jena, can we just relax for an hour? Let's just breathe, freshen up, and then we'll go meet the others."

Jena turns away.

"Andy has guards all over this compound," Jake says. "He's already started preparations."

Jena takes a deep breath. "Okay. Since we're here, I'll make use of the time."

She walks toward the bathroom and drops her bag, closes the door, and stares at herself in the bathroom mirror. She turns her head from side to side, as if she doesn't recognize herself. She remembers being back in the hotel room, where she dyed her hair red. She stared at herself then, as she stares at herself now.

Then Mike McNeil flashes into her consciousness, and she begins to breathe hard. She leans over the bathroom sink, thinking she might be sick. Shaking her head to vanquish the image of Mike McNeil, she turns on the faucets and splashes her face.

"Wake up Jena," she says to herself. "Now is not the time to fall apart."

Jake is standing near the bathroom door. He can hear Jena talking to herself. He taps on the door.

"Jena, are you okay?"

"Yes," she replies quietly. "I'll be out in a minute."

Jake eases away from the bathroom door and gazes at the astoundingly extravagant apartment. He makes his way to the bedroom and stares at the bed. He can't help but think of how spectacular it would be to make love to Jena in an actual bed, especially this one. He closes his eyes, fantasizing, and when he opens them, the real-live Jena is standing in front of him.

She puts her hand on his forehead, pretends to check his temperature. "You okay?"

"Yeah, I'm just thinking, that's all," Jake says in a calm voice.

"Thinking about what?" she teases him.

Jake knows better than to get too comfortable with the soft, playful Jena. In less than an hour, she will be a warrior, focused only on the mission.

"It's not important, Jena," he replies, backing away from her. "My turn to freshen up."

When he's gone, Jena stares briefly around her lavish bedroom. She walks to her closet, where she finds the weapons that were once a stark lesson in the reality of Moschi's missions and his vision for her. This time, she is not surprised.

Jake is standing behind her looking at the weapons, camouflage clothing, and other battle provisions.

"What is this?" Jake asks.

"What does it look like, Jake?"

"It looks like someone is going to wage an all-out war. That's what it looks like."

"In that case, you are absolutely right," Jena says, closing the closet door. She walks into the living room and sits on the couch. Looking at the confused Jake, she says, "I didn't know exactly what would be expected of me here—back when Moschi took me out of the prison. I knew I was going to be trained by Moschi, but the moment I opened that closet door, reality set in. And I wasn't sure I was ready to commit to that reality."

Jake sits next to Jena on the couch. "So, you were bought here to be a killer."

Jena shakes her head at Jake. "I was already a killer." She pauses and thinks back. "When Moschi and I were in the car together, he said I reminded him of someone he once loved: Maria. He told me his story—that he was an orphan and that he met Maria at a training camp."

She explains that Moschi and Maria fell in love and decided, and tried, to escape together. But Romli's people captured them and took Maria away from Moschi.

"Then they ordered Maria to kill her own mother," Jena says.

But Maria couldn't kill her mother and begged Moschi to do it for her, Jena says. Deciding that she could not run away from Romli, Maria faked her own death, leaving Moschi to think that Romli had killed her as punishment for refusing his order.

"One day, when I was in prison," Jena says, "the guard said I had a visitor. It was Moschi. I was shocked. I thought he was long gone, escaped to some foreign country."

Moschi made a bargain that would free her from prison.

Jena gazes into Jake's eyes. "Moschi told me that I was born for this. Born to be a killer. He told me I could come here and that he would train me, and I would work for him," she explains.

Jena says that Moschi arranged to get Jena out of prison—just as Jake and Ken had seen on the local news. In exchange, he would take responsibility for Jena's crimes in and around Maplesville.

"He even had surveillance tapes altered to make it look as if he had killed Mike McNeil," Jena continues. She stands and looks at Jake firmly. "The business of this business—Moschi's business, Pulue's business—is killing, high-tech espionage, and sex trafficking."

Jake reaches for her hand. She reaches back and allows herself to be pulled gently back to the couch. They sit as close as they possibly can to each other, enjoying the luxury of looking into each other's eyes.

"Jake, despite my best intentions, I moved from one bad situation to another," she says. "But if I could help save these women—women kidnapped against their will—and help them to go home … it wouldn't make up for what I've done, but at least it would be a good deed that might go toward all of the bad things I have done."

Jake touches her face.

"I want to take this rage and turn it into something good," Jena says.

"I love you," Jake says. "You are good. You are my best friend." Jake leans into kiss Jena's lips.

She pulls back. "I don't deserve you."

"Yes, you do," he says, kissing her and slowly caressing her body. He gently lays her back on the couch. "Now. Can I have you now?"

Jena whispers his name, lost in the moment.

A hard knock at the door brings them back to reality.

Jake is startled.

Jena is resigned.

"Time to meet!" Ken shouts from the other side of the door.

Jake gets up slowly, but Jena quickly grabs her bag. Jake follows.

Jena opens the door. "We're ready," she says and they both walk into the hallway.

Waiting, in addition to Ken, are Franklin, Mr. Tindale, and Denise. They all look at Jake like he's supposed to say something important.

Jake stammers, "Let's roll."

They move swiftly down the hall with a servant leading the way.

When they enter the main dining room, Andy has changed the dining room into a strategy table. More chairs have been added, and Andy has invited more guards to be part of the meeting. He greets Jena, and Jake stands beside her.

"Let's get started," Andy says as he leads Jena to the chair next to his.

Jake sits next to Jena.

Andy stands with his arms folded as everyone takes a seat.

Veronica strolls in and takes the seat on Andy's other side.

The room becomes quiet.

"Thank you all for joining us," Andy says. "Jena has brought us the news that Moschi has been killed. He was great a leader. Now we must protect what he built. This compound is not just a training ground. It is our home." He looks around the table. "Once Romli finds out that Moschi is dead, if he hasn't already, he will deem us weak and leaderless. He will send his wolves to attack us. They are probably on their way.

"Pulue is not here because he went out in search of Moschi. We have no idea whether he is alive or dead. He took two of our best men," Andy explains.

Jena gasps. She and her group had no idea that Pulue was missing—out looking for Moschi, who Jena knows is already dead.

"I was second-in-command to Pulue, who was second to Moschi," Andy says. "Now, I need someone to take my place in case I'm killed or incapacitated." He looks around the room. His gaze lands on Luis. "Luis, you are second-in-command to me. We do not know Pulue's fate. You will take my place if that becomes necessary." He pauses. "Until then, you will fight by my side so that you will be ready if you must take command."

Luis stands and nods to Andy. "I will be ready," says the transgender warrior.

Andy turns his attention to a strategy board at the front of the room. He picks up a pointer and shows the group each entrance to the compound.

"We are most vulnerable at the lake. It would be easy for them to attack us, especially at night or at dawn," Andy explains. "We must have several guards at this entry point and just inside the building in case they manage to get through."

Andy calls for Hero, the leader of one of the teams and the man Andy had talked to earlier about Pulue's mission in search of Moschi.

Hero steps forward.

"Your team will cover the entry point next to the lake," Andy says. "I want you to include Jena, Jake ... and Ken ... to be part of your team."

Hero nods obediently.

"You must ensure that Jena and her friends are properly armed and ready for an attack, if it happens. I know you are short-handed because we sent your men, Terrus and Bonquet, on the mission with Pulue."

Andy looks around the room. "It is bad fate that we will face this battle, if it comes, without our two original, and best, leaders and soldiers, Moschi and Pulue. We can only hope that they trained us well and that their faith in us is well-placed."

Andy dismisses Hero and the new team members and turns to his butler. "Sir James, your staff can expect to get little sleep."

CHAPTER TWENTY-NINE

A ndy stands before the team members remaining in the room.

"We are at war," he says, "therefore, everyone must be on full alert at all times." He directs Sir James to gather his staff to prepare food, beds, and medical supplies.

"Yes, sir," the butler says, as he leaves to begin his duties.

Andy calls Veronica to the front of the room.

She comes forward. "Yes, sir," she says.

"Your team will guard the front entrance and the roof. In addition to your regular teammates, you will include Franklin, Mr. Tindale, and Miss Denise," Andy orders.

Veronica's expression is unpleasant, but Andy ignores it.

"You will need to conduct the same preparations that I explained to Hero," he says. "Luis and I and the rest of the guards will secure the main compound." Andy's expression is stern and stoic. "Prepare yourselves. As of now, we are on full alert. Ensure coordination, cooperation, and structure."

Andy asks if anyone has questions. All are quiet, wearing their battle faces.

Veronica turns to face her teammates. "Let's go, team," she orders. She looks at Franklin. "You and the others, join us."

She leads her team to the front conference room to begin her leadership meeting. Her stride is strong, and her expression is without emotion.

When everyone is gathered in the room, she turns to face her team.

"I am Veronica," she says, using a dramatic inflection as she pronounces her name. "I am your leader, and you will take orders from me and no one else. Is this clear?"

Veronica's team members nod in agreement. But Franklin, Mr. Tindale, and Denise are fearful and doubting themselves. Mr. Tindale even reaches for Franklin's hand, but Franklin brushes his hand aside. Franklin turns to Mr. Tindale, who has terror written on his face.

Franklin whispers, "I understand. It's going to be okay."

Veronica sees Franklin whispering to Mr. Tindale.

"What I am saying is important," she says more loudly than necessary. "There will be silence while I am speaking."

Franklin and Mr. Tindale turn toward Veronica, blushing like they are children caught misbehaving.

Everyone in the room is embarrassed, except Veronica, and everyone quickly faces forward again.

"Leza!"

Veronica calls a team member to the front. Leza, a thin, pale young woman with blond hair, comes forward and stands beside Veronica.

"Leza is one of the top members of this team," Veronica says. "She is an expert shooter. She is highly trained in the use of the bow, knives, spears, and other sharp objects." She smiles. "Leza has been honored by our late leader Moschi as the best knife fighter in the entire compound."

Leza allows herself a bright smile.

"I have chosen Leza as my assistant," Veronica says. "She does not have command, yet, but I can't be in every sector. If she gives you an order, assume the order is from me."

She explains that Leza will train Franklin, Mr. Tindale, and Denise for battle. "This training may save your lives," she tells the newcomers firmly, but something in her expression betrays a hint of pleasure at the idea of what the three will face.

Leza lifts her chin in confidence. She walks through the group to Franklin.

"Are you ready?" she asks him. She turns to Mr. Tindale and Denise, eyeing them with a competitive, confident, and daring smile. "Follow me, all of you," she orders.

Franklin, Denise, and Mr. Tindale are taken to an isolated training area.

Meanwhile, Veronica continues to instruct her team.

———

Hero leads his team, including Jake, Jena, and Ken, to the lakeside entrance of the compound. Hero's brown hair and blue eyes sparkle in the sunlight. His strong physique is covered with armor.

"Welcome," Hero says sincerely. "My name is Hero, in honor of my father. We take our name very seriously." He pauses. "But first, I thank you for your hard work and dedication as team members. We have lost our great leader, Moschi, but we will never forget. We will fight to protect this compound, which is also our home."

Hero looks at Jena, Jake, and Ken. "Everyone, please welcome back Jena and welcome her friends, Jake and Ken."

Everyone turns to nod at the three.

"Now it time for us to prepare," Hero tells them. "Most of you have engaged in some sort of battle. Whether a battle is large or small, you must use all of your skills. Normally, within these walls, we are peaceful."

Jena wonders whether the "training" she endured could be considered peaceful. But she is silent.

"We went into the world to perform our missions, as we were trained and instructed," Hero says. "But Moschi and Pulue never wanted to provoke a war that brought battle to our compound, to the place where we live and train."

Hero explains that the team members protect the innocents within their walls, treat each other with respect, and earn luxury and respect in return.

"But the warriors who may be coming to our door are ruled by a ruthless man named Romli. He rules over the less fortunate. He has caused pain, wounds, and misfortune," he says. "We must fight, or he will make us his slaves."

He stops so that his message sinks in, then he calls a man forward.

"May I introduce Rightpoint, my second-in-command. If he gives an order, that order comes from me," Hero says. "Rightpoint's father was my best friend. We served many missions together."

Hero explains that Rightpoint's father, Daniel, was on a mission when they got word that Daniel's pregnant wife was suffering complications. The two men were granted leave so that Daniel could return to his wife. On their way home, they were attacked and had to hunker down in a cave. Hero was shot in the shoulder, so he had only one arm to fight their fierce enemy, but he was still able to wound the man who shot him. Their two foes had boxed them in and had plenty of ammunition—Hero and Daniel neared the end of their supply.

"The enemies had trapped us," he explains. "They were laughing at us. Two men raised their weapons to fire on us, but Daniel fired twice, killing both men. Even still, one of them shot Daniel before he fell. I did what I could to help Daniel, but the wound was too severe. He was losing too much blood. He died in my arms." Hero lowers his head in sadness and respect.

Hero explains that, because of his own wound, he couldn't carry Daniel's body back to the compound. But he was able to get back himself and send a team to retrieve the body.

"We gave Daniel a proper burial, a burial for a warrior," Hero says.

When Daniel's widow, Erin, gave birth, she asked her late husband's team to come help name the baby.

"We laughed, we joked, and we cried, and we came up with a worthy name for Daniel's son. Daniel was right-handed, and he used that hand to save my life," Hero recalls. "And so, this is his son, named Rightpoint."

Hero, smiling at the strong, handsome man who is really still a boy, turns to Jake, Jena, and Ken.

"Rightpoint will be your trainer while the rest of us take our positions. You will not train long. But you will train enough to defend yourselves and to defend another team member if needed," Hero says.

Hero tells Rightpoint to bring his trainees back in two hours.

Rightpoint smiles brightly and gathers Jena, Jake, and Ken, who all nods.

Jake moves closer to Jena so that Rightpoint knows that she is his.

Rightpoint leads them to the training room. Jena had trained here. She steps forward and scrutinizes the fighting platform above.

"You remember," he says to Jena.

Jena stares at him. "Yes, I do."

"We won't have time for those kinds of games," he says.

Jake and Ken tilt their heads, curious about the concrete platform high above them.

"What is that?" Ken asks, pointing at the platform.

"That is part of the initiation here," Jena says, involuntarily shivering at the memory of her fight and near-death on that platform. "That is where your strength, courage, and will to live are tested. That is where you may die. That is where I nearly died."

"Doesn't sound like the place for you, bro," Jake teases Ken.

Ken shoves his friend good-naturedly. "I could totally handle that."

"You say that, until you're up there. Then, everything you thought you knew about yourself changes." Jena looks upward and remembers her battle, where she almost lost everything, but won—and then was shot for her efforts. She turns to Ken. "The battle is fierce, and there is only one winner."

Jena walks toward Rightpoint. "With your permission, I will help you train them because I am ready."

Rightpoint nods and leads them into a smaller training area. "We will start in the shooting range."

"They need a little training in that area," Jena says.

Ken objects. "I know how to fire a weapon."

Jena and Rightpoint ignore him and lead Jake and Ken to a weapons-simulation area.

Leza is there, having just completed a training session with Denise, Franklin, and Mr. Tindale. Rightpoint bows his head slightly to Leza, who nods in return but keeps her team from interacting with Rightpoint's. She hurries her team to another training area, so that Franklin, Denise, and Mr. Tindale can't share their opinions and experiences.

Jake and Ken eye the room.

Rightpoint calls out the code, and the room is transformed into a simulated battleground.

Ken is mesmerized by the room's instant transformation. He circles the room like a kid at an amusement park.

Rightpoint calls out the same codeword, and the room returns to normal.

Ken is disappointed. "Hey, what happened?"

"I wanted to give you guys an overview," Rightpoint says as he leads Jake and Ken to a shelf full of training weapons that do not have ammunition. He grabs two and hands one to Jake and one to Ken.

Jena and Rightpoint watch Ken and Jake examine the weapons.

Jokester Ken pretends he's Rambo.

Rightpoint smiles but tells him to slow down. "Save your moves for the actual simulation."

Rightpoint looks at Jena and asks if she is ready. She says she is.

He turns to Jake and Ken. "Are you two ready?"

"Heck, yeah!" Ken yells.

"I'm ready, man," Jake says, trying to play it cool.

Rightpoint yells out the code word, and the simulation begins. He and Jena, who stand in an observation area, become invisible as Jake and Ken engage with the simulation. A realistic enemy appears to Jake and Ken. The two separate, trying not to get captured or killed. Simulated ammunition flies at the two newbies. Ken hits the floor, while Jake shoots back and rushes for cover. The simulation, which includes the voice of a team leader giving orders, can "see" the fighters by sensing their body heat. The sensor picks up Ken, and the simulated enemy runs toward him. Ken stands and begins to fire, while darting around for cover. He wounds one of the simulated enemies, who falls.

"Yes!" Ken yells out in exultation.

He quickly becomes quiet, thinking about the way video games work. The simulation can hear him, too.

Sure enough, the enemy's simulated voice calls out, "He's over here."

The sound of enemy boots fills the room and seems to race toward Ken. They fire, and he fires back, knocking down two more focs. He tries to take cover and manages to take down one of the enemy soldiers.

"Heck, yeah!" Jake yells out.

Jena smiles at Rightpoint.

Ken and Jake continue the battle until they get into the rhythm of the simulation. Both are fully engaged.

When the simulation ends, the lights come on, and Jake and Ken stop in their tracks and stare at one another. Ken gives Jake a high-five.

Rightpoint and Jena approach them. Jena gives Ken a congratulatory slug in the arm, and she hugs Jake and gives him a quick kiss on the cheek.

"That was great," Jena says.

"They need a little more training, but it was a pretty good start," Rightpoint says.

Next is training with the bow, he explains.

Ken and Jake look at each other in confusion.

"That's right, you guys are going to get some quick training on how to use a bow and arrow," Rightpoint says as he takes the weapons from Jake and Ken.

He returns them to the shelf and leads the trio to another room.

"This is the bow training room," he says. "We will be training with Leza's team. They have been waiting for us."

Leza is standing in front of her trainees, telling them how she came to be a fighter for Moschi and how she earned her knife-fighting award. She turns her attention to Rightpoint when he walks into the room.

"This is my colleague, one-time trainer, and friend, Rightpoint," she says.

Rightpoint smiles.

"Rightpoint and I have decided to train our teams together as we teach you to use the bow and arrow," Leza says. "The bow can be even more useful in an intense battle than a gun, and it might be your only weapon if you are unlucky enough to run out of ammunition."

Leza looks toward Franklin, then Mr. Tindale, who looks a little frazzled. She steps back to let Rightpoint speak.

Walking to the center of the room, he says, "Hello, to all of you. We are preparing for a possible battle, and you have agreed to fight with us."

He turns to Leza, who nods and says, "I'm ready to start."

"Let the bow-and-arrow game begin," Rightpoint says.

"Let the bow-and-arrow game begin," Leza repeats.

With their words, each station lights up, while the room lights dim.

There are seven simulation areas, each with a bow and arrows. The weapons are made from sturdy plastic.

Jena, who will lead the training, asks everyone to take a station. They all follow her, except Rightpoint and Leza, who stand to the side to provide instructions.

Jena steps into a space, and Jake takes the one next to her. Mr. Tindale takes the space on Jena's other side and smiles at her. The others take their places. They are ready to begin training. Leza and Rightpoint share a knowing smile.

"Team, the simulation is about to begin," Leza says.

An automated voice takes over. "Trainees, pick up your bow and then your arrow."

Jena, Jake, and Ken reach for their weapons. Mr. Tindale stares at Ken in fear, and Ken rolls his eyes but also motions to Mr. Tindale to pick up the bow and arrow. Mr. Tindale conquers his fear and picks up the weapon, as do Denise and Franklin.

The automated voice comes on again. "Take your bow and position it properly with your arrow. Stop and wait for an instructor to ensure your position is correct."

Mr. Tindale is nervous and struggles to keep his arrow straight. Leza stands behind him, showing him how to pull the arrow back and keep it in place. She waits patiently until Mr. Tindale can do it alone. She watches Ken, who looks back at her and grins, raising his eyebrows and showing off. He flexes his arm muscles, and she walks away, signaling approval. Rightpoint helps Denise angle her bow and arrow correctly. Denise catches on quickly and holds a sturdy pose. Jena checks on Jake, and Leza gets Franklin in proper formation. The instructors nod at each other. Rightpoint and Leza walk to their observation spot.

Rightpoint gives the signal. "Go."

The automated voice again takes over. "You have ten arrows. As each target appears, you must prevent him from reaching you. The closer you allow your target to get to you, the more chance he has to wound you or kill you. Aim at the center of your target." The voice pauses. "Start now."

Different characters appear in each simulation. Each character has a unique style. Peaceful. Warrior-like. Passive. Aggressive.

The trainees begin to shoot their arrows.

Jena, Jake, Ken, and even Denise seems to be doing well. Franklin struggles and curses under his breath. He looks at Denise and realizes that she is doing better than he is. She gives him a little extra motivation. He fires off three arrows, knocking down three enemy combatants in a row. Mr. Tindale is firing off good shots, too. Leza stands next to him and gives him a thumbs-up. He grins at her, feeling like a hero, but quickly turns his attention to the simulation.

Leza and Rightpoint meet again in the observation area, and they smile.

<hr />

The forest is quiet. Lero sits near his jeep and absentmindedly fiddles with sticks he picked up. Occasionally, he glances at Matty, who is sitting alone.

Both teams are settled into rest and prepare themselves to attack at dawn.

Matty catches Lero staring at her and turns away.

Lero walks toward Matty. She looks at him without emotion.

"Can I talk to you?" he asks.

"No," she answers bluntly.

"Please?" he asks again.

Matty stands and faces Lero. "What is it?" she asks impatiently.

"Can we go somewhere more private?" Lero asks.

Matty doesn't answer, but she walks away from him to a more secluded spot. Lero follows.

She turns to face him. "What is it?" she asks again.

Lero is stung and a little choked up. "We have a big mission ahead, Matty."

She cocks her head and begins to walk away.

"Please don't go," Lero pleads.

She comes back.

"Matty, you of all people know that I'm a hard son-of-a-b. I don't like to admit when I'm wrong, much less express love or affection," he says. "But I'm getting older, and this mission has me thinking a lot about you and me."

Matty grunts to rebuff him. "There is no 'you and me.'"

"If I can let down my guard, you can stop the tough act, too," Lero says, not unkindly. "I know you love me."

Matty is quiet.

"Please believe me when I tell you that I didn't know there was a feud between you and Chance," he explains. "Had I known, I might not have chosen her. I thought I saw something in her or maybe it was just my ego wanting to win." Lero kicks dirt around with one foot. "She has a hatred for Jena Parker. Maybe that's why I chose her. But I never intended to anger you."

Something in Lero's eyes keeps Matty from responding. "I'm ..." he hesitates. "I'm dying, Matty."

Matty is too shocked to say anything. Her anger at Lero is gone, replaced with emotions she can't immediately name.

Lero watches her as his news sinks in.

Matty takes small breaths. "What? What is it?" she asks.

"Cancer," Lero replies.

"When did you find out? Why didn't you tell me?" she asks.

Lero lets his head drop.

Matty looks up at the stars. She can't believe that she has been pushing this man away when they both know she loves him. A petty game? Pride? She returns her gaze to him and sees in his expression that he is broken, that his world has come crashing down. She thought he was heartless, a warrior made of steel. Now she sees so much more.

He begs for forgiveness. "I couldn't tell you when you were so angry. I deserved your anger, and I didn't want your pity."

Matty's eyes pool with tears.

"That night we argued? When I told you that I had never loved you? That I didn't want you anymore?" Lero asks. "What am I saying? Of course, you remember."

Yes, she thinks, of course she remembers. It's why she's barely spoken to him since.

"That was the day I found out about the cancer," Lero says, trying to hold his emotions in check.

Matty can't bear to watch his lips quiver. She turns away, and her own tears begin to fall.

"I was angry. I was in shock. And I wanted to take it out on someone, and that someone was you," Lero says. "I was wrong. I should have told you."

Matty turns back to him and nods. She's afraid to speak.

"We could have been together on those cold, lonely nights. I wanted so badly to hold you," he says.

She tries to stop her tears. But she can't. "How much time do you have?" she asks, her voice cracking.

Lero steps closer. "Not long." He touches her shoulders, afraid that she will pull away. "Maybe I will die in the battle. I'd rather go that way than let the cancer take me." He clears his throat. "That's why I had to tell you. If I die while fighting, I wanted you to know that I love you and that I never stopped loving you, and I never stopped wanting you."

Lero gently leans forward to kiss Matty on the forehead.

She doesn't stop him.

"I'll always love you," Lero says.

He won't let his emotions get the best of him. He gazes at her for a moment, then slowly walks away and out of Matty's sight.

Finally, Matty lets her tears flow freely. Death is a constant part of their lives, but this is different, something she'd never confronted before. She is grateful to Lero for telling her. This pain is not the same as the pain she felt when he rejected her and the pain she felt when she spurned his attention again and again. Oh, how she now regrets the hate and resentment she felt then. She feels the love rushing back in a way she can never again deny.

———

Matty's and Lero's teams sleep while they take shifts watching Moschi's compound. When it's almost dawn, those who are on duty quietly wake those who are sleeping. The teams move steadily, calmly, and quietly as they gather their weapons and battle gear. Matty scans the group for Lero but doesn't see him, so she continues getting ready. Just as she is about to pick up her pack and weapons, she turns to see Lero standing right beside her. They look at each other for mere seconds, and he smiles at her.

"It's time," he says simply, and walks away to take charge of his team.

CHAPTER THIRTY

Matty watches Lero walk away and tries to hold back her tears and steel her face against emotion. Now that she knows the truth, it's hard for her to pretend. She remembers their first kiss, the first time he touched her. He seemed so ruthless but was so gentle when they made love. She thinks about the first time he told her that he loved her and explained that they had to hide their relationship, especially from Romli. Romli would have separated them or had one or both of them killed.

Chance looks at Matty and notices that Matty seems sad. Chance manages to turn away before Matty catches her watching.

Paula sees Chance and decides to distract her from Matty. She approaches Chance and catches her off-guard. She tries to strike up a conversation.

"This is a big mission," Paula says.

Chance rolls her eyes at Paula's inane comment. "Yeah," she replies.

"What are the chances of us both being named second-in-command of the teams?" Paula says, still trying to engage Chance.

Chance is not the slightest bit interested in talking to Paula. She looks away and continues packing her equipment, while keeping an eye on Matty.

Paula wants to get under Chance's skin. She also wants Chance to know that she sees Chance spying on Matty. She steps around Chance and blocks her view of Matty.

"Hey, Chance," she says. "Did you hear me say how odd it is that we are both second-in-command?"

Chance gives Paula a nasty look, but Paula keeps talking. "Me second to Matty, and you second to Lero. Who would have thought?"

"Why are you talking to me?" Chance says. "We're not friends."

Paula nods toward Matty. "You just seem awfully interested in our team," Paula says, dropping the friendly pretense.

"And you seem very interested in what I'm doing," Chance barks back.

"Like it or not, Chance, we're teammates," Paula says with authority. "We've been given responsibilities. Maybe you should take the mission more seriously … and spend less time checking out the team leader." She walks away, satisfied that Chance got the message.

"Hey, Paula," Chance calls out.

Paula turns.

"Watch your back. Anything can happen in battle," Chance threatens.

Paula understands that she's just gotten a warning shot. She smirks and as she walks away to finish packing, she says, "You do the same."

Sharon approaches Paula. "What was that about?"

"You know as well as I do," Paula says. "Chance is her own team. Ever since I met her, back when we were both in prison, she's been self-serving."

Paula continues arranging her gear. "She was in a big fight, in prison, with Jena Parker."

"You know this Jena Parker?" Sharon asks.

"Yeah, it's really strange," Paula says. "Jena Parker was my cellmate back at the prison in Maplesville. She was released before Romli's people kidnapped me. I don't know how Jena's involved with these people—or why they want to capture her."

"It must be something pretty bad," Sharon says.

"That's the truth. Anyway, there was a big fight between Chance and Jena. But there was already bad blood between them, all the way back to high school," Paula says, stooping to pick up a knife that had fallen out of her bag.

Sharon is intrigued by Paula's story. "They went to high school together, and then they ended up in prison at the same time?"

"Yeah, pretty crazy," Paula replies, amused that she has gossip to share. "That fight in the prison cafeteria was like animals gone wild in a zoo." Paula looks up. "I never want to go back to those days. I want to see my daughter again someday, and I'm not going to let Chance or anyone else get in my way."

On the men's side of the camp, Lero asks Aeo if they are prepared.

"We're ready," Aeo says with authority. "I'm waiting for your instructions."

"Are the bows packed?" Lero asks. "And the boats, are they ready? You'll need to prepare those, as well as your swimming gear."

"Everything is in order and ready, sir," Aeo says.

"Let's make a final check, then," Lero says. "We must honor Romli and his orders."

Aeo nods and walks back to inspect the men and their gear.

Lero looks into the distance at Matty, who is also rounding up her team.

Matty is in command and looking tough as she paces back and forth. Her team members are standing in a straight line, watching as she passes them.

"Team, the time has come for us to engage in battle with our enemy. Romli has given us strict instructions, and every one of us will follow those orders until we are killed or taken captive," Matty says sternly. She stops in front of Paula. "You have been chosen to take my place if I cannot continue my duties. Are you ready?"

"Yes, ma'am," Paula says confidently.

Chance leans forward slightly to look at Paula. She's surprised to hear the fire in Paula's voice. Chance quickly stands at attention as Matty walks back down the line of fighters.

"Team get the boats ready. Sharon, make sure your swim gear is in order," Matty orders.

"Yes, ma'am," Sharon replies.

Everyone begins moving again. Boats are being taken from their storage space on top of the jeeps. Paddles are gathered. Everyone is focused on the battle ahead.

Aeo walks over, and he and Sharon discuss their swim. They shake hands and nod at each other. Then Aeo returns to Lero.

Lero looks at Matty and signals that his team is ready to move out. Matty raises her weapon signaling that she and her team are ready, as well. Team members carry their rucksacks on their backs and their weapons slung across their chests. Every pocket is filled with a knife or some kind of weapon or gear. Some lift the boats into the lake. Others stand guard and check the terrain.

Matty and Lero, and Paula, and Aeo walk into the center of the team. The others walk on either side of them and behind them.

All heads swivel, watching for the enemy, traps, and other obstacles.

They reach the lake, which is still miles away from the compound.

It's just before daybreak, and Lero and Matty signal their swimmers to gear up. They set their spears to the side and get dressed. They each have a small gun, secure in the pocket of the swimsuits. Then they ease into the cool water. Next, the four boats slip into the lake, and team members climb in with their gear.

Lero and Matty each sit in the middle of their boats, surrounded by team members.

Chance and Paula are in separate boats, which wait for the swimmers to get ahead, then the team members dip their paddles quietly into the water. The swimmers do their jobs like pros, signaling every few minutes that the boats can move forward. Everyone is quiet. The paddle strokes are smooth and steady.

The sun is rising along the horizon. Lero hopes to get close to the compound before full daylight.

———————

Leza and Rightpoint smile at each other in the training room that Moschi designed. They are pleased with the progress their amateurs have made.

Rightpoint says it is time for Jake, Jena, and Ken to join Hero and the rest of their team at the lake.

Leza announces that Franklin, Mr. Tindale, and Denise will join Veronica and her team.

Leaders and trainees, alike, look stoic, but Denise rushes to Jena and hugs her for what seems like a long time.

Leza isn't pleased, but she doesn't interfere.

Jena and Denise exchange another affectionate glance before Rightpoint leads Jena, Jake, and Ken out of the bow room, through the battle simulation area, and into the room with the raised platform. Jena can't help but stare at the concrete platform one more time.

They enter the labyrinth of hallways and finally reach the rest of the team near the compound entrance that is closest to the lake. Team members are eating protein bars and taking quick breaks as they wait to see what the day will bring.

Leza leads Franklin, Mr. Tindale, and Denise back through the rooms to join the rest of their team. She stops midway and turns to them.

"You guys did great today," she says. "You should be proud of yourselves, especially you, Mr. Tindale, because I know you doubted yourself."

The trainees smile at the unexpected praise.

"You have courage," Leza says, looking at Mr. Tindale and then at Franklin and Denise.

Leza walks them through the compound back to Veronica's team. She has some team members practicing their battle moves, while others rest and eat.

Veronica notices Leza and her team's arrival and approaches them, dismissing the three newcomers to eat and rest.

"How did training go?" Veronica asks.

Leza smiles. "Very well. They certainly have heart."

"I wasn't sure about that Mr. Tindale," Veronica says. "He seems a bit fragile."

Leza smiles. "He had a hard time grasping the bow and arrow, but he didn't give up. All things considered, he did fine."

———

Rightpoint leaves Jena, Jake, and Ken with the rest of the team and heads outside to find Hero. Hero is standing with binoculars, staring out over the lake. Rightpoint taps him on the shoulder.

"My son," Hero says, turning around. "You're done with training?"

"Yes," Rightpoint replies, smiling broadly. "It was interesting."

Hero smiles back. "I'm sure it was interesting." He turns and looks at the lake again.

"The water is still," Hero tells Rightpoint. "But I sense something out there." His expression is fierce. "We need to get people into position. I know they're coming. I know they're getting close."

Hero says he wants two boats of four people each in the lake.

Rightpoint says he will gear up and put together the boat crews.

Just as Rightpoint is about to leave, Hero tells him to stop.

"No," Hero says. "I will lead the team. I want you here, prepared to take the lead in case I don't return."

Rightpoint is bewildered.

"You're just like your father," Hero grins. Smart, brave, talented. … You even have his handsome looks. You are a leader, and I have every confidence in you."

Rightpoint beams. "Thank you, Hero. You have taught me everything I know. You're like a father to me. I would rather be on the water, but I will do as ordered."

Hero walks away to prepare for the mission.

Rightpoint gathers the boat teams. He pulls aside eight team members.

"You eight will be going out with our leader, Hero," he says, instructing the group to begin preparing their boats and gear immediately.

One team member takes charge and pushes the others to hurry. Rightpoint stands guard as the other team member's work. He walks inside and pulls Jena aside.

"May I speak to you?" he asks.

She nods, and they walk a short distance away from the others.

"Hero is going out with the boat teams to see if he can get a better look at anything happening on the lake," Rightpoint says.

Jena can tell that Rightpoint is concerned, and she asks why.

"Hero hasn't been well. I wanted to talk to someone who wasn't part of the team—I mean not a longtime member of the team. … You know what I mean," Rightpoint says, trying not to insult Jena. "I don't want Hero to know I'm worried about him." He stares into the distance, then looks back at Jena. "Can you take over the guard position? I need to talk to someone. I won't be gone long,"

Jena is confused but agrees.

Rightpoint dashes to the other side of the compound, where Andy is speaking to his team. Andy is just finishing when Rightpoint enters the room.

Andy approaches the young team member. "Is something wrong?"

"Yes and no," Rightpoint says. "Hero plans to join the boat teams that will provide surveillance on the lake."

Andy is attentive.

"We both know he's not well, but he insists that he will lead the teams. I thought maybe you could spare a team member to accompany him," Rightpoint says. "Perhaps Passionquest?"

"Of course," Andy says. "She's right over there. Why don't you speak to her?"

Rightpoint thanks Andy and approaches the young woman, who is one of the best.

She looks at him and smiles. "What brings you here?" she asks.

"Something is wrong with Hero again," Rightpoint says. "He's put himself in charge of the boat team that is going out onto the lake to look for the enemy." He pauses. "Will you go with him?"

She asks if Andy has approved, and Rightpoint assures her that Andy has agreed.

"Then I will go. Just let me gather my equipment," Passionquest replies.

Rightpoint thanks her profusely and leads her to the lakeside entrance.

"Where's Hero?" she asks when they arrive.

"He'll be out by the lake," he replies.

"I'll join him," Passionquest says, smiling at Rightpoint. "Everything will be fine. Try not to worry. I know you love him like a father. I will take care of him."

Rightpoint watches as she walks away and fondly remembers that they were once teenagers in love.

Soon, Jena interrupts his thoughts to ask if there is a problem.

Rightpoint quickly reassures her that everything is fine.

Jena watches Passionquest as she walks toward the door.

"Who is she?" Jena asks.

Rightpoint smiles. "That lovely, talented, and brave woman is Passionquest."

"Passionquest," Jena says. "That's an interesting name."

"She's an interesting person," Rightpoint says, suggesting that Jena and Passionquest are alike. "Strong, ambitious, fierce, and beautiful women."

Jena smiles. "Why, thank you."

Jake watches the two talk. He's not happy about the way Rightpoint is looking at Jena.

Jena turns the conversation back to the mission. "We don't even know when or where they will attack us."

"Don't despair, Jena. I have heard that you are a strong fighter. That's why Moschi and Pulue brought you here," Rightpoint says. "We may not know when they're going to strike, but we will be ready. Moschi told us that one day we would battle Romli's teams. He was certain of it." Rightpoint looks sad, but Jena understands.

Rightpoint goes on: "We didn't know that we would be fighting that battle without him. Every plan was made with Moschi in command and Pulue as second-in-command." He shakes his head. "Now, Pulue is out searching for Moschi, even though we know he is no longer with us."

"I suppose it's too dangerous to send a team to look for Pulue," Jena says.

"Yes," Rightpoint says. "I wish we could. But we must continue to prepare for war with Romli's forces."

Jena nods in agreement, but she still wonders why Rightpoint seems distracted at times.

"I will head back to the team until you give us further instructions," she says, watching Hero beginning to prepare for his mission on the water.

Several men and women are with him.

After the boats have been checked thoroughly, Hero nods and smiles at his team.

"Team are you ready?" he asks with authority.

"Yes, we are," they reply in unison.

One woman separates from the crowd and steps onto the boat with Hero.

"Passionquest," he says pleasantly. "Are you joining us?"

She smiles. "Hello, Hero. I am joining you." She hugs him affectionately. "Or shall I call you 'father'?"

Hero picks up his daughter, then gently puts her back down. "You shall call me father," Hero says before turning to look at two other team members. "They will call me Hero." He orders them to carry on, then quietly addresses his daughter. "This is a surprise."

They smile at one another.

"When I recruited team members, I did not envision that one of them would be my daughter," he says.

"I spoke to Rightpoint," she explains. "He is concerned about you, as I am. I insisted that I join you on this mission."

"I have led many missions—before and after you were born, sweet daughter," Hero says sincerely.

"Father, you are ill," she says, scolding him a bit.

"I am well enough, daughter." Hero stands his ground. "But let's not argue. The purpose of this mission is great. We must protect what Moschi has built, and we must protect our home." He looks into the sky. "This is where my beautiful Emily gave birth to you," he says as he looks at the stunning colors of the coming dawn. Sighing, he says, "Another angel, gone to heaven."

He is sad, and Passionquest looks away.

"Mother," she says softly.

"Yes, your beautiful mother," he replies.

Father and daughter clear their throats, wipe their eyes, and shake their arms a little to change the mood. Rightpoint is correct. A great battle is ahead.

Both boats are ready to move out. Hero gives the signal for the boats to begin heading into the lake as the sun rises above them.

———

Sharon and Aeo swim steadily ahead of the boats led by Lero and Matty.

All the rowers and swimmers are alert and pacing themselves.

Aeo is the first to see two boats in the distance. He signals to Sharon, then turns to swim back to Lero's boat.

"There are boats approaching us," Aeo whispers as he floats next to the boat.

Lero gives Matty the signal that the battle is about to begin.

Sharon and Aeo swim around to the back of the boats.

Lero doesn't want the enemy to see his boats until absolutely necessary. He picks up his binoculars and sees two boats approaching.

Lero stands and yells, "Enemy ahead!"

Aeo quickly puts on long-distance eyewear, and Lero hands him a bow and arrow.

While still wading in the lake, he fires one sure arrow straight at the man who appears to be leading the crews.

The arrow finds its mark.

The arrow flies straight Hero's chest, the point piercing his back. Blood gushes from his body.

Passionquest stares in shock.

"Father!" she screams. Her voice echoes over the lake.

She quickly helps move Hero to his side, while directing the boats to turn around; she stays low but takes charge.

"Turn these boats around! Now!" she orders, struggling to control her emotions as she tries to stop the blood pouring from Hero's chest. "Father, please hold on," she begs.

She takes off her shirt and ties it around the wound in the front and then pulls out a knife to break the arrow in Hero's back.

Hero can't move or speak.

"Hold on," she says. "Hold on. Hold on."

She knows she can't pull out the arrow. Hero would die instantly.

Passionquest knows there is no hope for her father. She sits low in the boat, holding Hero's head close to hers.

Hero musters enough strength to speak. Passionquest listens, but she can't understand because his voice is so weak.

"What is it, father?" she asks. "What are you trying to tell me?"

He is quiet, then: "I see your mother."

He takes his last breath.

Passionquest collapses onto her father's body, her eyes blind with tears of anger and pain. Hero lies perfectly still as she holds him.

The boats move as fast as possible back to the compound.

Two team members from each boat fire at Lero's and Matty's boats to slow them down, while two other team members paddle as fast as they can.

Passionquest collects herself and pulls out her radio to warn Rightpoint that they're returning to the compound in a state of emergency and that the enemy is not far behind. She reluctantly moves away from her father. She lays low, keeping hold of the radio.

The static doesn't waver. "Rightpoint," she calls. Then more static. "Rightpoint," she calls again, panicked.

Rightpoint finally answers.

Passionquest pauses, and her voice fades in and out. "We're headed back … the enemy …"

Rightpoint struggles to understand what she is saying.

Finally, her voice comes through clearly.

"The enemy is coming!" she yells. "The enemy is coming!"

The team keeps rowing, trying to reach the shore in time to join the others in defense of the compound.

Rightpoint finally understands and sounds the alarm.

"We will be ready!" he yells back to her.

Everyone in the compound moves into combat mode when they hear the alarm.

Rightpoint runs to Andy, who is already in uniform. Luis and the rest of Andy's team are dressed and ready to fight.

"Passionquest made the call," Rightpoint says, breathless and overcome.

He pauses and looks from Andy to Luis.

"Do you understand? Passionquest made the call. Not Hero," Rightpoint says as clearly as he can.

"That could only mean one thing," Andy says wearily. He looks at Luis. "Hero is injured, or he has been killed."

Rightpoint turns away, hoping for the best, but fearing the worst.

He tries to compose himself. "I must go back to lead my team."

"Go," Andy orders. He then turns to Luis. "Luis, you must ensure that our team is ready for combat."

Luis is ready. He nods and turns away to continue preparing their team.

Andy uses his codes as he walks through each area of the compound. Pulue had trained Andy well, even giving him the codes, which he shared with no one else. The codes work only at the sound of Andy's voice, arming the hidden technology designed for invasions—cameras, tripwires, floor spikes, and, of course, mounted weaponry.

Andy then walks through the compound yelling. Everything and everyone are in a state of emergency. Team members are scattered and preparing for battle.

Tammy appears behind Andy.

"What can I do?" she asks, walking quickly to keep up with him.

He stops. "Go to the roof and make sure the team is properly prepared, that all corners are secured. Then have Sir James' crew take food and water to the roof. We don't know how long they will be up there. I want every man and woman to have what they need."

"Yes, sir!" Tammy replies and takes off quickly.

Andy stops and calls out for her.

Tammy turns and stands still.

"We have sick men and women in the medical area, and we will have battle injuries before this is over," he says. "Make sure that equipment, supplies, medicine, and blankets are readily available." The list continues. "The children have to be protected. Get anyone not already on a combat team to help you."

Meanwhile, Rightpoint hurries back to the lakeside entrance.

"Our boats are coming back in a state of emergency!" he yells. "Take your stations immediately. The enemy will be upon us in moments. Be prepared to fight."

As Rightpoint walks through the groups of teammates, he grabs Jena and pulls her aside.

"Jena, there has been a casualty."

CHAPTER THIRTY-ONE

Rightpoint stares into Jena's eyes.

"What is it?" Jena asks frantically.

"I can't talk about it now," he says. His face is serious and uncharacteristically angry. He seems lost in Jena's eyes. "It's time for battle. It's time to fight for the compound that Moschi and Pulue built. It may be time for the ultimate sacrifice. I need you to take over for me here, inside, at the entrance. I must go to the shoreline to meet our boats before our enemy arrives."

Rightpoint sprints away, leaving her baffled—and in charge.

Jena sees that many are already preparing to battle Romli's army. She tries to gather her wits and notices Jake and Ken looking to her for guidance. The room seems to be closing in on her, testing her strength. She had trained for this, and yet she feels weak with waves of anxiety and impotence. She tries to focus and looks around the room, until she sees individuals instead of blurs. She taps into the power deep in her body and soul, and then she tries to pull it into her hands and feet and mind.

She finally gives Jake and Ken her first order.

"Jake, Ken … get your weapons … now," Jena says. "Join the other team members and prepare to defend your lives and the lives of those fighting next to you. Our boats are returning to shore, and Romli's boats are not far behind them."

They look at Jena, their mouths agape. They hear something they don't recognize in her voice. Ken and Jake look at each other and hustle off to the weapons room. A team member stands at the door, nodding as each person enters. People from the compound are grabbing guns, bows, knives, and other weapons that Jena's friends have never seen before. They look around the room as the rush of war weighs on them. No one in the room speaks to anyone else.

Ken takes the initiative and grabs some weapons. Jake does the same.

———

Rightpoint rushes to the shore. He brings team members to help get the boats to shore quickly … and, he is now certain, to help Passionquest carry Hero's body.

Boats finally reach the shore, and team members jump out and start dragging their boats on land.

Rightpoint steps onto Hero's boat and can't take his eyes away off of Hero's stiff body and the arrow piercing his chest. He heaves with sadness and anger. He looks at Passionquest's red eyes and swallows his emotions so that he can help lift Hero's body safely back into the compound.

Passionquest, Rightpoint, and another team member from the boat get Hero's body onto a stretcher. A team member is at each of the four corners, waiting to carry Hero's body. They move quickly to get the body inside. Passionquest and Rightpoint follow the stretcher.

Passionquest stops at the entry and turns to Rightpoint.

"You and Andy must lead. I need to be with my father," she says. And she turns away.

Rightpoint takes a moment to grieve his friend's death and then yells out to the team.

"Secure the area! The enemy is upon us!" Rightpoint yells. "I want every man and woman lined up on this shoreline."

———

Aeo has no way of knowing that his arrow has hit its mark, much less that it has killed one of his enemy's leaders. He hands the bow back to Lero.

"Well done," Lero says, looking through his binoculars at the enemy boats.

The swimmers move out in front of their own boats, as ordered by Romli's lieutenants, Matty and Lero. Aeo and Sharon swim until they see Moschi's followers lining the shoreline in front of their compound. They swim back to report to their leaders.

"They're all along the shore," Aeo tells Lero.

Sharon reports the same to Matty.

Lero signals that the boats should remain still until his order. He commands one of his rowers to take him to Matty's boat.

As Lero's boat slides to Matty's, he tells her, "They are all around the shoreline. I believe we must move to the backup plan."

Matty nods in agreement. "There is no other choice."

Lero calls to Aeo and Sharon.

"We will move closer," he tells them. "Proceed to the backup plan—the waterproof grenades."

Lero gives Aeo and Sharon each a backpack filled with highly explosive waterproof grenades, along with a grenade launcher for each.

"You have trained for this moment. Get as close as you can but stay out of their range and fire as many grenades as you can," he says. "We'll move in close behind the explosions."

Sharon and Aeo struggle to put on the backpacks and balance the grenade launchers. They put on high-tech goggles, which will allow them to see above or below the water.

They start swimming—one to the right, one to the left. The boats float slowly behind them.

Aeo looks up and can see through the water to the sky. He also has a clear view of the shore. He and Sharon are so stealthy, quiet, and well-equipped that they are virtually invisible to the enemy on the shore.

Shots fly from the enemy shoreline toward Lero's and Matty's boats. Everyone in the boats stays low to avoid being shot.

Sharon and Aeo can see each other under the water. They get as close as they can to the shore, and—in a move they've practiced—each throws two grenades toward the shore.

The grenades blast pockets of Moschi's people. Rightpoint and the people around him barely escape the explosives. Wounded team members help each other into the compound.

As the smoke clears, Romli's boats—helmed by Matty and Lero—have reached the shore of the compound.

Romli's fighters pour out of the boats and onto the grounds of the compound. Lero and Matty are among them.

Moschi's people fire shots from the roof, taking out two of Lero's men.

Lero and Matty signal that their soldiers should hug the sides of the compound since Moschi's people have retreated inside.

Lero slides away from the wall and fires upward at the roof, then quickly moves back to the wall. Other members of his team follow.

Two of Moschi's fighters fall from the roof and slam to the ground.

With Matty's and Lero's teams just outside their door, Andy stands in silence in the center of the room at the lakeside entrance. Luis stands to one side; Jena is on the other.

Veronica, Tammy Jake, Ken, Mr. Tindale, and Denise stand behind. Other team members are scattered around the room. Some guard the door, others line up against the inside wall, around the windows, and behind columns.

Andy looks around the room and tries to make eye contact with each person. His moment of truth is now—the stakes could not be higher. With Pulue gone and Moschi dead, Andy is responsible for every man, woman, and child.

Rightpoint makes his way to Andy. He pauses, then gives a status report.

"They're lined up against the wall of the compound," Rightpoint says. "It's only a matter of time before they use their explosives to get inside the building."

Andy steps aside slightly to speak to Rightpoint. "The exterior wall is explosive resistant."

"That is good," Rightpoint says. "I advise that we storm through the door and attack them all."

"That is logical," Andy says. "But I also think that is what they want us to do." He turns to the group. "Everyone stay in position until I give the order to attack. If we go to them, we will lose lives."

Veronica speaks up. "There are only a few of them, and we have a compound full of strong fighters."

Rightpoint advocates that they stay on the offensive. He is angry.

"They killed Hero. We can't allow them to take this compound that Moschi, Pulue, and all of us worked so hard to build. We can't allow Romli to make us his slaves," he argues passionately.

Andy stares at Rightpoint. "Do you honestly believe that Romli would send such a small team? This is just the beginning."

"So, let's kill them now," Rightpoint argues again. "All of them. We must avenge Hero's death."

Meanwhile, outside, Lero, Matty, and the rest of their team members wait.

Andy is correct. More of Romli's boats are flooding the lake.

Matty inches over to Lero. "They're not going to come out," she whispers.

Lero points to the lake, where at least ten more boats of team members are heading their way.

"I wondered when they were going to arrive," Matty says.

"It doesn't matter whether Moschi's people come out because soon, we're going in," Lero says.

The team on the roof sends word that more boats are arriving. Tammy rushes to Rightpoint and Andy to tell them.

"Their boats are lined up all the way across the lake," she says.

Andy's eyes catch fire. He knows now that action is their only option.

Luis, Veronica, Tammy, Rightpoint, Passionquest, Jena, Jake, Ken, Denise, Mr. Tindale, and Ken all surround Andy. All are worried.

Andy steps into the circle.

"Get word to all of the teams. Make sure all entries to the compound are secure. Teams that are not guarding entrances, or the roof, shall now take the battle to Romli's soldiers," he says. "They will get war."

Romli's boats are now at the compound shoreline. Teams of men and women jump from the boats, fully prepared and geared up for battle.

Luis has returned to his team on the roof. He and her teammates aim their weapons at the boats.

But Romli's team, led by Lero, is ready, too. They aim their weapons at the roof and the entrance.

The tension grows, and the standoff can't hold much longer.

"Fire!" Luis orders from above. Her team rains a fusillade down onto Romli's team.

Many of Romli's soldiers jump into the lake, others run for cover on one side or the other of the compound, and some are wounded.

Lero signals the teams into position.

Inside, Andy prepares to take his people to the lake entrance. He stands in front of the bulletproof door with Rightpoint's team.

The door opens, and Andy rushes out with at least one team behind him.

The battle spills out of control, a chaos of weapons, fists, and tactical fighting. A bloodbath.

Andy battles Lero.

The entry to the compound is now wide open.

Chance, Suzanne, and many of Lero's team members boldly enter.

The battle inside the compound begins.

Weapons fire. Everyone is engaged.

Chance spots Jena. Their eyes lock. The war between them has never abated. Now, it appears that it never will. The battle will continue as long as both are alive.

Wasting no time, the two race toward one another.

Jena jumps over a chair, smashing into Chance.

They both drop their weapons and gear. Everyone is battling around them, but the two women have eyes—and hate—for only each other. Chance and Jena are consumed with vengeance.

Jena doesn't waste any time. She jumps at Chance, channeling their fight back in the prison cafeteria, where inmates leaped, yelled, banged on tables, and cheered on.

This time, their teammates have other battles to worry about.

Chance takes the first swing. Jena manages to dodge the blow and tackles Chance. Jena holds Chance down and stares at her.

"We can stop this," Jena says.

Chance smirks and shoves back. "There's no going back now, Jena."

The entire compound is in battle. Some of the fighting is more brawl than tactics.

Andy and Lero are locked in a fight that has moved inside.

Lero feels his body getting weaker. He becomes dizzy and weak, the cancer eating inside him. Still, he fights fiercely.

Passionquest has found Matty, instinctively knowing that she is a leader of this foe. Passionquest's anger over the loss of her father rushes through her veins. She glares at Matty.

Both are prepared for battle—and for any outcome.

"You killed my father!" Passionquest says, seething. "Now you're going to pay the price for your army's vicious quest for power."

"We had no wish to kill your father," Matty says. "But it appears you live by the sword, and you will surely die by it."

They drop their weapons and lunge at one another.

Passionquest's face turns red. She wants to harness her pain and loss to destroy Matty. She remembers when her mother fought Romli's soldiers. The thought of losing both parents overwhelms her.

"You will die in the name of my parents," Passionquest says as she charges Matty and slams her against a wall. "What do you have to say now?"

Passionquest transitions into her tactical moves, but Matty is more than ready. She grabs Passionquest with a tight grip and swings her around to slam her into the same wall.

"I think, little girl, that you are in over your head," Matty says confidently.

Passionquest pushes back and frees herself from Matty's grip. With wild eyes, Passionquest grits her teeth. "We'll see," she spits back.

Their brutal struggle continues.

Throughout the compound, nothing is clear. From the rooftops to almost every corner of every room inside and outside the compound, there is battle. Everyone is fighting.

The combat between the two armies comes to a head.

The final, inevitable battle between the two armies—always envisioned as a war of weapons and missiles and technology—shifts. The idea of individuals fighting face-to-face was thought to be a thing of stories and rumors. But now personal engagement with the enemy is a reality, and technology has little to do with it. Muscle and determination replace illusions and distance.

On the roof, some of Luis' team fight to the bitter end. Some team members hang from the edge of the roof, while others fall to their deaths.

Members of both team's race throughout the compound, battling whoever they encounter. They fight until they can fight no more or until they are captured and taken to Romli's boats or to the basement prison in Moschi's compound.

It is clear that this is the fight of their lives, with one leader—Moschi—dead, and with the other leader—Romli—waiting back at his palace to be the ruler of all.

Lero manages to overthrow Andy, battling him through the halls of the compound.

Matty and Passionquest battle close by.

Ken, Jake, Mr. Tindale, Franklin, and Denise find themselves in the middle of a brawl. They have become soldiers.

Chance has gotten the advantage in her fight with Jena. She has her hands wrapped around Jena's neck.

Jena uses her strength to hold Chance back as best she can, but she feels the breath leaving her body as she struggles.

Chance stares at Jena with madness in every part of her body. "I hate you," she says, squeezing Jena's throat with every bit of her hate.

"You are the fire burning inside of me," Chance growls. "It will never go out until you are dead. I thought the fire would go out when I got rid of that back-stabbing Carol. But it was always you. I must destroy you!" Chance screeches. "You made me who I am!"

Jena's face turns red, then bluish, as she starts to lose consciousness, faintly hearing Chance's raving.

Images of the dead flash through Jena's mind: Miles McNeil, the hotel clerk, the doctor, and Jena's beloved mother, Kitty. The ghosts push Jena's strength to take over as the room becomes a blur.

She manages to lift her knees and push them deep into Chance's chest. She bashes Chance's face with her elbows. Blood gushes from Chance's mouth, and she falls backward, slamming to the floor.

Jena gasps for air and leans over Chance.

"You're pathetic," Jena says as she lands a hard blow to Chance's bleeding face, knocking Chance unconscious.

Jena stands tall, glaring at Chance, who is still breathing.

Jena thinks of her aunt and begins searching for her frantically. Out of the corner of her eye, she sees Denise struggling to fight off a man who seems more interested in pinning her against the wall than in fighting her. Jena races to her aunt and grabs the man by the neck, drags him to the floor, takes his weapon away, and points it at him. The man's eyes grow large. He holds his hands out so that Jena can see them. Jena tries to control her anger as she holds the weapon at the man's face. Denise stands behind her.

"So, you like harassing women?" Jena yells.

The scruffy man lays on the floor, afraid to move.

Two of Jena's teammates approach Jena. One points a weapon at the offender and nods to her. Jena notices that one of the men is Mr. Tindale, who looks at Jena, and she stares back at a man transformed.

"We'll take it from here," Mr. Tindale says in an authoritative tone.

Jena hands the enemy's weapon to Mr. Tindale and nods in agreement.

Mr. Tindale stands tall and nods back. He and the other member of the team take the enemy soldier to the compound's prison.

Jena turns to her aunt, who is still shaken. "I'm sorry. I should never have left you alone." Jena hugs her aunt and pulls her away from the chaos.

Denise kisses Jena's forehead. "I wanted to be here with you. Now that your father is gone, you're all I have. It's worth risking my life for my only niece. I owe it to my brother."

Jena and Denise share a moment as Jena remembers the night Miles McNeil shot her father. She remembers running to the McNeil household and finding her mother holding her father's bloody body.

In a fog, she sees the room of fighting people and, at the same time, her younger self is still full of shock and pain. The two worlds are colliding.

Jena grabs her aunt's arm, and they run through the room. She takes Denise to the weapons room, where Jena thinks Denise will be safe.

Guards are protecting the room, and if nothing else, Denise would have plenty of access to weapons.

Jena nudges aunt into the room. "Stay here, my sweet aunt," she says her eyes as wild as the day she went hunting for Miles McNeil. "I have things to do."

Denise nods. She sees the anger that has returned to Jena's soul.

Jena turns away from Denise. She leaves the room and closes the door to the room tightly.

Denise turns to face the others in the room. A young woman approaches her.

"Where is your weapon?" she asks.

Denise stutters. "Out there … somewhere … in the middle of the battle."

The guard retrieves a large weapon from a shelf and hands it to Denise.

"We're at war," the guard says. "And that means all of us."

Denise stares at the weapon. She doesn't want to take it, but she does. Denise wraps the straps around her shoulder. The guard nods in approval and returns to her assigned area.

Jena enters the room where most of the fighting is taking place. She is in a rage and ready to battle. She sees Chance, still unconscious. She sees Ken, Jake, Franklin, and Mr. Tindale in a fierce battle against an enemy team. Even with few skills, they seem to be holding their own. Mr. Tindale, the proper butler, is in a bloody fight with his opponent. One of his arms is bleeding, but he looks like he has been soldiering for years.

Suddenly, Jena is tackled from behind.

She falls hard. She stares at a big, burly man walking toward her. With all her strength, she stands and braces herself for what she knows will be a difficult fight.

The giant man picks her up and holds her in the air.

"What now, little girl?" he asks.

The odds against her, Jena remembers a maneuver she has used before. Dangling, she swings her legs and wraps them around the man's neck. He falls to the floor like shattered glass. Two of her teammates arrive to help.

Lero is holding his own, but feels his body getting weaker from his illness.

Passionquest and Matty fight close by. Their brawl is relentless and intense. Both women are committed to fighting to the death.

After a hard blow to the face, Lero begins to lean forward in a daze. Andy can tell that something, besides the fighting, is wrong. He backs away. He doesn't want to hit Lero again.

Distracted by Lero, Matty inadvertently gives Passionquest the advantage. Matty has to struggle to find her rhythm again. She succeeds in wrestling Passionquest to the floor, but she can still keep one eye on Lero.

Lero struggles to stand. His eyes blur and he stumbles backward and falls flat. Andy watches Lero, keeping his distance in case this is a trick. But Lero is not breathing. Andy kneels beside him and checks his pulse. There is none.

Matty immediately sees Lero fall. She throws Passionquest down and runs to him.

Andy pulls his weapon and points it at her.

Matty stops and stares at Lero. "You don't understand! He's sick. He has cancer!"

Andy sees the sorrow in Matty's eyes, and he is moved. "He's gone."

"What?" she asks, incredulous.

"He's gone," Andy repeats, gently. "He has no pulse."

"Save him!" she screams. She drops to the floor and tries to resuscitate the man she loves. She breaks apart as she realizes that Lero is gone.

Andy feels compassion for Matty as her tears fall onto Lero's shirt.

Nothing else exists for Matty in that moment.

Passionquest walks over and stands next to Andy.

Matty stands and addresses them both.

"Capture who you need to capture," she says, looking at Lero again. "This is Romli's senseless war. My mission is over. I don't have the strength or the heart to continue." She summons her meager energy and yells, "Retreat!"

Everyone suddenly stops.

Not quite ready to do the same, Andy orders his teams to capture as many of Romli's people as they can, but Romli's soldiers are fleeing. Still, Andy's soldiers heed Andy's order.

Suzanne, Sharon, Paula, Aeo, and others are captured along with Matty, who surrenders.

As the fight changes, Chance takes a deep breath and opens her eyes.

Jena is standing over her.

"Welcome back," Jena says.

CHAPTER THIRTY-TWO

Chance tries to get up. Jena reaches down to help her, but Chance swats away Jena's hand.

"I don't need your help," Chance mumbles.

"Of course not," Jena smirks.

Some of Romli's team members are still racing to escape, while others are being captured by Andy's teams and taken to the prison downstairs.

Matty sits in her enemy's home base and cradles Lero's body. She is silent, but the tears keep flowing. She was trained to be a woman of steel. But that woman seems like a different woman with a different life. She felt abandoned in every way, found love in the most unlikely place, under the most unlikely conditions. Now, that love has been taken away. She is broken, in a pit of pain after the loss of Lero. Yet, her grief makes her feel human again. She remembers the death of her son and how his death brought her here. She thought she only deserved to live without love.

Andy is moved to comfort this woman, though he doesn't even know her; she may still see him as the enemy and may blame him for Lero's death. Instead, he keeps his distance.

"The body must be taken to the medical ward. He can't stay here," he tells her gently.

She looks up at him with eyes that show her heartbreak.

"You can go with him," Andy says, trying to be kind.

Four team members step toward Matty. One gently moves her out of the way. Andy moves to her side and waits for an outburst, but she is mute with pain.

The four-member team picks up Lero's body and places it on a gurney. One pushes, and two others follow. The final team member approaches Matty.

"You can come with us and your loved one, or you can be escorted to the prison."

"I want to go with Lero," she replies.

The armed guard follows her to the medical ward but tells her she can stay with the body.

Mr. Tindale and another team member walk over to Chance and Jena.

"We'll take her," the team member says. He grabs Chance by her bruised arm.

"Careful," Jena says. "She's a bit sore right now."

And just like that, Chance is taken to the prison in the compound that Moschi built, the compound where Jena trained, the compound where Chance had hoped beyond hope to exact her revenge.

Jena watches through the glass door as Romli's team members flee.

She looks around the compound and sees broken furniture, shattered glass, abandoned weapons, busted walls, and blood everywhere.

Moschi's team—they still think of themselves that way, even though Moschi is dead—begin making their way to the main hall. Some are limping, others are being carried.

Franklin, Ken, and Jake are being treated in the medical ward.

The weapons room door is open, and Denise walks out, relieved, and unharmed. She takes the weapon from her shoulder and places it on the floor.

Andy, Passionquest, Veronica, Luis, and Tammy huddle in the hallway, where Lero fell. Andy scans the room and sees Jena. He waves her over to join them.

They all stand in a circle.

Andy steps forward. "We are lucky to be standing here with one another."

The others no in unison.

"Has anyone seen Rightpoint?" Andy asks, concerned.

"I'll go look for him," Passionquest says.

Rightpoint limps toward them. "May I join you?"

"Of course," Andy replies. "But do you need medical assistance first?"

Rightpoint declines. "I'll survive."

"Now that this bloody battle seems to be over, we must send a team to rescue Pulue," Andy says.

Everyone in the circle is silent.

"Surely by now, Romli has captured him. What can we possibly do?" Veronica asks bluntly. "Romli's people are on their way back to their home base. If we attack them there, they will be ready for us. It will be just another bloody war."

"Even so, we have we have to rescue him," Jena chimes in. "Maybe we should meet in the main dining room to sketch out a plan."

But first Jena explains that she'd like to check on her friends, Jake and Denise and the others.

Andy nods. "We'll meet in the dining room within the hour." He then says urgently, "We have no time to waste. We must get to Romli's compound before Pulue is killed or they decide to return and attack us again."

Andy walks away to check on his wounded team members.

A half-hour or so later, when the team returns to the dining room, they all look different than they had a few hours before. Everyone is bruised and bleeding. Some have their limbs wrapped or bandaged. One person is wearing a cast. Many are missing—too wounded to move, or worse.

Andy is sore but relatively unscathed.

"Our mission is not finished," he says. "It is possible that Pulue escaped or was not captured. Regardless, we must find him and the two teammates who went with him and bring them back where they belong."

Andy advises sending a team to Romli's compound.

"Don't you think they are already waiting for us?" Veronica asks. "Romli has many more soldiers than we do."

Jena, Jake, Ken, Franklin, Mr. Tindale, and Denise enter.

"I'm sorry we're late," Jena says. "My friends are pretty busted up."

Andy nods. "Thank you for the courage to stand with us in battle. We could not ask for more dedicated teammates."

Andy looks around the room at all of the men and women, all of them hurting.

"I honor all of you," he says. "Moschi would be proud of us. But we must move forward. I will lead a team to Romli's compound. We will search for Pulue and engage the enemy if needed."

Veronica sighs loudly. "Pulue is probably dead. Would he want us to look for him if it put our compound at risk?"

Many quietly nod in agreement as they sit at the table and in chairs scattered around the room.

"We can protect our compound using the technology and strategies that Pulue and Moschi taught us," Andy replies. "Besides, we won't take all of our fighters."

Jena steps forward and says adamantly, "We must also capture Romli."

Jena never fails to shock them, and most team members gasp audibly.

"I came here to tell you that Moschi had been killed and that Romli's army would certainly attack us," she explains. "But my goal is to take Romli back to the United States … to Maplesville.

He must face the consequences of his actions. The women and men who have suffered because of his criminal enterprise deserve justice."

No one says a word. They just stare at Jena.

Even Andy is puzzled. "What do you mean, Jena?"

Jena speaks louder.

"Women, mostly women, are being kidnapped from my hometown and brought here to be slaves and assassins," she explains. "It starts in my hometown—our hometown." She points to her Maplesville friends. "And it comes here—through Romli, Pulue, and Moschi. And it needs to end with justice, back in my town."

"Jena, you have information that we do not. We still do not understand," Andy says again.

"Well …" she says, trying to find a way to explain the complicated story. "Pulue and Moschi always told us that we were treated like royalty compared to those who work for Romli, right?"

She looks around the room, and people are nodding.

"Those people—actually, I can only speak of the women—who work for Romli are virtually slaves," she goes on. "They are kidnapped from the prison in my town—the prison I was in until Moschi rescued me—with the help of a corrupt warden and corrupt politicians and law enforcement and sold to Romli to serve him until they die."

She pauses to see if the people understand what she says, then defiantly, she goes on. "Many of the women downstairs, captured during the battle and jailed in our own compound, are from the same prison where I was held. And some of the women from my town—some of the women, and men, in this room—ended up in this compound, as well."

The room is quiet. Some people's mouths are open, as if they want to say something. Some gaze out, their eyes wide with disbelief.

"So, what are you proposing, exactly?" Veronica asks.

"The plan is explosive. It will uncover many secrets. And, yes, Veronica, it will be very dangerous," Jena says. "But Romli and others must be held accountable for their devious crimes, and the women they kidnapped deserve justice and a chance to go home."

"Are you really telling us that all of the fighters at Romli's compound are from the prison in your hometown?" Andy asks.

"No. Not all. Some may be there by choice, just like here. And the corruption has probably spread to villages throughout this region and to other towns in the United States," Jena says. "I'm sad to say that my beloved father may have been involved at one time, and my biological father was definitely involved. The corruption has made its way into every place where weak people are looking to make money off the backs of others."

Rightpoint, who is standing upright with the help of Passionquest, keeps his eyes on Passionquest and says, "For some of us, this is the only home we have ever known. For us, this is a hard, but benevolent, place. The place where we grew up. The place where our mothers and fathers lived and died."

Jena looks toward Luis, whose story is much like her own. But Luis looks away.

"I understand," Jena says, turning toward Rightpoint and Passionquest. "Moschi rescued me from the prison in Maplesville. Who knows what would have happened to me if he had not? He offered me the chance to come here and train to become an assassin. He gave me the opportunity to channel the darkness that coursed through my veins. And, yes, Rightpoint, the short time I was here was very hard—but nothing like the enslaved life I would have led in Romli's camp."

Andy speaks up, stopping a conversation that might go on and on.

"Jena, perhaps you and your friends would give us a chance to talk among ourselves," he says. "No offense intended."

Jena replies that she understands completely.

"Regardless of what you decide, thank you all for listening," Jena says, more calmly. "Thank you for allowing me and my friends into the compound. We are honored to have been of service to such good and brave people."

She scans the room and tries to make eye contact with as many of them as possible.

Before she leaves, she asks for one more favor, a private moment with Veronica. Veronica steps forward and she and Jena whisper briefly near the doorway.

Then Jena corrals her friends and guides them out of the dining room.

"We won't be long," Andy says. "We will bring you back as soon as possible."

Once outside the room, Jake pulls Jena into a big hug.

"That was very brave, my sweet love," he says.

Catching the spirit, and wanting to lighten the mood, Ken leads the entire Maplesville crew in a group hug. Soon, they are all laughing. Ken's mission is accomplished.

"Thank you all for believing in me," Jena tells her friends. "Thank you for coming to rescue me."

Franklin nods and grins. "Consider it research."

"I think we all had a piece of the puzzle," Ken says. "But none of us understood the scope of what was happening back home and that it reached this far."

Jena's Aunt Denise nods vigorously. "I met that Warden Peters. I knew something evil was afoot, but I never would have figured it out by myself."

Jena smiles at her people. She's overwhelmed with love for them.

"Okay, folks, see all of the fancy furniture in this hallway? I suggest you take advantage of these elegant sofas and chairs." She giggles a little. "Funny, I never see anyone sitting on them."

She barely finishes her sentence before Mr. Tindale and Ken plop down on the plush silk furnishings.

"I have something I need to do. Alone," Jena says. "I'm sorry. I won't be long."

She looks over her shoulder and sees the others pick places to relax. She won't be surprised if some of them are nodding off within seconds.

Jena heads to the medical ward, where she finds Matty, still grieving Lero.

Matty is standing over his body, tears streaming down her cheeks. She touches him, smoothing his hair and squeezing his hand. The medical team is patient and understands her need to spend a few more moments with someone who obviously meant a great deal to her. But Jena can't wait. She knows she needs this woman's help to make her plan work—if Andy and the others approve.

Matty feels Jena's presence behind her and turns to face the young woman.

"Do you know who I am?" Jena asks.

"I do," Matty says.

"And you are Matty, aren't you?" Jena asks. "I talked to Veronica, one of Moschi's and Pulue's fighters. She's done surveillance at Romli's camp."

"That's correct," Matty replies calmly. "Lero, lying here dead … he and I led teams for Romli. Lero was his second-in-command. We were ordered to lead the fighters who would destroy this compound—and also capture you, Jena Parker, and return you to Romli."

"Why does Romli care about me?" Jena asks.

"Romli blames you for Maria's death."

"I did not kill Maria, but that doesn't matter now. I was brought here from the prison in Maplesville, but I do not remember you," Jena says.

"I was taken before you came. Other women on my teams know you," Matty says. "But you're not here to introduce yourself."

Jena speaks softly out of respect. "No, I'm not."

"I know what you want," Matty says, without emotion. "And the answer is yes." Matty turns away from Jena and gazes at Lero as she speaks. "I will help you capture Romli and take down his evil empire." She sighs. "I have one request."

Jena nods.

"I want to be the one to kill Romli. I want to see the fear in his eyes. I want him to know that he is paying for the evil deeds he has done to women—women like me whose lives were ripped away from them," Matty says.

"I understand," Jena tells Matty.

Matty can't bear to look away from the lifeless Lero. "I love him," she says.

She touches Lero's face one more time, turns away from her lover and toward Jena and follows Jena out of the medical ward and back to her friends.

Jena is introducing Matty to Jake and the others when Andy opens the dining room door and gestures for them to enter.

They walk in with more than a little trepidation. Andy and the others may well turn down Jena's request for help.

Things don't get off to a good start when the teammates recognize Matty. Passionquest and Rightpoint seem on the brink of violence, or revolt.

"I'll explain," Jena says, a bit plaintively.

Andy stands in front of Jena. "We have decided to hear you out. Tell us what you propose."

Jena is relieved. Now the hard part begins. But she's ready to take charge.

"We must capture Romli and take him to Maplesville," Jena says. She gestures toward Matty. "Matty is one of the team leaders for Romli. She has agreed to lead us inside Romli's compound so we can capture him without a fight. The rest of his camp won't know he is gone until we are far away."

She pauses to let the plans sink in. "We will take some of the women who are imprisoned downstairs with us. We will convince some to help us and return them to Maplesville, where many were kidnapped on Romli's orders."

Jena asks that Andy, and the others provide support—on the ground at Romli's compound, in the air, and in Maplesville.

"Once we get to Maplesville, we must be one team."

Jena waits to hear what Andy will say.

"I will help you, of course," Andy says. "Our primary mission will be rescuing Pulue and his men. But we will also help you with your plan. No one will be forced to join."

"Veronica, Luis, and Tammy, will you join us?" Jena asks.

They stare at one another.

Veronica stands. "Yes, I will."

"As will I," Luis says.

Tammy echoes the same.

Jena smiles with gratitude.

"I will get you into Romli's compound," Matty tells the group. "I believe the team tasked with capturing Romli should be me, Jena, Paula—who is one of my people—and only one or two others."

Andy cuts in. "Then there's the issue of our leader, Pulue, and his teammates. They may have been captured. He left before the battle to search for Moschi." Andy gestures toward Jena. "He left before Jena told us that Moschi had been killed, that he and Maria had killed one another."

Matty nods in agreement. "Moschi's and Maria's bodies are at the compound. As for Pulue, he had not been taken before our mission began, but I can't say what happened after we left."

Jena gets nervous. "Trust me, I know this plan seems impossible."

Andy clears his throat. "It seems to me that we have several missions. We must bring Moschi's body back to our compound so that he can be honored in a manner in keeping with his accomplishments in life. And we must rescue Pulue and his team if he is at Romli's camp."

Passionquest and Rightpoint step forward.

"My father, and the man who was like a father to Rightpoint, died today in battle," Passionquest says, glaring at Matty for a split-second.

Rightpoint chimes in, "We will honor my father by setting out to recover Moschi's body and to rescue Pulue and the others. We'll take a jeep."

"Let it be so," Andy agrees.

"How many airplanes does this compound have?" Jena asks.

"We have two," replies Tammy.

"Good," Jena says. "We have one. So that will be three."

Jena asks if she can have radios from the compound, and Andy agrees.

Jena turns to Jake. "Jake, you will return to Franklin's plane with Ken, Franklin, Mr. Tindale, and Aunt Denise, plus two team members from here to guide you and help in case of trouble."

Tammy says she and Luis will prepare the aircraft at the compound.

"After we capture Romli, we will bring him to one of the planes here and then on to Maplesville. As I said, anyone who wants to return to the United States from here or from Romli's camp will join us," Jena says.

"If Andy agrees," she continues, "we will take all three planes to Maplesville, where I hope we will expose the prison, the warden, the police department, and anyone else involved in this horrible scheme." Then, with urgency, she says. "We should leave now."

"We will land as close as we can to the compound, then continue on foot," Andy says.

Matty speaks up. "There is a secret entrance to the compound, one that Romli doesn't know about. My team and I use it to move people around without Romli knowing." She takes a firm step forward. "I need one more thing. I want Lero's body returned to the United States so that I can bury him properly." She turns to Andy. "Will you find a way to bring his body to me?"

Andy agrees.

"Then I suggest we get started," Jena says.

"I will command a team in one plane," Andy orders. "Veronica will command the plane with Jena and Matty. Both planes will land outside of Romli's camp and leave for the United States together. Rightpoint and Passionquest will drive a convoy to recover Moschi's body and return Pulue to this compound."

Rightpoint and Passionquest ask that they be allowed to leave immediately, and Andy agrees.

Jena tells Andy that she and Matty will go to the prison downstairs and collect the women who will return with them on the plane. They will also free Paula, who will accompany them on the mission.

Veronica agrees to help.

"May we be excused?" Jena asks Andy.

He nods.

Veronica leads the way as the women make their way downstairs to the detention area where Chance, Sharon, Suzanne, Aeo, and many others are being held. The area floor is covered with blood. In some cells, prisoners are lying on the floor.

Veronica and Jena approach the guards.

Matty stays back, staring into the cells at her team members. They stare at her like she is a traitor.

Veronica speaks to the guard. "We are taking some of the prisoners."

The guard nods.

"I will tell you who to release, but keep them handcuffed for our safety," Veronica says.

Jena whispers to Veronica, telling her which prisoners should be released. Veronica points to Chance, Suzanne, Sharon, Aeo, and Paula, who is relieved to see Matty and Jena. The guards handcuff each prisoner and bring each one out of the cell to face Veronica, Jena, and Matty. The prisoners have no idea what is happening. Matty walks toward Paula. Jena whispers to Veronica that Matty and Paula will be fine together.

"The rest of you follow me," Veronica says. "Chance, Jena will guard you."

Chance glares at Jena with hate. Jena has a slight smirk on her face.

"You prisoners will understand more as we go along," Veronica says.

They slowly make their way out of the detention area and up the stairs, with extra guards in front and back. When they reach the main floor, Veronica addresses the prisoners again.

"We are all taking a little trip. We will be flying to an undisclosed location," she says. "Prisoners will be guarded until further notice."

She asks the guards to take the prisoners, including Chance, to one of the compound's planes.

Matty turns Paula over to the guards, but not before whispering in her ear. "You'll soon be free," she says.

Paula looks relieved and confused.

Aeo is angry.

Chance is defiant.

Suzanne and Sharon just follow orders.

Veronica checks on Luis and Tammy, who are gathering weapons and supplies. She asks them, as well as Matty and Jena, to join her in a final meeting with Andy and other team members who are joining the mission.

Jake and Ken and the others, along with two team members, have already left for Franklin's plane.

"We are ready to embark on the next mission," Veronica tells Andy.

"We're ready, as well," Tammy says.

Andy approaches Matty. "We have taken care of Lero's body. We will take him back to the United States on my plane."

"Thank you," Matty replies sincerely.

Veronica, Matty, and Jena walk away. It is clear now that there will be no turning back. They head to the plane that will take them to Romli's camp.

The prisoners get chained to their seats.

Jena stops in front of Chance and stares, then sits down next to Matty.

Veronica goes forward to speak to the pilot privately.

"Where are we headed?" the pilot asks.

"To the outskirts of Romli's compound," she replies. "Once we land, I will need you and the guards to ensure the prisoners do not escape. Andy will have his plane land near us. I need you to stay in communication with the other two pilots."

The pilot nods and asks when they will leave.

"Now," Veronica says firmly.

The plane lands nearly as quickly as it takes off.

When they are at a complete stop, Matty, Jena, and Veronica prepare to hike to Romli's camp. Chance watches them closely; she has a good idea of what's going on but says nothing. Matty looks at Paula and whispers to Veronica, who tells one of the guards to remove Paula's handcuffs and unlock her from her seat. Paula can't contain her relief.

Three of the team members follow the women off of the plane, leaving Suzanne, Aeo, Sharon, and Chance behind with more guards and the pilot.

Once they get to the wooded area, Matty gathers them together.

"They can't see us here," she whispers. "I have a secret pathway. Follow me."

Matty leads them to the tunnel entrance. She raises one finger to stop the group. She looks around and listens for any movement and then waves the group on. A little farther along, she stops and turns around. She motions for Jena and Veronica to join her.

"When I was first brought here, Romli would send for me, but he didn't want anyone to know that he had women in his room, so he had a secret entrance. They closed up the entry a long time ago," she explains. "But I started re-opening it a little bit at a time, in secret, because I was going to kill him myself. The entry leads straight to Romli's room."

Matty tells them that when she fell in love with Lero, she never made good on her vow to kill Romli.

"Now, here we are. Romli is up in that room all alone," she says, her eyes wide with excitement. "You don't how many nights I wanted to sneak in here and finish him off."

Veronica and Jena step back with the intensity of her passion.

"I think it's destiny that I'm the one to go in there to kill him," Matty says as she starts to walk forward.

"Wait," Jena whispers urgently. "We're not here to kill Romli. We're here to capture him and take him back to face the women whose lives he, and others, destroyed."

Veronica touches Matty's shoulder lightly and sympathetically.

"There will be a time for vengeance, but that time is not now," she says.

Veronica takes the strategic lead again.

"Matty, guide me and Jena and one of the guards to Romli's room. The others will stay here to keep watch for us," she says.

Matty nods, devastated that she will not be able to take her revenge. But she steps forward, weapon over her shoulder, and leads the tight group through a small cave and then down a dark tunnel. One side of the tunnel is bricked up, and a portion looks different from the rest. At ground level is a hole that doesn't even look large enough for a body.

Matty kneels and crawls into the tiny space. She motions for the other three to follow. She puts her finger to her lips and warns them to be quiet.

When she comes to the end of the tight, dark tunnel, she knows there is a hidden door, which she opens quietly. As she does, she sees Romli fast asleep in his bed.

She smiles and is still smiling as she motions the others forward. Just as they had all been trained, they use stealth and restraint to enter the room and surround Romli's bed. He doesn't even blink.

They point their weapons at Romli, and Matty puts her weapon right up to Romli's cheek. She takes a deep breath and shoves the barrel deeper into his cheek.

He quickly opens his eyes to see Matty standing over him, daring him to make a sound. He also sees three people he doesn't know.

"Now, you listen very closely," Matty hisses. "We are going on a little trip far away from this evil wonderland you've created."

As she distracts him, the team member sent by Andy uses one swift motion to stab Romli with a needle. Everyone watches as he drifts away. Ironic, Matty thinks, needle and serum are the tools they used to bring her here.

When Romli is completely limp, Matty and the others strap on their weapons so they can begin moving Romli's body. Jena and Veronica start to lift him and look at each other in dismay.

"This will be impossible. He's too heavy. We will never be able to drag him through that tunnel," Veronica says.

Matty stands tall. "We won't have to. A narcissistic man like Romli would always have a way out in an emergency. He'd have no qualms about leaving everyone else behind," she says. "Besides, Lero once told me that Romli can leave his room through a secret door that takes him into the woods."

Matty starts turning in circles, looking for something out of place.

"Lero didn't know the location of the door, so we just have to find it," she says.

All four begin examining the walls and floor.

Jena spies a large picture of Romli himself, but she can't find anything unusual behind or around it. Matty keeps looking and sees a smaller picture of Romli, smiling. He never smiles, she tells the others. She takes the photo out of its frame, and behind it is a picture of Maria.

"This is Maria," Matty tells the others.

Despite their precarious circumstances, the others can't help craning their necks to see the pretty woman who was the love of both Romli's and Moschi's lives.

When Matty pulls at the frame, it comes away from the wall and reveals a button. She presses it, and a shelf begins to move. The wall moves, revealing an elevator large enough for just two people.

Jena shakes her head. "Romli had an elevator made, just for himself." She steps forward and looks at the others. "If you three can jam Romli's body in here with me, I'll ride down and then send the elevator back so you all can follow."

Once they are out of Romli's room, they'll have to find a way to recover Moschi's body, Veronica says.

"It will be too dangerous for Passionquest and Rightpoint to infiltrate the compound without Matty's help," Veronica says.

"Is there anyone here who you trust to help with Moschi?" Jena asks.

Matty nods. "I'll go back through the crawl space and find people to take care of Mochi's body. There are many people who want to get out of here. I'll have them take Moschi's body back to his compound, where his people can prepare for his burial."

"The team is coming," Veronica says.

"My people will be able to move more quickly," Matty says. "Trust me. Trust has gotten us this far, hasn't it?"

The other three nod.

"I'll find people to carry Moschi home, and I'll release Pulue if he's here," Matty says. "You three take Romli and meet the others. They can help you carry him back to the plane."

Veronica grabs a couple of sturdy blankets they can use to carry or drag Romli back to the plane. By now, Andy's plane will be nearby, too.

"I've got to move quickly," Matty says. "Give me an hour to get back to the plane. Don't leave without me."

She leaves the room the way she came.

Veronica, Jena, and their team member scramble to get Romli into the elevator with Jena.

The elevator opens into a tunnel that will lead them into the woods.

Matty makes her way out to quickly speak to Paula and the others who are watching the entrance to the secret passage.

"We have Romli," Matty says.

Paula sighs with relief.

"Go about fifty yards out into the woods, and they'll run right into you. You can help them get Romli to the plane," Matty explains. "Go now and be quiet."

"What about you?" Paula asks.

"Don't worry," Matty says bravely. "I have a plan. You all just go."

She watches for a minute to make sure they are following her instructions and then follows another path that leads to another cave that leads to the back entrance of the men's quarters. Matty quickly sneaks into the quarters and to the bed of her old friend, Risata. She kneels and whispers his name, and then whispers again, before he wakes up and jumps.

He sees Matty and knows that he'd best be quiet.

"Matty, what are you doing here?" he asks.

"Romli has been captured, and Lero died in battle," Matty tells him.

"What?" Risata can't believe what he hears.

"It's true," Matty says. "I need your help."

"Anything," her friend replies.

"Have Pulue and two others been captured?" she asks.

"Yes," Risata says. "They are in the stockade."

Risata quietly gets out of bed and gets dressed. Matty asks him to take her to Pulue. Without further questions, Risata agrees readily.

"Follow me," he says.

They pass guards, but no one stops or questions them. After all, this is where they belong—or so the guards think—as they make their way to Pulue.

CHAPTER THIRTY-THREE

Matty stands in front of Pulue's cell with Risata.

"I'm here to free you and your men," Matty says to a bewildered Pulue. She continues, hoping to gain Pulue's trust. "I am Matty. Jena Parker and your teammate Andy sent me. Romli has been captured. I have joined Veronica, Andy, and your people to help Jena with her mission. It's very complicated—too complicated to explain now."

She sees bewilderment in Pulue's face, so she says, "My job is getting you out of here." Then she turns to Risata. "I need you to gather your most loyal and deserving team members."

Risata gives her a hard look. "That would be everyone in the compound."

"Even better," Matty says. "Just make sure someone goes to the women's quarters and gets the only woman still there. Her name is Tonya. She's injured and didn't go to battle with us."

Matty asks Risata to open the cell, and he turns the big key in the lock, and the door swings open.

"Thank you for your help, Risata," Matty says.

"Yes, thank you, sir," Pulue says. "And thank you, ma'am, whoever you are."

Matty smiles.

She turns to Risata. "After you gather your people, take this man and his two team members and Moschi's body and return them to Moschi's compound. You will be welcomed there." Matty turns to Pulue. "I was one of Romli's soldiers. We just waged war on your compound and were defeated."

"And you are here because …?" Pulue asks.

"It's a long story. If you know Jena Parker, perhaps you can imagine." Matty says, smiling a little. "Jena told your people a long story about how women are being kidnapped from her hometown and sold to people like Romli. I can attest that she is telling the truth because I am one of those women. Perhaps you, too, are aware that what she's saying is true."

Pulue sighs, entirely aware of Jena's history and the kidnapping scheme.

"She has an even more complicated plan to take Romli, some of your people, and some of the women who were kidnapped back to her town to see that Romli and the other perpetrators are punished," Matty says breathlessly.

Pulue nods, not as surprised as Matty expected. "I must go with you," he says.

Now Matty is taken aback.

Pulue tells his men to follow Risata and his people back to the compound, after securing Moschi's body so that they can take his remains with them.

"You may run into a team of people sent by Andy," Matty says. "If you do, just turn them around. They won't doubt your intent because you will have Moschi's body and Pulue's men with you."

Then, Risata leads Matty and Pulue out of the compound safely.

When they reach the outer edges of the compound, Matty looks at Risata with affection and concern.

"I will take care of everything, Matty," Risata says. "Don't worry."

Matty takes Risata's arm, gently.

"I can't say that you are safe. Even without Romli, this is a dangerous place," Matty says. "But you—and everyone you take with you—are free. You belong to no one. As I said, you will be welcomed at Pulue's compound, but you are no man's slave."

Pulue shakes Risata's hand. "What she says is true. You saved my life. I owe you a debt."

Risata and Matty grasp hands one more time, and then she and Pulue take off quickly in the direction of the plane. Once they are into the woods, Matty dials her radio into a channel the other members of the team are using.

"Mission accomplished," Matty speaks into the radio. "Pulue is free, and Moschi's body will be taken home. ... Copy that?" She speaks again, "Andy, come in?"

"Andy here," he answers.

"A loyal group of friends from Romli's camp will bring Moschi's body and Pulue's men to your compound. ... Copy?"

"Copy," Andy says. "I will turn our team around. Your people will be welcomed."

"Copy that," Matty says.

"This is Franklin. Copy."

"Copy," Veronica echoes.

"I'm on my way to you, Veronica. And I'm bringing someone with me," Matty says. "Copy?"

"Copy that," Jena replies. "We're safe back at home base, and we have the package. We're just waiting for you."

Andy shares the good news with Luis, Tammy, and their team, and then he directs the pilot to take off again, leaving Romli's territory to join Franklin.

Jena, Veronica, Paula, and their team, along with the prisoners, wait for Matty.

Franklin shares the good news with Jake, Ken, Denise, and Mr. Tindale. He kicks Chief Reyes lightly when he walks past him.

"Miss us?" he asks sarcastically.

Franklin tells the pilot to get the plane ready for flight.

Matty and Pulue reach Veronica's plane, and Jena is standing at the entry. She stares at Pulue.

"Hello, Jena," he says lightly.

Jena doesn't know what to say.

Pulue can't stop looking at the drugged Romli.

"I can't believe you captured him," Pulue says, shaking his head.

"Romli is at the heart of the evil," Jena says. "We're going back to where this started."

Pulue nods. "So, I hear."

"When this is settled, you can come back here if you please," Jena says. "All of you can come back if that's what you want. But I will be free, and, hopefully, justice will prevail."

Jena looks at Matty with gratitude. Then she looks at Veronica and Paula and the others.

"I can't thank you all enough," Jena says. "You believed in me and put your lives on the line. Now we're heading to Maplesville, where we will be joined by Andy, in one plane, and my friends, in Franklin's plane."

Without further discussion, the pilot's voice echoes through the airplane.

"Are we ready for takeoff?" he asks.

"Yes," Veronica says with confidence as two team members pull up the staircase and close the plane's door.

"Stay away from the radar," Veronica tells the pilot. "Head for the United States ... Maplesville."

"We'll have to make some stops," Jena says mysteriously. "Final destination, Luttonville County Penitentiary."

"Yes, ma'am," the pilot answers.

Veronica goes forward and tells her pilot to stay in touch with the pilots of the other two planes. Once contact is made and the route is set, Veronica tells him, he should use the scrambler so that radar towers can't track them.

The three pilots find a radio channel where they can communicate without being heard by anyone else.

"All planes are in the air and bound for Maplesville," the pilot announces over the intercom.

Jena calls Veronica over to sit next to her when she comes back to the main cabin.

"I need to make a special stop. The pilots need to land so you and I can get off," Jena says.

Veronica asks why.

"We have to pay someone a visit," Jena says vaguely. "Let's sleep for a couple of hours, and then I'll tell you about it."

***

When Jena sees that Veronica is awake, she grabs a bottle of water for everyone on the plane, then sits down again.

"Okay, where are we going?" Veronica asks.

"To the home of the mayor of Maplesville," Jena says.

Veronica doesn't even express surprise at this point.

"I need to see if you can clear the way for us to land next to his house without being seen, while the other planes circle us," Jena says.

Veronica takes a seat where she can't be overheard and makes a call to someone Moschi used when he was bringing planes in and out of the area.

After a while, Veronica comes back. She's frowning.

"No go," Veronica says. "Our contacts say that ever since you picked up Chief Reyes, Maplesville is swarming with police, detectives, and even the FBI." She shrugs. "There's no way to land without being discovered."

"Okay," Jena says, unconcerned.

Veronica looks at her sideways. "That's not the reaction I was expecting."

"We'll parachute in," Jena says, as if she's suggesting a day at the beach.

Veronica just shakes her head in disbelief, and Jena goes to the cockpit to pick a location where the two women can parachute in.

She shows the pilot where the house is located, and the two decide on an altitude and a good place for Veronica and Jena to land.

Veronica has already pulled out the parachute gear. She and Jena suit up.

Everyone on the plane is curious but stays quiet.

Romli is still out cold.

Paula is asleep with a huge smile on her face.

"Dreaming of her little girl," Jena thinks to herself. She and Paula have come a long way since they shared a prison cell.

Only Matty gets up to speak to Jena and Veronica.

"What's she talked you into now?" Matty asks Veronica.

They all smile.

"Matty, thank you. I'm sorry about Lero," Jena says.

Matty looks sad as she thinks of her lover. "Thank you, Jena. Whatever happens, we're free. I don't think that could have happened without you."

Veronica and Matty grasp hands.

"Thank you for rescuing Pulue and our men," Veronica says. "Thank you for trusting us."

She brings Matty in close. "If you don't hear from Jena and me, you are this team's leader. I've already told the pilot. I haven't told the others, but I don't think you'll have a problem." She pauses, then says, "Watch that Chance, though."

"Oh, I know all about that one," Matty agrees firmly. "Thank you. I will take care of our people if the need arises."

"You know what needs to happen at the prison, right?" Jena asks.

Matty nods.

Without further chit-chat, Veronica and Jena stand by the airplane's front exit.

"Everyone buckle up and hold onto your seats, the force of this air is going to try to suck you out," Veronica orders.

She points to three strong team members who will open the door and then close it as quickly as possible after they jump.

Small objects fly around the plane as the door opens.

Veronica gives Jena a thumb's up and jumps.

Jena follows.

The jump is long enough for both women to enjoy floating toward the earth.

Both land safely in an open, grassy area about a mile from the mayor's house.

Jena and Veronica drop their parachutes and put their rucksacks and weapons on their backs.

"Let's do it," Veronica says, amped up from her ride through the sky. "Lead the way."

When they reach the gate to the mayor's estate, Veronica uses the radio to give Andy, Franklin, and the pilots their status.

"We'll let you know when we have our target. Copy?" Veronica says.

"Copy that," Andy and Franklin reply.

Jake, Mr. Tindale, and Ken are staring at Franklin.

"You're really into this, aren't you?" Ken asks.

"You have to admit this whole thing makes for a great novel," Franklin replies. "My girl, Reda Jones, is going to finish up this story with a bang."

Mr. Tindale just shakes his head.

"Come on, who doesn't think this is a bestseller?" Franklin asserts.

No one answers, but he doesn't notice.

On the ground, Jena and Veronica have reached the back entrance to the mayor's house.

"This guy is living large, isn't he?" Veronica says.

"He's not counting pennies, that's for sure," Jena jokes, as she searches for a way in.

"Let's see. Where would the mayor be sleeping?" Jena asks.

They both look up.

"Top floor," Jena says. "You feel like climbing?"

"Wait," Veronica says. "What was it that Matty said? A narcissistic man wants a special entrance in and out."

Jena laughs out loud.

"Jena, look. Car lights," Veronica says.

A black stretch limousine pulls up in front of the mayor's door. The driver gets out, opens the door, and the mayor steps out dressed like he's come from a charity ball.

"Could we get any luckier?" Jena whispers.

The mayor stumbles a little, and the driver reaches out to help him. But the mayor is belligerent.

"Get your hands off of me," he grunts rudely as he tries to unlock his door.

Jena and Veronica watch but stay hidden in the shadows as the driver gets back into the limousine and pulls back onto the street.

The mayor finally manages to get into his house. The foyer lights come on. The upstairs lights go on next, then they go off.

"How much do you want to bet that he didn't lock that front door," Veronica says as they creep toward the entry.

She's right.

They walk right through the door and up the stairs to the master bedroom. The door is open. He's lying flat on his back, snoring with his mouth wide open. They smell alcohol on his breath.

Jena and Veronica stand over him.

"Oh, mayor," Jena calls in a sweet voice.

He's sound asleep.

"Mayor Cannon Russ," Jena calls again.

The mayor opens one eye and then squints at the two women.

Veronica points her weapon at him, as Jena leans closer.

"Are you wondering who I am?" Jena asks. "I'm Jena Parker."

With that, she punches the mayor hard enough to knock him out.

"He probably didn't even feel that" Jena says.

"Now what?" Veronica asks.

"We find his keys, get him into his car, and then we head to the prison to meet the others," Jena says. "This guy and the other scumbags will be right where they belong."

Up in the sky, Chance is getting rude.

"How much longer are we going to be stuck in this freakin' airplane?" she complains.

"Shut your mouth!" Matty yells back. "You're not in any position to ask any questions."

In Franklin's plane, Denise is staring at Chief Reyes.

Reyes is cranky and sore from being tied up for so long. He stares back at Denise.

"You know that your niece is evil, right?" Reyes snaps at her.

"If she's evil, then I don't even have words to describe you," Denise snaps back.

"That may be true, but I certainly wouldn't kill my own mother," Reyes says.

"Don't you say another word!" Ken demands. "The ones to blame for this trail of bodies are you, your buddies on the police force, Warden Peters, the mayor, and probably a few more of your cronies."

Ken looks at Jake for support.

"If it weren't for you, we wouldn't be here," Jake says.

Reyes, shooting Ken a dirty look and swearing under his breath, taunts, "You guys think you're winning."

"I'd say that's true," Ken pops back.

Reyes laughs out loud. Everyone on the airplane stares at him.

"You really have lost your mind," Franklin says.

"Nope," Reyes says. "I've got my whole mind."

The others aren't really interested in what Reyes has to say, but they can't help listening anyway.

"You guys actually think you're saving the day," Reyes says. "Truthfully, you did me a favor by kidnapping me. This is a lot bigger than Romli, Moschi, Pulue, the mayor, me … or the warden. Yeah, I'm a little beat up." He laughs even louder. "Heck, I'm real beat up. You're probably better off just killing me right now. But just know that you're not winning anything."

Jake, Ken, Mr. Tindale, and Franklin exchange knowing glances. Bolstered by each other's company, they nod, silently agreeing that Reyes is an idiot—not to mention a murderer.

"Something does tell me that there's more to this than we know," Ken whispers to Jake.

Back on the ground, Jena and Veronica have succeeded in getting the mayor into his own car. Jena is in the driver's seat. Veronica is in back in case the mayor wakes up. She gets back on the radio.

"We've got the package. Mission accomplished," Veronica says. "Copy?"

"Copy that," Franklin says.

"Who's the package?" Reyes asks.

Jena hears him. She'd enjoy telling him but doesn't want to say anything over the radio.

Reyes shrugs.

"Next stop, Luttonville County Penitentiary," Jena says into the radio. "Let's roll."

"Copy that," Franklin says.

"Copy that," Andy chimes in. "Get as close as you can, while still staying safe and out of sight."

"This is about to get good," Franklin says, as three planes and the mayor's car bear down on the prison.

Jake approaches Reyes. "This is your last chance, man. Who else is involved?"

Reyes laughs at Jake. "Kill me now, dude. I've got nothing to gain by telling what you think you already know."

Jake shakes his head. "Why can't you just do the right thing?"

"Because I was born wrong," Reyes yells back.

"Who else? Senators? Governors?" Jake pushes.

Reyes glares at Jake, and Jake looks toward Ken, Mr. Tindale, and Franklin, who are all listening.

"Like I said, this is way bigger than you guys think. I'm already a dead man. You guys are just playing along with the game," Reyes says in his sleaziest voice.

No one says a word, except Franklin, who is never at a loss for words.

"Stories never end, man," Franklin says. "Stories just go on and on." They all roll their eyes at Franklin. Franklin gives them all a dirty look. "It's not that I don't want this story to end. But there's always another plot, more characters."

Jake sits back and sighs deeply.

"We've come this far, we're going to keep rockin'," Franklin says, rubbing his chin and looking at Reyes. "Your character might just make it into another book."

Reyes looks the other way.

Jake's nerves get the best of him. He stands, holding onto his seat to keep his balance.

"This is no time to play, Franklin," he says. "We're about to take part in a battle that's worse than the one we just finished. I can't believe we're still alive." He moves toward Mr. Tindale. "Even your butler is a soldier now."

"Hey!" Mr. Tindale says, defending himself. "I worked my butt off to train as a gourmet chef. I've worked for some of the most important people in the world." He shrugs. "I took a salary cut and a cut in stature to work for Mr. Bosler here."

"Huh?" Franklin objects.

"No offense, sir," Mr. Tindale says. "I got married. I work in a peaceful place—well, usually peaceful. Some of my previous employers were smug and ungrateful."

"No offense taken, Mr. Tindale," Franklin says. "You took good care of my parents, and you've taken good care of me. I couldn't have asked for a better friend, employee, or family member."

Mr. Tindale blushes. "Thank you, sir."

Back on the ground, Jena is speeding down the highway.

"Slow down," Veronica says sternly. "We don't want to get stopped by the cops." Over the radio, she says, "All pilots, please provide your status." She learns that everyone is on schedule. "When you land, everyone, but the pilots, exits the plane. Wait for us to arrive. Everyone, follow Jena."

"Jena, we are ready," Franklin sounds back.

"We're ready to march," Andy says.

"We're a go here," Matty says.

A pilot cuts in. "We have to find a safe spot to land."

"Land on the grounds of the prison," Jena says.

"Too dangerous," the pilot insists.

"Make it happen," Jena demands. "We have to get as close as possible."

The airplanes land a few miles from the prison.

Jena pulls up right behind them.

So begins the effort of getting teams, weapons, and prisoners off the planes.

Matty wakes Romli. "Wake up, sleeping beauty."

Romli opens his eyes. "You betrayed me," he says immediately.

"That shouldn't be a surprise," she spits back at him. "Now get up."

Reyes remains defiant, yelling, "What are you maniacs doing?"

Meanwhile, in the mayor's car, where he is still knocked out, Jena addresses the teams.

"We're about three miles from the prison. We couldn't get the planes any closer," Jena says. "We'll shove Reyes and Romli into this car with the mayor. Aunt Denise, we'll need you to ride along and keep a gun on Reyes, and Mr. Tindale can ride with me, too, in the back seat."

The planes land. The mayor's SUV pulls up.

"Start walking, everyone," Andy commands. "Franklin, Jake, and Ken, you three keep a watch on Suzanne, Sharon, and Aeo. Matty, you cover Chance."

Chance gives Jena an evil stare, which Jena ignores.

"Let's go," Andy says to the group of twenty or so team members, not including those who are handcuffed.

In the mayor's big SUV, Veronica speeds toward the prison. Mr. Tindale sits in the back seat guarding Romli, who sits up front.

In the back seat, Jena taunts the mayor, who sits next to Denise.

"Oh, mayor," Jena says sweetly.

The mayor opens his eyes. "What's going on here?" he yells, startled, his eyes widening in disbelief when he recognizes his captor. "Jena Parker."

"That's right, I'm Jena Parker—*the* Jena Parker," she says.

"Veronica, pull over," Jena says. "Me and the mayor are going to make a phone call."

Veronica pulls over, and Jena and Mr. Tindale push and pull the mayor out of the SUV.

Franklin, walking toward the prison with the team, decides they need more manpower and pulls out his phone.

"I'm gonna call my boys," he says, calling Steve, Bobby, Allen, and Sam and asking them to meet him at the prison.

"No problem," Bobby says, without asking a single question.

Jena pulls out the mayor's phone, which she grabbed when they were in his bedroom.

"Call the warden," she says in her most threatening voice.

The mayor just stares at her.

"I said, dial the warden and tell him to meet you at the prison," she says again.

"He's already at the prison," Mayor Russ says. "He doesn't leave until midnight."

"Are you telling me the truth?" she asks, badgering him.

He refuses to answer.

She points her gun at his head.

"Yes. Yes, he's there," the mayor says.

Veronica parks as close to the prison as she can without being spotted. She dims the lights and turns off the car.

"This is how it's going to go down," Jena says. "Veronica, you and Denise keep Reyes and Romli close. If they run, just shoot them."

The mayor looks at Jena like she's crazy.

"Mr. Tindale, you stick with me, and we'll walk in with the mayor," she says. Jena turns to the mayor and pretends to be coy. "Now, Mayor Russ, I know that you understand the severity of this situation. This is no time to play hero. Just leave that part up to us."

Reyes eyes Jena through the rearview mirror. He looks into the mayor's panicked eyes.

"Jena, there are two guards pacing out front," Veronica says.

"Mr. Mayor, you and I and Mr. Tindale are going to walk to the front of the prison, and you are going to tell those two guards to stand down and give us their keys and weapons," Jena says.

"I've got a better idea," Veronica says. "I'll take care of it." She aims her weapon, fires two shots, and hits both guards. With a tinge of pride and sarcasm, she says, "I'm an expert, trained by the best teacher of assassins in the world—Moschi."

She looks at Mr. Tindale and commands, "Run and get the keys before the other guards figure out what's going on."

Mr. Tindale is still in shock from the gunshots.

"I said run," she yells.

Mr. Tindale runs.

"Holy crap," the mayor whispers.

Franklin and his team, Matty and her team and prisoners, and Andy and his team from the compound walk up just as Mr. Tindale runs back breathlessly with the keys and the guns.

Jena puts Andy and Matty in charge of dragging Romli into the prison. She asks Mr. Tindale and Luis to guard Reyes and bring him along.

Jena and the mayor enter the prison with the dead guards' keys—her friends, her teams, her enemies, and her prisoners walk behind her.

She knows exactly where she's going—to the office of Warden Phillip Peters.

They force the guards they encounter to hand over their weapons, keys, and radios. They take three of them prisoner.

"Knock on the door," Jena tells one of them.

He knocks.

"What is it!" the warden yells, impatient as ever.

The guard hesitates, opens the door, and hesitates again when he sees the desperation in the mayor's eyes.

"Uh …" the guard ad-libs. "It's just a situation I need to talk to you about."

"Come in," Peters says wearily.

Veronica pushes the guard out of the way and kicks in the door. She points her weapon at Warden Peters.

Jena motions for Andy and Matty to position Romli beside Peters and tells Luis and Mr. Tindale to do the same with Reyes. Jena pushes the mayor toward the others, who are standing in front of the window and behind the warden's desk.

All of Jena's friends have all of their guns aimed directly at their captives.

The warden's mouth is agape as team member after team member walks into the room.

Pulue walks in.

Paula enters, weapon drawn.

Jake, Denise, Ken, Mr. Tindale, and Franklin enter.

Other team members push Chance, Suzanne, Sharon, and Aeo into the room.

Everyone else surges in behind them.

"Keep your hands where I can see them!" Veronica yells at the warden and the mayor.

Romli and Reyes are still tied up at their wrists and ankles.

Jena turns to Andy and tells him to release the women prisoners. She turns to Suzanne, Sharon, Chance, and Paula, who is not handcuffed.

"You were all in prison here. Either you will join us and fight, or you will fall with the warden and our enemies," she warns. "You can fight and be free, or you can stay and leave your fate to these men."

The women all nod eagerly. They are happy to fight.

"Give me a gun. I'm with you guys," Aeo shouts.

Jena looks at Chance. "I know you hate me, but we must free all of the women in this prison. You know what it's like here."

"I'm with you," Suzanne says.

"Me, too," says Paula.

"Hell, yeah," Sharon echoes.

Chance and Jena just stare at one another.

"Open the cells. Let those women be free," Jena orders.

The warden looks ready to faint but still summons the strength to yell, "You can't do that!"

Jena turns to the warden. "Just watch us!"

Andy and Luis lead the way. Chance, Sharon, Suzanne, and Aeo are not given weapons, but eagerly follow the teams.

"We need to find the main switch that opens all of the cell doors," Andy tells one of the guards. "I think you know where we can find it."

With twenty or more weapons pointed at him, the guard leads them to the switch.

Andy pulls the lever.

But the guard also pulls the lever for a universal alarm, which will announce that there is a prison riot to all of the guards, the police department, and all law enforcement within a twenty-mile radius.

"Now why did you go and do that?" Andy snarls before shooting the guard dead.

Jena smiles when she hears the alarm.

The warden falls to his knees. "What have you done?" he asks plaintively.

"My guess is that one of your guys set it off, but it's fine with me," she says. "But what am *I* doing? I am righting a wrong. Every one of you had a part in falsely imprisoning women, kidnapping them, and then selling them to assassins in South America."

Jena waves her weapon around, pointing it at the mayor, then Reyes, then at the warden, and Romli.

"And it all started in this crazy town," Jena says. "These women became assassins, whores, servants, and slaves for ruthless men— and sold to those men by ruthless men here."

Pulue steps forward and says, "I am as guilty as these men. But Moschi started out honorably. He tried to help those who were trapped in this town. That's why he took Jena away."

He looks at Jena and remembers the last time he was in this office when he came to spirit Jena away for Moschi.

"But killers kill," Pulue goes on, looking from Veronica to Jena. "Moschi is martyred now. In the end, I can't say that he and I were so much different than Romli and others like him. We did not buy kidnapped women, and we treated our people like family."

He stops and after a long pause, he says gravely, "The house of Moschi stands proudly behind Jena Parker today, and we will accept whatever fate may come."

As Pulue is speaking, the entire police force, fire trucks, ambulances, and the local news crews are all pulling up to the front of the prison.

Jena, Matty, and Veronica look out the window from their vantage point in front of the warden and the others. They see a frenzy of blue and red flashing lights.

"What now?" Matty asks.

Jena turns to them. "We let the fighters fight," she says. "We would all join them, but we can't leave these vultures here alone."

The prison is in chaos. Prisoners roam the halls looking for exits.

Police officers are waiting outside. News reporters are on air, the cameras filming the entire scene. Their reporting emerges on television screens throughout the county.

Jesse—Sherry Paterson's sister and Jake's aunt—is watching it all unfold. She calls to Sherry to come watch.

"There's a prison break," Jesse says excitedly.

One news reporter is speaking: "We are told by sources inside the prison that Mayor Cannon Russ is being held hostage by the recently released Jena Parker, who was convicted and later exonerated of murder charges against her."

Sherry Paterson gasps at the sound of Jena Parker's name. She says Jena's name out loud. Then she screams Jake's name.

"Get your shoes!" Sherry yells at Jesse. "We're going to the prison!"

A nurse in Mike Fredmond's room in the Intensive Care Unit is watching the news coverage with her patient.

Mike, who has been recovering well, tries to stand.

"I need to get to the prison," he says earnestly.

Dr. Charter walks in and, motioning for Mike to stop, says, "Wait, we found something. I need to talk to you."

Mike sits down and stares at the doctor. "What?"

"You might want to get back in bed," the doctor advises.

Detective Dean Martin and his team are on the scene.

The "You bag 'em. We send 'em" brothers are on the phone with Franklin and say they're at the back door to the prison.

"The cops are in the front," Allen says. "What do we do?"

Franklin shouts so Allen can hear him. "It's crazy in here. It may not be safe."

"We're not scared," Allen says. "The brothers are never scared. We're coming in."

The inmates are attacking and fighting the guards. Years of abuse have taken a toll. The inmates want their tormentors to know what it's like to be kicked and punched.

The riot continues for hours.

Police officers, detectives, and fire crews try to get through the prison doors. But the doors are barricaded.

When Sherry and Jesse reach the prison, they push their way through the crowd and past the news reporters. Sherry brazenly walks toward the prison doors.

"Hey, lady, stand down!" one police officer shouts.

When she doesn't stop, he points his weapon at her.

"My son is in there!" Sherry shouts. "Come on, Jesse."

"Lady, I'm going to tell you one more time. If you don't move to the back of the crowd, I'm going to arrest you," he says.

Jesse pulls on Sherry's arm and yells over the din of the crowd. "I don't want to get shot today!"

In the warden's office, Jena turns to the four men she blames most for this web of deceit and pain—Romli, Mayor Cannon Russ, Warden Phillip Peters, and Chief Reyes.

Brandishing her gun at them one by one, she orders, "Start walking."

The four men look at each other.

"I said, start walking," Jena orders again.

They begin to move, in a line, slowly.

"Matty and Veronica, keep your weapons aimed at them," Jena says, then to the men: "Here's what comes next. The four of you are going to turn yourselves in to authorities. You're going to admit that you are guilty of many crimes and that this prison riot should be blamed on you, not the women."

Jena tells them that they must ask the state Department of Justice to review all of the cases of all of the women sent to this prison for the last twenty years.

"Women who were wrongly imprisoned, or victimized while they were here, will be released and compensated for all that has been taken from them and their families," she says, then demands loudly, "Am I clear?"

The men eye each other. They know that they face embarrassment, endless news coverage, prison, or even a bullet.

"Even if we do as you say, how do we stop this prison riot?" the warden asks. "You've started a war. These women aren't going to just stop fighting."

"They will stop for justice," Jena says. "Get on that intercom, warden, and turn yourself in."

The warden bows his head and looks at the men who stand with him.

He receives no help from any quarter.

Peters leans over his desk, hits a button, and speaks into the intercom, his voice echoing throughout the prison. A speaker is positioned outside, as well.

"This is Warden Peters," he says hesitantly. "I am speaking to my guards, to the police, to anyone who can hear my voice."

The fighting stops. Everyone, inside and out, is listening.

The news crews are still reporting.

"Again. This is Warden Phillip Peters. I have been warden of this penitentiary for thirty years. There has been …" he hesitates. "There has been wrong committed in many towns around this prison, including Maplesville." He stops. His mouth is so dry that he can barely continue.

"Women have been wrongfully imprisoned here," he continues. "Not all women are innocent, but many are. And many have been kidnapped from this prison and taken to South America."

The warden sees Romli and Reyes out of the corner of his eye and knows one or both of them would happily put a bullet in his head if they could.

"Families were told that their loved ones were dead, even though many were not."

Detective Martin stares at the police officers listening and wonders how many of them have taken part in this corruption.

"Mayor Russ, Chief Reyes, myself, and many law enforcement officers and prison guards have been involved. Miles McNeil, now deceased, and others were involved in the past. We aligned ourselves with criminal organizations in South America, including one man in this office, that enslave their own people and our people for their own self-interest."

He stops, clears his throat, and goes on with his confession and commands.

"I am asking that all women be set free from this prison— guilty or not—and that their cases be examined and adjudicated appropriately."

Jena and Matty don't realize that they have been holding their breath, not truly believing what is happening right in front of them. Matty's eyes are glassy with tears.

"I ask that all guards and prisoners please stand down. I am admitting guilt, in part, so that the violence can stop and that the process of justice can start in peace."

The warden takes his hand off the intercom button.

There is silence, inside and out.

"Let's go—all of you," Jena says.

The mayor, Romli, Reyes, and Peters all fall in line to be escorted out of the prison by Jena, Veronica, and Matty. They move in slow motion. Matty leads. Veronica and Jena follow. Pulue, they realize, has disappeared. They walk past guards and past rows and rows of women—some on their knees, crying, some glaring at the warden and Reyes.

Franklin, Jake, Ken, Mr. Tindale, Denise, Suzanne, Sharon, Aeo, Chance, Paula, and the brothers follow Jena out the prison doors.

Outside the prison, Paula runs to stand beside Matty and holds onto her while tears run down her cheeks.

It's usually police officers and guards who escort women in and out of these doors. Now the tables are turned.

Detective Martin and his men step forward to take the four offenders into custody.

Jena lays down her weapon, and many of her cohorts do the same.

News crews are everywhere, documenting the astounding procession.

One by one, women walk out the doors to freedom—some only temporarily, some for the rest of their lives.

Jake runs to Jena. He picks her up in the air and swings her around and around.

At last, she can feel the freedom. At last, she can hear the wheels of justice beginning to turn. At last, she can feel the darkness within her fade away.

"You did it, baby!" Jake yells at the top of his lungs. "I love you so much. We'll never be apart again."

CHAPTER THIRTY-FOUR

Jake lies in bed and opens his eyes slowly.

He can hear Jena downstairs, singing. "If I can't have you, I don't want nobody, baby ..." Her beautiful voice. He is so grateful for the sound. He can't count the number of times he could have lost her forever.

"I'll be right there," he yells to her as he runs down the stairs and opens the front door. The easy breeze caresses his cheeks, and he smiles—overwhelmed with love and happiness.

"I'll be right back, sweetheart, I'm just going to check the mail," he yells to his love.

He waves to neighbors, who all ask about Jena.

"She's great," he replies over and over. "Have a great day!"

Mail in hand, he looks at the beautiful morning one more time. He walks into the house, closes the door, and starts going through the mail. Jake opens an official-looking letter.

"Dear Mr. Jake Paterson: You are listed as the contact person for Miss Jena Parker. We regret to inform you that Miss Parker died yesterday. We attempted to reach you by phone but were not able to do so."

Jake runs to the kitchen, but it is empty. He runs from room to room calling Jena's name. Finally, he stands in the foyer screaming, heartbroken, as loud as he can, "Jena!"

He runs to the bathroom to splash water on his face. When he looks in the mirror, he sees an old man with gray hair and a knotted brow. He begins to shout again.

A nurse arrives, Jake thinks, from nowhere.

"Mr. Paterson, please try to be calm," she says kindly.

"Where's Jena? Where is my perfect Jena?" he begs.

He is sobbing one minute and calling Jena's name the next.

The nurse makes soothing noises and gently takes his hand.

"Mr. Paterson, we've talked about this. Jena died in prison many years ago from natural causes. Don't you remember the story you told me so many times?"

The older Jake sits still, the nurse sitting in a chair next to him.

"You told me you wrote Jena many times, but she never returned your letters," the nurse says. "You were devasted. You even tried to go see her at the prison hundreds of times, but she refused to see you. More ten years went by until you received a letter from her, still in the prison."

The older Jake, eyes filled with tears, stares up at the nurse in denial. He doesn't want to accept that years have gone by and he hadn't seen Jena since she went to prison. The nurse had read the letter to him many times, but he always asked her to stop before finishing.

With a grim face, Jake settles more deeply into the chair. "Would you read that letter... again?" he asks in a calm voice.

The nurse hesitates.

"Please," he pleads.

The nurse slowly stands up, walks to the nightstand next to his bed, where Jake keeps the letter, where he has always kept it, near a picture of him and Jena in high school. The two of them smiling after graduation.

The nurse picks up the envelope, opens it, and begins unfolding the letter.

She glances at Jake, who nods for her to proceed.

My Dearest Jake,

First, I want to tell you I love so much, and I think about you every single day! I miss you! Being away from you has been one of the hardest things I have ever had to do, but my own doings are worse, I know.

I am sorry I returned all your letters, but I knew I had to. I knew that if we began writing back and forth, you would never let me go. You would never live a life for yourself, so I felt I had to force that on you. Or, at least, I tried.

I know how stubborn you are.

You are so much gentler than I am. I long to kiss your sweet lips, to touch your body and see that incredibly beautiful smile of yours.

I think about the last time we made love and how special every single second of it was. You completed me in a way no other person on this Earth could.

Your happiness means everything to me, and I know that you love me just as much as I love you. I know it is your unconditional love that has shielded and protected me through all of this.

I felt at times I did not deserve such as wonderful and caring man, more than that: a friend I have known since we were little children playing without any of the worries of the world. You are my best friend and the love of my life.

You do not know how many times I have plotted to escape this place just to be with you for a moment. It has been so hard, my love, so hard. I have cried and even thought of taking my own life.

But I knew my soul must find some kind of resolution. That I had to take responsibility for all the worst parts of me, the evil. I have found the spirit of light, God's power, and prayed for forgiveness and mercy for my soul.

I know I cannot take back everything, but I have been doing my best to be a force of good. I am a true believer that we all are given the opportunity to become what it means to be a good person.

Chance and I have become good friends again. She, too, has come to her own revelation to find peace in her heart and soul. Whenever possible, Chance and I talk, pray, and help one another through this most different, yet redemptive, process for both of us.

She cries thinking about what she did to Carol. There are times I cannot console her because I'm still working through my own deeds, as well as my mother.

In prison, I have gained a lot of good skills. I cook, clean, make things that I never thought I could. And although I don't have any children, I get to see pictures of other inmates' children while they share their stories of missing them—and I fantasize about what you and I would be like as parents with kids running around. Kids that look like us, you, and me.

Most of all, I have gotten to know some good people, women with some of the most difficult stories to listen to, stories that come from passionate hearts seeking redemption for their souls, too.

I've have attended church services, singing spiritual and gospel songs. Sitting quietly listening to the words of the prison preacher, which I find to be comforting. I have become a spiritual mentor, learning the words of wisdom, helping others like me who felt like lost souls, abandoned, as we all seek a higher purpose than what this Earth has revealed to us.

I believe there is dark and light within all of us, yet we must choose which direction we want our souls to gravitate.

Inspired by our old friend, Franklin, that bizarre author, I have written poems. (I have enclosed a few with this letter.) The poems are expressive of my deep love for you. They are all for you. Every word and sentence are for you. I guess Franklin, as an author/writer, rubbed off on me, but the poems came about because I missed you so much that I had to find an outlet to express my emotions.

I have been to the prison medical ward a few times. There seems to be something wrong, a pain on my side, off and on. But I am all right.

I will write to you again, my sweet Jake. Just know I will love you always and forever.

Yours forever, Jena.

Jake listens as the nurse reads the letter. He hears Jena's voice, tears streaming down his face.

Suddenly, in the bright sunlight reflecting off of the bathroom mirror, he sees Jena.

Beautiful Jena, in a flowing white dress. Her hair caught by the breeze. She glows as a pure light angel just the way he saw her before.

Jena reaches her arms out to Jake to come to her.

Jake smiles and slowly lifts one of his hands to reach back. His spiritual body rises from the chair.

The young dashing Jake is standing with Jena. They stare into each other's eyes.

"Jena," he whispers. "My Jena, Jena …"

The older Jake's hand lies flat on his leg, his eyes closed listening to the nurse read the final words of Jena's letter.

The nurse returns the letter to its special place.

Jake's body slightly slouches in the chair, his head laid to the side.

The nurse hurries over to him, calls his name, but Jake does not answer. She checks his pulse.

A breeze swirls swiftly through the room.

The nurse stares at Jake, his pulse gone.

In that instant, bright sunlight shines through the window. Then a stunning, sparkling rainbow appeared.

.